TRISTRAM SHANDY

AN AUTHORITATIVE TEXT
THE AUTHOR ON THE NOVEL
CRITICISM

A NORTON CRITICAL EDITION

LAURENCE STERNE

TRISTRAM SHANDY

AN AUTHORITATIVE TEXT
THE AUTHOR ON THE NOVEL
CRITICISM

Edited by

HOWARD ANDERSON

MICHIGAN STATE UNIVERSITY

W · W · NORTON & COMPANY
New York   London

ACKNOWLEDGMENTS

Howard Anderson: from *PMLA*, 86 (1971), 966–73. Reprinted by permission of the Modern Language Association of America.

Wayne Booth: from *Modern Philology*, XIVIII (1951), 172–83. Copyright © 1951 The University of Chicago Press. Reprinted by permission of the University of Chicago Press and the author.

Sigurd Burkhardt: from *ELH*, 28 (1961), 70–88. Reprinted by permission of the Johns Hopkins University Press.

Lodwick Hartley: from *Laurence Sterne in the Twentieth Century*. Copyright © 1966 by The University Press of North Carolina. Reprinted by permission of the publisher.

J. Paul Hunter: from *Novel*, 4 (1971), 132–46. Reprinted by permission of the publisher and the author.

Douglas Jefferson: from *Essays in Criticism*, I (1951), 225–48. Reprinted by permission of the publisher.

Richard A. Lanham: from *Tristram Shandy and the Games of Pleasure*. Copyright © 1973 by The Regents of the University of California. Reprinted by permission of the University of California Press.

Jean-Jacques Mayoux: from *The Winged Skull* edited by Arthur Cash and John Stedmond. Copyright © 1971 by Kent State University Press. Reprinted by permission of the publishers.

Toby A. Olshin: from *Genre*, 4 (1971), 360–75. Reprinted by permission of the University of Oklahoma.

Charles Parish: from *College English*, 22 (December 1960), 143–50. Copyright © 1960 by the National Council of Teachers of English. Reprinted by permission of the publisher and the author.

William Bowman Piper: from *Laurence Sterne* by William Bowman Piper. Copyright © 1965 by Twayne Publishers, Inc. Reprinted with the permission of Twayne Publishers, a Division of G. K. Hall & Co., Boston.

Martin Price: from *To the Palace of Wisdom* (New York: Doubleday, 1964). Reprinted by permission of the author.

Copyright © 1980 by W. W. Norton & Company, Inc.

Library of Congress Cataloging in Publication Data
Sterne, Laurence, 1713–1768.
    Tristram Shandy: an authoritative text, backgrounds and sources, criticism.
    (A Norton critical edition)
    Bibliography: p.
    1. Sterne, Laurence, 1713–1768. The life and opinions of Tristram Shandy, gentleman. I. Anderson, Howard Peter. II. Title.
PR3714.T73A5   1979   823'.6   79–277
ISBN 0-393-01244-1
ISBN 0-393-95034-4 pbk.

W. W. Norton & Company, Inc., 500 Fifth Avenue, New York, N.Y. 10110
www.wwnorton.com

W. W. Norton & Company Ltd., Castle House, 75/76 Wells Street, London W1T 3QT

Contents

vi · *Contents*

Preface

Tristram Shandy was a sensation—first in England, then through all of Europe—from the time the first two volumes appeared in the winter of 1760. And despite Dr. Johnson's unflattering choice of the book to exemplify his dictum that "nothing odd can last," it maintained its renown (though at times somewhat dubiously) through the nineteenth century, to emerge in our own time as the most modern of eighteenth-century novels.

An explanation for such endurance is that it was from the beginning a paradoxical synthesis of the old and the new. Artfully constructed to confound its reader's expectations, it did so with the aim of revealing the infinite ways in which conventional ideas of all sorts have handcuffed our minds and imaginations. This aim, and the satiric attacks on pedantry (whether academic, medical, legal, or clerical) through which it is realized, link *Tristram Shandy* to a great tradition of learned wit that extends back through Swift to Burton, Cervantes, Erasmus, and Rabelais, and beyond to classical writers like Lucian and Petronius. Like these writers, Sterne probes the abstractions which pedants put in place of life, dilating on the humorous potential of such a process, but also revealing the appalling self-interest from which it originates.

But the world of *Tristram Shandy* is at the same time inhabited by characters of a kind new to the eighteenth century. In Tristram's father, Walter Shandy, and even more in his uncle Toby, Sterne created people who are as much dominated as any pedant by the "hobby-horses" that occupy their minds, but who are given life and freedom by the strength of their generous sympathy with one another and the world. Don Quixote had been something like this, and so had Fielding's Parson Adams. But in Uncle Toby, Sterne realized for the first time a character embodying the uniqueness, indeed the eccentricity, of every human being—alive and loveable in his individuality.

It is finally to Tristram himself, however, that the reader owes the humorous and humiliating process of self-revelation that is at the core of our experience with this novel. The narrator's insight into the ways in which our arbitrary and unexplored assumptions about fiction shape our lives speaks perhaps most strongly to concerns of twentieth-century readers—and writers. Like Joyce and Beckett, Sterne knows that our conception of what constitutes a real *story* has found its way into our perception of all experience. And the result is nearly always a failure to notice and value whatever reality does not coincide with our preconceptions about what is real. That leads, further, to disappointment in (or blind refusal to face) whatever cannot be reconciled with a narrow definition of the "beautiful." From the moment that Tristram Shandy begins *his* story where no one else ever began one, we are confronted with the challenge of an imagination that sees all of life, rather than just a part, as its natural habitat. Or to put it another way, Sterne's vision of art is large enough to be undaunted by any subject matter.

The various ways that *Tristram Shandy* has, from the first, drawn readers in and spoken to them, are suggested by the responses— contemporary and later—assembled in this edition. Like the other greatest novels of the eighteenth century (at least in this), *Tristram Shandy* raises nearly all the questions that matter in the study of fiction in whatever age. From the remote literary past that figures so largely as the ground from which the novel springs, to contemporary speculations on the interrelations between art and the culture as a whole, the essays collected here outline some of the most important of the various rewarding lines leading into this novel.

The present text follows the first London editions of *Tristram Shandy*, published between December 1759 and January 1767. Sterne changed publishers between the fourth and fifth volumes, from R. & J. Dodsley to T. Becket & P. A. Dehondt. There is no sign that Sterne, having been taken up so suddenly in the literary and social world of London, and indeed of Europe, ever made deliberate changes in the texts of the editions of the novel published during his life. It was in any case not long from the publication of the first volumes to the last (1759–67). Sterne died in March of 1768. I have amended obvious errors; typographical or otherwise, it is usually impossible to tell. So I have not corrected spelling, except to make it consistent where the lapses appear accidental; spelling was far less regularized in the eighteenth century than it is today. The long eighteenth-century *s* (more like an *f* in modern printing) has been changed, and the quotation marks that head every line in a speech of several lines have been eliminated. But Sterne is much inclined to spell words, especially odd words, differently from time to time, and those variations remain. Beginning with Volume VII, his printers sharply reduce the number of names and other words italicized; I have however regularized the last three volumes to conform to the first six.

No one could annotate *Tristram Shandy* since 1940 without owing a great debt to James Work. His edition of the novel is probably the chief reason for the novel's renewed popularity in the colleges and universities in our own time, and certainly that edition is largely responsible for the kind of interest that resulted in the recent essays published here. Among the editions that followed

Work's, Samuel Holt Monk's, in 1950, with an introduction that is indispensable to any critical evaluation of the novel, and Ian Watt's in 1965, with notes that make the novel available to all readers, and an introduction that could only have been written by the most authoritative critic of the English novel in the eighteenth century, have both contributed to my own.

HOWARD ANDERSON

Chronology of Sterne's Life

1713   Laurence Sterne born on November 24 at Clonmel, in Tipperary, Ireland.

1723–31   At school near Halifax, Yorkshire.

1731   Death of Sterne's father.

1733–37   Undergraduate at Jesus College, Cambridge.

1737   Graduated B.A.

1738   Ordained priest; vicar of Sutton on the Forest, near York.

1740   Graduated M.A.

1741   Prebendary, York Cathedral; married Elizabeth Lumley.

1743   Vicar of Stillington, a parish adjoining Sutton on the Forest; published in *The Gentleman's Magazine,* "The Unknown World. Verses occasioned by hearing a Pass-Bell."

1747   Published "The Case of Elijah and the Widow of Zarephath considered. A Charity Sermon." Lydia Sterne born (his only child to survive to adulthood).

1750   Published "The Abuses of Conscience: set forth in a Sermon," preached in the Cathedral Church of St. Peter's, York (and also included in *Tristram Shandy,* Vol. II).

1759   Published A *Political Romance*—later called *The History of a Good Warm Watch-Coat.*

1760   Published *Tristram Shandy,* Vols. I and II, with R. & J. Dodsley, London, January 1. In London for publication of second edition of first two volumes of *Tristram Shandy; The Sermons of Mr. Yorick,* Vols. I and II; and Vols. III and IV of *Tristram Shandy.* Accepted living of Coxwold in Yorkshire.

1761   Published *Tristram Shandy,* Vols. III and IV, then Vols. V and VI.

1762–66   Because of ill health, travelled between London, France, and Italy.

1765   Published *Tristram Shandy*, Vols. VII and VIII.

1766   Published *The Sermons of Mr. Yorick*, Vols. III and IV.

1767   Published *Tristram Shandy*, Vol. IX.

1768   Published *A Sentimental Journey*; died in London on March 18.

The Text of
Tristram Shandy

SIR,

NEVER poor Wight of a Dedicator had less hopes from his Dedication, than I have from this of mine; for it is written in a bye corner of the kingdom, and in a retired thatch'd house, where I live in a constant endeavour to fence against the infirmities of ill health, and other evils of life, by mirth; being firmly persuaded that every time a man smiles,—but much more so, when he laughs, that it adds something to this Fragment of Life.

I humbly beg, Sir, that you will honour this book by taking it——(not under your Protection,——it must protect itself, but)— into the country with you; where, if I am ever told, it has made you smile, or can conceive, it has beguiled you of one moment's pain——I shall think myself as happy as a minister of state;—— perhaps much happier than any one (one only excepted) that I have ever read or heard of.

I am, great Sir,
(and what is more to your Honour,)
I am, good Sir,
Your Well-wisher,
and most humble Fellow-Subject,
THE AUTHOR.

---

1. William Pitt was secretary of state when the first two volumes of *Tristram Shandy* were published. Their success encouraged Sterne to ask Pitt's permission to dedicate them to him, which he did in the second edition.

The
Life and Opinions
of
Tristram Shandy, Gent.

Volume I.

Ταράσσει τοὺς 'Ανθρώπους οὐ τὰ Πράγματα,
'Αλλὰ τὰ περὶ τῶν Πραγμάτων Δόγματα.[2]

Chapter I.

I Wish either my father or my mother, or indeed both of them, as they were in duty both equally bound to it, had minded what they were about when they begot me; had they duly consider'd how much depended upon what they were then doing;—that not only the production of a rational Being was concern'd in it, but that possibly the happy formation and temperature of his body, perhaps his genius and the very cast of his mind;—and, for aught they knew to the contrary, even the fortunes of his whole house might take their turn from the humours[3] and dispositions which were then uppermost:——Had they duly weighed and considered all this, and proceeded accordingly,——I am verily persuaded I should have made a quite different figure in the world, from that, in which the reader is likely to see me.——Believe me, good folks, this is not so inconsiderable a thing as many of you may think it;——you have all, I dare say, heard of the animal spirits, as how they are transfused from father to son, &c. &c.——and a great deal to that purpose:——Well, you may take my word, that nine parts in ten of a man's sense or his nonsense, his successes and miscarriages in this world depend upon their motions and activity, and the different tracks and trains you put them into; so that when they are once set

---

2. "It is not things that disturb men, but their judgments about things." From the *Encheiridion* of Epictetus, an ancient Greek Stoic philosopher who lived in Rome.
3. In ancient and medieval physiology, the humours were the four fluids of the body—blood, phlegm, choler, and black choler. One or another was believed to dominate in a person, who would accordingly be cheerful ("sanguine") if the blood was dominant, melancholy if the black choler, etc. The animal spirits were thought to carry through the nerves tiny particles upon which sensation and movement depended. Similarly, the sperm carries the homunculus ("little man") in conception.

a-going, whether right or wrong, 'tis not a halfpenny matter,——
away they go cluttering like hey-go-mad; and by treading the same
steps over and over again, they presently make a road of it, as plain
and as smooth as a garden-walk, which, when they are once used to,
the Devil himself sometimes shall not be able to drive them off it.
Pray, my dear, quoth my mother, *have you not forgot to wind up
the clock?*——*Good G*——! cried my father, making an exclamation, but taking care to moderate his voice at the same time,——
*Did ever woman, since the creation of the world, interrupt a man
with such a silly question?* Pray, what was your father saying?
——Nothing.

Chapter II.

——Then, positively, there is nothing in the question, that I
can see, either good or bad.——Then let me tell you, Sir, it was a
very unseasonable question at least,——because it scattered and dispersed the animal spirits, whose business it was to have escorted and
gone hand-in-hand with the HOMUNCULUS, and conducted him
safe to the place destined for his reception.

The HOMUNCULUS, Sir, in how-ever low and ludicrous a light he
may appear, in this age of levity, to the eye of folly or prejudice;
——to the eye of reason in scientifick research, he stands confess'd
——a BEING guarded and circumscribed with rights:——The
minutest philosophers, who, by the bye, have the most enlarged
understandings, (their souls being inversely as their enquiries) shew
us incontestably, That the HOMUNCULUS is created by the same
hand,——engender'd in the same course of nature,——endowed
with the same loco-motive powers and faculties with us:——That
he consists, as we do, of skin, hair, fat, flesh, veins, arteries, ligaments, nerves, cartilages, bones, marrow, brains, glands, genitals,
humours, and articulations;——is a Being of as much activity,——
and, in all sense of the word, as much and as truly our fellow-
creature as my Lord Chancellor of England.——He may be benefited, he may be injured,——he may obtain redress;——in a word,
he has all the claims and rights of humanity, which *Tully*,[4] *Puffen-
dorff*, or the best ethick writers allow to arise out of that state and
relation.

Now, dear Sir, what if any accident had befallen him in his way
alone?——or that, thro' terror of it, natural to so young a traveller,
my little gentleman had got to his journey's end miserably spent;
——his muscular strength and virility worn down to a thread;——
his own animal spirits ruffled beyond description,——and that in

4. Tully (or Cicero) was an ancient
Roman philosopher and Puffendorf a
seventeenth-century German, both of
whom wrote on legal theory.

this sad disorder'd state of nerves, he had laid down a prey to suddenly start, or a series of melancholy dreams and fancies for nine long, long months together.——I tremble to think what a foundation had been laid for a thousand weaknesses both of body and mind, which no skill of the physician or the philosopher could ever afterwards have set thoroughly to rights.

Chapter III.

TO my uncle Mr. *Toby Shandy* do I stand indebted for the preceding anecdote,[5] to whom my father, who was an excellent natural philosopher, and much given to close reasoning upon the smallest matters, had oft, and heavily, complain'd of the injury; but once more particularly, as my uncle *Toby* well remember'd, upon his observing a most unaccountable obliquity, (as he call'd it) in my manner of setting up my top, and justifying the principles upon which I had done it,——the old gentleman shook his head, and in a tone more expressive by half of sorrow than reproach,——he said his heart all along foreboded, and he saw it verified in this, and from a thousand other observations he had made upon me, That I should neither think nor act like any other man's child:——*But alas!* continued he, shaking his head a second time, and wiping away a tear which was trickling down his cheeks, *My Tristram's misfortunes began nine months before ever he came into the world.*

——My mother, who was sitting by, look'd up,——but she knew no more than her backside what my father meant,——but my uncle, Mr. *Toby Shandy*, who had been often informed of the affair,——understood him very well.

Chapter IV.

I Know there are readers in the world, as well as many other good people in it, who are no readers at all,——who find themselves ill at ease, unless they are let into the whole secret from first to last, of every thing which concerns you.

It is in pure compliance with this humour of theirs, and from a backwardness in my nature to disappoint any one soul living, that I have been so very particular already. As my life and opinions are likely to make some noise in the world, and, if I conjecture right, will take in all ranks, professions, and denominations of men what-

5. Since many of the stories Tristram tells took place before his own birth, Toby could be considered a "source" for much of the book.

ever,——be no less read than the *Pilgrim's Progress*[6] itself——and, in the end, prove the very thing which *Montaigne* dreaded his essays should turn out, that is, a book for a parlour-window;——I find it necessary to consult every one a little in his turn; and therefore must beg pardon for going on a little further in the same way: For which cause, right glad I am, that I have begun the history of myself in the way I have done; and that I am able to go on tracing every thing in it, as *Horace* says, *ab Ovo*.[7]

Horace, I know, does not recommend this fashion altogether: But that gentleman is speaking only of an epic poem or a tragedy;—— (I forget which)——besides, if it was not so, I should beg Mr. *Horace*'s pardon;——for in writing what I have set about, I shall confine myself neither to his rules, nor to any man's rules that ever lived.

To such, however, as do not choose to go so far back into these things, I can give no better advice, than that they skip over the remaining part of this Chapter; for I declare before hand, 'tis wrote only for the curious and inquisitive.

————————— Shut the door.—————————

I was begot in the night, betwixt the first *Sunday* and the first *Monday* in the month of *March*, in the year of our Lord one thousand seven hundred and eighteen. I am positive I was.——But how I came to be so very particular in my account of a thing which happened before I was born, is owing to another small anecdote known only in our own family, but now made publick for the better clearing up this point.

My father, you must know, who was originally a *Turky* merchant,[8] but had left off business for some years, in order to retire to, and die upon, his paternal estate in the county of——, was, I believe, one of the most regular men in every thing he did, whether 'twas matter of business, or matter of amusement, that ever lived. As a small specimen of this extreme exactness of his, to which he was in truth a slave,——he had made it a rule for many years of his life,——on the first *Sunday night* of every month throughout the whole year,——as certain as ever the *Sunday night* came,——to wind up a large house-clock which we had standing upon the back-stairs head, with his own hands:——And being somewhere between fifty and sixty years of age, at the time I have been speaking of,——

6. *Pilgrim's Progress*, one of the most popular books ever written, was published by John Bunyan in 1678.. Montaigne, the French essayist, wrote in the second half of the sixteenth century; this complaint appears in "Upon Some Verses of Virgil."

7. Horace, the ancient Roman poet, praises Homer for *not* beginning the *Iliad* from the emergence of Helen *ab ovo*—that is, from the egg of Leda, procreated by Zeus in the form of a swan (*Art of Poetry*, XI.146 ff.). Homer began instead "in the middle of things," during the Trojan War, in which Helen was involved.

8. A dealer in goods from the Near East.

he had likewise gradually brought some other little family concernments to the same period, in order, as he would often say to my
uncle *Toby*, to get them all out of the way at one time, and be no
more plagued and pester'd with them the rest of the month.

It was attended but with one misfortune, which, in a great measure, fell upon myself, and the effects of which I fear I shall carry
with me to my grave; namely, that, from an unhappy association of
ideas which have no connection in nature, it so fell out at length,
that my poor mother could never hear the said clock wound up,
——but the thoughts of some other things unavoidably popp'd into
her head,——& vice versâ:——which strange combination of ideas,
the sagacious *Locke*,[9] who certainly understood the nature of these
things better than most men, affirms to have produced more wry
actions than all other sources of prejudice whatsoever.

But this by the bye.

Now it appears, by a memorandum in my father's pocket-book,
which now lies upon the table, "That on *Lady-Day*,[1] which was on
the 25th of the same month in which I date my geniture,——my
father set out upon his journey to *London* with my eldest brother
Bobby, to fix him at *Westminster* school;" and, as it appears from
the same authority, "That he did not get down to his wife and
family till the *second week* in *May* following,"——it brings the
thing almost to a certainty. However, what follows in the beginning
of the next chapter puts it beyond all possibility of doubt.

——But pray, Sir, What was your father doing all *December*,
—*January*, and *February?*——Why, Madam,——he was all that
time afflicted with a Sciatica.[2]

Chapter V.

O N the fifth day of *November*, 1718, which to the æra fixed on,
was as near nine kalendar months as any husband could in
reason have expected,[3]——was I *Tristram Shandy*, Gentleman,
brought forth into this scurvy and disasterous world of ours.——I
wish I had been born in the Moon, or in any of the planets, (except
Jupiter or *Saturn*, because I never could bear cold weather) for it

9. John Locke's *Essay Concerning Human Understanding* (1690) had an important influence on *Tristram Shandy*
and on modern psychological theory. In
Book II, Chapter 33, Locke speaks of
the way that ideas having nothing logically in common can become associated
in our minds, and considers these individual associations a cause of the dangerous isolation of one person from
another. Sterne, however, devotes himself to tracing and understanding such
associations (which result in "hobby-
horses"), as well as the equally irrational but more universal ones triggered
by words like "nose."
1. March 25 is the Feast of the Annunci-
ation (of the birth of Christ) to the
Virgin Mary.
2. A neuralgic disease of the hip which
makes movement painful.
3. From the first Sunday of March to
the fifth of November is nearer eight
months.

could not well have fared worse with me in any of them (tho' I will not answer for V*enus*)⁴ than it has in this vile, dirty planet of ours,——which o' my conscience, with reverence be it spoken, I take to be made up of the shreds and clippings of the rest;——not but the planet is well enough, provided a man could be born in it to a great title or to a great estate; or could any how contrive to be called up to publick charges, and employments of dignity or power; ——but that is not my case;——and therefore every man will speak of the fair as his own market has gone in it;——for which cause I affirm it over again to be one of the vilest worlds that ever was made;——for I can truly say, that from the first hour I drew my breath in it, to this, that I can now scarce draw it at all, for an asthma⁵ I got in scating against the wind in *Flanders*;——I have been the continual sport of what the world calls Fortune; and though I will not wrong her by saying, She has ever made me feel the weight of any great or signal evil;——yet with all the good temper in the world, I affirm it of her, That in every stage of my life, and at every turn and corner where she could get fairly at me, the ungracious Duchess has pelted me with a set of as pitiful mis-adventures and cross accidents as ever small Hero sustained.

Chapter VI.

IN the beginning of the last chapter, I inform'd you exactly *when* I was born;——but I did not inform you, *how*. No; that particular was reserved entirely for a chapter by itself;——besides, Sir, as you and I are in a manner perfect strangers to each other, it would not have been proper to have let you into too many circum-stances relating to myself all at once.——You must have a little patience. I have undertaken, you see, to write not only my life, but my opinions also; hoping and expecting that your knowledge of my character, and of what kind of a mortal I am, by the one, would give you a better relish for the other: As you proceed further with me, the slight acquaintance which is now beginning betwixt us, will grow into familiarity; and that, unless one of us is in fault, will terminate in friendship.——O *diem præclarum!*⁶——then nothing which has touched me will be thought trifling in its nature, or tedious in its telling. Therefore, my dear friend and companion, if you should think me somewhat sparing of my narrative on my first setting out,——bear with me,——and let me go on, and tell my story my own way:——or if I should seem now and then to trifle upon the road,——or should sometimes put on a fool's cap with a

---

4. Because it is named for the goddess of love.
5. Sterne himself was much troubled by tuberculosis while writing *Tristram Shandy*.
6. "O wondrous day!"

bell to it, for a moment or two as we pass along,——don't fly off,——but rather courteously give me credit for a little more wisdom than appears upon my outside;——and as we jogg on, either laugh with me, or at me, or in short, do any thing,——only keep your temper.

Chapter VII.

IN the same village where my father and my mother dwelt, dwelt also a thin, upright, motherly, notable, good old body of a midwife, who, with the help of a little plain good sense, and some years full employment in her business, in which she had all along trusted little to her own efforts, and a great deal to those of dame nature,——had acquired, in her way, no small degree of reputation in the world;——by which word *world*, need I in this place inform your worship, that I would be understood to mean no more of it, than a small circle described upon the circle of the great world, of four *English* miles diameter, or thereabouts, of which the cottage where the good old woman lived, is supposed to be the centre.—— She had been left, it seems, a widow in great distress, with three or four small children, in her forty-seventh year; and as she was at that time a person of decent carriage,——grave deportment,——a woman moreover of few words, and withall an object of compassion, whose distress and silence under it call'd out the louder for a friendly lift: the wife of the parson of the parish was touch'd with pity; and having often lamented an inconvenience, to which her husband's flock had for many years been exposed, inasmuch, as there was no such thing as a midwife, of any kind or degree to be got at, let the case have been never so urgent, within less than six or seven long miles riding; which said seven long miles in dark nights and dismal roads, the country thereabouts being nothing but a deep clay, was almost equal to fourteen; and that in effect was sometimes next to having no midwife at all; it came into her head, that it would be doing as seasonable a kindness to the whole parish, as to the poor creature herself, to get her a little instructed in some of the plain principles of the business, in order to set her up in it. As no woman thereabouts was better qualified to execute the plan she had formed than herself, the Gentle-woman very charitably undertook it; and having great influence over the female part of the parish, she found no difficulty in effecting it to the utmost of her wishes. In truth, the parson join'd his interest with his wife's in the whole affair; and in order to do things as they should be, and give the poor soul as good a title by law to practise, as his wife had given by institution,——he chearfully paid the fees for the ordinary's licence himself, amounting, in the whole, to the sum of eighteen shillings and fourpence; so that, betwixt them both, the good woman was fully invested in the real and corporal possession of her office, together with all its *rights, members, and appurtenances whatsoever.*[7]

These last words, you must know, were not according to the old form in which such licences, faculties, and powers usually ran, which in like cases had heretofore been granted to the sisterhood. But it was according to a neat *Formula* of *Didius* his own devising, who having a particular turn for taking to pieces, and new framing over again, all kind of instruments in that way, not only hit upon this dainty amendment, but coax'd many of the old licensed matrons in the neighbourhood, to open their faculties afresh, in order to have this whim-wham of his inserted.

I own I never could envy *Didius* in these kinds of fancies of his:——But every man to his own taste.——Did not Dr. *Kunastrokius*,[8] that great man, at his leisure hours, take the greatest delight imaginable in combing of asses tails, and plucking the dead hairs out with his teeth, though he had tweezers always in his pocket? Nay, if you come to that, Sir, have not the wisest of men in all ages, not excepting *Solomon* himself,——have they not had their HOBBY-HORSES;[9]——their running horses,——their coins and their cockle-shells, their drums and their trumpets, their fiddles, their pallets,——their maggots and their butterflies?——and so long as a man rides his HOBBY-HORSE peaceably and quietly along the King's highway, and neither compels you or me to get up behind him,—— pray, Sir, what have either you or I to do with it?

Chapter VIII.

——*De gustibus non est disputandum;*[1]——that is, there is no disputing against HOBBY-HORSES; and, for my part, I seldom do; nor could I with any sort of grace, had I been an enemy to them at the bottom; for happening, at certain intervals and changes of the Moon, to be both fiddler and painter, according as the fly stings: ——Be it known to you, that I keep a couple of pads myself, upon which, in their turns, (nor do I care who knows it) I frequently ride out and take the air;—tho' sometimes, to my shame be it spoken, I take somewhat longer journies than what a wise man would think

---

7. Sterne regularly makes fun of the language overused by various professions—here a common legal formula. Didius, one of several pedantic lawyers who move in and out of Tristram Shandy's world, is commonly taken for a satiric version of Dr. Francis Topham, a frequent opponent of Sterne's in the church politics of York.
8. The name "Kunastrokius" is from the Latin *cunnus*, female genital. A well-known London physician, Dr. Richard Mead, was rumored to deserve the nickname.
9. Hobby-horses were originally figures in the old morris dances. Sterne's use of the term to refer to obsessive or fixed ideas derives from the child's toy: a stick with a horse's head attached.
1. "There's no disputing about tastes."

altogether right.——But the truth is,——I am not a wise man;—— and besides am a mortal of so little consequence in the world, it is not much matter what I do; so I seldom fret or fume at all about it: Nor does it much disturb my rest when I see such great Lords and tall Personages as hereafter follow;——such, for instance, as my Lord A, B, C, D, E, F, G, H, I, K, L, M, N, O, P, Q, and so on, all of a row, mounted upon their several horses;——some with large stirrups, getting on in a more grave and sober pace;——others on the contrary, tuck'd up to their very chins, with whips across their mouths, scouring and scampering it away like so many little party- colour'd devils astride a mortgage,——and as if some of them were resolved to break their necks.——So much the better——say I to myself;——for in case the worst should happen, the world will make a shift to do excellently well without them;——and for the rest,——why,——God speed them,——e'en let them ride on with- out any opposition from me; for were their lordships unhorsed this very night,——'tis ten to one but that many of them would be worse mounted by one half before tomorrow morning.

Not one of these instances therefore can be said to break in upon my rest.——But there is an instance, which I own puts me off my guard, and that is, when I see one born for great actions, and, what is still more for his honour, whose nature ever inclines him to good ones;——when I behold such a one, my Lord, like yourself, whose principles and conduct are as generous and noble as his blood, and whom, for that reason, a corrupt world cannot spare one moment; ——when I see such a one, my Lord, mounted, though it is but for a minute beyond the time which my love to my country has pre- scribed to him, and my zeal for his glory wishes,——then, my Lord, I cease to be a philosopher, and in the first transport of an honest impatience, I wish the HOBBY-HORSE, with all his fraternity, at the Devil.

My Lord,

"I Maintain this to be a dedication, notwithstanding its singular- ity in the three great essentials of matter, form and place: I beg, therefore, you will accept it as such, and that you will permit me to lay it, with the most respectful humility, at your Lordship's feet, ——when you are upon them,——which you can be when you please;——and that is, my Lord, when ever there is occasion for it, and I will add, to the best purposes too. I have the honour to be,
My Lord,
Your Lordship's most obedient,
and most devoted,
and most humble servant,
TRISTRAM SHANDY.

Chapter IX.

I Solemnly declare to all mankind, that the above dedication was made for no one Prince, Prelate, Pope, or Potentate,——Duke, Marquis, Earl, Viscount, or Baron of this, or any other Realm in Christendom;——nor has it yet been hawk'd about, or offered publickly or privately, directly or indirectly, to any one person or personage, great or small; but is honestly a true Virgin-Dedication untried on, upon any soul living.

I labour this point so particularly, merely to remove any offence or objection which might arise against it, from the manner in which I propose to make the most of it;——which is the putting it up fairly to publick sale; which I now do.

——Every author has a way of his own, in bringing his points to bear;——for my own part, as I hate chaffering and higgling for a few guineas in a dark entry;——I resolved within myself, from the very beginning, to deal squarely and openly with your Great Folks in this affair, and try whether I should not come off the better by it.

If therefore there is any one Duke, Marquis, Earl, Viscount, or Baron, in these his Majesty's dominions, who stands in need of a tight, genteel dedication, and whom the above will suit, (for by the bye, unless it suits in some degree, I will not part with it)——it is much at his service for fifty guineas;——which I am positive is twenty guineas less than it ought to be afforded for, by any man of genius.

My Lord, if you examine it over again, it is far from being a gross piece of daubing, as some dedications are. The design, your Lordship sees, is good, the colouring transparent,——the drawing not amiss;——or to speak more like a man of science,——and measure my piece in the painter's scale, divided into 20,——I believe, my Lord, the out-lines will turn out as 12,——the composition as 9,——the colouring as 6,——the expression 13 and a half,——and the design,——if I may be allowed, my Lord, to understand my own *design*, and supposing absolute perfection in designing, to be as 20,——I think it cannot well fall short of 19. Besides all this,——there is keeping in it, and the dark strokes in the Hobby-Horse, (which is a secondary figure, and a kind of back-ground to the whole) give great force to the principal lights in your own figure, and make it come off wonderfully;——and besides, there is an air of originality in the *tout ensemble*.[2]

Be pleased, my good Lord, to order the sum to be paid into the hands of Mr. *Dodsley*,[3] for the benefit of the author; and in the

---

2. "The whole thing."
3. James Dodsley was Sterne's publisher at the time.

next edition care shall be taken that this chapter be expunged, and your Lordship's titles, distinctions, arms and good actions, be placed at the front of the preceding chapter: All which, from the words, *De gustibus non est disputandum*, and whatever else in this book relates to HOBBY-HORSES, but no more, shall stand dedicated to your Lordship.——The rest I dedicate to the MOON, who, by the bye, of all the PATRONS or MATRONS I can think of, has most power to set my book a-going, and make the world run mad after it.

Bright Goddess,

If thou art not too busy with CANDID[4] and Miss CUNEGUND's affairs,——take *Tristram Shandy's* under thy protection also.

Chapter X.

WHatever degree of small merit, the act of benignity in favour of the midwife, might justly claim, or in whom that claim truly rested,——at first sight seems not very material to this history;——certain however it was, that the gentlewoman, the parson's wife, did run away at that time with the whole of it: And yet, for my life, I cannot help thinking but that the parson himself, tho' he had not the good fortune to hit upon the design first,——yet, as he heartily concurred in it the moment it was laid before him, and as heartily parted with his money to carry it into execution, had a claim to some share of it,——if not to a full half of whatever honour was due to it.

The world at that time was pleased to determine the matter otherwise.

Lay down the book, and I will allow you half a day to give a probable guess at the grounds of this procedure.

Be it known then, that, for about five years before the date of the midwife's licence, of which you have had so circumstantial an account,——the parson we have to do with, had made himself a country-talk by a breach of all decorum, which he had committed against himself, his station, and his office;——and that was, in never appearing better, or otherwise mounted, than upon a lean, sorry, jack-ass of a horse, value about one pound fifteen shillings; who, to shorten all description of him, was full brother to *Rosinante,*[5] as far as similitude congenial could make him; for he answered his description to a hair-breadth in every thing,——except that I do not

---

4. Leading characters in Voltaire's *Candide*, first published in 1757, but appearing in English the same year as these two volumes of *Tristram Shandy*.
5. The unimpressive steed ridden by Don Quixote de la Mancha in Cervantes' novel. He was ordinarily a model of chastity, but when he encountered some mares belonging to a group of Yanguesian water carriers, he was carried away by lust and got beaten for it.

remember 'tis any where said, that *Rosinante* was broken winded; and that, moreover, *Rosinante*, as is the happiness of most *Spanish* horses, fat or lean,——was undoubtedly a horse at all points.

I know very well that the Hero's horse was a horse of chaste deportment, which may have given grounds for a contrary opinion: But it is as certain at the same time, that *Rosinante*'s continency (as may be demonstrated from the adventure of the *Yanguesian* carriers) proceeded from no bodily defect or cause whatsoever, but from the temperance and orderly current of his blood.——And let me tell you, Madam, there is a great deal of very good chastity in the world, in behalf of which you could not say more for your life.

Let that be as it may, as my purpose is to do exact justice to every creature brought upon the stage of this dramatic work,——I could not stifle this distinction in favour of Don *Quixote*'s horse; ——in all other points the parson's horse, I say, was just such another,——for he was as lean, and as lank, and as sorry a jade, as Humility herself could have bestrided.

In the estimation of here and there a man of weak judgment, it was greatly in the parson's power to have helped the figure of this horse of his,——for he was master of a very handsome demi-peak'd saddle, quilted on the seat with green plush, garnished with a double row of silver-headed studs, and a noble pair of shining brass stirrups, with a housing altogether suitable, of grey superfine cloth, with an edging of black lace, terminating in a deep, black, silk fringe, *poudré d'or*,[6]——all which he had purchased in the pride and prime of his life, together with a grand embossed bridle, ornamented at all points as it should be.——But not caring to banter his beast, he had hung all these up behind his study door;——and, in lieu of them, had seriously befitted him with just such a bridle and such a saddle, as the figure and value of such a steed might well and truly deserve.

In the several sallies about his parish, and in the neighbouring visits to the gentry who lived around him,——you will easily comprehend, that the parson, so appointed, would both hear and see enough to keep his philosophy from rusting. To speak the truth, he never could enter a village, but he caught the attention of both old and young.——Labour stood still as he pass'd,——the bucket hung suspended in the middle of the well,——the spinning-wheel forgot its round,——even chuck-farthing and shuffle-cap[7] themselves stood gaping till he had got out of sight; and as his movement was not of the quickest, he had generally time enough upon his hands to

6. Powdered with gold.
7. Country games involving tossing or shaking coins.

make his observations,——to hear the groans of the serious,——
and the laughter of the light-hearted;——all which he bore with
excellent tranquility.——His character was,——he loved a jest in
his heart——and as he saw himself in the true point of ridicule, he
would say, he could not be angry with others for seeing him in a
light, in which he so strongly saw himself: So that to his friends,
who knew his foible was not the love of money, and who therefore
made the less scruple in bantering the extravagance of his humour,
——instead of giving the true cause,——he chose rather to join in
the laugh against himself; and as he never carried one single ounce
of flesh upon his own bones, being altogether as spare a figure as his
beast,——he would sometimes insist upon it, that the horse was as
good as the rider deserved;——that they were, centaur-like,——
both of a piece. At other times, and in other moods, when his spirits
were above the temptation of false wit,——he would say, he found
himself going off fast in a consumption; and, with great gravity,
would pretend, he could not bear the sight of a fat horse without a
dejection of heart, and a sensible alteration in his pulse; and that he
had made choice of the lean one he rode upon, not only to keep
himself in countenance, but in spirits.

At different times he would give fifty humorous and opposite
reasons for riding a meek-spirited jade of a broken-winded horse,
preferably to one of mettle;——for on such a one he could sit
mechanically, and meditate as delightfully *de vanitate mundi et fugâ
sæculi*,[8] as with the advantage of a death's head before him;——
that, in all other exercitations, he could spend his time, as he rode
slowly along,——to as much account as in his study;——that he
could draw up an argument in his sermon,——or a hole in his
breeches, as steadily on the one as in the other;——that brisk
trotting and slow argumentation, like wit and judgment, were two
incompatible movements.——But that upon his steed——he could
unite and reconcile every thing,——he could compose his sermon,
——he could compose his cough,——and, in case nature gave a
call that way, he could likewise compose himself to sleep.——In
short, the parson upon such encounters would assign any cause, but
the true cause,——and he with-held the true one, only out of a
nicety of temper, because he thought it did honour to him.

But the truth of the story was as follows: In the first years of this
gentleman's life, and about the time when the superb saddle and
bridle were purchased by him, it had been his manner, or vanity, or
call it what you will,——to run into the opposite extream.——In
the language of the county where he dwelt, he was said to have
loved a good horse, and generally had one of the best in the whole

---

8. "On the vanity of the world and the passing of time."

parish standing in his stable always ready for saddling; and as the nearest midwife, as I told you, did not live nearer to the village than seven miles, and in a vile country,——it so fell out that the poor gentleman was scarce a whole week together without some piteous application for his beast; and as he was not an unkind-hearted man, and every case was more pressing and more distressful than the last,——as much as he loved his beast, he had never a heart to refuse him; the upshot of which was generally this, that his horse was either clapp'd, or spavin'd, or greaz'd;——or he was twitter-bon'd, or broken-winded, or something, in short, or other had befallen him which would let him carry no flesh;——so that he had every nine or ten months a bad horse to get rid of,——and a good horse to purchase in his stead.

What the loss in such a balance might amount to, *communibus annis*,[9] I would leave to a special jury of sufferers in the same traffic, to determine;——but let it be what it would, the honest gentleman bore it for many years without a murmur, till at length, by repeated ill accidents of the kind, he found it necessary to take the thing under consideration; and upon weighing the whole, and summing it up in his mind, he found it not only disproportion'd to his other expences, but withall so heavy an article in itself, as to disable him from any other act of generosity in his parish: Besides this he considered, that, with half the sum thus galloped away, he could do ten times as much good;——and what still weighed more with him than all other considerations put together, was this, that it confined all his charity into one particular channel, and where, as he fancied, it was the least wanted, namely, to the child-bearing and child-getting part of his parish; reserving nothing for the impotent, ——nothing for the aged,——nothing for the many comfortless scenes he was hourly called forth to visit, where poverty, and sickness, and affliction dwelt together.

For these reasons he resolved to discontinue the expence; and there appeared but two possible ways to extricate him clearly out of it;——and these were, either to make it an irrevocable law never more to lend his steed upon any application whatever,——or else be content to ride the last poor devil, such as they had made him, with all his aches and infirmities, to the very end of the chapter.

As he dreaded his own constancy in the first,——he very chearfully betook himself to the second; and tho' he could very well have explain'd it, as I said, to his honour,——yet, for that very reason, he had a spirit above it; choosing rather to bear the contempt of his enemies, and the laughter of his friends, than undergo the pain of telling a story, which might seem a panegyric upon himself.

9. "In ordinary years."

I have the highest idea of the spiritual and refined sentiments of this reverend gentleman, from this single stroke in his character, which I think comes up to any of the honest refinements of the peerless knight of *La Mancha*, whom, by the bye, with all his follies, I love more, and would actually have gone further to have paid a visit to, than the greatest hero of antiquity.

But this is not the moral of my story: The thing I had in view was to shew the temper of the world in the whole of this affair.——For you must know, that so long as this explanation would have done the parson credit,——the devil a soul could find it out,——I suppose his enemies would not, and that his friends could not.——But no sooner did he bestir himself in behalf of the midwife, and pay the expences of the ordinary's licence to set her up,——but the whole secret came out; every horse he had lost, and two horses more than ever he had lost, with all the circumstances of their destruction, were known and distinctly remembered.——The story ran like wild-fire.——"The parson had a returning fit of pride which had just seized him; and he was going to be well mounted once again in his life; and if it was so, 'twas plain as the sun at noonday, he would pocket the expence of the licence, ten times told the very first year:——so that every body was left to judge what were his views in this act of charity."

What were his views in this, and in every other action of his life,——or rather what were the opinions which floated in the brains of other people concerning it, was a thought which too much floated in his own, and too often broke in upon his rest, when he should have been sound asleep.

About ten years ago this gentleman had the good fortune to be made entirely easy upon that score,——it being just so long since he left his parish,——and the whole world at the same time behind him,——and stands accountable to a judge of whom he will have no cause to complain.

But there is a fatality attends the actions of some men: Order them as they will, they pass thro' a certain medium which so twists and refracts them from their true directions——that, with all the titles to praise which a rectitude of heart can give, the doers of them are nevertheless forced to live and die without it.

Of the truth of which this gentleman was a painful example.——But to know by what means this came to pass,——and to make that knowledge of use to you, I insist upon it that you read the two following chapters, which contain such a sketch of his life and conversation, as will carry its moral along with it.——When this is done, if nothing stops us in our way, we will go on with the midwife.

Chapter XI.

YORICK was this parson's name,[1] and, what is very remarkable in it, (as appears from a most antient account of the family, wrote upon strong vellum, and now in perfect preservation) it had been exactly so spelt for near,——I was within an ace of saying nine hundred years;——but I would not shake my credit in telling an improbable truth, however indisputable in itself;——and therefore I shall content myself with only saying,——It had been exactly so spelt, without the least variation or transposition of a single letter, for I do not know how long; which is more than I would venture to say of one half of the best surnames in the kingdom; which, in a course of years, have generally undergone as many chops and changes as their owners.——Has this been owing to the pride, or to the shame of the respective proprietors?——In honest truth, I think, sometimes to the one, and sometimes to the other, just as the temptation has wrought. But a villainous affair it is, and will one day so blend and confound us all together, that no one shall be able to stand up and swear, "That his own great grand father was the man who did either this or that."

This evil had been sufficiently fenced against by the prudent care of the *Yorick's* family, and their religious preservation of these records I quote, which do further inform us, That the family was originally of *Danish* extraction, and had been transplanted into *England* as early as in the reign of *Horwendillus*, king of *Denmark*, in whose court it seems, an ancestor of this Mr. *Yorick's*, and from whom he was lineally descended, held a considerable post to the day of his death. Of what nature this considerable post was, this record saith not;——it only adds, That, for near two centuries, it had been totally abolished as altogether unnecessary, not only in that court, but in every other court of the Christian world.

It has often come into my head, that this post could be no other than that of the king's chief Jester;——and that *Hamlet's Yorick*, in our *Shakespear*, many of whose plays, you know, are founded upon authenticated facts,——was certainly the very man.

I have not the time to look into *Saxo-Grammaticus's Danish* history, to know the certainty of this;——but if you have leisure, and can easily get at the book, you may do it full as well yourself.

I had just time, in my travels through *Denmark* with Mr. *Nod-*

---

1. All that is left of Yorick in Shakespeare's *Hamlet* is his skull and the Prince's memory of his good humor. Sterne's wit combined with his black clothes and tubercular frame to identify him with Yorick (as well as Tristram) in social and literary circles. One of Shakespeare's sources for *Hamlet* was Saxo Grammaticus, a thirteenth-century Danish historian who speaks of King Horwendil and his son Amleth.

dy's eldest son, whom, in the year 1741, I accompanied as governor, riding along with him at a prodigious rate thro' most parts of *Europe*, and of which original journey perform'd by us two, a most delectable narrative will be given in the progress of this work. I had just time, I say, and that was all, to prove the truth of an observation made by a long sojourner in that country;——namely, "That nature was neither very lavish, nor was she very stingy in her gifts of genius and capacity to its inhabitants;——but, like a discreet parent, was moderately kind to them all; observing such an equal tenor in the distribution of her favours, as to bring them, in those points, pretty near to a level with each other; so that you will meet with few instances in that kingdom of refin'd parts; but a great deal of good plain houshold understanding amongst all ranks of people, of which every body has a share;" which is, I think, very right.

With us, you see, the case is quite different;——we are all ups and downs in this matter;——you are a great genius;——or 'tis fifty to one, Sir, you are a great dunce and a blockhead;——not that there is a total want of intermediate steps,——no,——we are not so irregular as that comes to;——but the two extremes are more common, and in a greater degree in this unsettled island, where nature, in her gifts and dispositions of this kind, is most whimsical and capricious; fortune herself not being more so in the bequest of her goods and chattels than she.

This is all that ever stagger'd my faith in regard to *Yorick*'s extraction, who, by what I can remember of him, and by all the accounts I could ever get of him, seem'd not to have had one single drop of *Danish* blood in his whole crasis; in nine hundred years, it might possibly have all run out:——I will not philosophize one moment with you about it; for happen how it would, the fact was this:——That instead of that cold phlegm and exact regularity of sense and humours, you would have look'd for, in one so extracted;——he was, on the contrary, as mercurial and sublimated a composition,——as heteroclite a creature in all his declensions;—— with as much life and whim, and *gaité de cœur*[2] about him, as the kindliest climate could have engendered and put together. With all this sail, poor *Yorick* carried not one ounce of ballast; he was utterly unpractised in the world; and, at the age of twenty-six, knew just about as well how to steer his course in it, as a romping, unsuspicious girl of thirteen: So that upon his first setting out, the brisk gale of his spirits, as you will imagine, ran him foul ten times in a day of some body's tackling; and as the grave and more slow-paced were oftenest in his way,——you may likewise imagine, 'twas with such he had generally the ill luck to get the most entangled.

2. "Gaiety of heart."

For aught I know there might be some mixture of unlucky wit at the bottom of such *Fracas:*——For, to speak the truth, *Yorick* had an invincible dislike and opposition in his nature to gravity;——not to gravity as such;——for where gravity was wanted, he would be the most grave or serious of mortal men for days and weeks together;——but he was an enemy to the affectation of it, and declared open war against it, only as it appeared a cloak for ignorance, or for folly; and then, whenever it fell in his way, however sheltered and protected, he seldom gave it much quarter.

Sometimes, in his wild way of talking, he would say, That gravity was an errant scoundrel; and he would add,——of the most dangerous kind too,——because a sly one; and that, he verily believed, more honest, well-meaning people were bubbled out of their goods and money by it in one twelve-month, than by pocket-picking and shop-lifting in seven. In the naked temper which a merry heart discovered, he would say, There was no danger,——but to itself:——whereas the very essence of gravity was design, and consequently deceit;——'twas a taught trick to gain credit of the world for more sense and knowledge than a man was worth; and that, with all its pretensions,——it was no better, but often worse, than what a *French* wit had long ago defined it,——*viz. A mysterious carriage of the body to cover the defects of the mind*,[3]——which definition of gravity, *Yorick*, with great imprudence, would say, deserved to be wrote in letters of gold.

But, in plain truth, he was a man unhackneyed and unpractised in the world, and was altogether as indiscreet and foolish on every other subject of discourse where policy is wont to impress restraint. *Yorick* had no impression but one, and that was what arose from the nature of the deed spoken of; which impression he would usually translate into plain *English* without any periphrasis,——and too oft without much distinction of either personage, time, or place;——so that when mention was made of a pitiful or an ungenerous proceeding,——he never gave himself a moment's time to reflect who was the Hero of the piece,——what his station,——or how far he had power to hurt him hereafter;——but if it was a dirty action,——without more ado,——The man was a dirty fellow,——and so on:——And as his comments had usually the ill fate to be terminated either in a *bon mot*,[4] or to be enliven'd throughout with some drollery or humour of expression, it gave wings to *Yorick's* indiscretion. In a word, tho' he never sought, yet, at the same time, as he seldom shun'd occasions of saying what came uppermost, and without much ceremony;——he had but too many temptations in life,

3. The passage is from the *Maxims* (1665) of François de la Rochefoucauld.
4. "Witty saying."

of scattering his wit and his humour,——his gibes and his jests about him.——They were not lost for want of gathering.

What were the consequences, and what was *Yorick*'s catastrophe thereupon, you will read in the next chapter.

Chapter XII.

THE *Mortgager* and *Mortgagée* differ the one from the other, not more in length of purse, than the *Jester* and *Jestée* do, in that of memory. But in this the comparison between them runs, as the scholiasts call it, upon all-four; which, by the bye, is upon one or two legs more, than some of the best of *Homer*'s can pretend to;—— namely, That the one raises a sum and the other a laugh at your expence, and think no more about it. Interest, however, still runs on in both cases;——the periodical or accidental payments of it, just serving to keep the memory of the affair alive; till, at length, in some evil hour,——pop comes the creditor upon each, and by demanding principal upon the spot, together with full interest to the very day, makes them both feel the full extent of their obligations.

As the reader (for I hate your *ifs*) has a thorough knowledge of human nature, I need not say more to satisfy him, that my Hero could not go on at this rate without some slight experience of these incidental mementos. To speak the truth, he had wantonly involved himself in a multitude of small book-debts of this stamp, which, notwithstanding *Eugenius*'s[5] frequent advice, he too much disregarded; thinking, that as not one of them was contracted thro' any malignancy;——but, on the contrary, from an honesty of mind, and a mere jocundity of humour, they would all of them be cross'd out in course.

Eugenius would never admit this; and would often tell him, that one day or other he would certainly be reckoned with; and he would often add, in an accent of sorrowful apprehension,——to the uttermost mite. To which *Yorick*, with his usual carelessness of heart, would as often answer with a pshaw!——and if the subject was started in the fields,——with a hop, skip, and a jump, at the end of it; but if close pent up in the social chimney corner, where the culprit was barricado'd in, with a table and a couple of arm chairs, and could not so readily fly off in a tangent,——*Eugenius* would then go on with his lecture upon discretion, in words to this purpose, though somewhat better put together.

Trust me, dear *Yorick*, this unwary pleasantry of thine will sooner or later bring thee into scrapes and difficulties, which no

---

5. The name comes from a Greek word meaning "well-born." Sterne refers to his friend John Hall Stevenson.

a... wit can extricate thee out of.——In these sallies, too oft, I see, it happens, that a person laugh'd at, considers himself in the light of a person injured, with all the rights of such a situation belonging to him; and when thou viewest him in that light too, and reckons up his friends, his family, his kindred and allies,——and musters up with them the many recruits which will list under him from a sense of common danger;——'tis no extravagant arithmetic to say, that for every ten jokes,——thou hast got a hundred enemies; and till thou hast gone on, and raised a swarm of wasps about thy ears, and art half stung to death by them, thou wilt never be convinced it is so.

I cannot suspect it in the man whom I esteem, that there is the least spur from spleen or malevolence of intent in these sallies. ——I believe and know them to be truly honest and sportive:—— But consider, my dear lad, that fools cannot distingush this,——and that knaves will not; and thou knowest not what it is, either to provoke the one, or to make merry with the other,——whenever they associate for mutual defence, depend upon it, they will carry on the war in such a manner against thee, my dear friend, as to make thee heartily sick of it, and of thy life too.

REVENGE from some baneful corner shall level a tale of dishonour at thee, which no innocence of heart or integrity of conduct shall set right.——The fortunes of thy house shall totter,——thy character, which led the way to them, shall bleed on every side of it,——thy faith questioned,——thy works belied,——thy wit forgotten,——thy learning trampled on. To wind up the last scene of thy tragedy, CRUELTY and COWARDICE, twin ruffians, hired and set on by MALICE in the dark, shall strike together at all thy infirmities and mistakes:——the best of us, my dear lad, lye open there,—— and trust me,——trust me, Yorick, *When to gratify a private appetite, it is once resolved upon, that an innocent and an helpless creature shall be sacrificed, 'tis an easy matter to pick up sticks enew from any thicket where it has strayed, to make a fire to offer it up with.*

Yorick scarce ever heard this sad vaticination of his destiny read over to him, but with a tear stealing from his eye, and a promissory look attending it, that he was resolved, for the time to come, to ride his tit[6] with more sobriety.——But, alas, too late!——a grand confederacy, with. ***** and ***** at the head of it, was form'd before the first prediction of it.——The whole plan of the attack, just as *Eugenius* had foreboded, was put in execution all at once, ——with so little mercy on the side of the allies,——and so little suspicion in *Yorick*, of what was carrying on against him,——that

_____

6. A small horse.

when he thought, good easy man! full surely preferment was o' ripening,[7]——they had smote his root, and then he fell, as many a worthy man had fallen before him.

Yorick, however, fought it out with all imaginable gallantry for some time; till, over-power'd by numbers, and worn out at length by the calamities of the war,——but more so, by the ungenerous manner in which it was carried on,——he threw down the sword; and though he kept up his spirits in appearance to the last,——he died, nevertheless, as was generally thought, quite broken hearted.

What inclined *Eugenius* to the same opinion, was as follows:

A few hours before *Yorick* breath'd his last, *Eugenius* stept in with an intent to take his last sight and last farewell of him: Upon his drawing *Yorick's* curtain, and asking how he felt himself, *Yorick*, looking up in his face, took hold of his hand,——and, after thanking him for the many tokens of his friendship to him, for which, he said, if it was their fate to meet hereafter,——he would thank him again and again,——he told him, he was within a few hours of giving his enemies the slip for ever.——I hope not, answered *Eugenius*, with tears trickling down his cheeks, and with the tenderest tone that ever man spoke,——I hope not, *Yorick*, said he.—— *Yorick* replied, with a look up, and a gentle squeeze of *Eugenius's* hand, and that was all,——but it cut *Eugenius* to his heart.—— Come,——come, *Yorick*, quoth *Eugenius*, wiping his eyes, and summoning up the man within him,——my dear lad, be comforted, ——let not all thy spirits and fortitude forsake thee at this crisis when thou most wants them;——who knows what resources are in store, and what the power of God may yet do for thee?——*Yorick* laid his hand upon his heart, and gently shook his head;——for my part, continued *Eugenius*, crying bitterly as he uttered the words, ——I declare I know not, *Yorick*, how to part with thee,——and would gladly flatter my hopes, added *Eugenius*, chearing up his voice, that there is still enough left of thee to make a bishop,—— and that I may live to see it.——I beseech thee, *Eugenius*, quoth *Yorick*, taking off his night-cap as well as he could with his left hand,——his right being still grasped close in that of *Eugenius*, ——I beseech thee to take a view of my head.——I see nothing that ails it, replied *Eugenius*. Then, alas! my friend, said *Yorick*, let me tell you, that 'tis so bruised and mis-shapen'd with the blows which ***** and *****, and some others have so unhandsomely given me in the dark, that I might say with *Sancho Pança*,[8] that should I recover, and "Mitres thereupon be suffer'd to rain down

7. Cardinal Wolsey uses some of these words in describing his fall from great power in Shakespeare's *Henry VIII* (III.ii.356–57).
8. Don Quixote's servant and compan-

ion; he was altogether earthier and more skeptical than his master. The mitres he refers to are the headgear of bishops. A cervantic tone is both funny and satiric.

from heaven as thick as hail, not one of 'em would fit it."——
Yorick's last breath was hanging upon his trembling lips ready to
depart as he uttered this;——yet still it was utter'd with something
of a *cervantick* tone;——and as he spoke it, *Eugenius* could perceive a stream of lambent fire lighted up for a moment in his
eyes;——faint picture of those flashes of his spirit, which (as
Shakespear said of his ancestor) were wont to set the table in a
roar!

Eugenius was convinced from this, that the heart of his friend
was broke; he squeez'd his hand,——and then walk'd softly out of
the room, weeping as he walk'd. *Yorick* followed *Eugenius* with his
eyes to the door,——he then closed them,——and never opened
them more.

He lies buried in a corner of his church-yard, in the parish of
———, under a plain marble slabb, which his friend *Eugenius*, by
leave of his executors, laid upon his grave, with no more than these
three words of inscription serving both for his epitaph and elegy.[9]

> Alas, poor YORICK!

Ten times in a day has *Yorick*'s ghost the consolation to hear his
monumental inscription read over with such a variety of plaintive
tones, as denote a general pity and esteem for him;——a foot-way
crossing the church-yard close by the side of his grave,——not a
passenger goes by without stopping to cast a look upon it,——and
sighing as he walks on,

Alas, poor Y O R I C K !

---

9. Hamlet's words to Yorick's skull (V.i.179–80).

Chapter XIII.

IT is so long since the reader of this rhapsodical work has been parted from the midwife, that it is high time to mention her again to him, merely to put him in mind that there is such a body still in the world, and whom, upon the best judgment I can form upon my own plan at present,——I am going to introduce to him for good and all: But as fresh matter may be started, and much unexpected business fall out betwixt the reader and myself, which may require immediate dispatch;——'twas right to take care that the poor woman should not be lost in the mean time;——because when she is wanted we can no way do without her.

I think I told you that this good woman was a person of no small note and consequence throughout our whole village and township;——that her fame had spread itself to the very out-edge and circumference of that circle of importance, of which kind every soul living, whether he has a shirt to his back or no,——has one surrounding him;——which said circle, by the way, whenever 'tis said that such a one is of great weight and importance in the *world*,—— I desire may be enlarged or contracted in your worship's fancy, in a compound-ratio of the station, profession, knowledge, abilities, height and depth (measuring both ways) of the personage brought before you.

In the present case, if I remember, I fixed it at about four or five miles, which not only comprehended the whole parish, but extended itself to two or three of the adjacent hamlets in the skirts of the next parish; which made a considerable thing of it. I must add, That she was, moreover, very well looked on at one large grange-house and some other odd houses and farms within two or three miles, as I said, from the smoke of her own chimney:——But I must here, once for all, inform you, that all this will be more exactly delineated and explain'd in a map, now in the hands of the engraver, which, with many other pieces and developments to this work, will be added to the end of the twentieth volume,——not to swell the work,——I detest the thought of such a thing;——but by way of commentary, scholium, illustration, and key to such passages, incidents, or inuendos as shall be thought to be either of private interpretation, or of dark or doubtful meaning after my life and my opinions shall have been read over, (now don't forget the meaning of the word) by all the *world*;——which, betwixt you and me, and in spight of all the gentlemen reviewers in *Great-Britain*, and of all that their worships shall undertake to write or say to the contrary, ——I am determined shall be the case.——I need not tell your worship, that all this is spoke in confidence.

Chapter XIV.

UPON looking into my mother's marriage settlement, in order to satisfy myself and reader in a point necessary to be clear'd up, before we could proceed any further in this history;——I had the good fortune to pop upon the very thing I wanted before I had read a day and a half straightforwards,——it might have taken me up a month;——which shews plainly, that when a man sits down to write a history,——tho' it be but the history of *Jack Hickathrift*[1] or *Tom Thumb*, he knows no more than his heels what lets and confounded hinderances he is to meet with in his way,——or what a dance he may be led, by one excursion or another, before all is over. Could a historiographer drive on his history, as a muleteer drives on his mule,——straight forward;——for instance, from *Rome* all the way to *Loretto*,[2] without ever once turning his head aside either to the right hand or to the left,——he might venture to foretell you to an hour when he should get to his journey's end;——but the thing is, morally speaking, impossible: For, if he is a man of the least spirit, he will have fifty deviations from a straight line to make with this or that party as he goes along, which he can no ways avoid. He will have views and prospects to himself perpetually solliciting his eye, which he can no more help standing still to look at than he can fly; he will moreover have various

Accounts to reconcile:

Anecdotes to pick up:

Inscriptions to make out:

Stories to weave in:

Traditions to sift:

Personages to call upon:

Panegyricks[3] to paste up at this door:

Pasquinades at that:——All which both the man and his mule are quite exempt from. To sum up all; there are archives at every stage to be look'd into, and rolls, records, documents, and endless genealogies, which justice ever and anon calls him back to stay the reading of:——In short, there is no end of it;——for my own part, I declare I have been at it these six weeks, making all the speed I possibly could,——and am not yet born:——I have just been able, and that's all, to tell you *when* it happen'd, but not *how*;——so that you see the thing is yet far from being accomplished.

These unforeseen stoppages, which I own I had no conception of

---

1. Tom (not Jack) Hickathrift is, like Tom Thumb, a figure in an English nursery rhyme.
2. From Rome to Loretto was the route of pilgrims visiting the Santa Casa, reputed to be the residence of the Virgin Mary miraculously transported from Nazareth to Loretto in 1294.
3. *Panegyrics* are elaborate formal praise; *pasquinades* are lampoons.

when I first set out;——but which, I am convinced now, will rather increase than diminish as I advance,——have struck out a hint which I am resolved to follow;——and that is,——not to be in a hurry;——but to go on leisurely, writing and publishing two volumes of my life every year;——which, if I am suffered to go on quietly, and can make a tolerable bargain with my bookseller, I shall continue to do as long as I live.

Chapter XV.

THE article in my mother's marriage settlement, which I told the reader I was at the pains to search for, and which, now that I have found it, I think proper to lay before him,——is so much more fully express'd in the deed itself, than ever I can pretend to do it, that it would be barbarity to take it out of the lawyer's hand: ——It is as follows.[4]

"𝕬𝖓𝖉 𝖙𝖍𝖎𝖘 𝕴𝖓𝖉𝖊𝖓𝖙𝖚𝖗𝖊 𝖋𝖚𝖗𝖙𝖍𝖊𝖗 𝖜𝖎𝖙𝖓𝖊𝖘𝖘𝖊𝖙𝖍, That the said *Walter Shandy*, merchant, in consideration of the said intended marriage to be had, and, by God's blessing, to be well and truly solemnized and consummated between the said *Walter Shandy* and *Elizabeth Mollineux* aforesaid, and divers other good and valuable causes and considerations him thereunto specially moving,——doth grant, covenant, condescend, consent, conclude, bargain, and fully agree to and with *John Dixon* and *James Turner*, Esqrs. the above-named trustees, &c.&c.——to wit,——That in case it should hereafter so fall out, chance, happen, or otherwise come to pass,——That the said *Walter Shandy*, merchant, shall have left off business before the time or times, that the said *Elizabeth Mollineux* shall, according to the course of nature, or otherwise, have left off bearing and bringing forth children;——and that, in consequence of the said *Walter Shandy* having so left off business, he shall, in despight, and against the free-will, consent, and good-liking of the said *Elizabeth Mollineux*,——make a departure from the city of *London*, in order to retire to, and dwell upon, his estate at *Shandy-Hall*, in the county of ———, or at any other country seat, castle, hall, mansion-house, messuage, or grainge-house, now purchased, or hereafter to be purchased, or upon any part or parcel thereof:——That then, and as often as the said *Elizabeth Mollineux* shall happen to be enceint with child or children severally and lawfully begot, or to be begotten, upon the body of the said *Elizabeth Mollineux* during her said coverture,——he the said *Walter Shandy* shall, at his own proper

4. The Shandy marriage contract parodies legal language that says the same thing as many different ways as possible in an attempt to keep slippery life under control. And with words like "coverture," "backsides," etc., Sterne allows for suggestive double meanings.

cost and charges, and out of his own proper monies, upon good and reasonable notice, which is hereby agreed to be within six weeks of her the said *Elizabeth Mollineux's* full reckoning, or time of supposed and computed delivery,——pay, or cause to be paid, the sum of one hundred and twenty pounds of good and lawful money, to *John Dixon* and *James Turner*, Esqrs. or assigns,——upon TRUST and confidence, and for and unto the use and uses, intent, end, and purpose following:——𝕿𝖍𝖆𝖙 𝖎𝖘 𝖙𝖔 𝖘𝖆𝖞,——That the said sum of one hundred and twenty pounds shall be paid into the hands of the said *Elizabeth Mollineux*, or to be otherwise applied by them the said trustees, for the well and truly hiring of one coach, with able and sufficient horses, to carry and convey the body of the said *Elizabeth Mollineux* and the child or children which she shall be then and there enceint and pregnant with,——unto the city of *London*; and for the further paying and defraying of all other incidental costs, charges, and expences whatsoever,——in and about, and for, and relating to her said intended delivery and lying-in, in the said city or suburbs thereof. And that the said *Elizabeth Mollineux* shall and may, from time to time, and at all such time and times as are here covenanted and agreed upon,——peaceably and quietly hire the said coach and horses, and have free ingress, egress, and regress throughout her journey, in and from the said coach, according to the tenor, true intent, and meaning of these presents, without any let, suit, trouble, disturbance, molestation, discharge, hinderance, forfeiture, eviction, vexation, interruption, or incumberance whatsoever.——And that it shall moreover be lawful to and for the said *Elizabeth Mollineux*, from time to time, and as oft or often as she shall well and truly be advanced in her said pregnancy, to the time heretofore stipulated and agreed upon,—— to live and reside in such place or places, and in such family or families, and with such relations, friends, and other persons within the said city of *London*, as she, at her own will and pleasure, notwithstanding her present coverture, and as if she was a *femme sole*[5] and unmarried,——shall think fit.——𝕬𝖓𝖉 𝖙𝖍𝖎𝖘 𝕴𝖓𝖉𝖊𝖓𝖙𝖚𝖗𝖊 𝖋𝖚𝖗𝖙𝖍𝖊𝖗 𝖜𝖎𝖙𝖓𝖊𝖘𝖘𝖊𝖙𝖍, That for the more effectually carrying of the said covenant into execution, the said *Walter Shandy*, merchant, doth hereby grant, bargain, sell, release, and confirm unto the said *John Dixon*, and *James Turner*, Esqrs. their heirs, executors, and assigns, in their actual possession now being, by virtue of an indenture of bargain and sale for a year to them the said *John Dixon* and *James Turner*, Esqrs. by him the said *Walter Shandy*, merchant, thereof made; which said bargain and sale for a year, bears date the day next before the date of these presents, and by force and virtue

5. "Single woman."

of the statute for transferring of uses into possession,——𝕬𝖑𝖑 that the manor and lordship of *Shandy* in the county of ———, with all the rights, members, and appurtenances thereof; and all and every the messuages, houses, buildings, barns, stables, orchards, gardens, backsides, tofts, crofts, garths, cottages, lands, meadows, feedings, pastures, marshes, commons, woods, underwoods, drains, fisheries, waters, and water-courses;——together with all rents, reversions, services, annuities, fee-farms, knights fees, views of frank-pledge, escheats, reliefs, mines, quarries, goods and chattels of felons and fugitives, felons of themselves, and put in exigent, deodands, free warrens, and all other royalties and seignories, rights and jurisdictions, privileges and hereditaments whatsoever,——𝕬𝖓𝖉 𝖆𝖑𝖘𝖔 the advowson, donation, presentation and free disposition of the rectory or parsonage of *Shandy* aforesaid, and all and every the tenths, tythes, glebe-lands"——In three words,——"My mother was to lay in, (if she chose it) in *London*."

But in order to put a stop to the practice of any unfair play on the part of my mother, which a marriage article of this nature too manifestly opened a door to, and which indeed had never been thought of at all, but for my uncle *Toby Shandy*;——a clause was added in security of my father, which was this:——"That in case my mother hereafter should, at any time, put my father to the trouble and expence of a *London* journey upon false cries and tokens;——that for every such instance she should forfeit all the right and title which the covenant gave her to the next turn;——but to no more,——and so on, *toties quoties*,[6] in as effectual a manner, as if such a covenant betwixt them had not been made."——This, by the way, was no more than what was reasonable;——and yet, as reasonable as it was, I have ever thought it hard that the whole weight of the article should have fallen entirely, as it did, upon myself.

But I was begot and born to misfortunes;——for my poor mother, whether it was wind or water,——or a compound of both,——or neither;——or whether it was simply the mere swell of imagination and fancy in her;——or how far a strong wish and desire to have it so, might mislead her judgment;——in short, whether she was deceived or deceiving in this matter, it no way becomes me to decide. The fact was this, That, in the latter end of *September*, 1717, which was the year before I was born, my mother having carried my father up to town much against the grain,——he peremptorily insisted upon the clause;——so that I was doom'd, by marriage articles, to have my nose squeez'd as flat to my face, as if the destinies had actually spun me without one.

6. "Every time."

How this event came about,——and what a train of vexatious disappointments, in one stage or other of my life, have pursued me from the mere loss, or rather compression, of this one single member,——shall be laid before the reader all in due time.

Chapter XVI.

MY father, as any body may naturally imagine, came down with my mother into the country, in but a pettish kind of a humour. The first twenty or five-and-twenty miles he did nothing in the world but fret and teaze himself, and indeed my mother too, about the cursed expence, which he said might every shilling of it have been saved;——then what vexed him more than every thing else was the provoking time of the year,——which, as I told you, was towards the end of *September*, when his wall-fruit, and green gages especially, in which he was very curious, were just ready for pulling:——"Had he been whistled up to *London*, upon a *Tom Fool's* errand in any other month of the whole year, he should not have said three words about it."

For the next two whole stages,[7] no subject would go down, but the heavy blow he had sustain'd from the loss of a son, whom it seems he had fully reckon'd upon in his mind, and register'd down in his pocket-book, as a second staff for his old age, in case *Bobby* should fail him. "The disappointment of this, he said, was ten times more to a wise man than all the money which the journey, &c. had cost him, put together,——rot the hundred and twenty pounds,—— he did not mind it a rush."

From *Stilton*, all the way to *Grantham*, nothing in the whole affair provoked him so much as the condolences of his friends, and the foolish figure they should both make at church the first *Sunday*; ——of which, in the satirical vehemence of his wit, now sharpen'd a little by vexation, he would give so many humorous and provoking descriptions,——and place his rib and self in so many tormenting lights and attitudes in the face of the whole congregation;——that my mother declared, these two stages were so truly tragi-comical, that she did nothing but laugh and cry in a breath, from one end to the other of them all the way.

From *Grantham*, till they had cross'd the *Trent*, my father was out of all kind of patience at the vile trick and imposition which he fancied my mother had put upon him in this affair.——"Certainly," he would say to himself, over and over again, "the woman could not be deceived herself;——if she could,——what weakness!"—— tormenting word! which led his imagination a thorny dance, and,

---

7. A stage is the distance one set of horses could pull a coach before being replaced with another set.

before all was over, play'd the duce and all with him;——for sure as ever the word *weakness* was uttered, and struck full upon his brain,——so sure it set him upon running divisions upon how many kinds of weaknesses there were;——that there was such a thing as weakness of the body,——as well as weakness of the mind,——and then he would do nothing but syllogize within himself for a stage or two together, How far the cause of all these vexations might, or might not, have arisen out of himself.

In short, he had so many little subjects of disquietude springing out of this one affair, all fretting successively in his mind as they rose up in it, that my mother, whatever was her journey up, had but an uneasy journey of it down.——In a word, as she complained to my uncle *Toby*, he would have tired out the patience of any flesh alive.

Chapter XVII.

THough my father travelled homewards, as I told you, in none of the best of moods,——pshaw-ing and pish-ing all the way down,——yet he had the complaisance to keep the worst part of the story still to himself;——which was the resolution he had taken of doing himself the justice, which my uncle *Toby*'s clause in the marriage settlement empowered him; nor was it till the very night in which I was begot, which was thirteen months after, that she had the least intimation of his design; when my father, happening, as you remember, to be a little chagrin'd and out of temper,——took occasion as they lay chatting gravely in bed afterwards, talking over what was to come,——to let her know that she must accommodate herself as well as she could to the bargain made between them in their marriage deeds; which was to lye-in of her next child in the country to balance the last year's journey.

My father was a gentleman of many virtues,——but he had a strong spice of that in his temper which might, or might not, add to the number.——'Tis known by the name of perseverance in a good cause,——and of obstinacy in a bad one: Of this my mother had so much knowledge, that she knew 'twas to no purpose to make any remonstrance,——so she e'en resolved to sit down quietly, and make the most of it.

Chapter XVIII.

AS the point was that night agreed, or rather determin'd, that my mother should lye-in of me in the country, she took her measures accordingly; for which purpose, when she was three days, or thereabouts, gone with child, she began to cast her eyes upon the

ィhom you have so often heard me mention; and before
ィwas well got round, as the famous Dr. *Maningham*[8] was
not to be had, she had come to a final determination in her mind,
——notwithstanding there was a scientifick operator within so near
a call as eight miles of us, and who, moreover, had expressly wrote
a five shillings book upon the subject of midwifery, in which he had
exposed, not only the blunders of the sisterhood itself,——but had
likewise superadded many curious improvements for the quicker
extraction of the fœtus in cross births, and some other cases of
danger which belay us in getting into the world; notwithstanding all
this, my mother, I say, was absolutely determined to trust her life
and mine with it, into no soul's hand but this old woman's only.
——Now this I like;——when we cannot get at the very thing we
wish,——never to take up with the next best in degree to it;——no;
that's pitiful beyond description;——it is no more than a week from
this very day, in which I am now writing this book for the edification of the world,——which is *March* 9, 1759,——that my dear,
dear *Jenny*[9] observing I look'd a little grave, as she stood cheapening a silk of five-and-twenty shillings a yard,——told the mercer,
she was sorry she had given him so much trouble;——and immediately went and bought herself a yard-wide stuff of ten-pence a
yard.——'Tis the duplication of one and the same greatness of soul;
only what lessen'd the honour of it somewhat, in my mother's case,
was, that she could not heroine it into so violent and hazardous an
extream, as one in her situation might have wish'd, because the old
midwife had really some little claim to be depended upon,——as
much, at least, as success could give her; having, in the course of
her practice of near twenty years in the parish, brought every mother's son of them into the world without any one slip or accident
which could fairly be laid to her account.

These facts, tho' they had their weight, yet did not altogether
satisfy some few scruples and uneasinesses which hung upon my
father's spirits in relation to this choice.——To say nothing of the
natural workings of humanity and justice,——or of the yearnings
of parental and connubial love, all which prompted him to leave as
little to hazard as possible in a case of this kind;——he felt himself
concern'd in a particular manner, that all should go right in the
present case;——from the accumulated sorrow he lay open to,
should any evil betide his wife and child in lying-in at *Shandy-
Hall*.——He knew the world judged by events, and would add to
his afflictions in such a misfortune, by loading him with the whole
blame of it.——"Alas o'day;——had Mrs. *Shandy*, poor gentle-

8. A famous obstetrician of the time.
9. Jenny may be a name for Catherine
Fourmantelle, a young singer whom
Sterne was interested in at the time.
"Cheapening" means bargaining for.

woman! had but her wish in going up to town just to lye-in and come down again;——which, they say, she begg'd and pray'd for upon her bare knees,——and which, in my opinion, considering the fortune which Mr. *Shandy* got with her,——was no such mighty matter to have complied with, the lady and her babe might both of 'em have been alive at this hour."

This exclamation, my father knew was unanswerable;——and yet, it was not merely to shelter himself,——nor was it altogether for the care of his offspring and wife that he seem'd so extremely anxious about this point;——my father had extensive views of things,——and stood, moreover, as he thought, deeply concern'd in it for the publick good, from the dread he entertained of the bad uses an ill-fated instance might be put to.

He was very sensible that all political writers upon the subject had unanimously agreed and lamented, from the beginning of Queen *Elizabeth*'s reign down to his own time, that the current of men and money towards the metropolis, upon one frivolous errand or another,——set in so strong,——as to become dangerous to our civil rights;——tho', by the bye,——a *current* was not the image he took most delight in,——a *distemper* was here his favourite metaphor, and he would run it down into a perfect allegory, by maintaining it was identically the same in the body national as in the body natural, where blood and spirits were driven up into the head faster than they could find their ways down;——a stoppage of circulation must ensue, which was death in both cases.

There was little danger, he would say, of losing our liberties by *French* politicks or *French* invasions;——nor was he so much in pain of a consumption from the mass of corrupted matter and ulcerated humours in our constitution,——which he hoped was not so bad as it was imagined;——but he verily feared, that in some violent push, we should go off, all at once, in a state-apoplexy;—— and then he would say, *The Lord have mercy upon us all.*

My father was never able to give the history of this distemper, ——without the remedy along with it.

"Was I an absolute prince," he would say, pulling up his breeches with both his hands, as he rose from his arm-chair, "I would appoint able judges, at every avenue of my metropolis, who should take cognizance of every fool's business who came there;——and if, upon a fair and candid hearing, it appeared not of weight sufficient to leave his own home, and come up, bag and baggage, with his wife and children, farmers sons, &c. &c. at his backside, they should be all sent back, from constable to constable, like vagrants as they were, to the place of their legal settlements. By this means I shall take care, that my metropolis totter'd not thro' its own weight;—— that the head be no longer too big for the body;——that the extreams, now wasted and pin'd in, be restored to their due share of nourishment, and regain, with it, their natural strength and beauty:——I would effectually provide, That the meadows and corn-fields, of my dominions, should laugh and sing;——that good chear and hospitality flourish once more;——and that such weight and influence be put thereby into the hands of the Squirality[1] of my kingdom, as should counterpoise what I perceive my Nobility are now taking from them.

"Why are there so few palaces and gentlemen's seats," he would ask, with some emotion, as he walked a-cross the room, "throughout so many delicious provinces in *France?* Whence is it that the few remaining *Chateaus* amongst them are so dismantled,——so unfurnished, and in so ruinous and desolate a condition?—— Because, Sir," (he would say) "in that kingdom no man has any country-interest to support;——the little interest of any kind, which any man has any where in it, is concentrated in the court, and the looks of the Grand Monarch; by the sun-shine of whose countenance, or the clouds which pass a-cross it, every *French* man lives or dies."

Another political reason which prompted my father so strongly to guard against the least evil accident in my mother's lying-in in the country,——was, That any such instance would infallibly throw a balance of power, too great already, into the weaker vessels of the gentry, in his own, or higher stations;——which, with the many other usurped rights which that part of the constitution was hourly establishing,——would, in the end, prove fatal to the monarchical system of domestick government established in the first creation of things by God.

In this point he was entirely of Sir *Robert Filmer's*[2] opinion, That the plans and institutions of the greatest monarchies in the eastern parts of the world, were, originally, all stolen from that admirable pattern and prototype of this household and paternal power;——which, for a century, he said, and more, had gradually been degenerating away into a mix'd government;——the form of which, however desirable in great combinations of the species,—— was very troublesome in small ones,——and seldom produced any thing, that he saw, but sorrow and confusion.

For all these reasons, private and publick, put together,——my father was for having the man-midwife by all means,——my mother by no means. My father begg'd and intreated, she would for

---

1. Squirearchy, the landed gentry. "The Grand Monarch," Louis XIV, has systematically weakened the French nobility by depriving them of the political support of their tenants and neighbors ("country interest") when he required their constant attendance at the Court.

2. Sir Robert Filmer articulated in the *Patriarcha* (1680) the theory that the state was a family and the king a father to whom loyalty was required.

once recede from her prerogative in this matter, and su⸍ choose for her;——my mother, on the contrary, insisted upon ᴴᵉ. privilege in this matter, to choose for herself,——and have no mortal's help but the old woman's.——What could my father do? He was almost at his wit's end;——talked it over with her in all moods; ——placed his arguments in all lights;——argued the matter with her like a christian,——like a heathen,——like a husband,——like a father,——like a patriot,——like a man:——My mother answered every thing only like a woman; which was a little hard upon her;——for as she could not assume and fight it out behind such a variety of characters,——'twas no fair match;——'twas seven to one.——What could my mother do?——She had the advantage (otherwise she had been certainly overpowered) of a small reinforcement of chagrine personal at the bottom which bore her up, and enabled her to dispute the affair with my father with so equal an advantage,——that both sides sung *Te Deum*.[3] In a word, my mother was to have the old woman,——and the operator was to have licence to drink a bottle of wine with my father and my uncle *Toby Shandy* in the back parlour,——for which he was to be paid five guineas.

I must beg leave, before I finish this chapter, to enter a caveat in the breast of my fair reader;——and it is this:——Not to take it absolutely for granted from an unguarded word or two which I have dropp'd in it,——"That I am a married man."——I own the tender appellation of my dear, dear *Jenny*,——with some other strokes of conjugal knowledge, interspersed here and there, might, naturally enough, have misled the most candid judge in the world into such a determination against me.——All I plead for, in this case, Madam, is strict justice, and that you do so much of it, to me as well as to yourself,——as not to prejudge or receive such an impression of me, till you have better evidence, than I am positive, at present, can be produced against me:——Not that I can be so vain or unreasonable, Madam, as to desire you should therefore think, that my dear, dear *Jenny* is my kept mistress;——no,——that would be flattering my character in the other extream, and giving it an air of freedom, which, perhaps, it has no kind of right to. All I contend for, is the utter impossibility for some volumes, that you, or the most penetrating spirit upon earth, should know how this matter really stands.——It is not impossible, but that my dear, dear *Jenny*! tender as the appellation is, may be my child.——Consider,——I was born in the year eighteen.——Nor is there any thing unnatural or extravagant in the supposition, that my dear *Jenny* may be my friend.——Friend!——My friend.——Surely, Madam, a friendship

---

3. "We Praise Thee Lord" is a traditional hymn of praise, often sung at the conclusion of wars or battles.

between the two sexes may subsist, and be supported without ———Fy! Mr. *Shandy:*———Without any thing, Madam, but that tender and delicious sentiment, which ever mixes in friendship, where there is a difference of sex. Let me intreat you to study the pure and sentimental parts of the best *French* Romances;———it will really, Madam, astonish you to see with what a variety of chaste expression this delicious sentiment, which I have the honour to speak of, is dress'd out.

Chapter XIX.

I Would sooner undertake to explain the hardest problem in Geometry, than pretend to account for it, that a gentleman of my father's great good sense,———knowing, as the reader must have observed him, and curious too, in philosophy,———wise also in political reasoning,———and in polemical (as he will find) no way ignorant,———could be capable of entertaining a notion in his head, so out of the common track,———that I fear the reader, when I come to mention it to him, if he is the least of a cholerick temper, will immediately throw the book by; if mercurial, he will laugh most heartily at it;———and if he is of a grave and saturnine cast, he will, at first sight, absolutely condemn as fanciful and extravagant; and that was in respect to the choice and imposition of Christian names, on which he thought a great deal more depended than what superficial minds were capable of conceiving.

His opinion, in this matter, was, That there was a strange kind of magick bias, which good or bad names, as he called them, irresistibly impress'd upon our characters and conduct.

The Hero of *Cervantes*[4] argued not the point with more seriousness,———nor had he more faith,———or more to say on the powers of Necromancy in dishonouring his deeds,———or on DULCINEA's name, in shedding lustre upon them, than my father had on those of TRISMEGISTUS or ARCHIMEDES, on the one hand,———or of NYKY and SIMKIN on the other. How many CÆSARS and POMPEYS, he would say, by mere inspiration of the names, have been render'd worthy of them? And how many, he would add, are there who might have done exceeding well in the world, had not their characters and spirits been totally depress'd and NICODEMUS'D into nothing.

---

4. Cervantes' hero, Don Quixote, bestows his devotion and the elegant name of Dulcinea upon a simple peasant girl. "Hermes Trismegistus" was the Greek name, meaning "thrice-great," for the Egyptian god Thoth; he was credited with writing the philosophical and theosophical *Hermetica*. Archimedes was an ancient Greek mathematician. "Nyky" and "Simkin" are nicknames for Nicholas, to be contrasted with the grand sort of nomenclature that Walter Shandy prefers. Nicodemus represents a weak or timid character because, according to St. John (3:1–12 and 7:45–53) he visited Christ by night but would not avow his faith publicly.

I see plainly, Sir, by your looks, (or as the case happen'd) my father would say,——that you do not heartily subscribe to this opinion of mine,——which, to those, he would add, who have not carefully sifted it to the bottom,——I own has an air more of fancy than of solid reasoning in it;——and yet, my dear Sir, if I may presume to know your character, I am morally assured, I should hazard little in stating a case to you,——not as a party in the dispute,——but as a judge, and trusting my appeal upon it to your own good sense and candid disquisition in this matter;——you are a person free from as many narrow prejudices of education as most men;——and, if I may presume to penetrate further into you,—— of a liberality of genius above bearing down an opinion, merely because it wants friends. Your son!——your dear son,——from whose sweet and open temper you have so much to expect.—— Your BILLY, Sir!——would you, for the world, have called him JUDAS?——Would you, my dear Sir, he would say, laying his hand upon your breast, with the genteelest address,——and in that soft and irresistible *piano*[5] of voice, which the nature of the *argumentum ad hominem* absolutely requires,——Would you, Sir, if a *Jew* of a godfather had proposed the name for your child, and offered you his purse along with it, would you have consented to such a desecration of him?——O my God! he would say, looking up, if I know your temper right, Sir,——you are incapable of it;——you would have trampled upon the offer;——you would have thrown the temptation at the tempter's head with abhorrence.

Your greatness of mind in this action, which I admire, with that generous contempt of money which you shew me in the whole transaction, is really noble;——and what renders it more so, is the principle of it;——the workings of a parent's love upon the truth and conviction of this very hypothesis, namely, That was your son called JUDAS,——The sordid and treacherous idea, so inseparable from the name, would have accompanied him thro' life like his shadow, and, in the end, made a miser and a rascal of him, in spite, Sir, of your example.

I never knew a man able to answer this argument.——But, indeed, to speak of my father as he was;——he was certainly irresistible, both in his orations and disputations;——he was born an orator;——θεοδίδακτος.[6]——Persuasion hung upon his lips, and the elements of Logick and Rhetorick were so blended up in him, ——and, withall, he had so shrewd a guess at the weaknesses and passions of his respondent,——that NATURE might have stood up and said,——"This man is eloquent." In short, whether he was on the weak or the strong side of the question, 'twas hazardous in

---

5. *Piano* is the musical term for "softly." To argue *ad hominem* ("to the man") is to appeal to personal prejudice.

6. "Taught by God."

either case to attack him:——And yet, 'tis strange, he had never read *Cicero*[7] nor *Quintilian de Oratore*, nor *Isocrates*, nor *Aristotle*, nor *Longinus* amongst the antients;——nor *Vossius*, nor *Skioppius*, nor *Ramus*, nor *Farnaby* amongst the moderns;——and what is more astonishing, he had never in his whole life the least light or spark of subtilty struck into his mind, by one single lecture upon *Crackenthorp* or *Burgerdicius*, or any *Dutch* logician or commentator;——he knew not so much as in what the difference of an argument *ad ignorantiam*, and an argument *ad hominem* consisted; so that I well remember, when he went up along with me to enter my name at *Jesus College* in ****,[8]——it was a matter of just wonder with my worthy tutor, and two or three fellows of that learned society,——that a man who knew not so much as the names of his tools, should be able to work after that fashion with 'em.

To work with them in the best manner he could, was what my father was, however, perpetually forced upon;——for he had a thousand little sceptical notions of the comick kind to defend,—— most of which notions, I verily believe, at first enter'd upon the footing of mere whims, and of a *vive la Bagatelle*;[9] and as such he would make merry with them for half an hour or so, and having sharpen'd his wit upon 'em, dismiss them till another day.

I mention this, not only as matter of hypothesis or conjecture upon the progress and establishment of my father's many odd opinions,——but as a warning to the learned reader against the indiscreet reception of such guests, who, after a free and undisturbed enterance, for some years, into our brains,——at length claim a kind of settlement there,——working sometimes like yeast; ——but more generally after the manner of the gentle passion, beginning in jest,——but ending in downright earnest.

Whether this was the case of the singularity of my father's notions,——or that his judgment, at length, became the dupe of his wit;——or how far, in many of his notions, he might, tho' odd, be absolutely right;——the reader, as he comes at them, shall decide. All that I maintain here, is, that in this one, of the influence of Christian names, however it gain'd footing, he was serious;——he was all uniformity;——he was systematical, and, like all systematick reasoners, he would move both heaven and earth, and twist and torture every thing in nature to support his hypothesis. In a word, I repeat it over again;——he was serious;——and, in consequence of it, he would lose all kind of patience whenever he saw

---

7. Tristram lists ancient and Renaissance authorities on logic and rhetoric. To argue *ad ignorantiam* is to take advantage of an opponent's ignorance of the subject.

8. Sterne went to Jesus College, Cambridge; there is one at Oxford, as well.
9. "Hurrah for frivolity."

people, especially of condition, who should have known better,——
as careless and as indifferent about the name they imposed upon
their child,——or more so, than in the choice of *Ponto* or *Cupid*
for their puppy dog.

This, he would say, look'd ill;——and had, moreover, this particular aggravation in it, *viz.* That when once a vile name was wrong-
fully or injudiciously given, 'twas not like the case of a man's
character, which, when wrong'd, might hereafter be clear'd;——
and, possibly, sometime or other, if not in the man's life, at least
after his death,——be, somehow or other, set to rights with the
world: But the injury of this, he would say, could never be undone;
——nay, he doubted even whether an act of parliament could reach
it:——He knew as well as you, that the legislature assum'd a power
over surnames;——but for very strong reasons, which he could
give, it had never yet adventured, he would say, to go a step further.

It was observable, that tho' my father, in consequence of this
opinion, had, as I have told you, the strongest likings and dislikings
towards certain names;——that there were still numbers of names
which hung so equally in the balance before him, that they were
absolutely indifferent to him. *Jack, Dick,* and *Tom* were of this
class: These my father call'd neutral names;——affirming of them,
without a satyr,[1] That there had been as many knaves and fools, at
least, as wise and good men, since the world began, who had in-
differently borne them;——so that, like equal forces acting against
each other in contrary directions, he thought they mutually destroyed each others effects; for which reason, he would often declare, He would not give a cherry-stone to choose amongst them.
Bob, which was my brother's name, was another of these neutral
kinds of Christian names, which operated very little either way; and
as my father happen'd to be at *Epsom,*[2] when it was given him,
——he would oft times thank Heaven it was no worse. *Andrew* was
something like a negative quantity in Algebra with him;——'twas
worse, he said, than nothing.——*William* stood pretty high:——
Numps again was low with him;—and *Nick,* he said, was the
DEVIL.

But, of all the names in the universe, he had the most unconquerable aversion for TRISTRAM;[3]——he had the lowest and most
contemptible opinion of it of any thing in the world,——thinking it
could possibly produce nothing in *rerum naturâ,*[4] but what was
extreamly mean and pitiful: So that in the midst of a dispute on the
subject, in which, by the bye, he was frequently involved,——he

---

1. That is, without being satirical.
2. Epsom is known both for its medicinal mineral springs and for horse racing, so Walter Shandy may have been either sick or losing money while he was there.
3. "The sad one."
4. "The nature of things."

would sometimes break off in a sudden and spirited EPIPHONEMA,[5] or rather EROTESIS, raised a third, and sometimes a full fifth, above the key of the discourse,——and demand it catagorically of his antagonist, Whether he would take upon him to say, he had ever remember'd,——whether he had ever read,——or even whether he had ever heard tell of a man, call'd *Tristram*, performing any thing great or worth recording?——No——, he would say,——TRISTRAM!——The thing is impossible.

What could be wanting in my father but to have wrote a book to publish this notion of his to the world? Little boots it to the subtle speculatist to stand single in his opinions,——unless he gives them proper vent:——It was the identical thing which my father did; ——for in the year sixteen, which was two years before I was born, he was at the pains of writing an express DISSERTATION simply upon the word *Tristram*,——shewing the world, with great candour and modesty, the grounds of his great abhorrence to the name.

When this story is compared with the title-page,——Will not the gentle reader pity my father from his soul?——to see an orderly and well-disposed gentleman, who tho' singular,——yet inoffensive in his notions,——so played upon in them by cross purposes;——to look down upon the stage, and see him baffled and overthrown in all his little systems and wishes; to behold a train of events perpetually falling out against him, and in so critical and cruel a way, as if they had purposedly been plann'd and pointed against him, merely to insult his speculations.——In a word, to behold such a one, in his old age, ill-fitted for troubles, ten times in a day suffering sorrow; ——ten times in a day calling the child of his prayers TRISTRAM! ——Melancholy dissyllable of sound! which, to his ears, was unison to *Nicompoop*, and every name vituperative under heaven.——By his ashes! I swear it,——if ever malignant spirit took pleasure, or busied itself in traversing the purposes of mortal man,——it must have been here;——and if it was not necessary I should be born before I was christened, I would this moment give the reader an account of it.

Chapter XX.

——How could you, Madam, be so inattentive in reading the last chapter? I told you in it, *That my mother was not a papist.*—— Papist! You told me no such thing, Sir. Madam, I beg leave to repeat it over again, That I told you as plain, at least, as words, by direct inference, could tell you such a thing.——Then, Sir, I must have miss'd a page.——No, Madam,——you have not miss'd a

---

5. An exclamatory phrase ending a discourse. "Erotesis" is a rhetorical question (a good example follows the reference).

Volume I. Chapter XX.

word.——Then I was asleep, Sir.——My pride, Madam, allow you that refuge.——Then, I declare, I know nothing at all about the matter.——That, Madam, is the very fault I lay to your charge; and as a punishment for it, I do insist upon it, that you immediately turn back, that is, as soon as you get to the next full stop, and read the whole chapter over again.

I have imposed this penance upon the lady, neither out of wantonness or cruelty, but from the best of motives; and therefore shall make her no apology for it when she returns back:——'Tis to rebuke a vicious taste which has crept into thousands besides herself,——of reading straight forwards, more in quest of the adventures, than of the deep erudition and knowledge which a book of this cast, if read over as it should be, would infallibly impart with them.——The mind should be accustomed to make wise reflections, and draw curious conclusions as it goes along; the habitude of which made *Pliny* the younger[6] affirm, "That he never read a book so bad, but he drew some profit from it." The stories of *Greece* and *Rome*, run over without this turn and application,——do less service, I affirm it, than the history of *Parismus* and *Parismenus*,[7] or of the Seven Champions of *England*, read with it.

————But here comes my fair Lady. Have you read over again the chapter, Madam, as I desired you?——You have: And did you not observe the passage, upon the second reading, which admits the inference?——Not a word like it! Then, Madam, be pleased to ponder well the last line but one of the chapter, where I take upon me to say, "It was *necessary* I should be born before I was christen'd." Had my mother, Madam, been a Papist, that consequence did not follow.[8]

It is a terrible misfortune for this same book of mine, but more so to the Republick of Letters;——so that my own is quite swallowed up in the consideration of it,——that this self-same vile pruriency

6. Pliny the Younger, an ancient Roman writer and statesman, actually makes this statement about his uncle, Pliny the Elder, not about himself (*Letters*, III.5).
7. These are all traditional English tales.
8. The *Romish* Rituals direct the baptizing of the child, in cases of danger, *before* it is born;—but upon this proviso, That some part or other of the child's body be seen by the baptizer:——But the Doctors of the *Sorbonne*, by a deliberation held amongst them, *April* 10, 1733,—have enlarged the powers of midwives, by determining, That tho' no part of the child's body should appear,—— that baptism shall, nevertheless, be administered to it by injection,—*par le moyen d'une petite Canulle*,——Anglice, *a squirt*. [By means of a small injection-pipe.—In English, a squirt.]—'Tis very strange that St *Thomas Aquinas*, who had so good a mechanical head, both for tying and untying the knots of school-divinity,—should, after so much pains bestowed upon this,—give up the point at last, as a second *La chose impossible* [The impossible thing.];—"*Infantes in maternis uteris existentes* (quoth St. *Thomas*) *baptizari possunt nullo modo.*" [Infants in maternal wombs cannot be baptized by any means."]—O *Thomas! Thomas!*

If the reader has the curiosity to see the question upon baptism, *by injection*, as presented to the Doctors of the *Sorbonne*,—with their consultation thereupon, it is as follows. [*Sterne's note.*]

for fresh adventures in all things, has got so strongly into our habit and humours,——and so wholly intent are we upon satisfying the impatience of our concupiscence that way,——that nothing but the gross and more carnal parts of a composition will go down:—— The subtle hints and sly communications of science fly off, like spirits, upwards;——the heavy moral escapes downwards; and both the one and the other are as much lost to the world, as if they were still left in the bottom of the ink-horn.

I wish the male-reader has not pass'd by many a one, as quaint and curious as this one, in which the female-reader has been detected. I wish it may have its effects;——and that all good people, both male and female, from her example, may be taught to think as well as read.

MEMOIRE presenté à Messieurs les Docteurs de SORBONNE.

UN *Chirurgien Accoucheur, represente à Messieurs les Doctueurs de Sorbonne, qu'il y a des cas, quoique trés rares, où une mere ne sçauroit accoucher, & même où l'enfant est tellement renfermé dans le sein de sa mere, qu'il ne fait paroître aucune partie de son corps, ce qui seroit un cas, suivant les Rituels, de lui conférer, du moins sous condition, le baptême. Le Chirurgien, qui consulte, prétend, par le moyen d'une* petite canulle, *de pouvoir baptiser immediatement l'enfant, sans faire aucun tort à la mere.*——Il *demande si ce moyen, qu'il vient de proposer, est permis & légitime, et s'il peut s'en servir dans le cas qu'il vient d'exposer.*

RESPONSE

LE *Conseil estime, que la question proposée souffre de grandes difficultés. Les Théologiens posent d'un côté pour principe, que le baptême, qui est une naissance spirituelle, suppose une premiere naissance; il faut être né dans le monde, pour renaître en* Jesus Christ, *comme ils l'enseignent.* S. Thomas, 3 part. quæst. 68. artic. II. *suit cette doctrine comme une verité constante; l'on ne peut, dit ce* S. Docteur, *baptiser les enfans qui sont renfermés dans le sein de leurs Meres, et* S. Thomas *est fondé sur ce, que les enfans ne sont point nés, & ne peuvent être comtpés parmi les autres hommes; d'où il conclud, qu'ils ne peuvent être l'object d'une action extérieure, pour recevoir par leur ministére, les sacremens nécessaires au salut:* Pueri in maternis uteris existentes nondum prodierunt in lucem ut cum aliis hominibus vitam ducant; unde non possunt subjici actioni humanæ, ut per eorum ministerium sacramenta recipiant ad salutem. *Les rituels ordonnent dans la pratique ce que les théologiens ont établi sur les mêmes matiéres, & ils deffendent tous d'une maniére uniforme de baptiser les enfans qui sont renfermés dans le sein de leurs meres, s'ils ne font paroître quelque partie de leurs corps. Le concours des théologiens, & des rituels, qui sont les règles des diocéses, paroît former une autorité qui termine la question presente; cependant le conseil de conscience considerant d'un côté, que le raisonnement des théologiens est uniquement fondé sur une raison de convenance, & que la deffense des rituels, suppose que l'on ne peut baptiser immediatement les enfans ainsi renfermés dans le sein de leurs meres, ce qui est contre la supposition presente; & d'un autre côté, considerant que les mêmes théologiens enseignent, que l'on peut risquer les sacremens qu' Jesus Christ a établis comme des moyens faciles, mais nécessaires pour sanctifier les hommes; & d'ailleurs estimant, que les enfans renfermés dans le sein de leurs meres, pourroient être capables de salut, parce qu'ils sont capables de damnation;——pour ces considerations, & en égard à l'exposé, suivant lequel on assure avoir trouvé un moyen certain de baptiser ces enfans ainsi renfermés, sans faire aucun tort à la mere, le Conseil estime que l'on pourroit se servir du moyen proposé, dans la confiance qu'il a, que Dieu n'a point laissé ces sortes d'enfans sans aucuns secours, & supposant, comme il est exposé, que le moyen dont il s'agit est propre à leur procurer le baptême; cependant comme il s'agiroit, en autorisant la pratique proposée, de changer une règle universellement établie, le Conseil croit que celui qui consulte doit s'addresser à son évêque, & à qui il appartient de juger de l'utilité, & du danger du moyen proposé, & comme, sous le bon plaisir de l'évêque, le conseil estime qu'il faudroit recourir au Pape, qui a le droit d'expliquer les règles de l'église, et d'y déroger dans le cas, où la loi ne sçauroit obliger, quelque sage & quelque utile que paroisse la maniére de baptiser dont il s'agit, le conseil ne pourroit l'approuver sans le concours de ces deux autorités. On conseille au moins à celui qui consulte, de s'addresser à son évêque, & de lui faire part de la presente décision, afin que, si le prelat entre dans les raisons sur lesquelles les docteurs soussignés s'appuyent, il puisse être autorisé dans le cas de nécessité, où il risqueroit trop d'attendre que la permission fût demandée & accordée d'employer le moyen qu'il propose si avantageux au salut de l'enfant. Au reste le conseil, en estimant que l'on pourroit s'en servir croit cependant, que si les enfans dont il s'agit, venoient au monde, contre l'esperance de ceux qui se seroient servis du même moyen, il seroit nécessaire de les baptiser* sous condition, *& en cela le conseil se conforme à tous les rituels, qui en autorisant le baptême d'un enfant qui fait paroître*

44 · *Tristram Shandy*

quelque partie de son corps, enjoignent néanmoins, & ordonnent de le baptiser sous condition, *s'il vient heureusement au monde.*
Déliberé en *Sorbonne,* le 10 Avril, 1733.

A. Le Moyne,
L. De Romigny,
De Marcilly.[9]

9. Sterne informs us in a note to the second edition that the passage is from Heinrich van Deventer, *Observations importantes sur le manuel des accouchemens* [*Important Observations on the Manual of Childbirth*], 1734. A translation follows:
> *Memorandum* presented to the
> Doctors of the *Sorbonne*
An obstetrician-surgeon shows to the Doctors of the *Sorbonne* that there are certain cases, although very rare, when a mother cannot find a way to deliver, or even when an infant is so enclosed in the womb of its mother that it does not allow the slightest part of its body to show, which would be a case, according to the Rituals, of conferring baptism upon it, at least conditionally. This consulting-surgeon claims to be able to baptize the infant directly, without harming the mother, by means of a *small nozzle*. But he asks if this method which he has just proposed, is permitted and legitimate and if he can use it in such a case as he has just described.
> *Reply*
The Council deems that the matter proposed presents great problems. The theologians, for their part, put down as a matter of principle that baptism, which is a spiritual birth, presupposes a prior birth; one must be born into the world to be reborn in *Jesus Christ,* according to their doctrines. S. *Thomas, part 3, question 68, article 11,* follows this doctrine as a steadfast truth; one cannot, says this Holy Doctor, baptize infants who are enclosed in the womb of their mothers, and S. *Thomas* is justified on this account, that such infants are not at all born and cannot be counted among other men; from this he concludes that they may not be the object of an exterior action, to receive by men's ministry the sacraments necessary for salvation: *Children existing in their mothers' wombs have not yet come forth into the light of day so that they may not live with other men; therefore, they cannot be subjected to any human action, so that they may not receive salvation through the sacraments of men's ministry.* The rituals prescribe in practice what the theologians have established in the same matters and they prohibit all in a uniform manner from baptizing infants enclosed in the wombs of their mother, if they don't let

appear some part of their bodies. The consistency between the theologians and the rituals which are the rules of the dioceses appear to constitute an authority which solves the present problem; however, in conscience, the council considering on the one hand that the argument of the theologians is only based on practical grounds and that the prohibition from rituals assumes that one cannot baptize directly infants thus enclosed in the wombs of their mothers, which is contrary to the present supposition; and, on the other hand, considering what the theologians themselves teach that risks may be hazarded to administer the sacraments established by *Jesus Christ* as easy but necessary means for sanctifying men; and considering besides that such infants enclosed in the wombs of their mothers may be capable of salvation because they are capable of damnation; for these considerations and with regard to the report, according to which it is certain that a method of baptizing these infants thus enclosed has been discovered, without doing any harm to their mothers, the council deems that the method proposed would be practicable, in the confidence that God has not at all left these kinds of infants without succor, and supposing, as it is reported, that the method at question is proper for procuring them baptism; however, as it would be a matter of changing a universally established rule, by authorizing the proposed practice, the Council believes that he who consults ought to address himself to his bishop and to whoever is fit to judge of the expediency and of the danger of the proposed method and so, with the good will of the bishop, the Council deems that it would be necessary to have recourse to the Pope who has the right of explicating the rules of the church and of modifying them in the event that the law would not know how to oblige, however wise and however expedient this method of baptism in question might appear, the Council could not approve it without the agreement of these two authorities. It is advised at least to the one who is consulting to address himself to his bishop and to make him a party to the decision so that, if the prelate enters into the reasons upon which the undersigned doctors rely, he could be authorized in a matter of neces-

Mr. *Tristram Shandy's compliments* to Messrs. *Le Moyne, De Romigny,* and *De Marcilly,* hopes they all rested well the night after so tiresome a consultation.——He begs to know, whether, after the ceremony of marriage, and before that of consummation, the baptizing all the HOMUNCULI at once, slap-dash, by *injection,* would not be a shorter and safer cut still; on condition, as above, That if the HOMUNCULI do well and come safe into the world after this, That each and every of them shall be baptized again (*sous condition.*[1])

——And provided, in the second place, That the thing can be done, which Mr. *Shandy* apprehends it may, *par le moyen d'une* petite canulle, and *sans faire aucun tort au pere.*[2]

Chapter XXI.

——I wonder what's all that noise, and running backwards and forwards for, above stairs, quoth my father, addressing himself, after an hour and a half's silence, to my uncle *Toby,*——who you must know, was sitting on the opposite side of the fire, smoking his social pipe all the time, in mute contemplation of a new pair of black-plush-breeches which he had got on;——What can they be doing brother? quoth my father,——we can scarce hear ourselves talk.

I think, replied my uncle *Toby,* taking his pipe from his mouth, and striking the head of it two or three times upon the nail of his left thumb, as he began his sentence,——I think, says he:——But to enter rightly into my uncle *Toby's* sentiments upon this matter, you must be made to enter first a little into his character, the outlines of which I shall just give you, and then the dialogue between him and my father will go on as well again.

——Pray what was that man's name,——for I write in such a hurry, I have no time to recollect or look for it,——who first made the observation, "That there was great inconstancy in our air and

---

sity when it would be too hazardous to wait for asking permission and accord for employing the method that he proposes as so advantageous for the salvation of the infant. Moreover, the Council, in deeming that it could be used, believes however that if the infants in question come forth into the world, contrary to the expectation of those who would make use of this same method, it would be necessary to baptize them *conditionally,* and, in this matter, the Council, which, in authorizing the baptism of an infant who shows some part of his body, conforms to all the Rituals, enjoins and ordains nevertheless baptizing it *condi-*

tionally, if it comes forth into the world successfully.

Deliberated at the Sorbonne, *10* April, *1733.*

A. LE MOYNE,
L. DE ROMIGNY,
DE MARCILLY.

1. Conditional baptism was the term for that bestowed upon a child who had alraedy been baptized, or who might be dead, or who was in such condition that its very humanity was in doubt. So "conditional baptism" became a kind of joke, suggesting someone was very ugly.
2. "By means of a *little nozzle,* and without doing any harm to the father."

climate?"[3] Whoever he was, 'twas a just and good observation in him.——But the corollary drawn from it, namely, "That it is this which has furnished us with such a variety of odd and whimsical characters;"——that was not his;——it was found out by another man, at least a century and a half after him:——Then again,—— that this copious store-house of original materials, is the true and natural cause that our Comedies are so much better than those of *France*, or any others that either have, or can be wrote upon the Continent;——that discovery was not fully made till about the middle of king *William's* reign,——when the great *Dryden*, in writing one of his long prefaces, (if I mistake not) most fortunately hit upon it. Indeed towards the latter end of queen *Anne*, the great *Addison* began to patronize the notion, and more fully explained it to the world in one or two of his Spectators;——but the discovery was not his.——Then, fourthly and lastly, that this strange irregularity in our climate, producing so strange an irregularity in our characters,——doth thereby, in some sort, make us amends, by giving us somewhat to make us merry with when the weather will not suffer us to go out of doors,——that observation is my own; ——and was struck out by me this very rainy day, *March* 26, 1759, and betwixt the hours of nine and ten in the morning.

Thus,——thus my fellow labourers and associates in this great harvest of our learning, now ripening before our eyes; thus it is, by slow steps of casual increase, that our knowledge physical, metaphysical, physiological, polemical, nautical, mathematical, ænigmatical, technical, biographical, romantical, chemical, and obstetrical, with fifty other branches of it, (most of 'em ending, as these do, in *ical*) have, for these two last centuries and more, gradually been creeping upwards towards that Ακμη[4] of their perfections, from which, if we may form a conjecture from the advances of these last seven years, we cannot possibly be far off.

When that happens, it is to be hoped, it will put an end to all kind of writings whatsoever;——the want of all kind of writing will put an end to all kind of reading;——and that in time, As *war begets poverty, poverty peace*,[5]——must, in course, put an end to all kind of knowledge,——and then——we shall have all to begin over again; or, in other words, be exactly where we started.

——Happy! thrice happy Times! I only wish that the æra of my begetting, as well as the mode and manner of it, had been a little alter'd,——or that it could have been put off with any convenience

3. The idea that the irregularity of the English climate contributes to the eccentricity of the inhabitants is an old one that reached great popularity in the century before *Trisram Shandy*. John Dryden brings it up in *An Essay of Dramatic Poesy* (1668), and Joseph Addison in his periodical *The Spectator*, No. 371 (1712), where he also mentions the siege of Namur.

4. "Acme."

5. These are lines from a popular song.

to my father or mother, for some twenty or five-and-twer
longer, when a man in the literary world might have sto _ _____
chance.——

But I forget my uncle *Toby*, whom all this while we have left
knocking the ashes out of his tobacco pipe.

His humour was of that particular species, which does honour to
our atmosphere; and I should have made no scruple of ranking him
amongst one of the first-rate productions of it, had not there appear'd too many strong lines in it of a family-likeness, which
shewed that he derived the singularity of his temper more from
blood, than either wind or water, or any modifications or combinations of them whatever: And I have, therefore, oft times wondered,
that my father, tho' I believe he had his reasons for it, upon his
observing some tokens of excentricity in my course when I was a
boy,——should never once endeavour to account for them in this
way; for all the SHANDY FAMILY were of an original character
throughout;——I mean the males,——the females had no character
at all,——except, indeed, my great aunt DINAH, who, about sixty
years ago, was married and got with child by the coachman, for
which my father, according to his hypothesis of Christian names,
would often say, She might thank her godfathers and godmothers.[6]

It will seem very strange,——and I would as soon think of dropping a riddle in the reader's way, which is not my interest to do, as
set him upon guessing how it could come to pass, that an event of
this kind, so many years after it had happened, should be reserved
for the interruption of the peace and unity, which otherwise so
cordially subsisted, between my father and my uncle *Toby*. One
would have thought, that the whole force of the misfortune should
have spent and wasted itself in the family at first,——as is generally
the case:——But nothing ever wrought with our family after the
ordinary way. Possibly at the very time this happened, it might have
something else to afflict it; and as afflictions are sent down for·our
good, and that as this had never done the SHANDY FAMILY any good
at all, it might lye waiting till apt times and circumstances should
give it an opportunity to discharge its office.——Observe, I determine nothing upon this.——My way is ever to point out to the
curious, different tracts of investigation, to come at the first springs
of the events I tell;——not with a pedantic *Fescue*,[7]——or in the
decisive Manner of *Tacitus*, who outwits himself and his reader;
——but with the officious humility of a heart devoted to the assistance merely of the inquisitive;——to them I write,——and by

6. Walter Shandy may have in mind
that her godparents should have remembered Genesis 34, where Dinah, daughter of Jacob and Leah, is defiled by
Shechem.

7. A *fescue* is a pointer used for directing the attention of children learning to
read. Tacitus was an ancient Roman historian whose style is sometimes so concise that his meaning becomes unclear.

them I shall be read,——if any such reading as this could be supposed to hold out so long, to the very end of the world.

Why this cause of sorrow, therefore, was thus reserved for my
father and uncle, is undetermined by me. But how and in what
direction it exerted itself, so as to become the cause of dissatisfac-
tion between them, after it began to operate, is what I am able to
explain with great exactness, and is as follows:

My uncle TOBY SHANDY, Madam, was a gentleman, who, with the
virtues which usually constitute the character of a man of honour
and rectitude,——possessed one in a very eminent degree, which is
seldom or never put into the catalogue; and that was a most extream and unparallel'd modesty of nature;——tho' I correct the
word nature, for this reason, that I may not prejudge a point which
must shortly come to a hearing; and that is, Whether this modesty
of his was natural or acquir'd.——Which ever way my uncle *Toby*
came by it, 'twas nevertheless modesty in the truest sense of it; and
that is, Madam, not in regard to words, for he was so unhappy as to
have very little choice in them,——but to things;——and this kind
of modesty so possess'd him, and it arose to such a height in him, as
almost to equal, if such a thing could be, even the modesty of a
woman: That female nicety, Madam, and inward cleanliness of
mind and fancy, in your sex, which makes you so much the awe of
ours.

You will imagine, Madam, that my uncle *Toby* had contracted all
this from this very source;——that he had spent a great part of his
time in converse with your sex; and that, from a thorough knowledge of you, and the force of imitation which such fair examples
render irresistable,——he had acquired this amiable turn of mind.

I wish I could say so,——for unless it was with his sister-in-law,
my father's wife and my mother,——my uncle *Toby* scarce exchanged three words with the sex in as many years;——no, he got
it, Madam, by a blow.——A blow!——Yes, Madam, it was owing
to a blow from a stone, broke off by a ball from the parapet of a
horn-work at the siege of *Namur*,[8] which struck full upon my uncle
Toby's groin.—Which way could that effect it? The story of that,
Madam, is long and interesting;——but it would be running my
history all upon heaps to give it you here.——'Tis for an episode
hereafter; and every circumstance relating to it in its proper place,
shall be faithfully laid before you:——'Till then, it is not in my
power to give further light into this matter, or say more than what I
have said already,——That my uncle *Toby* was a gentleman of
unparallel'd modesty, which happening to be somewhat subtilized

8. A horn work is a peculiarly-shaped
military barricade, probably selected by
Sterne to allow play on the sexual implications of "horn." Namur, in Flanders (southwest Belgium) was captured
by the Allied force of the British, Dutch,
and Germans under William III in August, 1695.

and rarified by the constant heat of a little family-pride,——they both so wrought together within him, that he could never bear to hear the affair of my aunt DINAH touch'd upon, but with the greatest emotion.——The least hint of it was enough to make the blood fly into his face;——but when my father enlarged upon the story in mixed companies, which the illustration of his hypothesis frequently obliged him to do,——the unfortunate blight of one of the fairest branches of the family, would set my uncle *Toby*'s honour and modesty o'bleeding; and he would often take my father aside, in the greatest concern imaginable, to expostulate and tell him, he would give him any thing in the world, only to let the story rest.

My father, I believe, had the truest love and tenderness for my uncle *Toby*, that ever one brother bore towards another, and would have done any thing in nature, which one brother in reason could have desir'd of another, to have made my uncle *Toby*'s heart easy in this, or any other point. But this lay out of his power.

——My father, as I told you, was a philosopher in grain,—— speculative,——systematical;——and my aunt *Dinah*'s affair was a matter of as much consequence to him, as the retrogradation of the planets to *Copernicus*:[9]——The backslidings of *Venus* in her orbit fortified the *Copernican* system, call'd so after his name; and the backslidings of my aunt *Dinah* in her orbit, did the same service in establishing my father's system, which, I trust, will for ever hereafter be call'd the *Shandean System*, after his.

In any other family dishonour, my father, I believe, had as nice a sense of shame as any man whatever;——and neither he, nor, I dare say, *Copernicus*, would have divulged the affair in either case, or have taken the least notice of it to the world, but for the obligations they owed, as they thought, to truth.——*Amicus Plato*, my father would say, construing the words to my uncle *Toby*, as he went along, *Amicus Plato*; that is, DINAH was my aunt;——*sed magis amica veritas*[1]——but TRUTH is my sister.

This contrariety of humours betwixt my father and my uncle, was the source of many a fraternal squabble. The one could not bear to hear the tale of family disgrace recorded,——and the other would scarce ever let a day pass to an end without some hint at it.

For God's sake, my uncle *Toby* would cry,——and for my sake, and for all our sakes, my dear brother *Shandy*,——do let this story of our aunt's and her ashes sleep in peace;——how can you,——

---

9. Nicolaus Copernicus was the Polish astronomer whose work in the early-sixteenth century established the foundation of modern astronomical theory. He argued that apparent retrogradation ("backsliding") of the planets is an illusion caused by the fact that some of them revolve around the sun more slowly than does the Earth.
1. "Plato is dear to me, but dearer still is truth."

how can you have so little feeling and compassion for the character of our family:——What is the character of a family to an hypothesis? my father would reply.——Nay, if you come to that——what is the life of a family:——The life of a family!——my uncle *Toby* would say, throwing himself back in his arm-chair, and lifting up his hands, his eyes, and one leg.——Yes the life,——my father would say, maintaining his point. How many thousands of 'em are there every year that come cast away, (in all civilized countries at least)——and consider'd as nothing but common air, in competition of an hypothesis. In my plain sense of things, my uncle *Toby* would answer,——every such instance is downright MURDER, let who will commit it.——There lies your mistake, my father would reply;——for, in *Foro Scientiæ*[2] there is no such thing as MURDER, ——'tis only DEATH, brother.

My uncle *Toby* would never offer to answer this by any other kind of argument, than that of whistling half a dozen bars of *Lillabullero*.[3]——You must know it was the usual channel thro' which his passions got vent, when any thing shocked or surprised him;——but especially when any thing, which he deem'd very absurd, was offered.

As not one of our logical writers, nor any of the commentators upon them, that I remember, have thought proper to give a name to this particular species of argument,——I here take the liberty to do it myself, for two reasons. First, That, in order to prevent all confusion in disputes, it may stand as much distinguished for ever, from every other species of argument,——as the *Argumentum ad Verecundiam*,[4] *ex Absurdo*, *ex Fortiori*, or any other argument whatsoever:——And, secondly, That it may be said by my children's children, when my head is laid to rest,——that their learned grandfather's head had been busied to as much purpose once, as other people's:——That he had invented a name,——and generously thrown it into the TREASURY of the *Ars Logica*, for one of the most unanswerable arguments in the whole science. And if the end of disputation is more to silence than convince,——they may add, if they please, to one of the best arguments too.

I do therefore, by these presents, strictly order and command,

2. "The forum (or field) of knowledge."
3. Protestants used this song, with its title drawn from what had originally been a Catholic slogan, as an infuriating taunt against their opponents in the Irish wars of the late seventeenth century.
4. *Argumentum ad Verecundiam*: "argument to modesty"; *ex Absurdo*: "from absurdity"; *ex Fortiori*: "from stronger reasons"; *Ars Logica*: "the art of logic"; *Argumentum Fistulatorium*: "argument of the (musical) pipe"; *Argumentum Baculinum*: "argument of the stick" (i.e., threat); *Argumentum ad Crumenam*: "argument to the purse" (i.e., to self-interest); *Argumentum Tripodium*: "argument to the third leg"; *Argumentum ad Rem*: "argument to the thing in hand." These are all terms used in classical logic, except fistulatorium ("whistle") and tripodium ("third leg"), which Sterne made up to serve his own purposes.

That it be known and distinguished by the name and t
Argumentum Fistulatorium, and no other;——and th
hereafter with the *Argumentum Baculinum,* and the *Ar*
ad Crumenam, and for ever hereafter be treated of in the same
chapter.

As for the *Argumentum Tripodium,* which is never used but by
the woman against the man;——and the *Argumentum ad Rem,*
which, contrarywise, is made use of by the man only against the
woman:——As these two are enough in conscience for one lecture;
——and, moreover, as the one is the best answer to the other,——
let them likewise be kept apart, and be treated of in a place by
themselves.

Chapter XXII.

THE learned Bishop *Hall,* I mean the famous Dr. *Joseph Hall,*
who was Bishop of *Exeter* in King *James* the first's reign, tells
us in one of his *Decads,* at the end of his divine art of meditation,
imprinted at *London,* in the year 1610, by *John Beal,* dwelling in
Aldergate-street, "That it is an abominable thing for a man to
commend himself;"——and I really think it is so.

And yet, on the other hand, when a thing is executed in a masterly kind of a fashion, which thing is not likely to be found out;
——I think it is full as abominable, that a man should lose the
honour of it, and go out of the world with the conceit of it rotting
in his head.

This is precisely my situation.

For in this long digression which I was accidentally led into, as
in all my digressions (one only excepted) there is a master-stroke of
digressive skill, the merit of which has all along, I fear, been overlooked by my reader,——not for want of penetration in him,——
but because 'tis an excellence seldom looked for, or expected indeed, in a digression;——and it is this: That tho' my digressions are
all fair, as you observe,——and that I fly off from what I am about,
as far and as often too as any writer in *Great Britain;* yet I constantly take care to order affairs so, that my main business does not
stand still in my absence.

I was just going, for example, to have given you the great out-
lines of my uncle *Toby's* most whimsical character;——when my
aunt *Dinah* and the coachman came a-cross us, and led us a vagary
some millions of miles into the very heart of the planetary system:
Notwithstanding all this, you perceive that the drawing of my uncle
Toby's character went on gently all the time;——not the great
contours of it,——that was impossible,——but some familiar
strokes and faint designations of it, were here and there touch'd in,

as we went along, so that you are much better acquainted with my uncle *Toby* now than you was before.

By this contrivance the machinery of my work is of a species by itself; two contrary motions are introduced into it, and reconciled, which were thought to be at variance with each other. In a word, my work is digressive, and it is progressive too,——and at the same time.

This, Sir, is a very different story from that of the earth's moving round her axis, in her diurnal rotation, with her progress in her elliptick orbit which brings about the year, and constitutes that variety and vicissitude of seasons we enjoy;——though I own it suggested the thought,——as I believe the greatest of our boasted improvements and discoveries have come from some such trifling hints.

Digressions, incontestably, are the sunshine;——they are the life, the soul of reading;——take them out of this book for instance, ——you might as well take the book along with them;——one cold eternal winter would reign in every page of it; restore them to the writer;——he steps forth like a bridegroom,——bids All hail; brings in variety, and forbids the appetite to fail.

All the dexterity is in the good cookery and management of them, so as to be not only for the advantage of the reader, but also of the author, whose distress, in this matter, is truely pitiable: For, if he begins a digression,——from that moment, I observe, his whole work stands stock-still;——and if he goes on with his main work, ——then there is an end of his digression.

——This is vile work.——For which reason, from the beginning of this, you see, I have constructed the main work and the adventitious parts of it with such intersections, and have so complicated and involved the digressive and progressive movements, one wheel within another, that the whole machine, in general, has been kept a-going;——and, what's more, it shall be kept a-going these forty years, if it pleases the fountain of health to bless me so long with life and good spirits.

Chapter XXIII.

I Have a strong propensity in me to begin this chapter very non-sensically, and I will not balk my fancy.——Accordingly I set off thus.

If the fixure of *Momus*'s glass,[5] in the human breast, according to the proposed emendation of that arch-critick, had taken place,

---

5. Momus is a Greek figure who personifies mockery. He criticized Hephaestus, the workman god, for not fitting a window into the breast of a model human being he made.

——first, This foolish consequence would certainly have followed, ——That the very wisest and the very gravest of us all, in one coin or other, must have paid window-money[6] every day of our lives.

And, secondly, That had the said glass been there set up, nothing more would have been wanting, in order to have taken a man's character, but to have taken a chair and gone softly, as you would to a dioptrical bee-hive, and look'd in,——view'd the soul stark naked;——observ'd all her motions,——her machinations;—— traced all her maggots from their first engendering to their crawling forth;——watched her loose in her frisks, her gambols, her capri-cios; and after some notice of her more solemn deportment, conse-quent upon such frisks, *&c.*——then taken your pen and ink and set down nothing but what you had seen, and could have sworn to: ——But this is an advantage not to be had by the biographer in this planet,——in the planet *Mercury* (belike) it may be so, if not better still for him;——for there the intense heat of the country, which is proved by computators, from its vicinity to the sun, to be more than equal to that of red hot iron,——must, I think, long ago have vitrified the bodies of the inhabitants, (as the efficient cause[7]) to suit them for the climate (which is the final cause); so that, betwixt them both, all the tenements of their souls, from top to bottom, may be nothing else, for aught the soundest philosophy can shew to the contrary, but one fine transparent body of clear glass (bating the umbilical knot);——so, that till the inhabitants grow old and tolerably wrinkled, whereby the rays of light, in passing through them, become so monstrously refracted,——or return re-flected from their surfaces in such transverse lines to the eye, that a man cannot be seen thro';——his soul might as well, unless, for more ceremony,——or the trifling advantage which the umbilical point gave her,——might, upon all other accounts, I say, as well play the fool out o'doors as in her own house.

But this, as I said above, is not the case of the inhabitants of this earth;——our minds shine not through the body, but are wrapt up here in a dark covering of uncrystalized flesh and blood; so that if we would come to the specifick characters of them, we must go some other way to work.

Many, in good truth, are the ways which human wit has been forced to take to do this thing with exactness.

Some, for instance, draw all their characters with wind instru-ments.——*Virgil* takes notice of that way in the affair of *Dido* and *Æneas*,[8]——but it is as fallacious as the breath of fame;——and,

6. A tax on windows when glass was a luxury.
7. Tristram is saying that heat consti-tutes the active force ("efficient cause") that would turn men to glass, making it possible for them to survive ("final cause" or purpose) on the planet Mer-cury.
8. In Book Four of the *Aeneid*, Virgil has Fame (sometimes as a trumpet) spread word of the love affair of Dido and Aeneas.

moreover, bespeaks a narrow genius. I am not ignorant that the *Italians* pretend to a mathematical exactness in their designations of one particular sort of character among them, from the *forte* or *piano*[9] of a certain wind instrument they use,——which they say is infallible.——I dare not mention the name of the instrument in this place;——'tis sufficient we have it amongst us,——but never think of making a drawing by it;——this is ænigmatical, and intended to be so, at least, *ad populum*:[1]——And therefore I beg, Madam, when you come here, that you read on as fast as you can, and never stop to make any inquiry about it.

There are others again, who will draw a man's character from no other helps in the world, but merely from his evacuations;——but this often gives a very incorrect out-line,——unless, indeed, you take a sketch of his repletions too; and by correcting one drawing from the other, compound one good figure out of them both.

I should have no objection to this method, but that I think it must smell too strong of the lamp,[2]——and be render'd still more operose, by forcing you to have an eye to the rest of his *Non-Naturals*.[3]——Why the most natural actions of a man's life should be call'd his Non-Naturals,——is another question.

There are others, fourthly, who disdain every one of these expedients;——not from any fertility of their own, but from the various ways of doing it, which they have borrowed from the honourable devices which the Pentagraphic Brethren[4] of the brush have shewn in taking copies.——These, you must know, are your great historians.

One of these you will see drawing a full-length character *against the light*;——that's illiberal,——dishonest,——and hard upon the character of the man who sits.

Others, to mend the matter, will make a drawing of you in the *Camera*;[5]——that is most unfair of all,——because, *there* you are sure to be represented in some of your most ridiculous attitudes.

To avoid all and every one of these errors, in giving you my uncle *Toby*'s character, I am determin'd to draw it by no mechanical help whatever;——nor shall my pencil be guided by any one wind instrument which ever was blown upon, either on this, or on the other

9. Loud or soft.
1. "To the people." Sterne may want us to think of the *castrati*, young boys castrated to sing soprano in Italian operas, but other kinds of physiological associations are just as much to the point.
2. Over-ingenious, requiring too much working out (by lamplight).
3. Air; meat and drink; sleep and waking; motion and rest; excretion and retention; affections of mind—six things seen by physicians as vital to life, but "non-natural" because they could become sources of disease.
4. Pentagraph, an instrument to copy prints and pictures mechanically, and in any proportion. [*Sterne's note.*]
5. The camera obscura, a darkened chamber or box containing a lens through which light passes to project a traceable image on a paper—an aid to amateur artists. Sterne invites other associations of the word *chamber*, as well.

side of the *Alps*;——nor will I consider either his repletions or his discharges,——or touch upon his Non-Naturals;——but, in a word, I will draw my uncle *Toby*'s character from his HOBBY-HORSE.

Chapter XXIV.

IF I was not morally sure that the reader must be out of all patience for my uncle *Toby*'s character,——I would here previously have convinced him, that there is no instrument so fit to draw such a thing with, as that which I have pitch'd upon.

A man and his HOBBY-HORSE, tho' I cannot say that they act and re-act exactly after the same manner in which the soul and body do upon each other: Yet doubtless there is a communication between them of some kind, and my opinion rather is, that there is something in it more of the manner of electrified bodies,——and that by means of the heated parts of the rider, which come immediately into contact with the back of the HOBBY-HORSE.——By long journies and much friction, it so happens that the body of the rider is at length fill'd as full of HOBBY-HORSICAL matter as it can hold;——so that if you are able to give but a clear description of the nature of the one, you may form a pretty exact notion of the genius and character of the other.

Now the HOBBY-HORSE which my uncle *Toby* always rode upon, was, in my opinion, an HOBBY-HORSE well worth giving a description of, if it was only upon the score of his great singularity; for you might have travelled from *York* to *Dover*,——from *Dover* to *Penzance* in *Cornwall*, and from *Penzance* to *York* back again, and not have seen such another upon the road; or if you had seen such a one, whatever haste you had been in, you must infallibly have stopp'd to have taken a view of him. Indeed, the gait and figure of him was so strange, and so utterly unlike was he, from his head to his tail, to any one of the whole species, that it was now and then made a matter of dispute,——whether he was really a HOBBY-HORSE or no: But as the Philosopher[6] would use no other argument to the sceptic, who disputed with him against the reality of motion, save that of rising up upon his legs, and walking a-cross the room; ——so would my uncle *Toby* use no other argument to prove his HOBBY-HORSE was a HOBBY-HORSE indeed, but by getting upon his back and riding him about;——leaving the world after that to determine the point as it thought fit.

In good truth, my uncle *Toby* mounted him with so much pleasure, and he carried my uncle *Toby* so well,——that he troubled his

---

6. Diogenes, the ancient Greek Cynic philosopher, countered abstract logical arguments against the possibility that motion exists by getting up and walking away.

head very little with what the world either said or thought about it.

It is now high time, however, that I give you a description of him:——But to go on regularly, I only beg you will give me leave to acquaint you first, how my uncle *Toby* came by him.

Chapter XXV.

THE wound in my uncle *Toby*'s groin, which he received at the siege of *Namur*, rendering him unfit for the service, it was thought expedient he should return to *England*, in order, if possible, to be set to rights.

He was four years totally confined,——part of it to his bed, and all of it to his room; and in the course of his cure, which was all that time in hand, suffer'd unspeakable miseries,——owing to a succession of exfoliations from the *os pubis*,[7] and the outward edge of that part of the *coxendix* called the *os ilium*,——both which bones were dismally crush'd, as much by the irregularity of the stone, which I told you was broke off the parapet,——as by its size,——(though it was pretty large) which inclined the surgeon all along to think, that the great injury which it had done my uncle *Toby*'s groin, was more owing to the gravity of the stone itself, than to the projectile force of it,——which he would often tell him was a great happiness.

My father at that time was just beginning business in *London*, and had taken a house;——and as the truest friendship and cordiality subsisted between the two brothers,——and that my father thought my uncle *Toby* could no where be so well nursed and taken care of as in his own house,——he assign'd him the very best apartment in it.——And what was a much more sincere mark of his affection still, he would never suffer a friend or an acquaintance to step into the house on any occasion, but he would take him by the hand, and lead him up stairs to see his brother *Toby* and chat an hour by his bed side.

The history of a soldier's wound beguiles the pain of it;——my uncle's visiters at least thought so, and in their daily calls upon him, from the courtesy arising out of that belief, they would frequently turn the discourse to that subject,——and from that subject the discourse would generally roll on to the siege itself.

These conversations were infinitely kind; and my uncle *Toby* received great relief from them, and would have received much more, but that they brought him into some unforeseen perplexities, which, for three months together, retarded his cure greatly; and if

---

7. *Os pubis*: "pubic bone"; *coxendix*: "hip bone"; *os ilium*: "a pelvic bone."

he had not hit upon an expedient to extricate himself o
verily believe they would have laid him in his grave.

What these perplexities of my uncle *Toby* were,———— ... .,...
sible for you to guess;————if you could,————I should blush; not as a
relation,————not as a man,————nor even as a woman,————but I
should blush as an author; inasmuch as I set no small store by
myself upon this very account, that my reader has never yet been
able to guess at any thing. And in this, Sir, I am of so nice and
singular a humour, that if I thought you was able to form the least
judgment or probable conjecture to yourself, of what was to come
in the next page,————I would tear it out of my book.

END of the First Volume.

Volume II.[1]

Chapter I.

I Have begun a new book, on purpose that I might have room enough to explain the nature of the perplexities in which my uncle *Toby* was involved, from the many discourses and interrogations about the siege of *Namur*, where he received his wound.

I must remind the reader, in case he has read the history of King *William*'s wars,——but if he has not,——I then inform him, that one of the most memorable attacks in that siege, was that which was made by the *English* and *Dutch* upon the point of the advanced counterscarp,[2] before the gate of *St. Nicolas*, which inclosed the great sluice or water-stop, where the *English* were terribly exposed to the shot of the counter-guard and demi-bastion of *St. Roch*: The issue of which hot dispute, in three words, was this; That the *Dutch* lodged themselves upon the counter-guard,——and that the *English* made themselves masters of the covered way before *St. Nicolas*'s gate, notwithstanding the gallantry of the *French* officers, who exposed themselves upon the glacis sword in hand.

As this was the principal attack of which my uncle *Toby* was an eye-witness at *Namur*,——the army of the besigers being cut off, by the confluence of the *Maes* and *Sambre*, from seeing much of each other's operations,——my uncle *Toby* was generally more eloquent and particular in his account of it; and the many perplexities he was in, arose out of the almost insurmountable difficulties he found in telling his story intelligibly, and giving such clear ideas of the differences and distinctions between the scarp and counterscarp,——the glacis and covered way,——the half-moon and ravelin,——as to make his company fully comprehend where and what he was about.

Writers themselves are too apt to confound these terms;——so

1. This volume was published with Vol. I in December 1759 and dated 1760.
2. These terms of fortification, used throughout the novel, are often exploited by Sterne for their sexual suggestiveness. *Counterscarp*: the outer slope of a wall or ditch. *Counterguard*: a narrow detached rampart placed immediately in front of an important work to protect it. *Demi-bastion*: a bastion with one face and one flank. (A bastion is a projecting part of a fortification in the form of a pentagon with longer and shorter sides called faces and flanks.) *Covered way*: an open corridor around the outworks, guarded by an embankment. *Scarp*: the inner side of the ditch beneath a rampart. *Glacis*: the sloping embankment approaching a covered way so that troops crossing it would be exposed to firing. *Half-moon*: a crescent-shaped outwork, protecting a bastion. *Ravelin*: an outwork consisting of two faces forming a salient angle, constructed beyond the main ditch of a fortification.

that you will the less wonder, if in his endeavours to explain them, and in opposition to many misconceptions, that my uncle *Toby* did oft times puzzle his visiters; and sometimes himself too.

To speak the truth, unless the company my father led up stairs were tolerably clear-headed, or my uncle *Toby* was in one of his best explanatory moods, 'twas a difficult thing, do what he could, to keep the discourse free from obscurity.

What rendered the account of this affair the more intricate to my uncle *Toby*, was this,——that in the attack of the counterscarp before the gate of *St. Nicolas*, extending itself from the bank of the *Maes*, quite up to the great water-stop;——the ground was cut and cross-cut with such a multitude of dykes, drains, rivulets, and sluices, on all sides,——and he would get so sadly bewilder'd and set fast amongst them, that frequently he could neither get backwards or forwards to save his life; and was oft times obliged to give up the attack upon that very account only.

These perplexing rebuffs gave my uncle *Toby Shandy* more perturbations than you would imagine; and as my father's kindness to him was continually dragging up fresh friends and fresh inquirers, ——he had but a very uneasy task of it.

No doubt my uncle *Toby* had great command of himself,——and could guard appearances, I believe, as well as most men;——yet any one may imagine, that when he could not retreat out of the ravelin without getting into the half-moon, or get out of the covered way without falling down the counterscarp, nor cross the dyke without danger of slipping into the ditch, but that he must have fretted and fumed inwardly:——He did so;——and these little and hourly vexations, which may seem trifling and of no account to the man who has not read *Hippocrates*,[3] yet, whoever has read *Hippocrates*, or Dr. *James Mackenzie*, and has considered well the effects which the passions and affections of the mind have upon the digestion,——(Why not of a wound as well as of a dinner?)—— may easily conceive what sharp paroxisms and exacerbations of his wound my uncle *Toby* must have undergone upon that score only.

——My uncle *Toby* could not philosophize upon it;——'twas enough he felt it was so,——and having sustained the pain and sorrows of it for three months together, he was resolved some way or other to extricate himself.

He was one morning lying upon his back in his bed, the anguish and nature of the wound upon his groin suffering him to lye in no other position, when a thought came into his head, that if he could purchase such a thing, and have it pasted down upon a board, as a large map of the fortifications of the town and citadel of *Namur*,

3. Hippocrates, "the Father of Medicine," was an ancient Greek physician; Mackenzie an eighteenth-century Scottish one.

with its environs, it might be a means of giving him ease.——I take notice of his desire to have the environs along with the town and citadel, for this reason,——because my uncle *Toby*'s wound was got in one of the traverses, about thirty toises[4] from the returning angle of the trench, opposite to the salient angle of the demi-bastion of *St. Roch;*——so that he was pretty confident he could stick a pin upon the identical spot of ground where he was standing in when the stone struck him.

All this succeeded to his wishes, and not only freed him from a world of sad explanations, but, in the end, it prov'd the happy means, as you will read, of procuring my uncle *Toby* his HOBBY-HORSE.

Chapter II.

THERE is nothing so foolish, when you are at the expence of making an entertainment of this kind, as to order things so badly, as to let your criticks and gentry of refined taste run it down: Nor is there any thing so likely to make them do it, as that of leaving them out of the party, or, what is full as offensive, of bestowing your attention upon the rest of your guests in so particular a way, as if there was no such thing as a critick (by occupation) at table.

——I guard against both; for, in the first place, I have left half a dozen places purposely open for them;——and, in the next place, I pay them all court,——Gentlemen, I kiss your hands,——I protest no company could give me half the pleasure,——by my soul I am glad to see you,——I beg only you will make no strangers of yourselves, but sit down without any ceremony, and fall on heartily.

I said I had left six places, and I was upon the point of carrying my complaisance so far, as to have left a seventh open for them,—— and in this very spot I stand on;——but being told by a critick, (tho' not by occupation,——but by nature) that I had acquitted myself well enough, I shall fill it up directly, hoping, in the mean time, that I shall be able to make a great deal of more room next year.

——How, in the name of wonder! could your uncle *Toby*, who, is seems, was a military man, and whom you have represented as no fool,——be at the. same time such a confused, pudding-headed, muddle-headed fellow, as——Go look.

So, Sir Critick, I could have replied; but I scorn it.——'Tis language unurbane,——and only befitting the man who cannot give clear and satisfactory accounts of things, or dive deep enough into the first causes of human ignorance and confusion. It is moreover

4. An old French measurement, just over six feet.

the reply valiant,[5]——and therefore I reject it; for tho' ⟍
have suited my uncle *Toby*'s character as a soldier excellent   ⸴
——and had he not accustomed himself, in such attacks, to whistle
the *Lillabullero,*——as he wanted no courage, 'tis the very answer
he would have given; yet it would by no means have done for me.
You see as plain as can be, that I write as a man of erudition;——
that even my similies, my allusions, my illustrations, my metaphors,
are erudite,——and that I must sustain my character properly, and
contrast it properly too,——else what would become of me? Why,
Sir, I should be undone;——at this very moment that I am going
here to fill up one place against a critick,——I should have made an
opening for a couple.

——Therefore I answer thus:

Pray, Sir, in all the reading which you have ever read, did you
ever read such a book as *Locke*'s Essay upon the Human Understanding?[6]——Don't answer me rashly,——because many, I know,
quote the book, who have not read it,——and many have read it
who understand it not:——If either of these is your case, as I write
to instruct, I will tell you in three words what the book is.——It is
a history.——A history! of who? what? where? when? Don't hurry
yourself.——It is a history-book, Sir, (which may possibly recommend it to the world) of what passes in a man's own mind; and if
you will say so much of the book, and no more, believe me, you
will cut no contemptible figure in a metaphysic circle.

But this by the way.

Now if you will venture to go along with me, and look down into
the bottom of this matter, it will be found that the cause of obscurity and confusion, in the mind of man, is three-fold.

Dull organs, dear Sir, in the first place. Secondly, slight and
transient impressions made by objects when the said organs are not
dull. And, thirdly, a memory like unto a sieve, not able to retain
what it has received.——Call down *Dolly* your chamber-maid, and
I will give you my cap and bell along with it, if I make not this
matter so plain that *Dolly* herself shall understand it as well as *Mal-
branch.*[7]——When *Dolly* has indited her epistle to *Robin,* and has
thrust her arm into the bottom of her pocket hanging by her right-
side;——take that opportunity to recollect that the organs and
faculties of perception, can, by nothing in this world, be so aptly
typified and explained as by that one thing which *Dolly*'s hand is in
search of.——Your organs are not so dull that I should inform you
——'tis an inch, Sir, of red seal-wax.

When this is melted and dropp'd upon the letter,———if *Dolly*

---

5. The reply or retort valiant is one of
the conventional responses to quarrelsome
provocation.
6. See note 9 in Vol. I., Chap. iv.
7. Malebranch was a seventeenth-century

French philosopher studied and criticized by Locke. Sterne's metaphor of the
ball of wax parodies Locke's description
of the way ideas are derived from experience.

fumbles too long for her thimble, till the wax is over harden'd, it will not receive the mark of her thimble from the usual impulse which was wont to imprint it. Very well: If *Dolly*'s wax, for want of better, is bees-wax or of a temper too soft,——tho' it may receive, ——it will not hold the impression, how hard soever *Dolly* thrusts against it; and last of all, supposing the wax good, and eke[8] the thimble, but applied thereto in careless haste, as her Mistress rings the bell;——in any one of these three cases, the print, left by the thimble, will be as unlike the prototype as a brass-jack.

Now you must understand that not one of these was the true cause of the confusion in my uncle *Toby*'s discourse; and it is for that very reason I enlarge upon them so long, after the manner of great physiologists,——to shew the world what it did *not* arise from.

What it did arise from, I have hinted above, and a fertile source of obscurity is it,——and ever will be,——and that is the unsteady uses of words which have perplexed the clearest and most exalted understandings.

It is ten to one (at *Arthur's*[9]) whether you have ever read the literary histories of past ages;——if you have,——what terrible battles, 'yclept logomachies,[1] have they occasioned and perpetuated with so much gall and ink-shed,——that a good natured man cannot read the accounts of them without tears in his eyes.

Gentle critick! when thou has weigh'd all this, and consider'd within thyself how much of thy own knowledge, discourse, and conversation has been pestered and disordered, at one time or other, by this, and this only:——What a pudder and racket in COUNCILS about οὐσία and ὑπόστασις,[2] and in the SCHOOLS of the learned about power and about spirit;——about essences, and about quintessences;——about substances, and about space.——What confusion in greater THEATRES from words of little meaning, and as indeterminate a sense;——when thou considers this, thou wilt not wonder at my uncle *Toby*'s perplexities,——thou wilt drop a tear of pity upon his scarp and his counterscarp;——his glacis and his covered-way;——his ravelin and his half-moon: 'Twas not by ideas, ——by heaven! his life was put in jeopardy by words.

Chapter III.

WHEN my uncle *Toby* got his map of *Namur* to his mind, he began immediately to apply himself, and with the utmost diligence, to the study of it; for nothing being of more

8. Also.
9. A London club.
1. *Yclept* is an old word for "called";

logomachies are wars of words.
2. The Greek words mean "essence."

importance to him than his recovery, and his recovery depending, as you have read, upon the passions and affections of his mind, it behoved him to take the nicest care to make himself so far master of his subject, as to be able to talk upon it without emotion.

In a fortnight's close and painful application, which, by the bye, did my uncle *Toby*'s wound, upon his groin, no good,——he was enabled, by the help of some marginal documents at the feet of the elephant,[3] together with *Gobesius*'s military architecture and pyroballogy, translated from the *Flemish*, to form his discourse with passable perspicuity; and before he was two full months gone,—— he was right eloquent upon it, and could make not only the attack of the advanced counterscarp with great order;——but having, by that time, gone much deeper into the art, than what his first motive made necessary,——my uncle *Toby* was able to cross the *Maes* and *Sambre*; make diversions as far as *Vauban*'s line, the abbey of *Salsines*, *&c.* and give his visiters as distinct a history of each of their attacks, as of that of the gate of *St. Nicolas*, where he had the honour to receive his wound.

But the desire of knowledge, like the thirst of riches, increases ever with the acquisition of it. The more my uncle *Toby* pored over his map, the more he took a liking to it;——by the same process and electrical assimilation, as I told you, thro' which I ween the souls of connoisseurs themselves, by long friction and incumbition, have the happiness, at length, to get all be-virtu'd,——be-pictur'd, ——be-butterflied, and be-fiddled.

The more my uncle *Toby* drank of this sweet fountain of science, the greater was the heat and impatience of his thirst, so that, before the first year of his confinement had well gone round, there was scarce a fortified town in *Italy* or *Flanders*, of which, by one means or other, he had not procured a plan, reading over as he got them, and carefully collating therewith the histories of their sieges, their demolitions, their improvements, and new works, all which he would read with that intense application and delight, that he would forget himself, his wound, his confinement, his dinner.

In the second year my uncle *Toby* purchased *Ramelli*[4] and *Cataneo*, translated from the *Italian*;——likewise *Stevinus, Marolis,* the Chevalier *de Ville, Lorini, Coehorn, Sheeter,* the Count *de Pagan*, the Marshal *Vauban*, Mons. *Blondel*, with almost as many more books of military architecture, as Don *Quixote* was found to have of chivalry, when the curate and barber invaded his library.

---

3. The feet of the elephant may refer to the kind of ornamental drawing often found on old maps. "Gobesius" may be Leonhard Gorecius, a sixteenth-century expert on gunnery.
4. Ramelli, Cataneo, and the others were sixteenth and seventeenth-century military writers. In *Don Quixote* (I.vi) the priest and the barber humorously question the Don in his library, where they find "a hundred large volumes."

Towards the beginning of the third year, which was in *August,* ninety-nine,[5] my uncle *Toby* found it necessary to understand a little of projectiles:——And having judged it best to draw his knowledge from the fountain-head, he began with N. *Tartaglia,* who it seems was the first man who detected the imposition of a canonball's doing all that mischief under the notion of a right line.—— This N. *Tartaglia* proved to my uncle *Toby* to be an impossible thing.

——Endless is the Search of Truth!

No sooner was my uncle *Toby* satisfied which road the cannonball did not go, but he was insensibly led on, and resolved in his mind to enquire and find out which road the ball did go: For which purpose he was obliged to set off afresh with old *Maltus,*[6] and studied him devoutly.——He proceeded next to *Gallileo* and *Torricellius,* wherein, by certain geometrical rules, infallibly laid down, he found the precise path to be a PARABOLA,——or else an HYPERBOLA,——and that the parameter, or *latus rectum,* of the conic section of the said path, was to the quantity and amplitude in a direct *ratio,* as the whole line to the sine of double the angle of incidence, form'd by the breech upon an horizontal plane;——and that the semi-parameter,——stop! my dear uncle *Toby,*——stop! ——go not one foot further into this thorny and bewilder'd track, ——intricate are the steps! intricate are the mases of this labyrinth! intricate are the troubles which the pursuit of this bewitching phantom, KNOWLEDGE, will bring upon thee.——O my uncle! fly—fly— fly from it as from a serpent.——Is it fit, good-natur'd man! Thou should'st sit up, with the wound upon thy groin, whole nights baking thy blood with hectic watchings?——Alas! 'twill exasperate thy symptoms,——check thy perspirations,——evaporate thy spirits, ——waste thy animal strength,——dry up thy radical moisture,[7] ——bring thee into a costive habit of body, impair thy health,—— and hasten all the infirmities of thy old age.——O my uncle! my uncle *Toby*.

Chapter IV.

I Would not give a groat for that man's knowledge in pencraft, who does not understand this,——That the best plain narrative in the world, tack'd very close to the last spirited apostrophe to my uncle *Toby,*——would have felt both cold and vapid upon the reader's palate;——therefore I forthwith put an end to the chapter, ——though I was in the middle of my story.

lthus, Gallileo, and Tor-
Renaissance authorities
:cially as it involves pro-

jectiles, trajectories, etc. *Latus rectum* means "straight line."
7. Radical moisture is the body's natural moisture. *Costive* means constipated.

——Writers of my stamp have one principle in common with painters.——Where an exact copying makes our pictures less striking, we choose the less evil; deeming it even more pardonable to trespass against truth, than beauty.——This is to be understood *cum grano salis;*[8] but be it as it will,——as the parallel is made more for the sake of letting the apostrophe cool, than any thing else,——'tis not very material whether upon any other score the reader approves of it or not.

In the latter end of the third year, my uncle *Toby* perceiving that the parameter and semi-parameter of the conic section, angered his wound, he left off the study of projectiles in a kind of a huff, and betook himself to the practical part of fortification only; the pleasure of which, like a spring held back, returned upon him with redoubled force.

It was in this year that my uncle began to break in upon the daily regularity of a clean shirt,——to dismiss his barber unshaven,—— and to allow his surgeon scarce time sufficient to dress his wound, concerning himself so little about it, as not to ask him once in seven times dressing how it went on: When, lo!——all of a sudden, for the change was as quick as lightening, he began to sigh heavily for his recovery,——complain'd to my father, grew impatient with the surgeon;——and one morning as he heard his foot coming up stairs, he shut up his books, and thrust aside his instruments, in order to expostulate with him upon the protraction of his cure, which, he told him, might surely have been accomplished at least by that time:——He dwelt long upon the miseries he had undergone, and the sorrows of his four years melancholy imprisonment;—— adding, that had it not been for the kind looks, and fraternal chearings of the best of brothers,——he had long since sunk under his misfortunes.——My father was by: My uncle *Toby's* eloquence brought tears into his eyes;——'twas unexpected.——My uncle *Toby*, by nature, was not eloquent;——it had the greater effect. ——The surgeon was confounded;——not that there wanted grounds for such, or greater, marks of impatience,——but 'twas unexpected too; in the four years he had attended him, he had never seen any thing like it in my uncle *Toby's* carriage; he had never once dropp'd one fretful or discontented word;——he had been all patience,——all submission.

——We lose the right of complaining sometimes by forbearing it;——but we oftner treble the force:——The surgeon was astonished;——but much more so, when he heard my uncle *Toby* go on, and peremptorily insist upon his healing up the wound directly,—— or sending for Monsieur *Ronjat*, the King's Serjeant-Surgeon, to do it for him.

8. With a grain of salt.

esire of life and health is implanted in man's nature;——the liberty and enlargement is a sister-passion to it: These my uncle *Toby* had in common with his species;——and either of them had been sufficient to account for his earnest desire to get well and out of doors;——but I have told you before that nothing wrought with our family after the common way;——and from the time and manner in which this eager desire shew'd itself in the present case, the penetrating reader will suspect there was some other cause or crotchet for it in my uncle *Toby*'s head:——There was so, and 'tis the subject of the next chapter to set forth what that cause and crotchet was. I own, when that's done, 'twill be time to return back to the parlour fire-side, where we left my uncle *Toby* in the middle of his sentence.

Chapter V.

WHEN a man gives himself up to the government of a ruling passion,——or, in other words, when his HOBBY-HORSE grows head-strong,——farewell cool reason and fair discretion!

My uncle *Toby*'s wound was near well, and as soon as the surgeon recovered his surprize, and could get leave to say as much—— he told him, 'twas just beginning to incarnate;[9] and that if no fresh exfoliation happen'd, which there was no signs of,——it would be dried up in five or six weeks. The sound of as many olympiads twelve hours before, would have convey'd an idea of shorter duration to my uncle *Toby*'s mind.——The succession of his ideas was now rapid,——he broil'd with impatience to put his design in execution;——and so, without consulting further with any soul living,——which, by the bye, I think is right, when you are predetermined to take no one soul's advice,——he privately ordered *Trim*, his man, to pack up a bundle of lint and dressings, and hire a chariot and four to be at the door exactly by twelve o'clock that day, when he knew my father would be upon 'Change.[1]——So leaving a bank-note upon the table for the surgeon's care of him, and a letter of tender thanks for his brother's,——he pack'd up his maps, his books of fortification, his instruments, &c.——and, by the help of a crutch on one side, and *Trim* on the other,——my uncle *Toby* embark'd for *Shandy-Hall*.

The reason, or rather the rise, of this sudden demigration, was as follows:

The table in my uncle *Toby*'s room, and at which, the night before this change happened, he was sitting with his maps, &c.

---

9. "Incarnate": flesh over, heal; "exfoliation": peeling off; "olympiad": four years.

1. That is, at the Royal Exchange, a center of mercantile trade.

about him,——being somewhat of the smallest, for that infinity of great and small instruments of knowledge which usually lay crouded upon it;——he had the accident, in reaching over his tobacco-box, to throw down his compasses, and in stooping to take the compasses up, with his sleeve he threw down his case of instruments and snuffers;——and as the dice took a run against him, in his endeavouring to catch the snuffers in falling,——he thrust Monsieur *Blondel* off the table and Count *de Pagan* o'top of him.

'Twas to no purpose for a man, lame as my uncle *Toby* was, to think of redressing all these evils by himself,——he rung his bell for his man *Trim*;——*Trim!* quoth my uncle *Toby*, pri'thee see what confusion I have here been making.——I must have some better contrivance, *Trim.*——Can'st not thou take my rule and measure the length and breadth of this table, and then go and bespeak me one as big again?——Yes, an' please your Honour, replied *Trim*, making a bow;——but I hope your Honour will be soon well enough to get down to your country seat, where,——as your Honour takes so much pleasure in fortification, we could manage this matter to a T.

I must here inform you, that this servant of my uncle *Toby's*, who went by the name of *Trim*, had been a Corporal in my uncle's own company,——his real name was *James Butler*,——but having got the nick-name of *Trim* in the regiment, my uncle *Toby*, unless when he happened to be very angry with him, would never call him by any other name.

The poor fellow had been disabled for the service, by a wound on his left knee by a musket-bullet, at the battle of *Landen*, which was two years before the affair of *Namur*;——and as the fellow was well beloved in the regiment, and a handy fellow into the bargain, my uncle *Toby* took him for his servant, and of excellent use was he, attending my uncle *Toby* in the camp and in his quarters as valet, groom, barber, cook, sempster,[2] and nurse; and indeed, from first to last, waited upon him and served him with great fidelity and affection.

My uncle *Toby* loved the man in return, and what attached him more to him still, was the similitude of their knowledge:——For Corporal *Trim*, (for so, for the future, I shall call him) by four years occasional attention to his Master's discourse upon fortified towns, and the advantage of prying and peeping continually into his Master's plans, &c. exclusive and besides what he gained Hobby-Horsically, as a body-servant, *Non Hobby-Horsical per se;*[3]—— had become no mean proficient in the science; and was thought, by the cook and chamber-maid, to know as much of the nature of strong-holds as my uncle *Toby* himself.

2. Tailor.   3. Not hobby-horsical in himself.

ave but one more stroke to give to finish Corporal *Trim*'s character,——and it is the only dark line in it.——The fellow lov'd to advise,——or rather to hear himself talk; his carriage, however, was so perfectly respectful, 'twas easy to keep him silent when you had him so; but set his tongue a-going,——you had no hold of him;——he was voluble;——the eternal interlardings of *your Honour*, with the respectfulness of Corporal *Trim*'s manner, interceeding so strong in behalf of his elocution,——that tho' you might have been incommoded,——you could not well be angry. My uncle *Toby* was seldom either the one or the other with him,——or, at least, this fault, in *Trim*, broke no squares[4] with 'em. My uncle *Toby*, as I said, loved the man;——and besides, as he ever looked upon a faithful servant,——but as a humble friend,——he could not bear to stop his mouth.——Such was Corporal *Trim*.

If I durst presume, continued *Trim*, to give your Honour my advice, and speak my opinion in this matter.——Thou art welcome, *Trim*, quoth my uncle *Toby*,——speak,——speak what thou thinkest upon the subject, man, without fear. Why then, replied *Trim*, (not hanging his ears and scratching his head like a country lout, but) stroking his hair back from his forehead, and standing erect as before his division.——I think, quoth *Trim*, advancing his left, which was his lame leg, a little forwards,——and pointing with his right hand open towards a map of *Dunkirk*, which was pinn'd against the hangings,——I think, quoth Corporal *Trim*, with humble submission to your Honour's better judgment,——that these ravelins, bastions, curtins, and hornworks make but a poor, contemptible, fiddle faddle piece of work of it here upon paper, compared to what your Honour and I could make of it, were we in the country by ourselves, and had but a rood, or a rood and a half of ground to do what we pleased with: As summer is coming on, continued *Trim*, your Honour might sit out of doors, and give me the nography——(call it ichnography, quoth my uncle)——of the town or citadel, your Honour was pleased to sit down before,—— and I will be shot by your Honour upon the glacis of it, if I did not fortify it to your Honour's mind.——I dare say thou would'st, *Trim*, quoth my uncle.——For if your Honour, continued the Corporal, could but mark me the polygon, with its exact lines and angles.——that I'could do very well, quoth my uncle.——I would begin with the fossé, and if your Honour could tell me the proper depth and breadth,——I can to a hair's breadth, *Trim*, replied my uncle,——I would throw out the earth upon this hand towards the town for the scarp,——and on that hand towards the campaign for the counterscarp,——very right, *Trim*, quoth my uncle *Toby*,——

---

4. **Did not offend.**

and when I had sloped them to your mind,——an' please your Honour, I would face the glacis, as the finest fortifications are done in *Flanders*, with sods,——and as your Honour knows they should be,——and I would make the walls and parapets with sods too;—— the best engineers call them gazons, *Trim*, said my uncle *Toby*;—— whether they are gazons or sods, is not much matter, replied *Trim*, your Honour knows they are ten times beyond a facing either of brick or stone;——I know they are, *Trim*, in some respects,—— quoth my uncle *Toby*, nodding his head;——for a cannon-ball enters into the gazon right onwards, without bringing any rubbish down with it, which might fill the fossé, (as was the case at *St. Nicolas's Gate*) and facilitate the passage over it.

Your Honour understands these matters, replied Corporal *Trim*, better than any officer in his Majesty's service;——but would your Honour please to let the bespeaking of the table alone, and let us but go into the country, I would work under your Honour's directions like a horse, and make fortifications for you something like a tansy,[5] with all their batteries, saps, ditches, and palisadoes, that it should be worth all the world's riding twenty miles to go and see it.

My uncle *Toby* blushed as red as scarlet as *Trim* went on;—— but it was not a blush of guilt,——of modesty,——or of anger; ——it was a blush of joy;——he was fired with Corporal *Trim's* project and description.——*Trim!* said my uncle *Toby*, thou hast said enough.——We might begin the campaign, continued *Trim*, on the very day that his Majesty and the Allies take the field, and demolish 'em town by town as fast as——*Trim*, quoth my uncle *Toby*, say no more.——Your Honour, continued *Trim*, might sit in your arm-chair, (pointing to it) this fine weather, giving me your orders, and I would——Say no more, *Trim*, quoth my uncle *Toby*. ——Besides, your Honour would get not only pleasure and good pastime,——but good air, and good exercise, and good health,—— and your Honour's wound would be well in a month. Thou hast said enough, *Trim*,——quoth my uncle *Toby* (putting his hand into his breeches-pocket)——I like thy project mightily;——and if your Honour pleases, I'll, this moment, go and buy a pioneer's spade to take down with us, and I'll bespeak a shovel and a pick-ax, and a couple of——Say no more, *Trim*, quoth my uncle *Toby*, leaping up upon one leg, quite overcome with rapture,——and thrusting a guinea into *Trim's* hand.—*Trim*, said my uncle *Toby*, say no more; ——but go down, *Trim*, this moment, my lad, and bring up my supper this instant.

Trim ran down and brought up his master's supper,——to no

---

5. Properly, perfectly.

purpose:——*Trim*'s plan of operation ran so in my uncle *Toby*'s head, he could not taste it.——*Trim*, quoth my uncle *Toby*, get me to-bed;——'twas all one.——Corporal *Trim*'s description had fired his imagination,——my uncle *Toby* could not shut his eyes.—— The more he consider'd it, the more bewitching the scene appeared to him;——so that, two full hours before day-light, he had come to a final determination, and had concerted the whole plan of his and Corporal *Trim*'s decampment.

My uncle *Toby* had a little neat country-house of his own, in the village where my father's estate lay at *Shandy*, which had been left him by an old uncle, with a small estate of about one hundred pounds a-year. Behind this house, and contiguous to it, was a kitchen-garden of about half an acre;——and at the bottom of the garden, and cut off from it by a tall yew hedge, was a bowling-green, containing just about as much ground as Corporal *Trim* wished for;——so that as *Trim* uttered the words, "A rood and a half of ground to do what they would with:"——This identical bowling-green instantly presented itself, and became curiously painted, all at once, upon the retina of my uncle *Toby*'s fancy;—— which was the physical cause of making him change colour, or at least, of heightening his blush to that immoderate degree I spoke of.

Never did lover post down to a belov'd mistress with more heat and expectation, than my uncle *Toby* did, to enjoy this self-same thing in private;——I say in private;——for it was sheltered from the house, as I told you, by a tall yew hedge, and was covered on the other three sides, from mortal sight, by rough holly and thickset flowering shrubs;——so that the idea of not being seen, did not a little contribute to the idea of pleasure pre-conceived in my uncle *Toby*'s mind.——Vain thought! however thick it was planted about, ——or private soever it might seem,——to think, dear uncle *Toby*, of enjoying a thing which took up a whole rood and a half of ground,——and not have it known!

How my uncle *Toby* and Corporal *Trim* managed this matter, ——with the history of their campaigns, which were no way barren of events,——may make no uninteresting underplot in the epitasis[6] and working up of this drama.——At present the scene must drop, ——and change for the parlour fire-side.

Chapter VI.

——What can they be doing, brother? said my father.——I think, replied my uncle *Toby*,——taking, as I told you, his pipe

---

6. In classical drama, the epitasis is the part in which the main action is developed.

from his mouth, and striking the ashes out of it as he
sentence;——I think, replied he,——it would not be amiss,
if we rung the bell.

Pray, what's all that racket over our heads, *Obadiah?*——quoth
my father;——my brother and I can scarce hear ourselves speak.

Sir, answer'd *Obadiah,* making a bow towards his left-shoulder,
——my Mistress is taken very badly;——and where's *Susannah*
running down the garden there, as if they were going to ravish
her?——Sir, she is running the shortest cut into the town, replied
Obadiah, to fetch the old midwife.——Then saddle a horse, quoth
my father, and do you go directly for Dr. *Slop,* the man-midwife,
with all our services,——and let him know your Mistress is fallen
into labour,——and that I desire he will return with you with all
speed.

It is very strange, says my father, addressing himself to my uncle
Toby, as *Obadiah* shut the door,——as there is so expert an operator as Dr. *Slop* so near——that my wife should persist to the very
last in this obstinate humour of hers, in trusting the life of my child,
who has had one misfortune already, to the ignorance of an old
woman;——and not only the life of my child, brother,——but her
own life, and with it the lives of all the children I might, peradventure, have begot out of her hereafter.

Mayhap, brother, replied my uncle *Toby,* my sister does it to save
the expence:——A pudding's end,——replied my father,——the
doctor must be paid the same for inaction as action,——if not
better,——to keep him in temper.

——Then it can be out of nothing in the whole world, quoth my
uncle *Toby,* in the simplicity of his heart,——but MODESTY:——
My sister, I dare say, added he, does not care to let a man come so
near her ****. I will not say whether my uncle *Toby* had compleated
the sentence or not;——'tis for his advantage to suppose he had,
——as, I think, he could have added no ONE WORD which would
have improved it.

If, on the contrary, my uncle *Toby* had not fully arrived at his
period's end,——then the world stands indebted to the sudden
snapping of my father's tobacco-pipe, for one of the neatest examples of that ornamental figure in oratory, which Rhetoricians stile
the *Aposiopesis.*[7]——Just heaven! how does the *Poco più* and the
Poco meno of the *Italian* artists;——the insensible, more or less,
determine the precise line of beauty in the sentence, as well as in the
statue! How do the slight touches of the chisel, the pencil, the pen,
the fiddle-stick, *et cætera,*——give the true swell, which gives the

---

7. *Aposiopesis* is a rhetorical term for
breaking off in mid-sentence as if unable or unwilling to go on. *Pocu più*
and *poco meno*: a little more, a little
less.

true pleasure!——O my countrymen!——be nice;——be cautious of your language;——and never, O! never let it be forgotten upon what small particles your eloquence and your fame depend.

——"My sister, mayhap, quoth my uncle *Toby*, does not choose to let a man come so near her ****." Make this dash,——'tis an Aposiopesis.——Take the dash away, and write *Backside*,——'tis Bawdy.——Scratch Backside out, and put *Cover'd-way* in,——'tis a Metaphor;——and, I dare say, as fortification ran so much in my uncle *Toby*'s head, that if he had been left to have added one word to the sentence,——that word was it.

But whether that was the case or not the case;——or whether the snapping of my father's tobacco-pipe so critically, happened thro' accident or anger,——will be seen in due time.

Chapter VII.

THO' my father was a good natural philosopher,——yet he was something of a moral philosopher too; for which reason, when his tobacco-pipe snapp'd short in the middle,——he had nothing to do,——as such,——but to have taken hold of the two pieces, and thrown them gently upon the back of the fire.——He did no such thing;——he threw them with all the violence in the world;—— and, to give the action still more emphasis,——he started up upon both his legs to do it.

This look'd something like heat;——and the manner of his reply to what my uncle *Toby* was saying prov'd it was so.

——"Not choose," quoth my father, (repeating my uncle *Toby*'s words) "to let a man come so near her——" By heaven, brother *Toby!* you would try the patience of a *Job*;——and I think I have the plagues of one already, without it.——Why?——Where? ——Wherein?——Wherefore?——Upon what account, replied my uncle *Toby*, in the utmost astonishment.——To think, said my father, of a man living to your age, brother, and knowing so little about women!——I know nothing at all about them,——replied my uncle *Toby*; and I think, continued he, that the shock I received the year after the demolition of *Dunkirk*, in my affair with widow *Wadman*;——which shock you know I should not have received, but from my total ignorance of the sex,——has given me just cause to say, That I neither know, nor do pretend to know, anything about 'em, or their concerns either.——Methinks, brother, replied my father, you might, at least, know so much as the right end of a woman from the wrong.

It is said in *Aristotle's Master-Piece*, "That when a man doth think of any thing which is past,——he looketh down upon the ground;——but that when he thinketh of something which is to come, he looketh up towards the heavens."[8]

My uncle *Toby*, I suppose, thought of neither,——for he look'd horizontally.——Right end,——quoth my uncle *Toby*, muttering the two words low to himself, and fixing his two eyes insensibly as he muttered them, upon a small crevice, form'd by a bad joint in the chimney-piece.——Right end of a woman!——I declare, quoth my uncle, I know no more which it is, than the man in the moon;—— and if I was to think, continued my uncle *Toby*, (keeping his eye still fix'd upon the bad joint) this month together, I am sure I should not be able to find it out.

Then brother *Toby*, replied my father, I will tell you.

Every thing in this world, continued my father (filling a fresh pipe)——every thing in this earthly world, my dear brother *Toby*, has two handles;——not always, quoth my uncle *Toby*;——at least, replied my father, every one has two hands,——which comes to the same thing.——Now, if a man was to sit down coolly, and consider within himself the make, the shape, the construction, com-at-ability, and convenience of all the parts which constitute the whole of that animal, call'd *Woman*, and compare them analogi-cally.——I never understood rightly the meaning of that word,—— quoth my uncle *Toby*.——ANALOGY, replied my father, is the cer-tain relation and agreement, which different——Here a Devil of a rap at the door snapp'd my father's definition (like his tobacco-pipe) in two,——and, at the same time, crushed the head of as notable and curious a dissertation as ever was engendered in the womb of speculation;——it was some months before my father could get an opportunity to be safely deliver'd of it:——And, at this hour, it is a thing full as problematical as the subject of the dissertation itself,——(considering the confusion and distresses of our domestic misadventures, which are now coming thick one upon the back of another) whether I shall be able to find a place for it in the third volume or not.

Chapter VIII.

IT is about an hour and a half's tolerable good reading since my uncle *Toby* rung the bell, when *Obadiah* was order'd to saddle a horse, and go for Dr. *Slop* the man-midwife;——so that no one can say, with reason, that I have not allowed *Obadiah* time enough, poetically speaking, and considering the emergency too, both to go

---

8. There is a work by that name, but the reference here seems to be to one called *Aristotle's Book of Problems*, where the question asked is: why does a man look to heaven when he imagines things, and to the earth when he muses on the past?

and come;——tho', morally and truly speaking, the man, perhaps, has scarce had time to get on his boots.

If the hypercritick will go upon this; and is resolved after all to take a pendulum, and measure the true distance betwixt the ringing of the bell, and the rap at the door;——and, after finding it to be no more than two minutes, thirteen seconds, and three fifths,—— should take upon him to insult over me for such a breach in the unity, or rather probability, of time;——I would remind him, that the idea of duration and of its simple modes, is got merely from the train and succession of our ideas,——and is the true scholastick pendulum,——and by which, as a scholar, I will be tried in this matter,——abjuring and detesting the jurisdiction of all other pendulums whatever.

I would, therefore, desire him to consider that it is but poor eight miles from *Shandy-Hall* to Dr. *Slop*, the man mid-wife's house;—— and that whilst *Obadiah* has been going those said miles and back, I have brought my uncle *Toby* from *Namur*, quite across all *Flanders*, into *England*:——That I have had him ill upon my hands near four years;——and have since travelled him and Corporal *Trim*, in a chariot and four, a journey of near two hundred miles down into *Yorkshire*;——all which put together, must have prepared the reader's imagination for the entrance of Dr. *Slop* upon the stage,——as much, at least, (I hope) as a dance, a song, or a concerto between the acts.

If my hypercritick is intractable,——alledging, that two minutes and thirteen seconds are no more than two minutes and thirteen seconds,——when I have said all I can about them;——and that this plea, tho' it might save me dramatically, will damn me biographically, rendering my book, from this very moment, a profess'd ROMANCE, which, before, was a book apocryphal:——If I am thus pressed.——I then put an end to the whole objection and controversy about it all at once,——by acquainting him, that *Obadiah* had not got above threescore yards from the stable-yard before he met with Dr. *Slop*;——and indeed he gave a dirty proof that he had met with him,——and was within an ace of giving a tragical one too.

Imagine to yourself;——but this had better begin a new chapter.

Chapter IX.

Imagine to yourself a little, squat, uncourtly figure of a Doctor *Slop*,[9] of about four feet and a half perpendicular height, with a

---

9. Dr. Slop caricatures John Burton, a talented but controversial physician of York, whose politics and religion (he was a Roman Catholic) infuriated Sterne. "Sesquipedality" means "a foot-and-a-half."

breadth of back, and a sesquipedality of belly, which might have done honour to a Serjeant in the Horse-Guards.

Such were the out-lines of Dr. *Slop*'s figure, which,——if you have read *Hogarth*'s analysis of beauty,[1] and if you have not, I wish you would;——you must know, may as certainly be caracatur'd, and convey'd to the mind by three strokes as three hundred.

Imagine such a one,——for such, I say, were the out-lines of Dr. *Slop*'s figure, coming slowly along, foot by foot, waddling thro' the dirt upon the vertebræ of a little diminutive pony, of a pretty colour;——but of strength,——alack!——scarce able to have made an amble of it, under such a fardel, had the roads been in an ambling condition.——They were not.——Imagine to yourself, *Obadiah* mounted upon a strong monster of a coach-horse, prick'd into a full gallop, and making all practicable speed the adverse way.

Pray, Sir, let me interest you a moment in this description.

Had Dr. *Slop* beheld *Obadiah* a mile off, posting in a narrow lane directly towards him, at that monstrous rate,——splashing and plunging like a devil thro' thick and thin, as he approach'd, would not such a phænomenon, with such a vortex of mud and water moving along with it, round its axis,——have been a subject of juster apprehension to Dr. *Slop* in his situation, than the *worst* of *Whiston*'s comets?[2]——To say nothing of the Nucleus; that is, of *Obadiah* and the coach-horse.——In my idea, the vortex alone of 'em was enough to have involved and carried, if not the Doctor, at least the Doctor's pony quite away with it. What then do you think must the terror and hydrophobia of Dr. *Slop* have been, when you read (which you are just going to do) that he was advancing thus warily along towards *Shandy-Hall*, and had approach'd to within sixty yards of it, and within five yards of a sudden turn, made by an acute angle of the garden wall,——and in the dirtiest part of a dirty lane,——when *Obadiah* and his coach-horse turn'd the corner, rapid, furious,——pop,——full upon him!——Nothing, I think, in nature, can be supposed more terrible, than such a Rencounter,—— so imprompt! so ill prepared to stand the shock of it as Dr. *Slop* was!

What could Dr. *Slop* do?——He cross'd himself + ——Pugh! ——but the Doctor, Sir, was a Papist.——No matter; he had better have kept hold of the pummel.——He had so;——nay, as it happen'd, he had better have done nothing at all;——for in crossing himself he let go his whip,——and in attempting to save his whip

---

1. William Hogarth was one of the most important English artists of the eighteenth century. He published the *Analysis of Beauty* in 1753; and when *Tristram Shandy* proved successful, Sterne asked

him to provide some illustrations.
2. William Whiston predicted that the world would be destroyed by comets passing close by.

betwixt his knee and his saddle's skirt, as it slipp'd, he lost his stirrup,——in losing which, he lost his seat;——and in the multitude of all these losses, (which, by the bye, shews what little advantage there is in crossing) the unfortunate doctor lost his presence of mind. So that, without waiting for *Obadiah's* onset, he left his pony to its destiny, tumbling off it diagonally, something in the stile and manner of a pack of wool, and without any other consequence from the fall, save that of being left, (as it would have been) with the broadest part of him sunk about twelve inches deep in the mire.

Obadiah pull'd off his cap twice to Dr. *Slop*;——once as he was falling,——and then again when he saw him seated.——Ill-timed complaisance!——had not the fellow better have stopp'd his horse, and got off and help'd him?——Sir, he did all that his situation would allow;——but the MOMENTUM of the coach-horse was so great, that *Obadiah* could not do it all at once;——he rode in a circle three times round Dr. *Slop*, before he could fully accomplish it any how;——and at the last, when he did stop his beast, 'twas done with such an explosion of mud, that *Obadiah* had better have been a league off. In short, never was a Dr. *Slop* so beluted,[3] and so transubstantiated, since that affair came into fashion.

Chapter X.

WHEN Dr. *Slop* entered the back parlour, where my father and my uncle *Toby* were discoursing upon the nature of women,——it was hard to determine whether Dr. *Slop's* figure, or Dr. *Slop's* presence, occasioned more surprize to them; for as the accident happened so near the house, as not to make it worth while for *Obadiah* to remount him,——*Obadiah* had led him in as he was, *unwiped, unappointed, unanealed,*[4] with all his stains and blotches on him.——He stood like *Hamlet's* ghost, motionless and speechless, for a full minute and a half, at the parlour door, (*Obadiah* still holding his hand) with all the majesty of mud. His hinder parts, upon which he had received his fall, totally besmear'd, ——and in every other part of him, blotched over in such a manner with *Obadiah's* explosion, that you would have sworn, (without mental reservation) that every grain of it had taken effect.

Here was a fair opportunity for my uncle *Toby* to have triumph'd over my father in his turn;——for no mortal, who had beheld Dr. *Slop* in that pickle, could have dissented from so much, at least, of my uncle *Toby's* opinion, "That mayhap his sister might not care to

---

3. Covered with mud (lute).
4. That is, without having received extreme unction or last rites in the Church.

Hamlet's father describes his own death as "unhousel'd, disappointed, unanel'd," (I.v.77).

let such a Dr. *Slop* come so near her ****" But it was the *Argumentum ad hominem*;[5] and if my uncle *Toby* was not very expert at it, you may think, he might not care to use it.——No; the reason was,——'twas not his nature to insult.

Dr. *Slop*'s presence, at that time, was no less problematical than the mode of it; tho', it is certain, one moment's reflection in my father might have solved it; for he had apprized Dr. *Slop* but the week before, that my mother was at her full reckoning; and as the doctor had heard nothing since, 'twas natural and very political too in him, to have taken a ride to *Shandy-Hall*, as he did, merely to see how matters went on.

But my father's mind took unfortunately a wrong turn in the investigation; running, like the hypercritick's, altogether upon the ringing of the bell and the rap upon the door,——measuring their distance,——and keeping his mind so intent upon the operation, as to have power to think of nothing else,——common-place infirmity of the greatest mathematicians! working with might and main at the demonstration, and so wasting all their strength upon it, that they have none left in them to draw the corollary, to do good with.

The ringing of the bell and the rap upon the door, struck likewise strong upon the sensorium of my uncle *Toby*,——but it excited a very different train of thoughts;——the two irreconcileable pulsations instantly brought *Stevinus*,[6] the great engineer, along with them, into my uncle *Toby*'s mind:——What business *Stevinus* had in this affair,——is the greatest problem of all;——it shall be solved,——but not in the next chapter.

Chapter XI.

WRiting, when properly managed, (as you may be sure I think mine is) is but a different name for conversation: As no one, who knows what he is about in good company, would venture to talk all;——so no author, who understands the just boundaries of decorum and good breeding, would presume to think all: The truest respect which you can pay to the reader's understanding, is to halve this matter amicably, and leave him something to imagine, in his turn, as well as yourself.

For my own part, I am eternally paying him compliments of this kind, and do all that lies in my power to keep his imagination as busy as my own.

'Tis his turn now;——I have given an ample description of Dr. *Slop*'s sad overthrow, and of his sad appearance in the back parlour; ——his imagination must now go on with it for a while.

---

5. An argument referring to personal character.

6. A Dutch Renaissance mathematician and engineer.

Let the reader imagine then, that Dr. *Slop* has told his tale;——
and in what words, and with what aggravations his fancy chooses:
——Let him suppose that *Obadiah* has told his tale also, and with
such rueful looks of affected concern, as he thinks will best contrast
the two figures as they stand by each other: Let him imagine, that
my father has stepp'd up stairs to see my mother:——And, to
conclude this work of imagination,——let him imagine the doctor
wash'd,——rubb'd down,——condoled with,——felicitated,——
got into a pair of *Obadiah*'s pumps, stepping forwards towards the
door, upon the very point of entering upon action.

Truce!——truce, good Dr. *Slop!*——stay thy obstetrick hand;
——return it safe into thy bosom to keep it warm;——little do'st
thou know what obstacles;——little do'st thou think what hidden
causes retard its operation!——Hast thou, Dr. *Slop*,——hast thou
been intrusted with the secret articles of this solemn treaty which
has brought thee into this place?——Art thou aware that, at this
instant, a daughter of *Lucina*[7] is put obstetrically over thy head?
Alas! 'tis too true.——Besides, great son of *Pilumnus!* what canst
thou do?——Thou hast come forth unarm'd;——thou hast left thy
tire tête,[8]——thy new-invented *forceps*,——thy *crotchet*,——thy
squirt, and all thy instruments of salvation and deliverance behind
thee.——By heaven! at this moment they are hanging up in a green
bays bag, betwixt thy two pistols, at thy bed's head!——Ring;——
call;——send *Obadiah* back upon the coach-horse to bring them
with all speed.

——Make great haste, *Obadiah*, quoth my father, and I'll give
thee a crown;——and, quoth my uncle *Toby*, I'll give him another.

Chapter XII.

YOUR sudden and unexpected arrival, quoth my uncle *Toby*,
addressing himself to Dr. *Slop* (all three of them sitting down
to the fire together, as my uncle *Toby* began to speak)——instantly
brought the great *Stevinus* into my head, who, you must know, is a
favourite author with me.——Then, added my father, making use
of the argument Ad *Crumenam*,[9]——I will lay twenty guineas to a
single crown piece, (which will serve to give away to *Obadiah* when
he gets back) that this same *Stevinus* was some engineer or other,
——or has wrote something or other, either directly or indirectly,
upon the science of fortification.

He has so,——replied my uncle *Toby*.——I knew it, said my
father;——tho', for the soul of me, I cannot see what kind of

---

7. Lucina, "who brings the light," was
the Roman goddess of childbirth. Pilumnus was the god of marriage, protector
of pregnant women and newborn infants.

8. French for "head-puller," or forceps.
A crotchet is a hook-like instrument used
in obstetrics.
9. Argument to the purse.

connection there can be betwixt Dr. *Slop*'s sudden coming, and a discourse upon fortification;———yet I fear'd it.———Talk of what we will, brother,———or let the occasion be never so foreign or unfit for the subject,———you are sure to bring it in: I would not, brother *Toby*, continued my father,———I declare I would not have my head so full of curtins and horn-works.———That, I dare say, you would not, quoth Dr. *Slop*, interrupting him, and laughing most immóderately at his pun.

Dennis the critick could not detest and abhor a pun, or the insinuation of a pun, more cordially than my father;———he would grow testy upon it at any time;———but to be broke in upon by one, in a serious discourse, was as bad, he would say, as a fillip upon the nose;———he saw no difference.

Sir, quoth my uncle *Toby*, addressing himself to Dr. *Slop*,———the curtins my brother *Shandy* mentions here, have nothing to do with bed-steads;———tho', I know, *Du Cange*[1] says, "That bed-curtains, in all probability, have taken their name from them;"———nor have the horn-works, he speaks of, any thing in the world to do with the horn-works of cuckoldom:———But the *curtin*, Sir, is the word we use in fortification, for that part of the wall or rampart which lies between the two bastions and joins them.———Besiegers seldom offer to carry on their attacks directly against the curtin, for this reason, because they are so well *flanked*; ('tis the case of other curtins, quoth Dr. *Slop*, laughing) however, continued my uncle *Toby*, to make them sure, we generally choose to place ravelins before them, taking care only to extend them beyond the fossé or ditch:———The common men, who know very little of fortification, confound the ravelin and the half-moon together,———tho' they are very different things;———not in their figure or construction, for we make them exactly alike in all points;———for they always consist of two faces, making a salient angle, with the gorges, not straight, but in form of a crescent.———Where then lies the difference? (quoth my father, a little testily)———In their situations, answered my uncle *Toby*:——— For when a ravelin, brother, stands before the curtin, it is a ravelin; and when a ravelin stands before a bastion, then the ravelin is not a ravelin;———it is a half-moon;———a half-moon likewise is a half-moon, and no more, so long as it stands before its bastion;———but was it to change place, and get before the curtin,———'twould be no longer a half-moon; a half-moon, in that case, is not a half-moon; ———'tis no more than a ravelin.———I think, quoth my father, that the noble science of defence has its weak sides,———as well as others.

———As for the horn-works (high! ho! sigh'd my father) which,

---

1. Du Cange, a seventeenth-century French philologist, composed a dictionary of middle and late Latin. Tradition-ally, a man whose wife had been unfaithful grows horns on his forehead.

continued my uncle *Toby*, my brother was speaking of, they are a very considerable part of an outwork;——they are called by the *French* engineers, *Ouvrage à corne*, and we generally make them to cover such places as we suspect to be weaker than the rest;——'tis form'd by two epaulments or demi-bastions,——they are very pretty, and if you will take a walk, I'll engage to shew you one well worth your trouble.——I own, continued my uncle *Toby*, when we crown them,——they are much stronger, but then they are very expensive, and take up a great deal of ground; so that, in my opinion, they are most of use to cover or defend the head of a camp; otherwise the double tenaille.——By the mother who bore us!——brother *Toby*, quoth my father, not able to hold out any longer,——you would provoke a saint;——here have you got us, I know not how, not only souse into the middle of the old subject again:——But so full is your head of these confounded works, that tho' my wife is this moment in the pains of labour,——and you hear her cry out,——yet nothing will serve you but to carry off the man-midwife.——*Accoucheur*,——if you please, quoth Dr. *Slop*.
——With all my heart, replied my father, I don't care what they call you,——but I wish the whole science of fortification, with all its inventors, at the Devil;——it has been the death of thousands, ——and it will be mine, in the end.——I would not, I would not, brother *Toby*, have my brains so full of saps, mines, blinds, gabions, palisadoes, ravelins, half-moons, and such trumpery, to be proprietor of *Namur*, and of all the towns in *Flanders* with it.

My uncle *Toby* was a man patient of injuries;——not from want of courage,——I have told you in the fifth[2] chapter of this second book, "That he was a man of courage:"——And will add here, that where just occasions presented, or called it forth,——I know no man under whose arm I would sooner have taken shelter; nor did this arise from any insensibility or obtuseness of his intellectual parts;——for he felt this insult of my father's as feelingly as a man could do;——but he was of a peaceful, placid nature,——no jarring element in it,——all was mix'd up so kindly within him; my uncle *Toby* had scarce a heart to retaliate upon a fly.

——Go,——says he, one day at dinner, to an over-grown one which had buzz'd about his nose, and tormented him cruelly all dinner-time,——and which, after infinite attempts, he had caught at last, as it flew by him;——I'll not hurt thee, says my uncle *Toby*, rising from his chair, and going a-cross the room, with the fly in his hand,——I'll not hurt a hair of thy head:——Go, says he, lifting up the sash, and opening his hand as he spoke, to let it escape;—— go poor Devil, get thee gone, why should I hurt thee?——This world surely is wide enough to hold both thee and me.

2. It's in the second chapter.

I was but ten years old when this happened; but whether it was, that the action itself was more in unison to my nerves at that age of pity, which instantly set my whole frame into one vibration of most pleasurable sensation;——or how far the manner and expression of it might go towards it;——or in what degree, or by what secret magick,——a tone of voice and harmony of movement, attuned by mercy, might find a passage to my heart, I know not;——this I know, that the lesson of universal good-will then taught and imprinted by my uncle *Toby*, has never since been worn out of my mind: And tho' I would not depreciate what the study of the *Literæ humaniores*,[3] at the university, have done for me in that respect, or discredit the other helps of an expensive education bestowed upon me, both at home and abroad since;——yet I often think that I owe one half of my philanthropy to that one accidental impression.

☞ This is to serve for parents and governors instead of a whole volume upon the subject.

I could not give the reader this stroke in my uncle *Toby*'s picture, by the instrument with which I drew the other parts of it,——that taking in no more than the mere HOBBY-HORSICAL likeness;——this is a part of his moral character. My father, in this patient endurance of wrongs, which I mention, was very different, as the reader must long ago have noted; he had a much more acute and quick sensibility of nature, attended with a little soreness of temper; tho' this never transported him to any thing which looked like malignancy; ——yet, in the little rubs and vexations of life, 'twas apt to shew itself in a drollish and witty kind of peevishness:——He was, however, frank and generous in his nature,——at all times open to conviction; and in the little ebullitions of this subacid humour towards others, but particularly towards my uncle *Toby*, whom he truly loved;——he would feel more pain, ten times told (except in the affair of my aunt *Dinah*, or where an hypothesis was concerned) than what he ever gave.

The characters of the two brothers, in this view of them, reflected light upon each other, and appear'd with great advantage in this affair which arose about *Stevinus*.

I need not tell the reader, if he keeps a HOBBY-HORSE,——that a man's HOBBY-HORSE is as tender a part as he has about him; and that these unprovoked strokes, at my uncle *Toby*'s could not be unfelt by him.——No;——as I said above, my uncle *Toby* did feel them, and very sensibly too.

Pray, Sir, what said he?——How did he behave?——O, Sir!—— it was great: For as soon as my father had done insulting his HOBBY-HORSE,——he turned his head, without the least emotion, from Dr. *Slop*, to whom he was addressing his discourse, and look'd up

---

3. "Humane letters," the humanities.

into my father's face, with a countenance spread over with so much good nature;——so placid;——so fraternal;——so inexpressibly tender towards him;——it penetrated my father to his heart: He rose up hastily from his chair, and seizing hold of both my uncle *Toby*'s hands as he spoke:——Brother *Toby*, said he,——I beg thy pardon;——forgive, I pray thee, this rash humour which my mother gave me.——My dear, dear brother, answer'd my uncle *Toby*, rising up by my father's help, say no more about it;——you are heartily welcome, had it been ten times as much, brother. But 'tis ungenerous, replied my father, to hurt any man;——a brother worse;——but to hurt a brother of such gentle manners,——so unprovoking,——and so unresenting;——'tis base:——By heaven, 'tis cowardly.——You are heartily welcome, brother, quoth my uncle *Toby*,——had it been fifty times as much.——Besides, what have I to do, my dear *Toby*, cried my father, either with your amusements or your pleasures, unless it was in my power (which it is not) to increase their measure?——Brother *Shandy*, answer'd my uncle *Toby*, looking wistfully in his face,——you are much mistaken in this point;——for you do increase my pleasure very much, in begetting children for the *Shandy* family at your time of life.—— But, by that, Sir, quoth Dr. *Slop*, Mr. *Shandy* increases his own. ——Not a jot, quoth my father.

Chapter XIII.

MY brother does it, quoth my uncle *Toby*, out of *principle.* ——In a family-way, I suppose, quoth Dr. *Slop*.——Pshaw! ——said my father,——'tis not worth talking of.

Chapter XIV.

AT the end of the last chapter, my father and my uncle *Toby* were left both standing, like *Brutus* and *Cassius*[4] at the close of the scene making up their accounts.

As my father spoke the three last words,——he sat down;—— my uncle *Toby* exactly followed his example, only, that before he took his chair, he rung the bell, to order Corporal *Trim*, who was in waiting, to step home for *Stevinus*;——my uncle *Toby*'s house being no further off than the opposite side of the way.

Some men would have dropp'd the subject of *Stevinus*;——but my uncle *Toby* had no resentment in his heart, and he went on with the subject, to shew my father that he had none.

Your sudden appearance, Dr. *Slop*, quoth my uncle, resuming the

4. For instance, the end of Act IV, scene ii, of Shakespeare's *Julius Caesar.*

discourse, instantly brought *Stevinus* into my head. (My father, you may be sure, did not offer to lay any more wagers upon *Stevinus*'s head)——Because, continued my uncle *Toby*, the celebrated sailing chariot, which belonged to Prince *Maurice*, and was of such wonderful contrivance and velocity, as to carry half a dozen people thirty *German* miles, in I don't know how few minutes,——was invented by *Stevinus*, that great mathematician and engineer.

You might have spared your servant the trouble, quoth Dr. *Slop*, (as the fellow is lame) of going for *Stevinus*'s account of it, because, in my return from *Leyden* thro' the *Hague*, I walked as far as *Schevling*, which is two long miles, on purpose to take a view of it.

——That's nothing, replied my uncle *Toby*, to what the learned *Peireskius* did, who walked a matter of five hundred miles, reckoning from *Paris* to *Schevling*, and from *Schevling* to *Paris* back again, in order to see it,——and nothing else.

Some men cannot bear to be out-gone.

The more fool *Peireskius*, replied Dr. *Slop*. But mark,——'twas out of no contempt of *Peireskius* at all;——but that *Peireskius*'s indefatigable labour in trudging so far on foot out of love for the sciences, reduced the exploit of Dr. *Slop*, in that affair, to nothing;——the more fool *Peireskius*, said he again:——Why so?—— replied my father, taking his brother's part, not only to make reparation as fast as he could for the insult he had given him, which sat still upon my father's mind;——but partly, that my father began really to interest himself in the discourse;——Why so?——said he. Why is *Peireskius*, or any man else, to be abused for an appetite for that, or any other morsel of sound knowledge? For, notwithstanding I know nothing of the chariot in question, continued he, the inventor of it must have had a very mechanical head; and tho' I cannot guess upon what principles of philosophy he has atchiev'd it;——yet certainly his machine has been constructed upon solid ones, be they what they will, or it could not have answer'd at the rate my brother mentions.

It answered, replied my uncle *Toby*, as well, if not better; for, as *Peireskius* elegantly expresses it, speaking of the velocity of its motion, *Tam citus erat, quam erat ventus*; which, unless I have forgot my Latin, is, *that it was as swift as the wind itself*.

But pray, Dr. *Slop*, quoth my father, interrupting my uncle (tho' not without begging pardon for it, at the same time) upon what principles was this self-same chariot set a-going?——Upon very pretty principles to be sure, replied Dr. *Slop*;——and I have often wondered, continued he, evading the question, why none of our Gentry, who live upon large plains like this of ours,——(especially they whose wives are not past child-bearing) attempt nothing of this

kind; for it would not only be infinitely expeditious upon sudden
calls, to which the sex is subject,——if the wind only served,——
but would be excellent good husbandry to make use of the winds,
which cost nothing, and which eat nothing, rather than horses,
which (the Devil take 'em) both cost and eat a great deal.

For that very reason, replied my father, "Because they cost nothing, and because they eat nothing,"——the scheme is bad;——it is
the consumption of our products, as well as the manufactures of
them, which gives bread to the hungry, circulates trade,——brings
in money, and supports the value of our lands;——and tho', I own,
if I was a Prince, I would generously recompense the scientifick
head which brought forth such contrivances;——yet I would as
peremptorily suppress the use of them.

My father here had got into his element,——and was going on as
prosperously with his dissertation upon trade, as my uncle *Toby* had
before, upon his of fortification;——but, to the loss of much sound
knowledge, the destinies in the morning had decreed that no dissertation of any kind should be spun by my father that day;——for as
he opened his mouth to begin the next sentence,

Chapter XV.

IN popp'd Corporal *Trim* with *Stevinus*:——But 'twas too late,
——all the discourse had been exhausted without him, and was
running into a new channel.

——You may take the book home again, *Trim*, said my uncle
Toby, nodding to him.

But pri'thee, Corporal, quoth my father, drolling,——look first
into it, and see if thou canst spy aught of a sailing chariot in it.

Corporal *Trim*, by being in the service, had learned to obey,——
and not to remonstrate;——so taking the book to a side-table, and
running over the leaves; an' please your Honour, said *Trim*, I can
see no such thing;——however, continued the Corporal, drolling a
little in his turn, I'll make sure work of it, an' please your Honour;
——so taking hold of the two covers of the book, one in each hand,
and letting the leaves fall down, as he bent the covers back, he gave
the book a good sound shake.

There is something fallen out, however, said *Trim*, an' please
your Honour; but it is not a chariot, or any thing like one:——
Pri'thee Corporal, said my father, smiling, what is it then?——I
think, answered *Trim*, stooping to take it up,——'tis more like a
sermon,——for it begins, with a text of scripture, and the chapter
and verse;——and then goes on, not as a chariot,——but like a sermon directly.

The company smiled.

I cannot conceive how it is possible, quoth my uncle *Toby*, for such a thing as a sermon to have got into my *Stevinus*.

I think 'tis a sermon, replied *Trim*;——but if it please your Honours, as it is a fair hand, I will read you a page;——for *Trim*, you must know, loved to hear himself read almost as well as talk.

I have ever a strong propensity, said my father, to look into things which cross my way, by such strange fatalities as these;—— and as we have nothing better to do, at least till *Obadiah* gets back, I should be obliged to you, brother, if Dr. *Slop* has no objection to it, to order the Corporal to give us a page or two of it,——if he is as able to do it, as he seems willing. An' please your Honour, quoth *Trim*, I officiated two whole campaigns in *Flanders*, as Clerk to the Chaplain of the Regiment.——He can read it, quoth my uncle *Toby*, as well as I can.——*Trim*, I assure you, was the best scholar in my company, and should have had the next Halberd,[5] but for the poor fellow's misfortune. Corporal *Trim* laid his hand upon his heart, and made an humble bow to his Master;——then laying down his hat upon the floor, and taking up the sermon in his left-hand, in order to have his right at liberty,——he advanced, nothing doubting, into the middle of the room, where he could best see, and be best seen by, his audience.

Chapter XVI.

——If you have any objection,——said my father, addressing himself to Dr. *Slop*: Not in the least, replied Dr. *Slop*;——for it does not appear on which side of the question it is wrote;——it may be a composition of a divine of our church, as well as yours,——so that we run equal risks.——'Tis wrote upon neither side, quoth *Trim*, for 'tis only upon *Conscience*, an' please your Honours.

Trim's reason put his audience into good humour,——all but Dr. *Slop*, who, turning his head about towards *Trim*, look'd a little angry.

Begin, *Trim*,——and read distinctly, quoth my father;——I will, an' please your Honour, replied the Corporal, making a bow, and bespeaking attention with a slight movement of his right hand.

Chapter XVII.

——But before the Corporal begins, I must first give you a description of his attitude,——otherwise he will naturally stand represented, by your imagination, in an uneasy posture,——stiff,

---

5. A *halberd* is a combination spear and axe, carried on a long pole; by the eighteenth century (as now) it was carried mostly for ceremonial occasions, and here suggests that Trim was in line for a promotion.

W.Hogarth inv.ᵗ   Vol.2.page 128.   S.Ravenet Sculp.ᵗ

——perpendicular,——dividing the weight of his body equally upon both legs;——his eye fix'd, as if on duty;——his look determined,——clinching the sermon in his left-hand, like his firelock:——In a word, you would be apt to paint *Trim*, as if he was standing in his platoon ready for action:——His attitude was as unlike all this as you can conceive.

He stood before them with his body swayed, and bent forwards just so far, as to make an angle of 85 degrees and a half upon the plain of the horizon;——which sound orators, to whom I address this, know very well, to be the true persuasive angle of incidence;——in any other angle you may talk and preach;——'tis certain,——and it is done every day;——but with what effect,——I leave the world to judge?

The necessity of this precise angle of 85 degrees and a half to a mathematical exactness,——does it not shew us, by the way,——how the arts and sciences mutually befriend each other?

How the duce Corporal *Trim*, who knew not so much as an acute angle from an obtuse one, came to hit it so exactly;——or whether it was chance or nature, or good sense or imitation, &c. shall be commented upon in that part of this cyclopædia of arts and sciences, where the instrumental parts of the eloquence of the senate, the pulpit, the bar, the coffee-house, the bed-chamber, and fire-side, fall under consideration.

He stood,——for I repeat it, to take the picture of him in at one view, with his body sway'd, and somewhat bent forwards,——his right leg firm under him, sustaining seven-eighths of his whole weight,——the foot of his left leg, the defect of which was no disadvantage to his attitude, advanced a little,——not laterally, nor forwards, but in a line betwixt them;——his knee bent, but that not violently,——but so as to fall within the limits of the line of beauty;[6]——and I add, of the line of science too;——for consider, it had one eighth part of his body to bear up;——so that in this case the position of the leg is determined,——because the foot could be no further advanced, or the knee more bent, than what would allow him mechanically, to receive an eighth part of his whole weight under it,——and to carry it too.

☞ This I recommend to painters;——need I add,——to orators?——I think not; for, unless they practise it,——they must fall upon their noses.

So much for Corporal *Trim*'s body and legs.——He held the sermon loosely,——not carelessly, in his left-hand, raised something above his stomach, and detach'd a little from his breast;——his right arm falling negligently by his side, as nature and the laws

---

6. According to Hogath, in particular, the line of beauty is a line in the form of a lengthened letter *S*.

of gravity order'd it,——but with the palm of it open and turned towards his audience, ready to aid the sentiment, in case it stood in need.

Corporal *Trim*'s eyes and the muscles of his face were in full harmony with the other parts of him;——he look'd frank,—— unconstrained,——something assured,——but not bordering upon assurance.

Let not the critick ask how Corporal *Trim* could come by all this; I've told him it shall be explained;——but so he stood before my father, my uncle *Toby*, and Dr. *Slop*,——so swayed his body, so contrasted his limbs, and with such an oratorical sweep throughout the whole figure,——a statuary might have modell'd from it;—— nay, I doubt whether the oldest Fellow of a College,——or the *Hebrew* Professor himself, could have much mended it.

Trim made a bow, and read as follows:

The S E R M O N .[7]

H E B R E W S xiii. 18.

——*For we* trust *we have a good Conscience.*——

"TRust!——Trust we have a good conscience!"
[Certainly, *Trim*, quoth my father, interrupting him, you give that sentence a very improper accent; for you curl up your nose, man, and read it with such a sneering tone, as if the Parson was going to abuse the Apostle.

He is, an' please your Honour, replied *Trim*. Pugh! said my father, smiling.

Sir, quoth Dr. *Slop*, *Trim* is certainly in the right; for the writer (who I perceive is a Protestant) by the snappish manner in which he takes up the Apostle, is certainly going to abuse him,——if this treatment of him has not done it already. But from whence, replied my father, have you concluded so soon Dr. *Slop*, that the writer is of our Church?——for aught I can see yet,——he may be of any Church:——Because, answered Dr. *Slop*, if he was of ours,——he durst no more take such a licence,——than a bear by his beard: ——If, in our communion, Sir, a man was to insult an Apostle, ——a saint,——or even the paring of a saint's nail,——he would have his eyes scratched out.——What, by the saint? quoth my uncle *Toby*. No, replied Dr. *Slop*,——he would have an old house over his head.[8] Pray is the Inquisition an antient building, answered my uncle *Toby*, or is it a modern one?——I know nothing of architec-

7. The sermon is one that Sterne had preached at the cathedral church of York, at the opening of the summer court sessions (assizes) in 1750. It had been pub-lished separately, but Sterne apparently liked it enough to want to use it again.
8. To have an old house over your head is to be in trouble.

ture, replied Dr. *Slop.*——An' please your Honours, quoth *Trim*, the Inquisition is the vilest——Pri'thee spare thy description, *Trim*, I hate the very name of it, said my father.——No matter for that, answered Dr. *Slop*,——it has its uses; for tho' I'm no great advocate for it, yet in such a case as this, he would soon be taught better manners; and I can tell him, if he went on at that rate, would be flung into the Inquisition for his pains. God help him then, quoth my uncle *Toby*. Amen, added *Trim*; for, heaven above knows, I have a poor brother who has been fourteen years a captive in it.——I never heard one word of it before, said my uncle *Toby*, hastily:——How came he there, *Trim?*——O, Sir! the story will make your heart bleed,——as it has made mine a thousand times; ——but it is too long to be told now;——your Honour shall hear it from first to last some day when I am working besides you in our fortifications;——but the short of the story is this:——That my brother *Tom* went over a servant to *Lisbon*,——and then married a *Jew's* widow, who kept a small shop, and sold sausages, which, some how or other, was the cause of his being taken in the middle of the night out of his bed, where he was lying with his wife and two small children, and carried directly to the Inquisition, where, God help him, continued *Trim*, fetching a sigh from the bottom of his heart,——the poor honest lad lies confined at this hour;——he was as honest a soul, added *Trim*, (pulling out his handkerchief) as ever blood warm'd.——

——The tears trickled down *Trim's* cheeks faster than he could well wipe them away:——A dead silence in the room ensued for some minutes.——Certain proof of pity!

Come, *Trim*, quoth my father, after he saw the poor fellow's grief had got a little vent,——read on,——and put this melancholy story out of thy head:——I grieve that I interrupted thee;——but pri'-thee begin the sermon again;——for if the first sentence in it is matter of abuse, as thou sayest, I have a great desire to know what kind of provocation the Apostle has given.

Corporal *Trim* wiped his face, and returning his handkerchief into his pocket, and, making a bow as he did it,——he began again.]

The SERMON.

HEBREWS xiii. 18.

——*For we* trust *we have a good Conscience.*——

"TRust! trust we have a good conscience! Surely if there is any thing in this life which a man may depend upon, and to the knowledge of which he is capable of arriving upon the most indisputable evidence, it must be this very thing,——whether he has a good conscience or no."

[I am positive I am right, quoth Dr. *Slop.*]

"If a man thinks at all, he cannot well be a stranger to the true state of this account;——he must be privy to his own thoughts and desires;——he must remember his past pursuits, and know certainly the true springs and motives, which, in general, have governed the actions of his life."

[I defy him, without an assistant, quoth Dr. *Slop.*]

"In other matters we may be deceived by false appearances; and, as the Wise Man complains, *hardly do we guess aright at the things that are upon the earth, and with labour do we find the things that are before us.*[9] But here the mind has all the evidence and facts within herself;——is conscious of the web she has wove;——knows its texture and fineness, and the exact share which every passion has had in working upon the several designs which virtue or vice had plann'd before her."

[The language is good, and I declare *Trim* reads very well, quoth my father.]

"Now,——as conscience is nothing else but the knowledge which the mind has within herself of this; and the judgment, either of approbation or censure, which it unavoidably makes upon the successive actions of our lives; 'tis plain you will say, from the very terms of the proposition,——whenever this inward testimony goes against a man, and he stands self-accused,——that he must necessarily be a guilty man.——And, on the contrary, when the report is favourable on his side, and his heart condemns him not;——that it is not a matter of *trust*, as the Apostle intimates,——but a matter of *certainty* and fact, that the conscience is good, and that the man must be good also."

[Then the Apostle is altogether in the wrong, I suppose, quoth Dr. *Slop*, and the Protestant divine is in the right. Sir, have patience, replied my father, for I think it will presently appear that *St. Paul* and the Protestant divine are both of an opinion.——As nearly so, quoth Dr. *Slop*, as East is to West;——but this, continued he, lifting both hands, comes from the liberty of the press.

It is no more, at the worst, replied my uncle *Toby*, than the liberty of the pulpit; for it does not appear that the sermon is printed, or ever likely to be.

Go on, *Trim*, quoth my father.]

"At first sight this may seem to be a true state of the case; and I make no doubt but the knowledge of right and wrong is so truly impressed upon the mind of man,——that did no such thing ever

---

9. Sterne's phrasing is not exact, but the passage parallels Ecclesiastes 8:17.

happen, as that the conscience of a man, by long habits of sin, might (as the scripture assures it may) insensibly become hard;——and, like some tender parts of his body, by much stress and continual hard usage, lose, by degrees, that nice sense and perception with which God and nature endow'd it.——Did this never happen;——or was it certain that self-love could never hang the least bias upon the judgment;——or that the little interests below, could rise up and perplex the faculties of our upper regions, and encompass them about with clouds and thick darkness:——Could no such thing as favour and affection enter this sacred COURT:——Did WIT disdain to take a bribe in it;——or was asham'd to shew its face as an advocate for an unwarrantable enjoyment.——Or, lastly, were we assured, that INTEREST stood always unconcern'd whilst the cause was hearing,——and that passion never got into the judgment-seat, and pronounc'd sentence in the stead of reason, which is supposed always to preside and determine upon the case. ——Was this truly so, as the objection must suppose;——no doubt then, the religious and moral state of a man would be exactly what he himself esteem'd it;——and the guilt or innocence of every man's life could be known, in general, by no better measure, than the degrees of his own approbation and censure.

"I own, in one case, whenever a man's conscience does accuse him, (as it seldom errs on that side) that he is guilty; and, unless in melancholy and hypocondriack cases, we may safely pronounce upon it, that there is always sufficient grounds for the accusation.

"But the converse of the proposition will not hold true;—— namely, that whenever there is guilt the conscience must accuse; and if it does not, that a man is therefore innocent.——This is not fact:——So that the common consolation which some good christian or other, is hourly administering to himself,——that he thanks God his mind does not misgive him; and that, consequently, he has a good conscience, because he has a quiet one,——is fallacious; ——and as current as the inference is, and as infallible as the rule appears at first sight, yet, when you look nearer to it, and try the truth of this rule upon plain facts,——you see it liable to so much error from a false application;——the principle upon which it goes so often perverted;——the whole force of it lost, and sometimes so vilely cast away, that it is painful to produce the common examples from human life which confirm the account.

"A man shall be vicious and utterly debauched in his principles; ——exceptionable in his conduct to the world; shall live shameless, in the open commission of a sin which no reason or pretence can justify;——a sin, by which, contrary to all the workings of humanity, he shall ruin for ever the deluded partner of his guilt;——rob her of her best dowry; and not only cover her own head with dishonour,———but involve a whole virtuous family in shame and sorrow for her sake.———Surely, you will think conscience must lead such a man a troublesome Life;———he can have no rest night or day from its reproaches.

"Alas! CONSCIENCE had something else to do, all this time, than break in upon him; as *Elijah* reproached the god *Baal,*———this domestick God *was either talking, or pursuing, or was in a journey, or peradventure he slept and could not be awoke.*[1]

"Perhaps HE was gone out in company with HONOUR to fight a duel;———to pay off some debt at play;———or dirty annuity, the bargain of his lust: Perhaps CONSCIENCE all this time was engaged at home, talking loud against petty larceny, and executing vengeance upon some such puny crimes as his fortune and rank in life secured him against all temptation of committing; so that he lives as merrily, [If he was of our church tho', quoth Dr. *Slop,* he could not]———sleeps as soundly in his bed;———and at last meets death as unconcernedly;———perhaps much more so than a much better man."

[All this is impossible with us, quoth Dr. *Slop,* turning to my father,———the case could not happen in our church.———It happens in ours, however, replied my father, but too often.———I own, quoth Dr. *Slop* (struck a little with my father's frank acknowledgment) ———that a man in the *Romish* church may live as badly;———but then he cannot easily die so.———'Tis little matter, replied my father, with an air of indifference,———how a rascal dies.———I mean, answer'd Dr. *Slop,* he would be denied the benefits of the last sacraments.———Pray, how many have you in all, said my uncle *Toby,*———for I always forget?———Seven, answered Dr. *Slop.*——— Humph!———said my uncle *Toby;*———tho' not accented as a note of acquiescence,———but as an interjection of that particular species of surprize, when a man, in looking into a drawer, finds more of a thing than he expected.———Humph! replied my uncle *Toby.* Dr. *Slop,* who had an ear, understood my uncle *Toby* as well as if he had wrote a whole volume against the seven sacraments.[2]——— Humph! replied Dr. *Slop,* (stating my uncle *Toby*'s argument over again to him)———Why, Sir, are there not seven cardinal virtues? ———Seven mortal sins?———Seven golden candle-sticks?———Seven heavens?———'Tis more than I know, replied my uncle *Toby.*——— Are there not seven wonders of the world?———Seven days of the creation?———Seven planets?———Seven plagues?———That there are, quoth my father, with a most affected gravity. But pri'thee, continued he, go on with the rest of thy characters, *Trim.*]

1. Elijah reproached the god Baal in I Kings 18:27.
2. Most Protestant denominations count only the Eucharist (or Holy Communion) and Baptism as sacraments. Roman Catholics have seven: Eucharist, Baptism, Confirmation, Marriage, Penance, Extreme Unction (Last Rites), and Holy Orders (monastic, etc.).

"Another is sordid, unmerciful, (here *Trim* waved
hand) a strait-hearted, selfish wretch, incapable either ⸺ private
friendship or publick spirit. Take notice how he passes by the widow and orphan in their distress, and sees all the miseries incident
to human life without a sigh or a prayer." [And please your Honours, cried *Trim*, I think this a viler man than the other.]

"Shall not conscience rise up and sting him on such occasions?
⸺No; thank God there is no occasion; *I pay every man his
own;*⸺*I have no fornication to answer to my conscience;*⸺*no
faithless vows or promises to make up;*⸺*I have debauched no
man's wife or child; thank God, I am not as other men, adulterers,
unjust, or even as this libertine, who stands before me.*

"A third is crafty and designing in his nature. View his whole
life;⸺'tis nothing but a cunning contexture of dark arts and
unequitable subterfuges, basely to defeat the true intent of all laws,
⸺plain dealing and the safe enjoyment of our several properties.
⸺You will see such a one working out a frame of little designs
upon the ignorance and perplexities of the poor and needy man;
⸺ shall raise a fortune upon the inexperience of a youth, or the
unsuspecting temper of his friend, who would have trusted him with
his life.

"When old age comes on, and repentance calls him to look back
upon this black account, and state it over again with his conscience,
⸺Conscience looks into the Statutes at Large;⸺finds no
express law broken by what he has done;⸺perceives no penalty
or forfeiture of goods and chattels incurred;⸺sees no scourge
waving over his head, or prison opening his gates upon him:⸺
What is there to affright his conscience?⸺Conscience has got
safely entrenched behind the Letter of the Law; sits there invulner-
able, fortified with **Cases** and **Reports** so strongly on all sides;⸺
that it is not preaching can dispossess it of its hold."

[Here Corporal *Trim* and my uncle *Toby* exchanged looks with
each other.⸺Aye,⸺aye, *Trim!* quoth my uncle *Toby*, shaking
his head,⸺these are but sorry fortifications, *Trim.*⸺O! very
poor work, answered *Trim*, to what your Honour and I make of
it.⸺The character of this last man, said Dr. *Slop*, interrupting
Trim, is more detestable than all the rest;⸺and seems to have
been taken from some pettifogging Lawyer amongst you:⸺
Amongst us, a man's conscience could not possibly continue so long
blinded;⸺three times in a year, at least, he must go to confession. Will that restore it to sight? quoth my uncle *Toby.*⸺Go on,
Trim, quoth my father, or *Obadiah* will have got back before thou
hast got to the end of thy sermon;⸺'tis a very short one, replied
Trim.⸺I wish it was longer, quoth my uncle *Toby*, for I like it
hugely.⸺*Trim* went on.]

"A fourth man shall want even this refuge;⸺shall break

through all this ceremony of slow chicane;——scorns the doubtful workings of secret plots and cautious trains to bring about his purpose:——See the bare-faced villain, how he cheats, lies, perjures, robs, murders.——Horrid!——But indeed much better was not to be expected, in the present case,——the poor man was in the dark!——his priest had got the keeping of his conscience;——and all he would let him know of it, was, That he must believe in the Pope;——go to Mass;——cross himself;——tell his beads;——be a good Catholick, and that this, in all conscience, was enough to carry him to heaven. What;——if he perjures!——Why;——he had a mental reservation in it.——But if he is so wicked and abandoned a wretch as you represent him;——if he robs,——if he stabs,——will not conscience, on every such act, receive a wound itself? Aye,——but the man has carried it to confession;——the wound digests there, and will do well enough, and in a short time be quite healed up by absolution. O Popery! what hast thou to answer for?——when, not content with the too many natural and fatal ways, thro' which the heart of man is every day thus treacherous to itself above all things;——thou has wilfully set open this wide gate of deceit before the face of this unwary traveller, too apt, God knows, to go astray of himself; and confidently speak peace to himself, when there is no peace.

"Of this the common instances which I have drawn out of life, are too notorious to require much evidence. If any man doubts the reality of them, or thinks it impossible for a man to be such a bubble to himself,——I must refer him a moment to his own reflections, and will then venture to trust my appeal with his own heart.

"Let him consider in how different a degree of detestation, numbers of wicked actions stand *there*, tho' equally bad and vicious in their own natures;——he will soon find that such of them, as strong inclination and custom have prompted him to commit, are generally dress'd out and painted with all the false beauties, which a soft and a flattering hand can give them;——and that the others, to which he feels no propensity, appear, at once, naked and deformed, surrounded with all the true circumstances of folly and dishonour.

"When *David*[3] surprized *Saul* sleeping in the cave, and cut off the skirt of his robe,——we read his heart smote him for what he had done:——But in the matter of *Uriah*, where a faithful and gallant servant, whom he ought to have loved and honoured, fell to make way for his lust,——where conscience had so much greater reason to take the alarm, his heart smote him not. A whole year had almost passed from the first commission of that crime, to the time *Nathan*

3. For David and Saul, see I Samuel 24: 3–5. For the story of David's desire for Bathsheba, his successful plot to have her husband (his friend) Uriah killed in battle, and for the reproach that Nathan tenders him in the parable of the ewe lamb, see II Samuel 11 and 12.

was sent to reprove him; and we read not once of the least sorrow or compunction of heart which he testified, during all that time, for what he had done.

"Thus conscience, this once able monitor,——placed on high as a judge within us, and intended by our maker as a just and equitable one too,——by an unhappy train of causes and impediments, takes often such imperfect cognizance of what passes,——does its office so negligently,——sometimes so corruptly,——that it is not to be trusted alone; and therefore we find there is a necessity, an absolute necessity of joining another principle with it to aid, if not govern, its determinations.

"So that if you would form a just judgment of what is of infinite importance to you not to be misled in,——namely, in what degree of real merit you stand either as an honest man, an useful citizen, a faithful subject to your king, or a good servant to your God,—— call in religion and morality.——Look,——What is written in the law of God?——How readest thou?——Consult calm reason and the unchangeable obligations of justice and truth;——what say they?

"Let CONSCIENCE determine the matter upon these reports;—— and then if thy heart condemns thee not, which is the case the Apostle supposes,——the rule will be infallible;" [Here Dr. *Slop* fell asleep] "*thou wilt have confidence towards God;*[4]——that is, have just grounds to believe the judgment thou has past upon thyself, is the judgment of God; and nothing else but an anticipation of that righteous sentence which will be pronounced upon thee hereafter by that Being, to whom thou art finally to give an account of thy actions.

"*Blessed is the man,* indeed then, as the author of the book of *Ecclesiasticus* expresses it, *who is not prick'd with the multitude of his sins: Blessed is the man whose heart hath not condemn'd him; whether he be rich, or whether he be poor, if he have a good heart,* (a heart thus guided and informed) *he shall at all times rejoice in a chearful countenance; his mind shall tell him more than seven watch-men that sit above upon a tower on high.*[5]——[A tower has no strength, quoth my uncle *Toby*, unless 'tis flank'd.] In the darkest doubts it shall conduct him safer than a thousand casuists, and give the state he lives in a better security for his behavior than all the clauses and restrictions put together, which law-makers are forced to multiply:——*Forced*, I say, as things stand; human laws not being a matter of original choice, but of pure necessity, brought in to fence against the mischievous effects of those consciences which are no law unto themselves; well intending, by the many

4. See I John 3:21.   5. See Ecclesiasticus 13:25–26, 14:1–2.

provisions made,——that in all such corrupt and misguided cases, where principles and the checks of conscience will not make us upright,——to supply their force, and, by the terrors of gaols and halters, oblige us to it."

[I see plainly, said my father, that this sermon has been composed to be preach'd at the Temple,[6]——or at some Assize.——I like the reasoning,——and am sorry that Dr. *Slop* has fallen asleep before the time of his conviction;——for it is now clear, that the Parson, as I thought at first, never insulted St. *Paul* in the least;—— nor has there been, brother, the least difference between them.—— A great matter, if they had differed, replied my uncle *Toby*,——the best friends in the world may differ sometimes.——True,—— brother *Toby*, quoth my father, shaking hands with him,——we'll fill our pipes, brother, and then *Trim* shall go on.

Well,——what do'st thou think of it? said my father, speaking to Corporal *Trim*, as he reach'd his tobacco-box.

I think, answered the Corporal, that the seven watch-men upon the tower, who, I suppose, are all centinels there,——are more, an' please your Honour, than were necessary;——and, to go on at that rate, would harrass a regiment all to pieces, which a commanding officer, who loves his men, will never do, if he can help it; because two centinels, added the Corporal, are as good as twenty.——I have been a commanding officer myself in the *Corps de Garde*[7] a hundred times, continued *Trim*, rising an inch higher in his figure, as he spoke,——and all the time I had the honour to serve his Majesty King *William*, in relieving the most considerable posts, I never left more than two in my life.——Very right, *Trim*, quoth my uncle *Toby*;——but you do not consider *Trim*, that the towers, in *Solomon*'s days, were not such things as our bastions, flank'd and defended by other works;——this, *Trim*, was an invention since *Solomon*'s death; nor had they horn-works, or ravelins before the curtin, in his time;——or such a fossé as we make with a cuvette in the middle of it, and with cover'd-ways and counterscarps pallisadoed along it, to guard against a *Coup de main*:[8]——So that the seven men upon the tower were a party, I dare say, from the *Corps de Garde*, set there, not only to look out, but to defend it.——They could be no more, an' please your Honour, than a Corporal's Guard.——My father smiled inwardly,——but not outwardly;—— the subject between my uncle *Toby* and Corporal *Trim* being rather too serious, considering what had happened, to make a jest of:—— So, putting his pipe into his mouth, which he had just lighted,—— he contented himself with ordering *Trim* to read on. He read on as follows:]

---

6. The Temple Church in London has associations with one of the three Inns of Court where lawyers train.

7. A unit of men on guard duty.
8. A "sweep of the hand," or surprise attack.

"To have the fear of God before our eyes, and, in our mutual dealings with each other, to govern our actions by the eternal measures of right and wrong:——The first of these will comprehend the duties of religion;——the second, those of morality, which are so inseparably connected together, that you cannot divide these two *tables*,[9] even in imagination, (tho' the attempt is often made in practice) without breaking and mutually destroying them both.

"I said the attempt is often made, and so it is;——there being nothing more common than to see a man who has no sense at all of religion,——and indeed has so much honesty as to pretend to none, who would take it as the bitterest affront, should you but hint at a suspicion of his moral character,——or imagine he was not conscientiously just and scrupulous to the uttermost mite.

"When there is some appearance that it is so,——tho' one is unwilling even to suspect the appearance of so amiable a virtue as moral honesty, yet were we to look into the grounds of it, in the present case, I am persuaded we should find little reason to envy such a one the honour of his motive.

"Let him declaim as pompously as he chooses upon the subject, it will be found to rest upon no better foundation than either his interest, his pride, his ease, or some such little and changeable passion as will give us but small dependence upon his actions in matters of great stress.

"I will illustrate this by an example.

"I know the banker I deal with, or the physician I usually call in [There is no need, cried Dr. *Slop*, (waking) to call in any physician in this case] to be neither of them men of much religion: I hear them make a jest of it every day, and treat all its sanctions with so much scorn, as to put the matter past doubt. Well;——notwithstanding this, I put my fortune into the hands of the one;——and what is dearer still to me, I trust my life to the honest skill of the other.

"Now, let me examine what is my reason for this great confidence.——Why, in the first place, I believe there is no probability that either of them will employ the power I put into their hands to my disadvantage;——I consider that honesty serves the purposes of this life:——I know their success in the world depends upon the fairness of their characters.——In a word,——I'm persuaded that they cannot hurt me, without hurting themselves more.

"But put it otherwise, namely, that interest lay, for once, on the other side; that a case should happen, wherein the one, without stain to his reputation, could secrete my fortune, and leave me naked in the world;——or that the other could send me out of it, and enjoy an estate by my death, without dishonour to himself or

<hr>

9. Sterne is alluding to the two tables of the Ten Commandments (Exodus 31–32).

his art:——In this case, what hold have I of either of them?——
Religion, the strongest of all motives, is out of the question:——
Interest, the next most powerful motive in the world, is strongly
against me:——What have I left to cast into the opposite scale to
balance this temptation?——Alas! I have nothing,——nothing
but what is lighter than a bubble.——I must lay at the mercy of
Honour, or some such capricious principle.——Strait security for
two of my most valuable blessings!——my property and my life.

"As, therefore, we can have no dependence upon morality without religion;——so, on the other hand, there is nothing better to be
expected from religion without morality; nevertheless, 'tis no prod-
igy to see a man whose real moral character stands very low, who
yet entertains the highest notion of himself, in the light of a religious man.

"He shall not only be covetous, revengeful, implacable,——but
even a-wanting in points of common honesty; yet, inasmuch as he
talks aloud against the infidelity of the age,——is zealous for some
points of religion,——goes twice a day to church;——attends the
sacraments,——and amuses himself with a few instrumental parts
of religion,——shall cheat his conscience into a judgment that, for
this, he is a religious man, and has discharged truly his duty to
God: And you will find that such a man, thro' force of this delu-
sion, generally looks down with spiritual pride upon every other
man who has less affectation of piety,——tho', perhaps, ten times
more moral honesty than himself.

"*This likewise is a sore evil under the sun;*[1] and, I believe there is
no one mistaken principle which, for its time, has wrought more
serious michiefs.——For a general proof of this,——examine
the history of the *Romish* church;——[Well, what can you make of
that? cried Dr. *Slop*]——see what scenes of cruelty, murders,
rapines, blood-shed, [They may thank their own obstinacy, cried
Dr. *Slop*] have all been sanctified by a religion not strictly governed
by morality.

"In how many kingdoms of the world, [Here *Trim* kept waving
his right-hand from the sermon to the extent of his arm, returning it
backwards and forwards to the conclusion of the Paragraph.]

"In how many kingdoms of the world has the crusading sword of
this misguided saint-errant spared neither age, or merit, or sex, or
condition?——and, as he fought under the banners of a religion
which set him loose from justice and humanity, he shew'd none;
mercilessly trampled upon both,——heard neither the cries of the
unfortunate, nor pitied their distresses.

[I have been in many a battle, an' please your Honour, quoth

---

1. A paraphrase of a frequent theme in Ecclesiastes, for example 5:13.

Trim, sighing, but never in so melancholy a one as this.———I would not have drawn a tricker in it, against these poor souls,———to have been made a general officer.———Why, what do you understand of the affair? said Dr. *Slop,* looking towards *Trim* with something more of contempt than the Corporal's honest heart deserved.——— What do you know, friend, about this battle you talk of?———I know, replied *Trim,* that I never refused quarter in my life to any man who cried out for it;———but to a woman or a child, continued *Trim,* before I would level my musket at them, I would lose my life a thousand times.———Here's a crown for thee, *Trim,* to drink with *Obadiah* to-night, quoth my uncle *Toby,* and I'll give *Obadiah* another too.———God bless your Honour, replied *Trim,*———I had rather these poor women and children had it.———Thou art an honest fellow, quoth my uncle *Toby.*———My father nodded his head, ———as much as to say,———and so he is.———

But pri'thee *Trim,* said my father, make an end,———for I see thou hast but a leaf or two left.]

Corporal *Trim* read on.

"If the testimony of past centuries in this matter is not sufficient, ———consider, at this instant, how the votaries of that religion are every day thinking to do service and honour to God, by actions which are a dishonour and scandal to themselves.

"To be convinced of this, go with me for a moment into the Prisons of the inquisition.———[God help my poor brother *Tom.*] ———Behold *Religion,* with *Mercy* and *Justice* chained down under her feet,———there sitting ghastly upon a black tribunal, propp'd up with racks and instruments of torment. Hark!———hark! what a piteous groan! [Here *Trim's* face turned as pale as ashes.] See the melancholy wretch who utter'd it"———[Here the tears began to trickle down] just brought forth to undergo the anguish of a mock trial, and endure the utmost pains that a studied system of cruelty has been able to invent.———[D—n them all, quoth *Trim,* his colour returning into his face as red as blood.]———Behold this helpless victim delivered up to his tormentors,———his body so wasted with sorrow and confinement.———[Oh! 'tis my brother, cried poor *Trim* in a most passionate exclamation, dropping the sermon upon the Ground, and clapping his hands together———I fear 'tis poor *Tom.* My father's and my uncle *Toby's* hearts yearn'd with sympathy for the poor fellow's distress,———even *Slop* himself acknowledged pity for him.———Why, *Trim,* said my father, this is not a history,——— 'tis a sermon thou art reading;———pri'thee begin the sentence again.]———Behold this helpless victim deliver'd up to his tormentors,———his body so wasted with sorrow and confinement, you will see every nerve and muscle as it suffers.

"Observe the last movement of that horrid engine! [I would

rather face a cannon, quoth *Trim*, stamping.]——See what convulsions it has thrown him into!——Consider the nature of the
posture in which he now lies stretched——what exquisite tortures
he endures by it!——[I hope 'tis not in *Portugal*.]——'Tis all nature can bear! Good God! see how it keeps his weary soul hanging
upon his trembling lips! [I would not read another line of it, quoth
Trim, for all this world;——I fear, an' please your Honours, all this
is in *Portugal*, where my poor brother *Tom* is. I tell thee, *Trim*,
again, quoth my father, 'tis not an historical account,——'tis a
description.——'Tis only a description, honest man, quoth *Slop*,
there's not a word of truth in it.——That's another story, replied
my father.——However, as *Trim* reads it with so much concern,
——'tis cruelty to force him to go on with it.——Give me hold of
the sermon, *Trim*,——I'll finish it for thee, and thou mayst go. I
must stay and hear it too, replied *Trim*, if your Honour will allow
me;——tho' I would not read it myself for a Colonel's pay.——
Poor *Trim*! quoth my uncle *Toby*. My father went on.]

"——Consider the nature of the posture in which he now lies
stretch'd,——what exquisite torture he endures by it!——'Tis all
nature can bear!——Good God! See how it keeps his weary soul
hanging upon his trembling lips,——willing to take its leave,——
but not suffered to depart!——Behold the unhappy wretch led back
to his cell! [Then, thank God, however, quoth *Trim*, they have not
killed him]——See him dragg'd out of it again to meet the flames,
and the insults in his last agonies, which this principle,——this
principle, that there can be religion without mercy, has prepared for
him. [Then, thank God,——he is dead, quoth *Trim*,——he is out
of his pain,——and they have done their worst at him.——O Sirs!
——Hold your peace, *Trim*, said my father, going on with the
sermon, lest *Trim* should incense Dr. *Slop*,——we shall never have
done at this rate.]

"The surest way to try the merit of any disputed notion is, to
trace down the consequences such a notion has produced, and compare them with the spirit of Christianity;——'tis the short and decisive rule which our Saviour hath left us, for these and such-like
cases, and it is worth a thousand arguments,——*By their fruits ye
shall know them*.[2]

"I will add no further to the length of this sermon, than, by two
or three short and independent rules deducible from it.

"*First*, Whenever a man talks loudly against religion,——always
suspect that it is not his reason, but his passions which have got the
better of his Creed. A bad life and a good belief are disagreeable

2. Matthew 7:20.

and troublesome neighbours, and where they separate, depend upon it, 'tis for no other cause but quietness sake.

"*Secondly*, When a man, thus represented, tells you in any particular instance,——That such a thing goes *against* his conscience,——always believe he means exactly the same thing, as when he tells you such a thing goes *against* his stomach;——a present want of appetite being generally the true cause of both.

"In a word,——trust that man in nothing, who has not a CONSCIENCE in every thing.

"And, in your own case, remember this plain distinction, a mistake in which has ruined thousands,——that your conscience is not a law:——No, God and reason made the law, and have placed conscience within you to determine;——not like an *Asiatick* Cadi,[3] according to the ebbs and flows of his own passions,——but like a *British* judge in this land of liberty and good sense, who makes no new law, but faithfully declares that law which he knows already written."

FINIS

Thou hast read the sermon extremely well, *Trim*, quoth my father.——If he had spared his comments, replied Dr. *Slop*, he would have read it much better. I should have read it ten times better, Sir, answered *Trim*, but that my heart was so full.——That was the very reason, *Trim*, replied my father, which has made thee read the sermon as well as thou hast done; and if the clergy of our church, continued my father, addressing himself to Dr. *Slop*, would take part in what they deliver, as deeply as this poor fellow has done,——as their compositions are fine, (I deny it, quoth Dr. *Slop*) I maintain it, that the eloquence of our pulpits, with such subjects to inflame it,——would be a model for the whole world:——But, alas! continued my father, and I own it, Sir, with sorrow, that, like *French* politicians in this respect, what they gain in the cabinet they lose in the field.——'Twere a pity, quoth my uncle, that this should be lost. I like the sermon well, replied my father,——'tis dramatic,——and there is something in that way of writing, when skilfully managed, which catches the attention.——We preach much in that way with us, said Dr. *Slop*.——I know that very well, said my father,——but in a tone and manner which disgusted Dr. *Slop*, full as much as his assent, simply, could have pleased him.——But in this, added Dr. *Slop*, a little piqued,——our sermons have greatly the advantage, that we never introduce any character into them below a patriarch or a patriarch's wife, or a martyr or a saint.——

---

3. A judge in Persia or Arabia.

There are some very bad characters in this, however, said my father, and I do not think the sermon a jot the worse for 'em.——But pray, quoth my uncle *Toby*,——who's can this be?——How could it get into my *Stevinus*? A man must be as great a conjurer as *Stevinus*, said my father, to resolve the second question:——The first, I think, is not so difficult;——for unless my judgment greatly deceives me,——I know the author, for 'tis wrote, certainly, by the parson of the parish.

The similitude of the stile and manner of it, with those my father constantly had heard preach'd in his parish-church, was the ground of his conjecture,——proving it as strongly, as an argument *a priori*[4] could prove such a thing to a philosophic mind, That it was *Yorick's* and no one's else:——It was proved to be so *a posteriori*, the day after, when *Yorick* sent a servant to my uncle *Toby's* house to enquire after it.

It seems that *Yorick*, who was inquisitive after all kinds of knowledge, had borrowed *Stevinus* of my uncle *Toby*, and had carelessly popp'd his sermon, as soon as he had made it, into the middle of *Stevinus*; and, by an act of forgetfulness, to which he was ever subject, he had sent *Stevinus* home, and his sermon to keep him company.

Ill-fated sermon! Thou wast lost, after this recovery of thee, a second time, dropp'd thro' an unsuspected fissure in thy master's pocket, down into a treacherous and tatter'd lining,——trod deep into the dirt by the left hind foot of his Rosinante, inhumanly stepping upon thee as thou falledst;——buried ten days in the mire, ——raised up out of it by a beggar, sold for a halfpenny to a parish-clerk,——transferred to his parson,——lost for ever to thy own, the remainder of his days,——nor restored to his restless MANES[5] till this very moment, that I tell the world the story.

Can the reader believe, that this sermon of *Yorick's* was preach'd at an assize, in the cathedral of *York*, before a thousand witnesses, ready to give oath of it, by a certain prebendary of that church, and actually printed by him when he had done,——and within so short a space as two years and three months after *Yorick's* death.—— *Yorick*, indeed, was never better served in his life!——but it was a little hard to male-treat him before, and plunder him after he was laid in his grave.

However, as the gentleman who did it, was in perfect charity with *Yorick*,——and, in conscious justice, printed but a few copies to give away;——and that, I am told, he could moreover have made as good a one himself, had he thought fit,——I declare I would not

4. *A priori*: deductively, before examination or analysis. *A posteriori*: inductively, based on experience.
5. The Roman spirit or ghost of the dead. It was believed that the Manes never slept quietly in the grave while its survivors left its wishes unfulfilled.

have published this anecdote to the world;——nor do I publish it with an intent to hurt his character and advancement in the church; ——I leave that to others;——but I find myself impell'd by two reasons, which I cannot withstand.

The first is, That, in doing justice, I may give rest to *Yorick's* ghost;——which, as the country people,——and some others, believe,——*still walks.*

The second reason is, That, by laying open this story to the world, I gain an opportunity of informing it,——That in case the character of parson *Yorick*, and this sample of his sermons is liked, ——that there are now in the possession of the *Shandy* family, as many as will make a handsome volume, at the world's service,—— and much good may they do it.

Chapter XVIII.

OBADIAH gain'd the two crowns without dispute; for he came in jingling, with all the instruments in the green bays bag we spoke of, slung across his body, just as Corporal *Trim* went out of the room.

It is now proper, I think, quoth Dr. *Slop* (clearing up his looks) as we are in a condition to be of some service to Mrs. *Shandy*, to send up stairs to know how she goes on.

I have ordered, answered my father, the old midwife to come down to us upon the least difficulty;——for you must know, Dr. *Slop*, continued my father, with a perplexed kind of a smile upon his countenance, that by express treaty, solemnly ratified between me and my wife, you are no more than an auxiliary in this affair, ——and not so much as that,——unless the lean old mother of a midwife above stairs cannot do without you.——Women have their particular fancies, and in points of this nature, continued my father, where they bear the whole burden, and suffer so much acute pain for the advantage of our families, and the good of the species,—— they claim a right of deciding, *en Soveraines*,[6] in whose hands, and in what fashion, they chuse to undergo it.

They are in the right of it,——quoth my uncle *Toby*. But, Sir, replied Dr. *Slop*, not taking notice of my uncle *Toby's* opinion, but turning to my father,——they had better govern in other points; ——and a father of a family, who wished its perpetuity, in my opinion, had better exchange this prerogative with them, and give up some other rights in lieu of it.——I know not, quoth my father, answering a little too testily, to be quite dispassionate in what he said,——I know not, quoth he, what we have left to give up, in lieu

6. "As sovereign queens."

of who shall bring our children into the world,——unless that,——
of who shall beget them.——One would almost give up any
thing, replied Dr. *Slop*.——I beg your pardon,——answered my
uncle *Toby*.——Sir, replied Dr. *Slop*, it would astonish you to
know what Improvements we have made of late years in all
branches of obstetrical knowledge, but particularly in that one single point of the safe and expeditious extraction of the *fœtus*,——
which has received such lights, that, for my part, (holding up his
hands) I declare I wonder how the world has——I wish, quoth my
uncle *Toby*, you had seen what prodigious armies we had in
Flanders.

Chapter XIX.

I Have dropp'd the curtain over this scene for a minute,——to remind you of one thing,——and to inform you of another.

What I have to inform you, comes, I own, a little out of its due
course;——for it should have been told a hundred and fifty pages
ago, but that I foresaw then 'twould come in pat hereafter, and be
of more advantage here than elsewhere.——Writers had need look
before them to keep up the spirit and connection of what they have
in hand.

When these two things are done,——the curtain shall be drawn
up again, and my uncle *Toby*, my father, and Dr. *Slop* shall go on
with their discourse, without any more interruption.

First, then, the matter which I have to remind you of, is this;
——that from the specimens of singularity in my father's notions in
the point of Christian-names, and that other point previous thereto,
——you was led, I think, into an opinion, (and I am sure I said as
much) that my father was a gentleman altogether as odd and
whimsical in fifty other opinions. In truth, there was not a stage in
the life of man, from the very first act of his begetting,——down to
the lean and slipper'd pantaloon in his second childishness,[7] but he
had some favourite notion to himself, springing out of it, as sceptical, and as far out of the high-way of thinking, as these two which
have been explained.

——Mr. *Shandy*, my father, Sir, would see nothing in the light in
which others placed it;——he placed things in his own light;——he
would weigh nothing in common scales;——no,——he was too
refined a researcher to lay open to so gross an imposition.——To
come at the exact weight of things in the scientific steel-yard, the
fulcrum, he would say, should be almost invisible, to avoid all
friction from popular tenets;——without this the minutiæ of

---

7. That is, the loose clothing of an invalid old man.

philosophy, which should always turn the balance, will have no weight at all.——Knowledge, like matter, he would affirm, was divisible *in infinitum*;[8]——that the grains and scruples were as much a part of it, as the gravitation of the whole world.——In a word, he would say, error was error,——no matter where it fell, ——whether in a fraction,——or a pound,——'twas alike fatal to truth, and she was kept down at the bottom of her well as inevitably by a mistake in the dust of a butterfly's wing,——as in the disk of the sun, the moon, and all the stars of heaven put together.

He would often lament that it was for want of considering this properly, and of applying it skilfully to civil matters, as well as to speculative truths, that so many things in this world were out of joint;——that the political arch was giving way;——and that the very foundations of our excellent constitution in church and state, were so sapp'd as estimators had reported.

You cry out, he would say, we are a ruined, undone people.—— Why?——he would ask, making use of the sorites or syllogism of *Zeno* and *Chrysippus*,[9] without knowing it belonged to them.—— Why? why are we a ruined people?——Because we are corrupted. ——Whence is it, dear Sir, that we are corrupted?——Because we are needy;——our poverty, and not our wills, consent.——And wherefore, he would add,——are we needy?——From the neglect, he would answer, of our pence and our halfpence:——Our bank-notes, Sir, our guineas,——nay our shillings, take care of them-selves.

'Tis the same, he would say, throughout the whole circle of the sciences;——the great, the established points of them, are not to be broke in upon.——The laws of nature will defend themselves;—— but error——(he would add, looking earnestly at my mother)—— error, Sir, creeps in thro' the minute-holes, and small crevices, which human nature leaves unguarded.

This turn of thinking in my father, is what I had to remind you of:——The point you are to be informed of, and which I have reserved for this place, is as follows:

Amongst the many and excellent reasons, with which my father had urged my mother to accept of Dr. *Slop*'s assistance preferably to that of the old woman,——there was one of a very singular nature; which, when he had done arguing the matter with her as a Christian, and came to argue it over again with her as a philos-opher, he had put his whole strength to, depending indeed upon it as his sheet anchor.——It failed him; tho' from no defect in the

8. Into an infinite number of parts.

9. A "syllogism" is a common form of argument in which a conclusion is drawn from two premises. A "sorites," then, is a series of syllogisms in which the conclu-sion of one syllogism becomes the prem-ise of another (not always legitimately). Zeno was the founder of the ancient Stoic school of philosophy, Chrysippus one of his followers.

argument itself; but that, do what he could, he was not able for his soul to make her comprehend the drift of it.——Cursed luck!—— said he to himself, one afternoon, as he walk'd out of the room, after he had been stating it for an hour and a half to her, to no manner of purpose;——cursed luck! said he, biting his lip as he shut the door,——for a man to be master of one of the finest chains of reasoning in nature,——and have a wife at the same time with such a head-piece, that he cannot hang up a single inference within side of it, to save his soul from destruction.

This argument, though it was intirely lost upon my mother,—— had more weight with him, than all his other arguments joined together:——I will therefore endeavour to do it justice,——and set it forth with all the perspicuity I am master of.

My father set out upon the strength of these two following axioms:

First, That an ounce of a man's own wit, was worth a tun of other people's; and,

Secondly, (Which, by the bye, was the ground-work of the first axiom,——tho' it comes last)——That every man's wit must come from every man's own soul,——and no other body's.

Now, as it was plain to my father, that all souls were by nature equal,——and that the great difference between the most acute and the most obtuse understanding,——was from no original sharpness or bluntness of one thinking substance above or below another,—— but arose merely from the lucky or unlucky organization of the body, in that part where the soul principally took up her residence, ——he had made it the subject of his enquiry to find out the identical place.

Now, from the best accounts he had been able to get of this matter, he was satisfied it could not be where *Des Cartes*[1] had fixed it, upon the top of the *pineal* gland of the brain; which, as he philosophised, formed a cushion for her about the size of a marrow pea;——tho' to speak the truth, as so many nerves did terminate all in that one place,——'twas no bad conjecture;——and my father had certainly fallen with that great philosopher plumb into the center of the mistake, had it not been for my uncle *Toby,* who rescued him out of it, by a story he told him of a *Walloon*[2] officer at the battle of *Landen,* who had one part of his brain shot away by a musket-ball,——and another part of it taken out after by a *French* surgeon; and, after all, recovered, and did his duty very well without it.

1. René Descartes shared the interest of other seventeenth-century philosophers in mental processes and the question of how we think and why we believe as we do. He located the physical position of the soul in the pineal gland.

2. The Walloons are people of mixed origins inhabiting the part of Belgium around Namur.

If death, said my father, reasoning with himself, is nothing but the separation of the soul from the body;——and if it is true that people can walk about and do their business without brains,—— then certes the soul does not inhabit there. Q. E. D.[3]

As for that certain, very thin, subtle, and very fragrant juice which *Coglionissimo Borri,* the great *Milaneze* physician,[4] affirms, in a letter to *Bartholine,* to have discovered in the cellulæ of the occipital parts of the cerebellum, and which he likewise affirms to be the principal seat of the reasonable soul (for, you must know, in these latter and more enlightened ages, there are two souls in every man living,——the one, according to the great *Metheglingius,* being called the *Animus,* the other the *Anima*);——as for this opinion, I say, of *Borri,*——my father could never subscribe to it by any means; the very idea of so noble, so refined, so immaterial, and so exalted a being as the *Anima,* or even the *Animus,* taking up her residence, and sitting dabbling, like a tad-pole, all day long, both summer and winter, in a puddle,——or in a liquid of any kind, how thick or thin soever, he would say, shock'd his imagination; he would scarce give the doctrine a hearing.

What, therefore, seem'd the least liable to objections of any, was, that the chief sensorium, or head-quarters of the soul, and to which place all intelligences were referred, and from whence all her mandates were issued,——was in, or near, the cerebellum,——or rather some-where about the *medulla oblongata,* wherein it was generally agreed by *Dutch* anatomists, that all the minute nerves from all the organs of the seven senses concentered, like streets and winding alleys, into a square.

So far there was nothing singular in my father's opinion,——he had the best of philosophers, of all ages and climates, to go along with him.——But here he took a road of his own, setting up another *Shandean* hypothesis upon these cornerstones they had laid for him;——and which said hypothesis equally stood its ground; whether the subtilty and fineness of the soul depended upon the temperature and clearness of the said liquor, or of the finer network and texture in the cerebellum itself; which opinion he favoured.

He maintained, that next to the due care to be taken in the act of propagation of each individual, which required all the thought in

3. *Quid Erat Demonstrandum*: "that which has been demonstrated" (used at the end of geometrical proofs to state that the original hypothesis has been proven).
4. *Soglionissimo* is the superlative of the Italian word for testicles (*coglione*). Joseph Francis Borri and Thomas Partholine were both seventeenth-century physicians. *Metheglingius* is probably derived from metheglin—a type of alcoholic drink made from honey. *Animus* and *anima*: in the androgynous vision of the Middle Ages, the former was a term for the rational soul, or the masculine aspect of the human psyche, while the latter described the feminine aspect— or life-giving principle.

the world, as it laid the foundation of this incomprehensible contexture in which wit, memory, fancy, eloquence, and what is usually meant by the name of good natural parts, do consist;——that next to this and his Christian-name, which were the two original and most efficacious causes of all;——that the third cause, or rather what logicians call the *Causa sine quâ non*,[5] and without which all that was done was of no manner of significance,——was the preservation of this delicate and fine-spun web, from the havock which was generally made in it by the violent compression and crush which the head was made to undergo, by the nonsensical method of bringing us into the world by that part foremost.

——This requires explanation.

My father, who dipp'd into all kinds of books, upon looking into *Lithopœdus Senonesis de Partu difficili*,[6] published by *Adrianus Smelvogt*, had found out, That the lax and pliable state of a child's head in parturition, the bones of the cranium having no sutures at that time, was such,——that by force of the woman's efforts, which, in strong labour-pains, was equal, upon an average, to a weight of 470 pounds averdupoise acting perpendicularly upon it;——it so happened that, in 49 instances out of 50, the said head was compressed and moulded into the shape of an oblong conical piece of dough, such as a pastry-cook generally rolls up in order to make a pye of.——Good God! cried my father, what havock and destruction must this make in the infinitely fine and tender texture of the cerebellum!——Or if there is such a juice as *Borri* pretends, ——is it not enough to make the clearest liquor in the world both feculent and mothery?

But how great was his apprehension, when he further understood, that this force, acting upon the very vertex of the head, not only injured the brain itself or cerebrum,——but that it necessarily squeez'd and propell'd the cerebrum towards the cerebellum, which was the immediate seat of the understanding.——Angels and Ministers of grace defend us! cried my father,——can any soul withstand this shock?——No wonder the intellectual web is so rent and tatter'd as we see it; and that so many of our best heads are no better than a puzzled skein of silk,——all perplexity,——all confusion within side.

---

5. The indispensible cause, ("without which nothing").

6. The author is here twice mistaken;——for *Lithopaedus* should be wrote thus, *Lithopaedii Senonensis Icon.* The second mistake is, that this *Lithopaedus* is not an author, but a drawing of a petrified child. The account of this, published by *Albosius*, 1580, may be seen at the end of *Cordaeus's* works in *Spachius*. Mr. *Tristram Shandy* has been led into this error, either from seeing *Litho-* paedus's name of late in a catalogue of learned writers in Dr. ——, or by mistaking *Lithopaedus* for *Trinecavellius*, ——from the too great similitude of names. [*Sterne's note.*] *De Partu Difficili* means "About Difficult Childbirth." This is one more of Sterne's games with Dr. Burton (Slop), for the whole passage plays on Burton's attack on Dr. Smellie (Smelvogt), who had mistaken *Lithopaedus*, in the *title*, for the author's name.

But when my father read on, and was let into the secr⌐,
when a child was turn'd topsy-turvy, which· was easy for an operator to do, and was extracted by the feet;——that instead of the
cerebrum being propell'd towards the cerebellum, the cerebellum,
on the contrary, was propell'd simply towards the cerebrum where it
could do no manner of hurt:——By heavens! cried he, the world is
in a conspiracy to drive out what little wit God has given us,——
and the professors of the obstetrick art are listed into the same
conspiracy.——What is it to me which end of my son comes foremost into the world, provided all goes right after, and his cerebellum escapes uncrushed?

It is the nature of an hypothesis, when once a man has conceived
it, that it assimilates every thing to itself as proper nourishment;
and, from the first moment of your begetting it, it generally grows
the stronger by every thing you see, hear, read, or understand. This
is of great use.

When my father was gone with this about a month, there was
scarce a phænomenon of stupidity or of genius, which he could not
readily solve by it;——it accounted for the eldest son being the
greatest blockhead in the family.——Poor Devil, he would say,——
he made way for the capacity of his younger brothers.——It unrid-
dled the observations of drivellers and monstrous heads,——
shewing, *a priori*, it could not be otherwise,——unless * * * * I
don't know what. It wonderfully explain'd and accounted for the
acumen of the *Asiatick* genius, and that sprightlier turn, and a more
penetrating intuition of minds, in warmer climates; not from the
loose and common-place solution of a clearer sky, and a more
perpetual sunshine, *&c.*——which, for aught he knew, might as well
rarify and dilute the faculties of the soul into nothing, by one
extreme,——as they are condensed in colder climates by the other;
——but he traced the affair up to its spring-head;——shew'd that,
in warmer climates, nature had laid 'a lighter tax upon the fairest
parts of the creation;——their pleasures more;——the necessity of
their pains less, insomuch that the pressure and resistance upon the
vertex was so slight, that the whole organization of the cerebellum
was preserved;——nay, he did not believe, in natural births, that so
much as a single thread of the net-work was broke or displaced,
——so that the soul might just act as she liked.

When my father had got so far,——what a blaze of light did the
accounts of the *Cæsarian* section,[7] and of the towering geniuses

---

7. Caesarean operations, agonizingly
painful and dangerous for the mother
before modern anaesthetics, were the
means of birth not only for Julius Caesar,
but also for the Roman generals Scipio
and Manilius (not Manlius). Hermes
Trismegistus is the name the Greeks gave
to the Egyptian god of wisdom, arts, and
sciences, Thoth. The mother of Edward
VI, Jane Seymour, died shortly after
giving birth to him, though not necessarily because of Caesarean damage.
The *os pubis* is the pubic bone; the *os
coxygis* comprises the four lowest bones
of the spine. The *epigastrium* is the upper
and middle abdomen; the *matrix* is the
womb.

who had come safe into the world by it, cast upon this hypothesis? Here you see, he would say, there was no injury done to the sensorium;——no pressure of the head against the pelvis;——no propulsion of the cerebrum towards the cerebellum, either by the *os pubis* on this side, or the *os coxcygis* on that;——and, pray, what were the happy consequences? Why, Sir, your *Julius Cæsar*, who gave the operation a name;——and your *Hermes Trismegistus*, who was born so before ever the operation had a name;——your *Scipio Africanus*; your *Manlius Torquatus*; our *Edward* the sixth,—— who, had he lived, would have done the same honour to the hypothesis:——These, and many more, who figur'd high in the annals of fame,——all came *side-way*, Sir, into the world.

This incision of the *abdomen* and *uterus*, ran for six weeks together in my father's head;——he had read, and was satisfied, that wounds in the *epigastrium*, and those in the *matrix*, were not mortal;——so that the belly of the mother might be opened extremely well to give a passage to the child.——He mentioned the thing one afternoon to my mother,——merely as a matter of fact; ——but seeing her turn as pale as ashes at the very mention of it, as much as the operation flattered his hopes,——he thought it as well to say no more of it,——contenting himself with admiring——what he thought was to no purpose to propose.

This was my father Mr. *Shandy*'s hypothesis; concerning which I have only to add, that my brother *Bobby* did as great honour to it (whatever he did to the family) as any one of the great heroes we spoke of:——For happening not only to be christen'd, as I told you, but to be born too, when my father was at *Epsom*,——being moreover my mother's *first* child,——coming into the world with his head *foremost*,——and turning out afterwards a lad of wonderful slow parts,——my father spelt all these together into his opinion; and as he had failed at one end,——he was determined to try the other.

This was not to be expected from one of the sisterhood, who are not easily to be put out of their way,——and was therefore one of my father's great reasons in favour of a man of science, whom he could better deal with.

Of all men in the world, Dr. *Slop* was the fittest for my father's purpose;——for tho' his new-invented forceps was the armour he had proved, and what he maintained, to be the safest instrument of deliverance,——yet, it seems, he had scattered a word or two in his book, in favour of the very thing which ran in my father's fancy; ——tho' not with a view to the soul's good in extracting by the feet, as was my father's system,——but for reasons merely obstetrical.

This will account for the coalition betwixt my father and Dr. *Slop*, in the ensuing discourse, which went a little hard against my uncle *Toby*.——In what manner a plain man, with nothing but common sense, could bear up against two such allies in science, ——is hard to conceive.——You may conjecture upon it, if you please,——and whilst your imagination is in motion, you may encourage it to go on, and discover by what causes and effects in nature it could come to pass, that my uncle *Toby* got his modesty by the wound he received upon his groin.——You may raise a system to account for the loss of my nose by marriage articles,—— and shew the world how it could happen, that I should have the misfortune to be called TRISTRAM, in opposition to my father's hypothesis, and the wish of the whole family, God-fathers and God-mothers not excepted.——These, with fifty other points left yet unraveled, you may endeavour to solve if you have time;——but I tell you before-hand it will be in vain,——for not the sage *Alquife*, the magician in Don *Belianis* of *Greece*,[8] nor the no less famous *Urganda*, the sorceress his wife, (were they alive) could pretend to come within a league of the truth.

The reader will be content to wait for a full explanation of these matters till the next year,——when a series of things will be laid open which he little expects.

END of the SECOND VOLUME.

---

8. Don Belianus is the central figure of this sixteenth-century Spanish romance.

Volume III.

Multitudinis imperitæ non formido judicia; meis tamen, rogo, parcant
opusculis———in quibus fuit propositi semper, a jocis ad seria, a seriis
vicissim ad jocos transire.

JOAN. SARESBERIENSIS,
Episcopus Lugdun.[1]

Chapter I.

———"I Wish, Dr. *Slop*," quoth my uncle *Toby* (repeating his
wish for Dr. *Slop* a second time, and with a degree of
more zeal and earnestness in his manner of wishing, than he had
wished it at first[2])———"I wish, Dr. *Slop*," quoth my uncle *Toby*,
"*you had seen what prodigious armies we had in Flanders.*"

My uncle *Toby*'s wish did Dr. *Slop* a disservice which his heart
never intended any man,———Sir, it confounded him———and
thereby putting his ideas first into confusion, and then to flight, he
could not rally them again for the soul of him.

In all disputes,———male or female,———whether for honour, for
profit or for love,———it makes no difference in the case;———
nothing is more dangerous, madam, than a wish coming sideways in
this unexpected manner upon a man: the safest way in general to
take off the force of the wish, is, for the party wished at, instantly to
get up upon his legs———and wish the *wisher* something in return, of
pretty near the same value,———so balancing the account upon the
spot, you stand as you were———nay sometimes gain the advantage
of the attack by it.

This will be fully illustrated to the world in my chapter of wishes.

Dr. *Slop* did not understand the nature of this defence;———he
was puzzled with it, and it put an entire stop to the dispute for four
minutes and half;———five had been fatal to it:———my father saw
the danger———the dispute was one of the most interesting disputes
in the world, "Whether the child of his prayers and endeavours
should be born without a head or with one:"———he waited to the
last moment to allow Dr. *Slop*, in whose behalf the wish was made,

---

1. "I do not fear the judgments of the
ignorant populace, yet I ask that they
spare my humble works—in which it
has always been my intention to pass
from jests to serious matters and from
the serious back again to jests." From
the *Policraticus* [Stateman's Book] of
John of Salisbury, a twelfth-century
churchman. The original does not speak
of moving back again to jests.
2. Vid. Vol. II. p. 159. [*Sterne's note*;
p. 104 in this edition.]

his right of returning it; but perceiving, I say, that he was confounded, and continued looking with that perplexed vacuity of eye
which puzzled souls generally stare with,——first in my uncle
Toby's face——then in his——then up——then down——then
east——east and by east, and so on,——coasting it along by the
plinth of the wainscot till he had got to the opposite point of the
compass,——and that he had actually begun to count the brass
nails upon the arm of his chair——my father thought there was no
time to be lost with my uncle *Toby*, so took up the discourse as
follows.

Chapter II.

"——WHAT prodigious armies you had in *Flanders!*"——
Brother *Toby*, replied my father, taking his wig from
off his head with his right hand, and with his *left* pulling out a
striped *India* handkerchief from his right coat pocket, in order to
rub his head, as he argued the point with my uncle *Toby*.——

——Now, in this I think my father was much to blame; and I
will give you my reasons for it.

Matters of no more seeming consequence in themselves than,
*"Whether my father should have taken off his wig with his right
hand or with his left,"*——have divided the greatest kingdoms, and
made the crowns of the monarchs who governed them, to totter
upon their heads.——But need I tell you, Sir, that the circumstances with which every thing in this world is begirt, give every
thing in this world its size and shape;——and by tightening it, or
relaxing it, this way or that, make the thing to be, what it is——
great——little——good——bad——indifferent or not indifferent,
just as the case happens.

As my father's *India* handkerchief was in his right coat pocket,
he should by no means have suffered his right hand to have got
engaged: on the contrary, instead of taking off his wig with it, as he
did, he ought to have committed that entirely to the left; and then,
when the natural exigency my father was under of rubbing his head,
call'd out for his handkerchief, he would have had nothing in the
world to have done, but to have put his right hand into his right
coat pocket and taken it out;——which he might have done without
any violence, or the least ungraceful twist in any one tendon or
muscle of his whole body.

In this case, (unless indeed, my father had been resolved to make
a fool of himself by holding the wig stiff in his left hand——or by
making some nonsensical angle or other at his elbow joint, or arm-
pit)——his whole attitude had been easy——natural——unforced:

Reynolds[3] himself, as great and gracefully as he paints, might have painted him as he sat.

Now, as my father managed this matter,——consider what a devil of a figure my father made of himself.

——In the latter end of Queen *Anne*'s reign, and in the beginning of the reign of King *George* the first——*"Coat pockets were cut very low down in the skirt."*——I need say no more——the father of mischief, had he been hammering at it a month, could not have contrived a worse fashion for one in my father's situation.

Chapter III.

IT was not an easy matter in any king's reign, (unless you were as lean a subject as myself) to have forced your hand diagonally, quite across your whole body, so as to gain the bottom of your opposite coat-pocket.——In the year, one thousand seven hundred and eighteen, when this happened, it was extremely difficult; so that when my uncle *Toby* discovered the transverse zig-zaggery of my father's approaches towards it, it instantly brought into his mind those he had done duty in, before the gate of St. *Nicholas*;——the idea of which drew off his attention so entirely from the subject in debate, that he had got his right hand to the bell to ring up *Trim*, to go and fetch his map of *Namur*, and his compasses and sector along with it, to measure the returning angles of the traverses of that attack,——but particularly of that one, where he received his wound upon his groin.

My father knit his brows, and as he knit them, all the blood in his body seemed to rush up into his face——my uncle *Toby* dismounted immediately.

——I did not apprehend your uncle *Toby* was o' horseback.——

Chapter IV.

A Man's body and his mind, with the utmost reverence to both I speak it, are exactly like a jerkin, and a jerkin's lining;—— rumple the one——you rumple the other. There is one certain exception however in this case, and that is, when you are so fortunate a fellow, as to have had your jerkin made of a gum-taffeta, and the body-lining to it, of a sarcenet or thin persian.[4]

Zeno,[5] *Cleanthes, Diogenes, Babylonius, Dyonisius Heracleotes, Antipater, Panætius* and *Possidonius* amongst the Greeks;—— *Cato*

and *Varro* and *Seneca* amongst the *Romans;*———*Pa*
Clemens Alexandrinus and *Montaigne* amongst the Chi—
a score and a half of good honest, unthinking, *Shandean* people as
ever lived, whose names I can't recollect,———all pretended that
their jerkins were made after this fashion,———you might have
rumpled and crumpled, and doubled and creased, and fretted and
fridged the outsides of them all to pieces;———in short, you might
have played the very devil with them, and at the same time, not one
of the insides of 'em would have been one button the worse, for all
you had done to them.

I believe in my conscience that mine is made up somewhat after
this sort:———for never poor jerkin has been tickled off, at such a
rate as it has been these last nine months together,[6]———and yet I
declare the lining to it,———as far as I am a judge of the matter, it is
not a three-penny piece the worse;———pell mell, helter skelter, ding
dong, cut and thrust, back stroke and fore stroke, side way and
long way, have they been trimming it for me:———had there been
the least gumminess in my lining,———by heaven! it had all of it
long ago been fray'd and fretted to a thread.

———You Messrs. the monthly Reviewers!———how could you cut
and slash my jerkin as you did?———how did you know, but you
would cut my lining too?

Heartily and from my soul, to the protection of that Being who
will injure none of us, do I recommend you and your affairs,———so
God bless you;———only next month, if any one of you should
gnash his teeth, and storm and rage at me, as some of you did last
MAY, (in which I remember the weather was very hot)———don't be
exasperated, if I pass it by again with good temper,———being determined as long as I live or write (which in my case means the
same thing) never to give the honest gentleman a worse word or a
worse wish, than my uncle *Toby* gave the fly which buzz'd about his
nose all *dinner time,*———"Go,———go poor devil," quoth he,
"———get thee gone,———why should I hurt thee? This world is
surely wide enough to hold both thee and me."

Chapter V.

ANY man, madam, reasoning upwards, and observing the prodigious suffusion of blood in my father's countenance,———by
means of which, (as all the blood in his body seemed to rush up
into his face, as I told you) he must have redden'd, pictorically and
scientintically speaking, six whole tints and a half, if not a full

6. In May 1760, Sterne published two volumes of sermons that came under heavy critical attack, especially because he published them under the facetious name of Parson Yorick.

octave above his natural colour:——any man, madam, but my
uncle *Toby*, who had observed this, together with the violent knitting of my father's brows, and the extravagant contortion of his
body during the whole affair,——would have concluded my father
in a rage; and taking that for granted,——had he been a lover of
such kind of concord as arises from two such instruments being put
into exact tune,——he would instantly have skrew'd up his, to the
same pitch;——and then the devil and all had broke loose——the
whole piece, madam, must have been played off like the sixth of
Avison Scarlatti[7]——*con furia,*——like mad.——Grant me patience!——What has *con furia,*——*con strepito,*——or any other
hurlyburly word whatever to do with harmony?

Any man, I say, madam, but my uncle *Toby*, the benignity of
whose heart interpreted every motion of the body in the kindest
sense the motion would admit of, would have concluded my father
angry and blamed him too. My uncle *Toby* blamed nothing but the
taylor who cut the pocket-hole;——so sitting still, till my father had
got his handkerchief out of it, and looking all the time up in his
face with inexpressible good will——my father at length went on as
follows.

Chapter VI.

——"WHAT prodigious armies you had in *Flanders!*"
——Brother *Toby*, quoth my father, I do believe
thee to be as honest a man, and with as good and as upright a heart
as ever God created;——nor is it thy fault, if all the children which
have been, may, can, shall, will or ought to be begotten, come with
their heads foremost into the world:——but believe me, dear *Toby*,
the accidents which unavoidably waylay them, not only in the article
of our begetting 'em,——though these in my opinion, are well
worth considering,——but the dangers and difficulties our children
are beset with, after they are got forth into the world, are enow,——
little need is there to expose them to unnecessary ones in their
passage to it.——Are these dangers, quoth my uncle *Toby*, laying
his hand upon my father's knee, and looking up seriously in his face
for an answer,——are these dangers greater now o' days, brother,
than in times past? Brother *Toby*, answered my father, if a child was
but fairly begot, and born alive, and healthy, and the mother did
well after it,——our forefathers never looked further.——My uncle
Toby instantly withdrew his hand from off my father's knee, reclined
his body gently back in his chair, raised his head till he could just

---

7. Charles Avison, an English composer,
published *Twelve Concertos* by Domenico
Scarlatti (1685–1757) in 1744. *Con strepito* means "very noisily."

see the cornish[8] of the room, and then directing the buccinatory musles along his cheeks, and the orbicular muscles around his lips to do their duty——he whistled *Lillabullero*.

Chapter VII.

W HILST my uncle *Toby* was whistling Lillabullero to my father,——Dr. *Slop* was stamping, and cursing and damning at *Obadiah* at a most dreadful rate;——it would have done your heart good, and cured you, Sir, for ever, of the vile sin of swearing to have heard him.——I am determined therefore to relate the whole affair to you.

When Dr. *Slop*'s maid delivered the green bays bag, with her master's instruments in it, to *Obadiah*, she very sensibly exhorted him to put his head and one arm through the strings, and ride with it slung across his body: so undoing the bow-knot, to lengthen the strings for him, without any more ado, she helped him on with it. However, as this, in some measure, unguarded the mouth of the bag, lest any thing should bolt out in galloping back at the speed *Obadiah* threatened, they consulted to take it off again; and in the great care and caution of their hearts, they had taken the two strings and tied them close (pursing up the mouth of the bag first) with half a dozen hard knots, each of which, *Obadiah*, to make all safe, had twitched and drawn together with all the strength of his body.

This answered all that *Obadiah* and the maid intended; but was no remedy against some evils which neither her or she foresaw. The instruments, it seems, as tight as the bag was tied above, had so much room to play in it, towards the bottom, (the shape of the bag being conical) that *Obadiah* could not make a trot of it, but with such a terrible jingle, what with the *tire-tête, forceps* and *squirt*, as would have been enough, had *Hymen*[9] been taking a jaunt that way, to have frightened him out of the country; but when *Obadiah* accelerated this motion, and from a plain trot assayed to prick his coach-horse into a full gallop——by heaven! Sir,——the jingle was incredible.

As *Obadiah* had a wife and three children——the turpitude of fornication, and the many other political ill consequences of this jingling, never once entered his brain,——he had however his objection, which came home to himself, and weighed with him, as it has oft-times done with the greatest patriots.——*"The poor fellow, Sir, was not able to hear himself whistle."*

8. Cornice.   9. The Greek god of marriage.

Chapter VIII.

A S *Obadiah* loved wind musick preferably to all the instrumental musick he carried with him,——he very considerately set his imagination to work, to contrive and to invent by what means he should put himself in a condition of enjoying it.

In all distresses (except musical) where small cords are wanted,——nothing is so apt to enter a man's head, as his hat-band:——the philosophy of this is so near the surface——I scorn to enter into it.

As *Obadiah's* was a mix'd case,——mark, Sirs,——I say, a mix'd case; for it was obstetrical,——*scrip*-tical, squirtical, papistical,——and as far as the coach-horse was concerned in it,——caball-istical[1]——and only partly musical;——*Obadiah* made no scruple of availing himself of the first expedient which offered;——so taking hold of the bag and instruments, and gripeing them hard together with one hand, and with the finger and thumb of the other, putting the end of the hat-band betwixt his teeth, and then slipping his hand down to the middle of it,——he tied and cross-tied them all fast together from one end to the other (as you would cord a trunk) with such a multiplicity of round-abouts and intricate cross turns, with a hard knot at every intersection or point where the strings met,——that Dr. *Slop* must have had three fifths of *Job's* patience at least to have unloosed them.——I think in my conscience, that had NATURE been in one of her nimble moods, and in humour for such a contest——and she and Dr. *Slop* both fairly started together ——there is no man living who had seen the bag with all that *Obadiah* had done to it,——and known likewise, the great speed the goddess can make when she thinks proper, who would have had the least doubt remaining in his mind——which of the two would have carried off the prize. My mother, madam, had been delivered sooner than the green bag infallibly——at least by twenty *knots.*——Sport of small accidents, *Tristram Shandy!* that thou art, and ever will be! had that trial been made for thee, and it was fifty to one but it had,——thy affairs had not been so depress'd——(at least by the depression of thy nose) as they have been; nor had the fortunes of thy house and the occasions of making them, which have so often presented themselves in the course of thy life, to thee, been so often, so vexatiously, so tamely, so irrecoverably abandoned——as thou has been forced to leave them!——but 'tis over,——all but the account of 'em, which cannot be given to the curious till I am got out into the world.

---

1. A pun: *cabalistic means* "occult" or "mysterious"; *caballus* is Latin for "horse."

Chapter IX.

G REAT wits jump: for the moment Dr. *Slop* cast his eyes upon his bag (which he had not done till the dispute with my uncle *Toby* about midwifery put him in mind of it)——the very same thought occurred.——'Tis God's mercy, quoth he, (to himself) that Mrs. *Shandy* has had so bad a time of it,——else she might have been brought to bed seven times told, before one half of these knots could have got untied.——But here, you must distinguish——the thought floated only in Dr. *Slop*'s mind, without sail or ballast to it, as a simple proposition; millions of which, as your worship knows, are every day swimming quietly in the middle of the thin juice of a man's understanding, without being carried backwards or forwards, till some little gusts of passion or interest drive them to one side.

A sudden trampling in the room above, near my mother's bed, did the proposition the very service I am speaking of. By all that's unfortunate, quoth Dr. *Slop*, unless I make haste, the thing will actually befall me as it is.

Chapter X.

I N the case of *knots*,——by which, in the first place, I would not be understood to mean slip-knots,[2]——because in the course of my life and opinions,——my opinions concerning them will come in more properly when I mention the catastrophe of my great uncle Mr. *Hammond Shandy*,——a little man,——but of high fancy: ——he rushed into the duke of *Monmouth*'s affair:——nor, secondly, in this place, do I mean that particular species of knots, called bow-knots;——there is so little address, or skill, or patience, required in the unloosing them, that they are below my giving any opinion at all about them.——But by the knots I am speaking of, may it please your reverences to believe, that I mean good, honest, devilish tight, hard knots, made *bona fide*, as *Obadiah* made his; ——in which there is no quibbling provision made by the duplication and return of the two ends of the strings through the annulus or noose made by the second *implication* of them——to get them slipp'd and undone by——I hope you apprehend me.

In the case of these *knots* then, and of the several obstructions, which, may it please your reverences, such knots cast in our way in getting through life——every hasty man can whip out his penknife and cut through them.——'Tis wrong. Believe me, Sirs, the most virtuous way, and which both reason and conscience dictate——is

2. That is, knots used in executions by hanging—a fate apparently suffered by Hammond Shandy for supporting the un- successful rebellion of the Duke of Monmouth against his uncle James II in 1685.

to take our teeth or our fingers to them.——Dr. *Slop* had lost his teeth—his favourite instrument, by extracting in a wrong direction, or by some misapplication of it, unfortunately slipping, he had formerly in a hard labour, knock'd out three of the best of them, with the handle of it:———he tried his fingers——alas! the nails of his fingers and thumbs were cut close.——The deuce take it! I can make nothing of it either way, cried Dr. *Slop*——The trampling over head near my mother's bed side increased.——Pox take the fellow! I shall never get the knots untied as long as I live.——My mother gave a groan——Lend me your penknife——I must e'en cut the knots at last - - - - - pugh! - - - psha! - - - Lord! I have cut my thumb quite across to the very bone——curse the fellow——if there was not another man midwife within fifty miles——I am undone for this bout——I wish the scoundrel hang'd——I wish he was shot——I wish all the devils in hell had him for a block-head———

My father had a great respect for *Obadiah*, and could not bear to hear him disposed of in such a manner——he had moreover some little respect for himself——and could as ill bear with the indignity offer'd to himself in it.

Had Dr. *Slop* cut any part about him, but his thumb——my father had pass'd it by——his prudence had triumphed: as it was, he was determined to have his revenge.

Small curses, Dr. *Slop*, upon great occasions, quoth my father, (condoling with him first upon the accident) are but so much waste of our strength and soul's health to no manner of purpose.——I own it, replied Dr. *Slop*.——They are like sparrow shot, quoth my uncle *Toby*, (suspending his whistling) fired against a bastion.—— They serve, continued my father, to stir the humours——but carry off none of their acrimony:——for my own part, I seldom swear or curse at all——I hold it bad——but if I fall into it, by surprize, I generally retain so much presence of mind (right, quoth my uncle *Toby*) as to make it answer my purpose——that is, I swear on, till I find myself easy. A wise and a just man however would always endeavour to proportion the vent given to these humours, not only to the degree of them stirring within himself——but to the size and ill intent of the offence upon which they are to fall.——"*Injuries come only from the heart*,"——quoth my uncle *Toby*. For this reason, continued my father, with the most *Cervantick*[3] gravity, I have the greatest veneration in the world for that gentleman, who, in distrust of his own discretion in this point, sat down and composed (that is at his leisure) fit forms of swearing suitable to all cases, from the lowest to the highest provocations which could

---

3. Cervantes is a master of the art of appearing serious and satirically humorous at the same time.

possibly happen to him,——which forms being well consider'd by him, and such moreover as he could stand to, he kept them ever by him on the chimney piece, within his reach, ready for use.——I never apprehended, replied Dr. *Slop*, that such a thing was ever thought of,——much less executed. I beg your pardon——answered my father; I was reading, though not using, one of them to my brother *Toby* this morning, whilst he pour'd out the tea—'tis here upon the shelf over my head;——but if I remember right, 'tis too violent for a cut of the thumb.——Not at all, quoth Dr. *Slop* ——the devil take the fellow.——Then answered my father, 'Tis much at your service, Dr. *Slop*——on condition you will read it aloud;——so rising up and reaching down a form of excommunication of the church of *Rome*, a copy of which, my father (who was curious in his collections) had procured out of the leger-book of the church of *Rochester*, writ by Ernulphus the bishop——with a most affected seriousness of look and voice, which might have cajoled Ernulphus himself,——he put it into Dr. *Slop*'s hands.—— Dr. *Slop* wrapt his thumb up in the corner of his handkerchief, and with a wry face, though without any suspicion, read aloud, as follows,——my uncle *Toby* whistling *Lillabullero*, as loud as he could, all the time.

Textus de Ecclesiâ Roffensi, per Ernulfum Episcopum.

CAP. XXV.

EXCOMMUNICATIO.[4]

EX auctoriate Dei omnipotentis, Patris, et Filij, et Spiritus Sancti, et sanctorum canonum, sanctæque et intemeratæ Virginis Dei genetricis Mariæ,

---

4. As the genuineness of the consultation upon the question of baptism, was doubted by some, and denied by others, ——'twas thought proper to print the original of this excommunication; for the copy of which Mr. *Shandy* returns thanks to the chapter clerk and chapter of *Rochester*. [*Sterne's note*.] Ernulfus was an actual twelfth-century Bishop of Rochester, and his curse does exist.

Chapter XI.

B Y the authority of God Almighty, the Father, Son, and Holy
Ghost, and of the holy canons, and of the undefiled Virgin
Mary, mother and patroness of our Saviour." I think there is no
necessity, quoth Dr. *Slop*, dropping the paper down to his knee, and
addressing himself to my father,——as you have read it over, Sir,
so lately, to read it aloud;——and as Captain *Shandy* seems to have
no great inclination to hear it,——I may as well read it to
myself. That's contrary to treaty, replied my father,——besides,
there is something so whimsical, especially in the latter part of it, I
should grieve to lose the pleasure of a second reading. Dr. *Slop* did
not altogether like it,——but my uncle *Toby* offering at that
instant to give over whistling, and read it himself to them;——
Dr. *Slop* thought he might as well read it under the cover of my
uncle *Toby*'s whistling,——as suffer my uncle *Toby* to read it
alone;——so raising up the paper to his face, and holding it quite
parallel to it, in order to hide his chagrin,——he read it aloud as
follows,——my uncle *Toby* whistling *Lillabullero*, though not
quite so loud as before.

————Atque omnium cœlestium virtutum, angelorum, arch-
angelorum, thronorum, dominationum, potestatuum, cherubin ac
seraphin, & sanctorum patriarchum, prophetarum, & omnium apos-
tolorum et evangelistarum, & sanctorum innocentum, qui in con-
spectu Agni soli digni inventi sunt canticum cantare novum, et
sanctorum martyrum, et sanctorum confessorum, et sanctarum virginum, atque omnium simul sanctorum et electorum Dei,————
vel os   s
Excommunicamus, et anathematizamus hunc furem, *vel* hunc male-
s
factorem, N. N. et a liminibus sanctæ Dei ecclesiæ sequestramus et
vel i   n
æternis suppliciis excruciandus, mancipetur, cum Dathan et Abiram,
et cum his qui dixerunt Domino Deo, Recede à nobis, scientiam
viarum tuarum nolumus: et sicut aquâ ignis extinguitur, sic extingua-
vel eorum   n
tur lucerna ejus in secula seculorum nisi respuerit, et ad satisfac-
n
tionem venerit. Amen.

os   os
Maledicat illum Deus Pater qui hominem creavit. Maledicat illum
os
Dei Filius qui pro homine passus est. Maledicat illum Spiritus
os
Sanctus qui in baptismo effusus est. Maledicat illum sancta crux,
quam Christus pro nostrâ salute hostem triumphans, ascendit.

os
Maledicat illum sancta Dei genetrix et perpetua Virgo Maria.
os
Maledicat illum sanctus Michael, animarum susceptor sacrarum.
os
Maledicant illum omnes angeli et archangeli, principatus et potes-
tates, omnisque militia cœlestis.

"By the authority of God Almighty, the Father, Son, and Holy Ghost, and of the undefiled Virgin *Mary*, 'mother and patroness of our Saviour, and of all the celestial virtues, angels, archangels, thrones, dominions, powers, cherubins and seraphins, and of all the holy patriarchs, prophets, and of all the apostles and evangelists, and of the holy innocents, who in the sight of the holy Lamb, are found worthy to sing the new song of the holy martyrs and holy confessors, and of the holy virgins, and of all the saints together, with the holy and elect of God.——May he," (*Obadiah*) "be damn'd," (for tying these knots.)——"We excommunicate, and anathematise him, and from the thresholds of the holy church of God Almighty we sequester him, that he may be tormented, disposed and delivered over with *Dathan* and *Abiram*, and with those who say unto the Lord God, Depart from us, we desire none of thy ways. And as fire is quenched with water, so let the light of him be put out for evermore, unless it shall repent him" (*Obadiah*, of the knots which he has tied) "and make satisfaction" (for them.) Amen.

"May the Father who created man, curse him.——May the Son who suffered for us, curse him.——May the Holy Ghost who was given to us in baptism, curse him (*Obadiah*.)——May the holy cross which Christ for our salvation triumphing over his enemies, ascended,——curse him.

"May the holy and eternal *Virgin Mary*, mother of God, curse him.——May St. *Michael* the advocate of holy souls, curse him. ——May all the angels and archangels, principalities and powers, and all the heavenly armies, curse him." [Our armies swore terribly in *Flanders*, cried my uncle *Toby*,——but nothing to this.——For my own part, I could not have a heart to curse my dog so.]

os
Maledicat illum patriarcharum et prophetarum laudabilis num-
os
erus. Maledicat illum sanctus Johannes præcursor et Baptista Christi, et sanctus Petrus, et sanctus Paulus, atque sanctus Andreas, omnesque Christi apostoli, simul et cæteri discipuli, quatuor quoque evangelistæ, qui sua prædicatione mundum universum converterunt.

os
Maledicat illum cuneus martyrum et confessorum mirificus, qui Deo bonis operibus placitus inventus est.

os
Maledicant illum sacrarum virginum chori, quæ mundi vana causa
os
honoris Christi respuenda contempserunt. Maledicant illum omnes sancti qui ab initio mundi usque in finem seculi Deo delecti inveniuntur.

os
Maledicant illum cœli et terra, et omnia sancta in eis manentia.

i   n   n
Maledictus sit ubicunque fuerit, sive in domo, sive in agro, sive in viâ, sive in semitâ, sive in silvâ, sive in aquâ, sive in ecclesiâ.

i   n
Maledictus sit vivendo, moriendo,————————————
————— ————— ————— ————— ————— —————
————— ————— ————— ————— ————— —————
————— ————— ————— ————— ————— —————

manducando, bibendo, esuriendo, sitiendo, jejunando, dormitando, dormiendo, vigilando, ambulando, stando, sedendo, jacendo, operando, quiescendo, mingendo, cacando, flebotomando.

May St. John the præ-cursor, and St. John the Baptist,[5] and St. Peter and St. Paul, and St. Andrew, and all other Christ's apostles, together curse him. And may the rest of his disciples and four evangelists, who by their preaching converted the universal world, ——and may the holy and wonderful company of martyrs and confessors, who by their holy works are found pleasing to God Almighty, curse him (*Obadiah.*)

"May the holy choir of the holy virgins, who for the honour of Christ have despised the things of the world, damn him.——May all the saints who from the beginning of the world to everlasting ages are found to be beloved of God, damn him.——May the heavens and earth, and all the holy things remaining therein, damn him," (*Obadiah*) "or her," (or whoever else had a hand in tying these knots.)

"May he (*Obadiah*) be damn'd wherever he be,——whether in the house or the stables, the garden or the field, or the highway, or in the path, or in the wood, or in the water, or in the church.—— May he be cursed in living, in dying." [Here my uncle *Toby* taking the advantage of a *minim*[6] in the second barr of his tune, kept whistling one continual note to the end of the sentence——Dr. *Slop* with his division of curses moving under him, like a running bass all the way.] "May he be cursed in eating and drinking, in being hungry, in being thirsty, in fasting, in sleeping, in slumbering, in walking, in standing, in sitting, in lying, in working, in resting, in pissing, in shitting, and in blood-letting."

5. A mistranslation: it should read "May St. John the Precursor and Baptizer of Christ. . . ."
6. A half-note.

      i   n
Maledictus sit in totis viribus corporis.
      i   n
Maledictus sit intus et exterius.
      i   n   i   n   i
Maledictus sit in capillis; maledictus sit in cerebro. Maledictus
n
sit in vertice, in temporibus, in fronte, in auriculis, in superciliis, in oculis, in genis, in maxillis, in naribus, in dentibus, mordacibus sive molaribus, in labiis, in guttere, in humeris, in harnis, in brachiis, in manubus, in digitis, in pectore, in corde, et in omnibus interioribus stomacho tenus, in renibus, in inguinibus, in femore, in genitalibus, in coxis, in genubus, in cruribus, in pedibus, et in unguibus.

Maledictus sit in totis compagibus membrorum, a vertice capitis, usque ad plantam pedis——non sit in eo sanitas.

Maledicat illum Christus Filius Dei vivi toto suæ majestatis imperio

"May he (*Obadiah*) be cursed in all the faculties of his body.

"May he be cursed inwardly and outwardly.——May he be cursed in the hair of his head.——May he be cursed in his brains, and in his vertex," (that is a sad curse, quoth my father) "in his temples, in his forehead, in his ears, in his eye-brows, in his cheeks, in his jaw-bones, in his nostrils, in his foreteeth and grinders, in his lips, in his throat, in his shoulders, in his wrists, in his arms, in his hands, in his fingers.

"May he be damn'd in his mouth, in his breast, in his heart and purtenance, down to the very stomach.

"May he be cursed in his reins, and in his groin," (God in heaven forbid, quoth my uncle *Toby*)——"in his thighs, in his genitals," (my father shook his head) "and in his hips, and in his knees, his legs, and feet, and toe-nails.

"May he be cursed in all the joints and articulations of his members, from the top of his head to the soal of his foot, may there be no soundness in him.

"May the Son of the living God, with all the glory of his Majesty"——[Here my uncle *Toby* throwing back his head, gave a monstrous, long, loud Whew——w——w——something betwixt the interjectional whistle of *Hey day!* and the word itself.——

——By the golden beard of *Jupiter*——and of *Juno*, (if her majesty wore one), and by the beards of the rest of your heathen worships, which by the bye was no small number, since what with the beards of your celestial gods, and gods aerial and aquatick,—— to say nothing of the beards of town-gods and country-gods, or of the celestial goddesses your wives, or of the infernal goddesses your

—et insurgat adversus illum cœlum cum omnibus virtutibus quæ in eo moventur ad *damnandum* eum, nisi penituerit et ad satisfactionem venerit. Amen. Fiat, fiat. Amen.

whores and concubines, (that is in case they wore 'em)——all which beards, as *Varro*[7] tells me, upon his word and honour, when mustered up together, made no less than thirty thousand effective beards upon the pagan establishment;——every beard of which claimed the rights and privileges of being stroked and sworn by,—— by all these beards together then,——I vow and protest, that of the two bad cassocks I am worth in the world, I would have given the better of them, as freely as ever *Cid Hamet*[8] offered his,——only to have stood by, and heard my uncle *Toby*'s accompanyment.]

——"Curse him," continued Dr. *Slop*,——"and may heaven with all the powers which move therein, rise up against him, curse and damn him (*Obadiah*) unless he repent and make satisfaction. Amen. So be it,——so be it. Amen."

I declare, quoth my uncle *Toby*, my heart would not let me curse the devil himself with so much bitterness.——He is the father of curses, replied Dr. *Slop*.——So am not I, replied my uncle.——But he is cursed, and damn'd already, to all eternity,——replied Dr. *Slop*.

I am sorry for it, quoth my uncle *Toby*.

Dr. *Slop* drew up his mouth, and was just beginning to return my uncle *Toby* the compliment of his Whu——u——u——or interjectional whistle,——when the door hastily opening in the next chapter but one——put an end to the affair.

7. A Roman scholar of the second century.
8. The fictitious Arab writer whom Cervantes claims as the source of much of what he "translates" in *Don Quixote*. At II.iv.48 he wishes he could give his best coat to see "the knight and the matron walk thus hand in hand from the chamber-door to the bed-side."

Chapter XII.

NOW don't let us give ourselves a parcel of airs, and pretend that the oaths we make free with in this land of liberty of ours are our own; and because we have the spirit to swear them, ——imagine that we have had the wit to invent them too.

I'll undertake this moment to prove it to any man in the world, except to a connoisseur;——though I declare I object only to a connoisseur in swearing,——as I would do to a connoisseur in painting, &c. &c. the whole set of 'em are so hung round and *befetish'd* with the bobs and trinkets of criticism,——or to drop my metaphor, which by the bye is a pity,——for I have fetch'd it as far as from the coast of *Guinea*;[9]——their heads, Sir, are stuck so full of rules and compasses, and have that eternal propensity to apply them upon all occasions, that a work of genius had better go to the devil at once, than stand to be prick'd and tortured to death by 'em.

——And how did *Garrick*[1] speak the soliloquy last night?—— Oh, against all rule, my Lord,——most ungrammatically! betwixt the substantive and the adjective, which should agree togeher in *number*, *case* and *gender*, he made a breach thus,——stopping, as if the point wanted settling;——and betwixt the nominative case, which your lordship knows should govern the verb, he suspended his voice in the epilogue a dozen times, three seconds and three fifths by a stop-watch, my Lord, each time.——Admirable grammarian!——But in suspending his voice——was the sense suspended likewise? Did no expression of attitude or countenance fill up the chasm?——Was the eye silent? Did you narrowly look?—— I look'd only at the stop-watch, my Lord.——Excellent observer!

And what of this new book the whole world makes such a rout about?——Oh! 'tis out of all plumb, my Lord,——quite an irregular thing!——not one of the angles at the four corners was a right angle.——I had my rule and compasses, &c. my Lord, in my pocket.——Excellent critic!

——And for the epick poem, your lordship bid me look at;—— upon taking the length, breadth, height, and depth of it, and trying them at home upon an exact scale of *Bossu's*,[2]——'tis out, my Lord, in every one of its dimensions.——Admirable connoisseur!

——And did you step in, to take a look at the grand picture, in your way back.——'Tis a melancholy daub! my Lord; not one principle of the *pyramid* in any one group!——and what a price!

9. That is, he's derived "befetish'd" from the use of fetishes by native tribes.
1. Again, Sterne's friend, the famous actor.
2. René le Bossu was a French critic of the seventeenth century whose very influential *Traité du poeme epique* tried to derive precise rules for the epic from classical examples.

——for there is nothing of the colouring of *Titian*,[3]——the expression of *Rubens*,——the grace of *Raphael*,——the purity of *Dominichino*, the *corregiescity* of *Corregio*,——the learning of *Poussin*,——the airs of *Guido*,——the taste of the *Carrachi's*,—— or the grand contour of *Angelo*.——Grant me patience, just heaven!

——Of all the cants which are canted in this canting world,—— though the cant of hypocrites may be the worst,——the cant of criticism is the most tormenting!

I would go fifty miles on foot, for I have not a horse worth riding on, to kiss the hand of that man whose generous heart will give up the reins of his imagination into his author's hands,——be pleased he knows not why, and cares not wherefore.

Great *Apollo*! if thou art in a giving humour,——give me,——I ask no more, but one stroke of native humour, with a single spark of thy own fire along with it,——and send *Mercury*, with the *rules and compasses*, if he can be spared, with my compliments to——no matter.

Now to any one else, I will undertake to prove, that all the oaths and imprecations, which we have been puffing off upon the world for these two hundred and fifty years last past, as originals,—— except St. *Paul's thumb*,——*God's flesh and God's fish*, which were oaths monarchical,[4] and, considering who made them, not much amiss; and as kings oaths, 'tis not much matter whether they were fish or flesh;——else, I say, there is not an oath, or at least a curse amongst them, which has not been copied over and over again out of *Ernulphus*, a thousand times: but, like all other copies, how infinitely short of the force and spirit of the original!——It is thought to be no bad oath,——and by itself passes very well—— "G—d damn you."——Set it beside *Ernulphus's*——"God Almighty the Father damn you,——God the Son damn you,——God the Holy Ghost damn you,"——you see 'tis nothing.——There is an orientality in his, we cannot rise up to: besides, he is more copious in his invention,——possess'd more of the excellencies of a swearer, ——had such a thorough knowledge of the human frame, its membranes, nerves, ligaments, knittings of the joints, and articulations, ——that when *Ernulphus* cursed,——no part escaped him.——'Tis true, there is something of a *hardness* in his manner,——and, as in *Michael Angelo*, a want of *grace*,——but then there is such a greatness of *gusto*!——

My father, who generally look'd upon every thing in a light very different from all mankind,——would, after all, never allow this to be an original.——He consider'd rather *Ernulphus's* anathema, as

---

3. Tristram names many of the best-known painters of the sixteenth and seventeenth centuries, and characterizes each in the trite manner of bad art criticism.

4. Richard III is said to have sworn frequently by St. Paul, and Charles II by " 'Od's fish" (a euphemism for "God's flesh").

an institute of swearing, in which, as he suspected, upon the decline of *swearing* in some milder pontificate, *Ernulphus*, by order of the succeeding pope, had with great learning and diligence collected together all the laws of it;——for the same reason that *Justinian*, in the decline of the empire, had ordered his chancellor *Tribonian* to collect the *Roman* or civil laws all together into one code or digest,——lest through the rust of time,——and the fatality of all things committed to oral tradition; they should be lost to the world for ever.

For this reason my father would oft-times affirm, there was not an oath, from the great and tremendous oath of *William* the Conqueror, (*By the splendour of God*) down to the lowest oath of a scavenger, (*Damn your eyes*) which was not to be found in *Ernulphus*.——In short, he would add,——I defy a man to swear *out* of it.

The hypothesis is, like most of my father's, singular and ingenius too;——nor have I any objection to it, but that it overturns my own.

Chapter XIII.

BLESS my soul!——my poor mistress is ready to faint,—— and her pains are gone,——and the drops are done,—— and the bottle of julap[5] is broke,——and the nurse has cut her arm,——(and I, my thumb, cried Dr. *Slop*) and the child is where it was, continued *Susannah*,——and the midwife has fallen backwards upon the edge of the fender, and bruised her hip as black as your hat.——I'll look at, quoth Dr. *Slop*.——There is no need of that, replied *Susannah*,——you had better look at my mistress,—— but the midwife would gladly first give you an account how things are, so desires you would go up stairs and speak to her this moment.

Human nature is the same in all professions.

The midwife had just before been put over Dr. *Slop's* head.—— He had not digested it.——No, replied Dr. *Slop*, 'twould be full as proper, if the midwife came down to me.——I like subordination, quoth my uncle *Toby*,——and but for it, after the reduction of *Lisle*, I know not what might have become of the garrison of *Ghent*, in the mutiny for bread, in the year Ten.——Nor, replied Dr. *Slop*, (parodying my uncle *Toby's* hobby-horsical reflection, though full as hobby-horsical himself)——do I know, Captain *Shandy*, what might have become of the garrison above stairs, in the mutiny and confusion I find all things are in at present, but for the subordination of fingers and thumbs to ******—— the application of which,

5. A drink seasoned with herbs.

Sir, under this accident of mine, comes in so *a propos*, that without it, the cut upon my thumb might have been felt by the *Shandy* family, as long as the *Shandy* family had a name.

Chapter XIV.

L ET us go back to the ******——— in the last chapter.
It is a singular stroke of eloquence (at least it was so, when eloquence flourished at *Athens* and *Rome*, and would be so now, did orators wear mantles) not to mention the name of a thing, when you had the thing about you, *in petto*,[6] ready to produce, pop, in the place you want it. A scar, an axe, a sword, a pink'd-doublet, a rusty helmet, a pound and a half of pot-ashes in an urn, or a three-halfpenny pickle pot,——but above all, a tender infant royally accoutred.——Tho' if it was too young, and the oration as long as *Tully*'s second *Philippick*,[7]——it must certainly have beshit the orator's mantle.——And then again, if too old,——it must have been unwieldy and incommodious to his action,——so as to make him lose by his child almost as much as he could gain by it.—— Otherwise, when a state orator has hit the precise age to a minute, ——hid his BAMBINO in his mantle so cunningly that no mortal could smell it,——and produced it so critically, that no soul could say, it came in by head and shoulders,——Oh, Sirs! it has done wonders.——It has open'd the sluices, and turn'd the brains, and shook the principles, and unhinged the politicks of half a nation.

These feats however are not to be done, except in those states and times, I say, where orators wore mantles,——and pretty large ones too, my brethren, with some twenty or five and twenty yards of good purple, superfine, marketable cloth in them,——with large flowing folds and doubles, and in a great stile of design.——All which plainly shews, may it please your worships, that the decay of eloquence, and the little good service it does at present, both within, and without doors, is owing to nothing else in the world, but short coats, and the disuse of *trunk-hose*.[8]——We can conceal nothing under ours, Madam, worth shewing.

Chapter XV.

D R. *Slop* was within an ace of being an exception to all this argumentation: for happening to have his green bays bag upon his knees, when he began to parody my uncle *Toby*,——'twas

---

6. "In the breast;" in secret.
7. The longest of Cicero's (Tully's) orations against Mark Antony. "Phillipic" is derived from the ancient Greek Demosthenes' attack on Phillip of Macedon.

8. The full, bag-like breeches extending from waist to thigh that were in fashion in the sixteenth and seventeenth (but not the eighteenth) centuries.

as good as the best mantle in the world to him: for which purpose, when he foresaw the sentence would end in his new invented *forceps*, he thrust his hand into the bag in order to have them ready to clap in, where your reverences took so much notice of the******, which had he managed,——my uncle *Toby* had certainly been overthrown: the sentence and the argument in that case jumping closely in one point, so like the two lines which form the salient angle of a raveline,——Dr. *Slop* would never have given them up;——and my uncle *Toby* would as soon have thought of flying, as taking them by force: but Dr. *Slop* fumbled so vilely in pulling them out, it took off the whole effect, and what was a ten times worse evil (for they seldom come alone in this life) in pulling out his *forceps*, his *forceps* unfortunately drew out the *squirt* along with it.

When a proposition can be taken in two senses,——'tis a law in disputation That the respondent may reply to which of the two he pleases, or finds most convenient for him.——This threw the advantage of the argument quite on my uncle *Toby*'s side.——"Good God!" cried my uncle *Toby*, "*are children brought into the world with a squirt?*"

Chapter XVI.

——UPON my honour, Sir, you have tore every bit of the skin quite off the back of both my hands with your forceps, cried my uncle *Toby*,——and you have crush'd all my knuckles into the bargain with them, to a jelly. 'Tis your own fault, said Dr. *Slop*,——you should have clinch'd your two fists together into the form of a child's head, as I told you, and sat firm.——I did so, answered my uncle *Toby*.——Then the points of my forceps have not been sufficiently arm'd, or the rivet wants closing——or else the cut on my thumb has made me a little aukward,——or possibly ——'Tis well, quoth my father, interrupting the detail of possibilities,——that the experiment was not first made upon my child's head piece.——It would not have been a cherry stone the worse, answered Dr. *Slop*. I maintain it, said my uncle *Toby*, it would have broke the cerebellum, (unless indeed the skull had been as hard as a granado[9]) and turned it all into a perfect posset. Pshaw! replied Dr. *Slop*, a child's head is naturally as soft as the pap of an apple;—— the sutures give way,——and besides, I could have extracted by the feet after.——Not you, said she.——I rather wish you would begin that way, quoth my father.

Pray do, added my uncle *Toby*.

9. Grenade.

Chapter XVII.

——AND pray, good woman, after all, will you take upon you to say, it may not be the child's hip, as well as the child's head?——'Tis most certainly the head, replied the midwife. Because, continued Dr. *Slop*, (turning to my father) as positive as these old ladies generally are,——'tis a point very difficult to know,——and yet of the greatest consequence to be known;——because, Sir, if the hip is mistaken for the head,——there is a possibility (if it is a boy) that the forceps * * * * * * *
* * * * * * * * * * * * * * * * * * *

——What the possibility was, Dr. *Slop* whispered very low to my father, and then to my uncle *Toby*.——There is no such danger, continued he, with the head.——No, in truth, quoth my father, ——but when your possibility has taken place at the hip,——you may as well take off the head too.

——It is morally impossible the reader should understand this, ——'tis enough Dr. *Slop* understood it;——so taking the green bays bag in his hand, with the help of *Obadiah*'s pumps, he tripp'd pretty nimbly, for a man of his size, across the room to the door,——and from the door was shewn the way, by the good old midwife, to my mother's apartment.

Chapter XVIII.

IT is two hours, and ten minutes,——and no more,——cried my father, looking at his watch, since Dr. *Slop* and *Obadiah* arrived,——and I know not how it happens, brother *Toby*,——but to my imagination it seems almost an age.

——Here——pray, Sir, take hold of my cap,——nay, take the bell along with it, and my pantoufles[1] too.——

Now, Sir, they are all at your service; and I freely make you a present of 'em, on condition, you give me all your attention to this chapter.

Though my father said, "*he knew not how it happen'd*,"——yet he knew very well, how it happen'd;——and at the instant he spoke it, was pre-determined in his mind, to give my uncle *Toby* a clear account of the matter by a metaphysical dissertation upon the subject of *duration and its simple modes*, in order to shew my uncle *Toby*, by what mechanism and mensurations in the brain it came to pass, that the rapid succession of their ideas, and the eternal scampering of discourse from one thing to another, since Dr. *Slop* had come into the room, had lengthened out so short a period, to so

---

1. Slippers.

inconceivable an extent.——"I know not how it happens,——cried my father,——but it seems an age."

——'Tis owing, entirely, quoth my uncle *Toby*, to the succession of our ideas.

My father, who had an itch in common with all philosophers, of reasoning upon every thing which happened, and accounting for it too,——proposed infinite pleasure to himself in this, of the succession of ideas, and had not the least apprehension of having it snatch'd out of his hands by my uncle *Toby*, who (honest man!) generally took every thing as it happened;——and who, of all men in the world, troubled his brain the least with abstruse thinking;——the ideas of time and space,——or how we came by those ideas,——or of what stuff they were made,——or whether they were born with us,——or we pick'd them up afterwards as we went along,——or whether we did it in frocks,——or not till we had got into breeches,——with a thousand other inquiries and disputes about INFINITY, PRESCIENCE, LIBERTY, NECESSITY, and so forth, upon whose desperate and unconquerable theories, so many fine heads have been turned and crack'd,——never did my uncle *Toby*'s the least injury at all; my father knew it,——and was no less surprised, than he was disappointed with my uncle's fortuitous solution.

Do you understand the theory of that affair? replied my father.

Not I, quoth my uncle.

——But you have some ideas, said my father, of what you talk about.——

No more than my horse, replied my uncle *Toby*.

Gracious heaven! cried my father, looking upwards, and clasping his two hands together,——there is a worth in thy honest ignorance, brother *Toby*,——'twere almost a pity to exchange it for a knowledge.——But I'll tell thee.——

To understand what *time* is aright, without which we never can comprehend *infinity*, insomuch as one is a portion of the other,——we ought seriously to sit down and consider what idea it is, we have of *duration*, so as to give a satisfactory account, how we came by it.——What is that to any body? quoth my uncle *Toby*.[2] *For if you will turn your eyes inwards upon your mind, continued my father, and observe attentively, you will perceive, brother, that whilst you and I are talking together, and thinking and smoaking our pipes: or whilst we receive successively ideas in our minds, we know that we do exist, and so we estimate the existence, or the continuation of the existence of ourselves, or any thing else commensurate to the suc-*

---

2. Vid Locke [*Sterne's note*]. He goes on to paraphrase *An Essay Concerning Human Understanding* I.xiv. 3, 4, 19, 9.

cession of any ideas in our minds, the duration of ourselves, or any such other thing co existing with our thinking,——*and so according to that preconceived*——You puzzle me to death, cried my uncle *Toby.*——

——'Tis owing to this, replied my father, that in our computations of *time*, we are so used to minutes, hours, weeks, and months, ——and of clocks (I wish there was not a clock in the kingdom) to measure out their several portions to us, and to those who belong to us,——that 'twill be well, if in time to come, the *succession of our ideas* be of any use or service to us at all.

Now, whether we observe it or no, continued my father, in every sound man's head, there is a regular succession of ideas of one sort or other, which follow each other in train just like——A train of artillery? said my uncle *Toby.*——A train of a fiddle stick!—— quoth my father,——which follow and succeed one another in our minds at certain distances, just like the images in the inside of a lanthorn turned round by the heat of a candle.——I declare, quoth my uncle *Toby*, mine are like a smoak-jack.[3]——Then, brother *Toby*, I have nothing more to say to you upon the subject, said my father.

Chapter XIX.

——WHAT a conjuncture was here lost!——My father in one of his best explanatory moods,——in eager pursuit of a metaphysic point into the very regions where clouds and thick darkness would soon have encompassed it about;——my uncle *Toby* in one of the finest dispositions for it in the world;—— his head like a smoak-jack;——the funnel unswept, and the ideas whirling round and round about in it, all obfuscated and darkened over with fuliginous matter!——By the tomb stone of *Lucian*[4]—— if it is in being,——if not, why then, by his ashes! by the ashes of my dear *Rabelais*, and dearer *Cervantes*,——my father and my uncle *Toby*'s discourse upon TIME and ETERNITY,——was a discourse devoutly to be wished for! and the petulancy of my father's humour in putting a stop to it, as he did, was a robbery of the *Ontologic treasury*, of such a jewel, as no coalition of great occasions and great men, are ever likely to restore to it again.

3. A contrivance for turning a roasting spit: the spit is connected to a wheel in the chimney so that rising gasses turn it.
4. Lucian, the Greek satirist and humorist of the second century, Rabelais, the great French comic writer of the sixteenth century, and Cervantes, the great Spanish humorist of the early seventeenth century, all contributed to Sterne's humorous mixture of the educational and the entertaining. Ontology is the branch of philosophy concerned with the essence of things or being.

Chapter XX.

THO' my father persisted in not going on with the discourse, ——yet he could not get my uncle *Toby*'s smoak-jack out of his head,——piqued as he was at first with it;——there was something in the comparison at the bottom, which hit his fancy; for which purpose resting his elbow upon the table, and reclining the right side of his head upon the palm of his hand,——but looking first stedfastly in the fire,——he began to commune with himself and philosophize about it: but his spirits being wore out with the fatigues of investigating new tracts, and the constant exertion of his faculties upon that variety of subjects which had taken their turn in the discourse,——the idea of the smoak-jack soon turned all his ideas upside down,——so that he fell asleep almost before he knew what he was about.

As for my uncle *Toby*, his smoak-jack had not made a dozen revolutions, before he fell asleep also.——Peace be with them both. ——Dr. *Slop* is engaged with the midwife, and my mother above stairs.——*Trim* is busy in turning an old pair of jack-boots into a couple of mortars to be employed in the siege of *Messina* next summer,——and is this instant boring the touch holes with the point of a hot poker.——All my heroes are off my hands;——'tis the first time I have had a moment to spare,——and I'll make use of it, and write my preface.

THE

Author's PREFACE.

NO, I'll not say a word about it,——here it is;——in publishing it,——I have appealed to the world,——and to the world I leave it;——it must speak for itself.

All I know of the matter is,——when I sat down, my intent was to write a good book; and as far as the tenuity of my understanding would hold out,——a wise, aye, and a discreet,——taking care only, as I went along, to put into it all the wit and the judgment (be it more or less) which the great author and bestower of them had thought fit originally to give me,——so that, as your worships see, ——'tis just as God pleases.

Now, *Agalastes*[5] (speaking dispraisingly) sayeth, That there

---

5. *Agalastes*: "he who never laughs." *Triptolemus*: in Greek myth, the inventor of agriculture, and giver of laws, and judge of the dead. *Phutatorius*: "copulator." Locke describes the functions of wit and judgment in the human mind in the *Essay Concerning Human Understanding* II.xi.2. He considers judgment —the capacity to distinguish one thing from another—the useful function; wit— which notices similarities even where they are not obvious—he considers at

may be some wit in it, for aught he knows,——but no judgment at all. And *Triptolemus* and *Phutatorius* agreeing thereto, ask, How is it possible there should? for that wit and judgment in this world never go together; inasmuch as they are two operations differing from each other as wide as east is from west.——So, says *Locke*, ——so are farting and hickuping, say I. But in answer to this, *Didius* the great church lawyer, in his code *de fartandi et illustrandi fallaciis*, doth maintain and make fully appear, That an illustration is no argument,——nor do I maintain the wiping of a looking-glass clean, to be a syllogism;——but you all, may it please your worships, see the better for it,——so that the main good these things do, is only to clarify the understanding, previous to the application of the argument itself, in order to free it from any little motes, or specks of opacular matter, which if left swimming therein, might hinder a conception and spoil all.

Now, my dear Anti-Shandeans, and thrice able critics, and fellow-labourers, (for to you I write this Preface)——and to you, most subtle statesmen and discreet doctors (do——pull off your beards) renowned for gravity and wisdom;——*Monopolos*[6] my politician, *Didius*, my counsel; *Kysarcius*, my friend;——*Phutatorius*, my guide;——*Gastripheres*, the preserver of my life; *Somnolentius*, the balm and repose of it,——not forgetting all others as well sleeping as waking,——ecclesiastical as civil, whom for brevity, but out of no resentment to you, I lump all together.——Believe me, right worthy,

My most zealous wish and fervant prayer in your behalf, and in my own too, in case the thing is not done already for us,——is, that the great gifts and endowments both of wit and judgment, with every thing which usually goes along with them,——such as memory, fancy, genius, eloquence, quick parts, and what not, may this precious moment without stint or measure, let or hinderance, be poured down warm as each of us could bear it,——scum and sediment an' all; (for I would not have a drop lost) into the several receptacles, cells, cellules, domiciles, dormitories, refectories, and spare places of our brains,——in such sort, that they might continue to be injected and tunn'd[7] into, according to the true intent and meaning of my wish, until every vessel of them, both great and small, be so replenished, saturated and fill'd up therewith, that no more, would it save a man's life, could possibly be got either in or out.

Bless us!——what noble work we should make!——how should I

---

best amusing, at worst destructively misleading (a doctrine with dangerous implications for literature). Didius's code translates: "of Farting and the Explanation of Deceptions."

6. *Monopolos*: "monopolist." *Kysarcius*: "Kiss arse." *Gastripheres*: "big-belly." *Somnolentius*: "the sleepy one."
7. A tun is a barrel.

tickle it off!——and what spirits should I find myself in, to be writing away for such readers!——and you,——just heaven!—— with what raptures would you sit and read,——but oh!——'tis too much,——I am sick,——I faint away deliciously at the thoughts of it!——'tis more than nature can bear!——lay hold of me,——I am giddy,——I am stone blind,——I'm dying,——I am gone.—— Help! Help! Help!——But hold,——I grow something better again, for I am beginning to foresee, when this is over, that as we shall all of us continue to be great wits,——we should never agree amongst ourselves, one day to an end:——there would be so much satire and sarcasm,——scoffing and flouting, with raillying and repartee- ing of it,——thrusting and parrying in one corner or another,—— there would be nothing but mischief amongst us.——Chaste stars! what biting and scratching, and what a racket and a clatter we should make, what with breaking of heads, and rapping of knuckles, and hitting of sore places,——there would be no such thing as living for us.

But then again, as we should all of us be men of great judgment, we should make up matters as fast as ever they went wrong; and though we should abominate each other, ten times worse than so many devils or devilesses, we should nevertheless, my dear crea- tures, be all courtesy and kindness,——milk and honey,——'twould be a second land of promise,——a paradise upon earth, if there was such a thing to be had,——so that upon the whole we should have done well enough.

All I fret and fume at, and what most distresses my invention at present, is how to bring the point itself to bear; for as your worships well know, that of these heavenly emanations of *wit* and *judgment*, which I have so bountifully wished both for your worships and myself,——there is but a certain *quantum* stored up for us all, for the use and behoof of the whole race of mankind; and such small *modicums* of 'em are only sent forth into this wide world, circulat- ing here and there in one by corner or another,——and in such narrow streams, and at such prodigious intervals from each other, that one would wonder how it holds out, or could be sufficient for the wants and emergencies of so many great states, and populous empires.

Indeed there is one thing to be considered, that in *Nova Zembla*, *North Lapland*, and in all those cold and dreary tracts of the globe, which lie more directly under the arctick and antarctick circles, ——where the whole province of a man's concernments lies for near nine months together, within the narrow compass of his cave, ——where the spirits are compressed almost to nothing,——and where the passions of a man, with every thing which belongs to them, are as frigid as the zone itself;——there the least quantity of *judgment* imaginable does the business,——and of *wit*,——there is a total and an absolute saving,——for as not one spark is wanted,——so not one spark is given. Angels and ministers of grace defend us! What a dismal thing would it have been to have governed a kingdom, to have fought a battle, or made a treaty, or run a match, or wrote a book, or got a child, or held a provincial chapter[8] there, with so *plentiful a lack* of wit and judgment about us! for mercy's sake! let us think no more about it, but travel on as fast as we can southwards into *Norway*,——crossing over *Swedeland*, if you please, through the small triangular province of *Angermania* to the lake of *Bothnia;* coasting along it through east and west *Bothnia*, down to *Carelia*, and so on, through all those states and provinces which border upon the far side of the *Gulf* of *Finland*, and the north east of the *Baltick*, up to *Petersbourg*, and just stepping into *Ingria;*——then stretching over directly from thence through the north parts of the *Russian* empire——leaving *Siberia* a little upon the left hand till we get into the very heart of *Russian* and *Asiatick Tartary.*

Now throughout this long tour which I have led you, you observe the good people are better off by far, than in the polar countries which we have just left:——for if you hold your hand over your eyes, and look very attentively, you may perceive some small glimmerings (as it were) of wit, with a comfortable provision of good plain *houshold* judgment, which taking the quality and quantity of it together, they make a very good shift with,——and had they more of either the one or the other, it would destroy the proper ballance betwixt them, and I am satisfied moreover they would want occasions to put them to use.

Now, Sir, if I conduct you home again into this warmer and more luxuriant island, where you perceive the spring tide of our blood and humours runs high,——where we have more ambition, and pride, and envy, and lechery, and other whoreson passions upon our hands to govern and subject to reason,——the *height* of our wit and the *depth* of our judgment, you see, are exactly proportioned to the *length* and *breadth* of our necessities,——and accordingly, we have them sent down amongst us in such a flowing kind of decent and creditable plenty, that no one thinks he has any cause to complain.

It must however be confessed on this head, that, as our air blows hot and cold,——wet and dry, ten times in a day, we have them in no regular and settled way;——so that sometimes for near half a century together, there shall be very little wit or judgment, either to be seen or heard of amongst us:——the small channels of them shall seem quite dried up,——then all of a sudden the sluices shall

---

8. The chapter made up of the canons of a cathedral.

break out, and take a fit of running again like fury,——you would think they would never stop:——and then it is, that in writing and fighting, and twenty other gallant things, we drive all the world before us.

It is by these observations, and a wary reasoning by analogy in that kind of argumentative process, which *Suidas*[9] calls *dialectick induction,*——that I draw and set up this position as most true and veritable.

That of these two luminaries, so much of their irradiations are suffered from time to time to shine down upon us; as he, whose infinite wisdom which dispenses every thing in exact weight and measure, knows will just serve to light us on our way in this night of our obscurity; so that your reverences and worships now find out, nor is it a moment longer in my power to conceal it from you, That the fervent wish in your behalf with which I set out, was no more than the first insinuating *How d'ye* of a caressing prefacer stifling his reader, as a lover sometimes does a coy mistress into silence. For alas! could this effusion of light have been as easily procured, as the exordium wished it——I tremble to think how many thousands for it, of benighted travellers (in the learned sciences at least) must have groped and blundered on in the dark, all the nights of their lives,——running their heads against posts, and knocking out their brains without ever getting to their journies end;——some falling with their noses perpendicularly into stinks,——others horizontally with their tails into kennels.[1] Here one half of a learned profession tilting full butt against the other half of it, and then tumbling and rolling one over the other in the dirt like hogs.——Here the brethren, of another profession, who should have run in opposition to each other, flying on the contrary like a flock of wild geese, all in a row the same way.——What confusion!——what mistakes!—— fiddlers and painters judging by their eyes and ears,——admirable! ——trusting to the passions excited in an air sung, or a story painted to the heart,——instead of measuring them by a quadrant.

In the foreground of this picture, a *statesman* turning the political wheel, like a brute, the wrong way round——*against* the stream of corruption,——by heaven!——instead of *with* it.

In this corner, a son of the divine *Esculapius*,[2] writing a book against predistination; perhaps worse,——feeling his patient's pulse, instead of his apothecary's——a brother of the faculty in the back ground upon his knees in tears,——drawing the curtains of a mangled victim to beg his forgiveness;——offering a fee,——instead of taking one.

9. Suidas was a Byzantine lexicographer of the tenth or eleventh century.
1. Stinks (or perhaps Tristram means sinks) and kennels are sewers and gutters.

2. The Greek god of healing. Tristram goes on to list acts appropriate to true physicians, but not to be expected from the corrupted profession.

In that spacious HALL, a coalition of the gown,[3] from all the barrs
of it, driving a damn'd, dirty, vexatious cause before them with all
their might and main, the wrong way;——kicking it *out* of the great
doors, instead of, *in,*——and with such fury in their looks, and
such a degree of inveteracy in their manner of kicking it, as if the
laws had been originally made for the peace and preservation of
mankind:——perhaps a more enormous mistake committed by
them still,——a litigated point fairly hung up;——for instance,
Whether *John o'Nokes* his nose, could stand in *Tom o'Stiles* his
face, without a trespass, or not,——rashly determined by them in
five and twenty minutes, which, with the cautious pro's and con's
required in so intricate a proceeding, might have taken up as many
months,——and if carried on upon a military plan, as your honours
know, an ACTION should be, with all the stratagems practicable
therein,——such as feints,——forced marches,——surprizes,——
ambuscades,——mask-batteries, and a thousand other strokes of
generalship which consist in catching at all advantages on both
sides,——might reasonably have lasted them as many years, finding
food and raiment all that term for a centumvirate[4] of the profession.

As for the clergy——No——If I say a word against them, I'll
be shot.——I have no desire,——and besides, if I had, ——I durst
not for my soul touch upon the subject,——with such weak nerves
and spirits, and in the condition I am in at present, 'twould be as
much as my life was worth, to deject and contrist myself with so
sad and melancholy an account,——and therefore, 'tis safer to
draw a curtain across, and hasten from it, as fast as I can, to the
main and principal point I have undertaken to clear up,——and
that is, How it comes to pass, that your men of least *wit* are
reported to be men of most *judgment.*——But mark,——I say,
reported to be,——for it is no more, my dear Sirs, than a report,
and which like twenty others taken up every day upon trust, I
maintain to be a vile and a malicious report into the bargain.

This by the help of the observations already premised, and I hope
already weighed and perpended by your reverences and worships, I
shall forthwith make appear.

I hate set dissertations,——and above all things in the world, 'tis
one of the silliest things in one of them, to darken your hypothesis
by placing a number of tall, opake words, one before another, in a
right line, betwixt your own and your reader's conception,——when
in all likelihood, if you had looked about, you might have seen
something standing, or hanging up, which would have cleared the
point at once,——"for what hinderance, hurt or harm, doth the

---

3. The profession of law. Again there
follows a list of generous and socially
useful actions unlikely in a selfish profession.
4. A hundred men.

laudable desire of knowledge bring to any man, if even from a sot, a pot, a fool, a stool, a winter-mittain, a truckle for a pully, the lid of a goldsmith's crucible, an oyl bottle, an old slipper, or a cane chair,"[5]——I am this moment sitting upon one. Will you give me leave to illustrate this affair of wit and judgment, by the two knobs on the top of the back of it,——they are fasten'd on, you see, with two pegs stuck slightly into two gimlet-holes, and will place what I have to say in so clear a light, as to let you see through the drift and meaning of my whole preface, as plainly as if every point and particle of it was made up of sun beams.

I enter now directly upon the point.

——Here stands *wit*,——and there stands *judgment*, close beside it, just like the two knobbs I'm speaking of, upon the back of this self same chair on which I am sitting.

——You see, they are the highest and most ornamental parts of its *frame*,——as wit and judgment ar͟e of *ours*,——and like them too, indubitably both made and fitted to go together, in order as we say in all such cases of duplicated embellishments,——*to answer one another.*

Now for the sake of an experiment, and for the clearer illustrating this matter,——let us for a moment, take off one of these two curious ornaments (I care not which) from the point or pinacle of the chair it now stands on;——nay, don't laugh at it.——But did you ever see in the whole course of your lives such a ridiculous business as this has made of it?——Why, 'tis as miserable a sight as a sow with one ear; and there is just as much sense and symmetry in the one, as in the other:——do,——pray, get off your seats, only to take a view of it.——Now would any man who valued his character a straw, have turned a piece of work out of his hand in such a condition?——nay, lay your hands upon your hearts, and answer this plain question, Whether this one single knobb which now stands here like a blockhead by itself, can serve any purpose upon earth, but to put one in mind of the want of the other;——and let me further ask, in case the chair was your own, if you would not in your consciences think, rather than be as it is, that it would be ten times better without any knobb at all.

Now these two knobs——or top ornaments of the mind of man, which crown the whole entablature,——being, as I said, wit and judgment, which of all others, as I have proved it, are the most needful,——the most priz'd,——the most calamitous to be without, and consequently the hardest to come at,——for all these reasons put together, there is not a mortal amongst us, so destitute of a love of good fame or feeding,——or so ignorant of what will do him good therein,——who does not wish and stedfastly resolve in his

---

5. The quotation is from Rabelais, III.16.

own mind, to be, or to be thought at least master of the one or the other, and indeed of both of them, if the thing seems any way feasible, or likely to be brought to pass.

Now your graver gentry having little or no kind of chance in aiming at the one,——unless they laid hold of the other,——pray what do you think would become of them?——Why, Sirs, in spight of all their *gravities*, they must e'en have been contented to have gone with their insides naked:——this was not to be borne, but by an effort of philosophy not to be supposed in the case we are upon,——so that no one could well have been angry with them, had they been satisfied with what little they could have snatched up and secreted under their cloaks and great perrywigs, had they not raised a *hue* and *cry* at the same time against the lawful owners.

I need not tell your worships, that this was done with so much cunning and artifice,——that the great *Locke*, who was seldom outwitted by false sounds,——was nevertheless bubbled here. The cry, it seems, was so deep and solemn a one, and what with the help of great wigs, grave faces, and other implements of deceit, was rendered so general a one against the *poor wits* in this matter, that the philosopher himself was deceived by it,——it was his glory to free the world from the lumber of a thousand vulgar errors;——but this was not of the number; so that instead of sitting down coolly, as such a philosopher should have done, to have examined the matter of fact before he philosophised upon it;——on the contrary, he took the fact for granted, and so joined in with the cry, and halloo'd it as boisterously as the rest.

This has been made the *Magna Charta* of stupidity ever since, ——but your reverences plainly see, it has been obtained in such a manner, that the title to it is not worth a groat;——which by the bye is one of the many and vile impositions which gravity and grave folks have to answer for hereafter.

As for great wigs, upon which I may be thought to have spoken my mind too freely,——I beg leave to qualify whatever has been unguardedly said to their dispraise or prejudice, by one general declaration——That I have no abhorrence whatever, nor do I detest and abjure either great wigs or long beards,——any further than when I see they are bespoke and let grow on purpose to carry on this self-same imposture——for any purpose,——peace be with them;—— ☞ mark only,——I write not for them.

Chapter XXI.

EVERY day for at least ten years together did my father resolve to have it mended,——'tis not mended yet;——no family but ours would have borne with it an hour,——and what is most astonishing, there was not a subject in the world upon which my father was so eloquent, as upon that of door-hinges.————And yet at the same time, he was certainly one of the greatest bubbles[6] to them, I think, that history can produce: his rhetoric and conduct were at perpetual handy-cuffs.————Never did the parlour-door open————but his philosophy or his principles fell a victim to it;————three drops of oyl with a feather, and a smart stroke of a hammer, had saved his honour for ever.

————Inconsistent soul that man is!————languishing under wounds, which he has the power to heal!————his whole life a contradiction to his knowledge!————his reason, that precious gift of God to him————(instead of pouring in oyl) serving but to sharpen his sensibilities,————to multiply his pains and render him more melancholy and uneasy under them!————poor unhappy creature, that he should do so!————are not the necessary causes of misery in his life enow, but he must add voluntary ones to his stock of sorrow;————struggle against evils which cannot be avoided, and submit to others, which a tenth part of the trouble they create him, would remove from his heart for ever?

By all that is good and virtuous! if there are three drops of oyl to be got, and a hammer to be found within ten miles of *Shandy-Hall*,————the parlour-door hinge shall be mended this reign.

Chapter XXII.

WHEN corporal *Trim* had brought his two mortars to bear, he was delighted with his handy-work above measure; and knowing what a pleasure it would be to his master to see them, he was not able to resist the desire he had of carrying them directly into his parlour.

Now next to the moral lesson I had in view in mentioning the affair of *hinges*, I had a speculative consideration arising out of it, and it is this.

Had the parlour-door open'd and turn'd upon its hinges, as a door should do————

————Or for example, as cleverly as our government has been turning upon its hinges,————(that is, in case things have all along gone well with your worship,————otherwise I give up my simile) ————in this case, I'say, there had been no danger either to master or man, in corporal *Trim*'s peeping in: the moment, he had beheld my father and my uncle *Toby* fast asleep,————the respectfulness of his carriage was such, he would have retired as silent as death, and left them both in their arm-chairs, dreaming as happy as he had found them: but the thing was morally speaking so very impracticable, that for the many years in which this hinge was suffered to be out

---

6. "Bubble": fool; "handy-cuffs": fisticuffs.

of order, and amongst the hourly grievances my father submitted to upon its account,——this was one; that he never folded his arms to take his nap after dinner, but the thoughts of being unavoidably awakened by the first person who should open the door, was always uppermost in his imagination, and so incessantly step'd in betwixt him and the first balmy presage of his repose, as to rob him, as he often declared, of the whole sweets of it.

"*When things move upon bad hinges*, an' please your lordships, *how can it be otherwise?*"

Pray what's the matter? Who is there? cried my father, waking, the moment the door began to creak.——I wish the smith would give a peep at that confounded hinge.——'Tis nothing, an' please your honour, said *Trim*, but two mortars I am bringing in.—— They shan't make a clatter with them here, cried my father hastily. ——If Dr. *Slop* has any drugs to pound, let him do it in the kitchen.——May it please your honour, cried *Trim*,——they are two mortar-pieces for a siege next summer, which I have been making out of a pair of jack-boots, which *Obadiah* told me your honour had left off wearing.——By heaven! cried my father, springing out of his chair, as he swore,——I have not one appointment belonging to me, which I set so much store by, as I do by these jack-boots,——they were our great-grandfather's, brother *Toby*,—— they were *hereditary*. Then I fear, quoth my uncle *Toby*, *Trim* has cut off the entail.[7]——I have only cut off the tops, an' please your honour, cried *Trim*.——I hate *perpetuities* as much as any man alive, cried my father,——but these jack-boots, continued he, (smiling, though very angry at the same time) have been in the family, brother, ever since the civil wars;——Sir *Roger Shandy* wore them at the battle of *Marston-Moor*.——I declare I would not have taken ten pounds for them.——I'll pay you the money, brother *Shandy*, quoth my uncle *Toby*, looking at the two mortars with infinite pleasure, and putting his hand into his breeches-pocket, as he viewed them.——I'll pay you the ten pounds this moment with all my heart and soul.——

Brother *Toby*, replied my father, altering his tone, you care not what money you dissipate and throw away, provided, continued he, 'tis but upon a SIEGE.——Have I not a hundred and twenty pounds a year, besides my half-pay? cried my uncle *Toby*.——What is that,——replied my father, hastily,——to ten pounds for a pair of jack-boots?——twelve guineas for your *pontoons*;——half as much for your *Dutch*-draw-bridge;——to say nothing of the train of little brass-artillery you bespoke last week, with twenty other preparations for the siege of *Messina*; believe me, dear brother *Toby*, continued my father, taking him kindly by the hand,——these military

---

7. To determine the succession to an estate ("in perpetuity"), preventing a successive owner from disposing of it as he pleases.

operations of yours are above your strength;——you mean well, brother,——but they carry you into greater expences than you were first aware of,——and take my word,——dear *Toby*, they will in the end quite ruin your fortune, and make a beggar of you.—— What signifies it if they do, brother, replied my uncle *Toby*, so long as we know 'tis for the good of the nation.——

My father could not help smiling for his soul;——his anger at the worst was never more than a spark,——and the zeal and simplicity of *Trim*,——and the generous (tho' hobby-horsical) gallantry of my uncle *Toby*, brought him into perfect good humour with them in an instant.

Generous souls!——God prosper you both, and your mortar-pieces too, quoth my father to himself.

Chapter XXIII.

ALL is quiet and hush, cried my father, at least above stairs,—— I hear not one foot stirring.——Prithee, *Trim*, who is in the kitchen? There is no one soul in the kitchen, answered *Trim*, making a low bow as he spoke, except Dr. *Slop*.——Confusion! cried my father, (getting up upon his legs a second time)——not one single thing has gone right this day! had I faith in astrology, brother, (which by the bye, my father had) I would have sworn some retrograde planet was hanging over this unfortunate house of mine, and turning every individual thing in it out of its place.—— Why, I thought Dr. *Slop* had been above stairs with my wife, and so said you.——What can the fellow be puzzling about in the kitchen? ——He is busy, an' please your honour, replied *Trim*, in making a bridge.——'Tis very obliging in him, quoth my uncle *Toby*;—— pray give my humble service to Dr. *Slop*, *Trim*, and tell him I thank him heartily.

You must know, my uncle *Toby* mistook the bridge as widely as my father mistook the mortars;——but to understand how my uncle *Toby* could mistake the bridge,——I fear I must give you an exact account of the road which led to it;——or to drop my metaphor, (for there is nothing more dishonest in an historian, than the use of one,)——in order to conceive the probability of this error in my uncle *Toby* aright, I must give you some account of an adventure of *Trim*'s, though much against my will. I say much against my will, only because the story, in one sense, is certainly out of its place here; for by right it should come in, either amongst the anecdotes of my uncle *Toby*'s amours with widow *Wadman*, in which corporal *Trim* was no mean actor,——or else in the middle of his and my uncle *Toby*'s campaigns on the bowling green,——for it will do very well in either place;——but then if I reserve it for either of those parts of my story,——I ruin the story I'm upon,——and if I tell it here——I anticipate matters, and ruin it there.

——What would your worships have me to do in this case?

——Tell it, Mr. *Shandy*, by all means.——You are a fool, *Tristram*, if you do.

O ye POWERS! (for powers ye are, and great ones too)——which enable mortal man to tell a story worth the hearing,——that kindly shew him, where he is to begin it,——and where he is to end it,——what he is to put into it,——and what he is to leave out, ——how much of it he is to cast into shade,——and whereabouts he is to throw his light!——Ye, who preside over this vast empire of biographical freebooters, and see how many scrapes and plunges your subjects hourly fall into;——will you do one thing?

I beg and beseech you, (in case you will do nothing better for us) that wherever, in any part of your dominions it so falls out, that three several roads meet in one point, as they have done just here, ——that at least you set up a guide-post, in the center of them, in mere charity to direct an uncertain devil, which of the three he is to take.

Chapter XXIV.

THO' the shock my uncle *Toby* received the year after the demolition of *Dunkirk*,[8] in his affair with widow *Wadman*, had fixed him in a resolution, never more to think of the sex,——or of aught which belonged to it;——yet corporal *Trim* had made no such bargain with himself. Indeed in my uncle *Toby*'s case there was a strange and unaccountable concurrence of circumstances which insensibly drew him in, to lay siege to that fair and strong citadel.——In *Trim*'s case there was a concurrence of nothing in the world, but of him and *Bridget* in the kitchen;——though in truth, the love and veneration he bore his master was such, and so fond was he of imitating him in all he did, that had my uncle *Toby* employed his time and genius in tagging of points,[9]——I am persuaded the honest corporal would have laid down his arms, and followed his example with pleasure. When therefore my uncle *Toby* sat down before the mistress,——corporal *Trim* incontinently took ground before the maid.

Now, my dear friend *Garrick*,[1] whom I have so much cause to esteem and honour,——(why, or wherefore, 'tis no matter)——can it escape your penetration,——I defy it,——that so many playwrights, and opificers of chit chat have ever since been working upon *Trim*'s and my uncle *Toby*'s pattern.——I care not what

8. Dunkirk was demolished in 1713 under an agreement reached in the Treaty of Utrecht (ending the Wars of the Spanish Succession which had for so long occu-pied Uncle Toby).
9. Putting tips on shoelaces.
1. Once again David Garrick, the actor. *Opificers*: fabricators.

Aristotle,[2] or *Pacuvius*, or *Bossu*, or *Ricaboni* say,——(though I never read one of them)——there is not a greater difference between a single-horse chair and madam *Pompadour's vis-à-vis*,[3] than betwixt a single amour, and an amour thus nobly doubled, and going upon all four, prancing throughout a grand drama.——Sir, a simple, single, silly affair of that kind,——is quite lost in five acts, ——but that is neither here or there.

After a series of attacks and repulses in a course of nine months on my uncle *Toby's* quarter, a most minute account of every particular of which shall be given in its proper place, my uncle *Toby*, honest man! found it necessary to draw off his forces, and raise the siege somewhat indignantly.

Corporal *Trim*, as I said, had made no such bargain either with himself——or with any one else,——the fidelity however of his heart not suffering him to go into a house which his master had forsaken with disgust,——he contented himself with turning his part of the siege into a blockade;——that is, he kept others off,—— for though he never after went to the house, yet he never met *Bridget* in the village, but he would either nod or wink, or smile, or look kindly at her,——or (as circumstances directed), he would shake her by the hand,——or ask her lovingly how she did,——or would give her a ribban,——and now and then, though never but when it could be done with decorum, would give *Bridget* a——

Precisely in this situation, did these things stand for five years; that is, from the demolition of *Dunkirk* in the year 13, to the latter end of my uncle *Toby's* campaign in the year 18, which was about six or seven weeks before the time I'm speaking of.——When *Trim*, as his custom was, after he had put my uncle *Toby* to bed, going down one moon-shiny night to see that every thing was right at his fortifications,——in the lane separated from the bowling-green with flowering shrubs and holly,——he espied his *Bridget*.

As the corporal thought there was nothing in the world so well worth shewing as the glorious works which he and my uncle *Toby* had made, *Trim* courteously and gallantly took her by the hand, and led her in: this was not done so privately, but that the foul-mouth'd trumpet of Fame carried it from ear to ear, till at length it reached my father's, with this untoward circumstance along with it, that my uncle *Toby's* curious draw-bridge, constructed and painted after the *Dutch* fashion, and which went quite across the ditch,—— was broke down, and some how or other crush'd all to pieces that very night.

My father, as you have observed, had no great esteem for my uncle *Toby's* hobby-horse,——he thought it the most ridiculous

2. The list names classical and Renaissance dramatists and dramatic theorists.
3. Mme. de Pompadour (1721–64) was a favorite mistress of Louis XV. A *vis-à-vis* ("face-to-face") is a carriage with facing seats.

horse that ever gentleman mounted, and indeed unless my uncle *Toby* vexed him about it, could never think of it once, without smiling at it,——so that it never could get lame or happen any mischance, but it tickled my father's imagination beyond measure; but this being an accident much more to his humour than any one which had yet befall'n it, it proved an inexhaustible fund of entertainment to him.——Well,——but dear *Toby!* my father would say, do tell us seriously how this affair of the bridge happened.—— How can you teaze me so much about it? my uncle *Toby* would reply,——I have told it you twenty times, word for word as *Trim* told it me.——Prithee, how was it then, corporal? my father would cry, turning to *Trim.*——It was a mere misfortune, an' please your honour,——I was shewing Mrs.[4] *Bridget* our fortifications, and in going too near the edge of the fossé, I unfortunately slip'd in.—— Very well *Trim!* my father would cry,——(smiling mysteriously, and giving a nod,——but without interrupting him)——and being link'd fast, an' please your honour, arm in arm with Mrs. *Bridget,* I dragg'd her after me, by means of which she fell backwards soss against the bridge,——and *Trim's* foot, (my uncle *Toby* would cry, taking the story out of his mouth) getting into the cuvette,[5] he tumbled full against the bridge too.——It was a thousand to one, my uncle *Toby* would add, that the poor fellow did not break his leg.——Ay truly! my father would say,——a limb is soon broke, brother *Toby,* in such encounters.——And so, an' please your honour, the bridge, which your honour knows was a very slight one, was broke down betwixt us, and splintered all to pieces.

At other times, but especially when my uncle *Toby* was so unfortunate as to say a syllable about cannons, bombs or petards,——my father would exhaust all the stores of his eloquence (which indeed were very great) in a panegyric upon the BATTERING-RAMS of the ancients,——the VINEA[6] which *Alexander* made use of at the siege of *Tyre.*——He would tell my uncle *Toby* of the CATAPULTÆ of the *Syrians* which threw such monstrous stones so many hundred feet, and shook the strongest bulwarks from their very foundation;—— he would go on and describe the wonderful mechanism of the BALLISTA, which *Marcellinus* makes so much rout about,——the terrible effects of the PYRABOLI,——which cast fire,——the danger of the TEREBRA and SCORPIO, which cast javelins.——But what are these, he would say, to the destructive machinery of corporal *Trim?* ——Believe me, brother *Toby,* no bridge, or bastion, or sally port that ever was constructed in this world, can hold out against such artillery.

My uncle *Toby* would never attempt any defence against the

---

4. Both married and unmarried women were addressed as "mistress" (Mrs.) until well into the eighteenth century.
5. A deep ditch.

6. A moveable sled used to protect besiegers of a fort or city. Marcellinus was a fourth-century Greek historian of Rome.

force of this ridicule, but that of redoubling the vehemence of smoaking his pipe; in doing which, he raised so dense a vapour one night after supper, that it set my father, who was a little phthisical, into a suffocating fit of violent coughing: my uncle *Toby* leap'd up without feeling the pain upon his groin,——and, with infinite pity, stood beside his brother's chair, tapping his back with one hand, and holding his head with the other, and from time to time, wiping his eyes with a clean cambrick handkerchief, which he pull'd out of his pocket.——The affectionate and endearing manner in which my uncle *Toby* did these little offices,——cut my father thro' his reins, for the pain he had just been giving him.——May my brains be knock'd out with a battering ram or a catapulta, I care not which, quoth my father to himself,——if ever I insult this worthy soul more.

Chapter XXV.

THE draw-bridge being held irreparable, *Trim* was ordered directly to set about another,——but not upon the same model; for cardinal *Alberoni's*[7] intrigues at that time being discovered, and my uncle *Toby* rightly foreseeing that a flame would inevitably break out betwixt *Spain* and the Empire, and that the operations of the ensuing campaign must in all likelihood be either in *Naples* or *Sicily*,——he determined upon an *Italian* bridge,—— (my uncle *Toby*, by the bye, was not far out in his conjectures)—— but my father, who was infinitely the better politician, and took the lead as far of my uncle *Toby* in the cabinet, as my uncle *Toby* took it of him in the field,——convinced him, that if the King of *Spain* and the Emperor went together by the ears, that *England* and *France* and *Holland* must, by force of their pre-engagements, all enter the lists too;——and if so, he would say, the combatants, brother *Toby*, as sure as we are alive, will fall to it again, pell-mell, upon the old prize-fighting stage of *Flanders*;——then what will you do with your *Italian* bridge?

——We will go on with it then, upon the old model, cried my uncle *Toby*.

When Corporal *Trim* had about half finished it in that stile,—— my uncle *Toby* found out a capital defect in it, which he had never thoroughly considered before. It turned, it seems, upon hinges at both ends of it, opening in the middle, one half of which turning to one side of the fossé, and the other, to the other; the advantage of which was this, that by dividing the weight of the bridge into two equal portions, it impowered my uncle *Toby* to raise it up or let it down with the end of his crutch, and with one hand, which, as his

7. Cardinal Alberoni for a time in the eighteenth century directed Spanish foreign policy.

garrison was weak, was as much as he could well spare,——but the disadvantages of such a construction were insurmountable,——for by this means, he would say, I leave one half of my bridge in my enemy's possession,——and pray of what use is the other?

The natural remedy for this, was no doubt to have his bridge fast only at one end with hinges, so that the whole might be lifted up together, and stand bolt upright,——but that was rejected for the reason given above.

For a whole week after he was determined in his mind to have one of that particular construction which is made to draw back horizontally, to hinder a passage; and to thrust forwards again to gain a passage,——of which sorts your worships might have seen three famous ones at *Spires* before its destruction,——and one now at *Brisac*, if I mistake not;——but my father advising my uncle *Toby*, with great earnestness, to have nothing more to do with thrusting bridges,——and my uncle foreseeing moreover that it would but perpetuate the memory of the corporal's misfortune,—— he changed his mind, for that of the marquis *d'Hôpital's* invention, which the younger *Bernouilli* has so well and learnedly described, as your worships may see,——*Act. Erud. Lips.* an. 1695,[8]——to these a lead weight is an eternal ballance, and keeps watch as well as a couple of centinels, inasmuch as the construction of them was a curve-line approximating to a cycloid,——if not a cycloid itself.

My uncle *Toby* understood the nature of a parabola as well as any man in *England*,——but was not quite such a master of the cycloid;——he talked however about it every day;——the bridge went not forwards.——We'll ask somebody about it, cried my uncle *Toby* to *Trim*.

Chapter XXVI.

WHEN *Trim* came in and told my father, that Dr. *Slop* was in the kitchen, and busy in making a bridge,——my uncle *Toby*,——the affair of the jack-boots having just then raised a train of military ideas in his brain,——took it instantly for granted that Dr. *Slop* was making a model of the marquis *d'Hôpital's* bridge.

——'Tis very obliging in him, quoth my uncle *Toby*;——pray give my humble service to Dr. *Slop*, *Trim*, and tell him I thank him heartily.

Had my uncle *Toby's* head been a *Savoyard's* box,[9] and my father peeping in all the time at one end of it,——it could not have given him a more distinct conception of the operations in my uncle *Toby's* imagination, than what he had; so notwithstanding the catapulta and battering-ram, and his bitter imprecation about them, he was just beginning to triumph.——

8. Abbreviation of *Acta Eruditorium* [Transactions of the Learned], Leipzig, 1695.
9. A hurdy-gurdy or hand organ.

When *Trim's* answer, in an instant, tore the laurel from his brows, and twisted it to pieces.

Chapter XXVII.

——THIS unfortunate draw-bridge of yours, quoth my father ——God bless your honour, cried *Trim*, 'tis a bridge for master's nose.——In bringing him into the world with his vile instruments, he has crush'd his nose, *Susannah* says, as flat as a pancake to his face, and he is making a false bridge with a piece of cotton and a thin piece of whalebone out of *Susannah's* stays, to raise it up.

——Lead me, brother *Toby*, cried my father, to my room this instant.

Chapter XXVIII.

FROM the first moment I sat down to write my life for the amusement of the world, and my opinions for its instruction, has a cloud insensibly been gathering over my father.——A tide of little evils and distresses has been setting in against him.——Not one thing, as he observed himself, has gone right: and now is the storm thicken'd, and going to break, and pour down full upon his head.

I enter upon this part of my story in the most pensive and melancholy frame of mind, that ever sympathetic breast was touched with.——My nerves relax as I tell it.——Every line I write, I feel an abatement of the quickness of my pulse, and of that careless alacrity with it, which every day of my life prompts me to say and write a thousand things I should not.——And this moment that I last dipp'd my pen into my ink, I could not help taking notice what a cautious air of sad composure and solemnity there appear'd in my manner of doing it.——Lord! how different from the rash jerks, and hare-brain'd squirts thou art wont, *Tristram*! to transact it with in other humours,——dropping thy pen,——spurting thy ink about thy table and thy books,——as if thy pen and thy ink, thy books and thy furniture cost thee nothing.

Chapter XXIX.

——I WON'T go about to argue the point with you,——'tis so, ——and I am persuaded of it, madam, as much as can be, "That both man and woman bear pain or sorrow, (and, for aught I know, pleasure too) best in a horizontal position."

The moment my father got up into his chamber, he threw himself prostrate across his bed in the wildest disorder imaginable, but at the same time, in the most lamentable attitude of a man borne down with sorrows, that ever the eye of pity dropp'd a tear for.——The palm of his right hand, as he fell upon the bed, receiving his fore-head, and covering the greatest part of both his eyes, gently sunk down with his head (his elbow giving way backwards) till his nose touch'd the quilt;——his left arm hung insensible over the side of the bed, his knuckles reclining upon the handle of the chamber pot, which peep'd out beyond the valance,——his right leg (his left being drawn up towards his body) hung half over the side of the bed, the edge of it pressing upon his shin-bone.——He felt it not. A fix'd, inflexible sorrow took possession of every line of his face.—— He sigh'd once,——heaved his breast often,——but utter'd not a word.

An old set-stitch'd chair, valanced and fringed around with party-colour'd worsted bobs, stood at the bed's head, opposite to the side where my father's head reclined.——My uncle *Toby* sat him down in it.

Before an affliction is digested,——consolation ever comes too soon;——and after it is digested,——it comes too late: so that you see, madam, there is but a mark between these two, as fine almost as a hair, for a comforter to take aim at: my uncle *Toby* was always either on this side, or on that of it, and would often say, He believed in his heart, he could as soon hit the longitude;[1] for this reason, when he sat down in the chair, he drew the curtain a little forwards, and having a tear at every one's service,——he pull'd out a cam-brick handkerchief,——gave a low sigh,——but held his peace.

Chapter XXX.

——" ALL *is not gain that is got into the purse.*"——So that not withstanding my father had the happiness of read-ing the oddest books in the universe, and had moreover, in himself, the oddest way of thinking, that ever man in it was bless'd with, yet it had this drawback upon him after all,——that it laid him open to some of the oddest and most whimsical distresses; of which this particular one which he sunk under at present is as strong an example as can be given.

No doubt, the breaking down of the bridge of a child's nose, by the edge of a pair of forceps,——however scientifically applied, ——would vex any man in the world, who was at so much pains in begetting a child, as my father was,——yet it will not account for the extravagance of his affliction, or will it justify the unchristian manner he abandoned and surrender'd himself up to it.

To explain this, I must leave him upon the bed for half an

---

1. No means had yet been found for determining longitude at sea.

hour,——and my good uncle *Toby* in his old fringed chair sitting beside him.

Chapter XXXI.

——I THINK it a very unreasonable demand,——cried my great grandfather, twisting up the paper, and throwing it upon the table.——By this account, madam, you have but two thousand pounds fortune, and not a shilling more,——and you insist upon having three hundred pounds a year jointure[2] for it.——

——"Because," replied my great grandmother, "you have little or no nose, Sir."——

Now, before I venture to make use of the word *Nose* a second time,——to avoid all confusion in what will be said upon it, in this interesting part of my story, it may not be amiss to explain my own meaning, and define, with all possible exactness and precision, what I would willingly be understood to mean by the term: being of opinion, that 'tis owing to the negligence and perverseness of writers, in despising this precaution, and to nothing else,——That all the polemical writings in divinity, are not as clear and demonstrative as those upon *a Will o' the Wisp*, or any other sound part of philosophy, and natural pursuit; in order to which, what have you to do, before you set out, unless you intend to go puzzling on to the day of judgment,——but to give the world a good definition, and stand to it, of the main word you have most occasion for,—— changing it, Sir, as you would a guinea, into small coin?——which done,——let the father of confusion puzzle you, if he can; or put a different idea either into your head, or your reader's head, if he knows how.

In books of strict morality and close reasoning, such as this I am engaged in,——the neglect is inexcusable; and heaven is witness, how the world has revenged itself upon me for leaving so many openings to equivocal strictures,——and for depending so much as I have done, all along, upon the cleanliness of my reader's imaginations.

——Here are two senses, cried *Eugenius*, as we walk'd along, pointing with the fore finger of his right hand to the word *Crevice*, in the fifty-second page of the second volume of this book of books,[3]——here are two senses,——quoth he.——And here are two roads, replied I, turning short upon him,——a dirty and a clean one,——which shall we take?——The clean,——by all means, replied *Eugenius*. *Eugenius*, said I, stepping before him, and laying my hand upon his breast,——to define——is to distrust.——Thus I triumph'd over *Eugenius*; but I triumph'd over him as I always do,

---

2. The annual income settled on a woman, payable should she be widowed.
3. P. 73 in this edition.

like a fool.——'Tis my comfort however, I am not an obstinate one; therefore

I define a nose, as follows,——intreating only beforehand, and beseeching my readers, both male and female, of what age, complexion, and condition soever, for the love of God and their own souls, to guard against the temptations and suggestions of the devil, and suffer him by no art or wile to put any other ideas into their minds, than what I put into my definition.——For by the word *Nose*, throughout all this long chapter of noses, and in every other part of my work, where the word *Nose* occurs,——I declare, by that word I mean a Nose, and nothing more, or less.

Chapter XXXII.

——"**B**ECAUSE," quoth my great grandmother, repeating the words again, ——"you have little or no nose, Sir"——

S'death! cried my great grandfather, clapping his hand upon his nose,——'tis not so small as that comes to; 'tis a full inch longer than my father's.——Now, my great grandfather's nose was for all the world like unto the noses of all the men, women, and children, whom *Pantagruel* found dwelling upon the island of ENNASIN.[4]——By the way, if you would know the strange way of getting a-kin amongst so flat-nosed a people,——you must read the book;——find it out yourself, you never can.——

——'Twas shaped, Sir, like an ace of clubs.

——'Tis a full inch, continued my great grandfather, pressing up the ridge of his nose with his finger and thumb; and repeating his assertion,——'tis a full inch longer, madam, than my father's——. You must mean your uncle's, replied my great grandmother.

——My great grandfather was convinced.——He untwisted the paper, and signed the article.

Chapter XXXIII.

——**W**HAT an unconscionable jointure, my dear, do we pay out of this small estate of ours, quoth my grandmother to my grandfather.

My father, replied my grandfather, had no more nose, my dear, saving the mark, than there is upon the back of my hand.——

——Now, you must know, that my great grandmother outlived my grandfather twelve years; so that my father had the jointure to

4. On the island of Ennasin, noses are shaped like the ace of clubs (Rabelais, IV.9).

pay, a hundred and fifty pounds half yearly——(on *Michaelmas*[5] and *Lady day*)——during all that time.

No man discharged pecuniary obligations with a better grace than my father.——And as far as the hundred pounds went, he would fling it upon the table, guinea by guinea, with that spirited jerk of an honest welcome, which generous souls, and generous souls only, are able to fling down money: but as soon as ever he enter'd upon the odd fifty,——he generally gave a loud *Hem!*—— rubb'd the side of his nose leisurely with the flat part of his fore finger,——inserted his hand cautiously betwixt his head and the cawl of his wig,——look'd at both sides of every guinea, as he parted with it,——and seldom could get to the end of the fifty pounds, without pulling out his handkerchief, and wiping his temples.

Defend me, gracious heaven! from those persecuting spirits who make no allowances for these workings within us.——Never,——O never may I lay down in their tents, who cannot relax the engine, and feel pity for the force of education, and the prevalence of opinions long derived from ancestors!

For three generations at least, this *tenet* in favour of long noses had gradually been taking root in our family.——Tradition was all along on its side, and Interest was every half year stepping in to strengthen it; so that the whimsicality of my father's brain was far from having the whole honour of this, as it had of almost all his other strange notions.——For in a great measure he might be said to have suck'd this in, with his mother's milk. He did his part however.——If education planted the mistake, (in case it was one) my father watered it, and ripened it to perfection.

He would often declare, in speaking his thoughts upon the subject, that he did not conceive how the greatest family in *England* could stand it out against an uninterrupted succession of six or seven short noses.——And for the contrary reason, he would generally add, That it must be one of the greatest problems in civil life, where the same number of long and jolly noses following one another in a direct line, did not raise and hoist it up into the best vacancies in the kindgom.——He would often boast that the *Shandy* family rank'd very high in king *Harry* the VIIIth's time, but owed its rise to no state engine,——he would say,——but to that only;——but that, like other families, he would add,——it had felt the turn of the wheel, and had never recovered the blow of my great grandfather's nose.——It was an ace of clubs indeed, he would cry, shaking his head,——and as vile a one for an unfortunate family, as ever turn'd up trumps.

---

5. The feast of St. Michael, September 29, marks the beginning of an English legal term, and the feast of the Annunci- ation (of the coming birth of Christ) to the Virgin Mary (Our Lady), March 25, another.

————Fair and softly, gentle reader!————where is thy fancy carrying thee?————If there is truth in man, by my great grandfather's nose, I mean the external organ of smelling, or that part of man which stands prominent in his face,————and which painters say, in good jolly noses and well-proportioned faces, should comprehend a full third,————that is, measuring downwards from the setting on of the hair.————

————What a life of it has an author, at this pass!

Chapter XXXIV.

IT is a singular blessing, that nature has form'd the mind of man with the same happy backwardness and renitency against conviction, which is observed in old dogs,————"of not learning new tricks."

What a shuttlecock of a fellow would the greatest philosopher that ever existed, be whisk'd into at once, did he read such books, and observe such facts, and think such thoughts, as would eternally be making him change sides!

Now, my father, as I told you last year, detested all this.————He pick'd up an opinion, Sir, as a man in a state of nature picks up an apple.————It becomes his own,————and if he is a man of spirit, he would lose his life rather than give it up.————

I am aware, that *Didius* the great civilian,[6] will contest this point; and cry out against me, Whence comes this man's right to this apple? *ex confesso*, he will say,————things were in a state of nature.————The apple, as much *Frank's* apple, as *John's*. Pray, Mr. *Shandy*, what patent has he to shew for it? and how did it begin to be his? was it, when he set his heart upon it? or when he gather'd it? or when he chew'd it? or when he roasted it? or when he peel'd? or when he brought it home? or when he digested?————or when he ———— — ? ————. For 'tis plain, Sir, if the first picking up of the apple, made it not his,————that no subsequent act could.

Brother *Didius, Tribonius* will answer,————(now *Tribonius* the civilian and church lawyer's beard being three inches and a half and three eighths longer than *Didius* his beard,————I'm glad he takes up the cudgels for me, so I give myself no further trouble about the answer.)————Brother *Didius, Tribonius* will say, it is a decreed case, as you may find it in the fragments of *Gregorius*[7] and *Hermogenes*'s codes, and in all the codes from *Justinian's* down to the codes of *Louis* and *Des Eaux*,————That the sweat of a man's brows, and the exsudations of a man's brains, are as much a man's own property, as the breeches upon his backside;————which said exsuda-

6. Civil lawyer. *Ex confesso*: confessedly.
7. The list is of legal codes assembled from Roman times down to the *Ordon-* *nance des eaux et forêts* adopted by Louis XIV in 1669 to develop French waterways and forests.

tions, &c. being dropp'd upon the said apple by the labour of finding it, and picking it up; and being moreover indissolubly wasted, and as indissolubly annex'd by the picker up, to the thing pick'd up, carried home, roasted, peel'd, eaten, digested, and so on;——'tis evident that the gatherer of the apple, in so doing, has mix'd up something which was his own, with the apple which was not his own, by which means he has acquired a property;——or, in other words, the apple is *John*'s apple.

By the same learned chain of reasoning my father stood up for all his opinions: he had spared no pains in picking them up, and the more they lay out of the common way, the better still was his title.——No mortal claim'd them: they had cost him moreover as much labour in cooking and digesting as in the case above, so that they might well and truely be said to be of his own goods and chattles.——Accordingly he held fast by 'em, both by teeth and claws,——would fly to whatever he could lay his hands on,——and in a word, would intrench and fortify them round with as many circumvallations and breast-works, as my uncle *Toby* would a citadel.

There was one plaguy rub in the way of this,——the scarcity of materials to make any thing of a defence with, in case of a smart attack; inasmuch as few men of great genius had exercised their parts in writing books upon the subject of great noses: by the trotting of my lean horse, the thing is incredible! and I am quite lost in my understanding when I am considering what a treasure of precious time and talents together has been wasted upon worse subjects,——and how many millions of books in all languages, and in all possible types and bindings, have been fabricated upon points not half so much tending to the unity and peace-making of the world. What was to be had, however, he set the greater store by; and though my father would oft-times sport with my uncle *Toby*'s library,——which, by the bye, was ridiculous enough,——yet at the very same time he did it, he collected every book and treatise which had been systematically wrote upon noses, with as much care as my honest uncle *Toby* had done those upon military architecture. ——'Tis true, a much less table would have held them,——but that was not thy transgression, my dear uncle.——

Here,——but why here,——rather than in any other part of my story,——I am not able to tell;——but here it is,——my heart stops me to pay to thee, my dear uncle *Toby*, once for all, the tribute I owe thy goodness.——Here let me thrust my chair aside, and kneel down upon the ground, whilst I am pouring forth the warmest sentiments of love for thee, and veneration for the excellency of thy character, that ever virtue and nature kindled in a nephew's bosom.——Peace and comfort rest for evermore upon thy head!——Thou envied'st no man's comforts,——insulted'st no man's opinions.——Thou blackened'st no man's character,——

devoured'st no man's bread: gently with faithful *Trim* behind thee, didst thou amble round the little circle of thy pleasures, jostling no creature in thy way;——for each one's sorrows, thou hadst a tear, ——for each man's need, thou hadst a shilling.

Whilst I am worth one, to pay a weeder,——thy path from thy door to thy bowling green shall never be grown up.——Whilst there is a rood and a half of land in the *Shandy* family, thy fortifications, my dear uncle *Toby*, shall never be demolish'd.

Chapter XXXV.

MY father's collection was not great, but to make amends, it was curious; and consequently, he was some time in making it; he had the great good fortune however to set off well, in getting *Bruscambille's*[8] prologue upon long noses, almost for nothing,——for he gave no more for *Bruscambille* than three half crowns; owing indeed to the strong fancy which the stall-man saw my father had for the book the moment he laid his hands upon it.——There are not three *Bruscambilles* in *Christendom*,——said the stall-man, except what are chain'd up in the libraries of the curious. My father flung down the money as quick as lightening, ——took *Bruscambille* into his bosom,——hyed home from *Piccadilly* to *Coleman*-street with it, as he would have hyed home with a treasure, without taking his hand once off from *Bruscambille* all the way.

To those who do not yet know of which gender *Bruscambille* is,——inasmuch as a prologue upon long noses might easily be done by either,——'twill be no objection against the simile,——to say, That when my father got home, he solaced himself with *Bruscambille* after the manner, in which, 'tis ten to one, your worship solaced yourself with your first mistress,——that is, from morning even unto night: which by the bye, how delightful soever it may prove to the inamorato,——is of little, or no entertainment at all, to by-standers.——Take notice, I go no farther with the simile, ——my father's eye was greater than his appetite,——his zeal greater than his knowledge,——he cool'd——his affections became divided,——he got hold of *Prignitz*,[9]——purchased *Scroderus*, *Andrea Parœus*, *Bouchet's* Evening Conferences, and above all, the great and learned *Hafen Slawkenbergius*; of which, as I shall have much to say by and bye,——I will say nothing now.

---

8. The stage name of Sieur Deslauriers, author of *Prologues as much Serious as Facetious*, 1610.
9. Prignitz and Scroderus seem to be invented names, but Paré and Bouchet published (in French) in the sixteenth century. Slawkenbergius derives from *Hafen*, colloquial German for chamber pot, and *Schackenberg*, for a pile of manure. Pamphagus and Cocles appear in Erasmus's *Colloquia Familiaria* [Familiar Discourses].

Chapter XXXVI.

OF all the tracts my father was at the pains to procure and study in support of his hypothesis, there was not any one wherein he felt a more cruel disappointment at first, than in the celebrated dialogue between *Pamphagus* and *Cocles*, written by the chaste pen of the great and venerable *Erasmus*, upon the various uses and seasonable applications of long noses.——————Now don't let Satan, my dear girl, in this chapter, take advantage of any one spot of rising-ground to get astride of your imagination, if you can any ways help it; or if he is so nimble as to slip on,——let me beg of you, like an unback'd filly, *to frisk it, to squirt it, to jump it, to rear it, to bound it,*——*and to kick it, with long kicks and short kicks,* till like *Tickletoby*'s mare, you break a strap or a crupper, and throw his worship into the dirt.——You need not kill him.——

——And pray who was *Tickletoby*'s mare?——'tis just as discreditable and unscholar-like a question, Sir, as to have asked what year (*ab urb. con.*[1]) the second Punic war broke out.——Who was *Tickletoby*'s mare![2]——Read, read, read, read, my unlearned reader! read,——or by the knowledge of the great saint *Paraleipomenon*——I tell you before-hand, you had better throw down the book at once; for without *much reading*, by which your reverence knows, I mean *much knowledge*, you will no more be able to penetrate the moral of the next marbled page (motly emblem of my work!) than the world with all its sagacity has been able to unravel the many opinions, transactions and truths which still lie mystically hid under the dark veil of the black one.

Chapter XXXVII.

"NIHIL *me pœnitet hujus nasi,*"[3] quoth *Pamphagus*;——that is,——"My nose has been the making of me."—————— "*Nec est cur pœniteat,*" replies *Cocles*; that is, "How the duce should such a nose fail?"

The doctrine, you see, was laid down by *Erasmus*, as my father wished it, with the utmost plainness; but my father's disappointment was, in finding nothing more from so able a pen, but the bare fact itself; without any of that speculative subtilty or ambidexterity of argumentation upon it, which heaven had bestow'd upon man on

---

1. *Ab urbe condita*, "from the founding of the city." 753 B.C., the date of its founding, was used for dating events in ancient Rome. The Second Punic War began in 535 *ab. urb. con.*
2. Tickletoby's (slang for penis) young mare in Rabelais, IV.13, had "never been leaped yet." *Paraleipomenon* is Greek for "things omitted."
3. Pamphagus says, "The nose does not displease me." Cocles replies, "Nor is there reason why it should displease you."

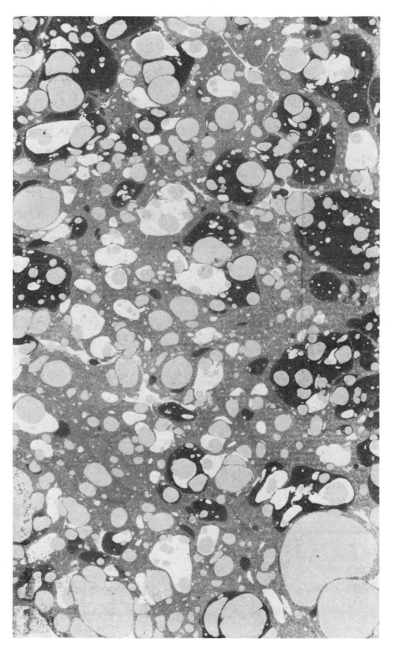

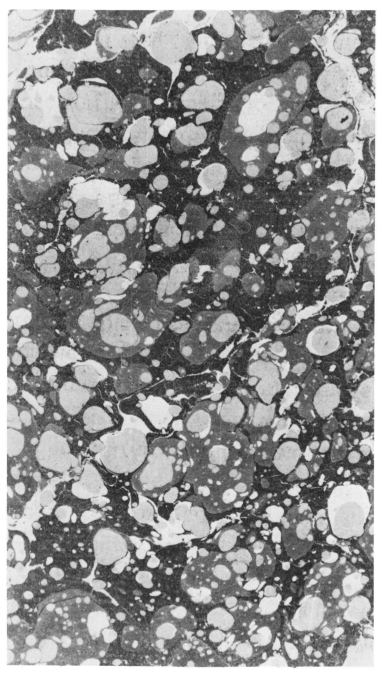

166

purpose to investigate truth and fight for her on all sides.——My father pish'd and pugh'd at first most terribly,——'tis worth something to have a good name. As the dialogue was of *Erasmus*, my father soon came to himself, and read it over and over again with great application, studying every word and every syllable of it thro' and thro' in its most strict and literal interpretation,——he could still make nothing of it, that way. Mayhaps there is more meant, than is said in it, quoth my father.——Learned men, brother *Toby*, don't write dialogues upon long noses for nothing.——I'll study the mystic and the allegoric sense,——here is some room to turn a man's self in, brother.

My father read on.——

Now, I find it needful to inform your reverences and worships, that besides the many nautical uses of long noses enumerated by *Erasmus*, the dialogist affirmeth that a long nose is not without its domestic conveniences also, for that in a case of distress,——and for want of a pair of bellows, it will do excellently well, *ad excitandum focum*,[4] (to stir up the fire.)

Nature had been prodigal in her gifts to my father beyond measure, and had sown the seeds of verbal criticism as deep within him, as she had done the seeds of all other knowledge,——so that he had got out his penknife, and was trying experiments upon the sentence, to see if he could not scratch some better sense into it.——I've got within a single letter, brother *Toby*, cried my father, of *Erasmus* his mystic meaning.——You are near enough, brother, replied my uncle, in all conscience.——Pshaw! cried my father, scratching on, ——I might as well be seven miles off.——I've done it,——said my father, snapping his fingers.——See, my dear brother *Toby*, how I have mended the sense.——But you have marr'd a word, replied my uncle *Toby*.——My father put on his spectacles,——bit his lip, ——and tore out the leaf in a passion.

Chapter XXXVIII.

O *Slawkenbergius*! thou faithful analyzer of my *Disgrázias*,[5] ——thou sad foreteller of so many of the whips and short turns, which in one stage or other of my life have come slap upon me from the shortness of my nose, and no other cause, that I am conscious of.——Tell me, *Slawkenbergius*! what secret impulse was it? what intonation of voice? whence came it? how did it sound in thy ears?——art thou sure thou heard'st it?——which first cried out to thee,——go,——go, *Slawkenbergius*! dedicate the labours of thy life,——neglect thy pastimes,——call forth all the powers and

4. Sterne changes the original slightly, from blowing to poking, for his own humorous purposes. And by "scratching a single letter" of *focum* Walter could turn it into either *locum* (place) or *ficum* (fig), either of which would add to the joke.
5. Disgraces.

faculties of thy nature,——macerate thyself in the service of mankind, and write a grand FOLIO for them, upon the subject of their noses.

How the communication was conveyed into *Slawkenbergius's* sensorium,——so that *Slawkenbergius* should know whose finger touch'd the key,——and whose hand it was that blew the bellows, ——as *Hafen Slawkenbergius* has been dead and laid in his grave above fourscore and ten years,——we can only raise conjectures.

Slawkenbergius was play'd upon, for aught I know, like one of *Whitefield's* disciples,[6]——that is, with such a distinct intelligence, Sir, of which of the two *masters* it was, that had been practising upon his *instrument,*——as to make all reasoning upon it needless.

——For in the account which *Hafen Slawkenbergius* gives the world of his motives and occasions for writing, and spending so many years of his life upon this one work——towards the end of his prolegomena, which by the bye should have come first,——but the bookbinder has most injudiciously placed it betwixt the analitical contents of the book, and the book itself,——he informs his reader, that ever since he had arrived at the age of discernment, and was able to sit down coolly, and consider within himself the true state and condition of man, and distinguish the main end and design of his being;——or,——to shorten my translation, for *Slawkenbergius's* book is in *Latin*, and not a little prolix in this passage,—— ever since I understood, quoth *Slawkenbergius*, any thing,——or rather *what was what,*——and could perceive that the point of long noses had been too loosely handled by all who had gone before; ——have I, *Slawkenbergius*, felt a strong impulse, with a mighty and unresistible call within me, to gird up myself to this undertaking.

And to do justice to *Slawkenbergius*, he has entered the list with a stronger lance, and taken a much larger career in it, than any one man who had ever entered it before him,——and indeed, in many respects, deserves to be *en-nich'd* as a prototype for all writers, of voluminous works at least, to model their books by,——for he has taken in, Sir, the whole subject,——examined every part of it, *dialectically,*——then brought it into full day; dilucidating it with all the light which either the collision of his own natural parts could strike,——or the profoundest knowledge of the sciences had impowered him to cast upon it,——collating, collecting and compiling,——begging, borrowing, and stealing, as he went along, all that had been wrote or wrangled thereupon in the schools and porticos of the learned: so that *Slawkenbergius* his book may properly be considered, not only as a model,——but as a thorough-

---

6. George Whitfield was an eighteenth-century Methodist and, like many of his followers, an enthusiastic pulpit orator.

stitch'd DIGEST and regular institute of *noses*; comprehending in it, all that is, or can be needful to be known about them.

For this cause it is, that I forebear to speak of so many (otherwise) valuable books and treatises of my father's collecting, wrote either, plump upon noses,——or collaterally touching them;—— such for instance as *Prignitz*, now lying upon the table before me, who with infinite learning, and from the most candid and scholarlike examination of above four thousand different skulls, in upwards of twenty charnel houses in *Silesia*, which he had rummaged,—— has informed us, that the mensuration and configuration of the osseous or boney parts of human noses, in any *given* tract of country, except *Crim Tartary*,[7] where they are all crush'd down by the thumb, so that no judgment can be formed upon them,——are much nearer alike, than the world imagines;——the difference amongst them, being, he says, a mere trifle, not worth taking notice of,——but that the size and jollity of every individual nose, and by which one nose ranks above another, and bears a higher price, is owing to the cartilagenous and muscular parts of it, into whose ducts and sinuses the blood and animal spirits being impell'd, and driven by the warmth and force of the imagination, which is but a step from it, (bating the case of ideots, whom *Prignitz*, who had lived many years in *Turky*, supposes under the more immediate tutelage of heaven)——it so happens, and ever must, says *Prignitz*, that the excellency of the nose is in a direct arithmetical proportion to the excellency of the wearer's fancy.

It is for the same reason, that is, because 'tis all comprehended in *Slawkenbergius*, that I say nothing likewise of *Scroderus* (*Andrea*) who all the world knows, set himself to oppugn *Prignitz* with great violence,——proving it in his own way, first, *logically* and then by a series of stubborn facts, "That so far was *Prignitz* from the truth, in affirming that the fancy begat the nose, that on the contrary,—— the nose begat the fancy."

——The learned suspected *Scroderus*, of an indecent sophism in this,——and *Prignitz* cried out aloud in the dispute, that *Scroderus* had shifted the idea upon him,——but *Scroderus* went on, maintaining his thesis.——

My father was just balancing within himself, which of the two sides he should take in this affair; when *Ambrose Paræus* decided it in a moment, and by overthrowing the systems, both of *Prignitz* and *Scroderus*, drove my father out of both sides of the controversy at once.

Be witness——

I don't acquaint the learned reader,——in saying it, I mention it only to shew the learned, I know the fact myself.——

7. Russian Crimea.

That this *Ambrose Parœus* was chief surgeon and nosemender to *Francis* the ninth of *France*, and in high credit with him and the two preceding, or succeeding kings (I know not which)——and that except in the slip he made in his story of *Taliacotius*'s noses,[8] and his manner of setting them on,——was esteemed by the whole college of physicians at that time, as more knowing in matters of noses, than any one who had ever taken them in hand.

Now *Ambrose Parœus* convinced my father, that the true and efficient cause of what had engaged so much the attention of the world, and upon which *Prignitz* and *Scroderus* had wasted so much learning and fine parts,——was neither this nor that,——but that the length and goodness of the nose was owing simply to the softness and flaccidity in the nurse's breast,——as the flatness and shortness of *puisne*[9] noses was, to the firmness and elastic repulsion of the same organ of nutrition in the hale and lively,——which, tho' happy for the woman, was the undoing of the child, inasmuch as his nose was so snubb'd, so rebuff'd, so rebated, and so refrigerated thereby, as never to arrive *ad mensuram suam legitimam*;[1] ——but that in case of the flaccidity and softness of the nurse or mother's breast,——by sinking into it, quoth *Parœus*, as into so much butter, the nose was comforted, nourish'd, plump'd up, refresh'd, refocillated, and set a growing for ever.

I have but two things to observe of *Parœus*; first, that he proves and explains all this with the utmost chastity and decorum of expression:——for which may his soul for ever rest in peace!

And, secondly, that besides the systems of *Prignitz* and *Scroderus*, which *Ambrose Parœus* his hypothesis effectually overthrew,—— it overthrew at the same time the system of peace and harmony of our family; and for three days together, not only embroiled matters between my father and my mother, but turn'd likewise the whole house and every thing in it, except my uncle *Toby*, quite upside down.

Such a ridiculous tale of a dispute between a man and his wife, never surely in any age or country got vent through the key-hole of a street-door!

My mother, you must know,——but I have fifty things more necessary to let you know first,——I have a hundred difficulties which I have promised to clear up, and a thousand distresses and domestic misadventures crouding in upon me thick and three-fold, one upon the neck of another,——a cow broke in (to-morrow morning) to my uncle *Toby*'s fortifications, and eat up two ratios[2] and half of dried grass, tearing up the sods with it, which faced his horn-work and covered way.——*Trim* insists upon being tried by a

8. Gaspar Tagliacozzi (1546–99) developed a method of grafting skin from the arm onto the nose.

9. A legal term meaning inferior.

1. At its normal size.

2. Rations.

court-martial,——the cow to be shot,——*Slop* to be *crucifix'd*,——
myself to be *tristram'd*, and at my very baptism made a martyr
of;——poor unhappy devils that we all are!——I want swaddling,
——but there is no time to be lost in exclamations.——I have left
my father lying across his bed, and my uncle *Toby* in his old
fringed chair, sitting beside him, and promised I would go back to
them in half an hour, and five and thirty minutes are laps'd already.
——Of all the perplexities a mortal author was ever seen in,——
this certainly is the greatest,——for I have *Hafen Slawkenbergius's*
folio, Sir, to finish——a dialogue between my father and my uncle
Toby, upon the solution of *Prignitz, Scroderus, Ambrose Paræus,
Ponocrates* and *Grangousier*[3] to relate,——a tale out of *Slawkenbergius* to translate, and all this in five minutes less, than no time at
all;——such a head!——would to heaven! my enemies only saw the
inside of it!

Chapter XXXIX.

THERE was not any one scene more entertaining in our family,
——and to do it justice in this point,——and I here put off
my cap and lay it upon the table close beside my ink-horn, on
purpose to make my declaration to the world concerning this one
article, the more solemn,——that I believe in my soul, (unless my
love and partiality to my understanding blinds me) the hand of the
supreme Maker and first Designer of all things, never made or put a
family together, (in that period at least of it, which I have sat down
to write the story of)——where the characters of it were cast or
contrasted with so dramatic a felicity as ours was, for this end; or in
which the capacities of affording such exquisite scenes, and the
powers of shifting them perpetually from morning to night, were
lodged and intrusted with so unlimited a confidence, as in the
SHANDY-FAMILY.

Not any one of these was more diverting, I say, in this whimsical
theatre of ours,——than what frequently arose out of this self-same
chapter of long noses,——especially when my father's imagination
was heated with the enquiry, and nothing would serve him but to
heat my uncle *Toby's* too.

My uncle *Toby* would give my father all possible fair play in this
attempt; and with infinite patience would sit smoking his pipe for
whole hours together, whilst my father was practising upon his
head, and trying every accessible avenue to drive *Prignitz* and
Scroderus's solutions into it.

Whether they were above my uncle *Toby's* reason,——or contrary to it,——or that his brain was like wet tinder, and no spark

3. In Rabelais, Grangousier is Gargantua's father, Ponocrates his tutor.

could possibly take hold,——or that it was so full of saps, mines, blinds, curtins, and such military disqualifications to his seeing clearly into *Prignitz* and *Scroderus*'s doctrines,——I say not,——let school-men——scullions, anatomists, and engineers, fight for it amongst themselves.——

'Twas some misfortune, I make no doubt, in this affair, that my father had every word of it to translate for the benefit of my uncle *Toby*, and render out of *Slawkenbergius*'s *Latin*, of which, as he was no great master, his translation was not always of the purest, ——and generally least so where 'twas most wanted,——this naturally open'd a door to a second misfortune;——that in the warmer paroxisms of his zeal to open my uncle *Toby*'s eyes——my father's ideas run on, as much faster than the translation, as the translation outmoved my uncle *Toby*'s;——neither the one or the other added much to the perspicuity of my father's lecture.

Chapter XL.

THE gift of ratiocination and making syllogisms,——I mean in man,——for in superior classes of beings, such as angels and spirits,——'tis all done, may it please your worships, as they tell me, by INTUITION;——and beings inferior, as your worships all know,——syllogize by their noses: though there is an island swiming in the sea, although not altogether at its ease, whose inhabitants, if my intelligence deceives me not, are so wonderfully gifted, as to syllogize after the same fashion, and oft-times to make very well out too:——but that's neither here nor there——

The gift of doing it as it should be, amongst us,——or the great and principal act of ratiocination in man, as logicians tell us, is the finding out the agreement or disagreement of two ideas one with another, by the intervention of a third; (called the *medius terminus*[4]) just as a man, as *Locke* well observes, by a yard, finds two mens nine-pin-alleys to be of the same length, which could not be brought together, to measure their equality, by *juxta-position*.

Had the same great reasoner looked on, as my father illustrated his systems of noses, and observed my uncle *Toby*'s deportment, ——what great attention he gave to every word,——and as oft as he took his pipe from his mouth, with what wonderful seriousness he contemplated the length of it,——surveying it transversely as he held it betwixt his finger and his thumb,——then foreright,—— then this way, and then that, in all its possible directions and fore-shortenings,——he would have concluded my uncle *Toby* had got hold of the *medius terminus*; and was syllogizing and measuring with it the truth of each hypothesis of long noses, in order as my

---

4. Middle term. Yard: a yard stick.

father laid them before him. This by the bye, was more than my father wanted,——his aim in all the pains he was at in these philosophic lectures,——was to enable my uncle *Toby* not to *discuss*, ——but *comprehend*——to *hold* the grains and scruples of learning,——not to *weigh* them.——My uncle *Toby*, as you will read in the next chapter, did neither the one or the other.

Chapter XLI.

'TIS a pity, cried my father one winter's night, after a three hours painful translation of *Slawkenbergius*,——'tis a pity, cried my father, putting my mother's thread-paper into the book for a mark, as he spoke——that truth, brother *Toby*, should shut herself up in such impregnable fastnesses, and be so obstinate as not to surrender herself sometimes up upon the closest siege.——

Now it happened then, as indeed it had often done before, that my uncle *Toby*'s fancy, during the time of my father's explanation of *Prignitz* to him,——having nothing to stay it there, had taken a short flight to the bowling-green;——his body might as well have taken a turn there too,——so that with all the semblance of a deep school-man intent upon the *medius terminus*,——my uncle *Toby* was in fact as ignorant of the whole lecture, and all its pro's and con's, as if my father had been translating *Hafen Slawkenbergius* from the *Latin* tongue into the *Cherokeè*. But the word *siege*, like a talismanic power, in my father's metaphor, wafting back my uncle *Toby*'s fancy, quick as a note could follow the touch,——he open'd his ears,——and my father observing that he took his pipe out of his mouth, and shuffled his chair nearer the table, as with a desire to profit,——my father with great pleasure began his sentence again, ——changing only the plan, and dropping the metaphor of the siege of it, to keep clear of some dangers my father apprehended from it.

'Tis a pity, said my father, that truth can only be on one side, brother *Toby*,——considering what ingenuity these learned men have all shewn in their solutions of noses.——Can noses be dissolved? replied my uncle *Toby*.——

——My father thrust back his chair,——rose up,——put on his hat,——took four long strides to the door,——jerked it open,—— thrust his head half way out,——shut the door again,——took no notice of the bad hinge,——returned to the table,——pluck'd my mother's thread-paper out of *Slawkenbergius*'s book,——went hastily to his bureau,——walk'd slowly back, twisting my mother's thread-paper about his thumb,——unbutton'd his waistcoat,—— threw my mother's thread-paper into the fire,——bit her sattin pincushion in two, fill'd his mouth with bran,——confounded it;—— but mark!——the oath of confusion was levell'd at my uncle *Toby*'s brain,——which was e'en confused enough already,——the curse came charged only with the bran,——the bran, may it please your honours,——was no more than powder to the ball.

'Twas well my father's passions lasted not long; for so long as they did last, they led him a busy life on't, and it is one of the most unaccountable problems that ever I met with in my observations of human nature, that nothing should prove my father's mettle so much, or make his passions go off so like gun-powder, as the un-expected strokes his science met with from the quaint simplicity of my uncle *Toby*'s questions.——Had ten dozen of hornets stung him behind in so many different places all at one time,——he could not have exerted more mechanical functions in fewer seconds,——or started half so much, as with one single *quære*[5] of three words unseasonably popping in full upon him in his hobbyhorsical career.

'Twas all one to my uncle *Toby*,——he smoaked his pipe on, with unvaried composure,——his heart never intended offence to his brother,——and as his head could seldom find out where the sting of it lay,——he always gave my father the credit of cooling by himself.——He was five minutes and thirty-five seconds about it in the present case.

By all that's good! said my father, swearing, as he came to him-self, and taking the oath out of *Ernulphus*'s digest of curses,—— (though to do my father justice it was a fault (as he told Dr. *Slop* in the affair of *Ernulphus*) which he as seldom committed as any man upon earth.)——By all that's good and great! brother *Toby*, said my father, if it was not for the aids of philosophy, which befriend one so much as they do,——you would put a man beside all temper.——Why, by the *solutions* of noses, of which I was telling you, I meant as you might have known, had you favoured me with one grain of attention, the various accounts which learned men of different kinds of knowledge have given the world, of the causes of short and long noses.——There is no cause but one, replied my uncle *Toby*,——why one man's nose is longer than another's, but because that God pleases to have it so.——That is *Grangousier*'s solution, said my father.——'Tis he, continued my uncle *Toby*, looking up, and not regarding my father's interruption, who makes us all, and frames and puts us together in such forms and propor-tions, and for such ends, as is agreeable to his infinite wisdom.—— 'Tis a pious account, cried my father, but not philosophical,—— there is more religion in it than sound science. 'Twas no inconsistent part of my uncle *Toby*'s character,——that he feared God, and reverenced religion.——So the moment my father finished his remark,——my uncle *Toby* fell a whistling *Lillabullero*, with more zeal (though more out of tune) than usual.——

What is become of my wife's thread-paper?

5. Query.

Chapter XLII.

N O matter,——as an appendage to seamstressy, the thread-paper might be of some consequence to my mother,——of none to my father, as a mark in *Slawkenbergius*. *Slawkenbergius* in every page of him was a rich treasury of inexhaustible knowledge to my father,——he could not open him amiss; and he would often say in closing the book, that if all the arts and sciences in the world, with the books which treated of them, were lost,——should the wisdom and policies of governments, he would say, through disuse, ever happened to be forgot, and all that statesmen had wrote, or caused to be written, upon the strong or the weak sides of courts and kingdoms, should they be forgot also,——and *Slawkenbergius* only left,——there would be enough in him in all conscience, he would say, to set the world a-going again. A treasure therefore was he indeed! an institute of all that was necessary to be known of noses, and every thing else,——at *matin*, noon, and vespers was *Hafen Slawkenbergius* his recreation and delight: 'twas for ever in his hands,——you would have sworn, Sir, it had been a canon's prayer-book,——so worn, so glazed, so contrited and attrited was it with fingers and with thumbs in all its parts, from one end even unto the other.

I am not such a bigot to *Slawkenbergius*, as my father;——there is a fund in him, no doubt; but in my opinion, the best, I don't say the most profitable, but the most amusing part of *Hafen Slawken-bergius*, is his tales,——and, considering he was a *German*, many of them told not without fancy:——these take up his second book, containing nearly one half of his folio, and are comprehended in ten decads, each decad containing ten tales.——Philosophy is not built upon tales; and therefore 'twas certainly wrong in *Slawkenbergius* to send them into the world by that name;——there are a few of them in his eighth, ninth, and tenth decads, which I own seem rather playful and sportive, than speculative,——but in general they are to be looked upon by the learned as a detail of so many independent facts, all of them turning round somehow or other upon the main hinges of his subject, and collected by him with great fidelity, and added to his work as so many illustrations upon the doctrines of noses.

As we have leisure enough upon our hands,——if you give me leave, madam, I'll tell you the ninth tale of his tenth decad.

THE END OF THE THIRD VOLUME.

Volume IV.

SLAWKENBERGII
FABELLA[1]

VESPERA quâdam frigidulâ, posteriori in parte mensis Augusti, peregrinus, mulo fusco colore insidens, manticâ a tergo, paucis indusijs, binis calceis, braccisque sericis coccinejs repletâ, Argentoratum ingressus est.

Militi eum percontanti, quum portus intraret, dixit, se apud Nasorum promontorium fuisse, Francofurtum proficisci, et Argentoratum, transitu ad fines Sarmatiæ mensis intervallo, reversurum.

Miles peregrini in faciem suspexit——Di boni, nova forma nasi!

At multum mihi profuit, inquit peregrinus, carpum amento extrahens, e quo pependit acinaces: Loculo manum inseruit; & magnâ cum urbanitate, pilei parte anteriore tactâ manu sinistrâ, ut extendit dextram, militi florinum dedit et processit.

Dolet mihi, ait miles, tympanistam nanum et valgum alloquens, virum adeo urbanum vaginam perdidisse; itinerari haud poterit nudâ acinaci, neque vaginam toto Argentorato, habilem inveniet.——
Nullam unquam habui, respondit peregrinus respiciens,——seque comiter inclinans——hoc more gesto, nudam acinacem elevans, mulo lentò progrediente, ut nasum tueri possim.

Non immerito, benigne peregrine, respondit miles.
Nihili œstimo, ait ille tympanista, e pergamenâ factitius est.

---

1. As *Hafen Slawkenbergius de Nasis* is extremely scarce, it may not be unacceptable to the learned reader to see the specimen of a few pages of his original; I will make no reflection upon it, but that his story-telling Latin is much more concise than his philosophic——and, I think, has more of Latinity in it. [*Sterne's note*.] Tristram takes some liberties with the "story-telling Latin" in his translation, exploiting wherever possible its sexually suggestive potential.

Volume IV.

SLAWKENBERGIUS'S
TALE

IT was one cool refreshing evening, at the close of a very sultry day, in the latter end of the month of *August*, when a stranger, mounted upon a dark mule, with a small cloak-bag behind him, containing a few shirts, a pair of shoes, and a crimson-sattin pair of breeches, entred the town of *Strasburg*.

He told the centinel, who questioned him as he entered the gates, that he had been at the promontory of NOSES——was going on to *Frankfort*——and should be back again at *Strasburg* that day month, in his way to the borders of *CrimTartary*.

The centinel looked up into the stranger's face——never saw such a nose in his life!

——I have made a very good venture of it, quoth the stranger—so slipping his wrist out of the loop of a black ribban, to which a short scymetar was hung: He put his hand into his pocket, and with great courtesy touching the forepart of his cap with his left-hand, as he extended his right——he put a florin into the centinel's hand, and passed on.

It grieves me, said the centinel, speaking to a little dwarfish bandy-leg'd drummer, that so courteous a soul should have lost his scabbard——he cannot travel without one to his scymetar, and will not be able to get a scabbard to fit it in all *Strasburg.*——I never had one, replied the stranger, looking back to the centinel, and putting his hand up to his cap as he spoke——I carry it, continued he, thus——holding up his naked scymetar, his mule moving on slowly all the time, on purpose to defend my nose.

It is well worth it, gentle stranger, replied the centinel.

——'Tis not worth a single stiver,[2] said the bandy-leg'd drummer—'tis a nose of parchment.

2. A Dutch coin that, like a groat, came to be nearly worthless.

Prout christianus sum, inquit miles, nasus ille, ni sexties major sit, meo esset conformis.
Crepitare audivi ait tympanista.
Mehercule! sanguinem emisit, respondit miles.
Miseret me, inquit tympanista, qui non ambo tetigimus!

Eodem temporis puncto, quo hæc res argumentata fuit inter militem et tympanistam, disceptabatur ibidem tubicine & uxore suâ, qui tunc accesserunt, et peregrino prætereunte, restiterunt.

Quantus nasus! æque longus est, ait tubicina, ac tuba.

Et ex eodem metallo, ait tubicen, velut sternutamento audias.

Tantum abest, respondit illa, quod fistulam dulcedine vincit.
Æneus est, ait tubicen.
Nequaquam, respondit uxor.
Rursum affirmo, ait tubicen, quod æneus est.
Rem penitus explorabo; prius, enim digito tangam, ait uxor, quam dormivero.
Mulus peregrini, gradu lento progressus est, ut unumquodque verbum controversiæ, non tantum inter militem et tympanistam, verum etiam inter tubicinem et uxorem ejus, audiret.
Nequaquam, ait ille, in muli collum fræna demittens, & manibus ambabus in pectus positis, (mulo lentè progrediente) nequaquam ait ille, respiciens, non necesse est ut res isthæc dilucidata foret. Minime gentium! meus nasus nunquam tangetur, dum spiritus hos reget artus——ad quid agendum? ait uxor burgomagistri.

Peregrinus illi non respondit. Votum faciebat tunc temporis sancto Nicolao, quo facto, sinum dextram inserens, e quâ negligenter pependit acinaces, lento gradu processit per plateam Argentorati latam quæ ad diversorium templo ex adversum ducit.

Peregrinus mulo descendens stabulo includi, & manticam inferri jussit: quâ apertâ et coccineis sericis femoralibus extractis cum ar-

As I am a true catholic——except that it is six times as big——
'tis a nose, said the centinel, like my own.

——I heard it crackle, said the drummer.

By dunder, said the centinel, I saw it bleed.

What a pity, cried the bandy-legg'd drummer, we did not both
touch it!

At the very time that this dispute was maintaining by the centinel
and the drummer——was the same point debating betwixt a trumpeter and a trumpeter's wife, who were just then coming up, and
had stopped to see the stranger pass by.

Benedicity!³——What a nose! 'tis as long, said the trumpeter's
wife, as a trumpet.

And of the same mettle, said the trumpeter, as you hear by its
sneezing.

——'Tis as soft as a flute, said she.

——'Tis brass, said the trumpeter.

——'Tis a pudding's end——said his wife.

I tell thee again, said the trumpeter, 'tis a brazen nose.

I'll know the bottom of it, said the trumpeter's wife, for I will
touch it with my finger before I sleep.

The stranger's mule moved on at so slow a rate, that he heard
every word of the dispute, not only betwixt the centinel and the
drummer; but betwixt the trumpeter and the trumpeter's wife.

No! said he, dropping his reins upon his mule's neck, and laying
both his hands upon his breast, the one over the other in a saint-like
position (his mule going on easily all the time) No! said he, looking
up,——I am not such a debtor to the world——slandered and
disappointed as I have been——as to give it that conviction——no!
said he, my nose shall never be touched whilst heaven gives me
strength——To do what? said a burgomaster's wife.

The stranger took no notice of the burgomaster's wife————
he was making a vow to saint *Nicolas*;⁴ which done, having un-
crossed his arms with the same solemnity with which he crossed
them, he took up the reins of his bridle with his left-hand, and
putting his right-hand into his bosom, with his scymetar hanging
loosely to the wrist of it, he rode on as slowly as one foot of the
mule could follow another thro' the principal streets of *Strasburg*,
till chance brought him to the great inn in the market-place over-
against the church.

The moment the stranger alighted, he ordered his mule to be led
into the stable, and his cloak-bag to be brought in; then opening,
and taking out of it, his crimson-satin breeches, with a silver-fringed
——(appendage to them, which I dare not translate)——he put his

---

3. "Bless me!"
4. St. Nicolas is not only the original

of Santa Claus, but also the patron of
wandering scholars.

genteo laciniato Περιζοματὲ, *his sese induit, statimque, acinaci in manu, ad forum deambulavit.*

Quod ubi peregrinus esset ingressus, uxorem tubicinis obviam euntem aspicit; illico cursum flectit, metuens ne nasus suus exploraretur, atque ad diversorium regressus est——exuit se vestibus; braccas coccineas sericas manticæ imposuit mulumque educi jussit.

Francofurtum proficiscor, ait ille, et Argentoratum quatuor abhinc hebdomadis revertar.
Bene curasti hoc jumentum (ait) muli faciem manu demulcens ——me, manticamque meam, plus sexcentis mille passibus portavit.

Longa via est! respondet hospes, nisi plurimum esset negoti.—— Enimvero ait peregrinus a nasorum promontorio redij, et nasum speciosissimum, egregiosissimumque quem unquam quisquam sortitus est, acquisivi!

Dum peregrinus hanc miram rationem, de seipso reddit, hospes et uxor ejus, oculis intentis, peregrini nasum contemplantur——Per sanctos, sanctasque omnes, ait hospitis uxor, nasis duodecim maximis, in toto Argentorato major est!——estne ait illa mariti in aurem insusurrans, nonne est nasus prægrandis?

Dolus inest, anime mi, ait hospes——nasus est falsus.——

Verus est, respondit uxor.——
Ex abiete factus est, ait ille, terebinthinum olet——
Carbunculus inest, ait uxor.
Mortuus est nasus, respondit hospes.
Vivus est, ait illa,——& si ipsa vivam tangam.

Votum feci sancto Nicolao, ait peregrinus, nasum meum intactum fore usque ad——Quodnam tempus? illico respondit illa.

Minime tangetur, inquit ille (manibus in pectus compositis) usque ad illam horam——Quam horam? ait illa.——Nullam, respondit peregrinus, donec pervenio, ad—Quem locum,—— obsecro? ait illa—Peregrinus nil respondens mulo conscenso discessit.

breeches, with his fringed cod-piece[5] on, and forthwith with his short scymetar in his hand, walked out to the grand parade.

The stranger had just taken three turns upon the parade, when he perceived the trumpeter's wife at the opposite side of it——so turn-ing short, in pain lest his nose should be attempted, he instantly went back to his inn——undressed himself, packed up his crimson-sattin breeches, &c. in his cloak-bag, and called for his mule.

I am going forwards, said the stranger, for *Franckfort*——and shall be back at *Strasburg* this day month.

I hope, continued the stranger, stroking down the face of his mule with his left-hand as he was going to mount it, that you have been kind to this faithful slave of mine——it has carried me and my cloak-bag, continued he, tapping the mule's back, above six hundred leagues.

——'Tis a long journey, Sir, replied the master of the inn—— unless a man has great business.——Tut! tut! said the stranger, I have been at the promontory of Noses; and have got me one of the goodliest and jolliest, thank heaven, that ever fell to a single man's lot.

Whilst the stranger was giving this odd account of himself, the master of the inn and his wife kept both their eyes fixed full upon the stranger's nose——By saint *Radagunda*,[6] said the inn-keeper's wife to herself, there is more of it than in any dozen of the largest noses put together in all *Strasburg!* is it not, said she, whispering her husband in his ear, is it not a noble nose?

'Tis an imposture, my dear, said the master of the inn——'tis a false nose.——

'Tis a true nose, said his wife.——

'Tis made of fir-tree, said he,——I smell the turpentine.————

There's a pimple on it, said she.

'Tis a dead nose, replied the inn-keeper.

'Tis a live nose, and if I am alive myself, said the inn-keeper's wife, I will touch it.

I have made a vow to saint *Nicolas* this day, said the stranger, that my nose shall not be touched till——Here the stranger, sus-pending his voice, looked up——Till when? said she hastily.

It never shall be touched, said he, clasping his hands and bringing them close to his breast, till that hour.——What hour? cried the inn-keeper's wife.——Never!——never! said the stranger, never till I am got——For heaven sake into what place? said she.——The stranger rode away without saying a word.

5. A flap or bag to cover the opening at the front of the tight trunk hose fash-ionable in the sixteenth and seventeenth centuries. The Greek word that Tristram declines to translate means "a girdle."
6. St. Radegunde was an extremely pious Queen of the Franks in the sixth century.
She is patron saint of Jesus College, Cambridge, where Sterne took his degree. Tristram speaks in Vol. VIII, Chap. xvii, of "the pricks which enter'd the flesh of St. *Radagunda* in the desert" when she retreated there to mortify her flesh.

The stranger had not got half a league on his way towards *Frank-fort*, before all the city of *Strasburg* was in an uproar about his nose. The *Compline*-bells[7] were just ringing to call the *Strasburgers* to their devotions, and shut up the duties of the day in prayer:——— no soul in all *Strasburg* heard 'em———the city was like a swarm of bees———men, women, and children (the *Compline*-bells tinkling all the time) flying here and there———in at one door, out at another———this way and that way———long ways and cross ways———up one street, down another street———in at this ally, out at that——— did you see it? did you see it? did you see it? O! did you see it?———who saw it? who did see it? for mercy's sake, who saw it?

Alack o'day! I was at vespers!———I was washing, I was starch-ing, I was scouring, I was quilting———God help me! I never saw it———I never touch'd it!———would I had been a centinel, a bandy-leg'd drummer, a trumpeter, a trumpeter's wife, was the general cry and lamentation in every street and corner of *Strasburg*.

Whilst all this confusion and disorder triumphed throughout the great city of *Strasburg*, was the courteous stranger going on as gently upon his mule in his way to *Frankfurt*, as if he had had no concern at all in the affair———talking all the way he rode in broken sentences, sometimes to his mule———sometimes to himself———sometimes to his Julia.

O Julia, my lovely Julia!———nay I cannot stop to let thee bite that thistle———that ever the suspected tongue of a rival should have robbed me of enjoyment when I was upon the point of tasting it.———

———Pugh!———'tis nothing but a thistle———never mind it——— thou shalt have a better supper at night.———

———Banish'd from my country———my friends———from thee.———

Poor devil, thou'rt sadly tired with thy journey!———come———get on a little faster———there's nothing in my cloak-bag but two shirts———a crimson-sattin pair of breeches, and a fringed———Dear Julia!

———But why to *Frankfort*?———is it that there is a hand unfelt, which secretly is conducting me through these meanders and unsus-pected tracts?———

———Stumbling! by saint *Nicolas*! every step———why at this rate we shall be all night in getting in———

———To happiness———or am I to be the sport of fortune and slander———destined to be driven forth unconvicted———unheard ———untouched———if so, why did I not stay at *Strasburg*, where justice———but I had sworn!———Come, thou shalt drink———to *St.*

---

7. Compline is the seventh and last of the canonical hours at which religious services are performed during the day.

Nicolas——O *Julia!*——What dost thou prick up thy ears at? ——'tis nothing but a man, &c.——

The stranger rode on communing in this manner with his mule and *Julia*——till he arrived at his inn, where, as soon as he arrived, he alighted——saw his mule, as he had promised it, taken good care of——took off his cloak-bag, with his crimson-sattin breeches, &c. in it——called for an omelet to his supper, went to his bed about twelve o'clock, and in five minutes fell fast asleep.

It was about the same hour when the tumult in *Strasburg* being abated for that night,——the *Strasburgers* had all got quietly into their beds——but not like the stranger, for the rest either of their minds or bodies; queen *Mab*,[8] like an elf as she was, had taken the stranger's nose, and without reduction of its bulk, had that night been at the pains of slitting and dividing it into as many noses of different cuts and fashions, as there were heads in *Strasburg* to hold them. The abbess of *Quedlingberg*,[9] who, with the four great dignitaries of her chapter, the prioress, the deaness, the sub-chantress, and senior canoness, had that week come to *Strasburg* to consult the university upon a case of conscience relating to their placket holes ——was ill all the night.

The courteous stranger's nose had got perched upon the top of the pineal gland of her brain, and made such rousing work in the fancies of the four great dignitaries of her chapter, they could not get a wink of sleep the whole night thro' for it——there was no keeping a limb still amongst them——in short, they got up like so many ghosts.

The penitentiaries of the third order of saint *Francis*——the nuns of mount *Calvary*——the *Præmonstratenses*——the *Clunienses*[1] ——the *Carthusians*, and all the severer orders of nuns who lay that night in blankets or hair-cloth, were still in a worse condition than the abbess of *Quedlingberg*——by tumbling and tossing, and tossing and tumbling from one side of their beds to the other the whole night long——the several sisterhoods had scratch'd and mawl'd themselves all to death——they got out of their beds almost flead[2] alive——every body thought saint *Antony* had visited them for probation with his fire——they had never once, in short, shut their eyes the whole night long from vespers to matins.

---

8. The "fairies' midwife," who delivers man's brain of dreams. Cf. Mercutio's great description of her in *Romeo and Juliet* I.iv.
9. The abbess of the convent in this town in Prussian Saxony had unusual ecclesiastical powers.
1. *Hafen Slawkenbergius* means the Benedictine nuns of *Cluny*, founded in the year 940, by *Odo*, abbé de *Cluny*.

[*Sterne's note.* Tristram lists religious orders both very old and more recent. The Benedictine monastery at Cluny was founded in 910 A.D., though the first convent of that order was actually not established until the next century.]
2. That is, flayed or scratched until they looked as if they had erysipelas, or "St. Anthony's fire."

The nuns of saint *Ursula* acted the wisest——they never attempted to go to bed at all.

The dean of *Strasburg*, the prebendaries, the capitulars[3] and
domiciliars (capitularly assembled in the morning to consider the
case of butter'd buns) all wished they had followed the nuns of
saint *Ursula's* example.————In the hurry and confusion every
thing had been in the night before, the bakers had all forgot to lay
their leaven——there were no butter'd buns to be had for breakfast
in all *Strasburg*——the whole close[4] of the cathedral was in one
eternal commotion——such a cause of restlessness and disquietude,
and such a zealous inquiry into the cause of that restlessness, had
never happened in *Strasburg*, since *Martin Luther*, with his doctrines, had turned the city up-side down.

If the stranger's nose took this liberty of thrusting itself thus into
the dishes[5] of religious orders, &c. what a carnival did his nose
make of it, in those of the laity!——'tis more than my pen, worn to
the stump as it is, has power to describe; tho' I acknowledge, (*cries*
Slawkenbergius, *with more gaiety of thought than I could have
expected from him*) that there is many a good simile now subsisting
in the world which might give my countrymen some idea of it; but
at the close of such a folio as this, wrote for their sakes, and in
which I have spent the greatest part of my life——tho' I own to
them the simile is in being, yet would it not be unreasonable in
them to expect I should have either time or inclination to search for
it? Let it suffice to say, that the riot and disorder it occasioned in the
Strasburgers fantacies was so general——such an overpowering
mastership had it got of all the faculties of the *Strasburgers* minds
——so many strange things, with equal confidence on all sides, and
with equal eloquence in all places, were spoken and sworn to concerning it, that turned the whole stream of all discourse and wonder
towards it——every soul, good and bad——rich and poor——
learned and unlearned——doctor and student——mistress and
maid——gentle and simple——nun's flesh and woman's flesh in
Strasburg spent their time in hearing tidings about it——every eye
in *Strasburg* languished to see it——every finger——every thumb
in *Strasburg* burned to touch it.

Now what might add, if any thing may be thought necessary to
add to so vehement a desire——was this, that the centinel, the
bandy-legg'd drummer, the trumpeter, the trumpeter's wife, the

---

3. Capitulars are the clergy comprising
a cathedral chapter. Domiciliars, also
members, did not have voting rights in
chapter. The group is assembled, presumably, for breakfast; but "butter'd
buns" is old slang for loose women.
4. Enclosure.
5. Mr. *Shandy's* compliments to orators

——is very sensible that *Slawkenbergius*
has here changed his metaphor——which
he is very guilty of;——that as a trans-
lator, Mr. *Shandy* has all along done
what he could to make him stick to
it——but that here 'twas impossible.
[*Sterne's note.*]

burgo-master's widow, the master of the inn, and the master of the inn's wife, how widely soever they all differed every one from another in their testimonies and descriptions of the stranger's nose ——they all agreed together in two points——namely, that he was gone to *Frankfort*, and would not return to *Strasburg* till that day month; and secondly, whether his nose was true or false, that the stranger himself was one of the most perfect paragons of beauty ——the finest made man!——the most genteel!——the most generous of his purse——the most courteous in his carriage that had ever entered the gates of *Strasburg*——that as he rode, with his scymetar slung loosely to his wrist, thro' the streets——and walked with his crimson-sattin breeches across the parade——'twas with so sweet an air of careless modesty, and so manly withal——as would have put the heart in jeopardy (had his nose not stood in his way) of every virgin who had cast her eyes upon him.

I call not upon that heart which is a stranger to the throbs and yearnings of curiosity, so excited, to justify the abbess of *Quedling-berg*, the prioress, the deaness and subchantress for sending at noonday for the trumpeter's wife: she went through the streets of *Strasburg* with her husband's trumpet in her hand;——the best apparatus the straitness of the time would allow her, for the illustration of her theory——she staid no longer than three days.

The centinel and the bandy-legg'd drummer!——nothing on this side of old *Athens* could equal them! they read their lectures under the city gates to comers and goers, with all the pomp of a *Chrysippus*[6] and a *Crantor* in their porticos.

The master of the inn, with his ostler on his left-hand, read his also in the same stile,——under the portico or gateway of his stable-yard——his wife, hers more privately in a back room: all flocked to their lectures; not promiscuously——but to this or that, as is ever the way, as faith and credulity marshal'd them——in a word, each *Strasburger* came crouding for intelligence——and every *Strasburger* had the intelligence he wanted.

'Tis worth remarking, for the benefit of all demonstrators in natural philosophy, *&c.* that as soon as the trumpeter's wife had finished the abbess of *Quedlinberg's*[7] private lecture, and had begun to read in public, which she did upon a stool in the middle of the great parade——she incommoded the other demonstrators mainly, by gaining incontinently the most fashionable part of the city of *Strasburg* for her auditory——But when a demonstrator in

6. An ancient Greek follower of Zeno, the Stoic philosopher. Crantor, another ancient Greek, was an early commentator on Plato's philosophy.
7. As earlier in the case of Frankfort, Sterne (or his printer) here shifts the spelling of the town's name slightly, and the change prevails through the rest of the tale. Consistency in spelling was not a great concern even among the most literate until toward the end of the eighteenth century.

philosophy (cries *Slawkenbergius*) has a *trumpet* for an apparatus, pray what rival in science can pretend to be heard besides him?

Whilst the unlearned, thro' these conduits of intelligence, were all busied in getting down to the bottom of the well, where TRUTH keeps her little court————were the learned in their way as busy in pumping her up thro' the conduits of dialect[8] induction————they concerned themselves not with facts————they reasoned————

Not one profession had thrown more light upon this subject than the faculty[9]————had not all their disputes about it run into the affair of Wens and œdematous swellings, they could not keep clear of them for their bloods and souls————the stranger's nose had nothing to do either with wens or œdematous swellings.

It was demonstrated however very satisfactorily, that such a ponderous mass of heterogenious matter could not be congested and conglomerated to the nose, whilst the infant was *in Utero*,[1] without destroying the statical balance of the fœtus, and throwing it plump upon its head nine months before the time.————

————The opponents granted the theory————they denied the consequences.

And if a suitable provision of veins, arteries, *&c.* said they, was not laid in, for the due nourishment of such a nose, in the very first stamina and rudiments of its formation before it came into the world (bating the case of Wens) it could not regularly grow and be sustained afterwards.

This was all answered by a dissertation upon nutriment, and the effect which nutriment had in extending the vessels, and in the increase and prolongation of the muscular parts to the greatest growth and expansion imaginable————In the triumph of which theory, they went so far as to affirm, that there was no cause in nature, why a nose might not grow to the size of the man himself.

The respondents satisfied the world this event could never happen to them so long as a man had but one stomach and one pair of lungs————For the stomach, said they, being the only organ destined for the reception of food, and turning it into chyle,————and the lungs the only engine of sanguification————it could possibly work off no more, than what the appetite brought it: or admitting the possibility of a man's overloading his stomach, nature had set bounds however to his lungs————the engine was of a determined size and strength, and could elaborate but a certain quantity in a given time————that is, it could produce just as much blood as was sufficient for one single man, and no more; so that, if there was as much nose as man————they proved a mortification must necessarily

8. Dialectical.
9. Members of a profession—in this case, the medical.
1. Uterus.

ensue; and forasmuch as there could not be a support for both, that the nose must either fall off from the man, or the man inevitably fall off from his nose.

Nature accommodates herself to these emergencies, cried the opponents—else what do you say to the case of a whole stomach ——a whole pair of lungs, and but *half* a man, when both his legs have been unfortunately shot off?——

He dies of a plethora,[2] said they——or must spit blood, and in a fortnight or three weeks go off in a consumption——

——It happens otherways——replied the opponents.——

It ought not, said they.

The more curious and intimate inquirers after nature and her doings, though they went hand in hand a good way together, yet they all divided about the nose at last, almost as much as the faculty itself.

They amicably laid it down, that there was a just and geometrical arrangement and proportion of the several parts of the human frame to its several destinations, offices, and functions, which could not be transgressed but within certain limits——that nature, though she sported——she sported within a certain circle;——and they could not agree about the diameter of it.

The logicians stuck much closer to the point before them than any of the classes of the literati;——they began and ended with the word nose; and had it not been for a *petitio principii*,[3] which one of the ablest of them ran his head against in the beginning of the combat, the whole controversy had been settled at once.

A nose, argued the logician, cannot bleed without blood——and not only blood——but blood circulating in it to supply the phænomenon with a succession of drops——(a stream being but a quicker succession of drops, that is included, said he)——Now death, continued the logician, being nothing but the stagnation of the blood——

I deny the definition——Death is the separation of the soul from the body, said his antagonist——Then we don't agree about our weapon, said the logician——Then there is an end of the dispute, replied the antagonist.

The civilians[4] were still more concise; what they offered being more in the nature of a decree——than a dispute.

——Such a monstrous nose, said they, had it been a true nose, could not possibly have been suffered in civil society——and if false——to impose upon society with such false signs and tokens, was a still greater violation of its rights, and must have had still less mercy shewn it.

---

2. That is, too much blood.
3. A logical fallacy, like begging the question.
4. Civil lawyers.

The only objection to this was, that if it proved any thing, it proved the stranger's nose was neither true nor false.

This left room for the controversy to go on. It was maintained by the advocates of the ecclesiastic court, that there was nothing to inhibit a decree, since the stranger *ex mero motu*[5] had confessed he had been at the Promontory of Noses, and had got one of the goodliest, *&c. &c.*——To this it was answered, it was impossible there should be such a place as the Promontory of Noses, and the learned be ignorant where it lay. The commissary of the bishop of *Strasburg* undertook the advocates, explained this matter in a treatice upon proverbial phrases, shewing them, that the Promontory of Noses was a mere allegoric expression, importing no more than that nature had given him a long nose: in proof of which, with great learning, he cited the underwritten authorities,[6] which had decided the point incontestably, had it not appeared that a dispute about some franchises of dean and chapter-lands had been determined by it nineteen years before.

It happened——I must not say unluckily for Truth, because they were giving her a lift another way in so doing; that the two universities of *Strasburg*——the *Lutheran*, founded in the year 1538 by *Jacobus Sturmius*, counsellor of the senate,——and the *Popish*, founded by *Leopold*, arch-duke of *Austria*, were, during all this time, employing the whole depth of their knowledge (except just what the affair of the abbess of *Quedlinburg*'s placket-holes required)——in determining the point of *Martin Luther*'s damnation.

The *Popish* doctors had undertaken to demonstrate *a priori*; that from the necessary influence of the planets on the twenty-second day of *October* 1483——when the moon was in the twelfth house ——*Jupiter*, *Mars*, and *Venus* in the third, the *Sun*, *Saturn*, and *Mercury* all got together in the fourth——that he must in course, and unavoidably be a damn'd man——and that his doctrines, by a direct corollary, must be damn'd doctrines too.

By inspection into his horoscope, where five planets were in coition all at once with scorpio[7] (in reading this my father would

5. Of his own accord.
6. Nonnulli ex nostratibus eadem loquendi formulâ utun.⋅Quinimo et Logistae & Canonistae——Vid. Parce Barne Jas in d. L. Provincial. Constitut. de conjec. vid. Vol. Lib. 4. Titul. I. N. 7. quâ etiam in re conspir. Om. de Promontorio Nas. Tichmak. ff. d. tit. 3. fol. 189. passim. Vid. Glos. de contrahend. empt. &c. nec non J. Scrudr. in cap. ſ. refut. ff. per totum Cum his cons. Rever. J. Tubal, Sentent. & Prov. cap. 9 ff. II, 12. obiter. V. et Librum, cui Tit. de Terris & Phras. Belg. ad finem, cum Comment. N. Bardy

Belg. Vid. Scrip. Argentotarens. de Antiq. Ecc. in Episc. Archiv. fid. coll. per Von Jacobum Koinshoven Folio Argent. 1583, praecip. ad finem Quibus add. Rebuff in L. obvenire de Signif. Nom. ff. fol. & de Jure, Gent. & Civil. de protib. aliena feud. per federa, test. Joha. Luxius in prolegom. quem velim vidaes, de Analy. Cap. 1, 2, 3. Vid Idea. [*Sterne's note.*] A parody of pedantic footnotes.
7. Haec mira, satisque horrenda. Planetarum coitio sub Scorpio Asterismo in nonâ coeli statione, quam Arabes re-

always shake his head) in the ninth house which the *Arabians* allotted to religion———it appeared that *Martin Luther* did not care one stiver about the matter———and that from the horoscope directed to the conjunction of *Mars*———they made it plain likewise he must die cursing and blaspheming———with the blast of which his soul (being steep'd in guilt) sailed before the wind, into the lake of hell fire.

The little objection of the *Lutheran* doctors to this, was, that it must certainly be the soul of another man, born *Oct.* 22, 83, which was forced to sail down before the wind in that manner———inasmuch as it appeared from the register of *Islaben* in the county of *Mansfelt*, that *Luther* was not born in the year 1483, but in 84; and not on the 22d day of *October*, but on the 10th of *November*, the eve of *Martinmas*-day, from whence he had the name of *Martin*.

[———I must break off my translation for a moment; for if I did not, I know I should no more be able to shut my eyes in bed, than the abbess of *Quedlinburg*———It is to tell the reader, that my father never read this passage of *Slawkenbergius* to my uncle *Toby* but with triumph———not over my uncle *Toby*, for he never opposed him in it———but over the whole world.

———Now you see, brother *Toby*, he would say, looking up, "that christian names are not such indifferent things;"———had *Luther* here been called by any other name but *Martin*, he would have been damned to all eternity———Not that I look upon *Martin*, he would add, as a good name———far from it———'tis something better than a neutral, and but a little———yet little as it is, you see it was of some service to him.

My father knew the weakness of this prop to his hypothesis, as well as the best logician could shew him———yet so strange is the weakness of man at the same time, as it fell in his way, he could not for his life but make use of it; and it was certainly for this reason, that though there are many stories in *Hafen Slawkenbergius*'s Decads full as entertaining as this I am translating, yet there is not one amongst them which my father read over with half the delight

---

ligioni deputabant efficit Martinum Lutherum sacrilegum hereticum, christianae religionis hostem acerrimum atqбe prophanum, ex horoscopi directione ad Martis coitum, [ir] religiosissimus obiit, ejus Anima scelestissima ad infernos navigavit———ab Alecto, Tisiphone et Megaera flagellis igneis cruciata perenniter.———Lucas Gauricus in Tractatu astrologico de præteritis multorum hominum accidentibus per genituras examinatis. [*Sterne's note.*] The passage is drawn from the entry on Luther in Bayle's Dictionary: "This is sufficiently miraculous and horrifying. The conjunction of

five planets under Scorpio in the ninth house of the heavens, which the Arabs ascribe to religion, made Martin Luther a sacrilegious heretic, a very bitter and profane enemy to the Christian religion; from the direction of the horoscope to the conjunction of Mars, it is clear that he died a very irreligious man, whose most wicked soul sailed to hell———where Alecto, Tisiphone and Magera forever flagellate him with fiery whips."——— Lucas Gauricus's *Astrological Treatise on the Past Accidents of Many Men, by Means of an Examination of their Nativities.*

——it flattered two of his strangest hypotheses together——his NAMES and his NOSES——I will be bold to say, he might have read all the books in the *Alexandrian* library,[8] had not fate taken other care of them, and not have met with a book or a passage in one, which hit two such nails as these upon the head at one stroke.]

The two universities of *Strasburg* were hard tugging at this affair of *Luther's* navigation. The Protestant doctors had demonstrated, that he had not sailed right before the wind, as the Popish doctors had pretended; and as every one knew there was no sailing full in the teeth of it,——they were going to settle, in case he had sailed, how many points he was off; whether *Martin* had doubled the cape, or had fallen upon a lee-shore; and no doubt, as it was an enquiry of much edification, at least to those who understood this sort of NAVIGATION, they had gone on with it in spite of the size of the stranger's nose, had not the size of the stranger's nose drawn off the attention of the world from what they were about——it was their business to follow.——

The abbess of *Quedlinburg* and her four dignitaries was no stop; for the enormity of the stranger's nose running full as much in their fancies as their case of conscience——The affair of their placket-holes kept cold——In a word, the printers were ordered to distribute their types——all controversies dropp'd.

'Twas a square cap with a silk tassel upon the crown of it[9]——to a nut shell——to have guessed on which side of the nose the two universities would split.

'Tis above reason, cried the doctors on one side.

'Tis below reason, cried the others.

'Tis faith, cried one.

'Tis a fiddle-stick, said the other.

'Tis possible, cried the one.

'Tis impossible, said the other.

God's power is infinite, cried the Nosarians, he can do any thing.

He can do nothing, replied the Antinosarians, which implies contradictions.

He can make matter think, said the Nosarians.

As certainly as you can make a velvet cap out of a sow's ear, replied the Antinosarians.

He can make two and two five, replied the Popish doctors.——

'Tis false, said their opponents.——

Infinite power is infinite power, said the doctors who maintained the *reality* of the nose.——It extends only to all possible things, replied the *Lutherans*.

8. The greatest library of the ancient world, established during the time the Greek Ptolemy family ruled Egypt, and traditionally believed to have been de-stroyed when Caesar was besieged in Alexandria.
9. An academic cap.

By God in heaven, cried the Popish doctors, he can make a nose, if he thinks fit, as big as the steeple of *Strasburg.*

Now the steeple of *Strasburg* being the biggest and the tallest church-steeple to be seen in the whole world, the Antinosarians denied that a nose of 575 geometrical feet in length could be worn, at least by a middle-siz'd man———The Popish doctors swore it could———The *Lutheran* doctors said No;———it could not.

This at once started a new dispute, which they pursued a great way upon the extent and limitation of the moral and natural attributes of God———That controversy led them naturally into *Thomas Aquinas*,[1] and *Thomas Aquinas* to the devil.

The stranger's nose was no more heard of in the dispute———it just served as a frigate to launch them into the gulph of school-divinity,———and then they all sailed before the wind.

Heat is in proportion to the want of true knowledge.

The controversy about the attributes, &c. instead of cooling, on the contrary had inflamed the *Strasburgers* imaginations to a most inordinate degree———The less they understood of the matter, the greater was their wonder about it———they were left in all the distresses of desire unsatisfied   saw their doctors, the *Parchmentarians*, the *Brassarians*, the *Turpentarians*, on one side———the Popish doctors on the other, like *Pantagruel* and his companions in quest of the oracle of the bottle, all embarked and out of sight.[2]

———The poor *Strasburgers* left upon the beach!

———What was to be done?———No delay———the uproar increased———every one in disorder———the city gates set open.———

Unfortunate *Strasburgers*! was there in the store-house of nature ———was there in the lumber-rooms of learning———was there in the great arsenal of chance, one single engine left undrawn forth to torture your curiosities, and stretch your desires, which was not pointed by the hand of fate to play upon your hearts?———I dip not my pen into my ink to excuse the surrender of yourselves———'tis to write your panegyrick. Shew me a city so macerated with expectation———who neither eat, or drank, or slept, or prayed, or hearkened to the calls either of religion or nature for seven and twenty days together, who could have held out one day longer.

On the twenty-eighth the courteous stranger had promised to return to *Strasburg.*

Seven thousand coaches (*Slawkenbergius* must certainly have made some mistake in his numerical characters) 7000 coaches——— 15000 single horse chairs———20000 waggons, crouded as full as

1. The thirteenth-century Italian theologian, a most important medieval philosopher.

2. Pantagruel sets off for "the Oracle of Bacbuc, alias the Holy Bottle" in Rabelais, IV.1.

they could all hold with senators, counsellors, syndicks[3]——
beguines, widows, wives, virgins, canons, concubines, all in their
coaches——The abbess of *Quedlinburg*, with the prioress, the
deaness and sub-chantress leading the procession in one coach, and
the dean of *Strasburg*, with the four great dignitaries of his chapter
on her left-hand——the rest following higglety-pigglety as they
could; some on horseback——some on foot——some led——some
driven——some down the *Rhine*——some this way——some that
——all set out at sun-rise to meet the courteous stranger on the
road.

Haste we now towards the catastrophe of my tale[4]——I say
Catastrophe (cries *Slawkenbergius*) inasmuch as a tale, with parts
rightly disposed, not only rejoiceth (*gaudet*) in the *Catastrophe* and
Peripeitia of a DRAMA, but rejoiceth moreover in all the essential
and integrant parts of it——it has its *Protasis, Epitasis, Catastasis*,
its *Catastrophe* or *Peripeitia* growing one out of the other in it, in
the order *Aristotle* first planted them——without which a tale had
better never be told at all, says *Slawkenbergius*, but be kept to a
man's self.

In all my ten tales, in all my ten decads, have I, *Slawkenbergius*,
tied down every tale of them as tightly to this rule, as I have done
this of the stranger and his nose.

——From his first parley with the centinel, to his leaving the city
of *Strasburg*, after pulling off his crimson-sattin pair of breeches, is
the *Protasis* or first entrance——where the characters of the *Per-
sonæ Dramatis* are just touched in, and the subject slightly begun.

The *Epitasis*, wherein the action is more fully entered upon and
heightened, till it arrives at its state or height called the *Catastasis*,
and which usually takes up the 2d and 3d act, is included within
that busy period of my tale, betwixt the first night's uproar about
the nose, to the conclusion of the trumpeter's wife's lectures upon it
in the middle of the grand parade; and from the first embarking of
the learned in the dispute——to the doctors finally sailing away,
and leaving the *Strasburgers* upon the beach in distress, is the *Catastasis* or the ripening of the incidents and passions for their bursting
forth in the fifth act.

This commences with the setting out of the *Strasburgers* in the
Frankfort road, and terminates in unwinding the labyrinth and
bringing the hero out of a state of agitation (as *Aristotle* calls it) to
a state of rest and quietness.

---

3. *Syndics*: government officials. *Beguines*: members of a lay sisterhood,
often nurses.
4. The catastrophe or *peripetia* (as it is
usually spelled) of a tragedy occurs

when the fortunes of the protagonist turn
finally for the worse. *Prostasis*: introductory action. *Epistasis*: developing
action. *Catastasis*: climax. *Personae
dramatis*: characters in the play.

This, says *Hafen Slawkenbergius*, constitutes the catastrophe or peripeitia of my tale——and that is the part of it I am going to relate.

We left the stranger behind the curtain asleep——he enters now upon the stage.

——What dost thou prick up thy ears at?——'tis nothing but a man upon a horse——was the last word the stranger uttered to his mule. It was not proper then to tell the reader, that the mule took his master's word for it; and without any more *ifs* or *ands*, let the traveller and his horse pass by.

The traveller was hastening with all diligence to get to *Strasburg* that night——What a fool am I, said the traveller to himself, when he had rode about a league farther, to think of getting into *Strasburg* this night——*Strabsurg!*——the great *Strasburg!*—— *Strasburg*, the capital of all *Alsatia*! *Strasburg*, an imperial city! *Strasburg*, a sovereign state! *Strasburg*, garrisoned with five thousand of the best troops in all the world!——Alas! if I was at the gates of *Strasburg* this moment, I could not gain admittance into it for a ducat,——nay a ducat and half——'tis too much——better go back to the last inn I have passed——than lie I know not where ——or give I know not what. The traveller, as he made these reflections in his mind, turned his horse's head about, and three minutes after the stranger had been conducted into his chamber, he arrived at the same inn.

——We have bacon in the house, said the host, and bread—— and till eleven o'clock this night had three eggs in it——but a stranger, who arrived an hour ago, has had them dressed into an omlet, and we have nothing.——

——Alas! said the traveller, harrassed as I am, I want nothing but a bed——I have one as soft as is in *Alsatia*, said the host.

——The stranger, continued he, should have slept in it, for 'tis my best bed, but upon the score of his nose——He has got a defluxion, said the traveller——Not that I know, cried the host—— But 'tis a camp-bed, and *Jacinta*, said he, looking towards the maid, imagined there was not room in it to turn his nose in——Why so? cried the traveller starting back——It is so long a nose, replied the host——The traveller fixed his eyes upon *Jacinta*, then upon the ground——kneeled upon his right knee——had just got his hand laid upon his breast——Trifle not with my anxiety, said he, rising up again——'Tis no trifle, said *Jacinta*, 'tis the most glorious nose! ——The traveller fell upon his knee again——laid his hand upon his breast——then said he, looking up to heaven! thou hast conducted me to the end of my pilgrimage——'Tis *Diego!*

The traveller was the brother of the *Julia*, so often invoked that night by the stranger as he rode from *Strasburg* upon his mule; and was come, on her part, in quest of him. He had accompanied his sister from *Valadolid* across the *Pyrenean* mountains thro' *France*, and had many an entangled skein to wind off in pursuit of him thro' the many meanders and abrupt turnings of a lover's thorny tracks.

——*Julia* had sunk under it——and had not been able to go a step farther than to *Lyons*, where, with the many disquietudes of a tender heart, which all talk of——but few feel——she sicken'd, but had just strength to write a letter to *Diego*; and having conjured her brother never to see her face till he had found him out, and put the letter into his hands, *Julia* took to her bed.

Fernandez (for that was her brother's name)——tho' the camp-bed was as soft as any one in *Alsace*, yet he could not shut his eyes in it.——As soon as it was day he rose, and hearing *Diego* was risen too, he enter'd his chamber, and discharged his sister's commission.

The letter was as follows:

"Seig.⁵ Diego.

"Whether my suspicions of your nose were justly excited or not—'tis not now to inquire——it is enough I have not had firmness to put them to farther tryal.

"How could I know so little of myself, when I sent my *Duena* to forbid your coming more under my lattice? or how could I know so little of you, *Diego*, as to imagine you would not have staid one day in *Valadolid* to have given ease to my doubts?——Was I to be abandoned, *Diego*, because I was deceived? or was it kind to take me at my word, whether my suspicions were just or no, and leave me, as you did, a prey to much uncertainty and sorrow?

"In what manner *Julia* has resented this——my brother, when he puts this letter into your hands, will tell you: He will tell you in how few moments she repented of the rash message she had sent you——in what frantic haste she flew to her lattice, and how many days and nights together she leaned immoveably upon her elbow, looking thro' it towards the way which *Diego* was wont to come.

"He will tell you, when she heard of your departure——how her spirits deserted her——how her heart sicken'd——how piteously she mourn'd——how low she hung her head. O *Diego*! how many weary steps has my brother's pity led me by the hand languishing to trace out yours! how far has desire carried me beyond strength——and how oft have I fainted by the way, and sunk into his arms, with only power to cry out——O my *Diego*!

"If the gentleness of your carriage has not belied your heart, you will fly to me, almost as fast as you fled from me——haste as you

5. Seigneur.

will, you will arrive but to see me expire.———'Tis a bitter draught, *Diego*, but oh! 'tis embitter'd still more by dying *un*———."

She could proceed no farther.

Slawkenbergius supposes the word intended was *unconvinced*, but her strength would not enable her to finish her letter.

The heart of the courteous *Diego* overflowed as he read the letter———he ordered his mule forthwith and *Fernandez*'s horse to be saddled; and as no vent in prose is equal to that of poetry in such conflicts———chance, which as often directs us to remedies as to *diseases*, having thrown a piece of charcoal into the window——— *Diego* availed himself of it, and whilst the ostler was getting ready his mule, he eased his mind against the wall as follows.

ODE

Harsh and untuneful are the notes of love,
   Unless my Julia strikes the key,
Her hand alone can touch the part,
   Whose dulcet move-
     -ment charms the heart,
And governs all the man with sympathetic sway.

              2d.

O *Julia*

The lines were very natural———for they were nothing at all to the purpose, says *Slawkenbergius*, and 'tis a pity there were no more of them; but whether it was that Seig. *Diego* was slow in composing verses———or the ostler quick in saddling mules———is not averred; certain it was, that *Diego*'s mule and *Fernandez*'s horse were ready at the door of the inn, before *Diego* was ready for his second stanza; so without staying to finish his ode, they both mounted, sallied forth, passed the *Rhine*, traversed *Alsace*, shaped their course towards *Lyons*, and before the *Strasburgers* and the abbess of *Quedlinberg* had set out on their cavalcade, had *Fernandez*, *Diego*, and his *Julia*, crossed the *Pyrenean* mountains, and got safe to *Valadolid*.

'Tis needless to inform the geographical reader, that when *Diego* was in *Spain*, it was not possible to meet the courteous stranger in the *Frankfort* road; it is enough to say, that of all restless desires, curiosity being the strongest———the *Strasburgers* felt the full force of it; and that for three days and nights they were tossed to and fro in the *Frankfort* road, with the tempestuous fury of this passion, before they could submit to return home———When alas! an event was prepared for them, of all others the most grievous that could befal a free people.

As this revolution of the *Strasburgers* affairs is often spoken of, and little understood, I will, in ten words, says *Slawkenbergius*, give the world an explanation of it, and with it put an end to my tale.

Every body knows of the grand system of Universal Monarchy, wrote by order of Mons. *Colbert*, and put in manuscript into the hands of *Louis* the fourteenth, in the year 1664.[6]

'Tis as well known, that one branch out of many of that system, was the getting possession of *Strasburg*, to favour an entrance at all times into *Suabia*, in order to disturb the quiet of *Germany*——and that in consequence of this plan, *Strasburg* unhappily fell at length into their hands.

It is the lot of few to trace out the true springs of this and such like revolutions——The vulgar look too high for them——Statesmen look too low——Truth (for once) lies in the middle.

What a fatal thing is the popular pride of a free city! cries one historian——The *Strasburgers* deemed it a diminution of their freedom to receive an imperial garrison——and so fell a prey to a *French* one.

The fate, says another, of the *Strasburgers*, may be a warning to all free people to save their money————They anticipated their revenues——brought themselves under taxes, exhausted their strength, and in the end became so weak a people, they had not strength to keep their gates shut, and so the *French* pushed them open.

Alas! alas! cries *Slawkenbergius*, 'twas not the *French*——'twas CURIOSITY pushed them open————The *French* indeed, who are ever upon the catch, when they saw the *Strasburgers*, men, women, and children, all marched out to follow the stranger's nose——each man followed his own, and marched in.

Trade and manufactures have decayed and gradually grown down ever since——but not from any cause which commercial heads have assigned; for it is owing to this only, that Noses have ever so run in their heads, that the *Strasburgers* could not follow their business.

Alas! alas! cries *Slawkenbergius*, making an exclamation——it is not the first——and I fear will not be the last fortress that has been either won——or lost by Noses.

The END of

Slawkenbergius's TALE.

---

6. Colbert was Finance Minister to Louis XIV, and one of his most influential advisors. Sterne is parodying the way that traditional tales are often shaped (or distorted) to explain complex historical events.

Chapter I.

W ITH all this learning upon Noses running perpetually in my father's fancy——with so many family prejudices ——and ten decads of such tales running on for ever along with them——how was it possible with such exquisite——was it a true nose?——That a man with such exquisite feelings as my father had, could bear the shock at all below stairs——or indeed above stairs, in any other posture, but the very posture I have described.

——Throw yourself down upon the bed, a dozen times—— taking care only to place a looking-glass first in a chair on one side of it, before you do it——But was the stranger's nose a true nose ——or was it a false one?

To tell that before-hand, madam, would be to do injury to one of the best tales in the christian world; and that is the tenth of the tenth decad which immediately follows this.

This tale, crieth *Slawkenbergius* somewhat exultingly, has been reserved by me for the concluding tale of my whole work; knowing right well, that when I shall have told it, and my reader shall have read it thro'——'twould be even high time for both of us to shut up the book; inasmuch, continues *Slawkenbergius*, as I know of no tale which could possibly ever go down after it.

——'Tis a tale indeed!

This sets out with the first interview in the inn at *Lyons*, when *Fernandez* left the courteous stranger and his sister *Julia* alone in her chamber, and is overwritten,

The I N T R I C A C I E S

of

Diego and Julia.

Heavens! thou art a strange creature *Slawkenbergius!* what a whimsical view of the involutions of the heart of woman hast thou opened! how this can ever be translated, and yet if this specimen of *Slawkenbergius's* tales, and the exquisitiveness of his moral should please the world——translated shall a couple of volumes be.—— Else, how this can ever be translated into good *English*, I have no sort of conception.——There seems in some passages to want a sixth sense to do it rightly.——What can he mean by the lambent pupilability of slow, low, dry chat, five notes below the natural tone,——which you know, madam, is little more than a whisper? The moment I pronounced the words, I could perceive an attempt towards a vibration in the strings, about the region of the heart.

——The brain made no acknowledgment.——There's often no good understanding betwixt 'em.——I felt as if I understood it.—— I had no ideas.——The movement could not be without cause.—— I'm lost. I can make nothing of it,——unless, may it please your worships, the voice, in that case being little more than a whisper, unavoidably forces the eyes to approach not only within six inches of each other——but to look into the pupils——is not that dangerous?——But it can't be avoided——for to look up to the cieling, in that case the two chins unavoidably meet——and to look down into each others laps, the foreheads come into immediate contact, which at once puts an end to the conference——I mean to the sentimental part of it.——What is left, madam, is not worth stooping for.

Chapter II.

MY father lay stretched across the bed as still as if the hand of death had pushed him down, for a full hour and a half, before he began to play upon the floor with the toe of that foot which hung over the bed-side; my uncle *Toby's* heart was a pound lighter for it.——In a few moments, his left-hand, the knuckles of which had all the time reclined upon the handle of the chamberpot, came to its feeling——he thrust it a little more within the valance——drew up his hand, when he had done, into his bosom ——gave a hem!——My good uncle *Toby*, with infinite pleasure, answered it; and full gladly would have ingrafted a sentence of consolation upon the opening it afforded; but having no talents, as I said, that way, and fearing moreover that he might set out with something which might make a bad matter worse, he contented himself with resting his chin placidly upon the cross of his crunch.

  Now whether the compression shortened my uncle *Toby's* face into a more pleasureable oval,——or that the philanthropy of his heart, in seeing his brother beginning to emerge out of the sea of his afflictions, had braced up his muscles,——so that the compression upon his chin only doubled the benignity which was there before, is not hard to decide.——My father, in turning his eyes, was struck with such a gleam of sun-shine in his face, as melted down the sullenness of his grief in a moment.

  He broke silence as follows.

Chapter III.

DID ever man, brother *Toby*, cried my father, raising himself up upon his elbow, and turning himself round to the opposite side of the bed where my uncle *Toby* was sitting in his old fringed chair, with his chin resting upon his crutch——did ever a poor unfortunate man, brother *Toby*, cried my father, receive so many lashes?——The most I ever saw given, quoth my uncle *Toby*, (ringing the bell at the bed's head for *Trim*) was to a grenadier, I think in *Makay's*[7] regiment.

——Had my uncle *Toby* shot a bullet thro' my father's heart, he could not have fallen down with his nose upon the quilt more suddenly.

Bless me! said my uncle *Toby*.

Chapter IV.

W AS it *Makay's* regiment, quoth my uncle *Toby*, where the poor grenadier was so unmercifully whipp'd at *Bruges* about the ducats?——O Christ! he was innocent! cried *Trim* with a deep sigh.——And he was whipp'd, may it please your honour, almost to death's door.——They had better have shot him outright as he begg'd, and he had gone directly to heaven, for he was as innocent as your honour.——I thank thee, *Trim*, quoth my uncle *Toby*. I never think of his, continued *Trim*, and my poor brother *Tom*'s misfortunes, for we were all three school-fellows, but I cry like a coward.——Tears are no proof of cowardice, *Trim*.——I drop them oft-times myself, cried my uncle *Toby*.——I know your honour does, replied *Trim*, and so am not ashamed of it myself. ——But to think, may it please your honour, continued *Trim*, a tear stealing into the corner of his eye as he spoke——to think of two virtuous lads with hearts as warm in their bodies, and as honest as God could make them——the children of honest people, going forth with gallant spirits to seek their fortunes in the world——and fall into such evils!——poor *Tom*! to be tortured upon a rack for nothing——but marrying a *Jew*'s widow who sold sausages——honest *Dick Johnson*'s soul to be scourged out of his body, for the ducats another man put into his knapsack!——O!——these are misfortunes, cried *Trim*,——pulling out his handkerchief——these are misfortunes, may it please your honour, worth lying down and crying over.

——My father could not help blushing.

'Twould be a pity, *Trim*, quoth my uncle *Toby*, thou shouldst ever feel sorrow of thy own——thou feelest it so tenderly for others.——Alack-o-day, replied the corporal, brightening up his face——your honour knows I have neither wife or child——I can have no sorrows in this world.——My father could not help smiling.——As few as any man, *Trim*, replied my uncle *Toby*; nor

---

7. Hugh MacKay was one of the British commanders in Flanders.

can I see how a fellow of thy light heart can suffer, but from the distress of poverty in thy old age——when thou art passed all services, *Trim*,——and hast out-lived thy friends——An' please your honour, never fear, replied *Trim* chearily——But I would have thee never fear, *Trim*, replied my uncle; and therefore, continued my uncle *Toby*, throwing down his crutch, and getting up upon his legs as he uttered the word *therefore*——in recompence, *Trim*, of thy long fidelity to me, and that goodness of thy heart I have had such proofs of——whilst thy master is worth a shilling——thou shalt never ask elsewhere, *Trim*, for a penny. *Trim* attempted to thank my uncle *Toby*,——but had not power——tears trickled down his cheeks faster than he could wipe them off——He laid his hands upon his breast——made a bow to the ground, and shut the door.

——I have left *Trim* my bowling-green, cried my uncle *Toby* ——My father smiled——I have left him moreover a pension, continued my uncle *Toby*——My father looked grave.

Chapter V.

IS this a fit time, said my father to himself, to talk of PENSIONS and GRENADIERS?

Chapter VI.

WHEN my uncle *Toby* first mentioned the grenadier, my father, I said, fell down with his nose flat to the quilt, and as suddenly as if my uncle *Toby* had shot him; but it was not added, that every other limb and member of my father instantly relapsed with his nose into the same precise attitude in which he lay first described; so that when corporal *Trim* left the room, and my father found himself disposed to rise off the bed,——he had all the little preparatory movements to run over again, before he could do it. ——Attitudes are nothing, madam,——'tis the transition from one attitude to another——like the preparation and resolution of the discord into harmony, which is all in all.

For which reason my father played the same jig over again with his toe upon the floor——pushed the chamber-pot still a little farther within the valance——gave a hem——raised himself up upon his elbow——and was just beginning to address himself to my uncle *Toby*——when recollecting the unsuccessfulness of his first effort in that attitude,——he got upon his legs, and in making the third turn across the room, he stopped short before my uncle *Toby*; and laying the three first fingers of his right-hand in the palm of his left, and stooping a little, he addressed himself to my uncle *Toby* as follows.

Chapter VII.

WHEN I reflect, brother *Toby*, upon MAN; and take a view of that dark side of him which represents his life as open to so many causes of trouble——when I consider, brother *Toby*, how oft we eat the bread of affliction, and that we are born to it, as to the portion of our inheritance——I was born to nothing, quoth my uncle *Toby*, interrupting my father——but my commission. Zooks!⁸ said my father, did not my uncle leave you a hundred and twenty pounds a year?——What could I have done without it? replied my uncle *Toby*.——That's another concern, said my father testily——But I say, *Toby*, when one runs over the catalogue of all the cross reckonings and sorrowful *items* with which the heart of man is overcharged, 'tis wonderful by what hidden resources the mind is enabled to stand it out, and bear itself up, as it does against the impositions laid upon our nature.——'Tis by the assistance of Almighty God, cried my uncle *Toby*, looking up, and pressing the palms of his hands close together——'tis not from our own strength, brother *Shandy*——a sentinel in a wooden centry-box, might as well pretend to stand it out against a detachment of fifty men,—— we are upheld by the grace and the assistance of the best of Beings.

——That is cutting the knot, said my father, instead of untying it.——But give me leave to lead you, brother *Toby*, a little deeper into this mystery.

With all my heart, replied my uncle *Toby*.

My father instantly exchanged the attitude he was in, for that in which *Socrates* is so finely painted by *Raffael* in his school of *Athens*;⁹ which your connoisseurship knows is so exquisitely imagined, that even the particular manner of the reasoning of *Socrates* is expressed by it——for he holds the fore-finger of his left-hand between the fore-finger and the thumb of his right, and seems as if he was saying to the libertine he is reclaiming——"*You grant me this*——and this: and this, and this, I don't ask of you——they follow of themselves in course."

So stood my father, holding fast his fore-finger betwixt his finger and his thumb, and reasoning with my uncle *Toby* as he sat in his old fringed chair, valanced around with partycoloured worsted bobs ——O *Garrick*! what a rich scene of this would thy exquisite powers make! and how gladly would I write such another to avail myself of thy immortality, and secure my own behind it.

---

8. "God's hooks"—i.e., the nails that fastened Christ to the cross.

9. Raphael's fresco painting of Athenian philosophers is in the Vatican.

Chapter VIII.

THOUGH man is of all others the most curious vehicle, said my father, yet at the same time 'tis of so slight a frame and so totteringly put together, that the sudden jerks and hard jostlings it unavoidably meets with in this rugged journey, would overset and tear it to pieces a dozen times a day——was it not, brother *Toby*, that there is a secret spring within us——Which spring, said my uncle *Toby*, I take to be Religion.——Will that set my child's nose on? cried my father, letting go his finger, and striking one hand against the other——It makes every thing straight for us, answered my uncle *Toby*——Figuratively speaking, dear *Toby*, it may, for aught I know, said my father; but the spring I am speaking of, is that great and elastic power within us of counterbalancing evil, which like a secret spring in a well-ordered machine, though it can't prevent the shock——at least it imposes upon our sense of it.

Now, my dear brother, said my father, replacing his fore-finger, as he was coming closer to the point,——had my child arrived safe into the world, unmartyr'd in that precious part of him——fanciful and extravagant as I may appear to the world in my opinion of christian names, and of that magic bias which good or bad names irresistably impress upon our characters and conducts——heaven is witness! that in the warmest transports of my wishes for the prosperity of my child, I never once wished to crown his head with more glory and honour, than what GEORGE or EDWARD would have spread around it.[1]

But alas! continued my father, as the greatest evil has befallen him——I must counteract and undo it with the greatest good.

He shall be christened *Trismegistus*, brother.

I wish it may answer——replied my uncle *Toby*, rising up.

Chapter IX.

WHAT a chapter of chances, said my father, turning himself about upon the first landing, as he and my uncle *Toby* were going down stairs——what a long chapter of chances do the events of this world lay open to us! Take pen and ink in hand, brother *Toby*, and calculate it fairly——I know no more of calculations than this balluster, said my uncle *Toby*, (striking short of it with his crutch, and hitting my father a desperate blow souse upon his shin-bone)——'Twas a hundred to one——cried my uncle

---

1. These are the names of the reigning monarch, George III, and of his brother the Duke of York, who had taken Sterne up socially after the success of the first volumes of *Tristram Shandy*. The name Trismegistus ("thrice-greatest") was given by the Greeks to the Egyptian god Thoth, who was associated with all knowledge and mysterious wisdom.

Toby.——I thought, quoth my father, (rubbing his shin) you had known nothing of calculations, brother *Toby.*——'Twas a meer chance, said my uncle *Toby*——Then it adds one to the chapter ——replied my father.

The double success of my father's repartees tickled off the pain of his shin at once——it was well it so fell out——(chance! again) ——or the world to this day had never known the subject of my father's calculation——to guess it——there was no chance—— What a lucky chapter of chances has this turned out! for it has saved me the trouble of writing one express, and in truth I have enow[2] already upon my hands without it——Have not I promised the world a chapter of knots? two chapters upon the right and the wrong end of a woman? a chapter upon whiskers? a chapter upon wishes?——a chapter of noses?——No, I have done that——a chapter upon my uncle *Toby*'s modesty: to say nothing of a chapter upon chapters, which I will finish before I sleep——by my great grandfather's whiskers, I shall never get half of 'em through this year.

Take pen and ink in hand, and calculate it fairly, brother *Toby*, said my father, and it will turn out a million to one, that of all the parts of the body, the edge of the forceps should have the ill luck just to fall upon and break down that one part, which should break down the fortunes of our house with it.

It might have been worse, replied my uncle *Toby*——I don't comprehend, said my father——Suppose the hip had presented, replied my uncle *Toby*, as Dr. *Slop* foreboded.

My father reflected half a minute——looked down——touched the middle of his forehead slightly with his finger——

——True, said he.

Chapter X.

IS it not a shame to make two chapters of what passed in going down one pair of stairs? for we are got no farther yet than to the first landing, and there are fifteen more steps down to the bottom; and for aught I know, as my father and my uncle *Toby* are in a talking humour, there may be as many chapters as steps;——let that be as it will, Sir, I can no more help it than my destiny:——A sudden impulse comes across me——drop the curtain, *Shandy*—— I drop it——Strike a line here across the paper, *Tristram*——I strike it——and hey for a new chapter!

The duce of any other rule have I to govern myself by in this affair——and if I had one——as I do all things out of all rule——I

2. Enow, enough.

would twist it and tear it to pieces, and throw it into the fire when I had done———Am I warm? I am, and the cause demands it———a pretty story! is a man to follow rules———or rules to follow him?

Now this, you must know, being my chapter upon chapters, which I promised to write before I went to sleep, I thought it meet to ease my conscience entirely before I lay'd down, by telling the world all I knew about the matter at once: Is not this ten times better than to set out dogmatically with a sententious parade of wisdom, and telling the world a story of a roasted horse———that chapters relieve the mind———that they assist———or impose upon the imagination———and that in a work of this dramatic cast they are as necessary as the shifting of scenes———with fifty other cold conceits, enough to extinguish the fire which roasted him.———O! but to understand this, which is a puff at the fire of *Diana*'s[3] temple———you must read *Longinus*———read away———if you are not a jot the wiser by reading him the first time over———never fear———read him again———*Avicenna* and *Licetus*, read *Aristotle*'s metaphysicks forty times through a piece, and never understood a single word.———But mark the consequence———*Avicenna* turned out a desperate writer at all kinds of writing———for he wrote books *de omni scribili*; and for *Licetus* (*Fortunio*) though all the world knows he was born a fœtus,[4] of no more than five inches and a half

3. Diana, the coolly virginal goddess of the moon. In the treatise of the Greek Longinus, *On the Sublime*, coldness is one of the rhetorical failings described. Avicenna (980–1037), the great Arabian physician-philosopher, wrote books of many different subjects (*de omni scribili*). Licetus (1577–1657), an Italian physician, was called Fortunio after his good fortune in surviving a premature birth.

4. Ce Faetus n'étoit pas plus grand que la paume de la main; mais son pere l'ayant éxaminé en qualité de Médecin, & ayant trouvé que c'étoit quelque chose de plus qu'un Embryon, le fit transporter tout vivant à Rapallo, où il le fit voir à Jerôme Bardi & à d'autres Médecins du lieu. On trouva qu'il ne lui manquoit rien d'essentiel à la vie; & son pere pour faire voir de quelle éxpérience, entreprit d'achever l'ouvrage de la Nature, & de travailler à la formation de l'Enfant avec le même artifice que celui dont on se sert pour faire éclorre les Poulets en Egypte. Il instruisit une Nourrice de tout ce qu'elle avoit à faire, & ayant fait mettre son fils dans un four proprement accommodé, il reussit à l'élever et à lui faire prendre ses accroissemens nécessaires, par l'uniformité d'une chaleur étrangère mesurée éxàctement sur les dégrés d'un Thermomètre, ou d'un autre instrument équivalent. (Vide Mich.

Giustinian, ne gli Scritt. Liguri à Cart. 223.488.)

On auroit toujours été très satisfait de l'indusrie d'un Pere si expérimenté dans l'Art de la Génération, quand il n'auroit pû prolonger la vie à son fils que pour quelques mois, ou pour peu d'années. Mais quand on se represente que l'Enfant a vécu pres de quatre-vingts ans, & qu'il a composé quatre-vingts Ouvrages différents tous fruits d'une longue lecture,———il faut convenir que tout ce qui est incroyable n'est pas toujours faux, & que le Vraisemblance n'est pas toujours du côté de la Verité. Il n'avoit que dix-neuf ans lorsqu'il composa Gonopsychanthropologia de Origine Animae humanae. (Les Enfans celebres. revus & corrigés par M. De la Monnoye de l'Académie Francoise.) [*Sterne's note.*] This passage, taken from Baillet's *Des Enfans devenus celebres par leurs etudes et par leurs ecrits* [Children who have become Famous by their Studies and by their Writings], may be translated: "This foetus was no bigger than the palm of the hand; but its father having examined it in his capacity of physician, and having found that it was something more than an embryo, had it carried living to Rapallo, where he showed it to Jerome Bardi and other physicians of the place. They found that it did not lack anything essential to life; and the father, to make

in length, yet he grew to that astonishing height in literature, as to write a book with a title as long as himself——the learned know I mean his *Gonopsychanthropologia,* upon the origin of the human soul.

So much for my chapter upon chapters, which I hold to be the best chapter in my whole work; and take my word, whoever reads it, is full as well employed, as in picking straws.

Chapter XI.

W E shall bring all things to rights, said my father, setting his foot upon the first step from the landing——This *Trismegistus,* continued my father, drawing his leg back, and turning to my uncle *Toby*——was the greatest (*Toby*) of all earthly beings——he was the greatest king——the greatest lawgiver—— the greatest philosopher——and the greatest priest——and engineer——said my uncle *Toby.*——

——In course, said my father.

Chapter XII.

___ A ND how does your mistress? cried my father, taking the same step over again from the landing, and calling to *Susannah,* whom he saw passing by the foot of the stairs with a huge pin-cushion in her hand——how does your mistress? As well, said *Susannah,* tripping by, but without looking up, as can be expected——What a fool am I! said my father, drawing his leg back again——let things be as they will, brother *Toby,* 'tis ever the precise answer——And how is the child, pray?——No answer. And where is doctor *Slop?* added my father, raising his voice aloud, and looking over the ballusters——*Susannah* was out of hearing.

Of all the riddles of a married life, said my father, crossing the landing, in order to set his back against the wall, whilst he pro-

---

a trial of his skill and experience, undertook to complete the work of Nature, and to work at the development of the infant with the same contrivance which serves to hatch chickens in Egypt: He instructed a nurse in all she had to do, and having placed his son in an oven properly arranged, he succeeded in raising him and in making him grow in the necessary way by the uniformity of an artificial heat measured exactly on the degrees of a thermometer, or of another equivalent instrument. (See Mich. Giustinian in the *Writers of Liguria,* 273.488.) People would always have been very satisfied with the industry of a father so experienced in the art of generation, if he had only been able to prolong the life of his son for a matter of a few months or years. But when one bears in mind that the infant lived for almost 80 years, and that he composed 80 different works which were all the products of a long course of reading, one is bound to agree that not everything which is unbelievable is always untrue, and that *apparent plausibility is not always on the side of truth.* He was only 19 years old when he composed *Gonopsychanthropologia, de Origine Animae humanae* [Greek and Latin for "the Origin of the Human Soul"]. (*Famous Children,* revised and corrected by M. De la Monnoye of the French Academy.)"

pounded it to my uncle *Toby*——of all the puzzling riddles, said he, in a marriage state,——of which you may trust me, brother *Toby*, there are more asses loads than all *Job*'s stock of asses could have carried[5]——there is not one that has more intricacies in it than this——that from the very moment the mistress of the house is brought to bed, every female in it, from my lady's gentlewoman down to the cinder-wench, becomes an inch taller for it; and give themselves more airs upon that single inch, than all their other inches put together.

I think rather, replied my uncle *Toby*, that 'tis we who sink an inch lower.——If I meet but a woman with child——I do it—— 'Tis a heavy tax upon that half of our fellow-creatures, brother *Shandy*, said my uncle *Toby*——'Tis a piteous burden upon 'em, continued he, shaking his head.——Yes, yes, 'tis a painful thing ——said my father, shaking his head too——but certainly since shaking of heads came into fashion, never did two heads shake together, in concert, from two such different springs.

God bless ⎫ 'em all————said my uncle *Toby* and my father,
Duce take ⎭ each to himself.

Chapter XIII.

HOLLA!——you chairman![6]——here's sixpence——do step into that bookseller's shop, and call me a *day-tall* critick. I am very willing to give any one of 'em a crown to help me with his tackling, to get my father and my uncle *Toby* off the stairs, and to put them to bed.——

——'Tis even high time; for except a short nap, which they both got whilst *Trim* was boring the jack-boots——and which, by the bye, did my father no sort of good upon the score of the bad hinge——they have not else shut their eyes, since nine hours before the time that doctor *Slop* was led into the back parlour in that dirty pickle by *Obadiah*.

Was every day of my life to be as busy a day as this,——and to take up,——truce——

I will not finish that sentence till I have made an observation upon the strange state of affairs between the reader and myself, just as things stand at present——an observation never applicable before to any one biographical writer since the creation of the world, but to myself——and I believe will never hold good to any other, until its final destruction——and therefore, for the very novelty of it alone, it must be worth your worships attending to.

5. See Job 1:3, 42:12 for the account of how his wealth (including his asses) increased after God had put him through his trials.

6. A sedan-chair carrier. A day-tall critic is one whose work is counted (talleyed) by the day—that is, by quantity not quality.

I am this month one whole year older than I was this time twelve-month; and having got, as you perceive, almost into the middle of my fourth volume——and no farther than to my first day's life—— 'tis demonstrative that I have three hundred and sixty-four days more life to write just now, than when I first set out; so that instead of advancing, as a common writer, in my work with what I have been doing at it——on the contrary, I am just thrown so many volumes back——was every day of my life to be as busy a day as this——And why not?——and the transactions and opinions of it to take up as much description——And for what reason should they be cut short? as at this rate I should just live 364 times faster than I should write——It must follow, an' please your worships, that the more I write, the more I shall have to write——and consequently, the more your worships read, the more your worships will have to read.

Will this be good for your worships eyes?

It will do well for mine; and, was it not that my OPINIONS will be the death of me, I perceive I shall lead a fine life of it out of this self-same life of mine; or, in other words, shall lead a couple of fine lives together.

As for the proposal of twelve volumes a year, or a volume a month, it no way alters my prospect——write as I will, and rush as I may into the middle of things, as *Horace* advises,[7]——I shall never overtake myself——whipp'd and driven to the last pinch, at the worst I shall have one day the start of my pen——and one day is enough for two volumes——and two volumes will be enough for one year.——

Heaven prosper the manufactures of paper under this propitious reign, which is now open'd to us,——as I trust its providence will prosper every thing else in it that is taken in hand.——

As for the propagation of Geese[8]——I give myself no concern ——Nature is all bountiful——I shall never want tools to work with.

——So then, friend! you have got my father and my uncle *Toby* off the stairs, and seen them to bed?——And how did you manage it?——You dropp'd a curtain at the stairs foot——I thought you had no other way for it——Here's a crown for your trouble.

Chapter XIV.

THEN reach me my breeches off the chair, said my father to *Susannah*——There is not a moment's time to dress you, Sir, cried *Susannah*——the child is as black in the face as my——As

---

7. Tristram discussed Horace's advice in Vol. I, Chap. iv.
8. For quill pens.

your, what? said my father, for like all orators, he was a dear searcher into comparisons——Bless me, Sir, said *Susannah*, the child's in a fit——And where's Mr. *Yorick*——Never where he should be, said *Susannah*, but his curate's in the dressing-room, with the child upon his arm, waiting for the name——and my mistress bid me run as fast as I could to know, as captain *Shandy* is the godfather, whether it should not be called after him.

Were one sure, said my father to himself, scratching his eye-brow, that the child was expiring, one might as well compliment my brother *Toby* as not——and 'twould be a pity, in such a case, to throw away so great a name as *Trismegistus* upon him——But he may recover.

No, no,——said my father to *Susannah*, I'll get up——There is no time, cried *Susannah*, the child's as black as my shoe. *Trismegistus*, said my father——But stay——thou art a leaky vessel, *Susannah*, added my father; canst thou carry *Trismegistus* in thy head, the length of the gallery without scattering——Can I? cried *Susannah*, shutting the door in a huff——If she can, I'll be shot, said my father, bouncing out of bed in the dark, and groping for his breeches.

Susannah ran with all speed along the gallery.

My father made all possible speed to find his breeches.

Susannah got the start, and kept it——'Tis *Tris*——something, cried *Susannah*——There is no christian name in the world, said the curate, beginning with *Tris*——but *Tristram*. Then 'tis *Tristram-gistus*, quoth *Susannah*.

——There is no *gistus* to it, noodle!——'tis my own name, re-plied the curate, dipping his hand as he spoke into the bason—— *Tristram!* said he, &c. &c. &c. &c. so *Tristram* was I called, and *Tristram* shall I be to the day of my death.

My father followed *Susannah* with his night-gown across his arm, with nothing more than his breeches on, fastened through haste with but a single button, and that button through haste thrust only half into the button-hole.

——She has not forgot the name, cried my father, half opening the door——No, no, said the curate, with a tone of intelligence ——And the child is better, cried *Susannah*——And how does your mistress? As well, said *Susannah*, as can be expected——Pish! said my father, the button of his breeches slipping out of the button-hole——So that whether the interjection was levelled at *Susannah*, or the button-hole,——whether pish was an interjection of con-tempt or an interjection of modesty, is a doubt, and must be a doubt till I shall have time to write the three following favorite chapters, that is, my chapter of *chamber-maids*——my chapter of *pishes*, and my chapter of *button-holes*.

W. Hogarth inv.ᵗ   F. Ravenet sculp.

All the light I am able to give the reader at present is this, that the moment my father cried Pish! he whisk'd himself about——and with his breeches held up by one hand, and his night-gown thrown across the arm of the other, he returned along the gallery to bed, something slower than he came.

Chapter XV.

I Wish I could write a chapter upon sleep.

A fitter occasion could never have presented itself, than what this moment offers, when all the curtains of the family are drawn ——the candles put out——and no creature's eyes are open but a single one, for the other has been shut these twenty years, of my mother's nurse.

It is a fine subject!

And yet, as fine as it is, I would undertake to write a dozen chapters upon button-holes, both quicker and with more fame than a single chapter upon this.

Button-holes!——there is something lively in the very idea of 'em ——and trust me, when I get amongst 'em——You gentry with great beards——look as grave as you will——I'll make merry work with my button-holes——I shall have 'em all to myself——'tis a maiden subject——I shall run foul of no man's wisdom or fine sayings in it.

But for sleep——I know I shall make nothing of it before I begin——I am no dab at your fine sayings in the first place——and in the next, I cannot for my soul set a grave face upon a bad matter, and tell the world——'tis the refuge of the unfortunate——the enfranchisement of the prisoner——the downy lap of the hopeless, the weary and the broken-hearted; nor could I set out with a lye in my mouth, by affirming, that of all the soft and delicious functions of our nature, by which the great Author of it, in his bounty, has been pleased to recompence the sufferings wherewith his justice and his good pleasure has wearied us,——that this is the chiefest (I know pleasures worth ten of it) or what a happiness it is to man, when the anxieties and passions of the day are over, and he lays down upon his back, that his soul shall be so seated within him, that which ever way she turns her eyes, the heavens shall look calm and sweet above her——no desire——or fear——or doubt that troubles the air, nor any difficulty pass'd, present, or to come, that the imagination may not pass over without offence, in that sweet secession.

——"God's blessing, said *Sancho Panca*, be upon the man who first invented this self-same thing called sleep——it covers a man all over like a cloak."[9] Now there is more to me in this, and it speaks warmer to my heart and affections, than all the dissertations squeez'd out of the heads of the learned together upon the subject.

——Not that I altogether disapprove of what *Montaigne* advances upon it——'tis admirable in its way.——(I quote by memory.)[1]

The world enjoys other pleasures, says he, as they do that of sleep, without tasting or feeling it as it slips and passes by——We should study and ruminate upon it, in order to render proper thanks to him who grants it to us——for this end I cause myself to be disturbed in my sleep, that I may the better and more sensibly relish it——And yet I see few, says he again, who live with less sleep when need requires; my body is capable of a firm, but not of a violent and sudden agitation——I evade of late all violent exercises ——I am never weary with walking——but from my youth, I never liked to ride upon pavements. I love to lie hard and alone, and even without my wife——This last word may stagger the faith of the world——but remember, "La Vraisemblance (as *Baylet* says in the affair of *Liceti*) n'est pas toujours du Côté de la Verité."[2] And so much for sleep.

Chapter XVI.

IF my wife will but venture him——brother *Toby, Trismegistus* shall be dress'd and brought down to us, whilst you and I are getting our breakfasts together.——

——Go, tell *Susannah, Obadiah,* to step here.

She is run up stairs, answered *Obadiah,* this very instant, sobbing and crying, and wringing her hands as if her heart would break.——

We shall have a rare month of it, said my father, turning his head from *Obadiah,* and looking wistfully in my uncle *Toby's* face for some time——we shall have a devilish month of it, brother *Toby,* said my father, setting his arms a-kimbo, and shaking his head; fire, water, women, wind——brother *Toby!*——'Tis some misfortune, quoth my uncle *Toby*——That it is, cried my father,——to have so many jarring elements breaking loose, and riding triumph in every corner of a gentleman's house——Little boots it to the peace of a family, brother *Toby,* that you and I possess ourselves, and sit here silent and unmoved,——whilst such a storm is whistling over our heads.——

——And what's the matter, *Susannah?* They have called the

9. The allusion is to *Don Quixote,* II.iv. 68.
1. The passage is loosely quoted from Montaigne's essay "Of Experience."

2. The reference is to the note Sterne just provided on Licetus: "What appears real isn't always on the side of truth."

child *Tristram*———and my mistress is just got out of an hysterick fit about it———No!———'tis not my fault, said *Susannah*———I told him it was *Tristram-gistus*.

———Make tea for yourself, brother *Toby*, said my father, taking down his hat———but how different from the sallies and agitations of voice and members which a common reader would imagine!

———For he spake in the sweetest modulation———and took down his hat with the gentlest movement of limbs, that ever affliction harmonized and attuned together.

———Go to the bowling-green for corporal *Trim*, said my uncle *Toby*, speaking to *Obadiah*, as soon as my father left the room.

Chapter XVII.

WHEN the misfortune of my NOSE fell so heavily upon my father's head,———the reader remembers that he walked instantly up stairs, and cast himself down upon his bed; and from hence, unless he has a great insight into human nature, he will be apt to expect a rotation of the same ascending and descending movements from him, upon this misfortune of my NAME;———no.

The different weight, dear Sir,———nay even the different package of two vexations of the same weight,———makes a very wide difference in our manners of bearing and getting through with them.——— It is not half an hour ago, when (in the great hurry and precipitation of a poor devil's writing for daily bread) I threw a fair sheet, which I had just finished, and carefully wrote out, slap into the fire, instead of the foul one.

Instantly I snatch'd off my wig, and threw it perpendicularly, with all imaginable violence, up to the top of the room———indeed I caught it as it fell———but there was an end of the matter; nor do I think any thing else in *Nature*, would have given such immediate ease: She, dear Goddess, by an instantaneous impulse, in all *provoking cases*, determines us to a sally of this or that member———or else she thrusts us into this or that place, or posture of body, we know not why———But mark, madam, we live amongst riddles and mysteries———the most obvious things, which come in our way, have dark sides, which the quickest sight cannot penetrate into; and even the clearest and most exalted understandings amongst us find ourselves puzzled and at a loss in almost every cranny of nature's works; so that this, like a thousand other things, falls out for us in a way, which tho' we cannot reason upon it,———yet we find the good of it, may it please your reverences and your worships———and that's enough for us.

Now, my father could not lie down with this affliction for his life——nor could he carry it up stairs like the other——He walked composedly out with it to the fish-pond.

Had my father leaned his head upon his hand, and reasoned an hour which way to have gone——reason, with all her force, could not have directed him to any thing like it: there is something, Sir, in fish-ponds——but what it is, I leave to system builders and fish pond diggers betwixt 'em to find out——but there is something, under the first disorderly transport of the humours, so unaccountably becalming in an orderly and a sober walk towards one of them, that I have often wondered that neither *Pythagoras*, nor *Plato*, nor *Solon*, nor *Licurgus*, nor *Mahomet*, nor any of your noted lawgivers, ever gave order about them.[3]

Chapter XVIII.

YOUR honour, said *Trim*, shutting the parlour door before he began to speak, has heard, I imagine, of this unlucky accident ——O yes, *Trim*! said my uncle *Toby*, and it gives me great concern——I am heartily concerned too, but I hope your honour, replied *Trim*, will do me the justice to believe, that it was not in the least owing to me——To thee——*Trim*!——cried my uncle *Toby*, looking kindly in his face——'twas *Susannah's* and the curate's folly betwixt them——What business could they have together, an' please your honour, in the garden?——In the gallery, thou meanest, replied my uncle *Toby*.

Trim found he was upon a wrong scent, and stopped short with a low bow——Two misfortunes, quoth the corporal to himself, are twice as many at least as are needful to be talked over at one time,——the mischief the cow has done in breaking into the fortifications, may be told his honour hereafter——*Trim's* casuistry and address, under the cover of his low bow, prevented all suspicion in my uncle *Toby*, so he went on with what he had to say to *Trim* as follows.

——For my own part, *Trim*, though I can see little or no difference betwixt my nephew's being called *Tristram* or *Trismegistus*——yet as the thing sits so near my brother's heart, *Trim*, ——I would freely have given a hundred pounds rather than it should have happened——A hundred pounds, an' please your honour, replied *Trim*, ——I would not give a cherry-stone to boot ——Nor would I, *Trim*, upon my own account, quoth my uncle *Toby*——but my brother, whom there is no arguing with in this case——maintains that a great deal more depends, *Trim*, upon

---

3. These men are most famous as philosophers, statesmen, and religious leaders, but they also wrote on the law.

christian names, than what ignorant people imagine;——for he says there never was a great or heroic action performed since the world began by one called *Tristram*——nay he will have it, *Trim*, that a man can neither be learned, or wise, or brave——'Tis all a fancy, an' please your honour——I fought just as well, replied the corporal, when the regiment called me *Trim*, as when they called me *James Butler*——And for my own part, said my uncle *Toby*, though I should blush to boast of myself, *Trim*,——yet had my name been *Alexander*,[4] I could have done no more at *Namur* than my duty——Bless your honour! cried *Trim*, advancing three steps as he spoke, does a man think of his christian name when he goes upon the attack?——Or when he stands in the trench, *Trim*? cried my uncle *Toby*, looking firm——Or when he enters a breach? said *Trim*, pushing in between two chairs——Or forces the lines? cried my uncle, rising up, and pushing his crutch like a pike——Or facing a platoon, cried *Trim*, presenting his stick like a firelock—— Or when he marches up the glacis, cried my uncle *Toby*, looking warm and setting his foot upon his stool.——

Chapter XIX.

MY father was returned from his walk to the fish-pond—— and opened the parlour-door in the very height of the attack, just as my uncle *Toby* was marching up the glacis——*Trim* recovered his arms——never was my uncle *Toby* caught riding at such a desperate rate in his life! Alas! my uncle *Toby*! had not a weightier matter called forth all the ready eloquence of my father ——how hadst thou then and thy poor HOBBY-HORSE too have been insulted!

My father hung up his hat with the same air he took it down; and after giving a slight look at the disorder of the room, he took hold of one of the chairs which had formed the corporal's breach, and placing it over-against my uncle *Toby*, he sat down in it, and as soon as the tea-things were taken away and the door shut, he broke out in a lamentation as follows.

MY FATHER'S LAMENTATION

IT is in vain longer, said my father, addressing himself as much to *Ernulphus's* curse, which was laid upon the corner of the chimney-piece,——as to my uncle *Toby* who sat under it——it is in vain longer, said my father, in the most querulous monotone imaginable, to struggle as I have done against this most uncom-

4. That is, Alexander the Great, who conquered the known world.

fortable of human persuasions——I see it plainly, that either for my own sins, brother *Toby*, or the sins and follies of the *Shandy*-family, heaven has thought fit to draw forth the heaviest of its artillery against me; and that the prosperity of my child is the point upon which the whole force of it is directed to play——Such a thing would batter the whole universe about our ears, brother *Shandy*, said my uncle *Toby*,——if it was so——Unhappy *Tristram*! child of wrath! child of decrepitude! interruption! mistake! and discontent! What one misfortune or disaster in the book of embryotic evils, that could unmechanize thy frame, or entangle thy filaments! which has not fallen upon thy head, or ever thou camest into the world——what evils in thy passage into it!——What evils since!——produced into being, in the decline of thy father's days ——when the powers of his imagination and of his body were waxing feeble——when radical heat and radical moisture,[5] the elements which should have temper'd thine, were drying up; and nothing left to found thy stamina in, but negations——'tis pitiful——brother *Toby*, at the best, and called out for all the little helps that care and attention on both sides could give it. But how were we defeated! You know the event, brother *Toby*,——'tis too melancholy a one to be repeated now,——when the few animal spirits[6] I was worth in the world, and with which memory, fancy, and quick parts should have been convey'd,——were all dispersed, confused, confounded, scattered, and sent to the devil.——

Here then was the time to have put a stop to this persecution against him;——and tried an experiment at least——whether calmness and serenity of mind in your sister, with a due attention, brother *Toby*, to her evacuations and repletions——and the rest of her non-naturals,[7] might not, in a course of nine months gestation, have set all things to rights.——My child was bereft of these!—— What a teazing life did she lead herself, and consequently her fœtus too, with that nonsensical anxiety of hers about lying in in town? I thought my sister submitted with the greatest patience, replied my uncle *Toby*——I never heard her utter one fretful word about it——She fumed inwardly, cried my father; and that, let me tell you, brother, was ten times worse for the child——and then! what battles did she fight with me, and what perpetual storms about the midwife——There she gave vent, said my uncle *Toby*——Vent! cried my father, looking up——

But what was all this, my dear *Toby*, to the injuries done us by my child's coming head foremost into the world, when all I wished

---

5. Basic heat and moisture.
6. The animal spirits, passing through the nerves, were thought to provide energy for the faculties Walter names.
7. Air, food and drink, sleep and waking, motion and rest, excretion and retention, affections of mind—six things seen by physicians as vital to life, but "non-natural" because they can become sources of disease.

in this general wreck of his frame, was to have saved this little casket unbroke, unrifled——

With all my precautions, how was my system turned topside turvy in the womb with my child! his head exposed to the hand of violence, and a pressure of 470 pounds averdupois weight acting so perpendicularly upon its apex——that at this hour 'tis ninety *per Cent.* insurance, that the fine network of the intellectual web be not rent and torn to a thousand tatters.

——Still we could have done.——Fool, coxcomb, puppy—— give him but a NOSE——Cripple, Dwarf, Driviller, Goosecap—— (shape him as you will) the door of Fortune stands open——O *Licetus! Licetus!* had I been blest with a fœtus five inches long and a half, like thee——fate might have done her worst.

Still, brother *Toby*, there was one cast of the dye left for our child after all——O *Tristram! Tristram! Tristram!*

We will send for Mr. *Yorick*, said my uncle *Toby*.

——You may send for whom you will, replied my father.

Chapter XX.

WHAT a rate have I gone on at, curvetting and frisking it away, two up and two down for four volumes together, without looking once behind, or even on one side of me, to see whom I trod upon!——I'll tread upon no one,——quoth I to my-self when I mounted——I'll take a good rattling gallop; but I'll not hurt the poorest jack-ass upon the road——So off I set——up one lane——down another, through this turn-pike——over that, as if the arch-jockey of jockeys had got behind me.

Now ride at this rate with what good intention and resolution you may,——'tis a million to one you'll do some one a mischief, if not yourself——He's flung——he's off——he's lost his seat——he's down——he'll break his neck——see!——if he has not galloped full amongst the scaffolding of the undertaking[8] criticks!——he'll knock his brains out against some of their posts——he's bounced out!——look——he's now riding like a madcap full tilt through a whole crowd of painters, fiddlers, poets, biographers, physicians, lawyers, logicians, players, schoolmen, churchmen, statesmen, sol-diers, casuists, connoisseurs, prelates, popes, and engineers—— Don't fear, said I——I'll not hurt the poorest jack-ass upon the king's high-way——But your horse throws dirt; see you've splash'd a bishop[9]——I hope in God, 'twas only *Ernulphus*, said I——But

---

8. Ambitious—or interfering.
9. The Bishop of Gloucester, William Warburton, was for a time Sterne's friend and patron, but the relationship cooled when the Bishop offered literary advice that the author ignored.

you have squirted full in the faces of Mess. *Le Moyne, De Romigny,* and *De Marcilly,* doctors of the Sorbonne——That was last year, replied I——But you have trod this moment upon a king.—— Kings have bad times on't, said I, to be trod upon by such people as me.

You have done it, replied my accuser.

I deny it, quoth I, and so have got off, and here am I standing with my bridle in one hand, and with my cap in the other, to tell my story——And what is it? You shall hear in the next chapter.

Chapter XXI.

A S *Francis* the first of *France* was one winterly night warming himself over the embers of a wood fire, and talking with his first minister of sundry things for the good of the state[1]——it would not be amiss, said the king, stirring up the embers with his cane, if this good understanding betwixt ourselves and *Switzerland* was a little strengthened——There is no end, Sire, replied the minister, in giving money to these people——they would swallow up the treasury of *France*——Poo! poo! answered the king——there are more ways, Mons. *le Premier*, of bribing states, besides that of giving money——I'll pay *Switzerland* the honour of standing god-father for my next child——Your majesty, said the minister, in so doing, would have all the grammarians in *Europe* upon your back; ——*Switzerland*, as a republick, being a female, can in no construction be godfather——She may be godmother, replied *Francis,* hastily——so announce my intentions by a courier to morrow morning.

I am astonished, said *Francis* the First, (that day fortnight) speaking to his minister as he entered the closet, that we have had no answer from *Switzerland*——Sire, I wait upon you this moment, said Mons. *le Premier*, to lay before you my dispatches upon that business.——They take it kindly? said the king——They do, Sire, replied the minister, and have the highest sense of the honour your majesty has done them——but the republick, as godmother, claims her right in this case, of naming the child.

In all reason, quoth the king——she will christen him *Francis*, or *Henry*, or *Louis*, or some name that she knows will be agreeable to us. Your majesty is deceived, replied the minister——I have this hour received a dispatch from our resident, with the determination of the republick on that point also——And what name has the

---

1. Vide Menagiana, vol. I. [*Sterne's note.* It refers to the collected opinions of Gilles Ménage, a seventeenth-century French philologist, from which the following anecdote is drawn.]

republick fixed upon for the Dauphin?[2]——*Shadrach, Mesech,* and *Abed-nego,* replied the minister——By saint *Peter's* girdle, I will have nothing to do with the *Swiss,* cried *Francis* the First, pulling up his breeches and walking hastily across the floor.

Your majesty, replied the minister calmly, cannot bring yourself off.

We'll pay them in money——said the king.

Sire, there are not sixty thousand crowns in the treasury, answered the minister——I'll pawn the best jewel in my crown, quoth *Francis* the First.

Your honour stands pawn'd already in this matter, answered Monsieur *le Premier.*

Then, Mons. *le Premier,* said the king, by——we'll go to war with 'em.

Chapter XXII.

ALBEIT, gentle reader, I have lusted earnestly, and endeavoured carefully (according to the measure of such slender skill as God has vouchsafed me, and as convenient leisure from other occasions of needful profit and healthful pastime have permitted) that these little books, which I here put into thy hands, might stand instead of many bigger books——yet have I carried myself towards thee in such fanciful guise of careless disport, that right sore am I ashamed now to entreat thy lenity seriously——in beseeching thee to believe it of me, that in the story of my father and his christennames,——I had no thoughts of treading upon *Francis* the First ——nor in the affair of the nose——upon *Francis* the Ninth[3]—— nor in the character of my uncle *Toby*——of characterizing the militiating spirits of my country——the wound upon his groin, is a wound to every comparison of that kind,——nor by *Trim,*——that I meant the duke of Ormond[4]——or that my book is wrote against predestination, or free will, or taxes——If 'tis wrote against any thing,——'tis wrote, an' please your worships, against the spleen; in order, by a more frequent and a more convulsive elevation and depression of the diaphragm, and the succussations of the intercostal and abdominal muscles in laughter, to drive the *gall* and other *bitter juices* from the gall bladder, liver and sweet-bread of his majesty's subjects, with all the inimicitious passions which belong to them, down into their duodenums.

2. The traditional title of the heir to the French throne.
3. There was no Francis IX, as Sterne certainly knew; but Francis I had a large nose and probably died of syphilis, which traditionally attacks nasal tissue.
4. Since both Trim and the Duke were named James Butler, and since the Duke was a general, satire was suspected by many readers.

Chapter XXIII.

———B UT can the thing be undone, *Yorick?* said my father——— for in my opinion, continued he, it cannot. I am a vile canonist, replied *Yorick*———but of all evils, holding suspense to be the most tormenting, we shall at least know the worst of this matter. I hate these great dinners[5]———said my father———The size of the dinner is not the point, answered *Yorick*———we want, Mr. *Shandy,* to dive into the bottom of this doubt, whether the name can be changed or not———and as the beards of so many commissaries, officials, advocates, proctors, registers, and of the most able of our school-divines, and others, are all to meet in the middle of one table, and *Didius* has so pressingly invited you,———who in your distress would miss such an occasion? All that is requisite, continued *Yorick,* is to apprize *Didius,* and let him manage a conversation after dinner so as to introduce the subject———Then my brother *Toby,* cried my father, clapping his two hands together, shall go with us.

———Let my old tye wig, quoth my uncle *Toby,* and my laced regimentals, be hung to the fire all night, *Trim.*

Chapter XXV.

———N O doubt, Sir———there is a whole chapter wanting here ———and a chasm of ten pages made in the book by it ———but the book-binder is neither a fool, or a knave, or a puppy ———nor is the book a jot more imperfect, (at least upon that score)———but, on the contrary, the book is more perfect and complete by wanting the chapter, than having it, as I shall demonstrate to your reverences in this manner———I question first by the bye, whether the same experiment might not be made as successfully upon sundry other chapters———but there is no end, an' please your reverences, in trying experiments upon chapters———we have had enough of it———So there's an end of that matter.

But before I begin my demonstration, let me only tell you, that the chapter which I have torn out, and which otherwise you would all have been reading just now, instead of this,———was the description of my father's, my uncle *Toby's,* *Trim's,* and *Obadiah's* setting out and journeying to the visitations at ****.

We'll go in the coach, said my father———Prithee, have the arms been altered, *Obadiah?*———It would have made my story much

---

5. The bishop of a diocese makes annual visitations to the parishes; Walter and Yorick have been invited to a visitation dinner, by Dedius the Canon lawyer, which can provide occasion for consulting about the possibility of rebaptising Tristram.

better, to have begun with telling you, that at the time my mother's arms were added to the *Shandy's*, when the coach was repainted upon my father's marriage, it had so fallen out, that the coach-painter, whether by performing all his works with the left-hand, like *Turpilius* the *Roman*, or *Hans Holbein* of *Basil*——or whether 'twas more from the blunder of his head than hand——or whether, lastly, it was from the sinister turn, which every thing relating to our family was apt to take——It so fell out, however, to our re-proach, that instead of the *bend dexter*,[6] which since *Harry* the Eighth's reign was honestly our due——a *bend sinister*, by some of these fatalities, had been drawn quite across the field of the *Shandy*-arms. 'Tis scarce credible that the mind of so wise a man as my father was, could be so much incommoded with so small a matter. The word coach——let it be whose it would——or coach-man, or coach-horse, or coach-hire, could never be named in the family, but he constantly complained of carrying this vile mark of Illegitimacy upon the door of his own; he never once was able to step into the coach, or out of it, without turning round to take a view of the arms, and making a vow at the same time, that it was the last time he would ever set his foot in it again, till the *bend-sinister* was taken out——but like the affair of the hinge, it was one of the many things which the *Destinies* had set down in their books——ever to be grumbled at (and in wiser families than ours)——but never to be mended.

——Has the *bend-sinister* been brush'd out, I say? said my father ——There has been nothing brush'd out, Sir, answered *Obadiah*, but the lining. We'll go o'horse-back, said my father, turning to *Yorick*——Of all things in the world, except politicks, the clergy know the least of heraldry, said *Yorick*——No matter for that, cried my father——I should be sorry to appear with a blot in my escutcheon before them——Never mind the *bend-sinister*, said my uncle *Toby*, putting on his tye-wig——No, indeed, said my father, ——you may go with my aunt *Dinah* to a visitation with a *bend-sinister*, if you think fit——My poor uncle *Toby* blush'd. My father was vexed at himself——No——my dear brother *Toby*, said my father, changing his tone——but the damp of the coach-lining about my loins, may give me the Sciatica again, as it did *December*, *January*, and *February* last winter——so if you please you shall ride my wife's pad——and as you are to preach, *Yorick*, you had better make the best of your way before,——and leave me to take care of my brother *Toby*, and to follow at our own rates.

Now the chapter I was obliged to tear out, was the description of

6. A band across a coat of arms from top right (*dexter*) to lower left; a band from top left (*sinister*) could be used to show that the bearer of the shield was illegitimate, or descended from an illegitimate branch of the family.

this cavalcade, in which Corporal *Trim* and *Obadiah,* upon two coach-horses a-breast, led the way as slow as a patrole——whilst my uncle *Toby,* in his laced regimentals and tye-wig, kept his rank with my father, in deep roads and dissertations alternately upon the advantage of learning and arms, as each could get the start.

——But the painting of this journey, upon reviewing it, appears to be so much above the stile and manner of any thing else I have been able to paint in this book, that it could not have remained in it, without depreciating every other scene; and destroying at the same time that necessary equipoise and balance, (whether of good or bad) betwixt chapter and chapter, from whence the just proportions and harmony of the whole work results. For my own part, I am but just set up in the business, so know little about it——but, in my opinion, to write a book is for all the world like humming a song——be but in tune with yourself, madam, 'tis no matter how high or how low you take it.

——This is the reason, may it please your reverences, that some of the lowest and flattest compositions pass off very well——(as *Yorick* told my uncle *Toby* one night) by siege——My uncle *Toby* looked brisk at the sound of the word *siege,* but could make neither head or tail of it.

I'm to preach at court next Sunday, said *Homenas*[7]——run over my notes——so I humm'd over doctor *Homenas's* notes——the modulation's very well—'twill do, *Homenas,* if it holds on at this rate——so on I humm'd——and a tolerable tune I thought it was; and to this hour, may it please your reverences, had never found out how low, how flat, how spiritless and jejune it was, but that all of a sudden, up started an air in the middle of it, so fine, so rich, so heavenly——it carried my soul up with it into the other world; now had I, (as *Montaigne* complained in a parallel accident[8])——had I found the declivity easy, or the ascent accessible——certes I had been outwitted——Your notes, *Homenas,* I should have said, are good notes,——but it was so perpendicular a precipice——so wholly cut off from the rest of the work, that by the first note I humm'd, I found myself flying into the other world, and from thence discovered the vale from whence I came, so deep, so low, and dismal, that I shall never have the heart to descend into it again.

☞ A dwarf who brings a standard along with him to measure his own size——take my word, is a dwarf in more articles than one——And so much for tearing out of chapters.

---

7. *Homenas* means homilist (preacher) and was the name of a Bishop in Rabelais, IV.48–54.

8. In the essay "Of the Education of Children."

Chapter XXVI.

——— SEE if he is not cutting it all into slips, and giving them about him to light their pipes!———'Tis abominable, answered *Didius*; it should not go unnoticed, said doctor *Kysarcius* ———☞ he was of the *Kysarcij* of the low countries.

Methinks, said *Didius* half rising from his chair, in order to remove a bottle and a tall decanter, which stood in a direct line betwixt him and *Yorick*———you might have spared this sarcastick stroke, and have hit upon a more proper place, Mr. *Yorick*———or at least upon a more proper occasion to have shewn your contempt of what we have been about: If the Sermon is of no better worth than to light pipes with———'twas certainly, Sir, not good enough to be preached before so learned a body; and if 'twas good enough to be preached before so learned a body———'twas certainly, Sir, too good to light their pipes with afterwards.

———I have got him fast hung up, quoth *Didius* to himself, upon one of the two horns of my dilemma—let him get off as he can.

I have undergone such unspeakable torments, in bringing forth this sermon, quoth *Yorick*, upon this occasion,———that I declare, *Didius*, I would suffer martyrdom———and if it was possible my horse with me, a thousand times over, before I would sit down and make such another: I was delivered of it at the wrong end of me———it came from my head instead of my heart———and it is for the pain it gave me, both in the writing and preaching of it, that I revenge myself of it, in this manner.———To preach, to shew the extent of our reading, or the subtleties of our wit———to parade it in the eyes of the vulgar with the beggarly accounts of a little learning, tinseled over with a few words which glitter, but convey little light and less warmth———is a dishonest use of the poor single half hour in a week which is put into our hands—'Tis not preaching the gospel———but ourselves———For my own part, continued *Yorick*, I had rather direct five words point blank to the heart———

As *Yorick* pronounced the word *point blank*, my uncle *Toby* rose up to say something upon projectiles———when a single word, and no more, uttered from the opposite side of the table, drew every one's ears towards it———a word of all others in the dictionary the last in that place to be expected———a word I am ashamed to write ———yet must be written———must be read;———illegal——— uncanonical———guess ten thousand guesses, multiplied into themselves———rack———torture your invention for ever, you're where you was———In short, I'll tell it in the next chapter.

Chapter XXVII.

Z OUNDS!⁹

————————————————Z——ds! cried *Phutatorius*, partly to himself——
and yet high enough to be heard——and what seemed odd, 'twas
uttered in a construction of look, and in a tone of voice, somewhat
between that of a man in amazement, and of one in bodily pain.

One or two who had very nice ears, and could distinguish the
expression and mixture of the two tones as plainly as a *third* or a
fifth, or any other chord in musick——were the most puzzled and
perplexed with it——the *concord* was good in itself——but then
'twas quite out of the key, and no way applicable to the subject
started;——so that with all their knowledge, they could not tell
what in the world to make of it.

Others who knew nothing of musical expression, and merely lent
their ears to the plain import of the *word*, imagined that *Phutatorius*, who was somewhat of a cholerick spirit, was just going to
snatch the cudgels out of *Didius*'s hands, in order to bemawl *Yorick*
to some purpose——and that the desperate monosyllable Z——ds
was the exordium to an oration, which, as they judged from the
sample, presaged but a rough kind of handling of him; so that my
uncle *Toby*'s good nature felt a pang for what *Yorick* was about to
undergo. But seeing *Phutatorius* stop short, without any attempt or
desire to go on——a third party began to suppose, that it was no
more than an involuntary respiration, casually forming itself into
the shape of a twelve-penny oath[1]——without the sin or substance
of one.

Others, and especially one or two who sat next him, looked upon
it on the contrary, as a real and substantial oath propensly formed
against *Yorick*, to whom he was known to bear no good liking——
which said oath, as my father philosophized upon it, actually lay
fretting and fuming at that very time in the upper regions of *Phutatorius*'s purtenance; and so was naturally, and according to the due
course of things, first squeezed out by the sudden influx of blood,
which was driven into the right ventricle of *Phutatorius*'s heart, by
the stroke of surprize which so strange a theory of preaching had
excited.

How finely we argue upon mistaken facts!

There was not a soul busied in all these various reasonings upon
the monosyllable which *Phutatorius* uttered,——who did not take
this for granted, proceeding upon it as from an axiom, namely, that

9. Short for "God's wounds."
1. Oaths were finable offenses under an
act of Parliament in the reign of George

II; a twelve-penny one was not very
serious.

Phutatorius's mind was intent upon the subject of debate which was arising between *Didius* and *Yorick*; and indeed as he looked first towards the one, and then towards the other, with the air of a man listening to what was going forwards,——who would not have thought the same? But the truth was, that *Phutatorius* knew not one word or one syllable of what was passing——but his whole thoughts and attention were taken up with a transaction which was going forwards at that very instant within the precincts of his own *Galligaskins*,[2] and in a part of them, where of all others he stood most interested to watch accidents: So that notwithstanding he looked with all the attention in the world, and had gradually skrewed up every nerve and muscle in his face, to the utmost pitch the instrument would bear, in order, as it was thought, to give a sharp reply to *Yorick*, who sat over-against him——Yet I say, was *Yorick* never once in any one domicile of *Phutatorius's* brain——but the true cause of his exclamation lay at least a yard below.

This I will endeavour to explain to you with all imaginable decency.

You must be informed then, that *Gastripheres*,[3] who had taken a turn into the kitchen a little before dinner, to see how things went on——observing a wicker-basket of fine chesnuts standing upon the dresser, had ordered that a hundred or two of them might be roasted and sent in, as soon as dinner was over——*Gastripheres* inforcing his orders about them, that *Didius*, but *Phutatorius* especially, were particularly fond of 'em.

About two minutes before the time that my uncle *Toby* interrupted *Yorick's* harangue——*Gastripheres's* chesnuts were brought in——and as *Phutatorius's* fondness for 'em, was uppermost in the waiter's head, he laid them directly before *Phutatorius*, wrapt up hot in a clean damask napkin.

Now whether it was physically impossible, with half a dozen hands all thrust into the napkin at a time——but that some one chesnut, of more life and rotundity than the rest, must be put in motion——it so fell out, however, that one was actually sent rolling off the table; and as *Phutatorius* sat straddling under——it fell perpendicularly into that particular aperture of *Phutatorius's* breeches, for which, to the shame and indelicacy of our language be it spoke, there is no chaste word throughout all *Johnson's* dictionary ——let it suffice to say——it was that particular aperture, which in all good societies, the laws of decorum do strictly require, like the temple of *Janus* (in peace at least) to be universally shut up.[4]

The neglect of this punctilio in *Phutatorius* (which by the bye

2. Breeches.
3. The "paunch-carrier"—as always, interested in food.

4. The temple of Janus, an ancient god who guarded Rome in time of war, opened only in times of military action.

should be a warning to all mankind) had opened a door to this accident.——

——Accident, I call it, in compliance to a received mode of speaking,———but in no opposition to the opinion either of *Acrites*[5] or *Mythogeras* in this matter; I know they were both prepossessed and fully persuaded of it——and are so to this hour, That there was nothing of accident in the whole event——but that the chesnut's taking that particular course, and in a manner of its own accord——and then falling with all its heat directly into that one particular place, and no other——was a real judgment upon *Phutatorius*, for that filthy and obscene treatise *de Concubinis retinendis*,[6] which *Phutatorius* had published about twenty years ago——and was that identical week going to give the world a second edition of.

It is not my business to dip my pen in this controversy——much undoubtedly may be wrote on both sides of the question——all that concerns me as an historian, is to represent the matter of fact, and render it credible to the reader, that the hiatus in *Phutatorius*'s breeches was sufficiently wide to receive the chesnut;——and that the chesnut, some how or other, did fall perpendicularly and piping hot into it, without *Phutatorius*'s perceiving it, or any one else at that time.

The genial warmth which the chesnut imparted, was not undelectable for the first twenty or five and twenty seconds,——and did no more than gently solicit *Phutatorius*'s attention towards the part:———But the heat gradually increasing, and in a few seconds more getting beyond the point of all sober pleasure, and then advancing with all speed into the regions of pain,——the soul of *Phutatorius*, together with all his ideas, his thoughts, his attention, his imagination, judgment, resolution, deliberation, ratiocination, memory, fancy, with ten batallions of animal spirits, all tumultuously crouded down, through different defiles and circuits, to the place in danger, leaving all his upper regions, as you may imagine, as empty as my purse.

With the best intelligence which all these messengers could bring him back, *Phutatorius* was not able to dive into the secret of what was going forwards below, nor could he make any kind of conjecture, what the devil was the matter with it: However, as he knew not what the true cause might turn out, he deemed it most prudent, in the situation he was in at present, to bear it, if possible, like a stoick; which, with the help of some wry faces and compursions of the mouth, he had certainly accomplished, had his imagination continued neuter——but the sallies of the imagination are ungov-

5. An undiscerning person. *Mythogeras*: Story-carrier.
6. *Of Keeping Concubines*.

ernable in things of this kind——a thought instantly darted into his mind, that tho' the anguish had the sensation of glowing heat——it might, notwithstanding that, be a bite as well as a burn; and if so, that possibly a *Newt* or an *Asker*, or some such detested reptile, had crept up, and was fastening his teeth——the horrid idea of which, with a fresh glow of pain arising that instant from the chestnut, seized *Phutatorius* with a sudden panick, and in the first terrifying disorder of the pasion it threw him, as it has done the best generals upon earth, quite off his guard;——the effect of which was this, that he leapt incontinently up, uttering as he rose that interjection of surprise so much discanted upon, with the aposiopestick break after it, marked thus, Z——ds——which, though not strictly canonical, was still as little as any man could have said upon the occasion;——and which, by the bye, whether canonical or not, *Phutatorius* could no more help than he could the cause of it.

Though this has taken up some time in the narrative, it took up little more time in the transaction, than just to allow time for *Phutatorius* to draw forth the chestnut, and throw it down with violence upon the floor——and for *Yorick*, to rise from his chair, and pick the chestnut up.

It is curious to observe the triumph of slight incidents over the mind:——What incredible weight they have in forming and governing our opinions, both of men and things,——that trifles light as air, shall waft a belief into the soul, and plant it so immoveably within it,——that *Euclid's* demonstrations, could they be brought to batter it in breach, should not all have power to overthrow it.

Yorick, I said, picked up the chestnut which *Phutatorius's* wrath had flung down——the action was trifling——I am ashamed to account for it——he did it, for no reason, but that he thought the chestnut not a jot worse for the adventure——and that he held a good chestnut worth stooping for.——But this incident, trifling as it was, wrought differently in *Phutatorius's* head: He considered this act of *Yorick's*, in getting off his chair, and picking up the chestnut, as a plain acknowledgment in him, that the chestnut was originally his,——and in course, that it must have been the owner of the chestnut, and no one else, who could have plaid him such a prank with it: What greatly confirmed him in this opinion, was this, that the table being parallelogramical and very narrow, it afforded a fair opportunity for *Yorick*, who sat directly over-against *Phutatorius*, of slipping the chestnut in——and consequently that he did it. The look of something more than suspicion, which *Phutatorius* cast full upon *Yorick* as these thoughts arose, too evidently spoke his opinion——and as *Phutatorius* was naturally supposed to know more of the matter than any person besides, his opinion at once became the general one;——and for a reason very different from any which have been yet given——in a little time it was put out of all manner of dispute.

When great or unexpected events fall out upon the stage of this sublunary world——the mind of man, which is an inquisitive kind of a substance, naturally takes a flight, behind the scenes, to see what is the cause and first spring of them——The search was not long in this instance.

It was well known that *Yorick* had never a good opinion of the treatise which *Phutatorius* had wrote *de Concubinis retinendis*, as a thing which he feared had done hurt in the world——and 'twas easily found out, that there was a mystical meaning in *Yorick's* prank——and that his chucking the chesnut hot into *Phutatorius's* *** *****, was a sarcastical fling at his book——the doctrines of which, they said, had inflamed many an honest man in the same place.

This conceit awaken'd *Somnolentus*——made *Agelastes* smile ——and if you can recollect the precise look and air of a man's face intent in finding out a riddle——it threw *Gastripheres's* into that form——and in short was thought by many to be a master-stroke of arch-wit.

This, as the reader has seen from one end to the other, was as groundless as the dreams of philosophy: *Yorick*, no doubt, as *Shakespear* said of his ancestor———*"was a man of jest,"*[7] but it was temper'd with something which withheld him from that, and many other ungracious pranks, of which he as undeservedly bore the blame;——but it was his misfortune all his life long to bear the imputation of saying and doing a thousand things of which (unless my esteem blinds me) his nature was incapable. All I blame him for——or rather, all I blame and alternately like him for, was that singularity of his temper, which would never suffer him to take pains to set a story right with the world, however in his power. In every ill usage of that sort, he acted precisely as in the affair of his lean horse——he could have explained it to his honour, but his spirit was above it; and besides he ever looked upon the inventor, the propagator and believer of an illiberal report alike so injurious to him,——he could not stoop to tell his story to them——and so trusted to time and truth to do it for him.

This heroic cast produced him inconveniences in many respects ——in the present, it was followed by the fixed resentment of *Phutatorius*, who, as *Yorick* had just made an end of his chesnut, rose up from his chair a second time, to let him know it——which indeed he did with a smile; saying only——that he would endeavour not to forget the obligation.

---

7. Hamlet describes Yorick as "a fellow of infinite jest" (V.i.202).

But you must mark and carefully separate and distinguish these two things in your mind.

——The smile was for the company.

——The threat was for *Yorick*.

Chapter XXVIII.

——C AN you tell me, quoth *Phutatorius*, speaking to *Gas-tripheres* who sat next to him,——for one would not apply to a surgeon in so foolish an affair,——can you tell me, *Gastripheres*, what is best to take out the fire?——Ask *Eugenius*, said *Gastripheres*——That greatly depends, said *Eugenius*, pretending ignorance of the adventure, upon the nature of the part——If it is a tender part, and a part which can conveniently be wrapt up ——It is both the one and the other, replied *Phutatorius*, laying his hand as he spoke, with an emphatical nod of his head, upon the part in question, and lifting up his right leg at the same time to ease and ventilate it——If that is the case, said *Eugenius*, I would advise you, *Phutatorius*, not to tamper with it by any means; but if you will send to the next printer, and trust your cure to such a simple thing as a soft sheet of paper just come off the press——you need do nothing more than twist it round——The damp paper, quoth *Yorick* (who sat next to his friend *Eugenius*) though I know it has a refreshing coolness in it——yet I presume is no more than the vehicle——and that the oil and lamp-black with which the paper is so strongly impregnated, does the business——Right, said *Eugenius*, and is of any outward application I would venture to recommend the most anodyne and safe.

Was it my case, said *Gastripheres*, as the main thing is the oil and lamp-black, I should spread them thick upon a rag, and clap it on directly. That would make a very devil of it, replied *Yorick*——And besides, added *Eugenius*, it would not answer the intention, which is the extreame neatness and elegance of the prescription, which the faculty[8] hold to be half in half——for consider, if the type is a very small one, (which it should be) the sanative particles, which come into contact in this form, have the advantage of being spread so infinitely thin and with such a mathematical equality (fresh paragraphs and large capitals excepted) as no art or management of the spatula can come up to. It falls out very luckily, replied *Phutatorius*, that the second edition of my treatise *de Concubinis retinendis*, is at this instant in the press——You may take any leaf of it, said *Eugenius*——No matter which——provided, quoth *Yorick*, there is no bawdry in it——

---

8. That is, the medical faculty.

They are just now, replied *Phutatorius*, printing off the ninth chapter——which is the last chapter but one in the book——Pray what is the title to that chapter, said *Yorick*, making a respectful bow to *Phutatorius* as he spoke————I think, answered *Phutatorius*, 'tis that, *de re concubinariâ*.[9]

For heaven's sake keep out of that chapter, quoth *Yorick*.

——By all means——added *Eugenius*.

Chapter XXIX.

—— NOW, quoth *Didius*, rising up, and laying his right-hand with his fiingers spread upon his breast——had such a blunder about a christian-name happened before the reformation ————(It happened the day before yesterday, quoth my uncle *Toby* to himself) and when baptism was administer'd in *Latin*——('Twas all in *English*, said my uncle)————Many things might have coincided with it, and upon the authority of sundry decreed cases, to have pronounced the baptism null, with a power of giving the child a new name—Had a priest, for instance, which was no uncommon thing, through ignorance of the *Latin* tongue, baptized a child of Tom-o'Stiles, *in nomino patriæ & filia & spiritum sanctos*,[1]—— the baptism was held null——I beg your pardon, replied *Kysarcius*, ——in that case, as the mistake was only in the *terminations*, the baptism was valid——and to have rendered it null, the blunder of the priest should have fallen upon the first syllable of each noun ————and not, as in your case, upon the last.——

My father delighted in subtleties of this kind, and listen'd with infinite attention.

Gastripheres, for example, continued *Kysarcius*, baptizes a child of *John Stradling*'s in *Gomine* gatris, &c. &c. instead of *in Nomine patris*, &c.——Is this a baptism? No,——say the ablest canonists; inasmuch as the radix of each word is hereby torn up, and the sense and meaning of them removed and changed quite to another object; for *Gomine* does not signify a name, nor *gatris* a father——What do they signify? said my uncle *Toby*——Nothing at all——quoth *Yorick*————Ergo, such a baptism is null, said *Kysarcius*——In course, answered *Yorick*, in a tone two parts jest and one part earnest——

But in the case cited, continued *Kysarcius*, where *patrim* is put for *patris*, *filia* for *filij*, and so on——as it is a fault only in the declension, and the roots of the words continue untouch'd, the inflexions of their branches, either this way or that, does not in any

---

9. Of something concerning concubinage.
1. "In the name of the Father and of the Son and of the Holy Ghost," but with the wrong declensional endings in Latin.

sort hinder the baptism, inasmuch as the same sense continues in the words as before——But then, said *Didius*, the intention of the priest's pronouncing them grammatically, must have been proved to have gone along with it——Right, answered *Kysarcius*; and of this, brother *Didius*, we have an instance in a decree of the decretals of Pope *Leo* the IIId.[2]——But my brother's child, cried my uncle *Toby*, has nothing to do with the Pope——'tis the plain child of a Protestant gentleman, christen'd *Tristram* against the wills and wishes both of its father and mother, and all who are a-kin to it——

If the wills and wishes, said *Kysarcius*, interrupting my uncle *Toby*, of those only who stand related to Mr. *Shandy*'s child, were to have weight in this matter, Mrs. *Shandy*, of all people, has the least to do in it——My uncle *Toby* lay'd down his pipe, and my father drew his chair still closer to the table to hear the conclusion of so strange an introduction.

It has not only been a question, captain *Shandy*, amongst the[3] best lawyers and civilians in this land, continued *Kysarcius*, "Whether the mother be of kin to her child,"——but after much dispassionate enquiry and jactitation of the arguments on all sides, ——it has been adjudged for the negative,——namely, "That the mother is not of kin to her child."[4] My father instantly clapp'd his hand upon my uncle *Toby*'s mouth, under colour of whispering in his ear——the truth was, he was alarmed for *Lillabullero*——and having a great desire to hear more of so curious an argument——he begg'd my uncle *Toby*, for heaven's sake, not to disappoint him in it——My uncle *Toby* gave a nod——resumed his pipe, and contenting himself with whistling *Lillabullero* inwardly——*Kysarcius*, *Didius*, and *Triptolemus* went on with the discourse as follows.

This determination, continued *Kysarcius*, how contrary soever it may seem to run to the stream of vulgar ideas, yet had reason strongly on its side; and has been put out of all manner of dispute from the famous case, known commonly by the name of the Duke of *Suffolk*'s case:——It is cited in *Brook*, said *Triptolemus*—— And taken notice of by Lord *Coke*,[5] added *Didius*——And you may find it in *Swinburn* on Testaments, said *Kysarcius*.

The case, Mr. *Shandy*, was this.

In the reign of *Edward* the Sixth, *Charles* duke of *Suffolk* having issue a son by one venter, and a daughter by another venter, made his last will, wherein he devised goods to his son, and died; after

2. Probably Innocent III.

3. Vid. Swinburn on Testaments, Part 7. §8. [*Sterne's note.*] *A Treatise of Testaments and Last Wills* by Henry Swinburne provides the sixteenth-century law case that is described here.

4. Vid. Brook Abridg. Tit. Administr.

N. 47. [*Sterne's note.*] He refers to Sir Robert Broke, *La Graunde abridgement*, which is cited in Swinburne.

5. Sir Edward Coke (1552–1634), a legal theorist frequently and importantly cited in law cases.

whose death the son died also——but without will, without wife, and without child——his mother and his sister by the father's side (for she was born of the former venter) then living. The mother took the administration of her son's goods, according to the statute of the 21st of *Harry* the Eighth, whereby it is enacted, That in case any person die intestate, the administration of his goods shall be committed to the next of kin.

The administration being thus (surreptitiously) granted to the mother, the sister by the father's side commenced a suit before the Ecclesiastical Judge, alledging, 1st, That she herself was next of kin; and 2dly, That the mother was not of kin at all to the party deceased; and therefore pray'd the court, that the administration granted to the mother might be revoked, and be committed unto her, as next of kin to the deceased, by force of the said statute.

Hereupon, as it was a great cause, and much depending upon its issue——and many causes of great property likely to be decided in times to come, by the precedent to be then made——the most learned, as well in the laws of this realm, as in the civil law, were consulted together, whether the mother was of kin to her son, or no.——Whereunto not only the temporal lawyers—but the church-lawyers——the juris-consulti[6]——the juris-prudentes——the civilians——the advocates——the commissaries——the judges of the consistory and prerogative courts of *Canterbury* and *York*, with the master of the faculties, were all unanimously of opinion, That the mother was not of[7] kin to her child——

And what said the duchess of *Suffolk* to it? said my uncle *Toby.*

The unexpectedness of my uncle *Toby's* question, confounded *Kysarcius* more than the ablest advocate——He stopp'd a full minute, looking in my uncle *Toby's* face without replying——and in that single minute *Triptolemus* put by him, and took the lead as follows.

'Tis a ground and principle in the law, said *Triptolemus*, that things do not ascend, but descend in it; and I make no doubt 'tis for this cause, that however true it is, that the child may be of the blood or seed of its parents——that the parents, nevertheless, are not of the blood and seed of it; inasmuch as the parents are not begot by the child, but the child by the parents——For so they write, *Liberi sunt de sanguine patris & matris, sed pater et mater non sunt de sanguine liberorum.*[8]

——But this, *Triptolemus*, cried *Didius*, proves too much——for from this authority cited it would follow, not only what indeed is

6. Law counselors; "juris-prudentes": those learned in the law.

7. Mater non numeratur inter consanguineos. Bald. in ult. C. de Verb. signific. [*Sterne's note.*] It refers to an Italian authority cited—in Latin—by Swinburne.

8. Children are of the blood of their father and mother, but the father and mother are not of the blood of their children.

granted on all sides, that the mother is not of kin to her child——
but the father likewise——It is held, said *Triptolemus*, the better
opinion; because the father, the mother, and the child, though they
be three persons, yet are they but (*una caro*[9]) one flesh; and
consequently no degree of kindred——or any method of acquiring
one *in nature*——There you push the argument again too far, cried
Didius——for there is no prohibition *in nature*, though there is in
the levitical law,[1]——but that a man may beget a child upon his
grandmother——in which case, supposing the issue a daughter, she
would stand in relation both of——But who ever thought, cried
Kysarcius, of laying with his grandmother?———The young gentleman, replied *Yorick*, whom *Selden*[2] speaks of——who not only
thought of it, but justified his intention to his father by the argument drawn from the law of retaliation——"You lay'd, Sir, with
my mother, said the lad——why may not I lay with yours?"——
'Tis the *Argumentum commune*,[3] added *Yorick*.——'Tis as good,
replied *Eugenius*, taking down his hat, as they deserve.

The company broke up——

Chapter XXX.

——AND pray, said my uncle *Toby*, leaning upon *Yorick*, as he
and my father were helping him leisurely down the
stairs——don't be terrified, madam, this stair-case conversation is
not so long as the last——And pray, *Yorick*, said my uncle *Toby*,
which way is this said affair of *Tristram* at length settled by these
learned men? Very satisfactorily, replied *Yorick*; no mortal, Sir, has
any concern with it——for Mrs. *Shandy* the mother is nothing at
all akin to him——and as the mother's is the surest side——Mr.
Shandy, in course, is still less than nothing———In short, he is not
as much akin to him, Sir, as I am——

——That may well be, said my father, shaking his head.

——Let the learned say what they will, there must certainly,
quoth my uncle *Toby*, have been some sort of consanguinity betwixt
the duchess of *Suffolk* and her son——

The vulgar are of the same opinion, quoth *Yorick*, to this hour.

Chapter XXXI.

THOUGH my father was hugely tickled with the subtleties of
these learned discourses——'twas still but like the anointing
of a broken bone———The moment he got home, the weight of

9. Vide Brooke Abridg. tit. Administr.
N.47. [*Sterne's note.*]
1. That is, in the Biblical book Leviticus
18:6ff.

2. John Selden (1584–1654), an English
jurist, in *Table Talk*.
3. Argument common to either side.

his afflictions returned upon him but so much the heavier, as is ever the case when the staff we lean on slips from under us——He became pensive——walked frequently forth to the fish-pond——let down one loop of his hat——sigh'd often——forebore to snap—— and, as the hasty sparks of temper, which occasion snapping, so much assist perspiration and digestion, as *Hippocrates* tells us——he had certainly fallen ill with the extinction of them, had not his thoughts been critically drawn off, and his health rescued by a fresh train of disquietudes left him, with a legacy of a thousand pounds by my aunt *Dinah*——

My father had scarce read the letter, when taking the thing by the right end, he instantly begun to plague and puzzle his head how to lay it out mostly to the honour of his family——A hundred and fifty odd projects took possession of his brains by turns——he would do this, and that, and t'other——He would go to *Rome*—— he would go to law——he would buy stock——he would buy *John Hobson*'s farm——he would new fore-front his house, and add a new wing to make it even——There was a fine water-mill on this side, and he would build a wind-mill on the other side of the river in full view to answer it——But above all things in the world, he would inclose the great *Ox-moor*, and send out my brother *Bobby* immediately upon his travels.

But as the sum was *finite*, and consequently could not do every thing——and in truth very few of these to any purpose,——of all the projects which offered themselves upon this occasion, the two last seemed to make the deepest impression; and he would infallibly have determined upon both at once, but for the small inconvenience hinted at above, which absolutely put him under a necessity of deciding in favour either of the one or the other.

This was not altogether so easy to be done; for though 'tis certain my father had long before set his heart upon this necessary part of my brother's education, and like a prudent man had actually determined to carry it into execution, with the first money that returned from the second creation of actions in the *Missisippi*-scheme,[4] in which he was an adventurer——yet the *Ox-moor*, which was a fine, large, whinny,[5] undrained, unimproved common, belonging to the *Shandy*-estate, had almost as old a claim upon him: He had long and affectionately set his heart upon turning it likewise to some account.

But having never hitherto been pressed with such a conjuncture of things, as made it necessary to settle either the priority or justice of their claims,——like a wise man he had refrained entering into

4. A stock-venture establishing a vast colonial trading company; established in 1717, it failed in 1720, with disastrous results for many investors.
5. Covered with gorse, a rough plant.

any nice or critical examination about them: So that upon the dismission of every other project at this crisis,———the two old projects, the Ox-MOOR and my BROTHER, divided him again; and so equal a match were they for each other, as to become the occasion of no small contest in the old gentleman's mind,———which of the two should be set o'going first.

———People may laugh as they will———but the case was this.

It had ever been the custom of the family, and by length of time was almost become a matter of common right, that the eldest son of it should have free ingress, egress, and regress into foreign parts before marriage,———not only for the sake of bettering his own private parts, by the benefit of exercise and change of so much air———but simply for the mere delectation of his fancy, by the feather put into his cap, of having been abroad———*tantum valet,* my father would say, *quantum sonat.*[6]

Now as this was a reasonable, and in course a most christian indulgence———to deprive him of it, without why or wherefore,——— and thereby make an example of him, as the first *Shandy* unwhirl'd about *Europe* in a post-chaise, and only because he was a heavy lad———would be using him ten times worse than a *Turk.*

On the other hand, the case of the *Ox-moor* was full as hard.

Exclusive of the original purchase-money, which was eight hundred pounds———it had cost the family eight hundred pounds more in a law-suit about fifteen years before———besides the Lord knows what trouble and vexation.

It had been moreover in possession of the *Shandy*-family ever since the middle of the last century; and though it lay full in view before the house, bounded on one extremity by the water-mill, and on the other by the projected wind-mill spoken of above,———and for all these reasons seemed to have the fairest title of any part of the estate to the care and protection of the family———yet by an unaccountable fatality, common to men, as well as the ground they tread on,———it had all along most shamefully been overlook'd; and to speak the truth of it, had suffered so much by it, that it would have made any man's heart have bled (*Obadiah* said) who understood the value of land, to have rode over it, and only seen the condition it was in.

However, as neither the purchasing this tract of ground———nor indeed the placing of it where it lay, were either of them, properly speaking, of my father's doing———he had never thought himself any way concerned in the affair———till the fifteen years before, when the breaking out of that cursed law-suit mentioned above (and which had arose about its boundaries)———which being alto-

6. It's worth as much as it sounds like.

gether my father's own act and deed, it naturally awakened every other argument in its favour; and upon summing them all up together, he saw, not merely in interest, but in honour, he was bound to do something for it——and that now or never was the time.

I think there must certainly have been a mixture of ill-luck in it, that the reasons on both sides should happen to be so equally balanced by each other; for though my father weigh'd them in all humours and conditions——spent many an anxious hour in the most profound and abstracted meditation upon what was best to be done——reading books of farming one day——books of travels another——laying aside all passion whatever—viewing the arguments on both sides in all their lights and circumstances—— communing every day with my uncle *Toby*——arguing with *Yorick*, and talking over the whole affair of the *Ox-moor* with *Obadiah* ——yet nothing in all that time appeared so strongly in behalf of the one, which was not either strictly applicable to the other, or at least so far counterbalanced by some consideration of equal weight, as to keep the scales even.

For to be sure, with proper helps, and in the hands of some people, tho' the *Ox-moor* would undoubtedly have made a different appearance in the world from what it did, or ever would do in the condition it lay——yet every title of this was true, with regard to my brother *Bobby*——let *Obadiah* say what he would.——

In point of interest——the contest, I own, at first sight, did not appear so undecisive betwixt them; for whenever my father took pen and ink in hand, and set about calculating the simple expence of paring and burning, and fencing in the *Ox-moor*, &c. &c.—— with the certain profit it would bring him in return——the latter turned out so prodigiously in his way of working the account, that you would have sworn the *Ox-moor* would have carried all before it. For it was plain he should reap a hundred lasts of rape,[7] at twenty pounds a last, the very first year——besides an excellent crop of wheat the year following——and the year after that, to speak within bounds, a hundred——but, in all likelihood, a hundred and fifty——if not two hundred quarters of pease and beans ——besides potatoes without end——But then, to think he was all this while breeding up my brother like a hog to eat them—— knocked all on the head again, and generally left the old gentleman in such a state of suspense——that, as he often declared to my uncle *Toby*——he knew no more than his heels what to do.

No body, but he who has felt it, can conceive what a plaguing thing it is to have a man's mind torn asunder by two projects of equal strength, both obstinately pulling in a contrary direction at

---

7. A plant used as sheep fodder.

the same time: For to say nothing of the havock, which by a certain consequence is unavoidably made by it all over the finer system of the nerves, which you know convey the animal spirits and more subtle juices from the heart to the head, and so on——It is not to be told in what a degree such a wayward kind of friction works upon the more gross and solid parts, wasting the fat and impairing the strength of a man every time as it goes backwards and forwards.

My father had certainly sunk under this evil, as certainly as he had done under that of my CHRISTIAN NAME——had he not been rescued out of it as he was out of that, by a fresh evil————the misfortune of my brother *Bobby*'s death.

What is the life of man! Is it not to shift from side to side?———— from sorrow to sorrow?————to button up one cause of vexation! ————and unbutton another!

Chapter XXXII.

FROM this moment I am to be considered as heir-apparent to the *Shandy* family——and it is from this point properly, that the story of my LIFE and my OPINIONS sets out; with all my hurry and precipitation I have but been clearing the ground to raise the building——and such a building do I foresee it will turn out, as never was planned, and as never was executed since *Adam*. In less than five minutes I shall have thrown my pen into the fire, and the little drop of thick ink which is left remaining at the bottom of my ink-horn, after it——I have but half a score things to do in the time——I have a thing to name——a thing to lament——a thing to hope——a thing to promise, and a thing to threaten——I have a thing to suppose——a thing to declare——a thing to conceal——a thing to chuse, and a thing to pray for.————This chapter, there-fore, I *name* the chapter of THINGS————and my next chapter to it, that is, the first chapter of my next volume, if I live, shall be my chapter upon WHISKERS, in order to keep up some sort of connec-tion in my works.

The thing I lament is, that things have crowded in so thick upon me, that I have not been able to get into that part of my work, towards which, I have all the way, looked forwards, with so much earnest desire; and that is the campaigns, but especially the amours of my uncle *Toby*, the events of which are of so singular a nature, and so Cervantick a cast, that if I can so manage it, as to convey but the same impressions to every other brain, which the occur-rences themselves excite in my own——I will answer for it the book shall make its way in the world, much better than its master has done before it——Oh *Tristram*! *Tristram*! can this but be once brought about——the credit, which will attend thee as an author, shall counterbalance the many evils which have befallen thee as a man——thou wilt feast upon the one——when thou hast lost all sense and remembrance of the other!——·

No wonder I itch so much as I do, to get at these amours—— They are the choicest morsel of my whole story! and when I do get at 'em——assure yourselves, good folks,——(nor do I value whose squeamish stomach takes offence at it) I shall not be at all nice in the choice of my words;——and that's the thing I have to *declare*.

——I shall never get all through in five minutes, that I fear—— and the thing I *hope* is, that your worships and reverences are not offended——if you are, depend upon't I'll give you something, my good gentry, next year, to be offended at——that's my dear *Jenny's* way——but who my *Jenny* is——and which is the right and which the wrong end of a woman, is the thing to be *concealed*——it shall be told you the next chapter but one, to my chapter of button-holes,——and not one chapter before.

And now that you have just got to the end of these four volumes ——the thing I have to *ask* is, how you feel your heads? my own akes dismally——as for your healths, I know, they are much better——True *Shandeism*, think what you will against it, opens the heart and lungs, and like all those affections which partake of its nature, it forces the blood and other vital fluids of the body to run freely thro' its channels, and makes the wheel of life run long and chearfully round.

Was I left like *Sancho Pança*, to chuse my kingdom, it should not be maritime——or a kingdom of blacks to make a penny of[8]—— no, it should be a kingdom of hearty laughing subjects: And as the bilious and more saturnine passions, by creating disorders in the blood and humours, have as bad an influence, I see, upon the body politick as body natural——and as nothing but a habit of virtue can fully govern those passions, and subject them to reason——I should add to my prayer——that God would give my subjects grace to be as WISE as they were MERRY; and then should I be the happiest monarch, and they the happiest people under heaven——

And so, with this moral for the present, may it please your worships and your reverences, I take my leave of you till this time twelve-month, when (unless this vile cough kills me in the mean time) I'll have another pluck at your beards, and lay open a story to the world you little dream of.

FINIS

8. Sancho stays with Don Quixote for a long time in hope of rewards like those Tristram mentions, at the same time gradually coming to love his master.

Volume V.

Dixero si quid fortè jocosius, hoc mihi juris
Cum venia dabis.———
                                        HOR.

—Si quis calumnietur levius esse quam decet theologum, aut mordacius
quam deceat Christianum—non Ego, sed Democritus dixit.—
                                        ERASMUS.[1]

To the Right Honourable

J O H N ,

Lord Viscount Spencer.[2]

My Lord,

I Humbly beg leave to offer you these two Volumes; they are the best my talents, with such bad health as I have, could produce: ———had providence granted me a larger stock of either, they had been a much more proper present to your Lordship.

I beg your Lordship will forgive me, if, at the same time I dedicate this work to you, I join Lady SPENCER, in the liberty I take of inscribing the story of *Le Fever* in the sixth volume to her name; for which I have no other motive, which my heart has informed me of, but that the story is a humane one.

I am,
My Lord,
Your Lordship's
Most devoted,
And most humble Servant,
LAUR. STERNE.

---

1. The sentences from Horace (*Satires*, I.iv.104–5) and from Erasmus ("Letter to Sir Thomas More," prefatory to *Moriae Encomium* [The Praise of Folly]) are both presented here as paraphrased by Thomas Burton in "Democritus Junior to the Reader,"—his Preface to *The Anatomy of Melancholy*. Horace: "If I say anything too facetious, you will grant it to me indulgently." Erasmus: "Should anyone judge my writings harshly as being in a lighter vein than suits a theologian, or more biting than is appropriate to a Christian—not I, but Democritus said it."

2. A Great-grandson of the Duke of Marlborough who figures so largely in the campaigns of Toby and Trim, Lord Spencer was Sterne's friend and patron.

Chapter I.

IF it had not been for those two mettlesome tits, and that mad-cap of a postilion, who drove them from Stilton to Stamford, the thought had never entered my head. He flew like lightning—— there was a slope of three miles and a half——we scarce touched the ground——the motion was most rapid——most impetuous—— 'twas communicated to my brain——my heart partook of it——By the great God of day, said I, looking towards the sun, and thrusting my arm out of the forewindow of the chaise, as I made my vow, "I will lock up my study door the moment I get home, and throw the key of it ninety feet below the surface of the earth, into the draw-well at the back of my house."[3]

The London waggon confirmed me in my resolution: it hung tottering upon the hill, scarce progressive, drag'd——drag'd up by eight *heavy beasts*——"by main strength!——quoth I, nodding—— but your betters draw the same way——and something of every bodies!——O rare!"

Tell me, ye learned, shall we for ever be adding so much to the *hulk*——so little to the *stock?*

Shall we for ever make new books, as apothecaries make new mixtures, by pouring only out of one vessel into another?

Are we for ever to be twisting, and untwisting the same rope? for ever in the same track——for ever at the same pace?

Shall we be destined to the days of eternity, on holy-days, as well as working-days, to be shewing the *relicks of learning*, as monks do the relicks of their saints——without working one——one single miracle with them?

Who made MAN, with powers which dart him from earth to heaven in a moment——that great, that most excellent, and most noble creature of the world——the *miracle* of nature, as Zoroaster[4] in his book περὶ φύσεως called him——the SHEKINAH of the divine presence, as Chrysostom——the *image* of God, as Moses——the *ray* of divinity, as Plato——the *marvel* of *marvels*, as Aristotle—— to go sneaking on at this pitiful——pimping——pettifogging rate?

I scorn to be as abusive as Horace upon the occasion——but if there is no catachresis[5] in the wish, and no sin in it, I wish from my

3. Tristram vows to throw away the key to his study to avoid borrowing from other writers (which he has just done twice in his epigraphs without acknowledging Burton as his source)—and borrows the form of the vow itself from Burton, again in "Democritus Junior to the Reader."
4. Zoroaster (or Zarathustra) was the founder of the ancient Persian religion which flourished in the sixth and seventh centuries B.C. The book referred to is *On Nature. Shekinah* is the Hebrew word for the manifestation of God, and St. John Chrysostom a fourth-century Greek Christian.
5. A "catachresis" is a misuse of words. In his *Epistles* I.xix.1–20, Horace attacks those who misuse them by being mere servile imitators—as Sterne is (consciously) doing in this passage of quotations.

soul, that every imitator in *Great Britain, France,* and *Ireland,* had the farcy for his pains; and that there was a good farcical house, large enough to hold——aye——and sublimate them, *shag-rag and bob-tail,* male and female, all together: and this leads me to the affair of *Whiskers*——but, by what chain of ideas——I leave as a legacy in *mort main*[6] to Prudes and Tartufs, to enjoy and make the most of.

Upon Whiskers.

I'm sorry I made it——'twas as inconsiderate a promise as ever entered a man's head——A chapter upon whiskers! alas! the world will not bear it——'tis a delicate world——but I knew not of what mettle it was made——nor had I ever seen the underwritten fragment; otherwise, as surely as noses are noses, and whiskers are whiskers still; (let the world say what it will to the contrary) so surely would I have steered clear of this dangerous chapter.

The Fragment.

* * * * * * * * *
* * * * * * * * *

* *——You are half asleep, my good lady, said the old gentleman, taking hold of the old lady's hand and giving it a gentle squeeze, as he pronounced the word *Whiskers*——shall we change the subject? By no means, replied the old lady——I like your account of these matters: so throwing a thin gauze handkerchief over her head, and leaning it back upon the chair with her face turned towards him, and advancing her two feet as she reclined herself——I desire, continued she, you will go on.

The old gentleman went on as follows.——Whiskers! cried the queen of *Navarre,*[7] dropping her knotting-ball, as *La Fosseuse* uttered the word——Whiskers; madam, said *La Fosseuse,* pinning the ball to the queen's apron, and making a courtesy as she repeated it.

La Fosseuse's voice was naturally soft and low, yet 'twas an articulate voice: and every letter of the word *whiskers* fell distinctly upon the queen of *Navarre's* ear—Whiskers! cried the queen, laying a greater stress upon the word, and as if she had still distrusted her ears——Whiskers; replied *La Fosseuse,* repeating the word a third time——There is not a cavalier, madam, of his age in *Navarre,*

6. *Mort main* means literally "dead hand"; it refers to the kind of perpetual possession of property granted to religious and some other institutions. A "Tartuf" (after the leading figure in Mo- liere's play) is a hypocrite, particularly a religious one.
7. Margaret, Queen of Navarre, whose sixteenth-century court is the setting for this story.

continued the maid of honour, pressing the page's interest upon the queen, that has so gallant a pair——Of what? cried *Margaret,* smiling——Of whiskers, said *La Fosseuse,* with infinite modesty.

The word whiskers still stood its ground, and continued to be made use of in most of the best companies throughout the little kingdom of *Navarre,* notwithstanding the indiscreet use which *La Fosseuse* had made of it: the truth was, *La Fosseuse* had pronounced the word, not only before the queen, but upon sundry other occasions at court, with an accent which always implied something of a mystery——And as the court of *Margaret,* as all the world knows, was at that time a mixture of gallantry and devotion ——and whiskers being as applicable to the one, as the other, the word naturally stood its ground——it gain'd full as much as it lost; that is, the clergy were for it——the laity were against it——and for the women,——*they* were divided.——

The excellency of the figure and mien of the young Sieur *De Croix,* was at that time beginning to draw the attention of the maids of honour towards the terras before the palace gate, where the guard was mounted. The Lady *de Baussiere* fell deeply in love with him,   *La Battarelle* did the same——it was the finest weather for it, that ever was remembered in *Navarre*——*La Guyol, La Maronette, La Sabatiere,* fell in love with the Sieur *de Croix* also——*La Rebours* and *La Fosseuse* knew better——*De Croix* had failed in an attempt to recommend himself to *La Rebours*; and *La Rebours* and *La Fosseuse* were inseparable.

The queen of *Navarre* was sitting with her ladies in the painted bow-window, facing the gate of the second court, as *De Croix* passed through it——He is handsome, said the Lady *Baussiere.* ——He has a good mien, said *La Battarelle.*——He is finely shaped, said *La Guyol.*——I never saw an officer of the horse-guards in my life, said *La Maronette,* with two such legs——Or who stood so well upon them, said *La Sabatiere*——But he has no whiskers, cried *La Fosseuse*——Not a pile, said *La Rebours.*

The queen went directly to her oratory, musing all the way, as she walked through the gallery, upon the subject; turning it this way and that way in her fancy——*Ave Maria* +——what can *La Fosseuse* mean? said she, kneeling down upon the cushion.

La Guyol, La Batterelle, La Maronette, La Sabatiere, retired instantly to their chambers——Whiskers! said all four of them to themselves, as they bolted their doors on the inside.

The Lady *Carnavallette* was counting her beads with both hands, unsuspected under her farthingal[8]——from St. *Antony* down to St. *Ursula* inclusive, not a saint passed through her fingers without

---

8. A hooped petticoat.

whiskers; St. *Francis*, St. *Dominick*, St. *Bennet*, St. *Basil*, St. *Bridget*, had all whiskers.

The Lady *Baussiere* had got into a wilderness of conceits,[9] with moralizing too intricately upon *La Fosseuse*'s text——She mounted her palfry, her page followed her——the host passed by——the lady *Baussiere* rode on.

One denier, cried the order of mercy——one single denier, in behalf of a thousand patient captives, whose eyes look towards heaven and you for their redemption.

——The Lady *Baussiere* rode on.

Pity the unhappy, said a devout, venerable, hoary-headed man, meekly holding up a box, begirt with iron, in his withered hands ——I beg for the unfortunate——good, my lady, 'tis for a prison ——for an hospital——'tis for an old man——a poor man undone by shipwreck, by suretyship,[1] by fire——I call God and all his angels to witness——'tis to cloath the naked——to feed the hungry—— 'tis to comfort the sick and the broken hearted.

——The Lady *Baussiere* rode on.

A decayed kinsman bowed himself to the ground.

——The Lady *Baussiere* rode on.

He ran begging bare-headed on one side of her palfry, conjuring her by the former bonds of friendship, alliance, consanguinity, &c. ——Cousin, aunt, sister, mother——for virtue's sake, for your own, for mine, for Christ's sake remember me——pity me.

——The Lady *Baussiere* rode on.

Take hold of my whiskers, said the Lady *Baussiere*——The page took hold of her palfry. She dismounted at the end of the terrace.

There are some trains of certain ideas which leave prints of themselves about our eyes and eye-brows; and there is a consciousness of it, somewhere about the heart, which serves but to make these etchings the stronger——we see, spell, and put them together without a dictionary.

Ha, ha! hee, hee! cried *La Guyol* and *La Sabatiere*, looking close at each others prints——Ho, ho! cried *La Batterelle* and *Maronette*, doing the same:——Whist! cried one——st, st,——said a second, ——hush, quoth a third——poo, poo, replied a fourth—— gramercy! cried the Lady *Carnavallette*;——'twas she who bewhisker'd St. *Bridget*.

La Fosseuse drew her bodkin from the knot of her hair, and having traced the outline of a small whisker, with the blunt end of it, upon one side of her upper lip, put it into *La Rebours*'s hand—— *La Rebours* shook her head.

9. That is, of metaphors, or images summoned up by a man's whiskers. *Host* means the Communion bread, which should be acknowledged (as the Body of Christ), but she is occupied with other thoughts.
1. By guaranteeing a friend's loan (standing surety) he has lost money.

The Lady *Baussiere* cough'd thrice into the inside of her muff
——*La Guyol* smiled—Fy, said the Lady *Baussiere*. The queen of
Navarre touched her eye with the tip of her fore finger——as much
as to say, I understand you all.

'Twas plain to the whole court the word was ruined: *La Fosseuse*
had given it a wound, and it was not the better for passing through
all these defiles——It made a faint stand, however, for a few
months; by the expiration of which, the Sieur *De Croix*, finding it
high time to leave *Navarre* for want of whiskers——the word in
course became indecent, and (after a few efforts) absolutely unfit
for use.

The best word, in the best language of the best world, must have
suffered under such combinations.————The curate of *d'Estella*
wrote a book against them, setting forth the dangers of accessory
ideas, and warning the *Navarois* against them.

Does not all the world know, said the curate *d'Estella* at the
conclusion of his work, that Noses ran the same fate some centuries
ago in most parts of *Europe*, which Whiskers have now done in the
kingdom of *Navarre*——The evil indeed spread no further then,
——but have not beds and bolsters, and night-caps and chamber-
pots stood upon the brink of destruction ever since? Are not
trouse,[2] and placket-holes, and pump-handles——and spigots and
faucets, in danger still, from the same association?——Chastity, by
nature the gentlest of all affections——give it but its head——'tis
like a ramping and a roaring lion.

The drift of the curate *d'Estella*'s argument was not understood.
——They ran the scent the wrong way.——The world bridled his
ass at the tail.——And when the *extreams* of DELICACY, and the
beginnings of CONCUPISCENCE, hold their next provincial chapter
together, they may decree that bawdy also.

Chapter II.

WHEN my father received the letter which brought him the
melancholy account of my brother *Bobby*'s death, he was
busy calculating the expence of his riding post[3] from *Calais* to
Paris, and so on to *Lyons*.

'Twas a most inauspicious journey; my father having had every
foot of it to travel over again, and his calculation to begin afresh,
when he had almost got to the end of it, by *Obadiah*'s opening the
door to acquaint him the family was out of yeast——and to ask

2. Tight trousers; a placket-hole in a
skirt opens into a pocket.
3. That is, the expense of renting horses
from one stop to another on his European tour.

whether he might not take the great coach-horse early in the morning, and ride in search of some.——With all my heart, *Obadiah*, said my father, (pursuing his journey)——take the coach-horse, and welcome.——But he wants a shoe, poor creature! said *Obadiah*.——Poor creature! said my uncle *Toby*, vibrating the note back again, like a string in unison. Then ride the *Scotch* horse, quoth my father hastily.——He cannot bear a saddle upon his back, quoth *Obadiah*, for the whole world.——The devil's in that horse; then take PATRIOT, cried my father, and shut the door.—— PATRIOT is sold, said *Obadiah*.——Here's for you! cried my father, making a pause, and looking in my uncle *Toby*'s face, as if the thing had not been a matter of fact.——Your worship ordered me to sell him last *April*, said *Obadiah*.——Then go on foot for your pains, cried my father.——I had much rather walk than ride, said *Obadiah*, shutting the door.

What plagues! cried my father, going on with his calculation. ——But the waters are out, said *Obadiah*,——opening the door again.

Till that moment, my father, who had a map of *Sanson's*,[4] and a book of the post roads before him, had kept his hand upon the head of his compasses, with one foot of them fixed upon *Nevers*, the last stage he had paid for——purposing to go on from that point with his journey and calculation, as soon as *Obadiah* quitted the room; but this second attack of *Obadiah's*, in opening the door and laying the whole country under water, was too much.——He let go his compasses——or rather with a mixed motion betwixt accident and anger, he threw them upon the table; and then there was nothing for him to do, but to return back to *Calais* (like many others) as wise as he had set out.

When the letter was brought into the parlour, which contained the news of my brother's death, my father had got forwards again upon his journey to within a stride of the compasses of the very same stage of *Nevers*.——By your leave, Mons. *Sanson*, cried my father, striking the point of his compasses through *Nevers* into the table,——and nodding to my uncle *Toby*, to see what was in the letter,——twice of one night is too much for an *English* gentleman and his son, Mons. *Sanson*, to be turned back from so lousy a town as *Nevers*,——what think'st thou, *Toby*, added my father in a sprightly tone.——Unless it be a garrison town, said my uncle *Toby*,——for then——I shall be a fool, said my father, smiling to himself, as long as I live.——So giving a second nod——and keeping his compasses still upon *Nevers* with one hand, and holding his book of the post-roads in the other——half calculating and half

4. A seventeenth-century mapmaker.

listening, he leaned forwards upon the table with both elbows, as my uncle *Toby* hummed over the letter.

———— ———— ———— ———— ———— ———— ———— ————

———— ———— ———— ———— ———— ———— ———— ————

———— ———— ———— ———— ————he's gone! said my uncle *Toby.* ————Where————Who? cried my father.————My nephew, said my uncle *Toby.*————What————without leave————without money———— without governor?[5] cried my father in amazement. No:————he is dead, my dear brother, quoth my uncle *Toby.*————Without being ill? cried my father again.————I dare say not, said my uncle *Toby,* in a low voice, and fetching a deep sigh from the bottom of his heart, he has been ill enough, poor lad! I'll answer for him————for he is dead.

When *Agrippina* was told of her son's death, *Tacitus*[6] informs us, that not being able to moderate the violence of her passions, she abruptly broke off her work————My father stuck his compasses into *Nevers,* but so much the faster.————What contrarieties! his, indeed, was matter of calculation————*Agrippina's* must have been quite a different affair; who else could pretend to reason from history?

How my father went on, in my opinion, deserves a chapter to itself.————

Chapter III.

———— ———— A nd a chapter it shall have, and a devil of a one too————so look to yourselves.

'Tis either *Plato,* or *Plutarch,* or *Seneca,* or *Xenophon,* or *Epictetus,* or *Theophrastus,* or *Lucian*————or some one perhaps of later date————either *Cardan,* or *Budæus,* or *Petrarch,* or *Stella*————or possibly it may be some divine or father of the church, St. *Austin,* or St. *Cyprian,* or *Barnard,* who affirms that it is an irresistable and natural passion to weep for the loss of our friends or children———— and *Seneca*[7] (I'm positive) tells us somewhere, that such griefs evacuate themselves best by that particular channel.————And accordingly we find, that *David*[8] wept for his son *Absolom*———— *Adrian* for his *Antinous*————*Niobe* for her children, and that *Apol-*

---

5. It was usual for a young man to take along a tutor on his European travels.
6. Agrippina wept for her stepson, whom her son Nero had poisoned, according to the *Annales* of the Roman historian Tacitus.
7. It was Seneca the Elder (c. 54 B.C.– 39 A.D.) who said this in his *Controversiae* [Disputes] (V.30).
8. David wept for his son Absalom,

killed while rebelling against him (II Samuel 18:3–19:4). The emperor Hadrian grieved when his favorite, Antinous, committed suicide. In Greek myth, Niobe wept for her children (killed by the gods Apollo and Artemis) even after Zeus had turned her to stone. In the *Phaedo,* Plato describes the meeting of Socrates and his two friends immediately after Socrates drank the poisoned cup.

Iodorus and *Crito* both shed tears for *Socrates* before his death.

My father managed his affliction otherwise; and indeed differently from most men either ancient or modern; for he neither wept it away, as the *Hebrews* and the *Romans*——or slept it off, as the *Laplanders*——or hang'd it, as the *English*, or drowned it, as the *Germans*——nor did he curse it, or damn it, or excommunicate it, or rhyme it, or lillabullero it.——

——He got rid of it, however.

Will your worships give mé leave to squeeze in a story between these two pages?

When *Tully*[9] was bereft of his dear daughter *Tullia*, at first he laid it to his heart,——he listened to the voice of nature, and modulated his own unto it.——O my *Tullia*! my daughter! my child!——still, still, still,——'twas O my *Tullia*!——my *Tullia*! Methinks I see my *Tullia*, I hear my *Tullia*, I talk with my *Tullia*.

——But as soon as he began to look into the stores of philosophy, and consider how many excellent things might be said upon the occasion——no body upon earth can conceive, says the great orator, how happy, how joyful it made me.

My father was as proud of his eloquence as MARCUS TULLIUS CICERO could be for his life, and for aught I am convinced of to the contrary at present, with as much reason: it was indeed his strength ——and his weakness too.——His strength——for he was by nature eloquent,——and his weakness——for he was hourly a dupe to it; and provided an occasion in life would but permit him to shew his talents, or say either a wise thing, a witty, or a shrewd one—— (bating the case of a systematick misfortune)——he had all he wanted.——A blessing which tied up my father's tongue, and a misfortune which set it loose with a good grace, were pretty equal: sometimes, indeed, the misfortune was the better of the two; for instance, where the pleasure of the harangue was as *ten*, and the pain of the misfortune but as *five*——my father gained half in half, and consequently was as well again off, as it never had befallen him.

This clue will unravel, what otherwise would seem very inconsistent in my father's domestick character; and it is this, that in the provocations arising from the neglects and blunders of servants, or other mishaps unavoidable in a family, his anger, or rather the duration of it, eternally ran counter to all conjecture.

My father had a favourite little mare, which he had consigned over to a most beautiful Arabian horse, in order to have a pad out of her for his own riding: he was sanguine in all his projects; so

9. Cicero (Tully) does speak of writing his now-lost *De Consolatione* to help him deal with his grief at the death of his daughter, But Tristram overstates the relief it provided.

talked about his pad every day with as absolute a security, as if it had been reared, broke,——and bridled and saddled at his door ready for mounting. By some neglect or other in *Obadiah*, it so fell out, that my father's expectations were answered with nothing better than a mule, and as ugly a beast of the kind as ever was produced.

My mother and my uncle *Toby* expected my father would be the death of *Obadiah*——and that there never would be an end of the disaster.——See here! you rascal, cried my father, pointing to the mule, what you have done!——It was not me, said *Obadiah*.—— How do I know that? replied my father.

Triumph swam in my father's eyes, at the repartee——the *Attic* salt[1] brought water into them——and so *Obadiah* heard no more about it.

Now let us go back to my brother's death.

Philosophy has a fine saying for every thing.——For *Death* it has an entire set; the misery was, they all at once rushed into my father's head, that 'twas difficult to string them together, so as to make any thing of a consistent show out of them.——He took them as they came.[2]

" 'Tis an inevitable chance——the first statute in *Magnâ Chartâ* ——it is an everlasting act of parliament, my dear brother,——*All must die.*

"If my son could not have died, it had been matter of wonder, ——not that he is dead."

"Monarchs and princes dance in the same ring with us."

"——*To die*, is the great debt and tribute due unto nature: tombs and monuments, which should perpetuate our memories, pay it themselves; and the proudest pyramid of them all, which wealth and science have erected, has lost its apex, and stands obtruncated in the traveller's horizon." (My father found he got great ease, and went on)——"Kingdoms and provinces, and towns and cities, have they not their periods? and when those principles and powers, which at first cemented and put them together, have performed their several evolutions, they fall back."——Brother *Shandy*, said my uncle *Toby*, laying down his pipe at the word *evolutions*——Revolutions, I meant, quoth my father,——by heaven! I meant revolutions, brother *Toby*——evolutions is nonsense.——'Tis not nonsense—— said my uncle *Toby*.——But is it not nonsense to break the thread of such a discourse, upon such an occasion? cried my father——do not——dear *Toby*, continued he, taking him by the hand, do not ——do not, I beseech thee, interrupt me at this crisis.——My uncle *Toby* put his pipe into his mouth.

1. That is, his stinging wit.
2. In fact, once again, largely as they come out of Burton's *Anatomy of Melancholy*.

"Where is *Troy* and *Mycenæ*, and *Thebes* and *Delos*, and *Persepolis* and *Agrigentum*"——continued my father, taking up his book of post-roads, which he had laid down.——"What is become, brother *Toby*, of *Nineveh* and *Babylon*, of *Cizicum* and *Mitylenæ*? The fairest towns that ever the sun rose upon, are now no more: the names only are left, and those (for many of them are wrong spelt) are falling themselves by piece-meals to decay, and in length of time will be forgotten, and involved with every thing in a perpetual night: the world itself, brother *Toby*, must——must come to an end.

"Returning out of *Asia*, when I sailed from *Ægina* towards *Megara*," (*when can this have been? thought my uncle Toby*) "I began to view the country round about. *Ægina* was behind me, *Megara* was before, *Pyræus* on the right hand, *Corinth* on the left.——What flourishing towns now prostrate upon the earth! Alas! alas! said I to myself, that man should disturb his soul for the loss of a child, when so much as this lies awfully buried in his presence——Remember, said I to myself again——remember thou art a man."——

Now my uncle *Toby* knew not that this last paragraph was an extract of *Servius Sulpicius's* consolatory letter to *Tully*.——He had as little skill, honest man, in the fragments, as he had in the whole pieces of antiquity.——And as my father, whilst he was concerned in the *Turky* trade, had been three or four different times in the *Levant*, in one of which he had staid a whole year and an half at *Zant*, my uncle *Toby* naturally concluded, that in some one of these periods he had taken a trip across the *Archipelago* into *Asia*; and that all this sailing affair with *Ægina* behind, and *Megara* before, and *Pyræus* on the right hand, &c. &c. was nothing more than the true course of my father's voyage and reflections.——'Twas certainly in his *manner*, and many an undertaking critick would have built two stories higher upon worse foundations.——And pray, brother, quoth my uncle *Toby*, laying the end of his pipe upon my father's hand in a kindly way of interruption——but waiting till he finished the account——what year of our Lord was this?——'Twas no year of our Lord, replied my father.——That's impossible, cried my uncle *Toby*.——Simpleton! said my father,——'twas forty years before Christ was born.

My uncle *Toby* had but two things for it; either to suppose his brother to be the wandering *Jew*,[3] or that his misfortunes had disordered his brain.——"May the Lord God of heaven and earth protect him and restore him," said my uncle *Toby*, praying silently for my father, and with tears in his eyes.

3. Who, according to legend, had been condemned to wander the earth forever because he abused Christ, urging him to go faster while carrying the Cross.

——My father placed the tears to a proper account, and went on with his harangue with great spirit.

"There is not such great odds, brother *Toby*, betwixt good and evil, as the world imagines"——(this way of setting off, by the bye, was not likely to cure my uncle *Toby*'s suspicions.)——"Labour, sorrow, grief, sickness, want, and woe, are the sauces of life."—— Much good may it do them——said my uncle *Toby* to himself.——

"My son is dead!——so much the better;——'tis a shame in such a tempest to have but one anchor."

"But he is gone for ever from us!——be it so. He is got from under the hands of his barber before he was bald——he is but risen from a feast before he was surfeited——from a banquet before he had got drunken."

"The *Thracians* wept when a child was born"——(and we were very near it, quoth my uncle *Toby*)——"and feasted and made merry when a man went out of the world; and with reason.—— Death opens the gate of fame, and shuts the gate of envy after it,——it unlooses the chain of the captive, and puts the bondsman's task into another man's hands."

"Shew me the man, who knows what life is, who dreads it, and I'll shew thee a prisoner who dreads his liberty."

Is it not better, my dear brother *Toby*, (for mark——our appetites are but diseases)——is it not better not to hunger at all, than to eat?——not to thirst, than to take physick to cure it?

Is it not better to be freed from cares and agues, from love and melancholy, and the other hot and cold fits of life, than like a galled traveller, who comes weary to his inn, to be bound to begin his journey afresh?

There is no terror, brother *Toby*, in its looks, but what it borrows from groans and convulsions——and the blowing of noses, and the wiping away of tears with the bottoms of curtains in a dying man's room.——Strip it of these, what is it——'Tis better in battle than in bed, said my uncle *Toby*.——Take away its herses, its mutes,[4] and its mourning,——its plumes, scutcheons, and other mechanic aids ——What is it?——*Better in battle!* continued my father, smiling, for he had absolutely forgot my brother *Bobby*——'tis terrible no way——for consider, brother *Toby*,——when we *are*——death is *not*;——and when death *is*——we are *not*. My uncle *Toby* laid down his pipe to consider the proposition; my father's eloquence was too rapid to stay for any man——away it went,——and hurried my uncle *Toby*'s ideas along with it.——

For this reason, continued my father, 'tis worthy to recollect, how little alteration in great men, the approaches of death have

---

4. Attendants hired to stand silently mournful at a funeral. Black plumes were used to decorate funeral horses.

made.——*Vespasian*[5] died in a jest upon his close stool—*Galba* with a sentence——*Septimius Severus* in a dispatch——*Tiberius* in dissimulation, and *Cæsar Augustus* in a compliment.——I hope, 'twas a sincere one——quoth my uncle *Toby*.
——'Twas to his wife,——said my father.

Chapter IV.

—— A nd lastly——for of all the choice anecdotes which history can produce of this matter, continued my father, ——this, like the gilded dome which covers in the fabrick—— crowns all.——
'Tis of *Cornelius Gallus*, the prætor——which I dare say, brother *Toby*, you have read.——I dare say I have not, replied my uncle.——He died, said my father, as * * * * * * * * * * * * * * * * * —— And if it was with his wife, said my uncle *Toby*——there could be no hurt in it.——That's more than I know——replied my father.

Chapter V.

M Y mother was going very gingerly in the dark along the passage which led to the parlour, as my uncle *Toby* pronounced the word *wife*.——'Tis a shrill, penetrating sound of itself, and *Obadiah* had helped it by leaving the door a little a-jar, so that my mother heard enough of it, to imagine herself the subject of the conversation: so laying the edge of her finger across her two lips ——holding in her breath, and bending her head a little downwards, with a twist of her neck——(not towards the door, but from it, by which means her ear was brought to the chink)——she listened with all her powers:——the listening slave, with the Goddess of Silence at his back, could not have given a finer thought for an intaglio.[6]
In this attitude I am determined to let her stand for five minutes: till I bring up the affairs of the kitchen (as *Rapin*[7] does those of the church) to the same period.

---

5. These were all emperors of Rome. Sitting on his chamber pot, Vespasian's last words were "Methinks I'm turning into a god." Galba advised his assassins to "Do your work, if this is better for the Roman people." Septimius Severus urged his servants to give him whatever paperwork waited to be read; Sterne plays on the word "dispatch" (messages, promptly). Tiberius tried to conceal his waning strength and appear to maintain his lecherous ways until death. Augustus died kissing his wife and reminding her of their happy life together.
6. That is, as a figure to be engraved in stone.
7. The French historian Rapin (1661–1725) was the author of a history of England in which he sums up the affairs of the Church in a special section at the end of each book.

Chapter VI.

THOUGH in one sense, our family was certainly a simple machine, as it consisted of a few wheels; yet there was thus much
to be said for it, that these wheels were set in motion by so many
different springs, and acted one upon the other from such a variety
of strange principles and impulses,——that though it was a simple
machine, it had all the honour and advantages of a complex one,
——and a number of as odd movements within it, as ever were
beheld in the inside of a *Dutch* silk-mill.

Amongst these there was one, I am going to speak of, in which,
perhaps, it was not altogether so singular, as in many others; and it
was this, that whatever motion, debate, harangue, dialogue, project,
or dissertation, was going forwards in the parlour, there was generally another at the same time, and upon the same subject, running
parallel along with it in the kitchen.

Now to bring this about, whenever an extraordinary message, or
letter, was delivered in the parlour,——or a discourse suspended till
a servant went out——or the lines of discontent were observed to
hang upon the brows of my father or mother——or, in short, when
any thing was supposed to be upon the tapis[8] worth knowing or
listening to, 'twas the rule to leave the door, not absolutely shut, but
somewhat a-jar——as it stands just now,——which, under covert
of the bad hinge, (and that possibly might be one of the many
reasons why it was never mended) it was not difficult to manage; by
which means, in all these cases, a passage was generally left, not
indeed as wide as the *Dardanells*, but wide enough, for all that, to
carry on as much of this windward trade, as was sufficient to save
my father the trouble of governing his house;——my mother at this
moment stands profiting by it.——*Obadiah* did the same thing, as
soon as he had left the letter upon the table which brought the news
of my brother's death; so that before my father had well got over
his surprize, and entered upon his harangue,——had *Trim* got upon
his legs, to speak his sentiments upon the subject.

A curious observer of nature, had he been worth the inventory of
all *Job*'s stock——though, by the bye, *your curious observers are
seldom worth a groat*——would have given the half of it, to have
heard Corporal *Trim* and my father, two orators so contrasted by
nature and education, haranguing over the same bier.

My father a man of deep reading——prompt memory——with
Cato, and *Seneca*, and *Epictetus*, at his fingers ends.——

The corporal——with nothing——to remember——of no deeper
reading than his muster-roll——or greater names at his finger's end,
than the contents of it.

8. Under discussion (literally, "on the tablecloth").

The one proceeding from period to period, by metaphor and allusion, and striking the fancy as he went along, (as men of wit and fancy do) with the entertainment and pleasantry of his pictures and images.

The other, without wit or antithesis, or point, or turn, this way or that; but leaving the images on one side, and the pictures on the other, going strait forwards as nature could lead him, to the heart. O *Trim!* would to heaven thou had'st a better historian!——would! ——thy historian had a better pair of breeches!——O ye criticks! will nothing melt you?

Chapter VII.

——M y young master in *London* is dead! said *Obadiah*.—— ——A green sattin night-gown[9] of my mother's, which had been twice scoured, was the first idea which *Obadiah*'s exclamation brought into *Susannah*'s head.——Well might *Locke* write a chapter upon the imperfections of words.[1]——Then, quoth *Susannah*, we must all go into mourning.——But note a second time: the word *mourning*, notwithstanding *Susannah* made use of it herself——failed also of doing its office; it excited not one single idea, tinged either with grey or black,——all was green.—— The green sattin night-gown hung there still.

——O! 'twill be the death of my poor mistress, cried *Susannah*. ——My mother's whole wardrobe followed.——What a procession! her red damask,——her orange-tawny,——her white and yellow lutestrings,[2]——her brown taffata,——her bone-laced caps, her bed-gowns, and comfortable under-petticoats.——Not a rag was left behind.——"No,——*she will never look up again*," said *Susannah*.

We had a fat foolish scullion——my father, I think, kept her for her simplicity;——she had been all autumn struggling with a dropsy.——He is dead! said *Obadiah*,——he is certainly dead!—— So am not I, said the foolish scullion.

——Here is sad news, *Trim!* cried *Susannah*, wiping her eyes as *Trim* step'd into the kitchen,——master *Bobby* is dead and *buried*, ——the funeral was an interpolation of *Susannah*'s,——we shall have all to go into mourning, said *Susannah*.

I hope not, said *Trim*.——You hope not! cried *Susannah* earnestly.——The mourning ran not in *Trim*'s head, whatever it did in *Susannah*'s.——I hope——said *Trim*, explaining himself, I hope in God the news is not true. I heard the letter read with my own ears, answered *Obadiah*; and we shall have a terrible piece of work

9. That is, evening dress.
1. *Essay Concerning Human Under-* *standing,* III.ix.
2. A shiny silk.

of it in stubbing the ox-moor.——Oh! he's dead, said *Susannah.*
——As sure, said the scullion, as I am alive.

I lament for him from my heart and my soul, said *Trim*, fetching
a sigh.——Poor creature!——poor boy! poor gentleman!

——He was alive last *Whitsontide*,[3] said the coachman.——
Whitsontide! alas! cried *Trim*, extending his right arm, and falling
instantly into the same attitude in which he read the sermon,——
what is *Whitsontide, Jonathan,* (for that was the coachman's name)
or *Shrovetide,* or any tide or time past, to this? Are we not here
now, continued the corporal, (striking the end of his stick perpendicularly upon the floor, so as to give an idea of health and sta-
bility)——and are we not——(dropping his hat upon the ground)
gone! in a moment!——'Twas infinitely striking! *Susannah* burst
into a flood of tears.——We are not stocks and stones.——*Jonathan, Obadiah,* the cook-maid, all melted.——The foolish fat scullion herself, who was scouring a fish-kettle upon her knees, was
rous'd with it.——The whole kitchen crouded about the corporal.

Now as I perceive plainly, that the preservation of our constitution in church and state,——and possibly the preservation of the
whole world——or what is the same thing, the distribution and
balance of its property and power, may in time to come depend
greatly upon the right understanding of this stroke of the corporal's
eloquence——I do demand your attention,——your worships and
reverences, for any ten pages together, take them where you will in
any other part of the work, shall sleep for it at your ease.

I said, "we were not stocks and stones"——'tis very well. I
should have added, nor are we angels, I wish we were,——but men
cloathed with bodies, and governed by our imaginations;——and
what a junketting piece of work of it there is, betwixt these and our
seven senses, especially some of them, for my own part, I own it, I
am ashamed to confess. Let it suffice to affirm, that of all the senses,
the eye, (for I absolutely deny the touch, though most of your
Barbati,[4] I know, are for it) has the quickest commerce with the
soul,——gives a smarter stroke, and leaves something more inexpressible upon the fancy, than words can either convey——or
sometimes get rid of.

——I've gone a little about——no matter, 'tis for health——let
us only carry it back in our mind to the mortality of *Trim*'s hat.

——"Are we not here now,——and gone in a moment?"——There
was nothing in the sentence——'twas one of your self-evident truths
we have the advantage of hearing every day; and if *Trim* had not

3. Whitsontide is Pentecost, celebrating
the descent of the Holy Spirit to the
disciples fifty days after Easter. Shrovetide is the three days before Ash Wednesday.

4. "Bearded ones" (philosophers).

trusted more to his hat than his head——he had made nothing at all of it.

——"Are we not here now;"——continued the corporal, "and are we not"——(dropping his hat plumb upon the ground——and pausing, before he pronounced the word)——"gone! in a moment?" The descent of the hat was as if a heavy lump of clay had been kneaded into the crown of it.——Nothing could have expressed the sentiment of mortality, of which it was the type and fore-runner, like it,——his hand seemed to vanish from under it,——it fell dead,——the corporal's eye fix'd upon it, as upon a corps,——and *Susannah* burst into a flood of tears.

Now——Ten thousand, and ten thousand times ten thousand (for matter and motion are infinite) are the ways by which a hat may be dropped upon the ground, without any effect.——Had he flung it, or thrown it, or cast it, or skimmed it, or squirted, or let it slip or fall in any possible direction under heaven,——or in the best direction that could be given to it,——had he dropped it like a goose——like a puppy——like an ass——or in doing it, or even after he had done, had he looked like a fool,——like a ninny——like a nicompoop——it had fail'd, and the effect upon the heart had been lost.

Ye who govern this mighty world and its mighty concerns with the *engines* of eloquence,——who heat it, and cool it, and melt it, and mollify it,——and then harden it again to *your purpose*——

Ye who wind and turn the passions with this great windlass,—— and, having done it, lead the owners of them, whither ye think meet——

Ye, lastly, who drive——and why not, Ye also who are driven, like turkeys to market, with a stick and a red clout——meditate ——meditate, I beseech you, upon *Trim's* hat.

Chapter VIII.

STAY——I have a small account to settle with the reader, before *Trim* can go on with his harangue.——It shall be done in two minutes.

Amongst many other book-debts, all of which I shall discharge in due time,——I own myself a debtor to the world for two items, ——a chapter upon *chamber-maids and button-holes*, which, in the former part of my work, I promised and fully intended to pay off this year: but some of your worships and reverences telling me, that the two subjects, especially so connected together, might endanger the morals of the world,——I pray the chapter upon chamber-maids and button-holes may be forgiven me,——and that they will accept of the last chapter in lieu of it; which is nothing, an't please your reverences, but a chapter of *chamber-maids, green-gowns, and old hats.*[5]

Trim took his off the ground,——put it upon his head,——and then went on with his oration upon death, in manner and form following.

Chapter IX.

——To us, *Jonathan,* who know not what want or care is—— who live here in the service of two of the best of masters ——(bating in my own case his majesty King *William* the Third, whom I had the honour to serve both in *Ireland* and *Flanders*)—— I own it, that from *Whitsontide* to within three weeks of *Christmas,* ——'tis not long——'tis like nothing;——but to those, *Jonathan,* who know what death is, and what havock and destruction he can make, before a man can well wheel about——'tis like a whole age.——O *Jonathan!* 'twould make a good-natured man's heart bleed, to consider, continued the corporal, (standing perpendicularly) how low many a brave and upright fellow has been laid since that time!——And trust me, *Susy,* added the corporal, turning to *Susannah,* whose eyes were swimming in water,——before that time comes round again,——many a bright eye will be dim.—— *Susannah* placed it to the right side of the page——she wept—— but she court'sied too.——Are we not, continued *Trim,* looking still at *Susannah*——are we not like a flower of the field——a tear of pride stole in betwixt every two tears of humiliation——else no tongue could have described *Susannah*'s affliction——is not all flesh grass?——'Tis clay,——'tis dirt.——They all looked directly at the scullion,——the scullion had just been scouring a fish-kettle.——It was not fair.——

——What is the finest face that ever man looked at!——I could hear *Trim* talk so for ever, cried *Susannah,*——what is it! (*Susannah* laid her hand upon *Trim*'s shoulder)——but corruption?—— *Susannah* took it off.

——Now I love you for this——and 'tis this delicious mixture within you which makes you dear creatures what you are——and he who hates you for it————all I can say of the matter, is—— That he has either a pumkin for his head——or a pippin for his heart,——and whenever he is dissected 'twill be found so.

Chapter X.

WHETHER *Susannah,* by taking her hand too suddenly from off the corporal's shoulder, (by the whisking about of her passions)——broke a little the chain of his reflections——

5. *Green-gowns*: slang for "whores"; *old hats*: slang for "female genitals."

Or whether the corporal began to be suspicious, he had got into the doctor's quarters, and was talking more like the chaplain than himself——

Or whether -
Or whether——for in all such cases a man of invention and parts may with pleasure fill a couple of pages with suppositions——which of all these was the cause, let the curious physiologist, or the curious any body determine——'tis certain, at least, the corporal went on thus with his harangue.

For my own part, I declare it, that out of doors, I value not death at all:——not this . . added the corporal, snapping his fingers, ——but with an air which no one but the corporal could have given to the sentiment.——In battle, I value death not this . . . and let him not take me cowardly, like poor *Joe Gibbins*, in scouring his gun.——What is he? A pull of a trigger——a push of a bayonet an inch this way or that——makes the difference.——Look along the line——to the right——see! *Jack's* down! well,——'tis worth a regiment of horse to him.——No——'tis *Dick*. Then *Jack's* no worse.——Never mind which,——we pass on,——in hot pursuit the wound itself which brings him is not felt,——the best way is to stand up to him,——the man who flies, is in ten times more danger than the man who marches up into his jaws.——I've look'd him, added the corporal, an hundred times in the face,——and know what he is.——He's nothing, *Obadiah*, at all in the field.——But he's very frightful in a house, quoth *Obadiah*.——I never mind it myself, said *Jonathan*, upon a coach-box.——It must, in my opinion, be most natural in bed, replied *Susannah*.——And could I escape him by creeping into the worst calf's skin that ever was made into a knapsack, I would do it there——said *Trim*——but that is nature.

——Nature is nature, said *Jonathan*.——And that is the reason, cried *Susannah*, I so much pity my mistress.——She will never get the better of it.——Now I pity the captain the most of any one in the family, answered *Trim*.——Madam will get ease of heart in weeping,——and the Squire in talking about it,——but my poor master will keep it all in silence to himself.——I shall hear him sigh in his bed for a whole month together, as he did for lieutenant *Le Fever*. An' please your honour, do not sigh so piteously, I would say to him as I laid besides him. I cannot help it, *Trim*, my master would say,——'tis so melancholy an accident——I cannot get it off my heart.——Your honour fears not death yourself.——I hope, *Trim*, I fear nothing, he would say, but the doing a wrong thing. ——Well, he would add, whatever betides, I will take care of *Le Fever's* boy.——And with that, like a quieting draught, his honour would fall asleep.

I like to hear *Trim's* stories about the captain, said *Susannah.*——
He is a kindly-hearted gentleman, said *Obadiah*, as ever lived.——
Aye,——and as brave a one too, said the corporal, as ever stept
before a platoon.——There never was a better officer in the king's
army,——or a better man in God's world; for he would march up
to the mouth of a cannon, though he saw the lighted match at the
very touch-hole,——and yet, for all that, he has a heart as soft as a
child for other people.——He would not hurt a chicken.——I
would sooner, quoth *Jonathan*, drive such a gentleman for seven
pounds a year——than some for eight.——Thank thee, *Jonathan!*
for thy twenty shillings,——as much, *Jonathan*, said the corporal,
shaking him by the hand, as if thou hadst put the money into my
own pocket.——I would serve him to the day of my death out of
love. He is a friend and a brother to me,——and could I be sure my
poor brother *Tom* was dead,——continued the corporal, taking out
his handkerchief,——was I worth ten thousand pounds, I would
leave every shilling of it to the captain.——*Trim* could not refrain
from tears at this testamentary proof he gave of his affection to his
master.——The whole kitchen was affected.——Do tell us this
story of the poor lieutenant, said *Susannah.*——With all my heart,
answered the corporal.

Susannah, the cook, *Jonathan*, *Obadiah*, and corporal *Trim*,
formed a circle about the fire; and as soon as the scullion had shut
the kitchen door,——the corporal begun.

Chapter XI.

I Am a *Turk* if I had not as much forgot my mother, as if Nature
had plaistered me up, and set me down naked upon the banks
of the river *Nile*, without one.[6]——Your most obedient servant,
Madam——I've cost you a great deal of trouble,——I wish it
may answer;——but you have left a crack in my back,——and
here's a great piece fallen off here before,——and what must I do
with this foot?——I shall never reach *England* with it.

For my own part I never wonder at any thing;——and so often
has my judgment deceived me in my life, that I always suspect it,
right or wrong,——at least I am seldom hot upon cold subjects. For
all this, I reverence truth as much as any body; and when it has
slipped us, if a man will but take me by the hand, and go quietly
and search for it, as for a thing we have both lost, and can neither
of us do well without,——I'll go to the world's end with him:——
But I hate disputes,——and therefore (bating religious points, or
such as touch society) I would almost subscribe to any thing which

6. The mud of the Nile was believed in ancient time to have powers of spontaneous
generation.

does not choak me in the first passage, rather than be drawn into one——But I cannot bear suffocation,——and bad smells worst of all.——For which reasons, I resolved from the beginning, That if ever the army of martyrs was to be augmented,——or a new one raised,——I would have no hand in it, one way or t'other.

Chapter XII.

——**B**UT to return to my mother.

My uncle *Toby*'s opinion, Madam, "that there could be no harm in *Cornelius Gallus*, the *Roman* prætor's lying with his wife;"—— or rather the last word of that opinion,——(for it was all my mother heard of it) caught hold of her by the weak part of the whole sex:——You shall not mistake me,——I mean her curiosity, ——she instantly concluded herself the subject of the conversation, and with that prepossession upon her fancy, you will readily conceive every word my father said, was accommodated either to herself, or her family concerns.

——Pray, Madam, in what street does the lady live, who would not have done the same?

From the strange mode of *Cornelius*'s death, my father had made a transition to that of *Socrates*, and was giving my uncle *Toby* an abstract of his pleading before his judges;——'twas irresistable: ——not the oration of *Socrates*,——but my father's temptation to it.——He had wrote the[7] Life of *Socrates* himself the year before he left off trade, which, I fear, was the means of hastening him out of it;——so that no one was able to set out with so full a sail, and in so swelling a tide of heroic loftiness upon the occasion, as my father was. Not a period in *Socrates*'s oration, which closed with a shorter word than *transmigration*, or *annihilation*,——or a worse thought in the middle of it than *to be*——*or not to be*,——the entering upon a new and untried state of things,——or, upon a long, a profound and peaceful sleep, without dreams, without disturbance;——*That we and our children were born to die*,——*but neither of us born to be slaves.*——No——there I mistake; that was part of *Eleazer*'s oration, as recorded by *Josephus* (*de Bell.Judaic.*)[8] ——*Eleazer* owns he had it from the philosophers of *India*; in all likelihood *Alexander* the Great, in his irruption into *India*, after he

7. This book my father would never consent to publish; 'tis in manuscript, with some other tracts of his, in the family, all, or most of which will be printed in due time. [*Sterne's note.*]
8. Josephus (37–c.95) wrote *The Wars* of *the Jews* (the Latin title abbreviated *de Bell, Judaic.*). In the rest of this chapter Sterne is playing with attempts in his time to trace Western culture to Eastern origins.

had over-run *Persia,* amongst the many things he stole,——stole that sentiment also; by which means it was carried, if not all the way by himself, (for we all know he died at *Babylon*) at least by some of his maroders, into *Greece,*——from *Greece* it got to *Rome,* ——from *Rome* to *France,*——and from *France* to *England:*—— So things come round.——

By land carriage I can conceive no other way.——

By water the sentiment might easily have come down the *Ganges* into the *Sinus Gangeticus,* or *Bay of Bengal,* and so into the *Indian Sea;* and following the course of trade, (the way from *India* by the *Cape of Good Hope* being then unknown) might be carried with other drugs and spices up the *Red Sea* to *Joddah,* the port of *Mekka,* or else to *Tor* or *Sues,* towns at the bottom of the gulf; and from thence by karrawans to *Coptos,* but three days journey distant, so down the *Nile* directly to *Alexandria,* where the SENTIMENT would be landed at the very foot of the great stair-case of the *Alexandrian* library,——and from that store-house it would be fetched.——Bless me! what a trade was driven by the learned in those days!

Chapter XIII.

——NOW my father had a way, a little like that of *Job's* (in case there ever was such a man——if not, there's an end of the matter.——

Though, by the bye, because your learned men find some difficulty in fixing the precise æra in which so great a man lived;—— whether, for instance, before or after the patriarchs, &c.——to vote, therefore, that he never lived *at all,* is a little cruel,——'tis not doing as they would be done by——happen that as it may)——My father, I say, had a way, when things went extremely wrong with him, especially upon the first sally of his impatience,——of wondering why he was begot,——wishing himself dead;——sometimes worse:——And when the provocation ran high, and grief touched his lips with more than ordinary powers,——Sir, you scarce could have distinguished him from *Socrates* himself.——Every word would breathe the sentiments of a soul disdaining life, and careless about all its issues; for which reason, though my mother was a woman of no deep reading, yet the abstract of *Socrates's* oration, which my father was giving my uncle *Toby,* was not altogether new to her.——She listened to it with composed intelligence, and would have done so to the end of the chapter, had not my father plunged (which he had no occasion to have done) into that part of the pleading where the great philosopher reckons up his connections, his alliances, and children; but renounces a security to be so won by working upon the passions of his judges.———"I have friends———I have relations,———I have three desolate children,"———says *Socrates*.⁹———

———Then, cried my mother, opening the door,———you have one more, Mr. *Shandy*, than I know of.

By heaven! I have one less,———said my father, getting up and walking out of the room.

Chapter XIV.

———They are *Socrates*'s children, said my uncle *Toby*. He has been dead a hundred years ago, replied my mother.

My uncle *Toby* was no chronologer———so not caring to advance a step but upon safe ground, he laid down his pipe deliberately upon the table, and rising up, and taking my mother most kindly by the hand, without saying another word, either good or bad, to her, he led her out after my father, that he might finish the ecclaircissement¹ himself.

Chapter XV.

HAD this volume been a farce, which, unless every one's life and opinions are to be looked upon as a farce as well as mine, I see no reason to suppose———the last chapter, Sir, had finished the first act of it, and then this chapter must have set off thus.

Ptr..r..r..ing———twing———twang———prut———trut———'tis a cursed bad fiddle.———Do you know whether my fiddle's in tune or no?———trut..prut..———They should be *fifths*.———'Tis wickedly strung———tr...a.e.i.o.u.-twang.———The bridge is a mile too high, and the sound-post absolutely down,———else———trut . . prut——— hark! 'tis not so bad a tone.———Diddle diddle, diddle diddle, diddle diddle, dum. There is nothing in playing before good judges,——— but there's a man there———no———not him with the bundle under his arm———the grave man in black.———'Sdeath! not the gentleman with the sword on.———Sir, I had rather play a *Caprichio*² to *Calliope* herself, than draw my bow across my fiddle before that very man; and yet, I'll stake my *Cremona* to a *Jew*'s trump, which is the greatest musical odds that ever were laid, that I will this moment stop three hundred and fifty leagues out of tune upon my fiddle, without punishing one single nerve that belongs to him.———Twaddle diddle, tweddle diddle,———twiddle diddle,———twoddle diddle,———twuddle diddle,———prut-trut———krish———krash———krush.

9. In Plato's *Apology*.
1. Enlightenment.
2. *Caprichio*: a lively piece of music.
Calliope: the muse of (serious) epic poetry. *Cremona*: a fine violin made in Cremona, Italy. *Jew's trump*: Jew's harp.

————I've undone you, Sir,————but you see he is no worse,———— and was *Apollo* to take his fiddle after me, he can make him no better.

Diddle diddle, diddle diddle, diddle diddle———hum———dum——— drum.

————Your worships and your reverences love musick———and God has made you all with good ears———and some of you play delightfully yourselves———trut-prut,———prut-trut.

O! there is———whom I could sit and hear whole days,———whose talents lie in making what he fiddles to be felt,———who inspires me with his joys and hopes, and puts the most hidden springs of my heart into motion.———If you would borrow five guineas of me, Sir,———which is generally ten guineas more than I have to spare ———or you, Messrs. Apothecary and Taylor, want your bills paying,———that's your time.

Chapter XVI.

THE first thing which entered my father's head, after affairs were a little settled in the family, and *Susannah* had got possession of my mother's green sattin night-gown,———was to sit down coolly, after the example of *Xenophon*,[3] and write a Tristra- pædia, or system of education for me; collecting first for that purpose his own scattered thoughts, counsels, and notions; and binding them together, so as to form an INSTITUTE for the govern- ment of my childhood and adolescence. I was my father's last stake———he had lost my brother *Bobby* entirely,———he had lost, by his own computation, full three fourths of me———that is, he had been unfortunate in his three first great casts for me———my geni- ture, nose, and name,———there was but this one left; and accord- ingly my father gave himself up to it with as much devotion as ever my uncle *Toby* had done to his doctrine of projectils.———The dif- ference between them was, that my uncle *Toby* drew his whole knowledge of projectils from *Nicholas Tartaglia*———My father spun his, every thread of it, out of his own brain,———or reeled and cross- twisted what all other spinners and spinsters had spun before him, that 'twas pretty near the same torture to him.

In about three years, or something more, my father had got advanced almost into the middle of his work.———Like all other writers, he met with disappointments.———He imagined he should be able to bring whatever he had to say, into so small a compass, that

3. The Greek historian (c.430–c.355 B.C.) discusses the education of Cyrus (founder of the Persian Empire) in his *Cyropaedia,* together with his own theories of educa- tion.

when it was finished and bound, it might be rolled up in my mother's hussive.[4]——Matter grows under our hands.——Let no man
say,——"Come——I'll write a *duodecimo*."

My father gave himself up to it, however, with the most painful
diligence, proceeding step by step in every line, with the same kind
of caution and circumspection (though I cannot say upon quite so
religious a principle) as was used by *John de la Casse*, the lord
archbishop of *Benevento*,[5] in compassing his *Galateo*; in which his
Grace of *Benevento* spent near forty years of his life; and when the
thing came out, it was not of above half the size or the thickness of
a *Rider*'s Almanack.——How the holy man managed the affair,
unless he spent the greatest part of his time in combing his whiskers,
or playing at *primero* with his chaplain,——would pose any mortal not let into the true secret;——and therefore 'tis worth explaining to the world, was it only for the encouragement of those few in
it, who write not so much to be fed——as to be famous.

I own had *John de la Casse*, the archbishop of *Benevento*, for
whose memory (notwithstanding his *Galateo*) I retain the highest
veneration,——had he been, Sir, a slender clerk——of dull wit——
slow parts——costive head, and so forth,——he and his *Galateo*
might have jogged on together to the age of *Methusalah* for me,
——the phænomenon had not been worth a parenthesis.——

But the reverse of this was the truth: *John de la Casse* was a
genius of fine parts and fertile fancy; and yet with all these great
advantages of nature, which should have pricked him forwards with
his *Galateo*, he lay under an impuissance at the same time of
advancing above a line and an half in the compass of a whole
summer's day: this disability in his Grace arose from an opinion he
was afflicted with,——which opinion was this,——*viz.* that whenever a Christian was writing a book (not for his private amusement,
but) where his intent and purpose was *bonâ fide*, to print and
publish it to the world, his first thoughts were always the temptations of the evil one.——This was the state of ordinary writers: but
when a personage of venerable character and high station, either in
church or state, once turned author,——he maintained, that from
the very moment he took pen in hand——all the devils in hell broke
out of their holes to cajole him.——'Twas Term-time with them,
——every thought, first and last, was captious;——how specious
and good soever,——'twas all one;——in whatever form or colour
it presented itself to the imagination,——'twas still a stroke of one
or other of 'em levelled at him, and was to be fenced off.——So
that the life of a writer, whatever he might fancy to the contrary,

4. A small sewing case. *Duodecimo*: a
small book made by folding the sheets
into twelve leaves.

5. An Italian poet and churchman of
the sixteenth century. His *Galateo* and
Rider's *Almanack* were small books.

was not so much a state of *composition*, as a state of *warfare*; and his probation in it, precisely that of any other man militant upon earth,——both depending alike, not half so much upon the degrees of his wit——as his resistance.

My father was hugely pleased with this theory of *John de la Casse*, archbishop of *Benevento*; and (had it not cramped him a little in his creed) I believe would have given ten of the best acres in the *Shandy* estate, to have been the broacher of it.——How far my father actually believed in the devil, will be seen, when I come to speak of my father's religious notions, in the progress of this work: 'tis enough to say here, as he could not have the honour of it, in the literal sense of the doctrine——he took up with the allegory of it;——and would often say, especially when his pen was a little retrograde, there was as much good meaning, truth, and knowledge, couched under the veil of *John de la Casse*'s parabolical representation,——as was to be found in any one poetic fiction, or mystick record of antiquity.——Prejudice of education, he would say, *is the devil*,——and the multitudes of them which we suck in with our mother's milk——*are the devil and all*.——We are haunted with them, brother *Toby*, in all our lucubrations and researches; and was a man fool enough to submit tamely to what they obtruded upon him,——what would his book be? Nothing,——he would add, throwing his pen away with a vengeance,——nothing but a farrago of the clack of nurses, and of the nonsense of the old women (of both sexes) throughout the kingdom.

This is the best account I am determined to give of the slow progress my father made in his *Tristra-pædia*; at which (as I said) he was three years and something more, indefatigably at work, and at last, had scarce compleated, by his own reckoning, one half of his undertaking: the misfortune was, that I was all that time totally neglected and abandoned to my mother; and what was almost as bad, by the very delay, the first part of the work, upon which my father had spent the most of his pains, was rendered entirely useless,——every day a page or two became of no consequence.——

——Certainly it was ordained as a scourge upon the pride of human wisdom, That the wisest of us all, should thus outwit ourselves, and eternally forego our purposes in the intemperate act of pursuing them.

In short, my father was so long in all his acts of resistance,—— or in other words,——he advanced so very slow with his work, and I began to live and get forwards at such a rate, that if an event had not happened,——which, when we get to it, if it can be told with decency, shall not be concealed a moment from the reader——I verily believe, I had put by my father, and left him drawing a sundial, for no better purpose than to be buried under ground.

Chapter XVII.

——'TWAS nothing,——I did not lose two drops of blood by it——'twas not worth calling in a surgeon, had he lived next door to us——thousands suffer by choice, what I did by accident.——Doctor *Slop* made ten times more of it, than there was occasion:——some men rise, by the art of hanging great weights upon small wires,——and I am this day (*August* the 10th, 1761) paying part of the price of this man's reputation.——O 'twould provoke a stone, to see how things are carried on in this world!—— The chamber-maid had left no ******* *** under the bed:—— Cannot you contrive, master, quoth *Susannah*, lifting up the sash with one hand, as she spoke, and helping me up into the window seat with the other,——cannot you manage, my dear, for a single time to **** *** ** *** ******?

I was five years old.——*Susannah* did not consider that nothing was well hung in our family,——so slap came the sash down like lightening upon us;——Nothing is left,——cried *Susannah*,—— nothing is left——for me, but to run my country.⁶——

My uncle *Toby*'s house was a much kinder sanctuary; and so *Susannah* fled to it.

Chapter XVIII.

WHEN *Susannah* told the corporal the misadventure of the sash, with all the circumstances which attended the *murder* of me,——(as she called it)——the blood forsook his cheeks;——all accessaries in murder, being principals,——*Trim*'s conscience told him he was as much to blame as *Susannah*,——and if the doctrine had been true, my uncle *Toby* had as much of the blood-shed to answer for to heaven, as either of 'em;——so that neither reason or instinct, separate or together, could possibly have guided *Susannah*'s steps to so proper an asylum. It is in vain to leave this to the Reader's imagination:——to form any kind of hypothesis that will render these propositions feasible, he must cudgel his brains sore,——and to do it without,——he must have such brains as no reader ever had before him.——Why should I put them either to tryal or to torture? 'Tis my own affair: I'll explain it myself.

Chapter XIX.

'TIS a pity, *Trim*, said my uncle *Toby*, resting with his hand upon the corporal's shoulder, as they both stood surveying their works,——that we have not a couple of field pieces to mount in the

6. That is, flee the country.

gorge of that new redoubt;——'twould secure the lines all along there, and make the attack on that side quite complete:——get me a couple cast, *Trim*.

Your honour shall have them, replied *Trim*, before to-morrow morning.

It was the joy of *Trim*'s heart,——nor was his fertile head ever at a loss for expedients in doing it, to supply my uncle *Toby* in his campaigns, with whatever his fancy called for; had it been his last crown, he would have sate down and hammered it into a paderero[7] to have prevented a single wish in his Master. The corporal had already,——what with cutting off the ends of my uncle *Toby*'s spouts——hacking and chiseling up the sides of his leaden gutters, ——melting down his pewter shaving bason,——and going at last, like *Lewis* the fourteenth, on to the top of the church,[8] for spare ends, &c.——he had that very campaign brought no less than eight new battering cannons, besides three demi-culverins into the field; my uncle *Toby*'s demand for two more pieces for the redoubt, had set the corporal at work again; and no better resource offering, he had taken the two leaden weights from the nursery window: and as the sash pullies, when the lead was gone, were of no kind of use, he had taken them away also, to make a couple of wheels for one of their carriages.

He had dismantled every sash window in my uncle *Toby*'s house long before, in the very same way,——though not always in the same order; for sometimes the pullies had been wanted, and not the lead,——so then he began with the pullies,——and the pullies being picked out, then the lead became useless,——and so the lead went to pot too.

——A great MORAL might be picked handsomly out of this, but I have not time——'tis enough to say, wherever the demolition began, 'twas equally fatal to the sash window.

Chapter XX.

THE corporal had not taken his measures so badly in this stroke of artilleryship, but that he might have kept the matter entirely to himself, and left *Susannah* to have sustained the whole weight of the attack, as she could;——true courage is not content with coming off so.——The corporal, whether as general or comptroller of the train,——'twas no matter,——had done that, without which, as he imagined, the misfortune could never have happened, ——at least in *Susannah's hands*;——How would your honours have behaved?——He determined at once, not to take shelter be-

---

7. A form of cannon used to propel scrap iron or stones.
8. Louis XIV often made the Church loan him money for his wars; but it was also common practice to melt down copper or lead church roofs and turn them into weapons or ammunition when other sources failed.

hind *Susannah,*——but to give it; and with this resolution upon his mind, he marched upright into the parlour, to lay the whole manœuvre before my uncle *Toby.*

My uncle *Toby* had just then been giving *Yorick* an account of the Battle of *Steenkirk,*[9] and of the strange conduct of count *Solmes* in ordering the foot to halt, and the horse to march where it could not act; which was directly contrary to the king's commands, and proved the loss of the day.

There are incidents in some families so pat to the purpose of what is going to follow,——they are scarce exceeded by the invention of a dramatic writer;——I mean of ancient days.——

Trim, by the help of his forefinger, laid flat upon the table, and the edge of his hand striking a-cross it at right angles, made a shift to tell his story so, that priests and virgins might have listened to it;——and the story being told,——the dialogue went on as follows.

Chapter XXI.

——I would be picquetted[1] to death, cried the corporal, as he concluded *Susannah's* story, before I would suffer the woman to come to any harm,——'twas my fault, an please your honour,——not hers.

Corporal *Trim,* replied my uncle *Toby,* putting on his hat which lay upon the table,——if any thing can be said to be a fault, when the service absolutely requires it should be done,——'tis I certainly who deserve the blame,——you obeyed your orders.

Had count *Solmes, Trim,* done the same at the battle of *Steenkirk,* said *Yorick,* drolling a little upon the corporal, who had been run over by a dragoon[2] in the retreat,——he had saved thee;——Saved! cried *Trim,* interrupting *Yorick,* and finishing the sentence for him after his own fashion,——he had saved five battalions, an please your reverence, every soul of them:——there was *Cutts's*[3] ——continued the corporal, clapping the forefinger of his right hand upon the thumb of his left, and counting round his hand,—— there was *Cutts's*——*Mackay's,*——*Angus's,*——*Graham's*——and *Leven's,* all cut to pieces;——and so had the *English* life-guards too, had it not been for some regiments upon the right, who marched up boldly to their relief, and received the enemy's fire in their faces, before any one of their own platoons discharged a musket,——they'll go to heaven for it,——added *Trim.*——*Trim* is right, said my uncle *Toby,* nodding to *Yorick,*——he's perfectly right. What signified his marching the horse, continued the cor-

---

9. An unsuccessful battle, headed by the Dutch Count Solmes, against the French in 1692.
1. A military punishment in which the victim is forced to stand on sharp stakes.
2. A mounted soldier armed with a carbine.
3. The names are those of commanders of regiments.

poral, where the ground was so strait, and the *French* had such a nation of hedges, and copses, and ditches, and fell'd trees laid this way and that to cover them; (as they always have.)——Count *Solmes* should have sent us,——we would have fired muzzle to muzzle with them for their lives.——There was nothing to be done for the horse:——he had his foot shot off however for his pains, continued the corporal, the very next campaign at *Landen.*—— Poor *Trim* got his wound there, quoth my uncle *Toby.*——'Twas owing, an please your honour, entirely to count *Solmes,*——had we drub'd them soundly at *Steenkirk,* they would not have fought us at *Landen.*——Possibly not,——*Trim,* said my uncle *Toby;*—— though if they have the advantage of a wood, or you give them a moment's time to intrench themselves, they are a nation which will pop and pop for ever at you.——There is no way but to march coolly up to them,——receive their fire, and fall in upon them, pell-mell——Ding dong, added *Trim.*——Horse and foot, said my uncle *Toby.*——Helter skelter, said *Trim.*——Right and left, cried my uncle *Toby.*——Blood an' ounds,[4] shouted the corporal;——the battle raged,——*Yorick* drew his chair a little to one side for safety, and after a moment's pause, my uncle *Toby* sinking his voice a note, ——resumed the discourse as follows.

Chapter XXII.

KING *William,* said my uncle *Toby,* addressing himself to Yorick, was so terribly provoked at count *Solmes* for disobeying his orders, that he would not suffer him to come into his presence for many months after.——I fear, answered *Yorick,* the squire[5] will be as much provoked at the corporal, as the King at the count. ——But 'twould be singularly hard in this case, continued he, if corporal *Trim,* who has behaved so diametrically opposite to count *Solmes,* should have the fate to be rewarded with the same disgrace; ——too oft in this world, do things take that train.——I would spring a mine, cried my uncle *Toby,* rising up,——and blow up my fortifications, and my house with them, and we would perish under their ruins, ere I would stand by and see it.——*Trim* directed a slight,——but a grateful bow towards his master,——and so the chapter ends.

Chapter XXIII.

——Then, *Yorick,* replied my uncle *Toby,* you and I will lead the way abreast,——and do you, corporal, follow a few paces behind us.——And *Susannah,* an' please your honour, said *Trim,* shall be put in the rear.——'Twas an excellent disposition,

4. An oath "By God's wounds."
5. Walter Shandy.

——and in this order, without either drums beating, or colours flying, they marched slowly from my uncle *Toby*'s house to *Shandy-hall*.

——I wish, said *Trim*, as they entered the door,——instead of the sash-weights, I had cut off the church-spout, as I once thought to have done.——You have cut off spouts enow, replied *Yorick*.——

Chapter XXIV.

AS many pictures as have been given of my father, how like him soever in different airs and attitudes,——not one, or all of them, can ever help the reader to any kind of preconception of how my father would think, speak, or act, upon any untried occasion or occurrence of life.——There was that infinitude of oddities in him, and of chances along with it, by which handle he would take a thing,——it baffled, Sir, all calculations.——The truth was, his road lay so very far on one side, from that wherein most men travelled,——that every object before him presented a face and section of itself to his eye, altogether different from the plan and elevation of it seen by the rest of mankind.——In other words, 'twas a different object,——and in course was differently considered:

This is the true reason, that my dear *Jenny* and I, as well as all the world besides us, have such eternal squabbles about nothing.——She looks at her outside,——I, at her in——. How is it possible we should agree about her value?

Chapter XXV.

'TIS a point settled,——and I mention it for the comfort of[6] *Confucius*, who is apt to get entangled in telling a plain story ——that provided he keeps along the line of his story,——he may go backwards and forwards as he will,——'tis still held to be no digression.

This being premised, I take the benefit of the *act of going backwards* myself.

Chapter XXVI.

FIFTY thousand pannier loads of devils——(not of the Archbishop of *Benevento*'s,——I mean of *Rabelais*'s devils[7]) with their tails chopped off by their rumps, could not have made so diabolical a scream of it, as I did——when the accident befell me:

6. Mr. *Shandy* is supposed to mean ***** *** ***, Esq; member for ******, ——and not the Chinese Legislator. [*Sterne's note.*] He is making fun of those determined to read specific references into his fiction.

7. Rabelais often refers to devils, notably in the Prologue to Book II.

it summoned up my mother instantly into the nursery,——so that *Susannah* had but just time to make her escape down the back stairs, as my mother came up the fore.

Now, though I was old enough to have told the story myself,—— and young enough, I hope, to have done it without malignity; yet *Susannah*, in passing by the kitchen, for fear of accidents, had left it in short-hand with the cook——the cook had told it with a commentary to *Jonathan*, and *Jonathan* to *Obadiah*; so that by the time my father had rung the bell half a dozen times, to know what was the matter above,——was *Obadiah* enabled to give him a particular account of it, just as it had happened.——I thought as much, said my father, tucking up his night-gown;——and so walked up stairs.

One would imagine from this——(though for my own part I somewhat question it)——that my father before that time, had actually wrote that remarkable chapter in the *Tristra-pædia*, which to me is the most original and entertaining one in the whole book; ——and that is the *chapter upon sash-windows*, with a bitter *Philippick* at the end of it, upon the forgetfulness of chambermaids.——I have but two reasons for thinking otherwise.

First, Had the matter been taken into consideration, before the event happened, my father certainly would have nailed up the sash-window for good an' all;——which, considering with what difficulty he composed books,——he might have done with ten times less trouble, than he could have wrote the chapter: this argument I foresee holds good against his writing the chapter, even after the event; but 'tis obviated under the second reason, which I have the honour to offer to the world in support of my opinion, that my father did not write the chapter upon sash-windows and chamber-pots, at the time supposed,——and it is this.

——That, in order to render the *Tristrapædia* complete,——I wrote the chapter myself.

Chapter XXVII.

MY father put on his spectacles——looked,——took them off,——put them into the case——all in less than a statutable minute; and without opening his lips, turned about, and walked precipitately down stairs: my mother imagined he had stepped down for lint and basilicon;[8] but seeing him return with a couple of folios under his arm, and *Obadiah* following him with a large reading desk, she took it for granted 'twas an herbal, and so drew him a chair to the bed side, that he might consult upon the case at his ease.

——If it be but right done,——said my father, turning to the *Section*——*de sede vel subjecto circumcisionis,*——for he had

8. Ointment.

brought up *Spencer de Legibus Hebræorum Ritualibus*⁹——and *Maimonides*, in order to confront and examine us altogether.——

——If it be but right done, quoth he:——Only tell us, cried my mother, interrupting him, what herbs.——For that, replied my father, you must send for Dr. *Slop*.

My mother went down, and my father went on, reading the section as follows.

```
    *    *    *    *    *    *    *    *    *    *    *    *
 *  *    *    *    *    *    *    *    *    *    *    *    *
 *  *    *    *    *    *——Very well,——said my father,
 *  *    *    *    *    *    *    *    *    *    *    *    *
 *  *    *    *    *    *    *    *    *    *    *    *    *
 *  *    *——nay, if it has that convenience——and so with-
```

out stopping a moment to settle it first in his mind, whether the *Jews* had it from the *Egyptians*, or the *Egyptians* from the *Jews*,—— he rose up, and rubbing his forehead two or three times across with the palm of his hand, in the manner we rub out the footsteps of care, when evil has trod lighter upon us than we foreboded,——he shut the book, and walked down stairs.——Nay, said he, mentioning the name of a different great nation upon every step as he set his foot upon it——if the EGYPTIANS,——the SYRIANS,——the PHOE-NICIANS,——the ARABIANS,——the CAPADOCIANS,¹——if the COL-CHI, and TROGLODYTES did it——if SOLON and PYTHAGORAS submitted,——what is TRISTRAM?——Who am I, that I should fret or fume one moment about the matter?

Chapter XXVIII.

DEAR *Yorick*, said my father smiling, (for *Yorick* had broke his rank with my uncle *Toby* in coming through the narrow entry, and so had stept first into the parlour)——this *Tristram* of ours, I find, comes very hardly by all his religious rites.——Never was the son of *Jew*, *Christian*, *Turk*, or *Infidel* initiated into them in so oblique and slovenly a manner.——But he is no worse, I trust, said *Yorick*.——There has been certainly, continued my father, the duce and all to do in some part or other of the ecliptic,² when this offspring of mine was formed.——That, you are a better judge of

9. This is not the John Spencer to whom Sterne dedicated this volume of *Tristram Shandy*, but rather a seventeenth-century churchman who wrote *On the Ritual Laws of the Hebrews* (with a section on circumcision). Maimonides (1135–1204), a great Jewish scholar, philosopher, and scientist, describes the reasons for circumcision in *Moreh Nebuchim*.
1. Capadocians lived in Asia Minor, the Colchi near the Caucasus mountains.

The Troglodytes were cave dwellers around the Red Sea.
2. The orbit of the sun. Trine and sextil aspects: numbers of degrees separating heavenly bodies in the zodiac. Lords of geniture: the astrological term for the heavenly body influencing a person from his birth. Bo-peep is the child's game. Sterne is describing a situation where all (astrological) order has broken down.

than I, replied *Yorick*.——Astrologers, quoth my father, know better than us both:——the trine and sextil aspects have jumped awry,——or the opposite of their ascendents have not hit it, as they should,——or the lords of the genitures (as they call them) have been at *bo-peep*,——or something has been wrong above, or below with us.

'Tis possible, answered *Yorick*.——But is the child, cried my uncle *Toby*, the worse?——The *Troglodytes* say not, replied my father.——And your theologists, *Yorick*, tell us——Theologically? said *Yorick*,——or speaking after the manner of apothecaries?[3] ——statesmen?[4]——or washer-women?[5]

——I'm not sure, replied my father,——but they tell us, brother *Toby*, he's the better for it.——Provided, said *Yorick*, you travel him into *Egypt*.——Of that, answered my father, he will have the advantage, when he sees the *Pyramids*.——

Now every word of this, quoth my uncle *Toby*, is *Arabick* to me.——I wish, said *Yorick*, 'twas so, to half the world.

——Ilus,[6] continued my father, circumcised his whole army one morning.——Not without a court martial? cried my uncle *Toby*.

——Though the learned, continued he, taking no notice of my uncle *Toby*'s remark, but turning to *Yorick*,——are greatly divided still who *Ilus* was;——some say *Saturn*;——some the supream Being;——others, no more than a brigadier general under *Pharoah-neco*.——Let him be who he will, said my uncle *Toby*, I know not by what article of war he could justify it.

The controvertists, answered my father, assign two and twenty different reasons for it:——others indeed, who have drawn their pens on the opposite side of the question, have shewn the world the futility of the greatest part of them.——But then again, our best polemic divines——I wish there was not a polemic divine, said *Yorick*, in the kingdom;——one ounce of practical divinity——is worth a painted ship load of all their reverences have imported these fifty years.——Pray, Mr. *Yorick*, quoth my uncle *Toby*,——do tell me what a polemic divine is.——The best description, captain *Shandy*, I have ever read, is a couple of 'em, replied *Yorick*, in the account of the battle fought single hands betwixt *Gymnast* and

---

3. Χαλεπῆς νόσου, καὶ δυσιάτου ἀπαλλαγὴ, ἣν ἄνθρακα καλοῦσιν.——PHILO. [*Sterne's note*.] He is quoting Philo Judaeus, an Alexandrian Jewish philosopher of the first century, whose work *De Circumcisione* is cited by Spencer: "A release from a terrible and painful disease, and hard to cure, which they call anthrax."

4. Τὰ τεμνόμενα τῶν ἐθνῶν πολυγονώτατα, καὶ πολυανθρωπότατα εἶναι. [*Sterne's note*.] Again Philo: "Nations practicing circumcision are the most prolific and populous."

5. Καθαριότητος εἵνεκεν.——BOCHART. [*Sterne's note*.] The source is not Bochart, but the *History* of Herodotus. It means "For the sake of cleanliness."

6. Ὁ Ἶλος, τὰ αἰδοῖα περιτέμνεται, ταὐτὸ ποιῆσαι καὶ τοὺς ἀμ' αὐτῷ συμμάχους καταναγκάσας.——SANCHUNIATHO. [*Sterne's note*.] Philo Byblius, a Phoenician grammarian of the first century, claimed to have translated the works of an ancient writer he called Sanchuniathon. The passage translates: "Ilus is circumcised and compels the allies with him to do the same."

captain *Tripet*;[7] which I have in my pocket.——I beg I may hear it, quoth my uncle *Toby* earnestly.——You shall, said *Yorick*.—— And as the corporal is waiting for me at the door,——and I know the description of a battle, will do the poor fellow more good than his supper,——I beg, brother, you'll give him leave to come in.—— With all my soul, said my father.——*Trim* came in, erect and happy as an emperour; and having shut the door, *Yorick* took a book from his right-hand coat pocket, and read, or pretended to read, as follows.

Chapter XXIX.

——"which words being heard by all the soldiers which were there, divers of them being inwardly terrified, did shrink back and make room for the assailant: all this did *Gymnast* very well remark and consider; and therefore, making as if he would have alighted from off his horse, as he was poising himself on the mounting side, he most nimbly (with his short sword by his thigh) shifting his feet in the stirrup and performing the stirrup-leather feat, whereby, after the inclining of his body downwards, he forthwith launched himself aloft into the air, and placed both his feet together upon the saddle, standing upright, with his back turned towards his horse's head, ——Now (said he) my case goes forward. Then suddenly in the same posture wherein he was, he fetched a gambol upon one foot, and turning to the left-hand, failed not to carry his body perfectly round, just into his former position, without missing one jot.—— Ha! said *Tripet*, I will not do that at this time,——and not without cause. Well, said *Gymnast*, I have failed,——I will undo this leap; then with a marvellous strength and agility, turning towards the right-hand, he fetched another frisking gambol as before; which done, he set his right-hand thumb upon the bow of the saddle, raised himself up, and sprung into the air, poising and upholding his whole weight upon the muscle and nerve of the said thumb, and so turned and whirled himself about three times: at the fourth, re- versing his body and overturning it upside-down, and foreside back, without *touching any thing*, he brought himself betwixt the horse's two ears, and then giving himself a jerking swing, he seated himself upon the crupper——"

(This can't be fighting, said my uncle *Toby*.——The corporal shook his head at it.——Have patience, said *Yorick*.)

"Then (*Tripet*) pass'd his right leg over his saddle, and placed himself *en croup*.[8]——But, said he, 'twere better for me to get into the saddle; then putting the thumbs of both hands upon the crupper

---

7. In Rabelais (I.35).   8. On the horse's rump.

before him, and thereupon leaning himself, as upon the only sup-
porters of his body, he incontinently turned heels over head in the
air, and straight found himself betwixt the bow of the saddle in a
tolerable seat; then springing into the air with a summerset, he
turned him about like a wind-mill, and made above a hundred
frisks, turns and demi-pommadas."⁹——Good God! cried *Trim*,
losing all patience,——one home thrust of a bayonet is worth it
all.——I think so too, replied *Yorick*.——
——I am of a contrary opinion, quoth my father.

Chapter XXX.

——No,——I think I have advanced nothing, replied my father,
making answer to a question which *Yorick* had taken the liberty to
put to him,——I have advanced nothing in the *Tristrapædia*, but
what is as clear as any one proposition in *Euclid*.——Reach me,
Trim, that book from off the scrutoir:¹ it has oft times been in my
mind, continued my father, to have read it over both to you, *Yorick*,
and to my brother *Toby*, and I think it a little unfriendly in
myself, in not having done it long ago:— shall we have a short
chapter or two now,——and a chapter or two hereafter, as occasions serve; and so on, till we get through the whole? My uncle
Toby and *Yorick* made the obeisance which was proper; and the
corporal, though he was not included in the compliment, laid his
hand upon his breast, and made his bow at the same time.——The
company smiled. *Trim*, quoth my father, has paid the full price for
staying out the *entertainment*.——He did not seem to relish the
play, replied *Yorick*.——'Twas a Tom-fool-battle, an' please your
reverence, of captain *Tripet's* and that other officer, making so
many summersets, as they advanced;——the *French* come on
capering now and then in that way,——but not quite so much.
 My uncle *Toby* never felt the consciousness of his existence with
more complacency than what the corporal's, and his own reflections, made him do at that moment;——he lighted his pipe,——
Yorick drew his chair closer to the table,——*Trim* snuff'd the
candle,——my father stir'd up the fire,——took up the book,——
cough'd twice, and begun.

Chapter XXXI.

THE first thirty pages, said my father, turning over the leaves,
——are a little dry; and as they are not closely connected
with the subject,——for the present we'll pass them by: 'tis a

9. A trick executed by vaulting on or
over a horse by placing one hand on the
saddle.
1. Escritoire, writing desk.

prefatory introduction, continued my father, or an introductory preface (for I am not determined which name to give it) upon political or civil government; the foundation of which being laid in the first conjunction betwixt male and female, for procreation of the species——I was insensibly led into it.——'Twas natural, said *Yorick*.

The original of society, continued my father, I'm satisfied is, what *Politian*[2] tells us, *i.e.* merely conjugal; and nothing more than the getting together of one man and one woman;——to which, (according to *Hesiod*) the philosopher adds a servant:——but supposing in the first beginning there were no men servants born——he lays the foundation of it, in a man,——a woman——and a bull.——I believe 'tis an ox, quoth *Yorick*, quoting the passage (οἶκον μὲν πρώτιστα, γυναῖκά τε, βοῦν τ' ἀροτῆρα.)——A bull must have given more trouble than his head was worth.——But there is a better reason still, said my father, (dipping his pen into his ink) for, the ox being the most patient of animals, and the most useful withal in tilling the ground for their nourishment,——was the properest instrument, and emblem too, for the new joined couple, that the creation could have associated with them.——And there is a stronger reason, added my uncle *Toby*, than them all for the ox.——My father had not power to take his pen out of his ink-horn, till he had heard my uncle *Toby*'s reason.——For when the ground was tilled, said my uncle *Toby*, and made worth inclosing, then they began to secure it by walls and ditches, which was the origin of fortification.——True, true; dear *Toby*, cried my father, striking out the bull, and putting the ox in his place.

My father gave *Trim* a nod, to snuff the candle, and resumed his discourse.

——I enter upon this speculation, said my father carelessly, and half shutting the book, as he went on,——merely to shew the foundation of the natural relation between a father and his child; the right and jurisdiction over whom he acquires these several ways——

1st, by marriage.

2d, by adoption.

3d, by legitimation.

And 4th, by procreation; all which I consider in their order.

I lay a slight stress upon one of them; replied *Yorick*——the act, especially where it ends there, in my opinion lays as little obligation upon the child, as it conveys power to the father.——You are wrong,——said my father argutely,[3] and for this plain reason   *

---

2. A fifteenth-century Italian writer. Hesiod is the ancient Greek poet; the passage is from his *Works and Days*: "First of all, a horse, a woman, and a ploughing ox."

3. Shrewdly.

*   *   *   *   *   *   *   *   *   *   *   *

*   *   *   *   *   *   *   . ——I own, added my father, that the offspring, upon this account, is not so under the power and jurisdiction of the *mother*.——But the reason, replied *Yorick*, equally holds good for her.——She is under authority herself, said my father:——and besides, continued my father, nodding his head and laying his finger upon the side of his nose, as he assigned his reason,——*she is not the principal agent*, Yorick.——In what? quoth my uncle *Toby*, stopping his pipe.——Though by all means, added my father (not attending to my uncle *Toby*) "The *son ought to pay her respect*," as you may read, Yorick, at large in the first book of the Institutes of *Justinian*, at the eleventh title and the tenth section.——I can read it as well, replied *Yorick*, in the Catechism.

Chapter XXXII.

*T*RIM can repeat every word of it by heart, quoth my uncle *Toby*. ——Pugh! said my father, not caring to be interrupted with *Trim*'s saying his Catechism. He can upon my honour, replied my uncle *Toby*.——Ask him, Mr. *Yorick*, any question you please.——

——The fifth Commandment, *Trim*——said *Yorick*, speaking mildly, and with a gentle nod, as to a modest Catechumen.[4] The corporal stood silent.——You don't ask him right, said my uncle *Toby*, raising his voice, and giving it rapidly like the word of command;——The fifth—— ——cried my uncle *Toby*.——I must begin with the first, an' please your honour, said the corporal.——

——*Yorick* could not forbear smiling.——Your reverence does not consider, said the corporal, shouldering his stick like a musket, and marching into the middle of the room, to illustrate his position, ——that 'tis exactly the same thing, as doing one's exercise in the field.——

"*Join your right hand to your* firelock," cried the corporal, giving the word of command, ar
ning the motion.——

"*Poise your firelock*," both adjutant and private
ɛ corporal, doing the duty still of
—

"*Rest your firelock*;"—
you see leads into anoth
the *first*——
notion, an' please your reverence,
f his honour will begin but with

THE FIRST—cried my
side—— *   *   ⅊
Toby, setting his hand upon his
*   *   *   *   *   *

*   *   *   *   ⅊
*   *   *

THE SECOND—cried m
Toby, waving his tobacco-pipe, as

---

4. A person learning the catechi

he would have done his sword at the head of a regiment.——The corporal went through his *manual* with exactness; and having *honoured his father and mother*, made a low bow, and fell back to the side of the room.

Every thing in this world, said my father, is big with jest,——and has wit in it, and instruction too,——if we can but find it out.

——Here is the *scaffold work* of INSTRUCTION, its true point of folly, without the BUILDING behind it.——

——Here is the glass for pedagogues, preceptors, tutors, governours, gerund-grinders and bear-leaders[5] to view themselves in, in their true dimensions.——

Oh! there is a husk and shell, *Yorick*, which grows up with learning, which their unskilfulness knows not how to fling away!

——SCIENCES MAY BE LEARNED BY ROTE, BUT WISDOM NOT.

Yorick thought my father inspired.——I will enter into obligations this moment, said my father, to lay out all my aunt *Dinah*'s legacy, in charitable uses (of which, by the bye, my father had no high opinion) if the corporal has any one determinate idea annexed to any one word he has repeated.——Prythee, *Trim*, quoth my father, turning round to him,——What do'st thou mean, by "*honouring thy father and mother?*"

Allowing them, an' please your honour, three halfpence a day out of my pay, when they grew old.——And didst thou do that, *Trim?* said *Yorick.*——He did indeed, replied my uncle *Toby.*——Then, *Trim*, said *Yorick*, springing out of his chair, and taking the corporal by the hand, thou art the best commentator upon that part of the *Decalogue*;[6] and I honour thee more for it, corporal *Trim*, than if thou hadst had a hand in the *Talmud* itself.

Chapter XXXIII.

O Blessed health! cried my father, making an exclamation, as he turned over the leaves to the next chapter,——thou art above all gold and treasure; 'tis thou who enlargest the soul,—— and openest all it's powers to receive instruction and to relish virtue.

——He that has thee, has little more to wish for;——and he that is so wretched as to want thee,——wants every thing with thee.

I have concentrated all that can be said upon this important head, said my father, into a very little room, therefore we'll read the chapter quite thro'.

My father read as follows.

"The whole secret of health depending upon the due contention

---

5. The tutors who accompanied young gentlemen on their travels.
6. The Ten Commandments. The Talmud is the book of Jewish civil and canonical law.

for mastery betwixt the radical heat and the radical moisture"——
You have proved that matter of fact, I suppose, above, said *Yorick*.
Sufficiently, replied my father.

In saying this, my father shut the book,——not as if he resolved
to read no more of it, for he kept his forefinger in the chapter:——
nor pettishly,——for he shut the book slowly; his thumb resting,
when he had done it, upon the upper-side of the cover, as his three
fingers supported the lower-side of it, without the least compressive
violence.——

I have demonstrated the truth of that point, quoth my father,
nodding to *Yorick*, most sufficiently in the preceding chapter.

Now could the man in the moon be told, that a man in the earth
had wrote a chapter, sufficiently demonstrating, That the secret of
all health depended upon the due contention for mastery betwixt the
radical heat and the *radical moisture*,——and that he had managed
the point so well, that there was not one single word wet or dry
upon radical heat or radical moisture, throughout the whole
chapter,——or a single syllable in it, *pro* or *con*, directly or indirectly, upon the contention betwixt these two powers in any part of
the animal œconomy——

"O thou eternal maker of all beings!"——he would cry, striking
his breast with his right hand, (in case he had one)——"Thou
whose power and goodness can enlarge the faculties of thy creatures
to this infinite degree of excellence and perfection,——What have
we MOONITES done?"

Chapter XXXIV.

WITH two strokes, the one at *Hippocrates*,[7] the other at
Lord *Verulam*, did my father atchieve it.

The stroke at the prince of physicians, with which he began, was
no more than a short insult upon his sorrowful complaint of the *Ars
longa*,——and *Vita brevis*.[8]——Life short, cried my father,——
and the art of healing tedious! And who are we to thank for both,
the one and the other, but the ignorance of quacks themselves,——
and the stage-loads of chymical nostrums, and peripatetic[9] lumber,
with which in all ages, they have first flatter'd the world, and at last
deceived it.

——O my lord *Verulam!* cried my father, turning from *Hippocrates*, and making his second stroke at him, as the principal of
nostrum-mongers, and the fittest to be made an example of to the

7. The Greek "father of medicine." Lord
Verulam is Francis Bacon (1561–1626),
the English scientist.

8. "Art is long, life is short," the first
of the *Aphorisms* of Hippocrates.
9. That is, derived from philosophy.

rest,——What shall I say to thee, my great lord *Verulam?* What shall I say to thy internal spirit,——thy opium,——thy salt-petre, ——thy greasy unctions,——thy daily purges,——thy nightly glis- ters, and succedaneums?[1]

——My father was never at a loss what to say to any man, upon any subject; and had the least occasion for the exordium of any man breathing: how he dealt with his lordship's opinion,——you shall see;——but when——I know not:——we must first see what his lordship's opinion was.

Chapter XXXV.

THE two great causes, which conspire with each other to shorten life, says lord *Verulam*, are first——

"The internal spirit, which like a gentle flame, wastes the body down to death:——And secondly, the external air, that parches the body up to ashes:——which two enemies attacking us on both sides of our bodies together, at length destroy our organs, and render them unfit to carry on the functions of life."[2]

This being the state of the case; the road to Longevity was plain; nothing more being required, says his lordship, but to repair the waste committed by the internal spirit, by making the substance of it more thick and dense, by a regular course of opiates on one side, and by refrigerating the heat of it on the other, by three grains and a half of salt-petre every morning before you got up.——

Still this frame of ours was left exposed to the inimical assaults of the air without;——but this was fenced off again by a course of greasy unctions, which so fully saturated the pores of the skin, that no spicula could enter;——nor could any one get out.——This put a stop to all perspiration, sensible and insensible, which being the cause of so many scurvy distempers——a course of glisters was requisite to carry off redundant humours,——and render the system compleat.

What my father had to say to my lord of *Verulam's* opiates, his salt-petre, and greasy unctions and glisters, you shall read,——but not to day——or to morrow: time presses upon me,——my reader is impatient——I must get forwards.——You shall read the chapter at your leisure, (if you chuse it) as soon as ever the *Tristrapœdia* is published.——

Sufficeth it at present, to say, my father levelled the hypothesis with the ground, and in doing that, the learned know, he built up and established his own.——

---

1. "Glisters": enemas; "succedaneums": inferior substitute remedies.

2. From Bacon's *Historia Vitae et Mortis* [History of Life and Death].

Chapter XXXVI.

THE whole secret of health, said my father, beginning the sentence again, depending evidently upon the due contention betwixt the radical heat and radical moisture within us;——the least imaginable skill had been sufficient to have maintained it, had not the schoolmen[3] confounded the task, merely (as *Van Helmont*, the famous chymist, has proved) by all along mistaking the radical moisture for the tallow and fat of animal bodies.

Now the radical moisture is not the tallow or fat of animals, but an oily and balsamous substance; for the fat and tallow, as also the phlegm or watery parts are cold; whereas the oily and balsamous parts are of a lively heat and spirit, which accounts for the observation of *Aristotle*, "*Quod omne animal post coitum est* triste."[4]

Now it is certain, that the radical heat lives in the radical moisture, but whether *vice versâ*, is a doubt: however, when the one decays, the other decays also; and then is produced, either an unnatural heat, which causes an unnatural dryness——or an unnatural moisture, which causes dropsies.——So that if a child, as he grows up, can but be taught to avoid running into fire or water, as either of 'em threaten his destruction,——'twill be all that is needful to be done upon that head.——

Chapter XXXVII.

THE description of the siege of *Jerico* itself, could not have engaged the attention of my uncle *Toby* more powerfully than the last chapter;——his eyes were fixed upon my father, throughout it;——he never mentioned radical heat and radical moisture, but my uncle *Toby* took his pipe out of his mouth, and shook his head; and as soon as the chapter was finished, he beckoned to the corporal to come close to his chair, to ask him the following question,——*aside.*—— *   *   *   *   *   *   *
*   *   *   *   *   *   *   *   * . It was at the siege of *Limerick*, an' please your honour, replied the corporal, making a bow.[5]

The poor fellow and I, quoth my uncle *Toby*, addressing himself to my father, were scarce able to crawl out of our tents, at the time the siege of *Limerick* was raised, upon the very account you mention.——Now what can have got into that precious noddle of thine, my dear brother *Toby?* cried my father, mentally.——By Heaven!

---

3. Medieval scholars and theologians. Van Helmont (1577–1644) was a Flemish physician.
4. "After coition all animals are sad."

5. William III had to stop his siege of Limerick (Ireland) in 1690 because of heavy rain.

continued he, communing still with himself, it would puzzle an
Œdipus[6] to bring it in point.——

I believe, an' please your honour, quoth the corporal, that if it
had not been for the quantity of brandy we set fire to every night,
and the claret and cinnamon with which I plyed your honour off;
——And the geneva,[7] *Trim*, added my uncle *Toby*, which did us
more good than all——I verily believe, continued the corporal, we
had both, an' please your honour, left our lives in the trenches, and
been buried in them too.——The noblest grave, corporal! cried my
uncle *Toby*, his eyes sparkling as he spoke, that a soldier could wish
to lie down in.——But a pitiful death for him! an' please your
honour, replied the corporal.

All this was as much *Arabick* to my father, as the rites of the
Colchi and *Troglodites* had been before to my uncle *Toby*; my
father could not determine whether he was to frown or smile.——

My uncle *Toby*, turning to *Yorick*, resumed the case at *Limerick*,
more intelligibly than he had begun it,——and so settled the point
for my father at once.

Chapter XXXVIII.

IT was was undoubtedly, said my uncle *Toby*, a great happiness for
myself and the corporal, that we had all along a burning fever,
attended with a most raging thirst, during the whole five and twenty
days the flux was upon us in the camp; otherwise what my brother
calls the radical moisture, must, as I conceive it, inevitably have got
the better.——My father drew in his lungs top-full of air, and
looking up, blew it forth again, as slowly as he possibly could.——

——It was heaven's mercy to us, continued my uncle *Toby*,
which put it into the corporal's head to maintain that due contention betwixt the radical heat and the radical moisture, by reinforc-
ing the fever, as he did all along, with hot wine and spices; whereby
the corporal kept up (as it were) a continual firing, so that the
radical heat stood its ground from the beginning to the end, and was
a fair match for the moisture, terrible as it was.——Upon my
honour, added my uncle *Toby*, you might have heard the contention
within our bodies, brother *Shandy*, twenty toises.[8]——If there was
no firing, said *Yorick*.

Well——said my father, with a full aspiration, and pausing a
while after the word——Was I a judge, and the laws of the country
which made me one permitted it, I would condemn some of the
worst malefactors, provided they had had their clergy —— ——
——*Yorick* foreseeing the sentence was likely to end with no sort

---

6. Who was able to solve the riddle of
the Sphinx.
7. Gin.

8. An old French measure: 6.395 English ft.

of mercy, laid his hand upon my father's breast, and begged he would respite it for a few minutes, till he asked the corporal a question. ——Prithee, *Trim*, said *Yorick*, without staying for my father's leave,——tell us honestly——what is thy opinion concerning this self-same radical heat and radical moisture?

With humble submission to his honour's better judgment, quoth the corporal, making a bow to my uncle *Toby*——Speak thy opinion freely, corporal, said my uncle *Toby*.——The poor fellow is my servant,——not my slave,——added my uncle *Toby*, turning to my father.——

The corporal put his hat under his left arm, and with his stick hanging upon the wrist of it, by a black thong split into a tassel about the knot, he marched up to the ground where he had performed his catechism; then touching his under jaw with the thumb and fingers of his right hand before he opened his mouth,——he delivered his notion thus.

Chapter XXXIX.

JUST as the corporal was humming, to begin——in waddled Dr. *Slop*.——'Tis not two-pence matter——the corporal shall go on in the next chapter, let who will come in.——

Well, my good doctor, cried my father sportively, for the transitions of his passions were unaccountably sudden,——and what has this whelp of mine to say to the matter?——

Had my father been asking after the amputation of the tail of a puppy-dog——he could not have done it in a more careless air: the system which Dr. *Slop* had laid down, to treat the accident by, no way allowed of such a mode of enquiry.——He sat down.

Pray, Sir, quoth my uncle *Toby*, in a manner which could not go unanswered,——in what condition is the boy?——'Twill end in a *phimosis*,[9] replied Dr. *Slop*.

I am no wiser than I was, quoth my uncle *Toby*,——returning his pipe into his mouth.——Then let the corporal go on, said my father, with his medical lecture.——The corporal made a bow to his old friend, Dr. *Slop*, and then delivered his opinion concerning radical heat and radical moisture, in the following words.

Chapter XL.

THE city of *Limerick*, the siege of which was begun under his majesty king *William* himself, the year after I went into the army——lies, an' please your honours, in the middle of a devilish

---

9. A contraction or inflammation of the foreskin.

wet, swampy country.——'Tis quite surrounded, said my uncle *Toby*, with the *Shannon*, and is, by its situation, one of the strongest fortified places in *Ireland.*——

I think this is a new fashion, quoth Dr. *Slop*, of beginning a medical lecture.——'Tis all true, answered *Trim.*——Then I wish the faculty would follow the cut of it, said *Yorick.*——'Tis all cut through, an' please your reverence, said the corporal, with drains and bogs; and besides, there was such a quantity of rain fell during the siege, the whole country was like a puddle,——'twas that, and nothing else, which brought on the flux, and which had like to have killed both his honour and myself; now there was no such thing, after the first ten days, continued the corporal, for a soldier to lie dry in his tent, without cutting a ditch round it, to draw off the water;——nor was that enough, for those who could afford it, as his honour could, without setting fire every night to a pewter dish full of brandy, which took off the damp of the air, and made the inside of the tent as warm as a stove.——

And what conclusion dost thou draw, Corporal *Trim*, cried my father, from all these premises?

I infer, an' please your worship, replied *Trim*, that the radical moisture is nothing in the world but ditch-water——and that the radical heat, of those who can go to the expence of it, is burnt brandy——the radical heat and moisture of a private man, an' please your honours, is nothing but ditch-water——and a dram of geneva——and give us but enough of it, with a pipe of tobacco, to give us spirits, and drive away the vapors[1]——we know not what it is to fear death.

I am at a loss, Captain *Shandy*, quoth Doctor *Slop*, to determine in which branch of learning your servant shines most, whether in physiology, or divinity.——*Slop* had not forgot *Trim*'s comment upon the sermon.——

It is but an hour ago, replied *Yorick*, since the corporal was examined in the latter, and pass'd muster with great honour.——

The radical heat and moisture, quoth Doctor *Slop*, turning to my father, you must know, is the basis and foundation of our being, ——as the root of a tree is the source and principle of its vegetation.——It is inherent in the seeds of all animals, and may be preserved sundry ways, but principally in my opinion by *consubstantials*, *impriments*, and *occludents.*[2]——Now this poor fellow, continued Dr. *Slop*, pointing to the corporal, has had the misfortune to have heard some superficial emperic[3] discourse upon this nice

1. Figuratively, a depression, low spirits.
2. Terms from Bacon's *History*: *consubstantials*: things of the same substance; *impriments*: things which impress or imprint; *occludents*: drugs which close up.
3. Empiric refers to learning by observation; by extension it can mean a quack doctor without formal training.

point.——That he has,——said my father.——Very likely, said my uncle.——I'm sure of it——quoth *Yorick.*——

Chapter XLI.

DOCTOR *Slop* being called out to look at a cataplasm he had ordered, it gave my father an opportunity of going on with another chapter in the *Tristra-pædia.*——Come! chear up, my lads; I'll shew you land——for when we have tugged through that chapter, the book shall not be opened again this twelve-month.—— Huzza!——

Chapter XLII.

——FIVE years with a bib under his chin;

Four years in traveling from Christ-cross-row[4] to *Malachi;*

A year and a half in learning to write his own name;

Seven long years and more τύπτω ing[5] it, at Greek and Latin;

Four years at his *probations* and his *negations*[6]——the fine statue still lying in the middle of the marble block,——and nothing done, but his tools sharpened to hew it out!——'Tis a piteous delay!——Was not the great *Julius Scaliger*[7] within an ace of never getting his tools sharpened at all?——Forty-four years old was he before he could manage his Greek;——and *Peter Damianus*, lord bishop of *Ostia*, as all the world knows, could not so much as read, when he was of man's estate.——And *Baldus* himself, as eminent as he turned out after, entered upon the law so late in life, that every body imagined he intended to be an advocate in the other world: no wonder, when *Eudamidas*, the son of *Archidamas*, heard *Xenocrates* at seventy-five disputing about *wisdom*, that he asked gravely,——*If the old man be yet disputing and enquiring concerning wisdom,*——*what time will he have to make use of it?*

Yorick listened to my father with great attention; there was a seasoning of wisdom unaccountably mixed up with his strangest whims, and he had sometimes such illuminations in the darkest of

4. Learning the alphabet was so called, from the arrangement of the letters in the shape of a cross in old primers. *Malachi*, the last book of the old Testament, was used as a text for the most advanced reading class.
5. "Working away at it"—the verb used as a paradigm in Greek grammars.
6. Studying logic.
7. Julius Scaliger (1484–1558) was a renowned literary and scientific writer, though he started late. Peter Damianus, (c. 1007–1072) became Cardinal-Bishop of Ostia though he began studies at thirty-eight. Pietro Baldi de Ubaldis (1327–1406) in fact received a law degree at seventeen. Eudamidas (c. 330 B.C.) was King of Sparta. Xenocrates (396–314 B.C.) was a philosopher and head of the Platonic Academy at Athens.

his eclipses, as almost attoned for them:——be wary, Sir, when you imitate him.

I am convinced, *Yorick*, continued my father, half reading and half discoursing, that there is a North-west passage[8] to the intellectual world; and that the soul of man has shorter ways of going to work, in furnishing itself with knowledge and instruction, than we generally take with it.——But alack! all fields have not a river or a spring running besides them;——every child, *Yorick*! has not a parent to point it out.

——The whole entirely depends, added my father, in a low voice, upon the *auxiliary verbs*, Mr. *Yorick*.

Had *Yorick* trod upon *Virgil's* snake,[9] he could not have looked more surprised.——I am surprised too, cried my father, observing it,——and I reckon it as one of the greatest calamities which ever befell the republick of letters, That those who have been entrusted with the education of our children, and whose business it was to open their minds, and stock them early with ideas, in order to set the imagination loose upon them, have made so little use of the auxiliary verbs in doing it, as they have done——So that, except *Raymond Lullius*,[1] and the elder *Pelegrini*, the last of which arrived to such perfection in the use of 'em, with his topics, that in a few lessons, he could teach a young gentleman to discourse with plausibility upon any subject, *pro* and *con*, and to say and write all that could be spoken or written concerning it, without blotting a word, to the admiration of all who beheld him.——I should be glad, said *Yorick*, interrupting my father, to be made to comprehend this matter. You shall, said my father.

The highest stretch of improvement a single word is capable of, is a high metaphor,——for which, in my opinion, the idea is generally the worse, and not the better;——but be that as it may,——when the mind has done that with it——there is an end,——the mind and the idea are at rest,——until a second idea enters;——and so on.

Now the use of the *Auxiliaries* is, at once to set the soul a going by herself upon the materials as they are brought her; and by the versability of this great engine, round which they are twisted, to open new tracks of enquiry, and make every idea engender millions.

You excite my curiosity greatly, said *Yorick*.

For my own part, quoth my uncle *Toby*, I have given it up.——The *Danes*, an' please your honour, quoth the corporal, who were

---

8. The looked-for shortcut across North America from the Atlantic to the Pacific.
9. In a poem attributed to Virgil called the *Culex* (Gnat), a gnat stings the speaker, waking him in time to avoid a snake.

1. Lull was a thirteenth-century Spanish missionary to the Arabs who urged the establishment of schools for missionary languages. Pellegrini was a seventeenth-century humanist whose system of predication Sterne parodies in this passage.

on the left at the siege of *Limerick*, were all auxiliaries.——And very good ones, said my uncle *Toby*.——But the auxiliaries, *Trim*, my brother is talking about,——I conceive to be different things.

——You do? said my father, rising up.

Chapter XLIII.

MY father took a single turn across the room, then sat down and finished the chapter.

The verbs auxiliary we are concerned in here, continued my father, are, *am; was; have; had; do; did; make; made; suffer; shall; should; will; would; can; could; owe; ought; used; or is wont.*—— And these varied with tenses, *present, past, future,* and conjugated with the verb *see,*——or with these questions added to them;——*Is it? Was it? Will it be? Would it be? May it be? Might it be?* And these again put negatively, *Is it not? Was it not? Ought it not?*—— Or affirmatively,——*It is; It was; It ought to be.* Or chronologically,——*Has it been always? Lately? How long ago?*——Or hypothetically,——*If it was; If it was not? What would follow?*—— If the *French* should beat the *English?* If the *Sun* go out of the *Zodiac?*

Now, by the right use and application of these, continued my father, in which a child's memory should be exercised, there is no one idea can enter his brain how barren soever, but a magazine[2] of conceptions and conclusions may be drawn forth from it.——Did'st thou ever see a white bear? cried my father, turning his head round to *Trim*, who stood at the back of his chair:——No, an' please your honour, replied the corporal.——But thou could'st discourse about one, *Trim*, said my father, in case of need?——How is it possible, brother, quoth my uncle *Toby*, if the corporal never saw one?——'Tis the fact I want; replied my father,——and the possibility of it, is as follows.

A WHITE BEAR! Very well. Have I ever seen one? Might I ever have seen one? Am I ever to see one? Ought I ever to have seen one? Or can I ever see one?

Would I had seen a white bear! (for how can I imagine it?)

If I should see a white bear, what should I say? If I should never see a white bear, what then?

If I never have, can, must or shall see a white bear alive; have I ever seen the skin of one? Did I ever see one painted?—described? Have I never dreamed of one?

Did my father, mother, uncle, aunt, brothers or sisters, ever see a

---

2. A warehouse, especially for military explosives.

white bear? What would they give? How would they behave? How would the white bear have behaved? Is he wild? Tame? Terrible? Rough? Smooth?

——Is the white bear worth seeing?——

——Is there no sin in it?——

Is it better than a BLACK ONE?

END OF THE FIFTH VOLUME.

Volume VI.

Chapter I.

————W E'LL not stop two moments, my dear Sir,——only, as we have got thro' these five volumes, (do, Sir, sit down upon a set——they are better than nothing) let us just look back upon the country we have pass'd through.——

————What a wilderness has it been! and what a mercy that we have not both of us been lost, or devoured by wild beasts in it.

Did you think the world itself, Sir, had contained such a number of Jack Asses?[1]——How they view'd and review'd us as we passed over the rivulet at the bottom of that little valley!——and when we climbed over that hill, and were just getting out of sight——good God! what a braying did they all set up together!

————Prithee, shepherd! who keeps all those Jack Asses? * * *

————Heaven be their comforter——What! are they never curried?——Are they never taken in in winter?——Bray bray—— bray. Bray on,——the world is deeply your debtor;——louder still ————that's nothing;——in good sooth, you are ill-used:——Was I a Jack Asse, I solemnly declare, I would bray in G-sol-re-ut from morning, even unto night.

Chapter II.

W HEN my father had danced his white bear backwards and forwards through half a dozen pages, he closed the book for good an' all,——and in a kind of triumph redelivered it into *Trim's* hand, with a nod to lay it upon the 'scrutoire where he found it.——*Tristram*, said he, shall be made to conjugate every word in the dictionary, backwards and forwards the same way;—— every word, *Yorick*, by this means, you see, is converted into a thesis or an hypothesis;——every thesis and hypothesis have an offspring of propositions;——and each proposition has its own consequences and conclusions; every one of which leads the mind on again, into fresh tracks of enquiries and doubtings.——The force of this engine, added my father, is incredible, in opening a child's head.——'Tis enough, brother *Shandy*, cried my uncle *Toby*, to burst it into a thousand splinters.——

1. Reviewers: Vols. III and IV of *Tristram Shandy* had been less well-received than the first two.

I presume, said *Yorick*, smiling,——it must be owing to this,——(for let logicians say what they will, it is not to be accounted for sufficiently from the bare use of the ten predicaments[2])—— That the famous *Vincent Quirino*,[3] amongst the many other astonishing feats of his childhood, of which the Cardinal *Bembo* has given the world so exact a story,——should be able to paste up in the publick schools at *Rome*, so early as in the eighth year of his age, no less than four thousand, five hundred, and sixty different theses, upon the most abstruse points of the most abstruse theology;——and to defend and maintain them in such sort, as to cramp and dumbfound his opponents.——What is that, cried my father, to what is told us of *Alphonsus Tostatus*, who, almost in his nurse's arms, learned all the sciences and liberal arts without being taught any one of them?——What shall we say of the great *Piereskius?*——That's the very man, cried my uncle *Toby*, I once told you of, brother *Shandy*, who walked a matter of five hundred miles, reckoning from *Paris* to *Schevling*, and from *Schevling* back again, merely to see *Stevinus's* flying chariot.——He was a very great man! added my uncle *Toby*; (meaning *Stevinus*)——He was so; brother *Toby*, said my father, (meaning *Piereskius*)——and had multiplied his ideas so fast, and increased his knowledge to such a prodigious stock, that, if we may give credit to an anecdote concerning him, which we cannot withhold here, without shaking the authority of all anecdotes whatever——at seven years of age, his father committed entirely to his care the education of his younger brother, a boy of five years old,——with the sole management of all his concerns.——Was the father as wise as the son? quoth my uncle *Toby*:——I should think not, said *Yorick*:——But what are these, continued my father——(breaking out in a kind of enthusiasm)——what are these, to those prodigies of childhood in *Grotius*,[4] *Scioppius, Heinsius, Politian, Pascal, Joseph Scaliger, Ferdinand de Cordouè*, and others——some of which left off their *substantial forms* at nine years old, or sooner, and went on reasoning without them;——others went through their classics at seven;——wrote tragedies at eight;——*Ferdinand de Cordouè* was so wise at nine,——'twas thought the Devil was in him;——and at *Venice* gave such proofs of his knowledge and goodness, that the monks imagined he was *Antichrist*, or nothing.——Others were masters of fourteen languages at ten,——finished the course of their rhetoric,

2. The ten categories that Aristotle believed all entities could be reduced to: substance, quantity, quality, relation, place, time, position, possession (condition), activity, and passivity.

3. Vincenzo Quirino and Pietro Bembo were humanist scholars of the Italian Renaissance. Alfonso Tostado was a Spanish theologian of the early fifteenth century.

4. These are figures from the Renaissance. Joseph Scaliger is the son of the Julius Scaliger mentioned in Vol. V, Chap. xlii. *Substantial forms* is the study of metaphysics.

poetry, logic, and ethics at eleven,——put forth their commentaries upon *Servius*[5] and *Martianus Capella* at twelve,——and at thirteen received their degrees in philosophy, laws, and divinity:——But you forget the great *Lipsius*, quoth *Yorick*, who composed a work[6] the day he was born;——They should have wiped it up, said my uncle *Toby*, and said no more about it.

Chapter III.

WHEN the cataplasm was ready, a scruple of *decorum* had unseasonably rose up in *Susannah's* conscience about holding the candle, whilst *Slop* tied it on; *Slop* had not treated *Susannah's* distemper with anodines,——and so a quarrel had ensued betwixt them.

——Oh! oh!——said *Slop*, casting a glance of undue freedom in *Susannah's* face, as she declined the office;——then, I think I know you, madam——You know me, Sir! cried *Susannah* fastidiously, and with a toss of her head, levelled evidently, not at his profession, but at the doctor himself,——you know me! cried *Susannah* again.

——Dr. *Slop* clapped his finger and his thumb instantly upon his nostrils;——*Susannah's* spleen was ready to burst at it;——'Tis false, said *Susannah*.——Come, come, Mrs. Modesty, said *Slop*, not a little elated with the success of his last thrust,——if you won't hold the candle, and look——you may hold it and shut your eyes:——That's one of your popish shifts, cried *Susannah*:——'Tis better, said *Slop*, with a nod, than no shift at all, young woman;——I defy you, sir, cried *Susannah*, pulling her shift sleeve below her elbow.

It was almost impossible for two persons to assist each other in a surgical case with a more splenetic cordiality.

Slop snatched up the cataplasm,——*Susannah* snatched up the

---

5. Servius's commentary on Virgil became itself the subject of further learned commentaries. Martianus Capella's encyclopedia of learning, *De Nuptiis Philologiae et Mercurii* [On the Marriage of Philology and Mercury], written in the fifth century, was also submitted to much commentary. Justus Lipsius was a sixteenth-century Flemish humanist.

6. Nous aurions quelque interêt, says *Baillet*, de montrer qu'il n' a rien de ridicule s'il étoit véritable, au moins dans le sense énigmatique que *Nicius Erythraeus* a tâché de lui donner. Cet auteur dit que pour comprendre comme *Lipse*, a pû composer un ouvrage le premier jour de sa vie, il faut s'imaginer, que ce premier jour n'est pas celui de sa naissance charnelle, mais celui au quel il a commencé d'user de la raison; il veut que

c'ait été à l'age de *neuf* ans; et il nous veut persuader que ce fut en cet âge, que *Lipse* fit un poème.——Le tour est ingenieux, &c. &c. [*Sterne's note.*] "We should have some interest, says *Baillet*, to show that there is nothing ridiculous if it is true, at least in the enigmatic sense that *Nicius Erythraeus* has tried to give it. This author says that to understand how Lipsius has been able to compose a work the first day of his life, it's necessary to imagine, that the first day is not that of his physical birth, but that in which he began to use his reason; he maintains that it was at the age of nine; and he wishes to persuade us that it was at this age that Lipsius created a poem.——The attempt is ingenious, etc., etc."

candle;——A little this way, said *Slop*; *Susannah* looking one way, and rowing another, instantly set fire to *Slop's* wig, which being somewhat bushy and unctuous withal, was burnt out before it was well kindled.——You impudent whore! cried *Slop*,——(for what is passion, but a wild beast)——you impudent whore, cried *Slop*, getting upright, with the cataplasm in his hand;——I never was the destruction of any body's nose, said *Susannah*,——which is more than you can say:——Is it?[7] cried *Slop*, throwing the cataplasm in her face;——Yes, it is, cried *Susannah*, returning the compliment with what was left in the pan.——

Chapter IV.

DOCTOR *Slop* and *Susannah* filed cross-bills against each other in the parlour; which done, as the cataplasm had failed, they retired into the kitchen to prepare a fomentation for me;——and whilst that was doing, my father determined the point as you will read.

Chapter V.

YOU see 'tis high time, said my father, addressing himself equally to my uncle *Toby* and *Yorick*, to take this young creature out of these women's hands, and put him into those of a private governor. *Marcus Antoninus* provided fourteen governors all at once to superintend his son *Commodus's* education,[8]——and in six weeks he cashiered five of them;——I know very well, continued my father, that *Commodus's* mother was in love with a gladiator at the time of her conception, which accounts for a great many of *Commodus's* cruelties when he became emperor;——but still I am of opinion, that those five whom *Antoninus* dismissed, did *Commodus's* temper in that short time, more hurt than the other nine were able to rectify all their lives long.

Now as I consider the person who is to be about my son, as the mirror in which he is to view himself from morning to night, and by which he is to adjust his looks, his carriage, and perhaps the inmost sentiments of his heart;——I would have one, *Yorick*, if possible, polished at all points, fit for my child to look into.——This is very good sense, quoth my uncle *Toby* to himself.

——There is, continued my father, a certain mien and motion of the body and all its parts, both in acting and speaking, which argues a man *well within*; and I am not at all surprized that *Gregory* of

7. Slop is implying that she may be carrying syphilis.
8. The benevolent emperor Marcus Aurelius Antoninus (A.D. 121–180) was succeeded by his cruel son, Commodus.

Nazianzum,[9] upon observing the hasty and untoward gestures of *Julian*, should foretel he would one day become an apostate;——or that *St. Ambrose*[1] should turn his *Amanuensis* out of doors, because of an indecent motion of his head, which went backwards and forwards like a flail;——or that *Democritus*[2] should conceive *Protagoras* to be a scholar, from seeing him bind up a faggot, and thrusting, as he did it, the small twigs inwards.——There are a thousand unnoticed openings, continued my father, which let a penetrating eye at once into a man's soul; and I maintain it, added he, that a man of sense does not lay down his hat in coming into a room,——or take it up in going out of it, but something escapes, which discovers him.

It is for these reasons, continued my father, that the governor I make choice of shall neither[3] lisp, or squint, or wink, or talk loud, or look fierce, or foolish;——or bite his lips, or grind his teeth, or speak through his nose, or pick it, or blow it with his fingers.——

He shall neither walk fast,——or slow, or fold his arms,——for that is laziness;——or hang them down,——for that is folly; or hide them in his pocket, for that is nonsense.——

He shall neither strike, or pinch, or tickle,——or bite, or cut his nails, or hawk, or spit, or snift, or drum with his feet or fingers in company;——nor (according to *Erasmus*[4]) shall he speak to any one in making water,——nor shall he point to carrion or excrement.——Now this is all nonsense again, quoth my uncle *Toby* to himself.——

I will have him, continued my father, cheerful, faceté,[5] jovial; at the same time, prudent, attentive to business, vigilant, acute, argute, inventive, quick in resolving doubts and speculative questions;—— he shall be wise and judicious, and learned:——And why not humble, and moderate, and gentle tempered, and good? said *Yorick:* ——And why not, cried my uncle *Toby*, free, and generous, and bountiful, and brave?——He shall, my dear *Toby*, replied my father, getting up and shaking him by his hand.——Then, brother *Shandy*, answered my uncle *Toby*, raising himself off the chair, and laying down his pipe to take hold of my father's other hand,——I humbly beg I may recommend poor *Le Fever*'s son to you;——a tear of joy of the first water sparkled in my uncle *Toby*'s eye,—— and another, the fellow to it, in the corporal's, as the proposition

---

9. St. Gregory of Nazianzus, though a friend of Julian when they were both students, attacked him when he became emperor, in two *Invectives* (c. A.D. 361).
1. A Church Father of the fourth century. *Amanuensis*: private secretary.
2. Protagoras was supposedly discovered and taken up by Democritus after he saw

him working as a laborer.
3. Vid. *Pellegrina*. [*Sterne's note.*] He refers to the Pellegrina spoken of in Vol. V, Chap. xlii.
4. This is a paraphrase of a passage in one of Erasmus's *Familiar Discourses.*
5. Good-humored.

was made;——you will see why when you read *Le Fever*'s story:
——fool that I was! nor can I recollect, (nor perhaps you) without
turning back to the place, what it was that hindered me from letting
the corporal tell it in his own words;——but the occasion is lost,
——I must tell it now in my own.

Chapter VI.

The Story of LE FEVER.

IT was some time in the summer of that year in which *Dendermond* was taken by the allies,[6]——which was about seven
years before my father came into the country,——and about as
many, after the time, that my uncle *Toby* and *Trim* had privately
decamped from my father's house in town, in order to lay some of
the finest sieges to some of the finest fortified cities in *Europe*——
when my uncle *Toby* was one evening getting his supper, with *Trim*
sitting behind him at a small sideboard,——I say, sitting——for in
consideration of the corporal's lame knee (which sometimes gave
him exquisite pain)——when my uncle *Toby* dined or supped
alone, he would never suffer the corporal to stand; and the poor
fellow's veneration for his master was such, that, with a proper
artillery, my uncle *Toby* could have taken *Dendermond* itself, with
less trouble than he was able to gain this point over him; for many a
time when my uncle *Toby* supposed the corporal's leg was at rest,
he would look back, and detect him standing behind him with the
most dutiful respect: this bred more little squabbles betwixt them,
than all other causes for five and twenty years together——But this
is neither here nor there——why do I mention it?——Ask my
pen,——it governs me,——I govern not it.

He was one evening sitting thus at his supper, when the landlord
of a little inn in the village came into the parlour with an empty
phial in his hand, to beg a glass or two of sack;[7] 'Tis for a poor
gentleman,——I think, of the army, said the landlord, who has
been taken ill at my house four days ago, and has never held up his
head since, or had a desire to taste any thing, till just now, that he
has a fancy for a glass of sack and a thin toast,——I *think*, says he,
taking his hand from his forehead, *it would comfort me.*——

——If I could neither beg, borrow, or buy such a thing,——
added the landlord,——I would almost steal it for the poor gentleman, he is so ill.——I hope in God he will still mend, continued
he——we are all of us concerned for him.

Thou art a good natured soul, I will answer for thee, cried my

6. 1706.   7. Sherry.

uncle *Toby*; and thou shalt drink the poor gentleman's health in a glass of sack thyself,——and take a couple of bottles with my service, and tell him he is heartily welcome to them, and to a dozen more if they will do him good.

Though I am persuaded, said my uncle *Toby*, as the landlord shut the door, he is a very compassionate fellow——*Trim*,——yet I cannot help entertaining a high opinion of his guest too; there must be something more than common in him, that in so short a time should win so much upon the affections of his host;——And of his whole family, added the corporal, for they are all concerned for him.——Step after him, said my uncle *Toby*,——do *Trim*,——and ask if he knows his name.

——I have quite forgot it, truly, said the landlord, coming back into the parlour with the corporal,——but I can ask his son again: ——Has he a son with him then? said my uncle *Toby*.——A boy, replied the landlord, of about eleven or twelve years of age;——but the poor creature has tasted almost as little as his father; he does nothing but mourn and lament for him night and day:——He has not stirred from the bedside these two days.

My uncle *Toby* laid down his knife and fork, and thrust his plate from before him, as the landlord gave him the account; and *Trim*, without being ordered, took away without saying one word, and in a few minutes after brought him his pipe and tobacco.

——Stay in the room a little, said my uncle *Toby*.——

Trim!——said my uncle *Toby*, after he lighted his pipe, and smoak'd about a dozen whiffs.——*Trim* came in front of his master and made his bow;——my uncle *Toby* smoak'd on, and said no more.——Corporal! said my uncle *Toby*——the corporal made his bow.——My uncle *Toby* proceeded no farther, but finished his pipe.

Trim! said my uncle *Toby*, I have a project in my head, as it is a bad night, of wrapping myself up warm in my roquelaure,[8] and paying a visit to this poor gentleman.——Your honour's roquelaure, replied the corporal, has not once been had on, since the night before your honour received your wound, when we mounted guard in the trenches before the gate of St. *Nicholas*;——and besides it is so cold and rainy a night, that what with the roquelaure, and what with the weather, 'twill be enough to give your honour your death, and bring on your honour's torment in your groin. I fear so; replied my uncle *Toby*, but I am not at rest in my mind, *Trim*, since the account the landlord has given me.——I wish I had not known so much of this affair,——added my uncle *Toby*,——or that I had known more of it:——How shall we manage it? Leave it, an't please your honour, to me, quoth the corporal;——I'll take my hat and

8. A knee-length cape.

stick and go to the house and reconnoitre, and act accordingly; and I will bring your honour a full account in an hour.——Thou shalt go, *Trim*, said my uncle *Toby*, and here's a shilling for thee to drink with his servant.——I shall get it all out of him, said the corporal, shutting the door.

My uncle *Toby* filled his second pipe; and had it not been, that he now and then wandered from the point, with considering whether it was not full as well to have the curtain of the tennaile[9] a straight line, as a crooked one,——he might be said to have thought of nothing else but poor *Le Fever* and his boy the whole time he smoaked it.

Chapter VII.

The Story of Le Fever *continued.*

IT was not till my uncle *Toby* had knocked the ashes out of his third pipe, that corporal *Trim* returned from the inn, and gave him the following account.

I despaired at first, said the corporal, of being able to bring back your honour any kind of intelligence concerning the poor sick lieutenant——Is he in the army then? said my uncle *Toby*——He is: said the corporal——And in what regiment? said my uncle *Toby* ——I'll tell your honour, replied the corporal, every thing straight forwards, as I learnt it.——Then, *Trim*, I'll fill another pipe, said my uncle *Toby*, and not interrupt thee till thou hast done; so sit down at thy ease, *Trim*, in the window seat, and begin thy story again. The corporal made his old bow, which generally spoke as plain as a bow could speak it——Your honour is good:——And having done that, he sat down, as he was ordered,——and begun the story to my uncle *Toby* over again in pretty near the same words.

I despaired at first, said the corporal, of being able to bring back any intelligence to your honour, about the lieutenant and his son; for when I asked where his servant was, from whom I made myself sure of knowing every thing which was proper to be asked,—— That's a right distinction, *Trim*, said my uncle *Toby*——I was answered, an' please your honour, that he had no servant with him;——that he had come to the inn with hired horses, which, upon finding himself unable to proceed, (to join, I suppose, the regiment) he had dismissed the morning after he came.——If I get better, my dear, said he, as he gave his purse to his son to pay the man,——we can hire horses from hence.——But alas! the poor

---

9. A protective outwork in a fortification.

gentleman will never get from hence, said the landlady to me,——
for I heard the death-watch[1] all night long;——and when he dies,
the youth, his son, will certainly die with him; for he is broken
hearted already.

I was hearing this account, continued the corporal, when the
youth came into the kitchen, to order the thin toast the landlord
spoke of;——but I will do it for my father myself, said the youth.
——Pray let me save you the trouble, young gentleman, said I,
taking up a fork for the purpose, and offering him my chair to sit
down upon by the fire, whilst I did it.——I believe, Sir, said he,
very modestly, I can please him best myself.——I am sure, said I,
his honour will not like the toast the worse for being toasted by an
old soldier.——The youth took hold of my hand, and instantly
burst into tears.——Poor youth! said my uncle *Toby*,——he has
been bred up from an infant in the army, and the name of a soldier,
Trim, sounded in his ears like the name of a friend;——I wish I had
him here.

——I never in the longest march, said the corporal, had so great
a mind to my dinner, as I had to cry with him for company:——
What could be the matter with me, an' please your honour? Nothing in the world, *Trim*, said my uncle *Toby*, blowing his nose,——
but that thou art a good natured fellow.

When I gave him the toast, continued the corporal, I thought it
was proper to tell him I was Captain *Shandy*'s servant, and that
your honour (though a stranger) was extremely concerned for his
father;——and that if there was any thing in your house or cellar
——(And thou might'st have added my purse too, said my uncle
Toby)——he was heartily welcome to it:——He made a very low
bow, (which was meant to your honour) but no answer,——for his
heart was full——so he went up stairs with the toast;——I warrant
you, my dear, said I, as I opened the kitchen door, your father will
be well again.——Mr. *Yorick*'s curate was smoking a pipe by the
kitchen fire,——but said not a word good or bad to comfort the
youth.——I thought it wrong; added the corporal——I think so
too, said my uncle *Toby*.

When the lieutenant had taken his glass of sack and toast, he felt
himself a little revived, and sent down into the kitchen, to let me
know, that in about ten minutes he should be glad if I would step
up stairs.——I believe, said the landlord, he is going to say his
prayers,——for there was a book laid upon the chair by his bedside,
and as I shut the door, I saw his son take up a cushion.——

I thought, said the curate, that you gentlemen of the army, Mr.
Trim, never said your prayers at all.——I heard the poor gentleman

---

1. A beetle whose clock-like sound suggests its name.

say his prayers last night, said the landlady, very devoutly, and with my own ears, or I could not have believed it.——Are you sure of it? replied the curate.——A soldier, an' please your reverence, said I, prays as often (of his own accord) as a parson;——and when he is fighting for his king, and for his own life, and for his honour too, he has the most reason to pray to God, of any one in the whole world——'Twas well said of thee, *Trim*, said my uncle *Toby*.—— But when a soldier, said I, an' please your reverence, has been standing for twelve hours together in the trenches, up to his knees in cold water,——or engaged, said I, for months together in long and dangerous marches;——harrassed, perhaps, in his rear to-day;—— harrassing others to-morrow;——detached here;——counter-manded there;——resting this night out upon his arms;——beat up in his shirt the next;——benumbed in his joints;——perhaps with-out straw in his tent to kneel on;——must say his prayers *how* and *when* he can.——I believe, said I,——for I was piqued, quoth the corporal, for the reputation of the army,——I believe, an' please your reverence, said I, that when a soldier gets time to pray,——he prays as heartily as a parson,——though not with all his fuss and hypocrisy.——Thou shouldst not have said that, *Trim*, said my uncle *Toby*,——for God only knows who is a hypocrite, and who is not:——At the great and general review of us all, corporal, at the day of judgment, (and not till then)——it will be seen who has done their duties in this world,——and who has not; and we shall be advanced, *Trim*, accordingly.——I hope we shall, said *Trim*. ——It is in the Scripture, said my uncle *Toby*; and I will shew it thee to-morrow:——In the mean time we may depend upon it, *Trim*, for our comfort, said my uncle *Toby*, that God Almighty is so good and just a governor of the world, that if we have but done our duties in it,——it will never be enquired into, whether we have done them in a red coat or a black one:——I hope not; said the corporal——But go on, *Trim*, said my uncle *Toby*, with thy story.

When I went up, continued the corporal, into the lieutenant's room, which I did not do till the expiration of the ten minutes,—— he was lying in his bed with his head raised upon his hand, with his elbow upon the pillow, and a clean white cambrick handkerchief beside it:——The youth was just stooping down to take up the cushion, upon which I supposed he had been kneeling,——the book was laid upon the bed,——and as he rose, in taking up the cushion with one hand, he reached out his other to take it away at the same time.——Let it remain there, my dear, said the lieutenant.

He did not offer to speak to me, till I had walked up close to his bed-side:——If you are Captain *Shandy*'s servant, said he, you must present my thanks to your master, with my little boy's thanks along with them, for his courtesy to me;——if he was of *Levens*'s

——said the lieutenant.——I told him your honour was——Then, said he, I served three campaigns with him in *Flanders*, and remember him,——but 'tis most likely, as I had not the honour of any acquaintance with him, that he knows nothing of me.——You will tell him, however, that the person his good nature has laid under obligations to him, is one *Le Fever*, a lieutenant in *Angus's*——but he knows me not,——said he, a second time, musing;——possibly he may my story——added he——pray tell the captain, I was the ensign at *Breda*,[2] whose wife was most unfortunately killed with a musket shot, as she lay in my arms in my tent.——I remember the story, an't please your honour, said I, very well.——Do you so? said he, wiping his eyes with his handkerchief,——then well may I.—— In saying this, he drew a little ring out of his bosom, which seemed tied with a black ribband about his neck, and kiss'd it twice—— Here, *Billy*, said he,——the boy flew across the room to the bedside,——and falling down upon his knee, took the ring in his hand, and kissed it too,——then kissed his father, and sat down upon the bed and wept.

I wish, said my uncle *Toby*, with a deep sigh,——I wish, *Trim*, I was asleep.

Your honour, replied the corporal, is too much concerned;—— shall I pour your honour out a glass of sack to your pipe?——Do, *Trim*, said my uncle *Toby*.

I remember, said my uncle *Toby*, sighing again, the story of the ensign and his wife, with a circumstance his modesty omitted;—— and particularly well that he, as well as she, upon some account or other, (I forget what) was universally pitied by the whole regiment; ——but finish the story thou art upon:——'Tis finished already, said the corporal,——for I could stay no longer,——so wished his honour a good night; young *Le Fever* rose from off the bed, and saw me to the bottom of the stairs; and as we went down together, told me, they had come from *Ireland*, and were on their route to join the regiment in *Flanders*.——But alas! said the corporal,—— the lieutenant's last day's march is over.——Then what is to become of his poor boy? cried my uncle *Toby*.

Chapter VIII.

The Story of LE FEVER *continued.*

IT was to my uncle *Toby*'s eternal honour,——though I tell it only for the sake of those, who, when coop'd in betwixt a natural and a positive law,[3] know not for their souls, which way in the

2. In the Netherlands.
3. The laws of nature vs. those instituted by man.

world to turn themselves——That notwithstanding my uncle *Toby* was warmly engaged at that time in carrying on the siege of *Dendermond*, parallel with the allies, who pressed theirs on so vigorously, that they scarce allowed him time to get his dinner——that nevertheless he gave up *Dendermond*, though he had already made a lodgment upon the counterscarp;——and bent his whole thoughts towards the private distresses at the inn; and, except that he ordered the garden gate to be bolted up, by which he might be said to have turned the siege of *Dendermond* into a blockade,——he left *Dendermond* to itself,——to be relieved or not by the *French* king, as the *French* king thought good; and only considered how he himself should relieve the poor lieutenant and his son.

——That king BEING, who is a friend to the friendless, shall recompence thee for this.

Thou hast left this matter short, said my uncle *Toby* to the corporal, as he was putting him to bed,——and I will tell thee in what, *Trim*.——In the first place, when thou madest an offer of my services to *Le Fever*,——as sickness and travelling are both expensive, and thou knowest he was but a poor lieutenant, with a son to subsist as well as himself, out of his pay,——that thou didst not make an offer to him of my purse; because, had he stood in need, thou knowest, *Trim*, he had been as welcome to it as myself.—— Your honour knows, said the corporal, I had no orders;——True, quoth my uncle *Toby*,——thou didst very right, *Trim*, as a soldier, ——but certainly very wrong as a man.

In the second place, for which, indeed, thou hast the same excuse, continued my uncle *Toby*,——when thou offeredst him whatever was in my house,——thou shouldst have offered him my house too:——A sick brother officer should have the best quarters, *Trim*, and if we had him with us,——we could tend and look to him:—— Thou art an excellent nurse thyself, *Trim*,——and what with thy care of him, and the old woman's, and his boy's, and mine together, we might recruit him again at once, and set him upon his legs.——

——In a fortnight or three weeks, added my uncle *Toby*, smiling, ——he might march.——He will never march, an' please your honour, in this world, said the corporal:——He will march; said my uncle *Toby*, rising up from the side of the bed, with one shoe off:——An' please your honour, said the corporal, he will never march, but to his grave:——He shall march, cried my uncle *Toby*, marching the foot which had a shoe on, though without advancing an inch,——he shall march to his regiment.——He cannot stand it, said the corporal;——He shall be supported, said my uncle *Toby*; ——He'll drop at last, said the corporal, and what will become of his boy?——He shall not drop, said my uncle *Toby*, firmly.——A-well-o'-day,——do what we can for him, said *Trim*, maintaining his point,——the poor soul will die:——He shall not die, by G—, cried my uncle *Toby*.

——The ACCUSING SPIRIT which flew up to heaven's chancery[4] with the oath, blush'd as he gave it in;——and the RECORDING ANGEL as he wrote it down, dropp'd a tear upon the word, and blotted it out for ever.

Chapter IX.

——M Y uncle *Toby* went to his bureau,——put his purse into his breeches pocket, and having ordered the corporal to go early in the morning for a physician,——he went to bed, and fell asleep.

Chapter X.

The Story of LE FEVER *concluded.*

T HE sun looked bright in the morning after, to every eye in the village but *Le Fever*'s and his afflicted son's; the hand of death press'd heavy upon his eye-lids,——and hardly could the wheel at the cistern turn round its circle,——when my uncle *Toby*, who had rose up an hour before his wonted time, entered the lieutenant's room, and without preface or apology, sat himself down upon the chair by the bed-side, and independantly of all modes and customs, opened the curtain in the manner an old friend and brother officer would have done it, and asked him how he did,——how he had rested in the night,——what was his complaint,——where was his pain,——and what he could do to help him:——and without giving him time to answer any one of the enquiries, went on and told him of the little plan which he had been concerting with the corporal the night before for him.——

——You shall go home directly, *Le Fever*, said my uncle *Toby*, to my house,——and we'll send for a doctor to see what's the matter,——and we'll have an apothecary,——and the corporal shall be your nurse;——and I'll be your servant, *Le Fever*.

There was a frankness in my uncle *Toby*,——not the *effect* of familiarity,——but the *cause* of it,——which let you at once into his soul, and shewed you the goodness of his nature; to this, there was something in his looks, and voice, and manner, superadded, which eternally beckoned to the unfortunate to come and take shelter under him; so that before my uncle *Toby* had half finished the kind offers he was making to the father, had the son insensibly

4. Where legal records are kept.

pressed up close to his knees, and had taken hold of the breast of his coat, and was pulling it towards him.———The blood and spirits of *Le Fever*, which were waxing cold and slow within him, and were retreating to their last citadel, the heart,———rallied back,——— the film forsook his eyes for a moment,———he looked up wishfully in my uncle *Toby*'s face,———then cast a look upon his boy,———and that *ligament*, fine as it was,———was never broken.———

Nature instantly ebb'd again,———the film returned to its place, ———the pulse fluttered———stopp'd———went on———throb'd——— stopp'd again———moved———stopp'd———shall I go on?———No.

Chapter XI.

I Am so impatient to return to my own story, that what remains of young *Le Fever*'s, that is, from this turn of his fortune, to the time my uncle *Toby* recommended him for my preceptor, shall be told in a very few words, in the next chapter.———All that is necessary to be added to this chapter is as follows.———

That my uncle *Toby*, with young *Le Fever* in his hand, attended the poor lieutenant, as chief mourners, to his grave.

That the governor of *Dendermond* paid his obsequies all military honours,———and that *Yorick*, not to be behind hand———paid him all ecclesiastic———for he buried him in his chancel:———And it appears likewise, he preached a funeral sermon over him———I say it *appears*,———for it was *Yorick*'s custom, which I suppose a general one with those of his profession, on the first leaf of every sermon which he composed, to chronicle down the time, the place, and the occasion of its being preached: to this, he was ever wont to add some short comment or stricture upon the sermon itself, seldom, indeed, much to its credit:———For instance, *This sermon upon the jewish dispensation———I don't like it at all;———Though I own there is a world of* WATER-LANDISH[5] *knowledge in it,———but 'tis all tritical, and most tritically put together.———This is but a flimsy kind of a composition; what was in my head when I made it?*

———N. B. *The excellency of this text is, that it will suit any sermon,———and of this sermon,———that it will suit any text.———*

———*For this sermon I shall be hanged,———for I have stolen the greatest part of it. Doctor* Paidagunes[6] *found me out.* ☞ *Set a thief to catch a thief.———*

On the back of half a dozen I find written, So, so, and no more ———and upon a couple *Moderato*; by which, as far as one may gather from *Altieri*'s *Italian* dictionary,———but mostly from the

---

5. A reference, with overtones of "outlandish," to a preacher named Daniel Waterland. *Tritical* compounds "trite" and "critical."

6. A female form of "pedagogue"; the reference is contemptuous of pedantry.

authority of a piece of green whipcord, which seemed to have been the unravelling of *Yorick's* whip-lash, with which he has left us the two sermons marked *Moderato,* and the half dozen of *So, so,* tied fast together in one bundle by themselves, ——one may safely suppose he meant pretty near the same thing.

There is but one difficulty in the way of this conjecture, which is this, that the *moderato's* are five times better than the *so, so's;*—— shew ten times more knowledge of the human heart;——have seventy times more wit and spirit in them;——(and, to rise properly in my climax)——discover a thousand times more genius;——and to crown all, are infinitely more entertaining than those tied up with them;——for which reason, whene'er *Yorick's dramatic* sermons are offered to the world, though I shall admit but one out of the whole number of the *so, so's,* I shall, nevertheless, adventure to print the two *moderato's*[7] without any sort of scruple.

What *Yorick* could mean by the words *lentamente,*——*tenutè,* ——*grave,*——and sometimes *adagio,*——as applied to theological compositions, and with which he has characterized some of these sermons, I dare not venture to guess.——I am more puzzled still upon finding *a l'octava alta!* upon one;——*Con strepito* upon the back of another;——*Siciliana* upon a third;——*Alla capella* upon a fourth;——*Con l'arco* upon this;——*Senza l'arco* upon that.—— All I know is, that they are musical terms, and have a meaning; ——and as he was a musical man, I will make no doubt, but that by some quaint application of such metaphors to the compositions in hand, they impressed very distinct ideas of their several characters upon his fancy,——whatever they may do upon that of others.

Amongst these, there is that particular sermon which has unaccountably led me into this digression——The funeral sermon upon poor *Le Fever,* who wrote out very fairly, as if from a hasty copy,——I take notice of it the more, because it seems to have been his favourite composition——It is upon mortality; and is tied lengthways and cross-ways with a yarn thrum, and then rolled up and twisted round with a half sheet of dirty blue paper,[8] which seems to have been once the cast cover of a general review, which to this day smells horribly of horse drugs.——Whether these marks of humiliation were designed,——I something doubt;——because at the end of the sermon, (and not at the beginning of it)——very different from his way of treating the rest, he had wrote——

Bravo!

---

7. *Moderato:* moderate. *Lentamente:* slowly. *Tenutè:* sustained. *Grave:* solemn. *Adagio:* slow. *L'octava alta:* in the high octave. *Con strepito:* exuberantly. *Siciliana:* as in a slow Sicilian dance. *Con l'arco:* with a bow. *Senza l'arco:* without the bow, i.e., pizzacato.

8. That is, the discarded (cast) cover of *The Critical Review,* which had published some unfavorable comments on Sterne, under the editorship of Dr. Tobias Smollett, who Tristram implies is a horse-doctor.

——Though not very offensively,——for it is at two inches, at least, and a half's distance from, and below the concluding line of the sermon, at the very extremity of the page, and in that right hand corner of it, which, you know, is generally covered with your thumb; and, to do it justice, it is wrote besides with a crow's quill so faintly in a small *Italian*[9] hand, as scarce to sollicit the eye towards the place, whether your thumb is there or not,——so that from the *manner of it*, it stands half excused; and being wrote moreover with very pale ink, diluted almost to nothing,——'tis more like a *ritratto* of the shadow of vanity, than of VANITY herself——of the two; resembling rather a faint thought of transient applause, secretly stirring up in the heart of the composer, than a gross mark of it, coarsely obtruded upon the world.

With all these extenuations, I am aware, that in publishing this, I do no service to *Yorick*'s character as a modest man;——but all men have their failings! and what lessens this still farther, and almost wipes it away, is this; that the word was struck through sometime afterwards (as appears from a different tint of the ink) with a line quite across it in this manner, ~~BRAVO~~—— as if he had retracted, or was ashamed of the opinion he had once entertained of it.

These short characters of his sermons were always written, excepting in this one instance, upon the first leaf of his sermon, which served as a cover to it; and usually upon the inside of it, which was turned towards the text;——but at the end of his discourse, where, perhaps, he had five or six pages, and sometimes, perhaps, a whole score to turn himself in,——he took a larger circuit, and, indeed, a much more mettlesome one;——as if he had snatched the occasion of unlacing himself with a few more frolicksome strokes at vice, than the straitness of the pulpit allowed.——These, though hussar-like, they skirmish lightly and out of all order, are still auxiliaries on the side of virtue——; tell me then, Mynheer Vander Blonederdon-dergewdenstronke,[1] why they should not be printed together?

Chapter XII.

WHEN my uncle *Toby* had turned every thing into money, and settled all accounts betwixt the agent of the regiment and *Le Fever*, and betwixt *Le Fever* and all mankind,—— there remained nothing more in my uncle *Toby*'s hands, than an old regimental coat and a sword; so that my uncle *Toby* found little or no opposition from the world in taking administration. The coat my uncle *Toby* gave the corporal;——Wear it, *Trim*, said my uncle *Toby*, as long as it will hold together, for the sake of the poor lieutenant——And this,——said my uncle *Toby*, taking up the

9. Italic script (not gothic). *Ritratto*: portrait.
1. Sterne's name for clumsy Dutch critics.

sword in his hand, and drawing it out of the scabbard as he spoke
——and this, *Le Fever*, I'll save for thee,——'tis all the fortune,
continued my uncle *Toby*, hanging it up upon a crook, and pointing
to it,——'tis all the fortune, my dear *Le Fever*, which God has left
thee; but if he has given thee a heart to fight thy way with it in the
world,——and thou doest it like a man of honour,——'tis enough
for us.

As soon as my uncle *Toby* had laid a foundation, and taught him
to inscribe a regular polygon in a circle, he sent him to a public
school, where, excepting *Whitsontide* and *Christmas*, at which times
the corporal was punctually dispatched for him,——he remained to
the spring of the year, seventeen; when the stories of the emperor's
sending his army into *Hungary* against the *Turks*, kindling a spark
of fire in his bosom, he left his *Greek* and *Latin* without leave, and
throwing himself upon his knees before my uncle *Toby*, begged his
father's sword, and my uncle *Toby*'s leave along with it, to go and
try his fortune under *Eugene*.[2]——Twice did my uncle *Toby* forget his wound, and cry out, *Le Fever*! I will go with thee, and thou
shalt fight beside me——And twice he laid his hand upon his groin,
and hung down his head in sorrow and disconsolation.——

My uncle *Toby* took down the sword from the crook, where it had
hung untouched ever since the lieutenant's death, and delivered it to
the corporal to brighten up;——and having detained *Le Fever* a
single fortnight to equip him, and contract for his passage to *Leg-
horn*,——he put the sword into his hand,——If thou art brave, *Le
Fever*, said my uncle *Toby*, this will not fail thee,——but Fortune,
said he, (musing a little)——Fortune may——And if she does,
——added my uncle *Toby*, embracing him, come back again to
me, *Le Fever*, and we will shape thee another course.

The greatest injury could not have oppressed the heart of *Le
Fever* more than my uncle *Toby*'s paternal kindness;——he parted
from my uncle *Toby*, as the best of sons from the best of fathers
——both dropped tears——and as my uncle *Toby* gave him his
last kiss, he slipped sixty guineas, tied up in an old purse of his
father's, in which was his mother's ring, into his hand,——and bid
God bless him.

Chapter XIII.

L E *Fever* got up to the Imperial army just time enough to try what
metal his sword was made of, at the defeat of the *Turk*'s
before *Belgrade*; but a series of unmerited mischances had pursued

2. Prince Eugene of Savoy (1663–1736),
one of the most brilliant generals of the
century, who had collaborated with Marlborough in some of his greatest victories,
commanded the forces of Charles VI
against the Turks in 1716–18.

him from that moment, and trod close upon his heels for four years together after: he had withstood these buffetings to the last, till sickness overtook him at *Marseilles,* from whence he wrote my uncle *Toby* word, he had lost his time, his services, his health, and, in short, every thing but his sword;——and was waiting for the first ship to return back to him.

As this letter came to hand about six weeks before *Susannah's* accident, *Le Fever* was hourly expected; and was uppermost in my uncle *Toby's* mind all the time my father was giving him and *Yorick* a description of what kind of a person he would chuse for a preceptor to me: but as my uncle *Toby* thought my father at first somewhat fanciful in the accomplishments he required, he forebore mentioning *Le Fever's* name,——till the character, by *Yorick's* interposition, ending unexpectedly, in one, who should be gentle tempered, and generous, and good, it impressed the image of *Le Fever,* and his interest upon my uncle *Toby* so forceably, he rose instantly off his chair; and laying down his pipe, in order to take hold of both my father's hands——I beg, brother *Shandy,* said my uncle *Toby,* I may recommend poor *Le Fever's* son to you——I beseech you, do, added *Yorick*——He has a good heart, said my uncle *Toby*——And a brave one too, an' please your honour, said the corporal.

——The best hearts, *Trim,* are ever the bravest, replied my uncle *Toby.*——And the greatest cowards, an' please your honour, in our regiment, were the greatest rascals in it.——There was serjeant *Kumbur,* and ensign——

——We'll talk of them, said my father, another time.

Chapter XIV.

WHAT a jovial and a merry world would this be, may it please your worships, but for that inextricable labyrinth of debts, cares, woes, want, grief, discontent, melancholy, large jointures, impositions, and lies!

Doctor *Slop,* like a son of a w——, as my father called him for it,——to exalt himself,——debased me to death,——and made ten thousand times more of *Susannah's* accident, than there was any grounds for; so that in a week's time, or less, it was in every body's mouth, *That poor Master Shandy* * * * * * * * * * * * * entirely.—— And FAME, who loves to double every thing,——in three days more, had sworn positively she saw it,——and all the world, as usual, gave credit to her evidence——"That the nursery window had not only *

*   *   *   *   *   ;——but that *   *   *   *   *
*   *   *   *   *   *   *   *   *   *   *   *
*   *   *   *   *   *   *'s also.''

Could the world have been sued like a BODY-CORPORATE,——my father had brought an action upon the case, and trounced it sufficiently; but to fall foul of individuals about it——as every soul who had mentioned the affair, did it with the greatest pity imaginable;——'twas like flying in the very face of his best friends:——And yet to acquiesce under the report, in silence——was to acknowledge it openly,——at least in the opinion of one half of the world; and to make a bustle again, in contradicting it,——was to confirm it as strongly in the opinion of the other half.——

——Was ever poor devil of a country gentleman so hampered? said my father.

I would shew him publickly, said my uncle *Toby*, at the market cross.

——'Twill have no effect, said my father.

Chapter XV.

——I'll put him, however, into breeches[3] said my father,——let the world say what it will.

Chapter XVI.

THERE are a thousand resolutions, Sir, both in church and state, as well as in matters, Madam, of a more private concern;—— which, though they have carried all the appearance in the world of being taken, and entered upon in a hasty, hare-brained, and unadvised manner, were, notwithstanding this, (and could you or I have got into the cabinet, or stood behind the curtain, we should have found it was so) weighed, poized, and perpended——argued upon——canvassed through——entered into, and examined on all sides with so much coolness, that the GODDESS of COOLNESS herself (I do not take upon me to prove her existence) could neither have wished it, or done it better.

Of the number of these was my father's resolution of putting me into breeches; which, though determined at once,——in a kind of huff, and a defiance of all mankind, had, nevertheless, been *pro'd* and *conn'd,* and judicially talked over betwixt him and my mother about a month before, in two several *beds of justice,*[4] which my

3. Children were often dressed alike, regardless of sex, until the age of five or six. Walter is determined to dress the boy in a way that will persuade the world that the window's fall did him no radical damage.
4. This was the name of the throne occupied by the King of France when he came before Parliament at certain times.

father had held for that purpose. I shall explain the nature of these beds of justice in my next chapter; and in the chapter following that, you shall step with me, Madam, behind the curtain, only to hear in what kind of manner my father and my mother debated between themselves, this affair of the breeches,——from which you may form an idea, how they debated all lesser matters.

Chapter XVII.

THE ancient *Goths* of *Germany*, who (the learned *Cluverius*[5] is positive) were first seated in the country between the *Vistula* and the *Oder*, and who afterwards incorporated the *Herculi*, the *Bugians*, and some other *Vandallick* clans to 'em,——had all of them a wise custom of debating every thing of importance to their state, twice; that is,——once drunk, and once sober:——Drunk ——that their counsels might not want vigour;——and sober—— that they might not want discretion.

Now my father being entirely a water-drinker,——was a long time gravelled almost to death, in turning this as much to his advantage, as he did every other thing, which the ancients did or said; and it was not till the seventh year of his marriage, after a thousand fruitless experiments and devices, that he hit upon an expedient which answered the purpose;——and that was when any difficult and momentous point was to be settled in the family, which required great sobriety, and great spirit too, in its determination,—— he fixed and set apart the first *Sunday* night in the month, and the *Saturday* night which immediately preceded it, to argue it over, in bed with my mother: By which contrivance, if you consider, Sir, with yourself,   *   *   *   *   *   *   *   *   *   *   *
*   *   *   *   *   *   *   *   *   *   *   *
*   *   *   *   *   *   *   *   *   *   *   *
*   *   *   *   *   *   *   *   *   *   *   *
*   *   *   *   *   *   *   *

These my father, humourously enough, called his *beds of justice*; ——for from the two different counsels taken in these two different humours, a middle one was generally found out, which touched the point of wisdom as well, as if he had got drunk and sober a hundred times.

It must not be made a secret of to the world, that this answers full as well in literary discussions, as either in military or conjugal; but it is not every author that can try the experiment as the *Goths* and *Vandals* did it——or if he can, may it be always for his body's

---

5. Philip Cluwer, a German geographer.

health; and to do it, as my father did it,——am I sure it would be always for his soul's.——

My way is this:——

In all nice and ticklish discussions,——(of which, heaven knows, there are but too many in my book)——where I find I cannot take a step without the danger of having either their worships or their reverences upon my back——I write one half *full*,——and t'other *fasting*;——or write it all full,——and correct it fasting;——or write it fasting,——and correct it full, for they all come to the same thing:——So that with a less variation from my father's plan, than my father's from the *Gothick*——I feel myself upon a par with him in his first bed of justice,——and no way inferior to him in his second.——These different and almost irreconcileable effects, flow uniformly from the wise and wonderful mechanism of nature,—— of which,——be her's the honour.——All that we can do, is to turn and work the machine to the improvement and better manufactury of the arts and sciences.——

Now, when I write full,——I write as if I was never to write fasting again as long as I live;——that is, I write free from the cares, as well as the terrors of the world.——I count not the number of my scars,——nor does my fancy go forth into dark entries and bye corners to antedate my stabs.——In a word, my pen takes its course; and I write on as much from the fullness of my heart, as my stomach.——

But when, an' please your honours, I indite fasting, 'tis a different history.——I pay the world all possible attention and respect,—— and have as great a share (whilst it lasts) of that understrapping virtue of discretion, as the best of you.——So that betwixt both, I write a careless kind of a civil, nonsensical, good humoured *Shandean* book, which will do all your hearts good——

——And all your heads too,——provided you understand it.

Chapter XVIII.

WE should begin, said my father, turning himself half round in bed, and shifting his pillow a little towards my mother's, as he opened the debate——We should begin to think, Mrs. *Shandy*, of putting this boy into breeches.——

We should so,——said my mother.——We defer it, my dear, quoth my father, shamefully.——

I think we do, Mr. *Shandy*,——said my mother.

——Not but the child looks extremely well, said my father, in his vests and tunicks.——

————He does look very well in them,——replied my mother.——

——And for that reason it would be almost a sin, added my father, to take him out of 'em.——

——It would so,——said my mother:——But indeed he is growing a very tall lad,——rejoin'd my father.

——He is very tall for his age, indeed,——said my mother.——

——I can not (making two syllables of it) imagine, quoth my father, who the duce he takes after.——

I cannot conceive, for my life,——said my mother.——

Humph!——said my father.

(The dialogue ceased for a moment.)

——I am very short myself,——continued my father, gravely.

You are very short, Mr. *Shandy*,——said my mother.

Humph! quoth my father to himself, a second time: in muttering which, he plucked his pillow a little further from my mother's,—— and turning about again, there was an end of the debate for three minutes and a half.

——When he gets these breeches made, cried my father in a higher tone, he'll look like a beast in 'em.

He will be very aukward in them at first, replied my mother.——

——And 'twill be lucky, if that's the worst on't, added my father.

It will be very lucky, answered my mother.

I suppose, replied my father,——making some pause first,—— he'll be exactly like other people's children.——

Exactly, said my mother.——

——Though I should be sorry for that, added my father: and so the debate stopped again.

——They should be of leather, said my father, turning him about again.——

They will last him, said my mother, the longest.

But he can have no linings to 'em, replied my father.——

He cannot, said my mother.

'Twere better to have them of fustian,[6] quoth my father.

Nothing can be better, quoth my mother.——

——Except dimity,——replied my father:——'Tis best of all,——replied my mother.

——One must not give him his death, however,——interrupted my father.

By no means, said my mother:——and so the dialogue stood still again.

I am resolved, however, quoth my father, breaking silence the fourth time, he shall have no pockets in them.——

——There is no occasion for any, said my mother.——

I mean in his coat and waistcoat,——cried my father.

6. Fustian is a coarse cotton twill fabric; dimity a fine, thin one.

——I mean so too,——replied my mother.

——Though if he gets a gig[7] or a top——Poor souls! it is a crown and a scepter to them,——they should have where to secure it.——

Order it as you please, Mr. *Shandy,* replied my mother.——

——But don't you think it right? added my father, pressing the point home to her.

Perfectly, said my mother, if it pleases you, Mr. *Shandy.*——

——There's for you! cried my father, losing temper——Pleases me!——You never will distinguish, Mrs. *Shandy,* nor shall I ever teach you to do it, betwixt a point of pleasure and a point of convenience.——This was on the *Sunday* night;——and further this chapter sayeth not.

Chapter XIX.

AFTER my father had debated the affair of the breeches with my mother,——he consulted *Albertus Rubenius*[8] upon it; and *Albertus Rubenius* used my father ten times worse in the consultation (if possible) than even my father had used my mother: For as *Rubenius* had wrote a quarto *express, De re Vestiaria Veterum,*——it was *Rubenius's* business to have given my father some lights.——On the contrary, my father might as well have thought of extracting the seven cardinal virtues out of a long beard,——as of extracting a single word out of *Rubenius* upon the subject.

Upon every other article of ancient dress, *Rubenius* was very communicative to my father;——gave him a full and satisfactory account of

    The Toga, or loose gown.

    The Chlamys.

    The Ephod.

    The Tunica, or Jacket.

    The Synthesis.

    The Pænula.

    The Lacema, with its Cucullus.

    Te Paludamentum.

    The Prætexta.

    The Sagum, or soldier's jerkin.

7. A spinning toy.

8. Albert Rubens (1614–57) was the son of the famous painter Peter Paul Rubens, and himself a writer and archeologist. His *De Re Vestiaria Veterum, Praecipue de Lato Clavo* [Of the Clothing of the Ancients, Particularly of the Latus Clavus] is a landmark of pedantry. *Chlamys*: a short woolen cloak. *Ephod*: a priestly garment worn at Hebrew religious ceremonies. *Synthesis*: a loose garment sometimes worn instead of the toga. *Paenula*: a full-length woolen cloak. *Lacema,* with *cucullus*: probably a *lacerna*, a military cloak, with a hood. *Paludamentum*: a military cloak. *Praetexta*: worn by Roman magistrates and free-born children. *Trabea*: robe of state.

The Trabea: of which, according to *Suetonius*,[9] there were three kinds.——

——But what are all these to the breeches? said my father.

Rubenius threw him down upon the counter all kinds of shoes which had been in fashion with the *Romans*.—— There was,

> The open shoe.
> The close shoe.
> The slip shoe.
> The wooden shoe.
> The soc.[1]
> The buskin.

And The military shoe with hobnails in it, which *Juvenal*[2] takes notice of.

There were, The clogs.
> The patins.
> The pantoufles.
> The brogues.
> The sandals, with latchets to them.

There was, The felt shoe.
> The linen shoe.
> The laced shoe.
> The braided shoe.
> The calceus incisus.

And The calceus rostratus.

Rubenius shewed my father how well they all fitted,——in what manner they laced on,——with what points, straps, thongs, lachets, ribands, jaggs, and ends.——

——But I want to be informed about the breeches, said my father.

Albertus Rubenius informed my father that the *Romans* manufactured stuffs of various fabricks,——some plain,——some striped,——others diapered throughout the whole contexture of the wool, with silk and gold——That linen did not begin to be in common use, till towards the declension of the empire, when the *Egyptians* coming to settle amongst them, brought it into vogue.

——That persons of quality and fortune distinguished themselves by the fineness and whiteness of their cloaths; which colour (next to purple, which was appropriated to the great offices) they most affected and wore on their birth-days and public rejoicings.——That it appeared from the best historians of those times, that they

---

9. A Roman historian of the second century.
1. *Soc*: a light shoe. *Patins*: overshoes constructed of wooden soles, supported by iron rings, to prevent sinking in mud. *Pantoufles*: slippers. *Calceus in-*

cisus: a cutwork shoe. *Calceus rostratus*: a hooked or pointed shoe.
2. Juvenal (c. 60–c. 127), was along with Horace, the greatest of Roman satirists. The reference here is to his *Satirae* XVI. 24–25.

frequently sent their cloaths to the fuller, to be cleaned and whit-ened;——but that the inferior people, to avoid that expence, gener-ally wore brown cloaths, and of a something coarser texture,——till towards the beginning of *Augustus*'s reign, when the slave dressed like his master, and almost every distinction of habiliment was lost, but the *Latus Clavus*.[3]

And what was the *Latus Clavus?* said my father.

Rubenius told him, that the point was still litigating amongst the learned:——That *Egnatius*,[4] *Sigonius, Bossius Ticinensis, Bayfius, Budæus, Salmasius, Lipsius, Lazius, Isaac Casaubon,* and *Joseph Scaliger,* all differed from each other,——and he from them: That some took it to be the button,——some the coat itself,——others only the colour of it:——That the great *Bayfius,* in his Wardrobe of the ancients, chap. 12.——honestly said, he knew not what it was,——whether a tibula,[5]——a stud,——a button,——a loop,——a buckle,——or clasps and keepers.——

——My father lost the horse, but not the saddle——They are *hooks and eyes,* said my father——and with hooks and eyes he ordered my breeches to be made.

Chapter XX.

WE are now going to enter upon a new scene of events.——

——Leave we then the breeches in the taylor's hands, with my father standing over him with his cane, reading him as he sat at work a lecture upon the *latus clavus,* and pointing to the precise part of the waistband, where he was determined to have it sewed on.——

Leave we my mother——(truest of all the *Poco-curante*'s[6] of her sex!)——careless about it, as about every thing else in the world which concerned her;——that is,——indifferent whether it was done this way or that,——provided it was but done at all.——

Leave we *Slop* likewise to the full profits of all my dishon-ours.——

Leave we poor *Le Fever* to recover, and get home from *Mar-seilles* as he can.——And last of all,——because the hardest of all——

Let us leave, if possible, *myself:*——But 'tis impossible,——I must go along with you to the end of the work.

---

3. Literally, *latus clavus* means "broad nail." It describes the wide purple stripe that distinguished the toga of a Roman senator.
4. All of these names are those of Ren-aissance scholars and historians.
5. Probably a misprint for *fibula,* a brooch or clasp.
6. "Little-caring"—from the name of a character in Voltaire's *Candide.*

Chapter XXI.

IF the reader has not a clear conception of the rood and the half of ground which lay at the bottom of my uncle *Toby*'s kitchen garden, and which was the scene of so many of his delicious hours, ——the fault is not in me,——but in his imagination;——for I am sure I gave him so minute a description, I was almost ashamed of it.

When FATE was looking forwards one afternoon, into the great transactions of future times,——and recollected for what purposes, this little plot, by a decree fast bound down in iron, had been destined,——she gave a nod to NATURE——'twas enough—— Nature threw half a spade full of her kindliest compost upon it, with just so *much* clay in it, as to retain the forms of angles and indentings,——and so *little* of it too, as not to cling to the spade, and render works of so much glory, nasty in foul weather.

My uncle *Toby* came down, as the reader has been informed, with plans along with him, of almost every fortified town in *Italy* and *Flanders*; so let the Duke of *Marlborough*, or the allies, have set down before what town they pleased, my uncle *Toby* was prepared for them.

His way, which was the simplest one in the world, was this; as soon as ever a town was invested——(but sooner when the design was known) to take the plan of it, (let it be what town it would) and enlarge it upon a scale to the exact size of his bowling-green; upon the surface of which, by means of a large role of packthread, and a number of small piquets driven into the ground, at the several angles and redans,[7] he transferred the lines from his papers; then taking the profile of the place, with its works, to determine the depths and slopes of the ditches,——the talus of the glacis, and the precise height of the several banquets, parapets, &c.——he set the corporal to work——and sweetly went it on:——The nature of the soil,——the nature of the work itself,——and above all, the good nature of my uncle *Toby* sitting by from morning to night, and chatting kindly with the corporal upon past-done deeds,——left LABOUR little else but the ceremony of the name.

When the place was finished in this manner, and put into a proper posture of defence,——it was invested,——and my uncle *Toby* and the corporal began to run their first parallel.[8]——I beg I may not be interrupted in my story, by being told, *That the first parallel should be at least three hundred toises distant from the main body of the place,——and that I have not left a single inch for it;*—— for my uncle *Toby* took the liberty of incroaching

---

7. A fortification with two faces forming an angle, but without protection from the rear (and so often placed against a river, etc.).

8. A trench in front of the fortification, and parallel to it.

upon his kitchen garden, for the sake of enlarging his works on the bowling green, and for that reason generally ran his first and second parallels betwixt two rows of his cabbages and his collyflowers; the conveniences and inconveniences of which will be considered at large in the history of my uncle *Toby*'s and the corporal's campaigns, of which, this I'm now writing is but a sketch, and will be finished, if I conjecture right, in three pages (but there is no guessing)——The campaigns themselves will take up as many books; and therefore I apprehend it would be hanging too great a weight of one kind of matter in so flimsy a performance as this, to rhapsodize them, as I once intended, into the body of the work—— surely they had better be printed apart,——we'll consider the affair ——so take the following sketch of them in the mean time.

Chapter XXII.

WHEN the town, with its works, was finished, my uncle *Toby* and the corporal began to run their first parallel ——not at random, or any how——but from the same points and distances the allies had begun to run theirs; and regulating their approaches and attacks, by the accounts my uncle *Toby* received from the daily papers,——they went on, during the whole siege, step by step with the allies.

When the duke of *Marlborough* made a lodgment,——my uncle *Toby* made a lodgment too.——And when the face of a bastion was battered down, or a defence ruined,——the corporal took his mattock and did as much,——and so on;——gaining ground, and making themselves masters of the works one after another, till the town fell into their hands.

To one who took pleasure in the happy state of others,——there could not have been a greater sight in the world, than, on a postmorning, in which a practicable breach had been made by the duke of *Marlborough*, in the main body of the place,——to have stood behind the horn-beam hedge, and observed the spirit with which my uncle *Toby*, with *Trim* behind him, sallied forth;——the one with the *Gazette* in his hand,——the other with a spade on his shoulder to execute the contents.——What an honest triumph in my uncle *Toby*'s looks as he marched up to the ramparts! What intense pleasure swimming in his eye as he stood over the corporal, reading the paragraph ten times over to him, as he was at work, lest, peradventure, he should make the breach an inch too wide,——or leave it an inch too narrow——But when the *chamade*[9] was beat, and the corporal helped my uncle up it, and followed with the colours in his hand, to fix them upon the ramparts——Heaven! Earth! Sea!——

---

9. A bugle or drum call for retreat or parley.

but what avails apostrophes?——with all your elements, wet or dry, ye never compounded so intoxicating a draught.

In this track of happiness for many years, without one interruption to it, except now and then when the wind continued to blow due west for a week or ten days together, which detained the *Flanders* mail, and kept them so long in torture,——but still 'twas the torture of the happy——In this track, I say, did my uncle *Toby* and *Trim* move for many years, every year of which, and sometimes every month, from the invention of either the one or the other of them, adding some new conceit or quirk of improvement to their operations, which always opened fresh springs of delight in carrying them on.

The first year's campaign was carried on from begining to end, in the plain and simple method I've related.

In the second year, in which my uncle *Toby* took *Liege* and *Ruremond*,[1] he thought he might afford the expence of four handsome draw-bridges, two of which I have given an exact description, in the former part of my work.

At the latter end of the same year he added a couple of gates with portcullises:——These last were converted afterwards into orgues,[2] as the better thing; and during the winter of the same year, my uncle *Toby*, instead of a new suit of cloaths, which he always had at *Christmas*, treated himself with a handsome sentry-box, to stand at the corner of the bowling-green, betwixt which point and the foot of the glacis, there was left a little kind of an esplanade for him and the corporal to confer and hold councils of war upon.

——The sentry-box was in case of rain.

All these were painted white three times over the ensuing spring, which enabled my uncle *Toby* to take the field with great splendour.

My father would often say to *Yorick*, that if any mortal in the whole universe had done such a thing, except his brother *Toby*, it would have been looked upon by the world as one of the most refined satyrs upon the parade and prancing manner, in which *Lewis* XIV, from the beginning of the war, but particularly that very year, had taken the field——But 'tis not my brother *Toby*'s nature, kind soul! my father would add, to insult any one.

——But let us go on.

Chapter XXIII.

I Must observe, that although in the first year's campaign, the word *town* is often mentioned,——yet there was no town at that time within the polygon; that addition was not made till the

---

1. Both cities fell in 1702.
2. A weapon created by putting several cannon side by side.

summer following the spring in which the bridges and sentry-box were painted, which was the third year of my uncle *Toby*'s campaigns,——when upon his taking *Amberg, Bonn,* and *Rhinberg,* and *Huy* and *Limbourg*,[3] one after another, a thought came into the corporal's head, that to talk of taking so many towns, *without one* TOWN *to show for it,*——was a very nonsensical way of going to work, and so proposed to my uncle *Toby,* that they should have a little model of a town built for them,——to be run up together of slit deals, and then painted, and clapped within the interior polygon to serve for all.

My uncle *Toby* felt the good of the project instantly, and instantly agreed to it, but with the addition of two singular improvements, of which he was almost as proud, as if he had been the original inventor of the project itself.

The one was to have the town built exactly in the stile of those, of which it was most likely to be the representative:——with grated windows, and the gable ends of the houses, facing the streets, &c. &c.——as those in *Ghent* and *Bruges,* and the rest of the towns in *Brabant* and *Flanders.*

The other was, not to have the houses run up together, as the corporal proposed, but to have every house independant, to hook on, or off, so as to form into the plan of whatever town they pleased. This was put directly into hand, and many and many a look of mutual congratulation was exchanged between my uncle *Toby* and the corporal, as the carpenter did the work.

——It answered prodigiously the next summer—the town was a perfect *Proteus*[4]——it was *Landen,* and *Trerebach,* and *Santvliet,* and *Drusen,* and *Hagenau,*——and then it was *Ostend* and *Menin,* and *Aeth* and *Dendermond.*

——Surely never did any TOWN act so many parts, since *Sodom* and *Gomorrah,*[5] as my uncle *Toby*'s town did.

In the fourth year, my uncle *Toby* thinking a town looked foolishly without a church, added a very fine one with a steeple.—— *Trim* was for having bells in it;——my uncle *Toby* said, the mettle had better be cast into cannon.

This led the way the next campaign for half a dozen brass field pieces,——to be planted three and three on each side of my uncle *Toby*'s sentry-box; and in a short time, these led the way for a train of somewhat larger,——and so on——(as must always be the case in hobby-horsical affairs) from pieces of half an inch bore, till it came at last to my father's jack boots.

---

3. These cities fell in 1703.
4. In classical myth, Proteus was a sea god who could change instantly to any form he wished. The cities listed here were captured 1704–06.
5. In Genesis 19, cities destroyed for their wickedness, particularly sexual perversion ("so many parts").

The next year, which was that in which *Lisle* was besieged,[6] and at the close of which both *Ghent* and *Bruges* fell into our hands, ——my uncle *Toby* was sadly put to it for *proper* ammunition;—— I say proper ammunition——because his great artillery would not bear powder; and 'twas well for the *Shandy* family they would not——For so full were the papers, from the beginning to the end of the siege, of the incessant firings kept up by the besiegers,—— and so heated was my uncle *Toby*'s imagination with the accounts of them, that he had infallibly shot away all his estate.

SOMETHING therefore was wanting, as a *succedaneum*, especially in one or two of the more violent paroxysms of the siege, to keep up something like a continual firing in the imagination,——and this *something*, the corporal, whose principal strength lay in invention, supplied by an entire new system of battering of his own,——with-out which, this had been objected to by military critics, to the end of the world, as one of the great *disiderata*[7] of my uncle *Toby*'s apparatus.

This will not be explained the worse, for setting off, as I generally do, at a little distance from the subject.

Chapter XXIV.

WITH two or three other trinkets, small in themselves, but of great regard, which poor *Tom*, the corporal's unfor-tunate brother, had sent him over, with the account of his marriage with the *Jew*'s widow——there was

A *Montero*-cap[8] and two *Turkish* tobacco pipes.

The *Montero*-cap I shall describe by and bye.——The *Turkish* tobacco pipes had nothing particular in them, they were fitted up and ornamented as usual, with flexible tubes of *Morocco* leather and gold wire, and mounted at their ends, the one of them with ivory,——the other with black ebony, tipp'd with silver.

My father, who saw all things in lights different from the rest of the world, would say to the corporal, that he ought to look upon these two presents more as tokens of his brother's nicety, than his affection.——*Tom* did not care, *Trim*, he would say, to put on the cap, or to smoak in the tobacco-pipe of a *Jew*.——God bless your honour, the corporal would say, (giving a strong reason to the contrary)——how can that be?——

The Montero-cap was scarlet, of a superfine *Spanish* cloth, died in grain, and mounted all round with furr, except about four inches in the front, which was faced with a light blue, slightly em-broidered,——and seemed to have been the property of a *Portu-guese* quartermaster, not of foot, but of horse, as the word denotes.

6. 1708.
7. "Desired things."

8. A Spanish rider's cap with ear flaps.

The corporal was not a little proud of it, as well for its own sake, as the sake of the giver, so seldom or never put it on but upon GALA-days; and yet never was a Montero-cap put to so many uses; for in all controverted points, whether military or culinary, provided the corporal was sure he was in the right,——it was either his *oath*, ——his *wager*,——or his *gift*.

——'Twas his gift in the present case.

I'll be bound, said the corporal, speaking to himself, to *give* away my Montero-cap to the first beggar who comes to the door, if I do not manage this matter to his honour's satisfaction.

The completion was no further off, than the very next morning; which was that of the storm of the counterscarp betwixt the *Lower Deule*, to the right, and the gate St. *Andrew*,——on the left, between St. *Magdalen*'s and the river.[9]

As this was the most memorable attack in the whole war,——the most gallant and obstinate on both sides,——and I must add the most bloody too, for it cost the allies themselves that morning above eleven hundred men,——my uncle *Toby* prepared himself for it with a more than ordinary solemnity.

The eve which preceded, as my uncle *Toby* went to bed, he ordered his ramallie wig,[1] which had laid inside out for many years in the corner of an old campaigning trunk, which stood by his bedside, to be taken out and laid upon the lid of it, ready for the morning;——and the very first thing he did in his shirt, when he had stepped out of bed, my uncle *Toby*, after he had turned the rough side outwards,——put it on:——This done, he proceeded next to his breeches, and having buttoned the waist-band, he forthwith buckled on his sword belt, and had got his sword half way in,——when he considered he should want shaving, and that it would be very inconvenient doing it with his sword on,——so took it off:——In assaying to put on his regimental coat and waistcoat, my uncle *Toby* found the same objection in his wig,——so that went off too:——So that what with one thing, and what with another, as always falls out when a man is in the most haste,——'twas ten o'clock, which was half an hour later than his usual time, before my uncle *Toby* sallied out.

Chapter XXV.

MY uncle *Toby* had scarce turned the corner of his yew hedge, which separated his kitchen garden from his bowling green, when he perceived the corporal had began the attack without him.——

9. Place names in the battle of Lille.
1. This kind of wig has a long braid tied at top and bottom; it was named for Ramillies, Belgium, where Marlborough defeated the French in 1706.

Let me stop and give you a picture of the corporal's apparatus; and of the corporal himself in the height of this attack just as it struck my uncle *Toby*, as he turned towards the sentry box, where the corporal was at work,——for in nature there is not such another,——nor can any combination of all that is grotesque and whimsical in her works produce its equal.

The corporal——

——Tread lightly on his ashes, ye men of genius,——for he was your kinsman:

Weed his grave clean, ye men of goodness,——for he was your brother.——Oh corporal! had I thee, but now,——now, that I am able to give thee a dinner and protection,——how would I cherish thee! thou should'st wear thy Montero-cap every hour of the day, and every day of the week,——and when it was worn out, I would purchase thee a couple like it:——But alas! alas! alas! now that I can do this, in spight of their reverences——the occasion is lost ——for thou art gone;——thy genius fled up to the stars from whence it came;——and that warm heart of thine, with all its generous and open vessels, compressed into a *clod of the valley*!

——But what——what is this, to that future and dreaded page, where I look towards the velvet pall, decorated with the military ensigns of thy master——the first——the foremost of created beings;——where, I shall see thee, faithful servant! laying his sword and scabbard with a trembling hand across his coffin, and then returning pale as ashes to the door, to take his mourning horse by the bridle, to follow his hearse, as he directed thee;——where—— all my father's systems shall be baffled by his sorrows; and, in spight of his philosophy, I shall behold him, as he inspects the lackered plate, twice taking his spectacles from off his nose, to wipe away the dew which nature has shed upon them——When I see him cast in the rosemary[2] with an air of disconsolation, which cries through my ears,——O *Toby*! in what corner of the world shall I seek thy fellow?

——Gracious powers! which erst have opened the lips of the dumb in his distress, and made the tongue of the stammerer speak plain——when I shall arrive at this dreaded page, deal not with me, then, with a stinted hand.

Chapter XXVI.

THE corporal, who the night before had resolved in his mind, to supply the grand *desideratum*, of keeping up something like an incessant firing upon the enemy during the heat of the

---

2. An herb associated with remembrance—here being thrown on the coffin.

attack,——had no further idea in his fancy at that time, than a contrivance of smoaking tobacco against the town, out of one of my uncle *Toby*'s six field pieces, which were planted on each side of his sentry-box; the means of effecting which occurring to his fancy at the same time, though he had pledged his cap, he thought it in no danger from the miscarriage of his projects.

Upon turning it this way, and that, a little in his mind, he soon began to find out, that by means of his two *Turkish* tobacco-pipes, with the supplement of three smaller tubes of wash-leather at each of their lower ends, to be tagg'd by the same number of tin pipes fitted to the touch holes, and sealed with clay next the cannon, and then tied hermetically with waxed silk at their several insertions into the *Morocco* tube,——he should be able to fire the six field pieces all together, and with the same ease as to fire one.——

——Let no man say from what taggs and jaggs hints may not be cut out for the advancement of human knowledge. Let no man who has read my father's first and second *beds of justice*, ever rise up and say again, from collision of what kinds of bodies, light may, or may not be struck out, to carry the arts and sciences up to perfection.——Heaven! thou knowest how I love them,——thou knowest the secrets of my heart, and that I would this moment give my shirt——Thou art a fool, *Shandy*, says *Eugenius*,——for thou hast but a dozen in the world,——and 'twill break thy set.——

No matter for that, *Eugenius*; I would give the shirt off my back to be burnt into tinder, were it only to satisfy one feverish enquirer, how many sparks at one good stroke, a good flint and steel could strike into the tail of it.——Think ye not that in striking these *in*,——he might, peradventure, strike something *out*? as sure as a gun.——

——But this project, by the bye.

The corporal sat up the best part of the night in bringing *his* to perfection; and having made a sufficient proof of his cannon, with charging them to the top with tobacco,——he went with contentment to bed.

Chapter XXVII.

THE corporal had slipped out about ten minutes before my uncle *Toby*, in order to fix his apparatus, and just give the enemy a shot or two before my uncle *Toby* came.

He had drawn the six field-pieces for this end, all close up together in front of my uncle *Toby*'s sentry-box, leaving only an interval of about a yard and a half betwixt the three, on the right and left, for the convenience of charging, &c.——and the sake possibly of two batteries, which he might think double the honour of one.

In the rear, and facing this opening, with his back to the door of the sentry-box, for fear of being flanked, had the corporal wisely taken his post:——He held the ivory pipe, appertaining to the battery on the right, betwixt the finger and thumb of his right hand,——and the ebony pipe tipp'd with silver, which appertained to the battery on the left, betwixt the finger and thumb of the other——and with his right knee fixed firm upon the ground, as if in the front rank of his platoon, was the corporal, with his montero-cap upon his head, furiously playing off his two cross batteries at the same time against the counterguard, which faced the counterscarp, where the attack was to be made that morning. His first intention, as I said, was no more than giving the enemy a single puff or two;——but the pleasure of the *puffs*, as well as the *puffing*, had insensibly got hold of the corporal, and drawn him on from puff to puff, into the very height of the attack, by the time my uncle *Toby* joined him.

'Twas well for my father, that my uncle *Toby* had not his will to make that day.

Chapter XXVIII.

MY uncle *Toby* took the ivory pipe out of the corporal's hand, ——looked at it for half a minute, and returned it.

In less than two minutes my uncle *Toby* took the pipe from the corporal again, and raised it half way to his mouth——then hastily gave it back a second time.

The corporal redoubled the attack,——my uncle *Toby* smiled, ——then looked grave,——then smiled for a moment,——then looked serious for a long time;——Give me hold of the ivory pipe, *Trim*, said my uncle *Toby*——my uncle *Toby* put it to his lips,—— drew it back directly,——gave a peep over the horn-beam[3] hedge; ——never did my uncle *Toby*'s mouth water so much for a pipe in his life.——My uncle *Toby* retired into the sentry-box with the pipe in his hand.——

——Dear uncle *Toby*! don't go into the sentry-box with the pipe,——there's no trusting a man's self with such a thing in such a corner.

Chapter XXIX.

I Beg the reader will assist me here, to wheel off my uncle *Toby*'s ordnance behind the scenes,——to remove his sentry-box, and clear the theatre, *if possible*, of horn-works and half moons, and

3. A kind of small beech tree.

get the rest of his military apparatus out of the way;——that done, my dear friend *Garrick*, we'll snuff the candles bright,—— sweep the stage with a new broom,——draw up the curtain, and exhibit my uncle *Toby* dressed in a new character, throughout which the world can have no idea how he will act: and yet, if pity be akin to love,——and bravery no alien to it, you have seen enough of my uncle *Toby* in these, to trace these family likenesses, betwixt the two passions (in case there is one) to your heart's content.

Vain science! thou assists us in no case of this kind——and thou puzzlest us in every one.

There was, Madam, in my uncle *Toby*, a singleness of heart which misled him so far out of the little serpentine tracks in which things of this nature usually go on; you can——you can have no conception of it: with this, there was a plainness and simplicity of thinking, with such an unmistrusting ignorance of the plies and foldings of the heart of woman;——and so naked and defenceless did he stand before you, (when a siege was out of his head) that you might have stood behind any one of your serpentine walks, and shot my uncle *Toby* ten times in a day, through his liver,[4] if nine times in a day, Madam, had not served your purpose.

With all this, Madam,——and what confounded every thing as much on the other hand, my uncle *Toby* had that unparalleled modesty of nature I once told you of, and which, by the bye, stood eternal sentry upon his feelings, that you might as soon——But where am I going? these reflections croud in upon me ten pages at least too soon, and take up that time, which I ought to bestow upon facts.

Chapter XXX.

OF the few legitimate sons of *Adam*, whose breasts never felt what the sting of love was,——(maintaining first, all mysogynists to be bastards)——the greatest heroes of ancient and modern story have carried off amongst them, nine parts in ten of the honour; and I wish for their sakes I had the key of my study out of my draw-well,[5] only for five minutes, to tell you their names— recollect them I cannot——so be content to accept of these, for the present, in their stead.——

There was the great king *Aldrovandus*, and *Bosphorus*, and

---

4. Traditionally, the organ most vulnerable to sexual feeling.
5. Since he cannot get his key to authorities out of the well where he claims to have thrown it, Tristram gives us a rather random list of men who had little use for women. Charles XII of Sweden is probably the only true misogynist here: when the King of Poland sent his beautiful mistress, the Countess of Königsmarck, to sue for peace in his behalf, Charles was impervious to her charms.

Capadocius, and *Dardanus,* and *Pontus,* and *Asius,*——to say nothing of the iron-hearted *Charles* the XIIth, whom the Countess of
K***** herself could make nothing of.——There was *Babylonicus,*
and *Mediterraneus,* and *Polixenes,* and *Persicus,* and *Prusicus,* not
one of whom (except *Capadocius* and *Pontus,* who were both a
little suspected) ever once bowed down his breast to the goddess
——The truth is, they had all of them something else to do——and
so had my uncle *Toby*——till Fate——till Fate I say, envying his
name the glory of being handed down to posterity with *Aldrovandus*'s and the rest,——she basely patched up the peace of *Utrecht.*[6]
——Believe me, Sirs, 'twas the worst deed she did that year.

Chapter XXXI.

AMONGST the many ill consequences of the treaty of *Utrecht,*
it was within a point of giving my uncle *Toby* a surfeit of
sieges; and though he recovered his appetite afterwards, yet *Calais*
itself left not a deeper scar in *Mary*'s heart, than *Utrecht* upon my
uncle *Toby*'s.[7] To the end of his life he never could hear *Utrecht*
mentioned upon any account whatever,——or so much as read an
article of news extracted out of the *Utrecht Gazette,* without fetching a sigh, as if his heart would break in twain.

My father, who was a great MOTIVE-MONGER, and consequently a
very dangerous person for a man to sit by, either laughing or
crying,——for he generally knew your motive for doing both, much
better than you knew it yourself——would always console my
uncle *Toby* upon these occasions, in a way, which shewed plainly,
he imagined my uncle *Toby* grieved for nothing in the whole affair,
so much as the loss of his *hobby-horse.*——Never mind, brother
Toby, he would say,——by God's blessing we shall have another
war break out again some of these days; and when it does,——the
belligerent powers, if they would hang themselves, cannot keep us
out of play.——I defy 'em, my dear *Toby,* he would add, to take
countries without taking towns,——or towns without sieges.

My uncle *Toby* never took this back-stroke of my father's at his
hobby-horse kindly.——He thought the stroke ungenerous; and the
more so, because in striking the horse, he hit the rider too, and in
the most dishonourable part a blow could fall; so that upon these
occasions, he always laid down his pipe upon the table with more
fire to defend himself than common.

I told the reader, this time two years, that my uncle *Toby* was not
eloquent; and in the very same page gave an instance to the con-

6. The treaty that ended the Wars of the
Spanish Succession, which had occupied
Toby for so long.
7. Queen Mary Tudor died in 1558, the
year that England finally lost Calais to
the French. She is supposed to have said
that the name of the city would be found
on her heart after she died.

trary:——I repeat the observation, and a fact which contradicts it again.——He was not eloquent,——it was not easy to my uncle *Toby* to make long harangues,——and he hated florid ones; but there were occasions where the stream overflowed the man, and ran so counter to its usual course, that in some parts my uncle *Toby*, for a time, was at least equal to *Tertullus*[8]——but in others, in my own opinion, infinitely above him.

My father was so highly pleased with one of these apologetical orations of my uncle *Toby*'s, which he had delivered one evening before him and *Yorick*, that he wrote it down before he went to bed.

I have had the good fortune to meet with it amongst my father's papers, with here and there an insertion of his own, betwixt two crooks, thus [   ], and is endorsed,

My brother TOBY'*s justification of his own principles and conduct in wishing to continue the war.*

I may safely say, I have read over this apologetical oration of my uncle *Toby*'s a hundred times, and think it so fine a model of defence,——and shews so sweet a temperament of gallantry and good principles in him, that I give it the world, word for word, (interlineations and all) as I find it.

Chapter XXXII.

My uncle TOBY'*s apologetical oration.*

I Am not insensible, brother *Shandy*, that when a man, whose profession is arms, wishes, as I have done, for war,——it has an ill aspect to the world;——and that, how just and right soever his motives and intentions may be,——he stands in an uneasy posture in vindicating himself from private views in doing it.

For this cause, if a soldier is a prudent man, which he may be, without being a jot the less brave, he will be sure not to utter his wish in the hearing of an enemy; for say what he will, an enemy will not believe him.——He will be cautious of doing it even to a friend,——lest he may suffer in his esteem:——But if his heart is overcharged, and a secret sigh for arms must have its vent, he will reserve it for the ear of a brother, who knows his character to the bottom, and what his true notions, dispositions, and principles of honour are: What, I *hope*, I have been in all these, brother *Shandy*, would be unbecoming in me to say:——much worse, I know, have

8. Tertullian is more likely who is meant, for he was a strong defender of the Christian Church in ancient Rome.

I been than I ought,——and something worse, perhaps, than I think: But such as I am, you, my dear brother *Shandy*, who have sucked the same breasts with me,——and with whom I have been brought up from my cradle,——and from whose knowledge, from the first hours of our boyish pastimes, down to this, I have concealed no one action of my life, and scarce a thought in it——Such as I am, brother, you must by this time know me, with all my vices, and with all my weaknesses too, whether of my age, my temper, my passions, or my understanding.

Tell me then, my dear brother *Shandy*, upon which of them it is, that when I condemned the peace of *Utrecht*, and grieved the war was not carried on with vigour a little longer, you should think your brother did it upon unworthy views; or that in wishing for war, he should be bad enough to wish more of his fellow creatures slain, ——more slaves made, and more families driven from their peaceful habitations, merely for his own pleasure:——Tell me, brother *Shandy*, upon what one deed of mine do you ground it? [*The devil a deed do I know of, dear* Toby, *but one for a hundred pounds, which I lent thee to carry on these cursed sieges.*]

If, when I was a school-boy, I could not hear a drum beat, but my heart beat with it——was it my fault?——Did I plant the propensity there?——did I sound the alarm within, or Nature?

When *Guy*, Earl of *Warwick*,[9] and *Parismus* and *Parismenus*, and *Valentine* and *Orson*, and the *Seven Champions of England* were handed around the school,——were they not all purchased with my own pocket money? Was that selfish, brother *Shandy*? When we read over the siege of *Troy*, which lasted ten years and eight months,——though with such a train of artillery as we had at *Namur*, the town might have been carried in a week——was I not as much concerned for the destruction of the *Greeks* and *Trojans* as any boy of the whole school? Had I not three strokes of a ferula given me, two on my right hand and one on my left, for calling *Helena*[1] a bitch for it? Did any one of you shed more tears for *Hector*? And when king *Priam* came to the camp to beg his body, and returned weeping back to *Troy* without it,——you know, brother, I could not eat my dinner.——

——Did that bespeak me cruel? Or because, brother *Shandy*, my blood flew out into the camp, and my heart panted for war,——was it a proof it could not ache for the distresses of war too?

O brother! 'tis one thing for a soldier to gather laurels,——and 'tis another to scatter cypress.——[*Who told thee, my dear* Toby, *that cypress was used by the ancients on mournful occasions?*]

9. Heroes of legends, popular in England from medieval times.
1. Helen's abduction by Paris (or seduction of him?) caused the Trojan War, in which Hector, the greatest of Trojan heroes, and son of Priam, was slain by Achilles.

——'Tis one thing, brother *Shandy*, for a soldier to hazard his own life——to leap first down into the trench, where he is sure to be cut in pieces:——'Tis one thing, from public spirit and a thirst of glory, to enter the breach the first man,——to stand in the foremost rank, and march bravely on with drums and trumpets, and colours flying about his ears:——'Tis one thing, I say, brother *Shandy*, to do this——and 'tis another thing to reflect on the miseries of war;——to view the desolations of whole countries, and consider the intolerable fatigues and hardships which the soldier himself, the instrument who works them, is forced (for six-pence a day, if he can get it) to undergo.

Need I be told, dear *Yorick*, as I was by you, in *Le Fever's* funeral sermon, *That so soft and gentle a creature, born to love, to mercy, and kindness, as man is, was not shaped for this?*——But why did you not add, *Yorick*,——if not by NATURE——that he is so by NECESSITY?——For what is war? what is it, *Yorick*, when fought as ours has been, upon principles of *liberty*, and upon principles of *honour*——what is it, but the getting together of quiet and harmless people, with their swords in their hands, to keep the ambitious and the turbulent within bounds? And heaven is my witness, brother *Shandy*, that the pleasure I have taken in these things,—— and that infinite delight, in particular, which has attended my sieges in my bowling green, has arose within me, and I hope in the corporal too, from the consciousness we both had, that in carrying them on, we were answering the great ends of our creation.

Chapter XXXIII.

I Told the Christian reader——I say *Christian*——hoping he is one——and if he is not, I am sorry for it——and only beg he will consider the matter with himself, and not lay the blame entirely upon this book,——

I told him, Sir——for in good truth, when a man is telling a story in the strange way I do mine, he is obliged continually to be going backwards and forwards to keep all tight together in the reader's fancy——which, for my own part, if I did not take heed to do more than at first, there is so much unfixed and equivocal matter starting up, with so many breaks and gaps in it,——and so little service do the stars afford, which, nevertheless, I hang up in some of the darkest passages, knowing that the world is apt to lose its way, with all the lights the sun itself at noon day can give it——and now, you see, I am lost myself!——

——But 'tis my father's fault; and whenever my brains come to be dissected, you will perceive, without spectacles, that he has left a large uneven thread, as you sometimes see in an unsaleable piece of

cambrick, running along the whole length of the web, and so un-
towardly, you cannot so much as cut out a * *, (here I hang up a
couple of lights again)——or a fillet,[2] or a thumb-stall, but it is
seen or felt.——

Quanto id diligentius in liberis procreandis cavendum, sayeth
Cardan.[3] All which being considered, and that you see 'tis morally
impracticable for me to wind this round to where I set out——

I begin the chapter over again.

Chapter XXXIV.

I Told the Christian reader in the beginning of the chapter which
preceded my uncle *Toby*'s apologetical oration,——though in
a different trope[4] from what I shall make use of now, That the
peace of *Utrecht* was within an ace of creating the same shyness
betwixt my uncle *Toby* and his hobby-horse, as it did betwixt the
queen and the rest of the confederating powers.

There is an indignant way in which a man sometimes dismounts
his horse, which as good as says to him, "I'll go afoot, Sir, all the
days of my life, before I would ride a single mile upon your back
again." Now my uncle *Toby* could not be said to dismount his horse
in this manner; for in strictness of language, he could not be said to
dismount his horse at all——his horse rather flung him——and
somewhat *viciously,* which made my uncle *Toby* take it ten times
more unkindly. Let this matter be settled by state jockies as they
like.——It created, I say, a sort of shyness betwixt my uncle *Toby*
and his hobby-horse.——He had no occasion for him from the
month of *March* to *November,* which was the summer after the
articles were signed, except it was now and then to take a short ride
out, just to see that the fortifications and harbour of *Dunkirk* were
demolished, according to stipulation.

The *French* were so backwards all that summer in setting about
that affair, and Monsieur *Tugghe,* the deputy from the magistrates
of *Dunkirk,* presented so many affecting petitions to the queen,——
beseeching her majesty to cause only her thunderbolts to fall upon
the martial works, which might have incurred her displeasure,——
but to spare——to spare the mole,[5] for the mole's sake; which, in
its naked situation, could be no more than an object of pity——and
the queen (who was but a woman) being of a pitiful disposition,
——and her ministers also, they not wishing in their hearts to have
the town dismantled, for these private reasons, * * * *

2. A ribbon; "thumb-stall": a protective
covering for the thumb.
3. "How much more careful we should
be in begetting our children." Girolamo
Cardan was a sixteenth-century Italian
mathematician, physician, and astrologer.
4. A figure of speech.
5. A mole is a pier, as well as a slang
term for penis.

* * * * * * * * * * * *
* * * * * * * * *———
  * * * * * * * * * * *
* * * * * * * * * * * *
* * * * *;so that the whole went heavily on with my uncle *Toby*; insomuch, that it was not within three full months, after he and the corporal had constructed the town, and put it in a condition to be destroyed, that the several commandants, commissaries, deputies, negotiators, and intendants, would permit him to set about it.———Fatal interval of inactivity!

The corporal was for beginning the demolition, by making a breach in the ramparts, or main fortifications of the town———No,———that will never do, corporal, said my uncle *Toby*, for in going that way to work with the town, the *English* garrison will not be safe in it an hour; because if the *French* are treacherous———They are as treacherous as devils, an' please your honour, said the corporal———It gives me concern always when I hear it, *Trim*, said my uncle *Toby*,———for they don't want personal bravery; and if a breach is made in the ramparts, they may enter it, and make themselves masters of the place when they please:———Let them enter it, said the corporal, lifting up his pioneer's spade in both his hands, as if he was going to lay about him with it,———let them enter, an' please your honour, if they dare.———In cases like this, corporal, said my uncle *Toby*, slipping his right hand down to the middle of his cane, and holding it afterwards truncheon-wise, with his forefinger extended,———'tis no part of the consideration of a commandant, what the enemy dare,———or what they dare not do; he must act with prudence. We will begin with the outworks both towards the sea and the land, and particularly with fort *Louis*, the most distant of them all, and demolish it first,———and the rest, one by one, both on our right and left, as we retreat towards the town;———then we'll demolish the mole,———next fill up the harbour,——— then retire into the citadel, and blow it up into the air; and having done that, corporal, we'll embark for *England*.———We are there, quoth the corporal, recollecting himself———Very true, said my uncle *Toby*———looking at the church.

Chapter XXXV.

A Delusive, delicious consultation or two of this kind, betwixt my uncle *Toby* and *Trim*, upon the demolition of *Dunkirk*,———for a moment rallied back the ideas of those pleasures, which were slipping from under him:———still———still all went on heavily ———the magic left the mind the weaker———STILLNESS, with SILENCE at her back, entered the solitary parlour, and drew their gauzy mantle over my uncle *Toby*'s head;——and LISTLESSNESS, with her lax fibre and undirected eye, sat quietly down beside him in his arm chair.——No longer *Amberg,* and *Rhinberg,* and *Limbourg,* and *Huy,* and *Bonn,* in one year,——and the prospect of *Landen,* and *Trerebach,* and *Drusen,* and *Dendermond,* the next, ——hurried on the blood:——No longer did saps, and mines, and blinds, and gabions, and palisadoes, keep out this fair enemy of man's repose:——No more could my uncle *Toby,* after passing the *French* lines, as he eat his egg at supper, from thence break into the heart of *France,*——cross over the *Oyes,* and with all *Picardie* open behind him, march up to the gates of *Paris,* and fall asleep with no-thing but ideas of glory:——No more was he to dream, he had fixed the royal standard upon the tower of the *Bastile,* and awake with it streaming in his head.

——Softer visions,——gentler vibrations stole sweetly in upon his slumbers;——the trumpet of war fell out of his hands,——he took up the lute, sweet instrument! of all others the most delicate! the most difficult!——how wilt thou touch it, my dear uncle *Toby?*

Chapter XXXVI.

NOW, because I have once or twice said, in my inconsiderate way of talking, That I was confident the following memoirs of my uncle *Toby*'s courtship of widow *Wadman,* whenever I got time to write them, would turn out one of the most compleat systems, both of the elementary and practical part of love and love-making, that ever was addressed to the world——are you to imag-ine from thence, that I shall set out with a description of *what love is?* whether part God and part Devil, as *Plotinus*[6] will have it——

——Or by a more critical equation, and supposing the whole of love to be as ten——to determine, with *Ficinus,* "*How many parts of it*——*the one,*——*and how many the other;*"—or whether it is *all of it one great Devil,* from head to tail, as *Plato*[7] has taken upon him to pronounce; concerning which conceit of his, I shall not offer my opinion:——but my opinion of *Plato* is this; that he appears, from this instance, to have been a man of much the same temper and way of reasoning with doctor *Baynyard,*[8] who being a great enemy to blisters, as imagining that half a dozen of 'em on at

6. Plotinus, the great third-century Greek Neoplatonist, envisions love as both a pure divine principle and as a spirit in-habiting individual souls, involved in passion and experience. The latter he calls a "daimon," not a devil. Marsilio Ficini, a fifteenth-century Italian philos-opher and physician, wrote a commentary on Plato.

7. Sterne again turns "daimon" into "devil," this time alluding to a speech in Plato's *Symposium.*
8. Edward Baynard, an English physician of the early eighteenth century, wrote a *History of Cold Bathing. Cantharides*: a preparation of powdered, dried Spanish flies used for raising blisters or as an aphrodisiac.

once, would draw a man as surely to his grave, as a herse and six——rashly concluded, that the Devil himself was nothing in the world, but one great bouncing *Cantharidis.*——

I have nothing to say to people who allow themselves this monstrous liberty in arguing, but what *Nazianzen* cried out (*that is polemically*) to *Philagrius*——

"'Εὐγε!" *O rare! 'tis fine reasoning, Sir, indeed!*——"ὅτι φιλοσοφεῖς ἐν Πάθεσι."⁹——*and most nobly do you aim at truth, when you philosophize about it in your moods and passions.*

Nor is it to be imagined, for the same reason, I should stop to enquire, whether love is a disease,——or embroil myself with *Rhasis*¹ and *Dioscorides*, whether the seat of it is in the brain or liver;——because this would lead me on, to an examination of the two very opposite manners, in which patients have been treated—— the one, of *Aætius*, who always begun with a cooling glyster of hempseed and bruised cucumbers;——and followed on with thin potations of water lillies and purslane——to which he added a pinch of snuff, of the herb *Hanea;*——and where *Aætius* durst venture it,——his topaz-ring.²

——The other, that of *Gordonius*,³ who (in his cap. 15. de *Amore*) directs they should be thrashed, "Ad putorem usque,"—— till they stink again.

These are disquisitions, which my father, who had laid in a great stock of knowledge of this kind, will be very busy with, in the progress of my uncle *Toby*'s affairs: I must anticipate thus much, That from his theories of love, (with which, by the way, he contrived to crucify my uncle *Toby*'s mind, almost as much as his amours themselves)——he took a single step into practice;——and by means of a camphorated cerecloth,⁴ which he found means to impose upon the taylor for buckram, whilst he was making my uncle *Toby* a new pair of breeches, he produced *Gordonius*'s effect upon my uncle *Toby* without the disgrace.

What changes this produced, will be read in its proper place: all that is needful to be added to the anecdote, is this,——That whatever effect it had upon my uncle *Toby*,——it had a vile effect upon the house;——and if my uncle *Toby* had not smoaked it down as he did, it might have had a vile effect upon my father too.

---

9. "Bravo! that you philosophize in your sufferings," is a more accurate translation than the one Tristram provides. The line comes from a letter written by St. Gregory of Nazianzus to his friend Philagrius.

1. Rhasis was a Persian medical writer of the tenth century. Dioscorides was an important Greek physician and author of the first century; Aetius another, of the sixth century.

2. Hanea is Sterne's version of the *agnus castus*, a shrub thought to promote chastity. Topazes were also supposed to be useful in cooling passions.

3. Bernard de Gordon was a French physician of the late thirteenth century.

4. A cerecloth is a bandage saturated with wax and medicines. Camphor was supposed to work in suppressing sexual passions.

Chapter XXXVII.

——'TWILL come out of itself by and bye.——All I contend for is, that I am not *obliged* to set out with a definition of what love is; and so long as I can go on with my story intelligibly, with the help of the word itself, without any other idea to it, than what I have in common with the rest of the world, why should I differ from it a moment before the time?——When I can get on no further,——and find myself entangled on all sides of this mystick labyrinth,——my Opinion will then come in, in course,——and lead me out.

At present, I hope I shall be sufficiently understood, in telling the reader, my uncle *Toby fell in love*:

——Not that the phrase is at all to my liking: for to say a man is *fallen* in love,——or that he is *deeply* in love,——or up to the ears in love,——and sometimes even *over head and ears in it*,—— carries an idiomatical kind of implication, that love is a thing *below* a man:——this is recurring again to *Plato*'s opinion, which, with all his divinityship,——I hold to be damnable and heretical;——and so much for that.

Let love therefore be what it will,——my uncle *Toby* fell into it.

——And possibly, gentle reader, with such a temptation——so wouldst thou: For never did thy eyes behold, or thy concupiscence covet any thing in this world, more concupiscible than widow *Wadman*.

Chapter XXXVIII.

TO conceive this right,——call for pen and ink——here's paper ready to your hand.——Sit down, Sir, paint her to your own mind——as like your mistress as you can——as unlike your wife as your conscience will let you——'tis all one to me——please but your own fancy in it.

——————Was ever any thing in Nature so sweet!——so exquisite!
——Then, dear Sir, how could my uncle *Toby* resist it?

Thrice happy book! thou wilt have one page, at least, within thy covers, which MALICE will not blacken, and which IGNORANCE cannot misrepresent.

Chapter XXXIX.

AS *Susannah* was informed by an express from Mrs. *Bridget,* of my uncle *Toby's* falling in love with her mistress, fifteen days before it happened,——the contents of which express, *Susannah* communicated to my mother the next day,——it has just given me an opportunity of entering upon my uncle *Toby's* amours a fortnight before their existence.

I have an article of news to tell you, Mr. *Shandy,* quoth my mother, which will surprise you greatly.——

Now my father was then holding one of his second beds of justice, and was musing within himself about the hardships of matrimony, as my mother broke silence.————

"——My brother *Toby,* quoth she, is going to be married to Mrs. *Wadman.*"

——Then he will never, quoth my father, be able to lie *diagonally* in his bed again as long as he lives.

It was a consuming vexation to my father, that my mother never asked the meaning of a thing she did not understand.

——That she is not a woman of science, my father would say ——is her misfortune—but she might ask a question.——

My mother never did.——In short, she went out of the world at last without knowing whether it turned *round,* or stood *still.*——My father had officiously told her above a thousand times which way it was,——but she always forgot.

For these reasons a discourse seldom went on much further betwixt them, than a proposition,——a reply, and a rejoinder; at the end of which, it generally took breath for a few minutes, (as in the affair of the breeches) and then went on again.

If he marries, 'twill be the worse for us,——quoth my mother.

Not a cherry-stone, said my father,——he may as well batter away his means upon that, as any thing else.

——To be sure, said my mother: so here ended the proposition, ——the reply,——and the rejoinder, I told you of.

It will be some amusement to him, too,——said my father.

A very great one, answered my mother, if he should have children.——

——Lord have mercy upon me,——said my father to himself
——— *   *   *   *   *   *   *   *   *   *   *

* * * * * * * * * * * *
* * * * * * * * * * * *
* * * * * * * * * * * *
* * * * * * * * *

Chapter XL.

I Am now beginning to get fairly into my work; and by the help of a vegitable diet, with a few of the cold seeds,[5] I make no doubt but I shall be able to go on with my uncle *Toby*'s story, and my own, in a tolerable straight line. Now,

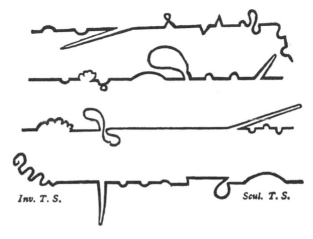

Inv. T. S.   *Scul. T. S.*

These were the four lines I moved in through my first, second, third, and fourth volumes.——In the fifth volume I have been very good,——the precise line I have described in it being this:

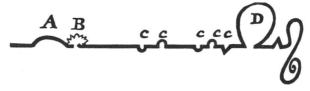

By which it appears, that except at the curve, marked A. where I took a trip to *Navarre*,——and the indented curve B. which is the short airing when I was there with the Lady *Baussiere* and her page,——I have not taken the least frisk of a digression, till *John de la Casse*'s devils led me the round you see marked D.——for as for *c c c c* they are nothing but parentheses, and the common *ins* and

5. As from cucumber, squash, etc.

outs incident to the lives of the greatest ministers of state; and when compared with what men have done,——or with my own trangressions at the letters A B D——they vanish into nothing.

In this last volume I have done better still——for from the end of *Le Fever*'s episode, to the beginning of my uncle *Toby*'s campaigns, ——I have scarce stepped a yard out of my way.

If I mend at this rate, it is not impossible——by the good leave of his grace of *Benevento*'s devils——but I may arrive hereafter at the excellency of going on even thus;

which is a line drawn as straight as I could draw it, by a writing-master's ruler, (borrowed for that purpose) turning neither to the right hand or to the left.

This *right line*,——the path-way for Christians to walk in! say divines[6]——

——The emblem of moral rectitude! says *Cicero*——

——The *best line!* say cabbage-planters——is the shortest line, says *Archimedes*, which can be drawn from one given point to another.——

I wish your ladyships would lay this matter to heart in your next birth-day suits![7]

——What a journey!

Pray can you tell me,——that is, without anger, before I write my chapter upon straight lines——by what mistake——who told them so——or how it has come to pass, that your men of wit and genius have all along confounded this line, with the line of GRAVITATION?

END of the SIXTH VOLUME.

---

6. "The right path of life" is a favorite formula of Cicero's. Archimedes, the Greek mathematician, made it the first assumption of his work *On the Sphere and Cylinder* that "Of all lines having the same extremities the straight line is the least."

7. Clothes worn at birthday celebrations, especially that of the monarch.

Volume VII.

Non enim excursus hic ejus, sed opus ipsum est.[1]
PLIN, Lib. quintus Epistola sexta.

Chapter I.

NO——I think, I said, I would write two volumes every year, provided the vile cough which then tormented me, and which to this hour I dread worse than the devil, would but give me leave ——and in another place——(but where, I can't recollect now) speaking of my book as a *machine*, and laying my pen and ruler down cross-wise upon the table, in order to gain the greater credit to it——I swore it should be kept a going at that rate these forty years if it pleased but the fountain of life to bless me so long with health and good spirits.

Now as for my spirits, little have I to lay to their charge——nay so very little (unless the mounting me upon a long stick, and playing the fool with me nineteen hours out of the twenty-four, be accusations) that on the contrary, I have much——much to thank 'em for: cheerily have ye made me tread the path of life with all the burdens of it (except its cares) upon my back; in no one moment of my existence, that I remember, have ye once deserted me, or tinged the objects which came in my way, either with sable, or with a sickly green; in dangers ye gilded my horizon with hope, and when DEATH himself knocked at my door——ye bad him come again; and in so gay a tone of careless indifference, did ye do it, that he doubted of his commission——

"——There must certainly be some mistake in this matter," quoth he.

Now there is nothing in this world I abominate worse, than to be interrupted in a story——and I was that moment telling *Eugenius* a most tawdry one in my way, of a nun who fancied herself a shell-fish, and of a monk damn'd for eating a muscle, and was shewing him the grounds and justice of the procedure——

"——Did ever so grave a personage get into so vile a scrape?" quoth Death. Thou hast had a narrow escape, *Tristram*, said *Eugenius*, taking hold of my hand as I finish'd my story——

---

1. "For this is not a digression (or excursion), but is itself the work." From the *Letters* of Pliny the Younger. This volume, even more than the others, sails off in an unexpected direction, drawing its matter from Sterne's own trip to France in 1762.

But there is no *living, Eugenius,* replied I, at this rate; for as this *son of a whore* has found out my lodgings——

——You call him rightly, said *Eugenius,*——for by sin, we are told, he enter'd the world——I care not which way he enter'd, quoth I, provided he be not in such a hurry to take me out with him——for I have forty volumes to write, and forty thousand things to say and do, which no body in the world will say and do for me, except thyself; and as thou seest he has got me by the throat (for *Eugenius* could scarce hear me speak across the table) and that I am no match for him in the open field, had I not better, whilst these few scatter'd spirits remain, and these two spider legs of mine (holding one of them up to him) are able to support me——had I not better, *Eugenius,* fly for my life? 'tis my advice, my dear *Tristram,* said *Eugenius*——then by heaven! I will lead him a dance he little thinks of——for I will gallop, quoth I, without looking once behind me to the banks of the *Garonne;* and if I hear him clattering at my heels——I'll scamper away to mount *Vesuvius*——from thence to *Joppa,* and from *Joppa* to the world's end, where, if he follows me, I pray God he may break his neck——

——He runs more risk *there,* said *Eugenius,* than thou.[2]

Eugenius's wit and affection brought blood into the cheek from whence it had been some months banish'd——'twas a vile moment to bid adieu in; he led me to my chaise——*Allons!*[3] said I; the post boy gave a crack with his whip——off I went like a cannon, and in half a dozen bounds got into *Dover.*

Chapter II.

NOW hang it! quoth I, as I look'd towards the *French* coast ——a man should know something of his own country too, before he goes abroad——and I never gave a peep into *Rochester* church, or took notice of the dock of *Chatham,* or visited St. *Thomas* at *Canterbury,*[4] though they all three laid in my way——

——But mine, indeed, is a particular case——

So without arguing the matter further with *Thomas o' Becket,* or any one else——I skip'd into the boat, and in five minutes we got under sail and scudded away like the wind.

Pray captain, quoth I, as I was going down into the cabin, is a man never overtaken by *Death* in this passage?

Why, there is not time for a man to be sick in it, replied he—— What a cursed lyar! for I am sick as a horse, quoth I, already—— what a brain!——upside down!——hey dey! the cells are broke

2. That is, the Devil will be punished there, but not Tristram.
3. "Let's go."
4. These are all towns on the road from London to Dover, where Tristram sails to France. Canterbury Cathedral contains the great shrine of the murdered St. Thomas Becket.

loose one into another, and the blood, and the lymph, and the nervous juices, with the fix'd and volatile salts, are all jumbled into one mass——good g—! every thing turns round in it like a thousand whirlpools——I'd give a shilling to know if I shan't write the clearer for it——

Sick! sick! sick! sick!——

——When shall we get to land? captain——they have hearts like stones——O I am deadly sick!——reach me that thing, boy——'tis the most discomfiting sickness——I wish I was at the bottom—— Madam! how is it with you? Undone! undone! un——O! undone! sir——What the first time?——No, 'tis the second, third, sixth, tenth time, sir,——hey-day——what a trampling over head!—— hollo! cabin boy! what's the matter——

The wind chopp'd about! s'Death![5]——then I shall meet him full in the face.

What luck!——'tis chopp'd about again, master——O the devil chop it——

Captain, quoth she, for heaven's sake, let us get ashore.

Chapter III.

IT is a great inconvenience to a man in a haste, that there are three distinct roads between *Calais* and *Paris*, in behalf of which there is so much to be said by the several deputies from the towns which lie along them, that half a day is easily lost in settling which you'll take.

First, the road by *Lisle* and *Arras*, which is the most about—— but most interesting, and instructing.

The second that by *Amiens*, which you may go, if you would see *Chantilly*——

And that by *Beauvais*, which you may go, if you will.

For this reason a great many chuse to go by *Beauvais*.

Chapter IV.

"NOW before I quit *Calais*," a travel-writer would say, "it would not be amiss to give some account of it."——Now I think it very much amiss——that a man cannot go quietly through a town, and let it alone, when it does not meddle with him, but that he must be turning about and drawing his pen at every kennel he crosses over, merely, o' my conscience, for the sake of drawing it; because, if we may judge from what has been wrote of these things, by all who have *wrote and gallop'd*——or who have *gallop'd and wrote*,

---

5. An oath on Christ's death.

which is a different way still; or who for more expedition than the rest, have *wrote-galloping*, which is the way I do at present—— from the great *Addison*[6] who did it with his satchel of school-books hanging at his a— and galling his beast's crupper at every stroke ——there is not a galloper of us all who might not have gone on ambling quietly in his own ground (in case he had any) and have wrote all he had to write, dry shod, as well as not.

For my own part, as heaven is my judge, and to which I shall ever make my last appeal——I know no more of *Calais*, (except the little my barber told me of it, as he was whetting his razor) than I do this moment of *Grand Cairo*; for it was dusky in the evening when I landed, and dark as pitch in the morning when I set out, and yet by merely knowing what is what, and by drawing this from that in one part of the town, and by spelling and putting this and that together in another——I would lay any travelling odds, that I this moment write a chapter upon *Calais* as long as my arm; and with so distinct and satisfactory a detail of every item, which is worth a stranger's curiosity in the town——that you would take me for the town clerk of *Calais* itself——and where, sir, would be the wonder? was not *Democritus*,[7] who laughed ten times more than I——town-clerk of *Abdera*? and was not (I forget his name) who had more discretion than us both, town-clerk of *Ephesus*?——it should be penn'd moreover, Sir, with so much knowledge and good sense, and truth, and precision——

——Nay——if you don't believe me, you may read the chapter for your pains.

Chapter V.

CALAIS, *Calatium, Calusium, Calesium*.[8] This town, if we may trust its archives, the authority of which I see no reason to call in question in this place——was *once* no more than a small village belonging to one of the first Counts *de Guines*; and as it boasts at present of no less than fourteen thousand inhabitants, exclusive of four hundred and twenty distinct families in the *basse ville*,[9] or suburbs——it must have grown up by little and little, I suppose, to it's present size.

Though there are four convents, there is but one parochial church in the whole town; I had not an opportunity of taking its

6. In his *Remarks on Several Parts of Italy*, the English writer Joseph Addison remarks that he liked to compare the places he visited with what had been said of them by classical authors.

7. Though Democritus ("the laughing philosopher") came from Abdera, he is not known to have been a city official. Heraclitus gave up a great deal more than the town clerkship of Ephesus to become a philosopher; he had been, nominally, the city's king.

8. These Latin names for Calais are part of Sterne's continuing parody of the standard pedantic guide book in this volume.

9. "Lower town."

exact dimensions, but it is pretty easy to make a tolerable conjecture of 'em——for as there are fourteen thousand inhabitants in the town, if the church holds them all, it must be considerably large ——and if it will not——'tis a very great pity they have not another——it is built in form of a cross, and dedicated to the Virgin *Mary*; the steeple which has a spire to it, is placed in the middle of the church, and stands upon four pillars elegant and light enough, but sufficiently strong at the same time——it is decorated with eleven altars, most of which are rather fine[1] than beautiful. The great altar is a masterpiece in its kind; 'tis of white marble, and as I was told near sixty feet high——had it been much higher, it had been as high as mount *Calvary* itself——therefore, I suppose it must be high enough in all conscience.

There was nothing struck me more than the great *Square*; tho' I cannot say 'tis either well paved or well built; but 'tis in the heart of the town, and most of the streets, especially those in that quarter, all terminate in it; could there have been a fountain in all *Calais*, which it seems there cannot, as such an object would have been a great ornament, it is not to be doubted, but that the inhabitants would have had it in the very centre of this square,—— not that it is properly a square,——because 'tis forty feet longer from east to west, than from north to south; so that the *French* in general have more reason on their side in calling them *Places* than *Squares*, which strictly speaking, to be sure they are not.

The town-house[2] seems to be but a sorry building, and not to be kept in the best repair; otherwise it had been a second great ornament to this place; it answers however its destination, and serves very well for the reception of the magistrates, who assemble in it from time to time; so that 'tis presumable, justice is regularly distributed.

I have heard much of it, but there is nothing at all curious in the *Courgain*; 'tis a distinct quarter of the town inhabited solely by sailors and fishermen; it consists of a number of small streets, neatly built and mostly of brick; 'tis extremely populous, but as that may be accounted for, from the principles of their diet,[3]——there is nothing curious in that neither.——A traveller may see it to satisfy himself——he must not omit however taking notice of *La Tour de Guet*,[4] upon any account; 'tis so called from its particular destination, because in war it serves to discover and give notice of the enemies which approach the place, either by sea or land;——but 'tis monstrous high, and catches the eye so continually, you cannot avoid taking notice of it, if you would.

It was a singular disappointment to me, that I could not have

1. I.e., grand.
2. City hall.
3. Seafood was sometimes thought to
stimulate sexuality.
4. Watchtower.

permission to take an exact survey of the fortifications, which are the strongest in the world, and which, from first to last, that is, from the time they were set about by *Philip* of *France* Count of *Bologne*, to the present war, wherein many reparations were made, have cost (as I learned afterwards from an engineer in *Gascony*)——above a hundred millions of livres. It is very remarkable that at the *Tête de Gravelenes*, and where the town is naturally the weakest, they have expended the most money; so that the outworks stretch a great way into the campaign,[5] and consequently occupy a large tract of ground.——However, after all that is *said* and *done*, it must be acknowledged that *Calais* was never upon any account so considerable from itself, as from its situation, and that easy enterance which it gave our ancestors upon all occasions into *France*: it was not without its inconveniences also; being no less troublesome to the *English* in those times, than *Dunkirk* has been to us, in ours; so that it was deservedly looked upon as the key to both kingdoms, which no doubt is the reason that there have arisen so many contentions who should keep it: of these, the siege of *Calais*, or rather the blockade (for it was shut up both by land and sea) was the most memorable, as it withstood the efforts of *Edward* the third a whole year, and was not terminated at last but by famine and extream misery; the gallantry of *Eustace de St. Pierre*,[6] who first offered himself a victim for his fellow citizens, has rank'd his name with heroes. As it will not take up above fifty pages, it would be injustice to the reader, not to give him a minute account of that romantic transaction, as well as of the siege itself, in *Rapin*'s own words:

Chapter VI.

——**B**UT courage! gentle reader!——I scorn it——'tis enough to have thee in my power——but to make use of the advantage which the fortune of the pen has now gained over thee, would be too much——No——! by that all powerful fire which warms the visionary brain, and lights the spirits through unworldly tracts! ere I would force a helpless creature upon this hard service, and make thee pay, poor soul! for fifty pages which I have no right to sell thee,——naked as I am, I would browse upon the mountains, and smile that the north wind brought me neither my tent or my supper.

——So put on, my brave boy! and make the best of thy way to *Boulogne*.

---

5. Countryside.

6. One of six "burgers of Calais" who offered themselves to Edward III as a sacrifice to prevent the massacre of the city after the long siege of 1346. They were saved by intervention of the queen. Rapin describes the siege in his *History of England*, mentioned earlier by Tristram.

Chapter VII.

——B OULOGNE!——hah!——so we are all got together——
debtors and sinners before heaven; a jolly set of us——
but I can't stay and quaff it off with you——I'm pursued myself
like a hundred devils, and shall be overtaken before I can well
change horses:——for heaven's sake, make haste——'Tis for high
treason, quoth a very little man, whispering as low as he could to a
very tall man that stood next him——Or else for murder; quoth the
tall man—Well thrown *Size-ace!*[7] quoth I. No; quoth a third, the
gentleman has been committing—— ——.

Ah! *ma chere fille!*[8] said I, as she tripp'd by, from her matins
——you look as rosy as the morning (for the sun was rising, and it
made the compliment the more gracious)——No; it can't be that,
quoth a fourth——(she made a curt'sy to me——I kiss'd my hand)
'tis debt; continued he: 'Tis certainly for debt; quoth a fifth; I
would not pay that gentleman's debts, quoth *Ace*, for a thousand
pounds; Nor would I, quoth *Size*, for six times the sum——Well
thrown, *Size-Ace*, again! quoth I;——but I have no debt but the
debt of NATURE,[9] and I want but patience of her, and I will pay her
every farthing I owe her——How can you be so hard-hearted,
MADAM, to arrest a poor traveller going along without molestation
to any one, upon his lawful occasions? do stop that death-looking,
long-striding scoundrel of a scare-sinner, who is posting after me
——he never would have followed me but for you——if it be but
for a stage, or two, just to give me start of him, I beseech you,
madam——do, dear lady——

——Now, in troth, 'tis a great pity, quoth mine *Irish* host, that
all this good courtship should be lost; for the young gentlewoman
has been after going out of hearing of it all along——.

——Simpleton! quoth I.

——So you have nothing *else* in *Boulogne* worth seeing?

——By Jasus! there is the finest SEMINARY for the HUMANI-
TIES——.

——There cannot be a finer; quoth I.

Chapter VIII.

W HEN the precipitancy of a man's wishes hurries on his
ideas ninety times faster than the vehicle he rides in——
woe be to truth! and woe be to the vehicle and its tackling (let 'em

---

7. Six-ace, in French; i.e., the lowest
and highest dice.
8. "Ah! my dear girl!" *Matins*: morning prayer.
9. That is, death. He later addresses
Mother Nature as "Madam."

be made of what stuff you will) upon which he breathes forth the disappointment of his soul!

As I never give general characters either of men or things in choler, *"the most haste, the worst speed;"* was all the reflection I made upon the affair, the first time it happen'd;——the second, third, fourth, and fifth time, I confined it respectively to those times, and accordingly blamed only the second, third, fourth, and fifth post-boy for it, without carrying my reflections further; but the event continuing to befall me from the fifth, to the sixth, seventh, eighth, ninth, and tenth time, and without one exception, I then could not avoid making a national reflection of it, which I do in these words;

That something is always wrong in a French post-chaise upon first setting out.

Or the proposition may stand thus.

A French postilion has always to alight before he has got three hundred yards out of town.

What's wrong now?——Diable![1]——a rope's broke!——a knot has slipt!——a staple's drawn!——a bolt's to whittle!——a tag, a rag, a jag, a strap, a buckle, or a buckle's tongue, want altering.——

Now true as all this is, I never think myself impower'd to ex-communicate thereupon either the post-chaise, or its driver——nor do I take it into my head to swear by the living G——, I would rather go a foot ten thousand times——or that I will be damn'd if ever I get into another——but I take the matter coolly before me, and consider, that some tag, or rag, or jag, or bolt, or buckle, or buckle's tongue, will ever be a wanting, or want altering, travel where I will——so I never chaff, but take the good and the bad as they fall in my road, and get on:——Do so, my lad! said I; he had lost five minutes already, in alighting in order to get at a luncheon of black bread which he had cramm'd into the chaise-pocket, and was re-mounted and going leisurely on, to relish it the better——Get on, my lad, said I, briskly——but in the most persuasive tone imag-inable, for I jingled a four and twenty sous piece against the glass, taking care to hold the flat side towards him, as he look'd back: the dog grinn'd intelligence from his right ear to his left, and behind his sooty muzzle discover'd such a pearly row of teeth, that *Sovereignty* would have pawn'd her jewels for them.——

Just heaven! $\left\{ \begin{array}{l} \text{What masticators!} \text{——} \\ \text{What bread!} \text{——} \end{array} \right.$

and so, as he finish'd the last mouthful of it, we enter'd the town of *Montreuil.*

---

1. "What the Devil!"

Chapter IX.

THERE is not a town in all *France*, which in my opinion, looks better in the map, than MONTREUIL;——I own, it does not look so well in the book of post roads; but when you come to see it——to be sure it looks most pitifully.

There is one thing however in it at present very handsome; and that is the inn-keeper's daughter: She has been eighteen months at *Amiens*, and six at *Paris*, in going through her classes; so knits, and sews, and dances, and does the little coquetries very well.——

——A slut![2] in running them over within these five minutes that I have stood looking at her, she has let fall at least a dozen loops in a white thread stocking——Yes, yes——I see, you cunning gipsy!——'tis long, and taper——you need not pin it to your knee—— and that 'tis your own——and fits you exactly.——

——That nature should have told this creature a word about a *statue's thumb!*——

——But as this sample is worth all their thumbs——besides I have her thumbs and fingers in at the bargain if they can be any guide to me,——and as *Janatone*[3] withal (for that is her name) stands so well for a drawing——may I never draw more, or rather may I draw like a draught-horse, by main strength all the days of my life,——if I do not draw her in all her proportions, and with as determin'd a pencil, as if I had her in the wettest drapery.——

——But your worships chuse rather that I give you the length, breadth, and perpendicular height of the great parish church, or a drawing of the fascade of the abbey of Saint *Austreberte* which has been transported from *Artois* hither——every thing is just I suppose as the masons and carpenters left them,——and if the belief in *Christ* continues so long, will be so these fifty years to come——so your worships and reverences, may all measure them at your leisures——but he who measures thee, *Janatone*, must do it now ——thou carriest the principles of change within thy frame; and considering the chances of a transitory life, I would not answer for thee a moment; and e'er twice twelve months are pass'd and gone, thou mayest grow out like a pumkin, and lose thy shapes——or, thou mayest go off like a flower, and lose thy beauty——nay, thou mayest go off like a hussy——and lose thyself.——I would not answer for my aunt *Dinah*, was she alive——'faith, scarce for her picture——were it but painted by *Reynolds*——

——But if I go on with my drawing, after naming that son of *Apollo*, I'll be shot——

2. The word had more affectionate, and fewer immoral, connotations in the eighteenth century than it has in the twentieth.

3. Like Jenny, a common name for a pretty girl. A wet drapery was sometimes used by models as a modest substitute for posing nude.

So you must e'en be content with the original; which if the evening is fine in passing thro' *Montreuil*, you will see at your chaise door, as you change horses: but unless you have as bad a reason for haste as I have——you had better stop:——She has a little of the *devote*:[4] but that, sir, is a terce to a nine in your favour——

——L— help me! I could not count a single point: so had been piqued, and repiqued, and capotted to the devil.

Chapter X.

ALL which being considered, and that Death moreover might be much nearer me than I imagined——I wish I was at *Abbeville*, quoth I, were it only to see how they card and spin—— so off we set.

[5]*de Montreuil à Nampont-poste et demi*[6]

de Nampont à *Bernay* - - - poste

de Bernay à *Nouvion* - - - poste

de Nouvion à ABBEVILLE poste

——but the carders and spinners were all gone to bed.

Chapter XI.

WHAT a vast advantage is travelling! only it heats one; but there is a remedy for that, which you may pick out of the next chapter.

Chapter XII.

WAS I in a condition to stipulate with death, as I am this moment with my apothecary, how and where I will take his glister——I should certainly declare against submitting to it before my friends; and therefore, I never seriously think upon the mode and manner of this great catastrophe, which generally takes up and torments my thoughts as much as the catastrophe itself, but I constantly draw the curtain across it with this wish, that the Disposer of all things may so order it, that it happen not to me in my own house——but rather in some decent inn——at home, I know it, ——the concern of my friends, and the last services of wiping my brows and smoothing my pillow, which the quivering hand of pale

4. Devout woman. *Terce to a nine*: a term indicating a slight advantage in the card game of piquet; to be piqued and repiqued is to be defeated—here, of course, with sexual innuendo.

5. Vid. Book of French post-roads, page

36. edition of 1762. [*Sterne's note*. He did in fact make use of the official French road guide, though no copy of that year's can be found.]

6. "From Montreuil to Nampont—a post [six miles] and a half."

affection shall pay me, will so crucify my soul, that I shall die of a distemper which my physician is not aware of: but in an inn, the few cold offices I wanted, would be purchased with a few guineas, and paid me with an undisturbed, but punctual attention—— but mark. This inn, should not be the inn at *Abbeville*——if there was not another inn in the universe, I would strike that inn out of the capitulation: so

Let the horses be in the chaise exactly by four in the morning ——Yes, by four, Sir,——or by *Genevieve!*[7] I'll raise a clatter in the house, shall wake the dead.

Chapter XIII.

"MAKE *them like unto a wheel*,"[8] is a bitter sarcasm, as all the learned know, against the *grand tour*, and that restless spirit for making it, which *David* prophetically foresaw would haunt the children of men in the latter days; and therefore, as thinketh the great bishop *Hall*,[9] 'tis one of the severest imprecations which *David* ever utter'd against the enemies of the Lord —— and, as if he had said, "I wish them no worse luck than always to be rolling about"——So much motion, continues he, (for he was very corpulent)——is so much unquietness; and so much of rest, by the same analogy, is so much of heaven.

Now, I (being very thin) think differently; and that so much of motion, is so much of life, and so much of joy——and that to stand still, or get on but slowly, is death and the devil——

Hollo! Ho!——the whole world's asleep!——bring out the horses ——grease the wheels——tie on the mail——and drive a nail into that moulding——I'll not lose a moment——

Now the wheel we are talking of, and *whereinto* (but not *whereunto*, for that would make an Ixion's wheel[1] of it) he curseth his enemies, according to the bishop's habit of body, should certainly be a post-chaise wheel, whether they were set up in *Palestine* at that time or not——and my wheel, for the contrary reasons, must as certainly be a cart-wheel groaning round its revolution once in an age; and of which sort, were I to turn commentator, I should make no scruple to affirm, they had great store in that hilly country.

I love the Pythagoreans (much more than ever I dare tell my dear *Jenny*) for their "χωρισμὸν ἀπὸ τοῦ Σώματος, εἰς τὸ Καλῶς Φιλοσοφεῖν"——[their] "*getting out of the body, in order to think*

---

7. St. Genevieve is one of the patron saints of Paris.
8. Psalms 83:13. While the Grand Tour of Europe was theoretically the capstone of a gentleman's education in the eighteenth century, it was often in fact an excuse for dissipation.

9. Joseph Hall, the same Bishop Hall mentioned in Vol. I. chap. xxiii, wrote *Quo Vadis? A Just Censure of Travel* (1617).
1. For his ingratitude to Zeus, Ixion was bound to a burning wheel eternally.

well."[2] No man thinks right whilst he is in it; blinded as he must be, with his congenial humours, and drawn differently aside, as the bishop and myself have been, with too lax or too tense a fibre——— REASON is, half of it, SENSE; and the measure of heaven itself is but the measure of our present appetites and concoctions———

———But which of the two, in the present case, do you think to be mostly in the wrong?

You, certainly: quoth she, to disturb a whole family so early.

Chapter XIV.

———But she did not know I was under a vow not to shave my beard till I got to *Paris*;———yet I hate to make mysteries of nothing; ———'tis the cold cautiousness of one of those little souls from which *Lessius* (*lib.* 13. *de moribus divinis, cap.* 24.)[3] hath made his estimate, wherein he setteth forth, That one *Dutch* mile,[4] cubically multiplied, will allow room enough, and to spare, for eight hundred thousand millions, which he supposes to be as great a number of souls (counting from the fall of *Adam*) as can possibly be damn'd to the end of the world.

From what he has made this second estimate———unless from the parental goodness of God———I don't know—I am much more at a loss what could be in *Franciscus Ribbera's*[5] head, who pretends that no less a space than one of two hundred *Italian* miles[6] multiplied into itself, will be sufficient to hold the like number———he certainly must have gone upon some of the old *Roman* souls, of which he had read, without reflecting how much, by a gradual and most tabid[7] decline, in a course of eighteen hundred years, they must unavoidably have shrunk, so as to have come, when he wrote, almost to nothing.

In *Lessius*'s time, who seems the cooler man, they were as little as can be imagined———

———We find them less *now*———

And next winter we shall find them less again; so that if we go on from little to less, and from less to nothing, I hesitate not one moment to affirm, that in half a century, at this rate, we shall have no souls at all; which being the period beyond which I doubt likewise of the existence of the Christian faith, 'twill be one advantage that both of 'em will be exactly worn out together.

Blessed *Jupiter!* and blessed every other heathen god and goddess!

2. Tristram speaks as if Pythagoras's distrust of the body applies specifically to sexuality. Hence it would be ungallant to discuss his ideas with Jenny.
3. A Jesuit theologian of the Renaissance; the work cited is *De Perfectionibis*

Moribusque Divinis [On Divine Customs].
4. Four and four-tenths English miles.
5. Another Renaissance Jesuit, author of *Apocalypsis*.
6. Nine-tenths of an English mile.
7. Wasting away.

for now ye will all come into play again, and with *Priapus*[8] at your tails——what jovial times!——but where am I? and into what a delicious riot of things am I rushing? I——I who must be cut short in the midst of my days, and taste no more of 'em than what I borrow from my imagination——peace to thee, generous fool! and let me go on.

Chapter XV.

——"So hating, I say, to make mysteries of *nothing*"——I intrusted it with the post-boy, as soon as ever I got off the stones; he gave a crack with his whip to balance the compliment; and with the thill-horse[9] trotting, and a sort of an up and a down of the other, we danced it along to *Ailly au clochers*, famed in days of yore for the finest chimes in the world; but we danced through it without music——the chimes being greatly out of order——(as in truth they were through all *France*).

And so making all possible speed, from
Ailly au clochers, I got to *Hixcourt*,
from *Hixcourt*, I got to *Pequignay*, and
from *Pequignay*, I got to AMIENS,
concerning which town I have nothing to inform you, but what I have informed you once before——and that was——that *Janatone* went there to school.

Chapter XVI.

IN the whole catalogue of those whiffling vexations which come puffing across a man's canvass, there is not one of a more teasing and tormenting nature, than this particular one which I am going to describe——and for which, (unless you travel with an avance-courier, which numbers do in order to prevent it)——there is no help: and it is this.

That be you in never so kindly a propensity to sleep——tho' you are passing perhaps through the finest country——upon the best roads,——and in the easiest carriage for doing it in the world—— nay was you sure you could sleep fifty miles straight forwards, without once opening your eyes——nay what is more, was you as demonstratively satisfied as you can be of any truth in *Euclid*, that you should upon all accounts be full as well asleep as awake—— nay perhaps better——Yet the incessant returns of paying for the horses at every stage,——with the necessity thereupon of putting

8. The Greek fertility god, symbolized by a phallus (and so Tristram's reference to being "cut short" may have double meaning).
9. The horse closest to the carriage.

your hand into your pocket, and counting out from thence, three livres fifteen sous (sous by sous) puts an end to so much of the project, that you cannot execute above six miles of it (or supposing it is a post and a half, that is but nine)——were it to save your soul from destruction.

——I'll be even with 'em, quoth I, for I'll put the precise sum into a piece of paper, and hold it ready in my hand all the way: "Now I shall have nothing to do" said I (composing myself to rest) "but to drop this gently into the post-boy's hat, and not say a word."——Then there wants two sous more to drink——or there is a twelve sous piece of *Louis* XIV, which will not pass——or livre and some odd liards to be brought over from the last stage, which Monsieur had forgot; which altercations (as a man cannot dispute very well asleep) rouse him: still is sweet sleep retrievable; and still might the flesh weigh down the spirit, and recover itself of these blows——but then, by heaven! you have paid but for a single post——whereas 'tis a post and a half; and this obliges you to pull out your book of post-roads, the print of which is so very small, it forces you to open your eyes, whether you will or no: then Monsieur *le Curé*[1] offers you a pinch of snuff——or a poor soldier shews you his leg——or a shaveling his box——or the priestesse of the cistern will water your wheels——they do not want it——but she swears by her *priesthood* (throwing it back) that they do:—— then you have all these points to argue, or consider over in your mind; in doing of which, the rational powers get so thoroughly awakened——you may get 'em to sleep again as you can.

It was entirely owing to one of these misfortunes, or I had pass'd clean by the stables of *Chantilly*[2]——

——But the postillion first affirming, and then persisting in it to my face, that there was no mark upon the two sous piece, I open'd my eyes to be convinced——and seeing the mark upon it, as plain as my nose——I leap'd out of the chaise in a passion, and so saw every thing at *Chantilly* in spite.——I tried it but for three posts and a half, but believe 'tis the best principle in the world to travel speedily upon; for as few objects look very inviting in that mood ——you have little or nothing to stop you; by which means it was that I pass'd through St. *Dennis*, without turning my head so much as on side towards the Abby——

——Richness of their treasury! stuff and nonsense!——bating their jewels, which are all false, I would not give three sous for any one thing in it, but *Jaidas*'s *lantern*?[3]——nor for that either, only as it grows dark, it might be of use.

---

1. The parish priest (not, as in English, his assistant). Shaveling is a derisive reference to a begging friar, with shaved head.

2. The site of a famous race track.
3. The cup and lantern used by Judas were supposed to be at the Abbey of St. Denis.

Chapter XVII.

CRACK, crack——crack, crack——crack, crack——so this is Paris! quoth I (continuing in the same mood)——and this is *Paris*!——humph!——*Paris*! cried I, repeating the name the third time——

The first, the finest, the most brilliant——

——The streets however are nasty;

But it looks, I suppose, better than it smells——crack, crack—— crack, crack——What a fuss thou makest!——as if it concern'd the good people to be inform'd, That a man with pale face, and clad in black, had the honour to be driven into *Paris* at nine o'clock at night, by a postilion in a tawny yellow jerkin turned up with red calamanco[4]——crack, crack——crack, crack——crack, crack—— I wish thy whip——

——But 'tis the spirit of thy nation; so crack——crack on.

Ha!——and no one gives the wall![5]——but in the SCHOOL of URBANITY herself, if the walls are besh-t——how can you do otherwise?

And prithee when do they light the lamps? What?——never in the summer months!——Ho! 'tis the time of sallads.——O rare! sallad and soup——soup and sallad——sallad and soup, *encore*——

——'Tis *too much* for sinners.

Now I cannot bear the barbarity of it; how can that unconscionable coachman talk so much bawdy to that lean horse? don't you see, friend, the streets are so villainously narrow, that there is not room in all *Paris* to turn a wheel-barrow? In the grandest city of the whole world, it would not have been amiss, if they had been left a thought wider; nay were it only so much in every single street, as that a man might know (was it only for satisfaction) on which side of it he was walking.

One——two——three——four——five——six——seven—— eight——nine——ten.——Ten cook's shops! and twice the number of barber's! and all within three minutes driving! one would think that all the cooks in the world on some great merry-meeting with the barbers, by joint consent had said——Come, let us all go live at *Paris*: the *French* love good eating——they are all *gourmands* ——we shall rank high; if their god is their belly——their cooks must be gentlemen: and forasmuch as *the periwig maketh the man*, and the periwig-maker maketh the periwig——*ergo*, would the barbers say, we shall rank higher still——we shall be above you all——

4. Glossy Flemish wool cloth.
5. Since the streets were often muddy, with sewage in a central gutter, it was polite to let others pass next to the wall; but in Paris, says Tristram, the walls themselves are filthy.

we shall be[6] *Capitouls* at least——*pardi!*[7] we shall all wear swords——

——And so, one would swear, (that is by candle-light,——but there is no depending upon it) they continue to do, to this day.

Chapter XVIII.

THE *French* are certainly misunderstood:——but whether the fault is theirs, in not sufficiently explaining themselves; or speaking with that exact limitation and precision which one would expect on a point of such importance, and which moreover, is so likely to be contested by us——or whether the fault may not be altogether on our side, in not understanding their language always so critically as to know "what they would be at"——I shall not decide; but 'tis evident to me, when they affirm, *"That they who have seen* Paris, *have seen every thing,"* they must mean to speak of those who have seen it by day-light.

As for candle-light——I give it up——I have said before, there was no depending upon it——and I repeat it again; but not because the lights and shades are too sharp——or the tints confounded—— or that there is neither beauty or keeping, &c. . . . for that's not truth——but it is an uncertain light in this respect, That in all the five hundred grand Hôtels,[8] which they number up to you in *Paris* ——and the five hundred good things, at a modest computation (for 'tis only allowing one good thing to a Hôtel) which by candle-light are best to be *seen, felt, heard and understood* (which, by the bye is a quotation from *Lilly*[9])——the devil a one of us out of fifty, can get our heads fairly thrust in amongst them.

This is no part of the *French* computation: 'tis simply this.

That by the last survey taken in the year one thousand seven hundred and sixteen, since which time there have been considerable augmentations, *Paris* doth contain nine hundred streets; (viz.)

In the quarter called the *City*——there are fifty three streets.

In St. *James* of the Shambles, fifty five streets.

In St. *Oportune*, thirty four streets.

In the quarter of the *Louvre*, twenty five streets.

In the *Palace Royal*, or St. *Honorius*, forty nine streets.

In *Mont. Martyr*, forty one streets.

In St. *Eustace*, twenty nine streets.

In the *Halles*, twenty seven streets.

In St. *Dennis*, fifty five streets.

In St. *Martin*, fifty four streets.

---

6. Chief Magistrate in Toulouse, &c. &c. &c. [*Sterne's note.*]
7. "By God!"
8. Great private houses of the upper classes.
9. William Lyly's Latin grammar book was standard in English schools from the sixteenth century.

In St. *Paul*, or the *Mortellerie*, twenty seven streets.
The *Greve*, thirty eight streets.
In St. *Avoy*, or the *Verrerie*, nineteen streets.
In the *Marais*, or the *Temple*, fifty two streets.
In St. *Antony*'s, sixty eight streets.
In the *Place Maubert*, eighty one streets.
In St. *Bennet*, sixty streets.
In St. *Andrews de Arcs*, fifty one streets.
In the quarter of the *Luxembourg*, sixty two streets.
And in that of St. Germain, fifty five streets, into any of which you
may walk; and that when you have seen them with all that belongs
to them, fairly by day-light——their gates, their bridges, their
squares, their statues - - - - and have crusaded it moreover through
all their parish churches, by no means omitting St. *Roche* and
Sulpice - - - and to crown all, have taken a walk to the four palaces,
which you may see either with or without the statues and pictures,
just as you chuse——

——Then you will have seen——

——but, 'tis what no one needeth to tell you, for you will read it
yourself upon the portico of the *Louvre*, in these words,

> [1] EARTH NO SUCH FOLKS!——NO FOLKS E'ER SUCH A TOWN
> As PARIS IS!——SING, DERRY, DERRY, DOWN.

The *French* have a *gay* way of treating every thing that is Great;
and that is all can be said upon it.

Chapter XIX.

IN mentioning the word *gay* (as in the close of the last chapter)
it puts one (*i.e.* an author) in mind of the word *spleen*
——especially if he has any thing to say upon it: not that by any
analysis——or that from any table of interest or genealogy, there
appears much more ground of alliance betwixt them, than betwixt
light and darkness, or any two of the most unfriendly opposites in
nature——only 'tis an undercraft of authors to keep up a good
understanding amongst words, as politicians do amongst men——
not knowing how near they may be under a necessity of placing
them to each other——which point being now gain'd, and that I
may place mine exactly to my mind, I write it down here——

SPLEEN.

1. Non Orbis gentem, non urbem gens habet ullam————ulla parem. [*Sterne's note.*] "The earth does not have any other such people, nor does any other people have such a city."

This, upon leaving *Chantilly*, I declared to be the best principle in the world to travel speedily upon; but I gave it only as matter of opinion, I still continue in the same sentiments——only I had not then experience enough of its working to add this, that though you do get on at a tearing rate, yet you get on but uneasily to yourself at the same time; for which reason I here quit it entirely, and for ever, and 'tis heartily at one's[2] service——it has spoiled me the digestion of a good supper, and brought on a bilious diarrhæa, which has brought me back again to my first principle on which I set out—— and with which I shall now scamper it away to the banks of the *Garonne*——

——No;——I cannot stop a moment to give you the character of the people——their genius——their manners——their customs ——their laws——their religion——their government——their manufactures——their commerce——their finances, with all the resources and hidden springs which sustain them: qualified as I may be, by spending three days and two nights amongst them, and during all that time, making these things the entire subject of my enquiries and reflections——

Still—still I must away——the roads are paved——the posts are short——the days are long——'tis no more than noon——I shall be at *Fontainbleau* before the king——

——Was he going there? not that I know——

Chapter XX.

NOW I hate to hear a person, especially if he be a traveller, complain that we do not get on so fast in *France* as we do in *England*; whereas we get on much faster, *consideratis considerandis*;[3] thereby always meaning, that if you weigh their vehicles with the mountains of baggage which you lay both before and behind upon them——and then consider their puny horses, with the very little they give them——'tis a wonder they get on at all: their suffering is most unchristian, and 'tis evident thereupon to me, that a *French* post-horse would not know what in the world to do, was it not for the two words ****** and ****** in which there is as much sustenance, as if you gave him a peck of corn: now as these words cost nothing, I long for my soul to tell the reader what they are; but here is the question——they must be told him plainly, and with the most distinct articulation, or it will answer no end——and yet to do it in that plain way——though their reverences may laugh at it in the bed-chamber——full well I wot, they will abuse it in the parlour: for which cause, I have been volving and revolving in my

2. Anyone's.
3. "Considering what must be considered."

fancy some time, but to no purpose, by what clean device or facete contrivance I might so modulate them, that whilst I satisfy *that ear* which the reader chuses to *lend* me——I might not dissatisfy the other which he keeps to himself.

——My ink burns my finger to try——and when I have—— 'twill have a worse consequence——it will burn (I fear) my paper.

——No;——I dare not——

But if you wish to know how the *abbess* of *Andoüillets*,[4] and a novice of her convent got over the difficulty (only first wishing myself all imaginable success)——I'll tell you without the least scruple.

Chapter XXI.

THE abbess of *Andoüillets*, which if you look into the large set of provincial maps now publishing at *Paris*, you will find situated amongst the hills which divide *Burgundy* from *Savoy*, being in danger of an *Anchylosis* or stiff joint (the *sinovid*[5] of her knee becoming hard by long matins) and having tried every remedy—— first, prayers and thanksgiving; then invocations to all the saints in heaven promiscuously——then particularly to every saint who had had ever a stiff leg before her——then touching it with all the reliques of the convent, principally with the thigh-bone of the man of *Lystra*, who had been impotent from his youth[6]——then wrapping it up in her veil when she went to bed——then cross-wise her rosary——then bringing in to her aid the secular arm, and anointing it with oils and hot fat of animals——then treating it with emollient and resolving fomentations——then with poultices of marsh-mallows, mallows, bonus Henricus,[7] white lillies and fenugreek——then taking the woods, I mean the smoak of 'em, holding her scapulary across her lap——then decoctions of wild chicory, water cresses, chervil, sweet cecily and cochlearia——and nothing all this while answering, was prevailed on at last to try the hot baths of *Bourbon*——so having first obtain'd leave of the visitor-general to take care of her existence——she ordered all to be got ready for her journey: a novice of the convent of about seventeen, who had been troubled with a whitloe[8] in her middle finger, by striking it constantly into the abbess's cast poultices, &c.——had gained such an interest, that overlooking a sciatical old nun, who might have

4. The French word for little sausage; Rabelais exploits its sexual implications in Book IV of *Gargantua and Pantagruel*, as Sterne does in his tale.
5. Sinovial (lubricating) fluid.
6. Acts 14:8–10; "impotent in his feet,"
he was healed by St. Paul.
7. "Good King Henry"—like all of these, a medicinal herb. A scapulary is a short shoulder-cape.
8. An inflammatory sore.

been set up for ever by the hot baths of *Bourbon, Margarita,* the little novice, was elected as the companion of the journey.

An old calesh,[9] belonging to the abbesse, lined with green frize, was ordered to be drawn out into the sun——the gardener of the convent being chosen muleteer, led out the two old mules to clip the hair from the rump-ends of their tails, whilst a couple of lay-sisters were busied, the one in darning the lining, and the other in sewing on the shreds of yellow binding, which the teeth of time had un-ravelled——the under-gardener dress'd the muleteer's hat in hot wine-lees[1]——and a taylor sat musically at it, in a shed overagainst the convent, in assorting four dozen of bells for the harness, whis-tling to each bell as he tied it on with a thong——

——The carpenter and the smith of *Andoüillets* held a council of wheels; and by seven, the morning after, all look'd spruce, and was ready at the gate of the convent for the hot-baths of *Bourbon*——two rows of the unfortunate stood ready there an hour before.

The abbess of *Andoüillets,* supported by *Margarita* the novice, advanced slowly to the calesh, both clad in white, with their black rosaries hanging at their breasts——

——There was a simple solemnity in the contrast: they entered the calesh; and nuns in the same uniform, sweet emblem of inno-cence, each occupied a window, and as the abbess and *Margarita* look'd up——each (the sciatical poor nun excepted)——each stream'd out the end of her veil in the air——then kiss'd the lilly hand which let it go: the good abbess and *Margarita* laid their hands saint-wise upon their breasts—look'd up to heaven——then to them——and look'd "God bless you, dear sisters."

I declare I am interested in this story, and wish I had been there.

The gardener, who I shall now call the muleteer, was a little, hearty, broad-set, good natured, chattering, toping[2] kind of a fel-low, who troubled his head very little with the *hows* and *whens* of life; so had mortgaged a month of his conventical wages in a bor-rachio, or leathern cask of wine, which he had disposed behind the calesh, with a large russet coloured riding coat over it, to guard it from the sun; and as the weather was hot, and he, not a niggard of his labours, walking ten times more than he rode——he found more occasions than those of nature, to fall back to the rear of his carriage; till by frequent coming and going, it had so happen'd, that all his wine had leak'd out at the *legal* vent of the borrachio, before one half of the journey was finish'd.

Man is a creature born to habitudes. The day had been sultry ——the evening was delicious——the wine was generous——the

9. A low-hooded carriage. Frieze is a woolen cloth with a nap.
1. That is, dyed it using the sediment at the bottom of the wine.
2. Drinking.

Burgundian hill on which it grew was steep——a little tempting bush³ over the door of a cool cottage at the foot of it, hung vibrating in full harmony with the passions——a gentle air rustled distinctly through the leaves——"Come——come, thirsty muleteer ——come in."

——The muleteer was a son of *Adam*. I need not say one word more. He gave the mules, each of 'em, a sound lash, and looking in the abbess's and *Margarita's* faces (as he did it)——as much as to say, "here I am"——he gave a second good crack——as much as to say to his mules, "get on"——so slinking behind, he enter'd the little inn at the foot of the hill.

The muleteer, as I told you, was a little, joyous, chirping fellow, who thought not of to-morrow, nor of what had gone before, or what was to follow it, provided he got but his scantling of Burgundy, and a little chit-chat along with it; so entering into a long conversation, as how he was chief gardener to the convent of *Andoüillets*, &c. &c. and out of friendship for the abbess and Mademoiselle *Margarita*, who was only in her noviciate, he had come along with them from the confines of *Savoy*, &c. - - &c. - - and as how she had got a white swelling by her devotions——and what a nation of herbs he had procured to mollify her humours, &c. &c. and that if the waters of *Bourbon* did not mend that leg——she might as well be lame of both——&c. &c. &c.——He so contrived his story as absolutely to forget the heroine of it——and with her, the little novice, and what was a more ticklish point to be forgot than both——the two mules; who being creatures that take advantage of the world, inasmuch as their parents took it of them⁴—— and they not being in a condition to return the obligation *downwards* (as men and women and beasts are)——they do it side-ways, and long-ways, and back-ways——and up hill, and down hill, and which way they can.——Philosophers, with all their ethics, have never considered this rightly——how should the poor muleteer then, in his cups, consider it at all? he did not in the least——'tis time we do; let us leave him then in the vortex of his element, the happiest and most thoughtless of mortal men——and for a moment let us look after the mules, the abbess, and *Margarita*.

By virtue of the muleteer's two last strokes, the mules had gone quietly on, following their own consciences up the hill, till they had conquer'd about one half of it; when the elder of them, a shrewd crafty old devil, at the turn of an angle, giving a side glance, and no muleteer behind them——

By my fig! said she, swearing, I'll go no further——And if I do, replied the other——they shall make a drum of my hide.——

And so with one consent they stopp'd thus——

---

3. A branch indicating a tavern.   4. That is, because mules are sterile.

Chapter XXII.

——Get on with you, said the abbess.

——Wh - - - - ysh——ysh——cried *Margarita.*

Sh - - - a——shu - u——shu - - u——sh - - aw——shaw'd the abbess.

—— Whu — v — w —— whew — w — w —— whuv'd *Margarita,* pursing up her sweet lips betwixt a hoot and a whistle.

Thump——thump——thump——obstreperated the abbess of *Andoüillets* with the end of her gold-headed cane against the bottom of the calesh——

——The old mule let a f——

Chapter XXIII.

WE are ruin'd and undone, my child, said the abbess to *Margarita*——we shall be here all night——we shall be plunder'd——we shall be ravish'd——

——We shall be ravish'd, said *Margarita*, as sure as a gun.

Sancta Maria! cried the abbess (forgetting the O!)——why was I govern'd by this wicked stiff joint? why did I leave the convent of *Andoüillets?* and why didst thou not suffer thy servant to go unpolluted to her tomb?

O my finger! my finger! cried the novice, catching fire at the word *servant*——why was I not content to put it here, or there, any where rather than be in this strait?

——Strait! said the abbess.

Strait——said the novice; for terrour had struck their understandings——the one knew not what she said——the other what she answer'd.

O my virginity! virginity! cried the abbess.

——inity!——inity! said the novice, sobbing.

Chapter XXIV.

MY dear mother, quoth the novice, coming a little to herself, ——there are two certain words, which I have been told will force any horse, or ass, or mule, to go up a hill whether he will or no; be he never so obstinate or ill-will'd, the moment he hears them utter'd, he obeys. They are words magic! cried the abbess, in the utmost horrour——No; replied *Margarita* calmly——but they are words sinful——What are they? quoth the abbess, interrupting her: They are sinful in the first degree, answered *Margarita,*——they are mortal——and if we are ravish'd and die unabsolved of them, we shall both——but you may pronounce them to me, quoth the abbess of *Andoüillets*——They cannot, my dear mother, said the novice, be pronounced at all; they will make all the blood in one's body fly up into one's face——But you' may whisper them in my ear, quoth the abbess.

Heaven! hadst thou no guardian angel to delegate to the inn at the bottom of the hill? was there no generous and friendly spirit unemploy'd——no agent in nature, by some monitory shivering, creeping along the artery which led to his heart, to rouze the mule-teer from his banquet?——no sweet minstrelsy to bring back the fair idea of the abbess and *Margarita*, with their black rosaries!

Rouse! rouse!——but 'tis too late——the horrid words are por-nounced this moment——

——and how to tell them——Ye, who can speak of every thing existing, with unpolluted lips——instruct me——guide me——

Chapter XXV.

ALL sins whatever, quoth the abbess, turning casuist in the dis-tress they were under, are held by the confessor of our convent to be either mortal or venial: there is no further division. Now a venial sin being the slightest and least of all sins,——being halved——by taking, either only the half of it, and leaving the rest——or, by taking it all, and amicably halving it betwixt yourself and another person——in course becomes diluted into no sin at all.

Now I see no sin in saying, *bou, bou, bou, bou, bou,* a hundred times together; nor is there any turpitude in pronouncing the syl-lable *ger, ger, ger, ger, ger,*[5] were it from our matins to our vespers: Therefore, my dear daughter, continued the abbess of *Andoüillets* ——I will say *bou,* and thou shalt say *ger*; and then alternately, as there is no more sin in *fou* then in *bou*——Thou shalt say *fou*—— and I will come in (like fa, sol, la, re, mi, ut, at our complines[6]) with *ter*. And accordingly the abbess, giving the pitch note, set off thus:

Abbess,　⎱Bou - - bou - - bou - -
Margarita, ⎰——ger, - - ger, - - ger

Margarita,⎱Fou - - fou - - fou - -
Abbess,　 ⎰——ter, - - ter, - - ter.

The two mules acknowledged the notes by a mutual lash of their tails; but it went no further.——'Twill answer by an' by, said the novice.

Abbess,　 ⎱Bou- bou- bou- bou- bou- bou-
Margarita,⎰——ger, ger, ger, ger, ger, ger.

---

5. *Bouger* means "to move" (budge), but Sterne's emphasis suggests we should hear *bougre*, "sodomist" ("bugger"). With *fouter* he has in mind *foutre*, "to copulate."

6. The last prayers of the day.

Quicker still, cried *Margarita*.
Fou, fou, fou, fou, fou, fou, fou, fou, fou.

Quicker still, cried *Margarita*.
Bou, bou, bou, bou, bou, bou, bou, bou, bou.

Quicker still——God preserve me! said the abbess——They do not understand us, cried *Margarita*——But the Devil does, said the abbess of *Andoüillets*.

Chapter XXVI.

WHAT a tract of country have I run!——how many degrees nearer to the warm sun am I advanced, and how many fair and goodly cities have I seen, during the time you have been reading, and reflecting, Madam, upon this story! There's FONTAIN-BLEAU, and SENS, and JOIGNY, and AUXERRE, and DIJON the capital of *Burgundy*, and CHALLON, and *Mâcon* the capital of the *Mâcon-ese*, and a score more upon the road to LYONS——and now I have run them over——I might as well talk to you of so many market-towns in the moon, as tell you one word about them: it will be this chapter at the least, if not both this and the next entirely lost, do what I will——

——Why, 'tis a strange story! *Tristram*.

————Alas! Madam, had it been upon some melancholy lecture of the cross——the peace of meekness, or the contentment of resignation——I had not been incommoded: or had I thought of writing it upon the purer abstractions of the soul, and that food of wisdom, and holiness, and contemplation, upon which the spirit of man (when separated from the body) is to subsist for ever——You would have come with a better appetite from it——

——I wish I never had wrote it: but as I never blot any thing out——let us use some honest means to get it out of our heads directly.

——Pray reach me my fool's cap——I fear you sit upon it, Madam——'tis under the cushion——I'll put it on——

Bless me! you have had it upon your head this half hour.—— There then let it stay, with a
Fa-ra diddle di
and a fa-ri diddle d
and a high-dum——dye-dum
    fiddle - - - dumb - c.
And now, Madam, we may venture, I hope, a little to go on.

Chapter XXVII.

——All you need say of *Fontainbleau* (in case you are ask'd) is, that it stands about forty miles (south *something*) from *Paris*, in the middle of a large forest——That there is something great in it——That the king goes there once, every two or three years, with his whole court, for the pleasure of the chase——and that during that carnival of sporting, any *English* gentleman of fashion (you need not forget yourself) may be accommodated with a nag or two, to partake of the sport, taking care only not to out-gallop the king——

Though there are two reasons why you need not talk loud of this to every one.

First, Because 'twill make the said nags the harder to be got; and

Secondly, 'Tis not a word of it true.——*Allons!*

As for Sens——you may dispatch it in a word————" *'Tis an archiepiscopal see.*"

For Joigny——the less, I think, one says of it, the better.

But for Auxerre——I could go on for ever: for in my *grand tour* through *Europe*, in which, after all, my father (not caring to trust me with any one) attended me himself, with my uncle *Toby*, and *Trim*, and *Obadiah*, and indeed most of the family, except my mother, who being taken up with a project of knitting my father a pair of large worsted breeches——(the thing is common sense) ——and she not caring to be put out of her way, she staid at home at Shandy Hall, to keep things right during the expedition; in which, I say, my father stopping us two days at *Auxerre*, and his researches being ever of such a nature, that they would have found fruit even in a desert——he has left me enough to say upon Auxerre: in short, wherever my father went——but 'twas more remarkably so, in this journey through *France* and *Italy*, than in any other stages of his life——his road seemed to lie so much on one side of that, wherein all other travellers had gone before him ——he saw kings and courts and silks of all colours, in such strange lights——and his remarks and reasonings upon the characters, the manners and customs of the countries we pass'd over, were so opposite to those of all other mortal men, particularly those of my uncle *Toby* and *Trim*——(to say nothing of myself)——and to crown all——the occurrences and scrapes which we were perpetually meeting and getting into, in consequence of his systems and opiniatry——they were of so odd, so mixed and tragicomical a contexture——That the whole put together, it appears of so different a shade and tint from any tour of *Europe*, which was ever executed——That I will venture to pronounce——the fault must be mine and mine only——if it be not read by all travellers and travel-readers, till travelling is no more,——or which comes to the same point——till the world, finally, takes it into its head to stand still.——

——But this rich bale is not to be open'd now; except a small thread or two of it, merely to unravel the mystery of my father's stay at AUXERRE.

——As I have mentioned it——'tis too slight to be kept suspended; and when 'tis wove in, there's an end of it.

We'll go, brother *Toby*, said my father, whilst dinner is coddling ——to the abby of Saint *Germain*, if it be only to see these bodies, of which monsieur *Seguier*[7] has given such a recommendation.—— I'll go see any body; quoth my uncle *Toby*; for he was all compliance thro' every step of the journey——Defend me! said my father ——they are all mummies——Then one need not shave; quoth my uncle *Toby*——Shave! no——cried my father——'twill be more like relations to go with our beards on——So out we sallied, the corporal lending his master his arm, and bringing up the rear, to the abby of Saint *Germain*.

Every thing is very fine, and very rich, and very superb, and very magnificent, said my father, addressing himself to the sacristan, who was a young brother of the order of *Benedictines*——but our curiosity has led us to see the bodies, of which monsieur *Seguier* has given the world so exact a description.——The sacristan made a bow, and lighting a torch first, which he had always in the vestry ready for the purpose; he led us into the tomb of St. *Heribald*—— This, said the sacristan, laying his hand upon the tomb, was a renowned prince of the house of *Bavaria*, who under the successive reigns of *Charlemagne*, *Louis le Debonair*, and *Charles the Bald*, bore a great sway in the government, and had a principal hand in bringing every thing into order and discipline——

Then he has been as great, said my uncle, in the field, as in the cabinet——I dare say he has been a gallant soldier——He was a monk——said the sacristan.

My uncle *Toby* and *Trim* sought comfort in each others faces ——but found it not: my father clapp'd both his hands upon his cod-piece, which was a way he had when any thing hugely tickled him; for though he hated a monk and the very smell of a monk worse than all the devils in hell——Yet the shot hitting my uncle *Toby* and *Trim* so much harder than him, 'twas a relative triumph; and put him into the gayest humour in the world.

——And pray what do you call this gentleman? quoth my father,

---

7. Bishop of Auxerre in the seventeenth century, he investigated the condition of the bodies of saints in the Abbey's tombs. Those named were former bishops of Auxerre.

rather sportingly: This tomb, said the young *Benedictine*, looking downwards, contains the bones of Saint MAXIMA, who came from *Ravenna* on purpose to touch the body——

——Of Saint MAXIMUS,[8] said my father, popping in with his saint before him—they were two of the greatest saints in the whole martyrology, added my father——Excuse me, said the sacristan ——————'twas to touch the bones of Saint *Germain* the builder of the abby——And what did she get by it? said my uncle *Toby* ——What does any woman get by it? said my father——MARTYR-DOME; replied the young *Benedictine*, making a bow down to the ground, and uttering the word with so humble, but decisive a cadence, it disarmed my father for a moment. 'Tis supposed, continued the *Benedictine*, that St. *Maxima* has lain in this tomb four hundred years, and two hundred before her canonization——'Tis but a slow rise, brother *Toby*, quoth my father, in this self same army of martyrs.——A desperate slow one, an' please your honour, said *Trim*, unless one could purchase[9]——I should rather sell out entirely, quoth my uncle *Toby*——I am pretty much of your opinion, brother *Toby*, said my father.

——Poor St. *Maxima*! said my uncle *Toby* low to himself, as we turn'd from her tomb: She was one of the fairest and most beautiful ladies either of *Italy* or *France*, continued the sacristan——But who the duce has got lain down here, besides her, quoth my father, pointing with his cane to a large tomb as we walked on——It is Saint *Optat*,[1] Sir, answered the sacristan——And properly is Saint *Optat* plac'd! said my father: And what is Saint *Optat*'s story? continued he. Saint *Optat*, replied the sacristan, was a bishop——

——I thought so, by heaven! cried my father, interrupting him ——Saint *Optat*!——how should Saint *Optat* fail? so snatching out his pocket-book, and the young *Benedictine* holding him the torch as he wrote, he set it down as a new prop to his system of christian names, and I will be bold to say, so disinterested was he in the search of truth, that had he found a treasure in St. *Optat*'s tomb, it would not have made him half so rich: 'Twas as successful a short visit as ever was paid to the dead; and so highly was his fancy pleas'd with all that had passed in it,——that he determined at once to stay another day in *Auxerre*.

——I'll see the rest of these good gentry to-morrow, said my father, as we cross'd over the square——And while you are paying that visit, brother *Shandy*, quoth my uncle *Toby*——the corporal and I will mount the ramparts.

---

8. Latin for "greatest" (or "largest").
9. That is, rise as one could in the army, by buying a commission.
1. Latin for "he chooses" (or "desires").

Chapter XXVIII.

——NOW this is the most puzzled skein of all——for in this last chapter, as far at least as it has help'd me through *Auxerre*, I have been getting forwards in two different journies together, and with the same dash of the pen——for I have got entirely out of *Auxerre* in this journey which I am writing now, and I am got half way out of *Auxerre* in that which I shall write hereafter——There is but a certain degree of perfection in every thing; and by pushing at something beyond that, I have brought myself into such a situation, as no traveller ever stood before me; for I am this moment walking across the market-place of *Auxerre* with my father and my uncle *Toby*, in our way back to dinner—— and I am this moment also entering *Lyons* with my post-chaise broke into a thousand pieces——and I am moreover this moment in a handsome pavillion built by *Pringello*,[2] upon the banks of the *Garonne*, which Mons. *Sligniac* has lent me, and where I now sit rhapsodizing all these affairs.

——Let me collect myself, and pursue my journey.

Chapter XXIX.

I Am glad of it, said I, settling the account with myself as I walk'd into *Lyons*——my chaise being all laid higgledy-piggledy with my baggage in a cart, which was moving slowly before me——I am heartily glad, said I, that 'tis all broke to pieces; for now I can go directly by water to *Avignon*, which will carry me on a hundred and twenty miles of my journey, and not cost me seven livres—— and from thence, continued I, bringing forwards the account, I can hire a couple of mules——or asses, if I like, (for no body knows me) and cross the plains of *Languedoc*, for almost nothing——I shall gain four hundred livres by the misfortune clear into my purse; and pleasure! worth——worth double the money by it. With what velocity, continued I, clapping my two hands together, shall I fly down the rapid *Rhone*, with the VIVARES on my right-hand, and DAUPHINY on my left, scarce seeing the ancient cities of VIENNE, *Valence*, and *Vivieres*. What a flame will it rekindle in the lamp, to snatch a blushing grape from the *Hermitage* and *Côte roti*,[3] as I shoot by the foot of them? and what a fresh spring in the blood! to behold upon the banks advancing and retiring, the castles of romance, whence courteous knights have whilome rescued the dis-

2. The same Don Pringello, the celebrated Spanish architect, of whom my cousin Antony has made such honourable mention in a scholium to the Tale inscribed to his name. Vid. p. 129, small edit. [*Sterne's note.*] His friend John Hall Stevenson (the Eugenius of *Tristram Shandy*, called Antony by his real-life friends) attributed a story in his *Crazy Tales* to an architect named Don Pringello.
3. Famous for their vineyards.

tress'd——and see vertiginous, the rocks, the mountains, the cataracts, and all the hurry which Nature is in with all her great works about her——

As I went on thus, methought my chaise, the wreck of which look'd stately enough at the first, insensibly grew less and less in its size; the freshness of the painting was no more——the gilding lost its lustre——and the whole affair appeared so poor in my eyes—— so sorry!——so contemptible! and, in a word, so much worse than the abbess of *Andoüillets'* itself——that I was just opening my mouth to give it to the devil——when a pert vamping chaise-undertaker, stepping nimbly across the street, demanded if Monsieur would have his chaise refitted——No, no, said I, shaking my head sideways——Would Monsieur chuse to sell it? rejoin'd the undertaker——With all my soul, said I——the iron work is worth forty livres——and the glasses worth forty more——and the leather you may take to live on.

——What a mine of wealth, quoth I, as he counted me the money, has this post chaise brought me in? And this is my usual method of book-keeping, at least with the disasters of life—— making a penny of every one of 'em as they happen to me——

——Do, my dear *Jenny*, tell the world for me, how I behaved under one, the most oppressive of its kind which could befall me as a man, proud, as he ought to be, of his manhood——

'Tis enough, said'st thou, coming close up to me, as I stood with my garters in my hand, reflecting upon what had *not* pass'd——'Tis enough, *Tristram*, and I am satisfied, said'st thou, whispering these words in my ear, **** ** **** *** ******;____**** ** ****——any other man would have sunk down to the center——

——Every thing is good for something, quoth I.

——I'll go into *Wales* for six weeks, and drink goat's-whey—— and I'll gain seven years longer life for the accident. For which reason I think myself inexcusable, for blaming Fortune so often as I have done, for pelting me all my life long, like an ungracious duchess, as I call'd her, with so many small evils: surely if I have any cause to be angry with her, 'tis that she has not sent me great ones——a score of good cursed, bouncing losses, would have been as good as a pension to me.

——One of a hundred a year, or so, is all I wish——I would not be at the plague of paying land tax for a larger.

Chapter XXX.

TO those who call vexations, VEXATIONS, as knowing what they are, there could not be a greater, than to be the best part of a day in *Lyons*, the most opulent and flourishing city in *France*, enriched with the most fragments of antiquity——and not be able to see it. To be withheld upon *any* account, must be a vexation; but to be withheld *by* a vexation——must certainly be, what philosophy justly calls

VEXATION

upon

VEXATION.

I had got my two dishes of milk coffee (which by the bye is excellently good for a consumption,[4] but you must boil the milk and coffee together——otherwise 'tis only coffee and milk)—— and as it was no more than eight in the morning, and the boat did not go off till noon, I had time to see enough of *Lyons* to tire the patience of all the friends I had in the world with it. I will take a walk to the cathedral, said I, looking at my list, and see the wonderful mechanism of this great clock of *Lippius* of *Basil,* in the first place——

Now, of all things in the world, I understand the least of mechanism——I have neither genius, or taste, or fancy——and have a brain so entirely unapt for every thing of that kind, that I solemnly declare I was never yet able to comprehend the principles of motion of a squirrel cage, or a common knife-grinder's wheel——tho' I have many an hour of my life look'd up with great devotion at the one——and stood by with as much patience as any christian ever could do, at the other——

I'll go see the surprising movements of this great clock, said I, the very first thing I do: and then I will pay a visit to the great library of the Jesuits, and procure, if possible, a sight of the thirty volumes of the general history of *China,* wrote (not in the *Tartarian*) but in the *Chinese* language, and in the *Chinese* character too.

Now I almost know as little of the *Chinese* language, as I do of the mechanism of *Lippius's* clock-work; so, why these should have jostled themselves into the two first articles of my list——I leave to the curious as a problem of Nature. I own it looks like one of her ladyship's obliquities; and they who court her, are interested in finding out her humour as much as I.

When these curiosities are seen, quoth I, half addressing myself to my *valet de place,*[5] who stood behind me——'twill be no hurt if WE go to the church of St. *Ireneus,* and see the pillar to which *Christ* was tied——and after that, the house where *Pontius Pilate* lived[6]——'Twas at the next town, said the *valet de place*——at

---

4. Tuberculosis.
5. Guide.
6. A house in Lyon once occupied by an Italian named Pilati came, through the confusion of names, to be known as that of Pontius Pilate. Sterne's source for this curiosity, as for others on these pages, is Jacob Spon's *Recherche des antiquités et curiosités de la ville de Lyon.*

Vienne; I am glad of it, said I, rising briskly from my chair, and walking across the room with strides twice as long as my usual pace——"for so much the sooner shall I be at the *Tomb of the two lovers.*"

What was the cause of this movement, and why I took such long strides in uttering this——I might leave to the curious too; but as no principle of clock-work is concern'd in it——'twill be as well for the reader if I explain it myself.

Chapter XXXI.

O! There is a sweet æra in the life of man, when, (the brain being tender and fibrillous, and more like pap than any thing else)——a story read of two fond lovers, separated from each other by cruel parents, and by still more cruel destiny——

Amandus[7]——He

Amanda——She——

each ignorant of the other's course,

He——east

She——west

Amandus taken captive by the *Turks*, and carried to the emperor of *Morocco*'s court, where the princess of *Morocco* falling in love with him, keeps him twenty years in prison, for the love of his *Amanda*——

She——(*Amanda*) all the time wandering barefoot, and with dishevell'd hair, o'er rocks and mountains enquiring for *Amandus* ——*Amandus! Amandus!*——making every hill and vally to echo back his name——

Amandus! Amandus!

at every town and city sitting down forlorn at the gate——Has *Amandus!*——has my *Amandus* enter'd?——till,——going round, and round, and round the world——chance unexpected bringing them at the same moment of the night, though by different ways, to the gate of *Lyons* their native city, and each in well known accents calling out aloud,

Is *Amandus* } still alive?
Is my *Amanda* }

they fly into each others arms, and both drop down dead for joy.

There is a soft æra in every gentle mortal's life, where such a story affords more *pabulum* to the brain, than all the *Frusts*,[8] and *Crusts*, and *Rusts* of antiquity, which travellers can cook up for it.

7. *Amandus* and *Amanda*: masculine and feminine forms of the Latin "one who must be loved."

8. Fragments.

————'Twas all that stuck on the right side of the cullender[9] in my own, of what *Spon* and others, in their accounts of *Lyons*, had *strained* into it; and finding, moreover, in some Itinerary, but in what God knows————That sacred to the fidelity of *Amandus* and *Amanda*, a tomb was built without the gates, where to this hour, lovers call'd upon them to attest their truths,————I never could get into a scrape of that kind in my life, but this *tomb of the lovers*, would some how or other, come in at the close————nay such a kind of empire had it establish'd over me, that I could seldom think or speak of *Lyons*————and sometimes not so much as see even a *Lyons-waistcoat*, but this remnant of antiquity would present itself to my fancy; and I have often said in my wild way of running on————tho' I fear with some irreverence————"I thought this shrine (neglected as it was) as valuable as that of *Mecca*,[1] and so little short, except in wealth, of the *Santa Casa* itself, that some time or other, I would go a pilgrimage (though I had no other business at *Lyons*) on purpose to pay it a visit."

In my list, therefore, of V*idenda*[2] at *Lyons*, this, tho' *last*————was not, you see, *least*; so taking a dozen or two of longer strides than usual across my room, just whilst it passed my brain, I walked down calmly into the *Basse Cour*,[3] in order to sally forth; and having called for my bill————as it was uncertain whether I should return to my inn, I had paid it————had moreover given the maid ten sous, and was just receiving the dernier[4] compliments of Monsieur *Le Blanc*, for a pleasant voyage down the *Rhône*————when I was stopped at the gate————

Chapter XXXII.

————'T WAS by a poor ass who had just turned in with a couple of large panniers upon his back, to collect eleemosunary turnip tops and cabbage-leaves; and stood dubious, with his two forefeet on the inside of the threshold, and with his two hinder feet towards the street, as not knowing very well whether he was to go in, or no.

Now, 'tis an animal (be in what hurry I may) I cannot bear to strike————there is a patient endurance of sufferings, wrote so unaffectedly in his looks and carriage, which pleads so mightily for him, that it always disarms me; and to that degree, that I do not like to speak unkindly to him: on the contrary, meet him where I will————whether in town or country————in cart or under panniers

---

9. *Cullender*: colander, strainer.
1. Mecca, the birthplace of Mahomet, is the most sacred Moslem shrine. The Santa Casa, home of the Virgin Mary, was supposed to have been transported from Nazareth to Loreto, Italy, by angels.
2. Things to see.
3. Lower court: stable yard.
4. "Last."

——whether in liberty or bondage——I have ever something civil to say to him on my part; and as one word begets another (if he has as little to do as I)——I generally fall into conversation with him; and surely never is my imagination so busy as in framing his responses from the etchings of his countenance——and where those carry me not deep enough——in flying from my own heart into his, and seeing what is natural for an ass to think——as well as a man, upon the occasion. In truth, it is the only creature of all the classes of beings below me, with whom I can do this: for parrots, jackdaws, &c.——I never exchange a word with them—nor with the apes, &c. for pretty near the same reason; they act by rote, as the others speak by it, and equally make me silent: nay my dog and my cat, though I value them both——(and for my dog he would speak if he could)——yet some how or other, they neither of them possess the talents for conversation——I can make nothing of a discourse with them, beyond the *proposition*, the *reply*, and *rejoinder*, which terminated my father's and my mother's conversations, in his beds of justice——and those utter'd——there's an end of the dialogue——

——But with an ass, I can commune for ever.

Come *Honesty*! said I,——seeing it was impracticable to pass betwixt him and the gate——art thou for coming in, or going out?

The ass twisted his head round to look up the street——

Well——replied I——we'll wait a minute for thy driver:

——He turned his head thoughtful about, and looked wistfully the opposite way——

I understand thee perfectly; answered I——if thou takest a wrong step in this affair, he will cudgel thee to death——Well! a minute is but a minute, and if it saves a fellow creature a drubbing, it shall not be set down as ill-spent.

He was eating the stem of an artichoke as this discourse went on, and in the little peevish contentions of nature betwixt hunger and unsavouriness, had dropt it out of his mouth half a dozen times, and pick'd it up again——God help thee, *Jack*! said I, thou hast a bitter breakfast on't——and many a bitter day's labour——and many a bitter blow, I fear, for its wages——'tis all——all bitterness to thee, whatever life is to others.——And now thy mouth, if one knew the truth of it, is as bitter, I dare say, as soot——(for he had cast aside the stem) and thou hast not a friend perhaps in all this world, that will give thee a macaroon.——In saying this, I pull'd out a paper of 'em, which I had just purchased, and gave him one——and at this moment that I am telling it, my heart smites me, that there was more of pleasantry in the conceit, of seeing *how* an ass would eat a macaroon——than of benevolence in giving him one, which presided in the act.

When the ass had eaten his macaroon, I press'd him to come in——the poor beast was heavy loaded——his legs seem'd to tremble under him——he hung rather backwards, and as I pull'd at his halter, it broke short in my hand——he look'd up pensive in my face——"Don't thrash me with it——but if you will, you may"—— If I do, said I, I'll be d——d.

The word was but one half of it pronounced, like the abbess of Andoüillets'——(so there was no sin in it)——when a person coming in, let fall a thundering bastinado upon the poor devil's crupper, which put an end to the ceremony.

                    Out upon it!
cried I——but the interjection was equivocal——and, I think, wrong placed too——for the end of an osier[5] which had started out from the contexture of the ass's pannier, had caught hold of my breeches pocket as he rush'd by me, and rent it in the most disastrous direction you can imagine——so that the

Out upon it! in my opinion, should have come in here——but this I leave to be settled by

The

REVIEWERS

of

MY BREECHES.

which I have brought over along with me for that purpose.

Chapter XXXIII.[6]

WHEN all was set to rights, I came down stairs again into the *basse cour* with my valet de place, in order to sally out towards the tomb of the two lovers, &c.——and was a second time stopp'd at the gate——not by the ass——but by the person who struck him; and who, by that time, had taken possession (as is not uncommon after a defeat) of the very spot of ground where the ass stood.

It was a commissary sent to me from the post-office, with a rescript in his hand for the payment of some six livres odd sous.

Upon what account? said I.——'Tis upon the part of the king, replied the commissary, heaving up both his shoulders——

——My good friend, quoth I——as sure as I am I——and you are you——

---

5. A piece of the caning from which the *pannier* (basket) was made.
6. In the first edition, this chapter is numbered XXXIV, and subsequent chapters in the volume are similarly advanced.

——And who are you? said he.—— ——Don't puzzle me; said I.

Chapter XXXIV.

——But it is an indubitable verity, continued I, addressing myself to the commissary, changing only the form of my asseveration—— that I owe the king of *France* nothing but my good-will; for he is a very honest man, and I wish him all health and pastime in the world——

Pardonnez moi[7]——replied the commissary, you are indebted to him six livres four sous, for the next post from hence to St. *Fons*, in your rout to *Avignion*——which being a post royal, you pay double for the horses and postillion——otherwise 'twould have amounted to no more than three livres, two sous——

——But I don't go by land; said I.

——You may if you please; replied the commissary——

Your most obedient servant——said I, making him a low bow——

The commissary, with all the sincerity of grave good breeding ——made me one, as low again.——I never was more disconcerted with a bow in my life.

——The devil take the serious character of these people! quoth I——(aside) they understand no more of IRONY than this——

The comparison was standing close by with his panniers——but something seal'd up my lips——I could not pronounce the name——

Sir, said I, collecting myself——it is not my intention to take post——

——But you may——said he, persisting in his first reply——you may take post if you chuse——

——And I may take salt to my pickled herring, said I, if I chuse——

——But I do not chuse——

——But you must pay for it, whether you do or no——

Aye! for the salt,[8] said I (I know)——

——And for the post too; added he. Defend me; cried I——

I travel by water——I am going down the *Rhône* this very after-noon——my baggage is in the boat——and I have actually paid nine livres for my passage——

C'est tout egal——'tis all one; said he.

Bon Dieu![9] what, pay for the way I go! and for the way I do *not* go!

7. "Excuse me."
8. There was a tax on salt in France.

9. "Good God!"

——*C'est tout egal*; replied the commissary——

——The devil it is! said I——but I will go to ten thousand Bastiles[1] first——

O *England*! *England*! thou land of liberty, and climate of good sense, thou tenderest of mothers—and gentlest of nurses, cried I, kneeling upon one knee, as I was beginning my apostrophè——

When the director of Madam *Le Blanc*'s conscience coming in at that instant, and seeing a person in black, with a face as pale as ashes, at his devotions——looking still paler by the contrast and distress of his drapery——ask'd, if I stood in want of the aids of the church——

I go by WATER——said I——and here's another will be for making me pay for going by OYL.[2]

Chapter XXXV.

AS I perceived the commissary of the post-office would have his six livres four sous, I had nothing else for it, but to say some smart thing upon the occasion, worth the money:

And so I set off thus——

——And pray Mr. commissary, by what law of courtesy is a defenceless stranger to be used just the reverse from what you use a *Frenchman* in this matter?

By no means; said he.

Excuse me; said I——for you have begun, sir, with first tearing off my breeches—and now you want my pocket——

Whereas——had you first taken my pocket, as you do with your own people——and then left me bare a—'d after——I had been a beast to have complain'd——

As it is——

——'Tis contrary to the *law of nature*.

——'Tis contrary to *reason*.

——'Tis contrary to the GOSPEL.

But not to this——said he——putting a printed paper into my hand.

PAR LE ROY.[3]

—— ——'Tis a pithy prolegomenon, quoth I——and so read on —— —— —— —— —— —— —— —— —— —— —— —— on ——

1. The great prison at Paris, which because of its many political prisoners became a focus for the hostility felt against the king and aristocracy before the French Revolution.

2. Because Tristram looks as though he is dying, the priest will want to give him Last Rites, anointing him with oil.

3. "By [order of] the King."

———By all which it appears, quoth I, having read it over, a little too rapidly, that if a man sets out in a post-chaise from *Paris*———he must go on travelling in one, all the days of his life———or pay for it.———Excuse me, said the commissary, the spirit of the ordinance is this———That if you set out with an intention of running post from *Paris* to *Avignon, &c.* you shall not change that intention or mode of travelling, without first satisfying the fermiers⁴ for two posts further than the place you repent at———and 'tis founded, continued he, upon this, that the REVENUES are not to fall short through your *fickleness*———

———O by heavens! cried I——— if fickleness is taxable in *France* ———we have nothing to do but to make the best peace with you we can———

AND SO THE PEACE WAS MADE;

———And if it is a bad one———as *Tristram Shandy* laid the corner stone of it—nobody but *Tristram Shandy* ought to be hanged.

Chapter XXXVI.

THOUGH I was sensible I had said as many clever things to the commissary as came to six livres four sous, yet I was determined to note down the imposition amongst my remarks before I retir'd from the place; so putting my hand into my coat pocket for my remarks———(which by the bye, may be a caution to travellers to take a little more care of *their* remarks for the future) "my remarks were *stolen*"———Never did sorry traveller make such a pother and racket about his remarks as I did about mine, upon the occasion.

Heaven! earth! sea! fire! cried I, calling in every thing to my aid but what I should———My remarks are stolen!———what shall I do?———Mr. commissary! pray did I drop any remarks as I stood besides you?———

You dropp'd a good many very singular ones; replied he——— Pugh! said I, those were but a few, not worth above six livres two sous———but these are a large parcel———He shook his head——— Monsieur *Le Blanc*! Madam *Le Blanc*! did you see any papers of mine?———you maid of the house! run up stairs———*François*! run up after her———

———I must have my remarks———they were the best remarks, cried I, that ever were made———the wisest———the wittiest——— What shall I do?———which way shall I turn myself?

---

4. *Fermiers* paid the crown a fixed sum to purchase the right to various lucra-tive monopolies—here the system of post-horses.

Sancho Pança, when he lost his ass's FURNITURE, did not exclaim more bitterly.[5]

Chapter XXXVII.

WHEN the first transport was over, and the registers of the brain were beginning to get a little out of the confusion into which this jumble of cross accidents had cast them——it then presently occurr'd to me, that I had left my remarks in the pocket of the chaise——and that in selling my chaise, I had sold my remarks along with it, to the chaise-vamper. I leave this void space that the reader may swear into it, any oath that he is most accustomed to——For my own part, if ever I swore a *whole* oath into a vacancy in my life, I think it was into that—— *** **** **, said I——and so my remarks through *France*, which were as full of wit, as an egg is full of meat, and as well worth four hundred guineas, as the said egg is worth a penny——Have I been selling here to a chaise-vamper——for four *Louis d'Ors*——and giving him a post-chaise (by heaven) worth six into the bargain; had it been to *Dodsley*, or *Becket*,[6] or any creditable bookseller, who was either leaving off business, and wanted a post-chaise——or who was beginning it——and wanted my remarks, and two or three guineas along with them——I could have borne it——but to a chaise-vamper!——shew me to him this moment *François*,——said I—— the valet de place put on his hat, and led the way——and I pull'd off mine, as I pass'd the commissary, and followed him.

Chapter XXXVIII.

WHEN we arrived at the chaise-vamper's house, both the house and the shop were shut up; it was the eighth of *September*, the nativity of the blessed Virgin *Mary*, mother of God——

——Tantarra-ra-tan-tivi——the whole world was going out a May-poling——frisking here——capering there——no body cared a button for me or my remarks; so I sat me down upon a bench by the door, philosophating upon my condition: by a better fate than usually attends me, I had not waited half an hour, when the mistress came in, to take the papilliotes[7] from off her hair, before she went to the May-poles——

The *French* women, by the bye, love May-poles, *à la folie*[8]—— that is, as much as their matins——give 'em but a May-pole, whether in *May*, *June*, *July*, or *September*——they never count the

---

5. *Don Quixote*, I.iii.9.
6. Sterne's publishers.
7. Curl-papers.
8. "Madly."

times——down it goes——'tis meat, drink, washing, and lodging to 'em——and had we but the policy, an' please your worships (as wood is a little scarce in *France*) to send them but plenty of May-poles——

The women would set them up; and when they had done, they would dance round them (and the men for company) till they were all blind.

The wife of the chaise-vamper step'd in, I told you, to take the papilliotes from off her hair——the toilet stands still for no man——so she jerk'd off her cap, to begin with them as she open'd the door, in doing which, one of them fell upon the ground——I instantly saw it was my own writing——

——O Seigneur![9] cried I——you have got all my remarks upon your head, Madam!——*J'en suis bien mortifiée*,[1] said she——'tis well, thinks I, they have stuck there—for could they have gone deeper, they would have made such confusion in a *French* woman's noddle——She had better have gone with it unfrizled, to the day of eternity.

Tenez[2]——said she——so without any idea of the nature of my suffering, she took them from her curls, and put them gravely one by one into my hat——one was twisted this way——another twisted that——ay! by my faith; and when they are published, quoth I,——

They will be worse twisted still.

Chapter XXXIX.

AND now for *Lippius*'s clock! said I, with the air of a man, who had got thro' all his difficulties——nothing can prevent us seeing that, and the *Chinese* history, &c. except the time, said *François*——for 'tis almost eleven——then we must speed the faster, said I, striding it away to the cathedral.

I cannot say, in my heart, that it gave me any concern in being told by one of the minor canons, as I was entering the west door, ——That *Lippius*'s great clock was all out of joints, and had not gone for some years——It will give me the more time, thought I, to peruse the *Chinese* history; and besides I shall be able to give the world a better account of the clock in its decay, than I could have done in its flourishing condition——

——And so away I posted to the college of the Jesuits.

Now it is with the project of getting a peep at the history of *China* in *Chinese* characters——as with many others I could mention, which strike the fancy only at a distance; for as I came nearer

9. "O Lord."   2. "Here you are."
1. "I'm very mortified."

and nearer to the point——my blood cool'd——the freak gradually went off, till, at length I would not have given a cherry-stone to have it gratified——The truth was, my time was short, and my heart was at the Tomb of the Lovers——I wish to God, said I, as I got the rapper in my hand, that the key of the library may be but lost; it fell out as well——

For all the JESUITS *had got the cholic*——and to that degree, as never was known in the memory of the oldest practitioner.[3]

Chapter XL.

AS I knew the geography of the Tomb of the Lovers, as well as if I had lived twenty years in *Lyons*, namely, that it was upon the turning of my right hand, just without the gate, leading to the *Fauxbourg de Vaise*——I dispatch'd *François* to the boat, that I might pay the homage I so long ow'd it, without a witness of my weakness.——I walk'd with all imaginable joy towards the place ——when I saw the gate which intercepted the tomb, my heart glowed within me——

——Tender and faithful spirits! cried I, addressing myself to *Amandus* and *Amanda*——long——long have I tarried to drop this tear upon your tomb——I come——I come——

When I came——there was no tomb to drop it upon.

What would I have given for my uncle *Toby* to have whistled, Lillo bullero!

Chapter XLI.

NO matter how, or in what mood——but I flew from the tomb of the lovers——or rather I did not fly *from* it——(for there was no such thing existing) and just got time enough to the boat to save my passage;——and e'er I had sailed a hundred yards, the *Rhône* and the *Saôn* met together, and carried me down merely betwixt them.

But I have described this voyage down the *Rhône*, before I made it——

——So now I am at *Avignion*——and as there is nothing to see[4] but the old house, in which the duke of *Ormond* resided, and nothing to stop me but a short remark upon the place, in three minutes you will see me crossing the bridge upon a mule, with *François* upon a horse with my portmanteau behind him, and the owner of both, striding the way before us with a long gun upon his

3. The Jesuits were suppressed as sub-versive by the government of France in 1764.

4. The anti-papist Tristram ignores the great Palace of Popes for which Avignon is famous.

shoulder, and a sword under his arm, least peradventure we should run away with his cattle. Had you seen my breeches in entering *Avignon,*——Though you'd have seen them better, I think, as I mounted——you would not have thought the precaution amiss, or found in your heart to have taken it, in dudgeon: for my own part, I took it most kindly; and determined to make him a present of them, when we got to the end of our journey, for the trouble they had put him to, of arming himself at all points against them.

Before I go further, let me get rid of my remark upon *Avignon,* which is this; That I think it wrong, merely because a man's hat has been blown off his head by chance the first night he comes to *Avignion,*——that he should therefore say, "*Avignion* is more subject to high winds than any town in all *France:*" for which reason I laid no stress upon the accident till I had inquired of the master of the inn about it, who telling me seriously it was so——and hearing moreover, the windyness of *Avignion* spoke of in the country about as a proverb——I set it down, merely to ask the learned what can be the cause——the consequence I saw——for they are all Dukes, Marquisses, and Counts, there——the duce a Baron, in all *Avignion*——so that there is scarce any talking to them, on a windy day.

Prithee friend, said I, take hold of my mule for a moment——for I wanted to pull off one of my jack-boots, which hurt my heel—— the man was standing quite idle at the door of the inn, and as I had taken it into my head, he was someway concerned about the house or stable, I put the bridle into his hand——so begun with my boot:——when I had finished the affair, I turned about to take the mule from the man, and thank him——

——But *Monsieur le Marquis* had walked in——

Chapter XLII.

I Had now the whole south of *France*, from the banks of the *Rhône* to those of the *Garonne* to traverse upon my mule at my own leisure——*at my own leisure*——for I had left Death, the lord knows——and He only——how far behind me——"I have followed many a man thro' *France*, quoth he——but never at this mettlesome rate"——Still he followed,——and still I fled him—— but I fled him chearfully——still he pursued——but like one who pursued his prey without hope——as he lag'd, every step he lost, softened his looks——why should I fly him at this rate?

So notwithstanding all the commissary of the post-office had said, I changed the *mode* of my travelling once more; and after so precipitate and rattling a course as I had run, I flattered my fancy with

thinking of my mule, and that I should traverse the rich plains of
Languedoc upon his back, as slowly as foot could fall.

There is nothing more pleasing to a traveller——or more terrible
to travel-writers, than a large rich plain; especially if it is without
great rivers or bridges; and presents nothing to the eye, but one
unvaried picture of plenty: for after they have once told you that
'tis delicious! or delightful! (as the case happens)——that the soil
was grateful, and that nature pours out all her abundance, &c. . . .
they have then a large plain upon their hands, which they know not
what to do with——and which is of little or no use to them but to
carry them to some town; and that town, perhaps of little more, but
a new place to start from to the next plain——and so on.

——This is most terrible work; judge if I don't manage my plains
better.

Chapter XLIII.

I Had not gone above two leagues and a half, before the man with
his gun, began to look at his priming.

I had three several times loiter'd *terribly* behind; half a mile at
least every time: once, in deep conference with a drum-maker, who
was making drums for the fairs of *Baucaira* and *Tarascone*——I
did not understand the principles——

The second time, I cannot so properly say, I stopp'd——for
meeting a couple of *Franciscans*[5] straiten'd more for time than myself, and not being able to get to the bottom of what I was about
——I had turn'd back with them——

The third, was an affair of trade with a gossip, for a hand basket
of *Provence* figs for four sous; this would have been transacted at
once; but for a case of conscience at the close of it; for when the
figs were paid for, it turn'd out, that there were two dozen of eggs
cover'd over with vine-leaves at the bottom of the basket——as I
had no intention of buying eggs——I made no sort of claim of
them——as for the space they had occupied—what signified it? I
had figs enow for my money——

——But it was my intention to have the basket——it was the
gossip's intention to keep it, without which, she could do nothing
with her eggs——and unless I had the basket, I could do as little
with my figs, which were too ripe already, and most of 'em burst at
the side: this brought on a short contention, which terminated in
sundry proposals, what we should both do——

——How we disposed of our eggs and figs, I defy you, or the
Devil himself, had he not been there (which I am persuaded he

5. Begging friars.

was) to form the least probable conjecture: You will read the whole of it———not this year, for I am hastening to the story of my uncle *Toby*'s amours———but you will read it in the collection of those which have arose out of the journey across this plain—— and which, therefore, I call my

PLAIN STORIES

How far my pen has been fatigued like those of other travellers, in this journey of it, over so barren a track———the world must judge———but the traces of it, which are now all set o' vibrating together this moment, tell me 'tis the most fruitful and busy period of my life; for as I had made no convention with my man with the gun as to time———by stopping and talking to every soul I met who was not in a full trot———joining all parties before me———waiting for every soul behind———hailing all those who were coming through cross roads———arresting all kinds of beggars, pilgrims, fid- dlers, fryars———not passing by a woman in a mulberry-tree without commending her legs, and tempting her into conversation with a pinch of snuff———In short, by seizing every handle, of what size or shape soever, which chance held out to me in this journey———I turned my *plain* into a *city*———I was always in company, and with great variety too; and as my mule loved society as much as myself, and had some proposals always on his part to offer to every beast he met———I am confident we could have passed through *Pall-Mall* or St. *James*'s-Street[6] for a month together, with fewer adventures—— and seen less of human nature.

O! there is that sprightly frankness which at once unpins every plait of a *Languedocian*'s dress———that whatever is beneath it, it looks so like the simplicity which poets sing of in better days———I will delude my fancy, and believe it is so.

'Twas in the road betwixt *Nismes* and *Lunel*, where there is the best *Muscatto* wine in all *France*, and which by the bye belongs to the honest canons of MONTPELLIER———and foul befall the man who has drank it at their table, who grudges them a drop of it.

———The sun was set———they had done their work; the nymphs had tied up their hair afresh———and the swains were preparing for a carousal———My mule made a dead point———'Tis the fife and tabourin, said I———I'm frighten'd to death, quoth he———They are running at the ring of pleasure, said I, giving him a prick———By saint *Boogar*, and all the saints at the backside of the door of purgatory, said he———(making the same resolution with the ab- besse of *Andoüillets*) I'll not go a step further———'Tis very well, sir, said I———I never will argue a point with one of your family, as

---

6. Busy and fashionable streets in London.

long as I live; so leaping off his back, and kicking off one boot into this ditch, and t'other into that——I'll take a dance, said I——so stay you here.

A sun-burnt daughter of Labour rose up from the groupe to meet me as I advanced towards them; her hair, which was a dark chestnut, approaching rather to a black, was tied up in a knot, all but a single tress.

We want a cavalier, said she, holding out both her hands, as if to offer them——And a cavalier ye shall have; said I, taking hold of both of them.

Hadst thou, *Nannette*, been array'd like a dutchesse!

——But that cursed slit in thy petticoat!

Nannette cared not for it.

We could not have done without you, said she, letting go one hand, with self-taught politeness, leading me up with the other.

A lame youth, whom *Apollo* had recompenced with a pipe, and to which he had added a tabourin of his own accord, ran sweetly over the prelude, as he sat upon the bank——Tie me up this tress instantly, said *Nannette*, putting a piece of string into my hand—— It taught me to forget I was a stranger——The whole knot fell down——We had been seven years acquainted.

The youth struck the note upon the tabourin——his pipe followed, and off we bounded——"the duce take that slit!"

The sister of the youth who had stolen her voice from heaven, sung alternately with her brother——'twas a *Gascoigne* roundelay.

VIVA LA JOIA!
FIDON LA TRISTESSA![7]

The nymphs join'd in unison, and their swains an octave below them——

I would have given a crown to have it sew'd up——*Nannette* would not have given a sous——*Viva la joia!* was in her lips—— *Viva la joia!* was in her eyes. A transient spark of amity shot across the space betwixt us——She look'd amiable!——Why could I not live and end my days thus? Just disposer of our joys and sorrows, cried I, why could not a man sit down in the lap of content here ——and dance, and sing, and say his prayers, and go to heaven with this nut brown maid? capriciously did she bend her head on one side, and dance up insiduous——Then 'tis time to dance off, quoth I; so changing only partners and tunes, I danced it away from *Lunel* to *Montpellier*——from thence to *Pesçnas, Beziers*——I danced it along through *Narbonne, Carcasson*, and *Castle Naudairy*, till at last I danced myself into *Perdrillo's*[8] pavillion, where pulling

---

7. "Long live joy! Down with sadness!"   8. Pringello's?

a paper of black lines, that I might go on straight forwards, without digression or parenthesis, in my uncle *Toby*'s amours——

I begun thus——

END of the SEVENTH VOLUME.

Volume VIII.[1]

Chapter I.

——BUT softly——for in these sportive plains, and under this genial sun, where at this instant all flesh is running out piping, fiddling, and dancing to the vintage, and every step that's taken, the judgment is surprised by the imagination, I defy, not withstanding all that has been said upon *straight lines*[2] in sundry pages of my book——I defy the best cabbage planter that ever existed, whether he plants backwards or forwards, it makes little difference in the account (except that he will have more to answer for in the one case than in the other)——I defy him to go on coolly, critically, and canonically, planting his cabbages one by one, in straight lines, and stoical distances, especially if slits in petticoats are unsew'd up——without ever and anon straddling out, or sidling into some bastardly digression——In *Freeze-land*, *Fog-land* and some other lands I wot of——it may be done——

But in this clear climate of fantasy and perspiration, where every idea, sensible and insensible, gets vent——in this land, my dear *Eugenius*——in this fertile land of chivalry and romance, where I now sit, unskrewing my ink-horn to write my uncle *Toby*'s amours, and with all the meanders of JULIA's track in quest of her DIEGO, in full view of my study window——if thou comest not and takest me by the hand——

What a work is it likely to turn out!

Let us begin it.

Chapter II.

IT is with LOVE as with CUCKOLDOM——
——But now I am talking of beginning a book, and have long had a thing upon my mind to be imparted to the reader, which if not imparted now, can never be imparted to him as long as I live (whereas the COMPARISON may be imparted to him any hour in the day)——I'll just mention it, and begin in good earnest.

The thing is this.

That of all the several ways of beginning a book which are now

1. Published with Vol. VII in January 1765.　　2. Vid. Vol. VI, p. 152. [*Sterne's note.*] P. 333 in this edition.

in practice throughout the known world, I am confident my own way of doing it is the best——I'm sure it is the most religious—— for I begin with writing the first sentence——and trusting to Almighty God for the second.

'Twould cure an author for ever of the fuss and folly of opening his street-door, and calling in his neighbours and friends, and kinsfolk, with the devil and all his imps, with their hammers and engines, &c. only to observe how one sentence of mine follows another, and how the plan follows the whole.

I wish you saw me half starting out of my chair, with what confidence, as I grasp the elbow of it, I look up——catching the idea, even sometimes before it half way reaches me——

I believe in my conscience I intercept many a thought which heaven intended for another man.

Pope and his Portrait[3] are fools to me——no martyr is ever so full of faith or fire——I wish I could say of good works too——but I have no

Zeal or Anger——or

Anger or Zeal——

And till gods and men agree together to call it by the same name ——the errantest TARTUFFE,[4] in science——in politics——or in religion, shall never kindle a spark within me, or have a worse word, or a more unkind greeting, than what he will read in the next chapter.

Chapter III.

——Bon jour!——good-morrow!——so you have got your cloak on betimes!——but 'tis a cold morning, and you judge the matter rightly——'tis better to be well mounted, than go o'foot——and obstructions in the glands are dangerous——And how goes it with thy concubine——thy wife——and thy little ones o'both sides? and when did you hear from the old gentleman and lady——your sister, aunt, uncle and cousins——I hope they have got better of their colds, coughs, claps, tooth-aches, fevers, stranguries, sciaticas, swellings, and sore-eyes.——What a devil of an apothecary! to take so much blood——give such a vile purge——puke——poultice—— plaister——night-draught——glister——blister?——And why so many grains of calomel? santa Maria! and such a dose of opium! periclitating, pardi![5] the whole family of ye, from head to tail—— By my great aunt *Dinah's* old black velvet mask! I think there was no occasion for it.

3. Vid. Pope's Portrait. [*Sterne's note.*] A number of portraits of the poet Alexander Pope show him receiving inspiration from above.

4. A religious hypocrite in Moliere's play by that name.
5. "Dangerous, by God!"

Now this being a little bald about the chin, by frequently putting off and on, *before* she was got with child by the coachman——not one of our family would wear it after. To cover the MASK afresh, was more than the mask was worth——and to wear a mask which was bald, or which could be half seen through, was as bad as having no mask at all——

This is the reason, may it please your reverences, that in all our numerous family, for these four generations, we count no more than one archbishop, a *Welch* judge, some three or four aldermen, and a single mountebank[6]——

In the sixteenth century, we boast of no less than a dozen alchymists.

Chapter IV.

"I T is with Love as with Cuckoldom"——the suffering party is at least the *third*, but generally the last in the house who knows any thing about the matter: this comes, as all the world knows, from having half a dozen words for one thing; and so long, as what in this vessel of the human frame, is *Love*——may be *Hatred*, in that——*Sentiment* half a yard higher——and *Nonsense* ————————no, Madam,——not there——I mean at the part I am now pointing to with my forefinger——how can we help ourselves?

Of all mortal, and immortal men too, if you please, who ever soliloquized upon this mystic subject, my uncle *Toby* was the worst fitted, to have push'd his researches, thro' such a contention of feelings; and he had infallibly let them all run on, as we do worse matters, to see what they would turn out——had not *Bridget*'s prenotification of them to *Susannah*, and *Susannah*'s repeated manifesto's thereupon to all the world, made it necessary for my uncle *Toby* to look into the affair.

Chapter V.

W HY weavers, gardeners, and gladiators——or a man with a pined[7] leg (proceeding from some ailment in the *foot*) ——should ever have had some tender nymph breaking her heart in secret for them, are points well and duely settled and accounted for, by ancient and modern physiologists.

A water-drinker, provided he is a profess'd one, and does it without fraud or covin, is precisely in the same predicament: not that, at first sight, there is any consequence, or shew of logic in it,

---

6. A wandering clown or quack (i.e., Tristram himself).
7. Wasted (as in "pining away").

"That a rill of cold water dribbling through my inward parts, should light up a torch in my *Jenny's*——"

——The proposition does not strike one; on the contrary it seems to run opposite to the natural workings of causes and effects——

But it shews the weakness and imbecility of human reason.

——"And in perfect good health with it?"

——The most perfect——Madam, that friendship herself could wish me——

——"And drink nothing!——nothing but water?"

——Impetuous fluid! the moment thou pressest against the floodgates of the brain——see how they give way!——

In swims CURIOSITY, beckoning to her damsels to follow——they dive into the centre of the current——

FANCY sits musing upon the bank, and with her eyes following the stream, turns straws and bulrushes into masts and bowsprits ——And DESIRE, with vest held up to the knee in one hand, snatches at them, as they swim by her, with the other——

O ye water-drinkers! is it then by this delusive fountain, that ye have so often governed and turn'd this world about like a mill-wheel——grinding the faces of the impotent——be-powdering their ribs——be-peppering their noses, and changing sometimes even the very frame and face of nature——

——If I was you, quoth *Yorick,* I would drink more water, *Eugenius.*——And, if I was you, *Yorick,* replied *Eugenius,* so would I.

Which shews they had both read *Longinus*[8]——

For my own part, I am resolved never to read any book but my own, as long as I live.

Chapter VI.

I Wish my uncle *Toby* had been a water-drinker; for then the thing had been accounted for, That the first moment Widow *Wadman* saw him, she felt something stirring within her in his favour——Something!——something.

——Something perhaps more than friendship——less than love ——something——no matter what——no matter where——I would not give a single hair off my mule's tail, and be obliged to pluck it off myself (indeed the villain has not many to spare, and is not a little vicious into the bargain) to be let by your worships into the secret——

But the truth is, my uncle *Toby* was not a water-drinker; he

8. A story told in a lost part of Longinus *On the Sublime,* and re-told elsewhere, describes how Alexander the Great was told by his advisor Parmenio that if he were Alexander he would accept the peace terms offered him by an enemy. Alexander answered that he would too— if he were Parmenio.

drank it neither pure nor mix'd, or any how, or any where, except fortuitously upon some advanced posts, where better liquor was not to be had——or during the time he was under cure; when the surgeon telling him it would extend the fibres, and bring them sooner into contact——my uncle *Toby* drank it for quietness sake.

Now as all the world knows, that no effect in nature can be produced without a cause and as it is as well known, that my uncle *Toby* was neither a weaver——a gardener, or a gladiator——unless as a captain, you will needs have him one——but then he was only a captain of foot——and besides the whole is an equivocation—— There is nothing left for us to suppose, but that my uncle *Toby*'s leg——but that will avail us little in the present hypothesis, unless it had proceeded from some ailment *in the foot*——whereas his leg was not emaciated from any disorder in his foot——for my uncle *Toby*'s leg was not emaciated at all. It was a little stiff and awkward, from a total disuse of it, for the three years he lay confined at my father's house in town; but it was plump and muscular, and in all other respects as good and promising a leg as the other.

I declare, I do not recollect any one opinion or passage of my life, where my understanding was more at a loss to make ends meet, and torture the chapter I had been writing, to the service of the chapter following it, than in the present case: one would think I took a pleasure in running into difficulties of this kind, merely to make fresh experiments of getting out of 'em——Inconsiderate soul that thou art! What! are not the unavoidable distresses with which, as an author and a man, thou art hemm'd in on every side of thee——are they, *Tristram*, not sufficient, but thou must entangle thyself still more?

Is it not enough that thou art in debt, and that thou hast ten cartloads of thy fifth and sixth volumes still——still unsold, and art almost at thy wit's ends, how to get them off thy hands.

To this hour art thou not tormented with the vile asthma thou gattest in skating against the wind in *Flanders*? and is it but two months ago, that in fit of laughter, on seeing a cardinal make water like a quirister[9] (with both hands) thou brakest a vessel in thy lungs, whereby, in two hours, thou lost as many quarts of blood; and hadst thou lost as much more, did not the faculty tell thee ——it would have amounted to a gallon?——

Chapter VII.

——But for heaven's sake, let us not talk of quarts of gallons ——let us take the story straight before us; it is so nice and intri-

---

9. Chorister; choir-boy.

cate a one, it will scarce bear the transposition of a single tittle; and some how or other, you have got me thrust almost into the middle of it——

——I beg we may take more care.

Chapter VIII.

MY uncle *Toby* and the corporal had posted down with so much heat and precipitation, to take possession of the spot of ground we have so often spoke of, in order to open their campaign as early as the rest of the allies; that they had forgot one of the most necessary articles of the whole affair; it was neither a pioneer's spade, a pick-ax, or a shovel——

——It was a bed to lie on: so that as *Shandy Hall* was at that time unfurnished; and the little inn where poor *Le Fever* died, not yet built; my uncle *Toby* was constrained to accept of a bed at Mrs. *Wadman's*, for a night or two, till corporal *Trim* (who to the character of an excellent valet, groom, cook, sempster, surgeon and engineer, superadded that of an excellent upholsterer too) with the help of a carpenter and a couple of taylors, constructed one in my uncle *Toby's* house.

A daughter of *Eve*, for such was widow *Wadman*, and 'tis all the character I intend to give of her——

——"*That she was a perfect woman;*"
had better be fifty leagues off——or in her warm bed——or playing with a case-knife——or any thing you please——than make a man the object of her attention, when the house and all the furniture is her own.

There is nothing in it out of doors and in broad day-light, where a woman has a power, physically speaking, of viewing a man in more lights than one——but here, for her soul, she see him in no light without mixing something of her own goods and chattels along with him——till by reiterated acts of such combinations, he gets foisted into her inventory——

——And then good night.

But this is not matter of SYSTEM; for I have delivered that above ——nor is it matter of BREVIARY[1]——for I make no man's creed but my own——nor matter of FACT——at least that I know of; but 'tis matter copulative and introductory to what follows.

Chapter IX.

I Do not speak it with regard to the coarseness or cleanness of them——or the strength of their gussets——but pray do not night-shifts differ from day-shifts as much in this particular, as in

---

1. A book of prayers, like those that Roman Catholic monks and nuns are to recite daily.

any thing else in the world; That they so far exceed the others in length, that when you are laid down in them, they fall almost as much below the feet, as the day-shifts fall short of them?

Widow *Wadman*'s night-shifts (as was the mode I suppose in King *William*'s and Queen *Anne*'s reigns) were cut however after this fashion; and if the fashion is changed, (for in *Italy* they are come to nothing)———so much the worse for the public; they were two Flemish ells[2] and a half in length; so that allowing a moderate woman two ells, she had half an ell to spare, to do what she would with.

Now from one little indulgence gain'd after another, in the many bleak and decemberly nights of a seven years widowhood, things had insensibly come to this pass, and for the two last years had got establish'd into one of the ordinances of the bed-chamber———That as soon as Mrs. *Wadman* was put to bed, and had got her legs stretched down to the bottom of it, of which she always gave *Bridget* notice———*Bridget* with all suitable decorum, having first open'd the bed-cloaths at the feet, took hold of the half ell of cloath we are speaking of, and having gently, and with both her hands, drawn it downwards to its furthest extension, and then contracted it again side long by four or five even plaits, she took a large corking pin out of her sleeve, and with the point directed towards her, pin'd the plaits all fast together a little above the hem; which done she tuck'd all in tight at the feet, and wish'd her mistress a good night.

This was constant, and without any other variation than this; that on shivering and tempestuous nights, when *Bridget* untuck'd the feet of the bed, *&c.* to do this———she consulted no thermometer but that of her own passions; and so performed it standing———kneeling——— or squatting, according to the different degrees of faith, hope, and charity, she was in, and bore towards her mistress that night. In every other respect the *etiquette* was sacred, and might have vied with the most mechanical one of the most inflexible bed-chamber in *Christendom.*

The first night, as soon as the corporal had conducted my uncle *Toby* up stairs, which was about ten———Mrs. *Wadman* threw herself into her arm chair, and crossing her left knee with her right, which formed a resting-place for her elbow, she reclin'd her cheek upon the palm of her hand, and leaning forwards, ruminated till midnight upon both sides of the question.

The second night she went to her bureau, and having ordered *Bridget* to bring her up a couple of fresh candles and leave them upon the table, she took out her marriage-settlement, and read it over with great devotion: and the third night (which was the last of my uncle *Toby*'s stay) when *Bridget* had pull'd down the night-shift, and was assaying to stick in the corking pin———

2. A Flemish ell is about twenty-seven inches.

——With a kick of both heels at once, but at the same time the most natural kick that could be kick'd in her situation——for supposing * * * * * * * * * to be the sun in its meridian, it was a north-east kick——she kick'd the pin out of her fingers——the *etiquette* which hung upon it, down——down it fell to the ground, and was shivered into a thousand atoms.

From all which it was plain that widow *Wadman* was in love with my uncle *Toby.*

Chapter X.

M Y uncle *Toby's* head at that time was full of other matters, so that it was not till the demolition of *Dunkirk*, when all the other civilities of *Europe* were settled, that he found leisure to return this.

This made an armistice (that is speaking with regard to my uncle *Toby*——but with respect to Mrs. *Wadman*, a vacancy)——of almost eleven years. But in all cases of this nature, as it is the second blow, happen at what distance of time it will, which makes the fray——I chuse for that reason to call these the amours of my uncle *Toby* with Mrs. *Wadman*, rather than the amours of Mrs. *Wadman* with my uncle *Toby.*

This is not a distinction without a difference.

It is not like the affair of *an old hat cock'd*——and *a cock'd old hat,*[3] about which your reverences have so often been at odds with one another——but there is a difference here in the nature of things——

And let me tell you, gentry, a wide one too.

Chapter XI.

N OW as widow *Wadman* did love my uncle *Toby*——and my uncle *Toby* did not love widow *Wadman*, there was nothing for widow *Wadman* to do, but to go on and love my uncle *Toby* ——or let it alone.

Widow *Wadman* would do neither the one or the other——

——Gracious heaven!——but I forget I am a little of her temper myself; for whenever it so falls out, which it sometimes does about the equinoxes, that an earthly goddess is so much this, and that, and t'other, that I cannot eat my breakfast for her——and that she careth not three halfpence whether I eat my breakfast or no——

——Curse on her! and so I send her to *Tartary*, and from *Tartary* to *Terra del Fuego*, and so on to the devil: in short there is not

3. A cocked hat is a three-cornered hat worn with the brims cocked, or turned up. Sterne is playing on slang terms: "an old hat" is a term for the female organs, "cock" for the male.

an infernal nitch where I do not take her divinityship and stick it.

But as the heart is tender, and the passions in these tides ebb and flow ten times in a minute, I instantly bring her back again; and as I do all things in extremes, I place her in the very centre of the milky-way——

Brightest of stars! thou wilt shed thy influence upon some one——

——The duce take her and her influence too——for at that word I lose all patience——much good may it do him!——By all that is hirsute and gashly![4] I cry, taking off my furr'd cap, and twisting it round my finger——I would not give sixpence for a dozen such!

——But 'tis an excellent cap too (putting it upon my head, and pressing it close to my ears)——and warm——and soft; especially if you stroke it the right way——but alas! that will never be my luck——(so here my philosophy is shipwreck'd again)

——No; I shall never have a finger in the pye (so here I break my metaphor)——

Crust and crumb

Inside and out

Top and bottom——I detest it, I hate it, I repudiate it——I'm sick at the sight of it——

'Tis all pepper,
     garlick,
     staragen,[5]
     salt, and
     devil's dung——by the great arch cook of cooks, who does nothing, I think, from morning to night, but sit down by the fire-side and invent inflammatory dishes for us, I would not touch it for the world——

O *Tristram! Tristram!* cried *Jenny.*

O *Jenny! Jenny!* replied I, and so went on with the twelfth chapter.

Chapter XII.

——"Not touch it for the world" did I say——
Lord, how I have heated my imagination with this metaphor!

Chapter XIII.

WHICH shews, let your reverences and worships say what you will of it (for as for *thinking*——all who *do* think ——think pretty much alike, both upon it and other matters)——
LOVE is certainly, at least alphabetically speaking, one of the most

---

4. Hairy and ghastly (and also gashlike).
5. Tarragon (the herb).

A gitating
B ewitching
C onfounded
D evilish affairs of life——the most
E xtravagant
F utilitous[6]
G alligaskinish
H andy-dandyish
I racundulous (there is no K to it) and
L yrical of all human passions: at the same time, the most
M isgiving
N innyhammering
O bstipating
P ragmatical
S stridulous
R idiculous——though by the bye the R should have gone first ——But in short 'tis of such a nature, as my father once told my uncle *Toby* upon the close of a long dissertation upon the subject ——"You can scarce," said he, "combine two ideas together upon it, brother *Toby*, without an hypallage"——What's that? cried my uncle *Toby*.

The cart before the horse, replied my father——

——And what has he to do there? cried my uncle *Toby*——

Nothing, quoth my father, but to get in——or let it alone.

Now widow *Wadman*, as I told you before, would do neither the one or the other.

She stood however ready harnessed and caparisoned[7] at all points to watch accidents.

Chapter XIV.

THE Fates, who certainly all foreknew of these amours of widow *Wadman* and my uncle *Toby*, had, from the first creation of matter and motion (and with more courtesy than they usually do things of this kind) established such a chain of causes and effects hanging so fast to one another, that it was scarce possible for my uncle *Toby* to have dwelt in any other house in the world, or to have occupied any other garden in *Christendom*, but the very house and garden which join'd and laid parallel to Mrs. *Wadman's*; this, with the advantage of a thickset arbour in Mrs. *Wadman's* garden, but planted in the hedge-row of my uncle *Toby's*, put all the occasions into her hands which Love-militancy wanted; she could ob-

6. *Futilitous*: futile. *Galligaskinish*: like galligaskins (breeches). *Iracundulous*: making irascible, bad-tempered. *Ninnyhammering*: making into a fool. *Obsti-* *pating*: constipating. *Striduolus*: strident, shrill.
7. Equipped and decorated.

serve my uncle *Toby*'s motions, and was mistress likewise of his councils of war; and as his unsuspecting heart had given leave to the corporal, through the mediation of *Bridget*, to make her a wicker gate of communication to enlarge her walks, it enabled her to carry on her approaches to the very door of the sentry-box; and sometimes out of gratitude, to make the attack, and endeavour to blow my uncle *Toby* up in the very sentry-box itself.

Chapter XV.

IT is a great pity——but 'tis certain from every day's observation of man, that he may be set on fire like a candle, at either end——provided there is a sufficient wick standing out; if there is not——there's an end of the affair; and if there is——by lighting it at the bottom, as the flame in that case has the misfortune generally to put out itself——there's an end of the affair again.

For my part, could I always have the ordering of it which way I would be burnt myself——for I cannot bear the thoughts of being burnt like a beast——I would oblige a housewife constantly to light me at the top; for then I should burn down decently to the socket; that is, from my head to my heart, from my heart to my liver, from my liver to my bowels, and so on by the meseraick veins and arteries, through all the turns and lateral insertions of the intestines and their tunicles[8] to the blind gut——

——I beseech you, doctor *Slop*, quoth my uncle *Toby*, interrupting him as he mentioned the *blind gut*, in a discourse with my father the night my mother was brought to bed of me——I beseech you, quoth my uncle *Toby*, to tell me which is the blind gut; for, old as I am, I vow I do not know to this day where it lies.

The *blind gut*, answered doctor *Slop*, lies betwixt the *Illion* and *Colon*——

——In a man? said my father.

——'Tis precisely the same, cried doctor *Slop*, in a woman—— That's more than I know; quoth my father.

Chapter XVI.

——And so to make sure of both systems, Mrs. *Wadman* predetermined to light my uncle *Toby* neither at this end or that; but like a prodigal's candle, to light him, if possible, at both ends at once.

Now, through all the lumber rooms of military furniture, including both of horse and foot, from the great arsenal of *Venice* to the *Tower* of *London* (exclusive) if Mrs. *Wadman* had been rum-

---

8. *Tunicles*: coverings. *Blind gut*: an intestine shaped like a pocket. *Illion*: the third part of the small intestine.

maging for seven years together, and with *Bridget* to help her, she could not have found any one *blind* or *mantelet*[9] so fit for her purpose, as that which the expediency of my uncle *Toby*'s affairs had fix'd up ready to her hands.

I believe I have not told you——but I don't know——possibly I have——be it as it will, 'tis one of the number of those many things, which a man had better do over again, than dispute about it——That whatever town or fortress the corporal was at work upon, during the course of their campaign, my uncle *Toby* always took care on the inside of his sentry-box, which was towards his left hand, to have a plan of the place, fasten'd up with two or three pins at the top, but loose at the bottom, for the conveniency of holding it up to the eye, *&c.* . . . as occasions required; so that when an attack was resolved upon, Mrs. *Wadman* had nothing more to do, when she had got advanced to the door of the sentry-box, but to extend her right hand; and edging in her left foot at the same movement, to take hold of the map or plan, or upright, or whatever it was, and with out-stretched neck meeting it half way,——to advance it towards her; on which my uncle *Toby*'s passions were sure to catch fire——for he would instantly take hold of the other corner of the map in his left hand, and with the end of his pipe, in the other, begin an explanation.

When the attack was advanced to this point;——the world will naturally enter into the reasons of Mrs. *Wadman*'s next stroke of generalship——which was, to take my uncle *Toby*'s tobacco-pipe out of his hand as soon as she possibly could; which, under one pretence or other, but generally that of pointing more distinctly at some redoubt or breast-work in the map, she would effect before my uncle *Toby* (poor soul!) had well march'd above half a dozen toises with it.

——It obliged my uncle *Toby* to make use of his forefinger.

The difference it made in the attack was this; That in going upon it, as in the first case, with the end of her forefinger against the end of my uncle *Toby*'s tobacco-pipe, she might have travelled with it, along the lines, from *Dan* to *Beersheba*, had my uncle *Toby*'s lines reach'd so far, without any effect: For as there was no arterial or vital heat in the end of the tobacco-pipe, it could excite no sentiment——it could neither give fire by pulsation——or receive it by sympathy——'twas nothing but smoak.

Whereas, in following my uncle *Toby*'s forefinger with hers, close thro' all the little turns and indentings of his works—pressing sometimes against the side of it——then treading upon it's nail—— then tripping it up——then touching it here——then there, and so on——it set something at least in motion.

9. A protective screen.

This, tho' slight skirmishing, and at a distance from the main body, yet drew on the rest; for here, the map usually falling with the back of it, close to the side of the sentry-box, my uncle *Toby*, in the simplicity of his soul, would lay his hand flat upon it, in order to go on with his explanation; and Mrs. *Wadman*, by a manœuvre as quick as thought, would as certainly place her's close besides it; this at once opened a communication, large enough for any sentiment to pass or repass, which a person skill'd in the elementary and practical part of love-making, has occasion for——

By bringing up her forefinger parallel (as before) to my uncle *Toby*'s——it unavoidably brought the thumb into action——and the forefinger and thumb being once engaged, as naturally brought in the whole hand. Thine, dear uncle *Toby*! was never now in it's right place——Mrs. *Wadman* had it ever to take up, or, with the gentlest pushings, protrusions, and equivocal compressions, that a hand to be removed is capable of receiving——to get it press'd a hair breadth of one side out of her way.

Whilst this was doing, how could she forget to make him sensible, that it was her leg (and no one's else) at the bottom of the sentry-box, which slightly press'd against the calf of his——So that my uncle *Toby* being thus attacked and sore push'd on both his wings——was it a wonder, if now and then, it put his centre into disorder?——

——The duce take it! said my uncle *Toby*.

Chapter XVII.

THESE attacks of Mrs. *Wadman*, you will readily conceive to be of different kinds; varying from each other, like the attacks which history is full of, and from the same reasons. A general looker on, would scarce allow them to be attacks at all——or if he did, would confound them all together——but I write not to them: it will be time enough to be a little more exact in my descriptions of them, as I come up to them, which will not be for some chapters; having nothing more to add in this, but that in a bundle of original papers and drawings which my father took care to roll up by themselves, there is a plan of *Bouchain*[1] in perfect preservation (and shall be kept so, whilst I have power to preserve any thing) upon the lower corner of which, on the right hand side, there is still remaining the marks of a snuffy finger and thumb, which there is all the reason in the world to imagine, were Mrs. *Wadman*'s; for the opposite side of the margin, which I suppose to have been my uncle *Toby*'s, is absolutely clean: This seems an authenticated record of

1. A fortress under siege by Louis XIV in 1711 and 1712.

one of these attacks; for there are vestigia of the two punctures partly grown up, but still visible on the opposite corner of the map, which are unquestionably the very holes, through which it has been pricked up in the sentry-box——

By all that is priestly! I value this precious relick, with it's *stigmata* and *pricks,* more than all the relicks of the *Romish* church ——always excepting, when I am writing upon these matters, the pricks which enter'd the flesh of St. *Radagunda* in the desert, which in your road from Fesse to Cluny, the nuns of that name will shew you for love.

Chapter XVIII.

I Think, an' please your honour, quoth *Trim,* the fortifications are quite destroyed——and the bason[2] is upon a level with the mole——I think so too; replied my uncle *Toby* with a sigh half suppress'd——but step into the parlour, *Trim,* for the stipulation ——it lies upon the table.

It has lain there these six weeks, replied the corporal, till this very morning that the old woman kindled the fire with it——

——Then, said my uncle *Toby,* there is no further occasion for our services. The more, an' please your honour, the pity, said the corporal; in uttering which he cast his spade into the wheel-barrow, which was beside him, with an air the most expressive of disconsolation that can be imagined, and was heavily turning about to look for his pick-ax, his pioneer's shovel, his picquets and other little military stores, in order to carry them off the field——when a heigh ho! from the sentry-box, which, being made of thin slit deal, reverberated the sound more sorrowfully to his ear, forbad him.

——No; said the corporal to himself, I'll do it before his honour rises to-morrow morning; so taking his spade out of the wheel-barrow again, with a little earth in it, as if to level something at the foot of the glacis——but with a real intent to approach nearer to his master, in order to divert him——he loosen'd a sod or two—— pared their edges with his spade, and having given them a gentle blow or two with the back of it, he sat himself down close by my uncle *Toby*'s feet, and began as follows.

Chapter XIX.

I T was a thousand pities——though I believe, an' please your honour, I am going to say but a foolish kind of a thing for a soldier——

2. "Bason": harbor; "mole": breakwater.

A soldier, cried my uncle *Toby*, interrupting the corporal, is no more exempt from saying a foolish thing, *Trim*, than a man of letters——But not so often; an' please your honour, replied the corporal——My uncle *Toby* gave a nod.

It was a thousand pities then, said the corporal, casting his eye upon *Dunkirk*, and the mole, as *Servius Sulpicius*,[3] in returning out of *Asia* (when he sailed from *Ægina* towards *Megara*) did upon *Corinth* and *Pyreus*——

——"It was a thousand pities, an' please your honour, to destroy these works——and a thousand pities to have let them stood."——

——Thou art right, *Trim*, in both cases; said my uncle *Toby*—— This, continued the corporal, is the reason, that from the beginning of their demolition to the end——I have never once whistled, or sung, or laugh'd, or cry'd, or talk'd of pass'd done deeds, or told your honour one story good or bad——

——Thou hast many excellencies, *Trim*, said my uncle *Toby*, and I hold it not the least of them, as thou happenest to be a story-teller, that of the number thou hast told me, either to amuse me in my painful hours, or divert me in my grave ones——thou hast seldom told me a bad one——

——Because, an' please your honour, except one of a *King of Bohemia and his seven castles*,——they are all true; for they are about myself——

I do not like the subject the worse, *Trim*, said my uncle *Toby*, on that score: But prithee what is this story? thou hast excited my curiosity.

I'll tell it your honour, quoth the corporal directly——Provided, said my uncle *Toby*, looking earnestly towards *Dunkirk* and the mole again——provided it is not a merry one; to such, *Trim*, a man should ever bring one half of the entertainment along with him; and the disposition I am in at present would wrong both thee, *Trim*, and thy story——It is not a merry one by any means, replied the corporal——Nor would I have it altogether a grave one, added my uncle *Toby*——It is neither the one nor the other, replied the corporal, but will suit your honour exactly——Then I'll thank thee for it with all my heart, cried my uncle *Toby*, so prithee begin it, *Trim*.

The corporal made his reverence; and though it is not so easy a matter as the world imagines, to pull off a lank montero-cap with grace——or a whit less difficult, in my conceptions, when a man is sitting squat upon the ground, to make a bow so teeming with respect as the corporal was wont, yet by suffering the palm of his right hand, which was towards his master, to slip backward upon

3. The Roman statesman whose remarks on the transciency of great cities Walter Shandy quoted to console himself on the death of his son Bobby.

the grass, a little beyond his body, in order to allow it the greater sweep——and by an unforced compression, at the same time, of his cap with the thumb and the two forefingers of his left, by which the diameter of the cap became reduced, so that it might be said, rather to be insensibly squeez'd——then pull'd off with a flatus——the corporal acquitted himself of both, in a better manner than the posture of his affairs promised; and having hemmed twice, to find in what key his story would best go, and best suit his master's humour ——he exchanged a single look of kindness with him, and set off thus.

The Story of the king of Bohemia
and his seven castles.

THERE was a certain king of Bo - - he———

As the corporal was entering the confines of *Bohemia*, my uncle *Toby* obliged him to halt for a single moment; he had set out bare-headed, having since he pull'd off his Montero-cap in the latter end of the last chapter, left it lying beside him on the ground.

——The eye of Goodness espieth all things——so that before the corporal had well got through the first five words of his story, had my uncle *Toby* twice touch'd his Montero-cap with the end of his cane, interrogatively——as much as to say, Why don't you put it on, *Trim? Trim* took it up with the most respectful slowness, and casting a glance of humiliation as he did it, upon the embroidery of the fore-part, which being dismally tarnish'd and fray'd moreover in some of the principal leaves and boldest parts of the pattern, he lay'd it down again betwixt his two feet, in order to moralize upon the subject.

——'Tis every word of it but too true, cried my uncle *Toby*, that thou art about to observe——

"*Nothing in this world, Trim, is made to last for ever.*"

——But when tokens, dear *Tom*, of thy love and remembrance wear out, said *Trim*, what shall we say?

There is no occasion, *Trim*, quoth my uncle *Toby*, to say any thing else; and was a man to puzzle his brains till Doom's day, I believe, *Trim*, it would be impossible.

The corporal perceiving my uncle *Toby* was in the right, and that it would be in vain for the wit of man to think of extracting a purer moral from his cap, without further attempting it, he put it on; and passing his hand across his forehead to rub out a pensive wrinkle, which the text and the doctrine between them had engender'd, he return'd, with the same look and tone of voice, to his story of the king of *Bohemia* and his seven castles.

The story of the king of Bohemia and
his seven castles, continued.

THERE was a certain king of *Bohemia,* but in whose reign,
except his own, I am not able to inform your honour——
I do not desire it of thee, *Trim,* by any means, cried my uncle
Toby.

——It was a little before the time, an' please your honour, when
giants were beginning to leave off breeding;——but in what year of
our Lord that was——

——I would not give a half-penny to know, said my uncle *Toby.*

——Only, an' please your honour, it makes a story look the
better in the face——

——'Tis thy own, *Trim,* so ornament it after thy own fashion;
and take any date, continued my uncle *Toby,* looking pleasantly
upon him——take any date in the whole world thou choosest, and
put it to——thou art heartily welcome——

The corporal bowed; for of every century, and of every year of
that century, from the first creation of the world down to *Noah's*
flood; and from *Noah's* flood to the birth of *Abraham*; through all
the pilgrimages of the patriarchs, to the departure of the *Israelites*
out of *Egypt*——and throughout all the Dynasties, Olympiads,
Urbecondita's, and other memorable epochas of the different nations of the world, down to the coming of Christ, and from thence
to the very moment in which the corporal was telling his story——
had my uncle *Toby* subjected this vast empire of time and all its
abysses at his feet; but as MODESTY scarce touches with a finger
what LIBERALITY offers her with both hands open——the corporal
contented himself with the very *worst year* of the whole bunch;
which, to prevent your honours of the Majority and Minority from
tearing the very flesh off your bones in contestation, 'Whether that
year is not always the last cast-year[4] of the last cast-almanack'——
I tell you plainly it was; but from a different reason than you wot
of——

——It was the year next him——which being the year of our
Lord seventeen hundred and twelve, when the duke of *Ormond* was
playing the devil in *Flanders*——the corporal took it, and set out
with it afresh on his expedition to *Bohemia.*

The story of the king of Bohemia and
his seven castles, continued.

4. "Cast": thrown away.

IN the year of our Lord one thousand seven hundred and twelve, there was, an' please your honour——

——To tell thee truly, *Trim*, quoth my uncle *Toby*, any other date would have pleased me much better, not only on account of the sad stain upon our history that year, in marching off our troops, and refusing to cover the siege of *Quesnoi*, though *Fagel* was carrying on the works with such incredible vigour——but likewise on the score, *Trim*, of thy own story; because if there are——and which, from what thou hast dropt, I partly suspect to be the fact——if there are giants in it——

There is but one, an' please your honour——

——'Tis as bad as twenty, replied my uncle *Toby*——thou should'st have carried him back some seven or eight hundred years out of harm's way, both of criticks and other people; and therefore I would advise thee, if ever thou tellest it again——

——If I live, an' please your honour, but once to get through it, I will never tell it again, quoth *Trim*, either to man, woman, or child——Poo——poo! said my uncle *Toby*——but with accents of such sweet encouragement did he utter it, that the corporal went on with his story with more alacrity than ever.

The story of the king of Bohemia and
his seven castles, continued.

THERE was, an' please your honour, said the corporal, raising his voice and rubbing the palms of his two hands cheerily together as he begun, a certain king of *Bohemia*——

——Leave out the date entirely, *Trim*, quoth my uncle *Toby*, leaning forwards, and laying his hand gently upon the corporal's shoulder to temper the interruption——leave it out entirely, *Trim*; a story passes very well without these niceties, unless one is pretty sure of 'em——Sure of 'em! said the corporal, shaking his head——

Right; answered my uncle *Toby*, it is not easy, *Trim*, for one, bred up as thou and I have been to arms, who seldom looks further forward than to the end of his musket, or backwards beyond his knapsack, to know much about this matter——God bless your honour! said the corporal, won by the *manner* of my uncle *Toby*'s reasoning, as much as by the reasoning itself, he has something else to do; if not on action, or a march, or upon duty in his garrison ——he has his firelock, an' please your honour, to furbish——his accoutrements to take care of——his regimentals to mend—— himself to shave and keep clean, so as to appear always like what he is upon the parade; what business, added the corporal triumphantly, has a soldier, an' please your honour, to know any thing at all of *geography*?

——Thou would'st have said *chronology*, *Trim*, said my uncle *Toby*; for as for geography, 'tis of absolute use to him; he must be acquainted intimately with every country and its boundaries where his profession carries him; he should know every town and city, and village and hamlet, with the canals, the roads, and hollow ways which lead up to them; there is not a river or a rivulet he passes, *Trim*, but he should be able at first sight to tell thee what is its name——in what mountains it takes its rise——what is its course ——how far it is navigable——where fordable——where not; he should know the fertility of every valley, as well as the hind who ploughs it; and be able to describe, or, if it is required, to give thee an exact map of all the plains and defiles, the forts, the acclivities, the woods and morasses, thro' and by which his army is to march; he should know their produce, their plants, their minerals, their waters, their animals, their seasons, their climates, their heats and cold, their inhabitants, their customs, their language, their policy, and even their religion.

Is it else to be conceived, corporal, continued my uncle *Toby*, rising up in his sentry-box, as he began to warm in this part of his discourse——how *Marlborough* could have marched his army from the banks of the *Maes* to *Belburg*; from *Belburg* to *Kerpenord*—— (here the corporal could sit no longer) from *Kerpenord*, *Trim*, to *Kalsaken*; from *Kalsaken* to *Newdorf*; from *Newdorf* to *Landenbourg*; from *Landenbourg* to *Mildenheim*; from *Mildenheim* to *Elchigen*; from *Elchigen* to *Gingen*; from *Gingen* to *Balmerchoffen*; from *Balmerchoffen* to *Skellenburg*, where he broke in upon the enemy's works; forced his passage over the *Danube*; cross'd the *Lech*——pushed on his troops into the heart of the empire, marching at the head of them through *Friburg*, *Hokenwert*, and *Schonevelt*, to the plains of *Blenheim*[5] and *Hochstet*?——Great as he was, corporal, he could not have advanced a step, or made one single day's march without the aids of *Geography*——As for *Chronology*, I own, *Trim*, continued my uncle *Toby*, sitting down again coolly in his sentry-box, that of all others, it seems a science which the soldier might best spare, was it not for the lights which that science must one day give him, in determining the invention of powder; the furious execution of which, renversing every thing like thunder before it, has become a new æra to us of military improvements, changing so totally the nature of attacks and defences both by sea

5. Blenheim was one of Marlborough's most impressive victories (1704). The other places are on his line of march into Austria.

and land, and awakening so much art and skill in doing it, that the world cannot be too exact in ascertaining the precise time of its discovery, or too inquisitive in knowing what great man was the discoverer, and what occasions gave birth to it.

I am far from controverting, continued my uncle *Toby*, what historians agree in, that in the year of our Lord 1380, under the reign of *Wenceslaus*, son of *Charles* the fourth——a certain priest, whose name was *Schwartz*,[6] shew'd the use of powder to the *Venetians*, in their wars against the *Genoese*; but 'tis certain he was not the first; because if we are to believe Don *Pedro* the bishop of *Leon*[7]——How came priests and bishops, an' please your honour, to trouble their heads so much about gun-powder?   God knows, said my uncle *Toby*——his providence brings good out of every thing——and he avers, in his chronicle of King *Alphonsus*, who reduced *Toledo*, That in the year 1343, which was full thirty seven years before that time, the secret of powder was well known, and employed with success, both by Moors and Christians, not only in their sea-combats, at that period, but in many of their most memorable sieges in *Spain* and *Barbary*——And all the world knows, that Friar *Bacon*[8] had wrote expressly about it, and had generously given the world a receipt to make it by, above a hundred and fifty years before even *Schwartz* was born——And that the *Chinese*, added my uncle *Toby*, embarass us, and all accounts of it still more, by boasting of the invention some hundreds of years even before him——

——They are a pack of liars, I believe, cried *Trim*——

——They are some how or other deceived, said my uncle *Toby*, in this matter, as is plain to me from the present miserable state of military architecture amongst them; which consists of nothing more than a fossé with a brick wall without flanks——and for what they give us as a bastion at each angle of it, 'tis so barbarously constructed, that it looks for all the world—— —— Like one of my seven castles, an' please your honour, quoth *Trim*.

My uncle *Toby*, tho' in the utmost distress for a comparison, most courteously refused *Trim*'s offer——till *Trim* telling him, he had half a dozen more in *Bohemia*, which he knew not how to get off his hands——my uncle *Toby* was so touch'd with the pleasantry of heart of the corporal——that he discontinued his dissertation upon gunpowder——and begged the corporal forthwith to go on with his story of the King of *Bohemia* and his seven castles.

---

6. A German monk said to have invented gunpowder around 1330.
7. Don *Pedro* was a twelfth-century bishop, so Toby probably means Peter Mexia, whose name is also mentioned in the article on gunpowder in Chambers's *Cyclopedia*.
8. Roger Bacon's thirteenth-century treatise *De Mirabili Potestate et Naturae* [Of the Marvelous Power of Art and Nature] contains a discussion of gunpowder.

The story of the king of Bohemia and
his seven castles, continued.

THIS *unfortunate* King of *Bohemia*, said *Trim*——Was he unfortunate then? cried my uncle *Toby*, for he had been so wrapt
up in his dissertation upon gun-powder and other military affairs,
that tho' he had desired the corporal to go on, yet the many interruptions he had given, dwelt not so strong upon his fancy, as to
account for the epithet——Was he *unfortunate* then, *Trim?* said my
uncle *Toby*, pathetically——The corporal, wishing first the *word*
and all its synonimas at the devil, forthwith began to run back in his
mind, the principal events in the King of *Bohemia's* story; from
every one of which, it appearing that he was the most fortunate
man that ever existed in the world——it put the corporal to a
stand: for not caring to retract his epithet——and less, to explain
it——and least of all, to twist his tale (like men of lore) to serve a
system——he looked up in my uncle *Toby's* face for assistance——
but seeing it was the very thing, my uncle *Toby* sat in expectation of
himself——after a hum and a haw, he went on——

The King of *Bohemia*, an' please your honour, replied the corporal, was *unfortunate*, as thus——That taking great pleasure and
delight in navigation and all sort of sea-affairs——and there *happening* throughout the whole kingdom of *Bohemia*, to be no sea-
port town whatever——

How the duce should there——*Trim?* cried my uncle *Toby*; for
Bohemia being totally inland, it could have happen'd no otherwise
——It might; said *Trim*, if it had pleased God——

My uncle *Toby* never spoke of the being and natural attributes of
God, but with diffidence and hesitation——

——I believe not, replied my uncle *Toby*, after some pause——
for being inland, as I said, and having *Silesia* and *Moravia* to the
east; *Lusatia* and *Upper Saxony* to the north; *Franconia* to the
west; and *Bavaria* to the south: *Bohemia* could not have been
propell'd to the sea, without ceasing to be *Bohemia*——nor could
the sea, on the other hand, have come up to *Bohemia*, without
overflowing a great part of *Germany*, and destroying millions of
unfortunate inhabitants who could make no defence against it——
Scandalous! cried *Trim*——Which would bespeak, added my uncle
Toby, mildly, such a want of compassion in him who is the father
of it——that, I think, *Trim*——the thing could have happen'd no
way.

The corporal made the bow of unfeigned conviction; and went on.

Now the King of *Bohemia* with his queen and courtiers *happening* one fine summer's evening to walk out——Aye! there the word
happening is right, *Trim*, cried my uncle *Toby*; for the King of

Bohemia and his queen might have walk'd out, or let it alone;——— 'twas a matter of contingency, which might happen, or not, just as chance ordered it.

King *William* was of an opinion, an' please your honour, quoth *Trim*, that every thing was predestined for us in this world; insomuch, that he would often say to his soldiers, that "every ball had it's billet." He was a great man, said my uncle *Toby*———And I believe, continued *Trim*, to this day, that the shot which disabled me at the battle of *Landen*, was pointed at my knee for no other purpose, but to take me out of his service, and place me in your honour's, where I should be taken so much better care of in my old age———It shall never, *Trim*, be construed otherwise, said my uncle *Toby*.

The heart, both of the master and the man, were alike subject to sudden overflowings;———a short silence ensued.

Besides, said the corporal, resuming the discourse———but in a gayer accent———if it had not been for that single shot, I had never, an' please your honour, been in love———

So, thou wast once in love, *Trim*! said my uncle *Toby*, smiling———

Souse! replied the corporal   over head and ears! an' please your honour. Prithee when? where?———and how came it to pass?

———I never heard one word of it before; quoth my uncle *Toby*: ———I dare say, answered *Trim*, that every drummer and serjeant's son in the regiment knew of it———Its high time I should———said my uncle *Toby*.

Your honour remembers with concern, said the corporal, the total rout and confusion of our camp and army at the affair of *Landen*; every one was left to shift for himself; and if it had not been for the regiments of *Wyndham*, *Lumley*, and *Galway*, which covered the retreat over the bridge of *Neerspeeken*, the king himself could scarce have gain'd it———he was press'd hard, as your honour knows, on every side of him———

Gallant mortal! cried my uncle *Toby*, caught up with enthusiasm ———this moment, now that all is lost, I see him galloping across me, corporal, to the left, to bring up the remains of the English horse along with him to support the right, and tear the laurel from *Luxembourg's*[9] brows, if yet 'tis possible———I see him with the knot of his scarfe just shot off, infusing fresh spirits into poor *Galway*'s regiment———riding along the line———then wheeling about, and charging *Conti* at the head of it———Brave! brave by heaven! cried my uncle *Toby*———he deserves a crown———As richly, as a thief a halter; shouted *Trim*.

9. Francois-Henri, Duc de Luxembourg (1628–95) was the victorious French commander at the battle of Landan. The other names are those of generals on the French and British sides.

My uncle *Toby* knew the corporal's loyalty;——otherwise the comparison was not at all to his mind——it did not altogether strike the corporal's fancy when he had made it——but it could not be recall'd——so he had nothing to do, but proceed.

As the number of wounded was prodigious, and no one had time to think of any thing, but his own safety——Though *Talmash*, said to my uncle *Toby*, brought off the foot with great prudence——But I was left upon the field, said the corporal. Thou wast so; poor fellow! replied my uncle *Toby*——So that it was noon the next day, continued the corporal, before I was exchanged, and put into a cart with thirteen or fourteen more, in order to be convey'd to our hospital.

There is no part of the body, an' please your honour, where a wound occasions more intolerable anguish than upon the knee——

Except the groin; said my uncle *Toby*. An' please your honour, replied the corporal, the knee, in my opinion, must certainly be the most acute, there being so many tendons and what-d'ye-call-'ems all about it.

It is for that reason, quoth my uncle *Toby*, that the groin is infinitely more sensible——there being not only as many tendons and what-d'ye-call-'ems (for I know their names as little as thou do'st)——about it——but moreover * * *——

Mrs. *Wadman*, who had been all the time in her arbour—— instantly stopp'd her breath——unpinn'd her mob[1] at the chin, and stood up upon one leg——

The dispute was maintained with amicable and equal force betwixt my uncle *Toby* and *Trim* for some time; till *Trim* at length recollecting that he had often cried at his master's sufferings, but never shed a tear at his own——was for giving up the point, which my uncle *Toby* would not allow——'Tis a proof of nothing, *Trim*, said he, but the generosity of thy temper——

So that whether the pain of a wound in the groin (cæteris paribus[2]) is greater than the pain of a wound in the knee——or

Whether the pain of a wound in the knee is not greater than the pain of a wound in the groin——are points which to this day remain unsettled.

Chapter XX.

THE anguish of my knee, continued the corporal, was excessive in itself; and the uneasiness of the cart, with the roughness of the roads which were terribly cut up——making bad still worse ——every step was death to me: so that with the loss of blood, and

1. That is, her mob-cap, tied at the chin and covering her ears.
2. "Other things being equal."

the want of care-taking of me, and a fever I felt coming on besides ——(Poor soul! said my uncle *Toby*) all together, an' please your honour, was more than I could sustain.

I was telling my sufferings to a young woman at a peasant's house, where our cart, which was the last of the line, had halted; they had help'd me in, and the young woman had taken a cordial out of her pocket and dropp'd it upon some sugar, and seeing it had cheer'd me, she had given it me a second and a third time——So I was telling her, an' please your honour, the anguish I was in, and was saying it was so intolerable to me, that I had much rather lie down upon the bed, turning my face towards one which was in the corner of the room——and die, than go on——when, upon her attempting to lead me to it, I fainted away in her arms. She was a good soul! as your honour, said the corporal, wiping his eyes, will hear.

I thought *love* had been a joyous thing, quoth my uncle *Toby*.

'Tis the most serious thing, an' please your honour (sometimes) that is in the world.

By the persuasion of the young woman, continued the corporal, the cart with the wounded men set off without me: she had assured them I should expire immediately if I was put into the cart. So when I came to myself——I found myself in a still quiet cottage, with no one but the young woman, and the peasant and his wife. I was laid across the bed in the corner of the room, with my wounded leg upon a chair, and the young woman beside me, holding the corner of her handkerchief dipp'd in vinegar to my nose with one hand, and rubbing my temples with the other.

I took her at first for the daughter of the peasant (for it was no inn)——so had offer'd her a little purse with eighteen florins, which my poor brother *Tom* (here *Trim* wip'd his eyes) had sent me as a token, by a recruit, just before he set out for *Lisbon*——

——I never told your honour that piteous story yet——here *Trim* wiped his eyes a third time.

The young woman call'd the old man and his wife into the room, to shew them the money, in order to gain me credit for a bed and what little necessaries I should want, till I should be in a condition to be got to the hospital——Come then! said she, tying up the little purse——I'll be your banker——but as that office alone will not keep me employ'd, I'll be your nurse too.

I thought by her manner of speaking this, as well as by her dress, which I then began to consider more attentively——that the young woman could not be the daughter of the peasant.

She was in black down to her toes, with her hair conceal'd under a cambrick border, laid close to her forehead: she was one of those kind of nuns, an' please your honour, of which, your honour

knows, there are a good many in *Flanders* which they let go loose
——By thy description, *Trim*, said my uncle *Toby*, I dare say she
was a young *Beguine*, of which there are none to be found any
where but in the *Spanish Netherlands*——except at *Amsterdam*
——they differ from nuns in this, that they can quit their cloister if
they choose to marry; they visit and take care of the sick by profession——I had rather, for my own part, they did it out of good-
nature.

——She often told me, quoth *Trim*, she did it for the love of
Christ——I did not like it.——I believe, *Trim*, we are both wrong,
said my uncle *Toby*——we'll ask Mr. *Yorick* about it to-night at
my brother *Shandy's*——so put me in mind; added my uncle *Toby*.

The young *Beguine*, continued the corporal, had scarce given
herself time to tell me "she would be my nurse," when she hastily
turned about to begin the office of one, and prepare something for
me——and in a short time——though I thought it a long one——
she came back with flannels, &c. &c. and having fomented my knee
soundly for a couple of hours, &c. and made me a thin basin of
gruel for my supper——she wish'd me rest, and promised to be with
me early in the morning.——She wish'd me, an' please your honour, what was not to be had. My fever ran very high that night——
her figure made sad disturbance within me——I was every moment
cutting the world in two——to give her half of it——and every
moment was I crying, That I had nothing but a knapsack and
eighteen florins to share with her——The whole night long was the
fair *Beguine*, like an angel, close by my bedside, holding back my
curtain and offering me cordials——and I was only awakened from
my dream by her coming there at the hour promised, and giving
them in reality. In truth, she was scarce ever from me, and so
accustomed was I to receive life from her hands, that my heart
sickened, and I lost colour when she left the room: and yet, continued the corporal (making one of the strangest reflections upon it
in the world)——

——"*It was not love*"——for during the three weeks she was
almost constantly with me, fomenting my knee with her hand, night
and day——I can honestly say, an' please your honour——that　＊
　＊　＊　＊　＊　＊　＊　＊　＊　＊　＊
＊　＊　＊　＊　＊　＊　once.

That was very odd, *Trim*, quoth my uncle *Toby*——
I think so too——said Mrs. *Wadman*.
It never did, said the corporal.

Chapter XXI.

——But 'tis no marvel, continued the corporal——seeing my
uncle *Toby* musing upon it——for Love, an' please your honour, is

exactly like war, in this; that a soldier, though he has escaped three weeks compleat o'*Saturday*-night,——may nevertheless be shot through his heart on *Sunday* morning——*It happened so here*, an' please your honour, with this difference only——that it was on *Sunday* in the afternoon, when I fell in love all at once with a sisserara[3]——it burst upon me, an' please your honour, like a bomb ——scarce giving me time to say, "God bless me."

I thought, *Trim*, said my uncle *Toby*, a man never fell in love so very suddenly.

Yes, an' please your honour, if he is in the way of it——replied *Trim*.

I prithee, quoth my uncle *Toby*, inform me how this matter happened.

——With all pleasure, said the corporal, making a bow.

Chapter XXII.

I Had escaped, continued the corporal, all that time from falling in love, and had gone on to the end of the chapter, had it not been predestined otherwise——there is no resisting our fate.

It was on a *Sunday*, in the afternoon, as I told your honour——

The old man and his wife had walked out——

Every thing was still and hush as midnight about the house——

There was not so much as a duck or a duckling about the yard——

——When the fair *Beguine* came in to see me.

My wound was then in a fair way of doing well——the inflammation had been gone off for some time, but it was succeeded with an itching both above and below my knee, so insufferable, that I had not shut my eyes the whole night for it.

Let me see it, said she, kneeling down upon the ground parallel to my knee, and laying her hand upon the part below it——It only wants rubbing a little, said the *Beguine*; so covering it with the bed cloaths, she began with the forefinger of her right-hand to rub under my knee, guiding her fore-finger backwards and forwards by the edge of the flannel which kept on the dressing.

In five or six minutes I felt slightly the end of the second finger ——and presently it was laid flat with the other, and she continued rubbing in that way round and round for a good while; it then came into my head, that I should fall in love——I blush'd when I saw how white a hand she had——I shall never, an' please your honour, behold another hand so white whilst I live——

——Not in that place: said my uncle *Toby*——

Though it was the most serious despair in nature to the corporal ——he could not forbear smiling.

---

3. Suddenly, arrestingly.

The young *Beguine*, continued the corporal, perceiving it was of great service to me——from rubbing, for some time, with two fingers——proceeded to rub at length, with three——till by little and little she brought down the fourth, and then rubb'd with her whole hand: I will never say another word, an' please your honour, upon hands again——but it was softer than satin——

——Prithee, *Trim*, commend it as much as thou wilt, said my uncle *Toby*; I shall hear thy story with the more delight——The corporal thank'd his master most unfeignedly; but having nothing to say upon the *Beguine*'s hand, but the same over again——he proceeded to the effects of it.

The fair *Beguine*, said the corporal, continued rubbing with her whole hand under my knee——till I fear'd her zeal would weary her——"I would do a thousand times more," said she, "for the love of Christ"——In saying which she pass'd her hand across the flannel, to the part above my knee, which I had equally complained of, and rubb'd it also.

I perceived, then, I was beginning to be in love——

As she continued rub-rub-rubbing——I felt it spread from under her hand, an' please your honour, to every part of my frame——

The more she rubb'd, and the longer strokes she took——the more the fire kindled in my veins——till at length, by two or three strokes longer than the rest——my passion rose to the highest pitch ——I seiz'd her hand——

——And then, thou clapped'st it to thy lips, *Trim*, said my uncle *Toby*——and madest a speech.

Whether the corporal's amour terminated precisely in the way my uncle *Toby* described it, is not material; it is enough that it contain'd in it the essence of all the love-romances which ever have been wrote since the beginning of the world.

Chapter XXIII.

As soon as the corporal had finished the story of his amour ——or rather my uncle *Toby* for him—Mrs. *Wadman* silently sallied forth from her arbour, replaced the pin in her mob, pass'd the wicker gate, and advanced slowly towards my uncle *Toby*'s sentry-box: the disposition which *Trim* had made in my uncle *Toby*'s mind, was too favourable a crisis to be let slipp'd——

——The attack was determin'd upon: it was facilitated still more by my uncle *Toby*'s having ordered the corporal to wheel off the pioneer's shovel, the spade, the pick-axe, the picquets, and other military stores which lay scatter'd upon the ground where *Dunkirk* stood——The corporal had march'd——the field was clear.

Now consider, sir, what nonsense it is, either in fighting, or writing, or any thing else (whether in rhyme to it, or not) which a man has occasion to do——to act by plan: for if ever Plan, independent of all circumstances, deserved registering in letters of gold (I mean in the archives of *Gotham*[4])——it was certainly the PLAN of Mrs *Wadman*'s attack of my uncle *Toby* in his sentry-box, BY PLAN——Now the Plan hanging up in it at this juncture, being the Plan of *Dunkirk*——and the tale of *Dunkirk* a tale of relaxation, it opposed every impression she could make: and besides, could she have gone upon it——the manœuvre of fingers and hands in the attack of the sentry-box, was so outdone by that of the fair *Beguine*'s in *Trim*'s story——that just then, that particular attack, however successful before——became the most heartless attack that could be made——

O! let woman alone for this. Mrs. *Wadman* had scarce open'd the wicker-gate, when her genius sported with the change of circumstances.

——She formed a new attack in a moment.

Chapter XXIV.

——I am half distracted, captain *Shandy*, said Mrs. *Wadman*, holding up her cambrick handkerchief to her left eye, as she approach'd the door of my uncle *Toby*'s sentry-box——a mote——or sand——or something——I know not what, has got into this eye of mine——do look into it——it is not in the white——

In saying which, Mrs. *Wadman* edged herself close in beside my uncle *Toby*, and squeezing herself down upon the corner of his bench, she gave him an opportunity of doing it without rising up————Do look into it——said she.

Honest soul! thou didst look into it with as much innocency of heart, as ever child look'd into a raree-shew-box;[5] and 'twere as much a sin to have hurt thee.

——If a man will be peeping of his own accord into things of that nature—I've nothing to say to it——

My uncle *Toby* never did: and I will answer for him, that he would have sat quietly upon a sopha from *June* to *January*, (which, you know, takes in both the hot and cold months) with an eye as fine as the *Thracian*[6] *Rodope*'s besides him, without being able to tell, whether it was a black or a blue one.

---

4. In legend the people of Gotham in Nottinghamshire pretended to be fools in order to prevent King John from settling there; so they are known as wise fools.
5. A small box with pictures to be seen through a lens.
6. Rodope Thracia tam inevitabili fas-

cino instructa, tan exacte oculis intuens attraxit, ut si in illam quis incidesset, fieri non posset, quin caperetur.——I know not who. [*Sterne's note.*] "Rhodopis of Thrace (a courtesan) had such an inevitable fascination and drew people to her so perfectly with her eyes when she looked at anyone, that if any-

The difficulty was to get my uncle *Toby*, to look at one, at all.
'Tis surmounted. And

I see him yonder with his pipe pendulous in his hand, and the
ashes falling out of it——looking——and looking——then rubbing
his eyes——and looking again, with twice the good nature that ever
Gallileo look'd for a spot in the sun.[7]

——In vain! for by all the powers which animate the organ——
Widow *Wadman*'s left eye shines this moment as lucid as her right
——there is neither mote, or sand, or dust, or chaff, or speck, or
particle of opake matter floating in it——there is nothing, my dear
paternal uncle! but one lambent delicious fire, furtively shooting out
from every part of it, in all directions, into thine——

——If thou lookest, uncle *Toby*, in search of this mote one
moment longer——thou art undone.

Chapter XXV.

AN eye is for all the world exactly like a cannon, in this respect;
That it is not so much the eye or the cannon, in themselves,
as it is the carriage of the eye——and the carriage of the cannon,
by which both the one and the other are enabled to do so much
execution. I don't think the comparison a bad one: However, as 'tis
made and placed at the head of the chapter, as much for use as
ornament, all I desire in return, is, that whenever I speak of Mrs.
Wadman's eyes (except once in the next period) that you keep it in
your fancy.

I protest, Madam, said my uncle *Toby*, I can see nothing whatever in your eye.

It is not in the white; said Mrs. *Wadman*: my uncle *Toby* look'd
with might and main into the pupil——

Now of all the eyes, which ever were created——from your own,
Madam, up to those of *Venus* herself, which certainly were as
venereal a pair of eyes as ever stood in a head——there never was
an eye of them all, so fitted to rob my uncle *Toby* of his repose, as
the very eye, at which he was looking——it was not, Madam, a
rolling eye——a romping or a wanton one——nor was it an eye
sparkling——petulant or imperious——of high claims and terrifying exactions, which would have curled at once that milk of human
nature, of which my uncle *Toby* was made up——but 'twas an eye
full of gentle salutations——and soft responses——speaking——

one met her, it was impossible for him
not to be captivated." Although Tris-
trim says he does not know the source
of the passage, it comes from Helio-
dorus, *An Aethiopian History*, a Greek
romance of the third century B.C. Sterne
took it (in this Latin version) from
Burton's *Anatomy of Melancholy*.
7. Galileo published *Letters on the Solar
Spots* in 1613, and was given credit for
their discovery.

not like the trumpet stop of some ill-made organ, in which many an eye I talk to, holds coarse converse——but whispering soft——like the last low accents of an expiring saint——"How can you live comfortless, captain *Shandy*, and alone, without a bosom to lean your head on——or trust your cares to?"

It was an eye——

But I shall be in love with it myself, if I say another word about it.

——It did my uncle *Toby*'s business.

Chapter XXVI.

THERE is nothing shews the characters of my father and my uncle *Toby*, in a more entertaining light, than their different manner of deportment, under the same accident——for I call not love a misfortune, from a persuasion, that a man's heart is ever the better for it——Great God! what must my uncle *Toby*'s have been, when 'twas all benignity without it.

My father, as appears from many of his papers, was very subject to this passion, before he married——but from a little subacid kind of drollish impatience in his nature, whenever it befell him, he would never submit to it like a christian; but would pish, and huff, and bounce, and kick, and play the Devil, and write the bitterest Philippicks against the eye that ever man wrote——there is one in verse upon some body's eye or other, that for two or three nights together, had put him by his rest; which in his first transport of resentment against it, he begins thus:

> "A Devil 'tis——and mischief such doth work
> As never yet did *Pagan, Jew*, or *Turk*."[8]

In short during the whole paroxism, my father was all abuse and foul language, approaching rather towards malediction——only he did not do it with as much method as *Ernulphus*——he was too impetuous; nor with *Ernulphus*'s policy——for tho' my father, with the most intolerant spirit, would curse both this and that, and every thing under heaven, which was either aiding or abetting to his love——yet never concluded his chapter of curses upon it, without cursing himself in at the bargain, as one of the most egregious fools and coxcombs, he would say, that ever was let loose in the world.

My uncle *Toby*, on the contrary, took it like a lamb——sat still and let the poison work in his veins without resistance——in the sharpest exacerbations of his wound (like that on his groin) he

---

8. This will be printed with my father's life of Socrates, &c. &c. [*Sterne's note.*] The passage is quoted in Burton's *Anat-omy of Melancholy*, and attributed to Robert Tofte.

never dropt one fretful or discontented word——he blamed neither heaven nor earth——or thought or spoke an injurious thing of any body, or any part of it; he sat solitary and pensive with his pipe—— looking at his lame leg——then whiffing out a sentimental heigh ho! which mixing with the smoak, incommoded no one mortal.

He took it like a lamb——I say.

In truth he had mistook it at first; for having taken a ride with my father, that very morning, to save if possible a beautiful wood, which the dean and chapter were hewing down to give to the poor;[9] which said wood being in full view of my uncle *Toby*'s house, and of singular service to him in his description of the battle of *Wynnendale*——by trotting on too hastily to save it——upon an uneasy saddle——worse horse, *&c. &c.* . . it had so happened, that the serous part of the blood had got betwixt the two skins, in the nethermost part of my uncle *Toby*——the first shootings of which (as my uncle *Toby* had no experience of love) he had taken for a part of the passion——till the blister breaking in the one case—— and the other remaining——my uncle *Toby* was presently convinced, that his wound was not a skin-deep-wound——but that it had gone to his heart.

Chapter XXVII.

THE world is ashamed of being virtuous——My uncle *Toby* knew little of the world; and therefore when he felt he was in love with widow *Wadman*, he had no conception that the thing was any more to be made a mystery of, than if Mrs. *Wadman*, had given him a cut with a gap'd[1] knife across his finger: Had it been otherwise——yet as he ever look'd upon *Trim* as a humble friend; and saw fresh reasons every day of his life, to treat him as such—— it would have made no variation in the manner in which he informed him of the affair.

"I am in love, corporal!" quoth my uncle *Toby*.

Chapter XXVIII.

IN love!——said the corporal——your honour was very well the day before yesterday, when I was telling your honour the story of the King of *Bohemia*——*Bohemia*! said my uncle *Toby* - - - musing a long time - - - What became of that story, *Trim*?

——We lost it, an' please your honour, somehow betwixt us—— but your honour was as free from love then, as I am——'twas, just

---

9. Mr. Shandy must mean the poor *in spirit*; inasmuch as they divided the mo- ney amongst themselves. [*Sterne's note.*]
1. Gaping, open.

whilst thou went'st off with the wheel-barrow——with Mrs. *Wad-man*, quoth my uncle *Toby*——She has left a ball here——added my uncle *Toby*——pointing to his breast——

——She can no more, an' please your honour, stand a siege, than she can fly——cried the corporal——

——But as we are neighbours, *Trim*,——the best way I think is to let her know it civilly first——quoth my uncle *Toby*.

Now if I might presume, said the corporal, to differ from your honour——

——Why else, do I talk to thee *Trim*: said my uncle *Toby*, mildly——

——Then I would begin, an' please your honour, with making a good thundering attack upon her, in return——and telling her civilly afterwards——for if she knows any thing of your honour's being in love, before hand——L—d help her!——she knows no more at present of it, *Trim*, said my uncle *Toby*——than the child unborn——

Precious souls!——

Mrs. *Wadman* had told it with all its circumstances, to Mrs. *Bridget* twenty-four hours before; and was at that very moment sitting in council with her, touching some slight misgivings with regard to the issue of the affair, which the Devil, who never lies dead in a ditch, had put into her head——before he would allow half time, to get quietly through her *te Deum*[2]——

I am terribly afraid, said widow *Wadman*, in case I should marry him *Bridget*——that the poor captain will not enjoy his health, with the monstrous wound upon his groin——

It may not, Madam, be so very large, replied *Bridget*, as you think——and I believe besides, added she——that 'tis dried up——

——I could like to know——merely for his sake, said Mrs. *Wadman*——

——We'll know the long and the broad of it, in ten days—— answered Mrs. *Bridget*, for whilst the captain is paying his addresses to you——I'm confident Mr. *Trim* will be for making love to me ——and I'll let him as much as he will——added *Bridget*——to get it all out of him——

The measures were taken at once——and my uncle *Toby* and the corporal went on with theirs.

Now, quoth the corporal, setting his left hand a kimbo, and giving such a flourish with his right, as just promised success—— and no more——if your honour will give me leave to lay down the plan of this attack——

——Thou wilt please me by it, *Trim*, said my uncle *Toby*, ex-

2. That is, her victory hymn.

ceedingly——and as I foresee thou must act in it as my *aid de camp*, here's a crown, corporal, to begin with, to steep[3] thy commission.

Then, an' please your honour, said the corporal (making a bow first for his commission)——we will begin with getting your honour's laced cloaths out of the great campaign-trunk, to be well-air'd, and have the blue and gold taken up at the sleeves——and I'll put your white ramallie-wig fresh into pipes[4]——and send for a taylor, to have your honour's thin scarlet breeches turn'd——

——I had better take the red plush ones, quoth my uncle *Toby*

——They will be too clumsy——said the corporal.

Chapter XXIX.

——Thou wilt get a brush and a little chalk[5] to my sword——
'Twill be only in your honour's way, replied *Trim*.

Chapter XXX.

——But your honour's two razors shall be new set——and I will get my Montero-cap furbish'd up, and put on poor lieutenant *Le Fever*'s regimental coat, which your honour gave me to wear for his sake——and as soon as your honour is clean shaved——and has got your clean shirt on, with your blue and gold, or your fine scarlet——sometimes one and sometimes t'other——and every thing is ready for the attack——we'll march up boldly, as if 'twas to the face of a bastion; and whilst your honour engages Mrs. *Wadman* in the parlour, to the right——I'll attack Mrs. *Bridget* in the kitchen, to the left; and having seiz'd that pass, I'll answer for it, said the corporal, snapping his fingers over his head——that the day is our own.

I wish I may but manage it right; said my uncle *Toby*——but I declare, corporal I had rather march up to the very edge of a trench——

——A woman is quite a different thing——said the corporal.

——I suppose so, quoth my uncle *Toby*.

Chapter XXXI.

IF any thing in this world, which my father said, could have provoked my uncle *Toby*, during the time he was in love, it was the perverse use my father was always making of an expression of

---

3. To buy a drink to "soak" the commission in.

4. Into curlers.

5. Chalk was used as metal polish.

Hilarion the hermit;[6] who, in speaking of his abstinence, his watchings, flagellations, and other instrumental parts of his religion——
would say——tho' with more facetiousness than became an hermit
——"That they were the means he used, to make his *ass* (meaning
his body) leave off kicking."

It pleased my father well; it was not only a laconick way of
expressing——but of libelling, at the same time, the desires and
appetites of the lower part of us; so that for many years of my
father's life, 'twas his constant mode of expression——he never
used the word *passions* once——but *ass* always instead of them
——So that he might be said truly, to have been upon the bones, or
the back of his own ass, or else of some other man's, during all that
time.

I must here observe to you, the difference betwixt

    My father's ass

    and my hobby-horse——in order to keep characters as sep-
arate as may be, in our fancies as we go along.

For my hobby-horse, if you recollect a little, is no way a vicious
beast; he has scarce one hair or lineament of the ass about him——
'Tis the sporting little filly-folly which carries you out for the
present hour——a maggot, a butterfly, a picture, a fiddle-stick——
an uncle *Toby*'s siege——or an *any thing*, which a man makes a
shift to get a stride on, to canter it away from the cares and
solicitudes of life——'Tis as useful a beast as is in the whole creation——nor do I really see how the world could do without it——

——But for my father's ass——oh! mount him——mount
him——mount him——(that's three times, is it not?)——mount
him not:——'tis a beast concupiscent——and foul befall the man,
who does not hinder him from kicking.

Chapter XXXII.

WELL! dear brother *Toby*, said my father, upon his first
seeing him after he fell in love——and how goes it with
your ASSE?

Now my uncle *Toby* thinking more of the *part* where he had had
the blister, than of *Hilarion*'s metaphor——and our preconceptions
having (you know) as great a power over the sounds of words as
the shapes of things, he had imagined, that my father, who was not
very ceremonious in his choice of words, had enquired after the
part by its proper name; so notwithstanding my mother, doctor
Slop, and Mr. *Yorick*, were sitting in the parlour, he thought it
rather civil to conform to the term my father had made use of than

6. St. Hilarion (c. 290–371) introduced monasteries in Palestine. This is another borrowing from Burton's *Anatomy*.

not. When a man is hemm'd in by two indecorums, and must commit one of 'em——I always observe——let him choose which he will, the world will blame him——so I should not be astonished if it blames my uncle *Toby.*

My A——e, quoth my uncle *Toby,* is much better——brother *Shandy*——My father had formed great expectations from his Asse in this onset; and would have brought him on again; but doctor *Slop* setting up an intemperate laugh——and my mother crying out L——bless us!——it drove my father's Asse off the field——and the laugh then becoming general——there was no bringing him back to the charge, for some time——

And so the discourse went on without him.

Every body, said my mother, says you are in love, brother *Toby* ——and we hope it is true.

I am as much in love, sister, I believe, replied my uncle *Toby,* as any man usually is——Humph! said my father——and when did you know it? quoth my mother——

——When the blister broke; replied my uncle *Toby.*

My uncle *Toby's* reply put my father into good temper——so he charged o'foot.

Chapter XXXIII.

AS the antients agree, brother *Toby,* said my father, that there are two different and distinct kinds of *love,* according to the different parts which are affected by it——the Brain or Liver ——I think when a man is in love, it behoves him a little to consider which of the two he is fallen into.

What signifies it, brother *Shandy,* replied my uncle *Toby,* which of the two it is, provided it will but make a man marry, and love his wife, and get a few children.

——A few children! cried my father, rising out of his chair, and looking full in my mother's face, as he forced his way betwixt her's and doctor *Slop's*——a few children! cried my father, repeating my uncle *Toby's* words as he walk'd to and fro'——

——"Not, my dear brother *Toby,* cried my father, recovering himself all at once, and coming close up to the back of my uncle *Toby's* chair——not that I should be sorry had'st thou a score——on the contrary I should rejoice——and be as kind, *Toby,* to every one of them as a father——

My uncle *Toby* stole his hand unperceived behind his chair, to give my father's a squeeze——

——Nay, moreover, continued he, keeping hold of my uncle *Toby's* hand——so much do'st thou possess, my dear *Toby,* of the milk of human nature, and so little of its asperities——'tis piteous the world is not peopled by creatures which resemble thee; and was I an *Asiatick* monarch, added my father, heating himself with his new project——I would oblige thee, provided it would not impair thy strength——or dry up thy radical moisture too fast——or weaken thy memory or fancy, brother *Toby*, which these gymnicks inordinately taken, are apt to do——else, dear *Toby*, I would procure thee the most beautiful women in my empire, and I would oblige thee, *nolens, volens*,[7] to beget for me one subject every month——

As my father pronounced the last word of the sentence——my mother took a pinch of snuff.

Now I would not, quoth my uncle *Toby*, get a child, *nolens, volens*, that is, whether I would or no, to please the greatest prince upon earth——

——And 'twould be cruel in me, brother *Toby*, to compell thee; said my father——but 'tis a case put to shew thee, that it is not thy begetting a child——in case thou should'st be able——but the system of Love and marriage thou goest upon, which I would set thee right in——

There is at least, said *Yorick*, a great deal of reason and plain sense in captain *Shandy*'s opinion of love; and 'tis amongst the ill spent hours of my life which I have to answer for, that I have read so many flourishing poets and rhetoricians in my time, from whom I never could extract so much——

I wish, *Yorick*, said my father, you had read *Plato*;[8] for there you would have learnt that there are two LOVES——I know there were two RELIGIONS, replied *Yorick*, amongst the ancients——one ——for the vulgar, and another for the learned; but I think ONE LOVE might have served both of them very well——

It could not; replied my father——and for the same reasons: for of these LOVES, according to *Ficinus*'s comment upon *Valesius*, the one is *rational*——

——the other is *natural*——

the first ancient——without mother——where *Venus* had nothing to do: the second, begotten of *Jupiter* and *Dione*——

——Pray brother, quoth my uncle *Toby*, what has a man who believes in God to do with this? My father could not stop to answer, for fear of breaking the thread of his discourse——

This latter, continued he, partakes wholly of the nature of *Venus*.

The first, which is the golden chain let down from heaven, excites to love heroic, which comprehends in it, and excites to the desire of philosophy and truth——the second, excites to *desire*, simply——

---

7. "Willing or unwilling."
8. In the *Symposium* Plato distinguishes between rational or heavenly love and the earthly kind. Ficinus and Velasius are commentators on Plato.

——I think the procreation of children as beneficial to the world, said *Yorick*, as the finding out the longitude——

——To be sure, said my mother, *love* keeps peace in the world——

——In the *house*——my dear, I own——

——It replenishes the earth; said my mother——

But it keeps heaven empty——my dear; replied my father.

——'Tis Virginity, cried *Slop*, triumphantly, which fills paradise. Well push'd nun! quoth my father.

Chapter XXXIV.

M Y father had such a skirmishing, cutting kind of a slashing way with him in his disputations, thrusting and ripping, and giving every one a stroke to remember him by in his turn—— that if there were twenty people in company——in less than half an hour he was sure to have every one of 'em against him.

What did not a little contribute to leave him thus without an ally, was, that if there was any one post more untenable than the rest, he would be sure to throw himself into it; and to do him justice, when he was once there, he would defend it so gallantly, that 'twould have been a concern, either to a brave man, or a good-natured one, to have seen him driven out.

Yorick, for this reason, though he would often attack him——yet could never bear to do it with all his force.

Doctor *Slop*'s VIRGINITY, in the close of the last chapter, had got him for once on the right side of the rampart; and he was beginning to blow up all the convents in *Christendom* about *Slop*'s ears, when corporal *Trim* came into the parlour to inform my uncle *Toby*, that his thin scarlet breeches, in which the attack was to be made upon Mrs. *Wadman*, would not do; for, that the taylor, in ripping them up, in order to turn them, had found they had been turn'd before ——Then turn them again, brother, said my father rapidly, for there will be many a turning of 'em yet before all's done in the affair——They are as rotten as dirt, said the corporal——Then by all means, said my father, bespeak a new pair, brother——for though I know, continued my father, turning himself to the company, that widow *Wadman* has been deeply in love with my brother *Toby* for many years, and has used every art and circumvention of woman to outwit him into the same passion, yet now that she has caught him——her fever will be pass'd it's height——

——She has gain'd her point.

In this case, continued my father, which *Plato*, I am persuaded, never thought of——Love, you see, is not so much a SENTIMENT as a SITUATION, into which a man enters, as my brother *Toby* would do, into a *corps*——no matter whether he loves the service or no——being once in it——he acts as if he did; and takes every step to shew himself a man of prowesse.

The hypothesis, like the rest of my father's, was plausible enough, and my uncle *Toby* had but a single word to object to it——in which *Trim* stood ready to second him——but my father had not drawn his conclusion——

For this reason, continued my father (stating the case over again) notwithstanding all the world knows, that Mrs. *Wadman affects* my brother *Toby*——and my brother *Toby* contrariwise *affects* Mrs. *Wadman*, and no obstacle in nature to forbid the music striking up this very night, yet will I answer for it, that this self-same tune will not be play'd this twelvemonth.

We have taken our measures badly, quoth my uncle *Toby*, looking up interrogatively in *Trim*'s face.

I would lay my Montero cap, said *Trim*——Now *Trim*'s Montero-cap, as I once told you, was his constant wager; and having furbish'd it up that very night, in order to go upon the attack——it made the odds look more considerable——I would lay, an' please your honour, my Montero-cap to a shilling——was it proper, continued *Trim* (making a bow) to offer a wager before your honours——

——There is nothing improper in it, said my father——'tis a mode of expression; for in saying thou would'st lay thy Montero-cap to a shilling——all thou meanest is this——that thou believest——

——Now, What do'st thou believe?

That widow *Wadman*, an' please your worship, cannot hold it out ten days——

And whence, cried *Slop*, jeeringly, hast thou all this knowledge of woman, friend?

By falling in love with a popish clergy-woman; said *Trim*.

'Twas a *Beguine*, said my uncle *Toby*.

Doctor *Slop* was too much in wrath to listen to the distinction; and my father taking that very crisis to fall in helter-skelter upon the whole order of *Nuns* and *Beguines*, a set of silly, fusty baggages ——*Slop* could not stand it——and my uncle *Toby* having some measures to take about his breeches——and *Yorick* about his fourth general division[9]——in order for their several attacks next day——the company broke up: and my father being left alone, and having half an hour upon his hands betwixt that and bed-time; he called for pen, ink, and paper, and wrote my uncle *Toby* the following letter of instructions.

9. That is, one of the main sections of his sermon.

My dear brother *Toby,*

WHAT I am going to say to thee, is upon the nature of women, and of love-making to them; perhaps it is as well for thee——tho' not so well for me——that thou hast occasion for a letter of instructions upon that head, and that I am able to write it to thee.

Had it been the good pleasure of him who disposes of our lots ——and thou no sufferer by the knowledge, I had been well content that thou should'st have dipp'd the pen this moment into the ink, instead of myself; but that not being the case—— ——Mrs. *Shandy* being now close besides me, preparing for bed——I have thrown together without order, and just as they have come into my mind, such hints and documents as I deem may be of use to thee; intending, in this, to give thee a token of my love; not doubting, my dear *Toby,* of the manner in which it will be accepted.

In the first place, with regard to all which concerns religion in the affair——though I perceive from a glow in my cheek, that I blush as I begin to speak to thee upon the subject, as well knowing, notwithstanding thy unaffected secrecy, how few of its offices thou neglectest——yet I would remind thee of one (during the continuance of thy courtship) in a particular manner, which I would not have omitted; and that is, never to go forth upon the enterprize, whether it be in the morning or the afternoon, without first recommending thyself to the protection of Almighty God, that he may defend thee from the evil one.

Shave the whole top of thy crown clean, once at least every four or five days, but oftner if convenient; lest in taking off thy wig before her, thro' absence of mind, she should be able to discover how much has been cut away by Time——how much by *Trim.*

——'Twere better to keep ideas of baldness out of her fancy.

Always carry it in thy mind, and act upon it, as a sure maxim, *Toby*——

"*That women are timid:*" And 'tis well they are——else there would be no dealing with them.

Let not thy breeches be too tight, or hang too loose about thy thighs, like the trunk-hose of our ancestors.

——A just medium prevents all conclusions.

Whatever thou has to say, be it more or less, forget not to utter it in a low soft tone of voice. Silence, and whatever approaches it, weaves dreams of midnight secrecy into the brain: For this cause, if thou canst help it, never throw down the tongs and poker.

Avoid all kinds of pleasantry and facetiousness in thy discourse with her, and do whatever lies in thy power at the same time, to keep from her all books and writings which tend thereto: there are,

some devotional tracts, which if thou canst entice her to read over
——it will be well: but suffer her not to look into *Rabelais,* or
Scarron,[1] or *Don Quixote*——

——They are all books which excite laughter; and thou knowest,
dear *Toby,* that there is no passion so serious, as lust.

Stick a pin in the bosom of thy shirt, before thou enterest her
parlour.

And if thou are permitted to sit upon the same sopha with her,
and she gives thee occasion to lay thy hand upon hers——beware
of taking it——thou can'st not lay thy hand on hers, but she will
feel the temper of thine. Leave that and as many other things as
thou canst, quite undetermined; by so doing, thou wilt have her
curiosity on thy side; and if she is not conquer'd by that, and thy
ASSE continues still kicking, which there is great reason to suppose
——Thou must begin, with first losing a few ounces of blood below
the ears, according to the practice of the ancient *Scythians,* who
cured the most intemperate fits of the appetite by that means.

Avicenna,[2] after this, is for having the part anointed with the
syrrup of hellebore, using proper evacuations and purges——and I
believe rightly. But thou must eat little oι no goat's flesh, nor red
deer——nor even foal's flesh by any means; and carefully abstain
——that is, as much as thou canst, from peacocks, cranes, coots,
didappers, and water-hens——

As for thy drink——I need not tell thee, it must be the infu-
sion of VERVAIN,[3] and the herb HANEA, of which *ælian* relates such
effects——but if thy stomach palls with it——discontinue it from
time to time, taking cucumbers, melons, purslane, water-lillies,
woodbine, and lettice, in the stead of them.

There is nothing further for thee, which occurs to me at
present——

——Unless the breaking out of a fresh war——So wishing every
thing, dear *Toby,* for the best,

I rest thy affectionate brother,

WALTER SHANDY

Chapter XXXV.

WHILST my father was writing his letter of instructions,
my uncle *Toby* and the corporal were busy in preparing
every thing for the attack. As the turning of the thin scarlet
breeches was laid aside (at least for the present) there was nothing

---

1. Paul Scarron, author of *Le Roman Comique* (1651–57).
2. The Arabian physician-philosopher.
3. Vervain and hanea were both sup-posed to be cooling herbs. Aelian (Clau-dius Aelianus) was a Roman rhetorician who wrote *De Natura Animalis* [On the Nature of Animals].

which should put it off beyond the next morning; so accordingly it was resolv'd upon, for eleven o'clock.

Come, my dear, said my father to my mother——'twill be but like a brother and sister, if you and I take a walk down to my brother *Toby's*——to countenance him in this attack of his.

My uncle *Toby* and the corporal had been accoutred both some time, when my father and mother enter'd, and the clock striking eleven, were that moment in motion to sally forth——but the account of this is worth more, than to be wove into the fag end of the eighth volume of such a work as this.——My father had no time but to put the letter of instructions into my uncle *Toby's* coat-pocket——and join with my mother in wishing his attack prosperous.

I could like, said my mother, to look through the key-hole out of *curiosity*——Call it by it's right name, my dear, quoth my father——

And look through the key-hole as long as you will.

END of the EIGHTH VOLUME.

Volume IX.

Si quid urbaniuſculè luſum a nobis, per Muſas et Charitas et omnium poetarum Numina, Ore te, ne me malè capias.[1]

A

DEDICATION

TO A

GREAT MAN.[2]

HAVING, *a priori*,[3] intended to dedicate *The Amours of my uncle Toby* to Mr. ***——I see more reasons, *a posteriori*,[4] for doing it to Lord *******.

I should lament from my soul, if this exposed me to the jealousy of their Reverences; because, *a posteriori*, in Court-latin, signifies, the kissing hands for preferment——or any thing else——in order to get it.

My opinion of Lord ******* is neither better nor worse, than it was of Mr. ***. Honours, like impressions upon coin, may give an ideal and local value to a bit of base metal; but Gold and Silver will pass all the world over without any other recommendation than their own weight.

The same good will that made me think of offering up half an hour's amusement to Mr. *** when out of place[5]—operates more forcibly at present, as half an hour's amusement will be more serviceable and refreshing after labour and sorrow, than after a philosophical repast.

Nothing is so perfectly *Amusement* as a total change of ideas; no ideas are so totally different as those of Ministers, and innocent Lovers: for which reason, when I come to talk of Statesmen and

---

1. "If we have joked with anything too facetiously, by the Muses and the Graces and the divine power of all the poets, I pray you, don't take it ill of me." (A letter from Julius Scaliger to Cardan, quoted in Burton's *Anatomy of Melancholy*, 3.1.1.1).
2. The "great man" is William Pitt, whom Sterne had dedicated his first two volumes to shortly after their very successful publication. In 1766, a year be-
fore Volume IX appeared, Pitt had become Earl of Chatham, as well as Prime Minister.
3. "From prior evidence," by deductive reasoning.
4. "From subsequent evidence"—and Sterne plays on other meanings of "posterior" as he goes on.
5. Pitt was out of office between 1761 and 1766.

421

Patriots, and set such marks upon them as will prevent confusion and mistakes concerning them for the future———I propose to dedicate that Volume to some gentle Shepherd,

> Whose Thoughts proud Science never taught to stray,
> Far as the Statesman's walk or Patriot-way;
> Yet *simple Nature* to his hopes had given
> Out of a cloud-capp'd head a humbler heaven;
> Some *untam'd* World in depth of woods embraced———
> Some happier Island in the watry-waste———
> And where admitted to that equal sky,
> His *faithful Dogs* should bear him company.[6]

In a word, by thus introducing an entire new set of objects to his Imagination, I shall unavoidably give a *Diversion* to his passionate and love-sick Contemplations. In the mean time,

I am

The AUTHOR.

Chapter I.

I CALL all the powers of time and chance, which severally check us in our careers in this world, to bear me witness, that I could never yet get fairly to my uncle *Toby*'s amours, till this very moment, that my mother's *curiosity*, as she stated the affair,———or a different impulse in her, as my father would have it———wished her to take a peep at them through the key-hole.

"Call it, my dear, by its right name, quoth my father, and look through the key-hole as long as you will."

Nothing but the fermentation of that little subacid humour, which I have often spoken of, in my father's habit, could have vented such an insinuation———he was however frank and generous in his nature, and at all times open to conviction; so that he had scarce got to the last word of this ungracious retort, when his conscience smote him.

My mother was then conjugally swinging with her left arm twisted under his right, in such wise, that the inside of her hand rested upon the back of his———she raised her fingers, and let them fall———it could scarce be call'd a tap; or if it was a tap———'twould have puzzled a casuist to say, whether 'twas a tap of remonstrance, or a tap of confession: my father, who was all sensibilities from head to foot, class'd it right———Conscience redoubled her blow———he turn'd his face suddenly the other way, and my mother supposing his body was about to turn with it in order to move

---

6. The lines are adapted from Pope's *Essay on Man*, I. 99–112.

homewards, by a cross movement of her right leg, keeping her left as its centre, brought herself so far in front, that as he turned his head, he met her eye———Confusion again! he saw a thousand reasons to wipe out the reproach, and as many to reproach himself ———a thin, blue, chill, pellucid chrystal with all its humours so at rest, the least mote or speck of desire might have been seen at the bottom of it, had it existed———it did not———and how I happened to be so lewd myself, particularly a little before the vernal and autumnal equinoxes———Heaven above knows———My mother ———madam———was so at no time, either by nature, by institution, or example.

A temperate current of blood ran orderly through her veins in all months of the year, and in all critical moments both of the day and night alike; nor did she superinduce the least heat into her humours from the manual effervescencies of devotional tracts, which having little or no meaning in them, nature is oft times obliged to find one———And as for my father's example! 'twas so far from being either aiding or abetting thereunto, that 'twas the whole business of his life to keep all fancies of that kind out of her head——— Nature had done her part, to have spared him this trouble; and what was not a little inconsistent, my father knew it———And here am I sitting, this 12th day of *August*, 1766, in a purple jerkin and yellow pair of slippers, without either wig or cap on, a most tragi-comical completion of his prediction, "That I should neither think, nor act like any other man's child, upon that very account."

The mistake of my father, was in attacking my mother's motive, instead of the act itself: for certainly key-holes were made for other purposes; and considering the act, as an act which interfered with a true proposition, and denied a key-hole to be what it was———it became a violation of nature; and was so far, you see, criminal.

It is for this reason, an' please your Reverances, That key-holes are the occasions of more sin and wickedness, than all other holes in this world put together.

———which leads me to my uncle *Toby*'s amours.

Chapter II.

THOUGH the Corporal had been as good as his word in putting my uncle *Toby*'s great ramallie-wig into pipes, yet the time was too short to produce any great effects from it: it had lain many years squeezed up in the corner of his old campaign trunk; and as bad forms are not so easy to be got the better of, and the use of candle-ends not so well understood, it was not so pliable a business as one would have wished. The Corporal with cheary eye and both arms extended, had fallen back perpendicular from it a score times, to inspire it, if possible, with a better air——had SPLEEN given a look at it, 'twould have cost her ladyship a smile——it curl'd every where but where the Corporal would have it; and where a buckle or two, in his opinion, would have done it honour, he could as soon have raised the dead.

Such it was——or rather such would it have seem'd upon any other brow; but the sweet look of goodness which sat upon my uncle *Toby*'s assimulated every thing around it so sovereignly to itself, and Nature had moreover wrote GENTLEMAN with so fair a hand in every line of his countenance, that even his tarnish'd gold-laced hat and huge cockade of flimsy taffeta became him; and though not worth a button in themselves, yet the moment my uncle *Toby* put them on, they became serious objects, and altogether seem'd to have been picked up by the hand of Science to set him off to advantage.

Nothing in this world could have co-operated more powerfully towards this, than my uncle *Toby*'s blue and gold——*had not Quantity in some measure been necessary to Grace*: in a period of fifteen or sixteen years since they had been made, by a total inactivity in my uncle *Toby*'s life, for he seldom went further than the bowling-green——his blue and gold had become so miserably too strait for him, that it was with the utmost difficulty the Corporal was able to get him into them: the taking them up at the sleeves, was of no advantage.——They were laced however down the back, and at the seams of the sides, &c. in the mode of King *William*'s reign; and to shorten all description, they shone so bright against the sun that morning, and had so metallick, and doughty an air with them, that had my uncle *Toby* thought of attacking in armour, nothing could have so well imposed upon his imagination.

As for the thin scarlet breeches, they had been unripp'd by the taylor between the legs, and left at *sixes and sevens*——

——Yes, Madam,——but let us govern our fancies. It is enough they were held impracticable the night before, and as there was no alternative in my uncle *Toby*'s wardrobe, he sallied forth in the red plush.

The Corporal had array'd himself in poor *Le Fevre*'s regimental coat; and with his hair tuck'd up under his Montero-cap, which he had furbish'd up for the occasion, march'd three paces distant from his master: a whiff of military pride had puff'd out his shirt at the wrist; and upon that in a black leather thong clipp'd into a tassel beyond the knot, hung the Corporal's stick——My uncle *Toby* carried his cane like a pike.

——It looks well at least; quoth my father to himself.

Chapter III.

MY uncle *Toby* turn'd his head more than once behind him, to see how he was supported by the Corporal; and the Corporal as oft as he did it, gave a slight flourish with his stick——but not vapouringly; and with the sweetest accent of most respectful encouragement, bid his honour "never fear."

Now my uncle *Toby* did fear; and grievously too: he knew not (as my father had reproach'd him) so much as the right end of a Woman from the wrong, and therefore was never altogether at his ease near any one of them——unless in sorrow or distress; then infinite was his pity; nor would the most courteous knight of romance have gone further, at least upon one leg, to have wiped away a tear from a woman's eye; and yet excepting once that he was beguiled into it by Mrs. *Wadman,* he had never looked steadfastly into one; and would often tell my father in the simplicity of his heart, that it was almost (if not alout[7]) as bad as talking bawdy.——

——And suppose it is? my father would say.

Chapter IV.

SHE cannot, quoth my uncle *Toby*, halting, when they had march'd up to within twenty paces of Mrs. *Wadman's* door ——she cannot, Corporal, take it amiss.——

——She will take it, an' please your honour, said the Corporal, just as the *Jew's* widow at *Lisbon* took it of my brother *Tom.*——

——And how was that? quoth my uncle *Toby*, facing quite about to the Corporal.

Your honour, replied the Corporal, knows of *Tom's* misfortunes; but this affair has nothing to do with them any further than this, That if *Tom* had not married the widow——or had it pleased God after their marriage, that they had but put pork into their sausages, the honest soul had never been taken out of his warm bed, and dragg'd to the inquisition——'Tis a cursed place——added the Corporal, shaking his head,——when once a poor creature is in, he is in, an' please your honour, for ever.

'Tis very true; said my uncle *Toby* looking gravely at Mrs. *Wadman's* house, as he spoke.

Nothing, continued the Corporal, can be so sad as confinement for life——or so sweet, an' please your honour, as liberty.

Nothing, *Trim*——said my uncle *Toby*, musing——

---

7. All out, completely.

Whilst a man is free——cried the Corporal, giving a flourish with his stick thus——

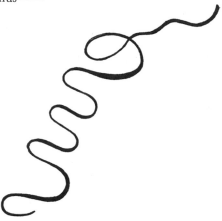

A thousand of my father's most subtle syllogisms could not have said more for celibacy.

My uncle *Toby* look'd earnestly towards his cottage and his bowling-green.

The Corporal had unwarily conjured up the Spirit of calculation with his wand; and he had nothing to do, but to conjure him down again with his story, and in this form of Exorcism, most un-ecclesiastically did the Corporal do it.

Chapter V.

AS *Tom*'s place, an' pleasure your honour, was easy——and the weather warm——it put him upon thinking seriously of settling himself in the world; and as it fell out about that time, that a *Jew* who kept a sausage shop in the same street, had the ill luck to die of a strangury,[8] and leave his widow in possession of a rousing trade——*Tom* thought (as every body in *Lisbon* was doing the best he could devise for himself) there could be no harm in offering her his service to carry it on: so without any introduction to the widow, except that of buying a pound of sausages at her shop——*Tom* set out——counting the matter thus within himself, as he walk'd along; that let the worst come of it that could, he should at least get a pound of sausages for their worth——but, if things went well, he should be set up; inasmuch as he should get not only a pound of sausages——but a wife——and a sausage-shop, an' please your honour, into the bargain.

8. A disease of the urinary organs.

Every servant in the family, from high to low, wish'd *Tom* success; and I can fancy, an' please your honour, I see him this moment with his white dimity waistcoat and breeches, and hat a little o' one side, passing jollily along the street, swinging his stick, with a smile and a chearful word for every body he met:———But alas! *Tom*! thou smilest no more, cried the Corporal, looking on one side of him upon the ground, as if he apostrophized him in his dungeon.

Poor fellow! said my uncle *Toby*, feelingly.

He was an honest, light-hearted lad, an' please your honour, as ever blood warm'd———

———Then he resembled thee, *Trim*, said my uncle *Toby*, rapidly.

The Corporal blush'd down to his fingers ends———a tear of sentimental bashfulness———another of gratitude to my uncle *Toby* ———and a tear of sorrow for his brother's misfortunes, started into his eye and ran sweetly down his cheek together; my uncle *Toby*'s kindled as one lamp does at another; and taking hold of the breast of *Trim*'s coat (which had been that of *Le Fevre*'s) as if to ease his lame leg, but in reality to gratify a finer feeling———he stood silent for a minute and a half; at the end of which he took his hand away, and the Corporal making a bow, went on with his story of his brother and the *Jew*'s widow.

Chapter VI.

WHEN *Tom*, an' please your honour, got to the shop, there was nobody in it, but a poor negro girl, with a bunch of white feathers slightly tied to the end of a long cane, flapping away flies———not killing them.———'Tis a pretty picture! said my uncle *Toby*———she had suffered persecution, *Trim*, and had learnt mercy———

———She was good, an' please your honour, from nature as well as from hardships; and there are circumstances in the story of that poor friendless slut[9] that would melt a heart of stone, said *Trim*; and some dismal winter's evening, when your honour is in the humour, they shall be told you with the rest of *Tom*'s story, for it makes a part of it———

Then do not forget, *Trim*, said my uncle *Toby*.

A Negro has a soul? an' please your honour, said the Corporal (doubtingly).

I am not much versed, Corporal, quoth my uncle *Toby*, in things of that kind; but I suppose, God would not leave him without one, any more than thee or me———

———It would be putting one sadly over the head of another, quoth the Corporal.

9. Again the word is used as a term of affection.

It would so; said my uncle *Toby*. Why then, an' please your honour, is a black wench to be used worse than a white one?

I can give no reason, said my uncle *Toby*——

——Only, cried the Corporal, shaking his head, because she has no one to stand up for her——

——'Tis that very thing, *Trim*, quoth my uncle *Toby*,——which recommends her to protection——and her brethren with her; 'tis the fortune of war which has put the whip into our hands *now*—— where it may be hereafter, heaven knows!——but be it where it will, the brave, *Trim*! will not use it unkindly.

——God forbid, said the Corporal.

Amen, responded my uncle *Toby*, laying his hand upon his heart.

The Corporal returned to his story, and went on——but with an embarrassment in doing it, which here and there a reader in this world will not be able to comprehend; for by the many sudden transitions all along, from one kind and cordial passion to another, in getting thus far on his way, he had lost the sportable key of his voice which gave sense and spirit to his tale: he attempted twice to resume it, but could not please himself; so giving a stout hem! to rally back the retreating spirits, and aiding Nature at the same time with his left arm a-kimbo on one side, and with his right a little extended, supporting her on the other——the Corporal got as near the note as he could; and in that attitude, continued his story.

Chapter VII.

AS *Tom*, an' please your honour, had no business at that time with the *Moorish* girl, he passed on into the room beyond to talk to the *Jew*'s widow about love——and his pound of sausages; and being, as I have told your honour, an open, cheary hearted lad, with his character wrote in his looks and carriage, he took a chair, and without much apology, but with great civility at the same time, placed it close to her at the table, and sat down.

There is nothing so awkward, as courting a woman, an' please your honour, whilst she is making sausages——So *Tom* began a discourse upon them; first gravely,——"as how they were made ——with what meats, herbs and spices"——Then a little gayly—— as, "With what skins——and if they never burst——Whether the largest were not the best"——and so on——taking care only as he went along, to season what he had to say upon sausages, rather under, than over;——that he might have room to act in——

It was owing to the neglect of that very precaution, said my uncle *Toby*, laying his hand upon *Trim*'s shoulder, That Count *de la Motte* lost the battle of *Wynendale*: he pressed too speedily into the wood; which if he had not done, *Lisle* had not fallen into our hands, nor *Ghent* and *Bruges*, which both followed her example; it was so late in the year, continued my uncle *Toby*, and so terrible a season came on, that if things had not fallen out as they did, our troops must have perished in the open field.——

——Why therefore, may not battles, an' please your honour, as well as marriages, be made in heaven?——My uncle *Toby* mused.——

Religion inclined him to say one thing, and his high idea of military skill tempted him to say another; so not being able to frame a reply exactly to his mind——my uncle *Toby* said nothing at all; and the Corporal finished his story.

As *Tom* perceived, an' please your honour, that he gained ground, and that all he had said upon the subject of sausages was kindly taken, he went on to help her a little in making them.—— First, by taking hold of the ring of the sausage whilst she stroked the forced meat down with her hand——then by cutting the strings into proper lengths, and holding them in his hand, whilst she took them out one by one——then, by putting them across her mouth, that she might take them out as she wanted them——and so on from little to more, till at last he adventured to tie the sausage himself, whilst she held the snout.——

——Now a widow, an' please your honour, always chuses a second husband as unlike the first as she can: so the affair was more than half settled in her mind before *Tom* mentioned it.

She made a feint however of defending herself, by snatching up a sausage:——*Tom* instantly laid hold of another——

But seeing *Tom's* had more gristle in it——

She signed the capitulation——and *Tom* sealed it; and there was an end of the matter.

Chapter VIII.

ALL womankind, continued *Trim*, (commenting upon his story) from the highest to the lowest, an' please your honour, love jokes; the difficulty is to know how they chuse to have them cut; and there is no knowing that, but by trying as we do with our artillery in the field, by raising or letting down their breeches, till we hit the mark.——

——I like the comparison, said my uncle *Toby*, better than the thing itself——

——Because your honour, quoth the Corporal, loves glory, more than pleasure.

I hope, *Trim*, answered my uncle *Toby*, I love mankind more than either; and as the knowledge of arms tends so apparently to the good and quiet of the world——and particularly that branch of it which we have practised together in our bowling-green, has no object but to shorten the strides of AMBITION, and intrench the lives and fortunes of the *few*, from the plunderings of the *many*———whenever that drum beats in our ears, I trust, Corporal, we shall neither of us want so much humanity and fellow-feeling as to face about and march.

In pronouncing this, my uncle *Toby* faced about, and march'd firmly as at the head of his company———and the faithful Corporal, shouldering his stick, and striking his hand upon his coat-skirt as he took his first step———march'd close behind him down the avenue.

———Now what can their two noddles be about? cried my father to my mother———by all that's strange, they are besieging Mrs. *Wadman* in form, and are marching round her house to mark out the lines of circumvallation.[1]

I dare say, quoth my mother———————————But stop, dear Sir———for what my mother dared to say upon the occasion———and what my father did say upon it———with her replies and his rejoinders, shall be read, perused, paraphrased, commented and discanted upon———or to say it all in a word, shall be thumb'd over by Posterity in a chapter apart———I say, by Posterity———and care not, if I repeat the word again———for what has this book done more than the Legation of Moses,[2] or the Tale of a Tub, that it may not swim down the gutter of Time along with them?

I will not argue the matter: Time wastes too fast: every letter I trace tells me with what rapidity Life follows my pen; the days and hours of it, more precious, my dear *Jenny*! than the rubies about thy neck, are flying over our heads like light clouds of a windy day, never to return more———every thing presses on———whilst thou art twisting that lock,———see! it grows grey; and every time I kiss thy hand to bid adieu, and every absence which follows it, are preludes to that eternal separation which we are shortly to make.———

———Heaven have mercy upon us both!

Chapter IX.

NOW, for what the world thinks of that ejaculation———I would not give a groat.

Chapter X.

MY mother had gone with her left arm twisted in my father's right, till they had got to the fatal angle of the old garden wall, where Doctor *Slop* was overthrown by *Obadiah* on the

---

1. Surrounding trenches.
2. *The Divine Legation of Moses Demonstrated on the Principles of a Religious Deist* (1737–41) is a serious theological work by Bishop Warburton. As the Bishop was already annoyed by rumors that he might figure as Tristram's tutor in the novel, he may have been further offended to have his work linked with an irreverent satire like Swift's *Tale of a Tub* (which at its publication in 1704 was dedicated to "Prince Posterity").

coach-horse: as this was directly opposite to the front of Mrs. *Wad-man*'s house, when my father came to it, he gave a look across; and seeing my uncle *Toby* and the Corporal within ten paces of the door, he turn'd about———"Let us just stop a moment, quoth my father, and see with what ceremonies my brother *Toby* and his man *Trim* make their first entry———it will not detain us, added my father, a single minute:"———No matter, if it be ten minutes, quoth my mother.

———It will not detain us half a one; said my father.

The Corporal was just then setting in with the story of his brother *Tom* and the *Jew*'s widow: the story went on———and on———it had episodes in it———it came back, and went on———and on again; there was no end of it———the reader found it very long———

———G— help my father! he pish'd fifty times at every new atti-tude, and gave the corporal's stick, with all its flourishings and danglings, to as many devils as chose to accept of them.

When issues of events like these my father is waiting for, are hanging in the scales of fate, the mind has the advantage of chang-ing the principle of expectation three times, without which it would not have power to see it out.

Curiosity governs the *first moment*; and the second moment is all œconomy to justify the expence of the first———and for the third, fourth, fifth, and six moments, and so on to the day of judgment———'tis a point of Honour.

I need not be told, that the ethic writers have assigned this all to Patience; but that Virtue methinks, has extent of dominion suffi-cient of her own, and enough to do in it, without invading the few dismantled castles which Honour has left him upon the earth.

My father stood it out as well as he could with these three auxiliaries to the end of *Trim*'s story; and from thence to the end of my uncle *Toby*'s panegyrick upon arms, in the chapter following it; when seeing, that instead of marching up to Mrs. *Wadman*'s door, they both faced about and march'd down the avenue diametrically opposite to his expectation———he broke out at once with that little subacid soreness of humour which, in certain situations, distin-guished his character from that of all other men.

Chapter XI.

———"NOW what can their two noddles be about?" cried my father - - &c. - - - -

I dare say, said my mother, they are making fortifications———

———Not on Mrs. *Wadman*'s premises! cried my father, step-ping back———

I suppose not: quoth my mother.

I wish, said my father, raising his voice, the whole science of fortification at the devil, with all its trumpery of saps, mines, blinds, gabions, fausse-brays and cuvetts————

————They are foolish things————said my mother.

Now she had a way, which by the bye, I would this moment give away my purple jerkin, and my yellow slippers into the bargain, if some of your reverences would imitate————and that was never to refuse her assent and consent to any proposition my father laid before her, merely because she did not understand it, or had no ideas to the principal word or term of art, upon which the tenet or proposition rolled. She contented herself with doing all that her godfathers and godmothers promised for her————but no more; and so would go on using a hard word twenty years together————and replying to it too, if it was a verb, in all its moods and tenses, without giving herself any trouble to enquire about it.

This was an eternal source of misery to my father, and broke the neck, at the first setting out, of more good dialogues between them, than could have done the most petulant contradiction————the few which survived were the better for the *cuvetts*[3]————

————"They are foolish things;" said my mother.

————Particularly the *cuvetts*; replied my father.

'Twas enough————he tasted the sweet of triumph————and went on.

————Not that they are, properly speaking, Mrs. *Wadman's* premises, said my father, partly correcting himself————because she is but tenant for life————

————That makes a great difference————said my mother————

————In a fool's head, replied my father————

Unless she should happen to have a child————said my mother————

————But she must persuade my brother *Toby* first to get her one————

————To be sure, Mr. *Shandy*, quoth my mother.

————Though if it comes to persuasion————said my father————Lord have mercy upon them.

Amen: said my mother, *piano*.

Amen: cried my father, *fortissimè*.

Amen: said my mother again————but with such a sighing cadence of personal pity at the end of it, as discomfited every fibre about my father————he instantly took out his almanack; but before he could untie it, *Yorick's* congregation coming out of church, became a full answer to one half of his business with it————and my mother telling him it was a sacrament day[4]————left him as little in

---

3. A "cuvette" is a trench, and also a kind of bed-pan.
4. The sacrament of Holy Communion was often celebrated only on the first Sunday of the month—the day Walter Shandy set aside for winding the clock, etc.

doubt, as to the other part——He put his almanack into his pocket.

The first Lord of the Treasury thinking of *ways and means,* could not have returned home, with a more embarrassed look.

Chapter XII.

UPON looking back from the end of the last chapter and sur-veying the texture of what has been wrote, it is necessary, that upon this page and the five following, a good quantity of heterogeneous matter be inserted, to keep up that just balance be-twixt wisdom and folly, without which a book would not hold together a single year: nor is it a poor creeping digression (which but for the name of, a man might continue as well going on in the king's highway) which will do the business——no; if it is to be a digression, it must be a good frisky one, and upon a frisky subject too, where neither the horse or his rider are to be caught, but by rebound.

The only difficulty, is raising powers suitable to the nature of the service: FANCY is capricious——WIT must not be searched for—— and PLEASANTRY (good-natured slut as she is) will not come in at a call, was an empire to be laid at her feet.

——The best way for a man, is to say his prayers——

Only if it puts him in mind of his infirmities and defects as well ghostly[5] as bodily——for that purpose, he will find himself rather worse after he has said them than before——for other purposes, better.

For my own part there is not a way either moral or mechanical under heaven that I could think of, which I have not taken with myself in this case: sometimes by addressing myself directly to the soul herself, and arguing the point over and over again with her upon the extent of her own faculties——

——I never could make them an inch the wider——

Then by changing my system, and trying what could be made of it upon the body, by temperance, soberness and chastity: These are good, quoth I, in themselves——they are good, absolutely;——they are good, relatively;——they are good for health——they are good for happiness in this world——they are good for happiness in the next——

In short, they were good for every thing but the thing wanted; and there they were good for nothing, but to leave the soul just as heaven made it: as for the theological virtues of faith and hope, they give it courage; but then that sniveling virtue of Meekness (as my father would always call it) takes it quite away again, so you are exactly where you started.

5. Spiritual.

Now in all common and ordinary cases, there is nothing which I have found to answer so well as this——

——Certainly, if there is any dependence upon Logic, and that I am not blinded by self-love, there must be something of true genius about me, merely upon this symptom of it, that I do not know what envy is: for never do I hit upon any invention or device which tendeth to the furtherance of good writing, but I instantly make it public; willing that all mankind should write as well as myself.

——Which they certainly will, when they think as little.

Chapter XIII.

NOW in ordinary cases, that is, when I am only stupid, and the thoughts rise heavily and pass gummous through my pen——

Or that I am got, I know not how, into a cold unmetaphorical vein of infamous writing, and cannot take a plumb-lift out of it *for my soul*; so must be obliged to go on writing like a *Dutch* commentator to the end of the chapter, unless something be done——

——I never stand confering with pen and ink one moment; for if a pinch of snuff or a stride or two across the room will not do the business for me——I take a razor at once; and having tried the edge of it upon the palm of my hand, without further ceremony, except that of first lathering my beard, I shave it off; taking care only if I do leave a hair, that it be not a grey one: this done, I change my shirt——put on a better coat——send for my last wig ——put my topaz ring[6] upon my finger; and in a word, dress myself from one end to the other of me, after my best fashion.

Now the devil in hell must be in it, if this does not do: for consider, Sir, as every man chuses to be present at the shaving of his own beard (though there is no rule without an exception) and unavoidably sits overagainst himself the whole time it is doing, in case he has a hand in it——the Situation, like all others, has notions of her own to put into the brain.——

——I maintain it, the conceits[7] of a rough-bearded man, are seven years more terse and juvenile for one single operation; and if they did not run a risk of being quite shaved away, might be carried up by continual shavings, to the highest pitch of sublimity——How *Homer* could write with so long a beard, I don't know——and as it makes against my hypothesis, I as little care——But let us return to the Toilet.

Ludovicus Sorbonensis makes this entirely an affair of the body

---

6. Topazes were supposed to calm the passions and senses.

7. That is, the conceptions or figures of speech.

(ἐξωτερικὴ πρᾶξις[8]) as he calls it——but he is deceived: the soul and body are joint-sharers in every thing they get: A man cannot dress, but his ideas get cloath'd at the same time; and if he dresses like a gentleman, every one of them stands presented to his imagination, genteelized along with him——so that he has nothing to do, but take his pen, and write like himself.

For this cause, when your honours and reverences would know whether I writ clean and fit to be read, you will be able to judge full as well by looking into my Laundress's bill, as my book: there was one single month in which I can make it appear, that I dirtied one and thirty shirts with clean writing; and after all, was more abus'd, curs'd, criticis'd and confounded, and had more mystic heads shaken at me, for what I had wrote in that one month, than in all the other months of that year put together.

——But their honours and reverences had not seen my *bills*.

Chapter XIV.

AS I never had any intention of beginning the Digression, I am making all this preparation for, till I come to the 15th chapter——I have this chapter to put to whatever use I think proper——I have twenty this moment ready for it——I could write my chapter of Button-holes in it——

Or my chapter of *Pishes*, which should follow them——

Or my chapter of *Knots*, in case their reverences have done with them——they might lead me into mischief: the safest way is to follow the tract of the learned, and raise objections against what I have been writing, tho' I declare beforehand, I know no more than my heels how to answer them.

And first, it may be said, there is a pelting kind of *thersitical*[9] satire, as black as the very ink 'tis wrote with——(and by the bye, whoever says so, is indebted to the muster-master general of the *Grecian* army, for suffering the name of so ugly and foul-mouth'd a man as *Thersites* to continue upon his roll——for it has furnished him with an epithet)——in these productions he will urge, all the personal washings and scrubbings upon earth do a sinking genius no sort of good——but just the contrary, inasmuch as the dirtier the fellow is, the better generally he succeeds in it.

To this, I have no other answer——at least ready——but that the Archbishop of *Benevento* wrote his *nasty* Romance of the *Galateo*,[1] as all the world knows, in a purple coat, waistcoat, and

---

8. "An external matter."
9. "Foul-mouthed" and vicious, like Thersites in the *Iliad*.
1. The *Galateo*, which Tristram has mentioned earlier deals with polite man-ners, so he may really be talking here of the *Capitoli de Forno*, a lascivious work of the Archbishop's. Purple is the color of an archbishop's costume.

purple pair of breeches; and that the penance set him of writing a commentary upon the book of the *Revelations*, as severe as it was look'd upon by one part of the world, was far from being deem'd so, by the other, upon the single account of that *Investment*.

Another objection, to all this remedy, is its want of universality; forasmuch as the shaving part of it, upon which so much stress is laid, by an unalterable law of nature excludes one half of the species entirely from its use: all I can say is, that female writers, whether of *England,* or of *France,* must e'en go without it———

As for the *Spanish* ladies———I am in no sort of distress———

Chapter XV.

T HE fifteenth chapter is come at last; and brings nothing with it but a sad signature of "How our pleasure slips from under us in this world;"

For in talking of my digression———I declare before heaven I have made it! What a strange creature is mortal man! said she.

'Tis very true, said I———but 'twere better to get all these things out of our heads, and return to my uncle *Toby.*

Chapter XVI.

W HEN my uncle *Toby* and the Corporal had marched down to the bottom of the avenue, they recollected their business lay the other way; so they faced about and marched up streight to Mrs. *Wadman's* door.

I warrant your honour; said the Corporal, touching his Montero-cap with his hand, as he passed him in order to give a knock at the door———My uncle *Toby,* contrary to his invariable way of treating his faithful servant, said nothing good or bad: the truth was, he had not altogether marshal'd his ideas; he wish'd for another conference, and as the Corporal was mounting up the three steps before the door———he hem'd twice———a portion of my uncle *Toby's* most modest spirits fled, at each expulsion, towards the Corporal; he stood with the rapper of the door suspended for a full minute in his hand, he scarce knew why. *Bridget* stood perdue[2] within, with her finger and her thumb upon the latch, benumb'd with expectation; and Mrs. *Wadman,* with an eye ready to be deflowered again, sat breathless behind the window-curtain of her bedchamber, watching their approach.

Trim! said my uncle *Toby*———but as he articulated the word, the minute expired, and *Trim* let fall the rapper.

---

2. Hidden.

My uncle *Toby* perceiving that all hopes of a conference were knock'd on the head by it————whistled Lillabullero.

Chapter XVII.

AS Mrs. *Bridget*'s finger and thumb were upon the latch, the Corporal did not knock as oft as perchance your honour's taylor———I might have taken my example something nearer home; for I owe mine, some five and twenty pounds at least, and wonder at the man's patience———

————But this is nothing at all to the world: only 'tis a cursed thing to be in debt; and there seems to be a fatality in the exchequers of some poor princes, particularly those of our house, which no Economy can bind down in irons: for my own part, I'm persuaded there is not any one prince, prelate, pope, or potentate, great or small upon earth, more desirous in his heart of keeping streight with the world than I am———or who takes more likely means for it. I never give above half a guinea———or walk with boots———or cheapen tooth-picks———or lay out a shilling upon a band-box the year round; and for the six months I'm in the country, I'm upon so small a scale, that with all the good temper in the world, I out-do *Rousseau*,[3] a bar length———for I keep neither man or boy, or horse, or cow, or dog, or cat, or any thing that can eat or drink, except a thin poor piece of a Vestal[4] (to keep my fire in) and who has generally as bad an appetite as myself———but if you think this makes a philosopher of me———I would not, my good people! give a rush for your judgments.

True philosophy———but there is no treating the subject whilst my uncle is whistling Lillabullero.

————Let us go into the house.

3. Jean-Jacques Rousseau, the eighteenth-century French philosopher who steadily urged a return to a simpler, more natural, life.

4. Vestal virgins historically guarded the flame at the temple of the Roman goddess of the hearth; Tristram is referring to his kitchen maid.

Chapter XVIII.

Chapter XIX.

Chapter XX.

——— * * * * * * * * * *
* * * * * * * * * * * *
* * * * * * * *

 * * * * * * * * * * *
* * * * * * * * * * * *
* * * * * * * * * * * *
* * * * * * * ———

——You shall see the very place, Madam; said my uncle *Toby*.

Mrs. *Wadman* blush'd——look'd towards the door——turn'd pale——blush'd slightly again——recovered her natural colour ——blush'd worse than ever; which for the sake of the unlearned reader, I translate thus——

"L—d! I cannot look at it——
What would the world say if I look'd at it?
I should drop down, if I look'd at it——
I wish I could look at it——
There can be no sin in looking at it.
——*I will look at it.*"

Whilst all this was running through Mrs. *Wadman's* imagination, my uncle *Toby* had risen from the sopha, and got to the other side of the parlour-door, to give *Trim* an order about it in the passage——
 * * * * * * * * * * *
* * * * *——I believe it is in the garret, said my uncle *Toby*——I saw it there, an' please your honour, this morning, answered *Trim*——Then prithee, step directly for it, *Trim*, said my uncle *Toby*, and bring it into the parlour.

The Corporal did not approve of the orders, but most chearfully obey'd them. The first was not an act of his will——the second was; so he put on his Montero cap, and went as fast as his lame knee would let him. My uncle *Toby* returned into the parlour, and sat himself down again upon the sopha.

——You shall lay your finger upon the place——said my uncle *Toby*.——I will not touch it, however, quoth Mrs. *Wadman* to herself.

This requires a second translation:——it shews what little knowledge is got by mere words——we must go up to the first springs.

Now in order to clear up the mist which hangs upon these three pages, I must endeavour to be as clear as possible myself.

Rub your hands thrice across your foreheads——blow your noses——cleanse your emunctories[5]——sneeze, my good people! ——God bless you——

Now give me all the help you can.

5. The bodily organs that give off waste.

Chapter XXI.

AS there are fifty different ends (counting all ends in——as well civil as religious) for which a woman takes a husband, she first sets about and carefully weighs, then separates and distinguishes in her mind, which of all that number of ends, is hers: then by discourse, enquiry, argumentation and inference, she investigates and finds out whether she has got hold of the right one—— and if she has——then, by pulling it gently this way and that way, she further forms a judgment, whether it will not break in the drawing.

The imagery under which *Slawkenbergius* impresses this upon his reader's fancy, in the beginning of his third Decad, is so ludicrous, that the honour I bear the sex, will not suffer me to quote it—— otherwise 'tis not destitute of humour.

"She first, saith *Slawkenbergius*, stops the asse, and holding his halter in her left hand (lest he should get away) she thrusts her right hand into the very bottom of his pannier to search for it—— For what?——you'll not know the sooner, quoth *Slawkenbergius*, for interrupting me——

"I have nothing, good Lady, but empty bottles;" says the asse.

"I'm loaded with tripes;" says the second.

——And thou are little better, quoth she to the third; for nothing is there in thy panniers but trunk-hose and pantofles——and so to the fourth and fifth, going on one by one through the whole string, till coming to the asse which carries it, she turns the pannier upside down, looks at it——considers it——samples it——measures it ——stretches it——wets it——dries it——then takes her teeth both to the warp and weft of it——

——Of what? for the love of Christ!

I am determined, answered *Slawkenbergius*, that all the powers upon earth shall never wring that secret from my breast.

Chapter XXII..

WE live in a world beset on all sides with mysteries and riddles——and so 'tis no matter——else it seems strange, that Nature, who makes every thing so well to answer its destination, and seldom or never errs, unless for pastime, in giving such forms and aptitudes to whatever passes through her hands, that whether she designs for the plough, the caravan, the cart——or whatever other creature she models, be it but an asse's foal, you are sure to have the thing you wanted; and yet at the same time should so eternally bungle it as she does, in making so simple a thing as a married man.

Whether it is in the choice of the clay——or that it is frequently spoiled in the baking; by an excess of which a husband may turn out too crusty (you know) on one hand——or not enough so, through defect of heat, on the other——or whether this great Artificer is not so attentive to the little Platonic exigencies *of that part* of the species, for whose use she is fabricating *this*——or that her Ladyship sometimes scarce knows what sort of a husband will do——I know not: we will discourse about it after supper.

It is enough, that neither the observation itself, or the reasoning upon it, are at all to the purpose——but rather against it; since with regard to my uncle *Toby's* fitness for the marriage state, nothing was ever better: she had formed him of the best and kindliest clay——had temper'd it with her own milk, and breathed into it the sweetest spirit——she had made him all gentle, generous and humane——she had fill'd his heart with trust and confidence, and disposed every passage which led to it, for the communication of the tenderest offices——she had moreover considered the other causes for which matrimony was ordained——

And accordingly   *   *   *   *   *   *   *   *
*   *   *   *   *   *   *   *   *   *   *   *
*   *   *   *   *   *   *   *   *   *   *   *
*   *   *   *

The DONATION was not defeated by my uncle *Toby's* wound.

Now this last article was somewhat apocryphal; and the Devil, who is the great disturber of our faiths in this world, had raised scruples in Mrs. *Wadman's* brain about it; and like a true devil as he was, had done his own work at the same time, by turning my uncle *Toby's* Virtue thereupon into nothing but *empty bottles, tripes, trunk-hose,* and *pantofles.*

Chapter XXIII.

MRS. *Bridget* had pawn'd all the little stock of honour a poor chambermaid was worth in the world, that she would get to the bottom of the affair in ten days; and it was built upon one of the most concessible *postulatum*[6] in nature: namely, that whilst my uncle *Toby* was making love to her mistress, the Corporal could find nothing better to do, than make love to her——"*And I'll let him as much as he will,*" said *Bridget,* "*to get it out of him.*"

Friendship has two garments; an outer, and an under one. *Bridget* was serving her mistress's interests in the one——and doing the thing which most pleased herself in the other; so had as many stakes depending upon my uncle *Toby's* wound, as the Devil himself

6. Postulates.

——Mrs. *Wadman* had but one——and as it possibly might be her last (without discouraging Mrs. *Bridget*, or discrediting her talents) was determined to play her cards herself.

She wanted not encouragement: a child might have look'd into his hand——there was such a plainness and simplicity in his playing out what trumps he had——with such an unmistrusting ignorance of the *ten-ace*[7]——and so naked and defenceless did he sit upon the same sopha with widow *Wadman,* that a generous heart would have wept to have won the game of him.

Let us drop the metaphor.

Chapter XXIV.

—— AND the story too——if you please: for though I have all along been hastening towards this part of it, with so much earnest desire, as well knowing it to be the choicest morsel of what I had to offer to the world, yet know that I am got to it, any one is welcome to take my pen, and go on with the story for me that will——I see the difficulties of the descriptions I'm going to give ——and feel my want of powers.

It is one comfort at least to me, that I lost some fourscore ounces of blood this week in a most uncritical fever which attacked me at the beginning of this chapter; so that I have still some hopes remaining, it may be more in the serous or globular parts of the blood, than in the subtile *aura* of the brain——be it which it will——an Invocation can do no hurt——and I leave the affair entirely to the *invoked,* to inspire or to inject me according as he sees good.

THE INVOCATION.

GENTLE Spirit of sweetest humour, who erst didst sit upon the easy pen of my beloved CERVANTES; Thou who glided'st daily through his lattice, and turned'st the twilight of his prison into noon-day brightness by thy presence——tinged'st his little urn of water with heaven-sent Nectar, and all the time he wrote of *Sancho* and his master, didst cast thy mystic mantle o'er his wither'd[8] stump, and wide extended it to all the evils of his life——

——Turn in hither, I beseech thee!——behold these breeches! ——they are all I have in the world——that piteous rent was given them at *Lyons*——

---

7. Holding two cards that bracket one held by the opponent—a great advantage.

8. He lost his hand at the battle of Lepanto. [*Sterne's note.*]

My shirts! see what a deadly schism has happen'd amongst 'em
——for the laps are in *Lombardy*, and the rest of 'em here——I
never had but six, and a cunning gypsey of a laundress at *Milan* cut
me off the *fore*-laps of five——To do her justice, she did it with
some consideration——for I was returning *out* of *Italy*.

And yet, notwithstanding all this, and a pistol tinder-box which
was moreover filch'd from me at *Sienna*, and twice that I pay'd five
Pauls[9] for two hard eggs, once at *Raddicoffini*, and a second time at
Capua——I do not think a journey through *France* and *Italy*, provided a man keeps his temper all the way, so bad a thing as some
people would make you believe: there must be *ups* and *downs*, or
how the duce should we get into vallies where Nature spreads so
many tables of entertainment.——'Tis nonsense to imagine they
will lend you their voitures[1] to be shaken to pieces for nothing; and
unless you pay twelve sous for greasing your wheels, how should
the poor peasant get butter to his bread?——We really expect too
much——and for the livre or two above par for your suppers and
bed——at the most they are but one shilling and ninepence halfpenny——who would embroil their philosophy for it? for heaven's
and for your own sake, pay it——pay it with both hands open,
rather than leave *Disappointment* sitting drooping upon the eye of
your fair Hostess and her Damsels in the gate-way, at your departure——and besides, my dear Sir, you get a sisterly kiss of each
of 'em worth a pound——at least I did——

——For my uncle *Toby*'s amours running all the way in my
head, they had the same effect upon me as if they had been my
own——I was in the most perfect state of bounty and good will;
and felt the kindliest harmony vibrating within me, with every oscillation of the chaise alike; so that whether the roads were rough or
smooth, it made no difference; every thing I saw, or had to do with,
touch'd upon some secret spring either of sentiment or rapture.

——They were the sweetest notes I ever heard; and I instantly let
down the fore-glass to hear them more distinctly——'Tis *Maria*;
said the postilion, observing I was listening——Poor *Maria*, continued he, (leaning his body on one side to let me see her, for he was
in a line betwixt us) is sitting upon a bank playing her vespers upon
her pipe, with her little goat beside her.

The young fellow utter'd this with an accent and a look so perfectly in tune to a feeling heart, that I instantly made a vow, I
would give him a four and twenty sous piece, when I got to
Moulins——

9. Paolo, a small Italian coin. The complaint here is part of Sterne's continuing
parody of Tobias Smollett's *Travels*

through France and Italy (1766).
1. Carriages.

————And who is *poor Maria*? said I.

The love and pity of all the villages around us; said the postillion ————it is but three years ago, that the sun did not shine upon so fair, so quick-witted and amiable a maid; and better fate did *Maria* deserve, than to have her Banns forbid,[2] by the intrigues of the curate of the parish who published them————

He was going on, when *Maria*, who had made a short pause, put the pipe to her mouth and began the air again————they were the same notes;————yet were ten times sweeter: It is the evening service to the Virgin, said the young man————but who has taught her to play it————or how she came by her pipe, no one knows; we think that Heaven has assisted her in both; for ever since she has been unsettled in her mind, it seems her only consolation————she has never once had the pipe out of her hand, but plays that *service* upon it almost night and day.

The postillion delivered this with so much discretion and natural eloquence, that I could not help decyphering something in his face above his condition, and should have sifted out his history, had not poor *Maria's* taken such full possession of me.

We had got up by this time almost to the bank where *Maria* was sitting: she was in a thin white jacket with her hair, all but two tresses, drawn up into a silk net, with a few olive leaves twisted a little fantastically on one side————she was beautiful; and if ever I felt the full force of an honest heart-ache, it was the moment I saw her————

————God help her! poor damsel! above a hundred masses, said the postillion, have been said in the several parish churches and convents around, for her,————but without effect; we have still hopes, as she is sensible for short intervals, that the Virgin at last will restore her to herself; but her parents, who know her best, are hopeless upon that score, and think her senses are lost for ever.

As the postillion spoke this, MARIA made a cadence so melancholy, so tender and querulous, that I sprung out of the chaise to help her, and found myself sitting betwixt her and her goat before I relapsed from my enthusiasm.

MARIA look'd wistfully for some time at me, and then at her goat ————and then at me————and then at her goat again, and so on, alternately————

————Well, *Maria*, said I softly————What resemblance do you find?

I do intreat the candid reader to believe me, that it was from the humblest conviction of what a *Beast* man is,————that I ask'd the question; and that I would not have let fallen an unseasonable

2. That is, to be forbidden to marry.

pleasantry in the venerable presence of Misery, to be entitled to all
the wit that ever *Rabelais* scatter'd——and yet I own my heart
smote me, and that I so smarted at the very idea of it, that I swore I
would set up for Wisdom and utter grave sentences the rest of my
days——and never——never attempt again to commit mirth with
man, woman, or child, the longest day I had to live.

As for writing nonsense to them——I believe, there was a reserve
——but that I leave to the world.

Adieu, *Maria!*——adieu, poor hapless damsel!——some time,
but not *now*, I may hear thy sorrows from thy own lips——but I
was deceived; for that moment she took her pipe and told me such a
tale of woe with it, that I rose up, and with broken and irregular
steps walk'd softly to my chaise.

——What an excellent inn at *Moulins!*

Chapter XXV.

WHEN we have got to the end of this chapter (but not
before) we must all turn back to the two blank chapters,
on the account of which my honour has lain bleeding this half
hour——I stop it, by pulling off one of my yellow slippers and
throwing it with all my violence to the opposite side of my room,
with a declaration at the heel of it——

——That whatever resemblance it may bear to half the chapters
which are written in the world, or, for aught I know, may be now
writing in it——that it was as casual as the foam of *Zeuxis* his
horse:[3] besides, I look upon a chapter which has, *only nothing in it*,
with respect; and considering what worse things there are in the
world——That it is no way a proper subject for satire——

——Why then was it left so? And here, without staying for my
reply, shall I be call'd as many blockheads, numsculs, doddypoles,
dunderheads, ninny-hammers, goosecaps, joltheads, nicompoops,
and sh--t-a-beds——and other unsavory appellations, as ever the
cake-bakers of *Lerné*, cast in the teeth of King *Gargantua's*
shepherds[4]——And I'll let them do it, as *Bridget* said, as much as
they please; for how was it possible they should foresee the necessity I was under of writing the 25th chapter of my book, before the
18th, &c.?

——So I don't take it amiss——All I wish is, that it may be a
lesson to the world, *"to let people tell their stories their own way."*

---

3. Zeuxis was an ancient Greek painter,
but it was another one, Nealces, who
created the appearance of foam on a
horse's mouth by throwing a sponge
at his painting.
4. Rabelais, I.25.

𝕿𝖍𝖊 𝕰𝖎𝖌𝖍𝖙𝖊𝖊𝖓𝖙𝖍 𝕮𝖍𝖆𝖕𝖙𝖊𝖗

AS Mrs. *Bridget* open'd the door before the Corporal had well given the rap, the interval betwixt that and my uncle *Toby*'s introduction into the parlour, was so short, that Mrs. *Wadman* had but just time to get from behind the curtain——lay a Bible upon the table, and advance a step or two towards the door to receive him.

My uncle *Toby* saluted Mrs. *Wadman*, after the manner in which women were saluted by men in the year of our Lord God one thousand seven hundred and thirteen——then facing about, he march'd up abreast with her to the sopha, and in three plain words ——thought not before he was sat down——nor after he was sat down——but as he was sitting down, told her, *"he was in love"* ——so that my uncle *Toby* strained himself more in the declaration than he needed.

Mrs. *Wadman* naturally looked down, upon a slit she had been darning up in her apron, in expectation every moment, that my uncle *Toby* would go on; but having no talents for amplification, and LOVE moreover of all others being a subject of which he was the least a master——When he had told Mrs. *Wadman* once that he loved her, he let it alone, and left the matter to work after its own way.

My father was always in raptures with this system of my uncle *Toby*'s, as he falsely called it, and would often say, that could his brother *Toby* to his processe have added but a pipe of tobacco—— he had wherewithal to have found his way, if there was faith in a *Spanish* proverb,[5] towards the hearts of half the women upon the globe.

My uncle *Toby* never understood what my father meant; nor will I presume to extract more from it, than a condemnation of an error which the bulk of the world lie under——but the *French*, every one of 'em to a man, who believe in it, almost as much as the REAL PRESENCE,[6] *"That talking of love, is making it."*

——I would as soon set about making a black-pudding by the same receipt.

Let us go on: Mrs. *Wadman* sat in expectation my uncle *Toby* would do so, to almost the first pulsation of that minute, wherein silence on one side or the other, generally becomes indecent: so edging herself a little more towards him, and raising up her eyes, sub-blushing, as she did it——she took up the gauntlet——or the

5. A number of Spanish proverbs suggest that love does not require many words.

6. The Roman Catholic doctrine that Christ is really and substantially present in the Communion bread and wine.

discourse (if you like it better) and communed with my uncle *Toby*, thus.

The cares and disquietudes of the marriage state, quoth Mrs. *Wadman*, are very great. I suppose so——said my uncle *Toby*: and therefore when a person, continued Mrs. *Wadman*, is so much at his ease as you are——so happy, captain *Shandy*, in yourself, your friends and your amusements——I wonder, what reasons can incline you to the state——

——They are written, quoth my uncle *Toby*, in the Common-Prayer Book.[7]

Thus far my uncle *Toby* went on warily, and kept within his depth, leaving Mrs. *Wadman* to sail upon the gulph as she pleased.

——As for children——said Mrs. *Wadman*——though a principal end perhaps of the institution, and the natural wish, I suppose, of every parent——yet do not we all find, they are certain sorrows, and very uncertain comforts? and what is there, dear sir, to pay one for the heart-aches——what compensation for the many tender and disquieting apprehensions of a suffering and defenceless mother who brings them into life? I declare, said my uncle *Toby*, smit with pity, I know of none; unless it be the pleasure which it has pleased God——

A fiddlestick! quoth she.

Chapter the Nineteenth

NOW there are such an infinitude of notes, tunes, cants, chants, airs, looks, and accents with which the word *fiddlestick* may be pronounced in all such causes as this, every one of 'em impressing a sense and meaning as different from the other, as *dirt* from *cleanliness*——That Casuists (for it is an affair of conscience on that score) reckon up no less than fourteen thousand in which you may do either right or wrong.

Mrs. *Wadman* hit upon the *fiddlestick*, which summoned up all my uncle *Toby*'s modest blood into his cheeks——so feeling within himself that he had somehow or other got beyond his depth, he stopt short; and without entering further either into the pains or pleasures of matrimony, he laid his hand upon his heart, and made an offer to take them as they were, and share them along with her.

When my uncle *Toby* had said this, he did not care to say it again; so casting his eye upon the Bible which Mrs. *Wadman* had laid upon the table, he took it up; and popping, dear soul! upon a

7. According to the Anglican Book of Common Prayer, marriage is ordained for three purposes: to bring children into the world, to provide an unsinful outlet for sexual passion, and for mutual comfort and help.

passage in it, of all others the most interesting to him——which was the siege of *Jericho*——he set himself to read it over——leaving his proposal of marriage, as he had done his declaration of love, to work with her after its own way. Now it wrought neither as an astringent or a loosener; nor like opium, or bark, or mercury, or buckthorn,[8] or any one drug which nature had bestowed upon the world——in short, it work'd not at all in her; and the cause of that was, that there was something working there before——Babbler that I am! I have anticipated what it was a dozen times; but there is fire still in the subject——allons.

Chapter XXVI.

IT is natural for a perfect stranger who is going from *London* to *Edinburgh,* to enquire before he sets out, how many miles to York; which is about the half way——nor does any body wonder, if he goes on and asks about the Corporation, &c.--

It was just as natural for Mrs. *Wadman,* whose first husband was all his time afflicted with a Sciatica, to wish to know how far from the hip to the groin; and how far she was likely to suffer more or less in her feelings, in the one case than in the other.

She had accordingly read *Drake's*[9] anatomy from one end to the other. She had peeped into *Wharton* upon the brain, and borrowed[1] *Graaf* upon the bones and muscles; but could make nothing of it.

She had reason'd likewise from her own powers—laid down theorems——drawn consequences, and come to no conclusion.

To clear up all, she had twice asked Doctor *Slop,* "if poor captain *Shandy* was ever likely to recover of his wound——?"

——He is recovered, Doctor *Slop* would say——

What! quite?

——Quite: madam——

But what do you mean by a recovery? Mrs. *Wadman* would say.

Doctor *Slop* was the worst man alive at definitions; and so Mrs. *Wadman* could get no knowledge: in short, there was no way to extract it, but from my uncle *Toby* himself.

There is an accent of humanity in an enquiry of this kind which lulls Suspicion to rest——and I am half persuaded the serpent got pretty near it, in his discourse with Eve; for the propensity in the sex to be deceived could not be so great, that she should have

8. A plant used as a cathartic.
9. James Drake (1667–1707) wrote *Anthropologia Nova, or a New System of Anatomy.* Thomas Wharton was a seventeenth-century anatomist; the reference is to his *Adenographia,* a treatise on glands.

1. This must be a mistake in Mr. Shandy; for Graaf wrote upon the pancreatick juice, and the parts of generation. [*Sterne's note.*] He refers to Regnier de Graaf, a seventeenth-century Dutch physician._

boldness to hold chat with the devil, without it——But there is an
accent of humanity——how shall I describe it?——'tis an accent
which covers the part with a garment, and gives the enquirer a right
to be as particular with it, as your body-surgeon.

"——Was it without remission?——

——Was it more tolerable in bed?

——Could he lie on both sides alike with it?

——Was he able to mount a horse?

——Was motion bad for it?" et cætera, were so tenderly spoke
to, and so directed towards my uncle *Toby*'s heart, that every item
of them sunk ten times deeper into it than the evils themselves——
but when Mrs. *Wadman* went round about by *Namur* to get at my
uncle *Toby*'s groin; and engaged him to attack the point of the
advanced counterscarp, and *pêle mêle* with the *Dutch* to take the
counterguard of St. *Roch* sword in hand——and then with tender
notes playing upon his ear, led him all bleeding by the hand out of
the trench, wiping her eye, as he was carried to his tent——Heaven!
Earth! Sea!——all was lifted up——the springs of nature rose
above their levels——an angel of mercy sat besides him on the
sopha——his heart glow'd with fire——and had he been worth a
thousand, he had lost every heart of them to Mrs. *Wadman*.

——And whereabouts, dear Sir, quoth Mrs. *Wadman*, a little
categorically, did you receive this sad blow?——In asking this question, Mrs. *Wadman* gave a slight glance towards the waistband of
my uncle *Toby*'s red plush breeches, expecting naturally, as the
shortest reply to it, that my uncle *Toby* would lay his fore-finger
upon the place——It fell out otherwise——for my uncle *Toby*
having got his wound before the gate of St. *Nicolas*, in one of the
traverses of the trench, opposite to the salient angle of the demi-
bastion of St. *Roch*; he could at any time stick a pin upon the
identical spot of ground where he was standing when the stone
struck him: this struck instantly upon my uncle *Toby*'s sensorium
——and with it, struck his large map of the town and citadel of
Namur and its environs, which he had purchased and pasted down
upon a board by the Corporal's aid, during his long illness——it
had lain with other military lumber in the garret ever since, and
accordingly the Corporal was detached into the garret to fetch it.

My uncle *Toby* measured off thirty toises, with Mrs. *Wadman*'s
scissars, from the returning angle before the gate of St. *Nicolas*; and
with such a virgin modesty laid her finger upon the place, that the
goddess of Decency, if then in being——if not, 'twas her shade——
shook her head, and with a finger wavering across her eyes——
forbid her to explain the mistake.

Unhappy Mrs. *Wadman*!——

——For nothing can make this chapter go off with spirit but an apostrophe to thee——but my heart tells me, that in such a crisis an apostrophe is but an insult in disguise, and ere I would offer one to a woman in distress——let the chapter go to the devil; provided any damn'd critick *in keeping*[2] will be but at the trouble to take it with him.

Chapter XXVII.

MY uncle *Toby*'s Map is carried down into the kitchen.

Chapter XXVIII.

—— AND here is the *Maes*——and this is the *Sambre;* said the Corporal, pointing with his right hand extended a little towards the map, and his left upon Mrs. *Bridget*'s shoulder ——but not the shoulder next him——and this, said he, is the town of *Namur*——and this the citadel——and there lay the *French*—— and here lay his honour and myself——and in this cursed trench, Mrs. *Bridget,* quoth the Corporal, taking her by the hand, did he receive the wound which crush'd him so miserably *here*——In pronouncing which he slightly press'd the back of her hand towards the part he felt for——and let it fall.

We thought, Mr. *Trim,* it had been more in the middle——said Mrs. *Bridget*——

That would have undone us for ever——said the Corporal.

——And left my poor mistress undone too——said *Bridget.*

The Corporal made no reply to the repartee, but by giving Mrs. *Bridget* a kiss.

Come——come——said *Bridget*——holding the palm of her left-hand parallel to the plane of the horizon, and sliding the fingers of the other over it, in a way which could not have been done, had there been the least wart or protuberance——'Tis every syllable of it false, cried the Corporal, before she had half finished the sentence——

——I know it to be fact, said *Bridget,* from credible witnesses.

———Upon my honour, said the Corporal, laying his hand upon his heart, and blushing as he spoke with honest resentment——'tis a story, Mrs. *Bridget,* as false as hell——Not, said *Bridget,* interrupting him, that either I or my mistress care a halfpenny about it, whether 'tis so or no———only that when one is married, one would chuse to have such a thing by one at least——

It was somewhat unfortunate for Mrs. *Bridget,* that she had

2. That is, "kept" by his publisher, and writing only to please him.

begun the attack with her manual exercise; for the Corporal instantly

* * * * * * * * * * * *

* * * * * * * * * * * *

* * * * * * * * * * * *

* * * *.

Chapter XXIX.

I T was like the momentary contest in the moist eye-lids of an *April* morning, "Whether *Bridget* should laugh or cry."

She snatch'd up a rolling-pin——'twas ten to one, she had laugh'd——

She laid it down——she cried; and had one single tear of 'em but tasted of bitterness, full sorrowful would the Corporal's heart have been that he had used the argument; but the Corporal understood the sex, a *quart major*[3] *to a terce* at least, better than my uncle *Toby*, and accordingly he assailed Mrs. *Bridget* after this manner.

I know, Mrs. *Bridget*, said the Corporal, giving her a most respectful kiss, that thou art good and modest by nature, and art withal so generous a girl in thyself, that if I know thee rightly, thou wouldst not wound an insect, much less the honour of so gallant and worthy a soul as my master, wast thou sure to be made a countess of——but thou hast been set on, and deluded, dear *Bridget*, as is often a woman's case, "to please others more than themselves——"

Bridget's eyes poured down at the sensations the Corporal excited.

——Tell me——tell me then, my dear *Bridget*, continued the Corporal, taking hold of her hand, which hung down dead by her side,——and giving a second kiss——whose suspicion has misled thee?

Bridget sobb'd a sob or two——then open'd her eyes——the Corporal wiped 'em, with the bottom of her apron——she then open'd her heart and told him all.

Chapter XXX.

M Y uncle *Toby* and the Corporal had gone on separately with their operations the greatest part of the campaign, and as effectually cut off from all communication of what either the one or the other had been doing, as if they had been separated from each other by the *Maes* or the *Sambre*.

My uncle *Toby*, on his side, had presented himself every afternoon in his red and silver, and blue and gold alternately, and

3. Considerably better—the difference is between a hand of cards including a run of the four highest in a suit, and one with a run of any three cards.

sustained an infinity of attacks in them, without knowing them to be attacks——and so had nothing to communicate——

The Corporal, on his side, in taking *Bridget*, by it had gain'd considerable advantages——and consequently had much to communicate——but what were the advantages——as well, as what was the manner by which he had seiz'd them, required so nice an historian that the Corporal durst not venture upon it; and as sensible as he was of glory, would rather have been contented to have gone bareheaded and without laurels for ever, than torture his master's modesty for a single moment——

——Best of honest and gallant servants!——But I have apostrophiz'd thee, *Trim!* once before——and could I apotheosize thee also (that is to say) with good company——I would do it *without ceremony* in the very next page.

Chapter XXXI.

N OW my uncle *Toby* had one evening laid down his pipe upon the table, and was counting over to himself upon his finger ends, (beginning at his thumb) all Mrs. *Wadman*'s perfections one by one; and happening two or three times together, either by omitting some, or counting others twice over to puzzle himself sadly before he could get beyond his middle finger——Prithee, *Trim!* said he, taking up his pipe again,——bring me a pen and ink: *Trim* brought paper also.

Take a full sheet——*Trim!* said my uncle *Toby*, making a sign with his pipe at the same time to take a chair and sit down close by him at the table. The Corporal obeyed——placed the paper directly before him——took a pen and dip'd it in the ink.

——She has a thousand virtues, *Trim!* said my uncle *Toby*——

Am I to set them down, an' please your honour? quoth the Corporal.

——But they must be taken in their ranks, replied my uncle *Toby*; for them all, *Trim*, that which wins me most, and which is a security for all the rest, is the compassionate turn and singular humanity of her character——I protest, added my uncle *Toby*, looking up, as he protested it, towards the top of the ceiling—— That was I her brother, *Trim*, a thousand fold, she could not make more constant or more tender enquiries after my sufferings—— though now no more.

The Corporal made no reply to my uncle *Toby*'s protestation, but by a short cough——he dip'd the pen a second time into the ink-horn; and my uncle *Toby*, pointing with the end of his pipe as close to the top of the sheet at the left hand corner of it, as he could get it——the Corporal wrote down the word

HUMANITY - - - - - - - - - - - - - - thus.

Prithee, Corporal, said my uncle *Toby*, as soon as *Trim* had done it——————how often does Mrs. *Bridget* enquire after the wound on the cap of thy knee, which thou received'st at the battle of *Landen*?

She never, an' please your honour, enquires after it at all.

That, Corporal, said my uncle *Toby*, with all the triumph the goodness of his nature would permit——————That shews the difference in the character of the mistress and maid——————had the fortune of war allotted the same mischance to me, Mrs. *Wadman* would have enquired into every circumstance relating to it a hundred times——————She would have enquired, an' please your honour, ten times as often about your honour's groin——————The pain, *Trim*, is equally excruciating,——————and Compassion has as much to do with the one as the other——————

——————God bless your honour! cried the Corporal——————what has a woman's compassion to do with a wound upon the cap of a man's knee? had your honour's been shot into ten thousand splinters at the affair of *Landen*, Mrs. *Wadman* would have troubled her head as little about it as *Bridget*; because, added the Corporal, lowering his voice and speaking very distinctly, as he assigned his reason——————

"The knee is such a distance from the main body——————whereas the groin, your honour knows, is upon the very *curtin* of the *place*."

My uncle *Toby* gave a long whistle——————but in a note which could scarce be heard across the table.

The Corporal had advanced too far to retire——————in three words he told the rest——————

My uncle *Toby* laid down his pipe as gently upon the fender, as if it had been spun from the unravellings of a spider's web——————

——————Let us go to my brother *Shandy*'s, said he.

Chapter XXXII.

THERE will be just time, whilst my uncle *Toby* and *Trim* are walking to my father's, to inform you, that Mrs. *Wadman* had, some moons before this, made a confident of my mother; and that Mrs. *Bridget*, who had the burden of her own, as well as her mistress's secret to carry, had got happily delivered of both to *Susannah* behind the garden-wall.

As for my mother, she saw nothing at all in it, to make the least bustle about——————but *Susannah* was sufficient by herself for all the ends and purposes you could possibly have, in exporting a family secret; for she instantly imparted it by signs to *Jonathan*——————and *Jonathan* by tokens to the cook, as she was basting a loin of mutton; the cook sold it with some kitchen-fat to the postillion for a groat, who truck'd it with the dairy maid for something of about the same value———and though whisper'd in the hay-loft, FAME caught the notes with her brazen trumpet and sounded them upon the house-top———In a word, not an old woman in the village or five miles round, who did not understand the difficulties of my uncle *Toby*'s siege, and what were the secret articles which had delay'd the surrender.———

My father, whose way was to force every event in nature into an hypothesis, by which means never man crucified TRUTH at the rate he did———had but just heard of the report as my uncle *Toby* set out; and catching fire suddenly at the trespass done his brother by it, was demonstrating to *Yorick*, notwithstanding my mother was sitting by———not only, "That the devil was in women, and that the whole of the affair was lust;" but that every evil and disorder in the world, of what kind or nature soever, from the first fall of *Adam*, down to my uncle *Toby*'s (inclusive) was owing one way or other to the same unruly appetite.

Yorick was just bringing my father's hypothesis to some temper, when my uncle *Toby* entering the room with marks of infinite benevolence and forgiveness in his looks, my father's eloquence rekindled against the passion———and as he was not very nice in the choice of his words when he was wroth———as soon as my uncle *Toby* was seated by the fire, and had filled his pipe, my father broke out in this manner.

Chapter XXXIII.

———THAT provision should be made for continuing the race of so great, so exalted and godlike a Being as man———I am far from denying———but philosophy speaks freely of every thing; and therefore I still think and do maintain it to be a pity, that it should be done by means of a passion which bends down the faculties, and turns all the wisdom, contemplations, and operations of the soul backwards———a passion, my dear, continued my father, addressing himself to my mother, which couples and equals wise men with fools, and makes us come out of caverns and hiding-places more like satyrs and four-footed beasts than men.

I know it will be said, continued my father (availing himself of the *Prolepsis*[4]) that in itself, and simply taken———like hunger, or thirst, or sleep———'tis an affair neither good or bad———or shameful or otherwise.———Why then did the delicacy of *Diogenes*[5] and *Plato* so recalcitrate against it? and wherefore, when we go about to make and plant a man, do we put out the candle? and for what reason is

---

4. To anticipate an argument and an-swer it in advance.
5. Diogenes, the Greek Cynic philos-opher, and Plato both discuss the de-structive effects of sexual passion.

it, that all the parts thereof——the congredients——the preparations——the instruments, and whatever serves thereto, are so held
as to be conveyed to a cleanly mind by no language, translation, or
periphrasis whatever?

——The act of killing and destroying a man, continued my father raising his voice——and turning to my uncle *Toby*——you
see, is glorious——and the weapons by which we do it are honourable——We march with them upon our shoulders——We strut
with them by our sides——We gild them——We carve them——
We in-lay them——We enrich them——Nay, if it be but a *scoun-
dril* cannon, we cast an ornament upon the breech of it.——

——My uncle *Toby* laid down his pipe to intercede for a better
epithet——and *Yorick* was rising up to batter the whole hypothesis
to pieces——

——When *Obadiah* broke into the middle of the room with a
complaint, which cried out for an immediate hearing.

The case was this:

My father, whether by ancient custom of the manor, or as im-
propriator of the great tythes,[6] was obliged to keep a Bull for the
service of the Parish, and *Obadiah* had led his cow upon a *pop-visit*
to him one day or other the preceeding summer——I say, one day
or other——because as chance would have it, it was the day on
which he was married to my father's housemaid——so one was a
reckoning to the other. Therefore when *Obadiah*'s wife was brought
to bed——*Obadiah* thanked God——

——Now, said *Obadiah*, I shall have a calf: so *Obadiah* went
daily to visit his cow.

She'll calve on Monday——on Tuesday——on Wednesday at the
farthest——

The cow did not calve——no——she'll not calve till next week
——the cow put it off terribly——till at the end of the sixth week
Obadiah's suspicions (like a good man's) fell upon the Bull.

Now the parish being very large, my father's Bull, to speak the
truth of him, was no way equal to the department; he had, however,
got himself, somehow or other, thrust into employment——and as
he went through the business with a grave face, my father had a
high opinion of him.

——Most of the townsmen, an' please your worship, quoth
Obadiah, believe that 'tis all the Bull's fault——

——But may not a cow be barren? replied my father, turning to
Doctor *Slop*.

It never happens: said Dr. *Slop*, but the man's wife may have
come before her time naturally enough——Prithee has the child
hair upon his head?——added Dr. *Slop*——

6. The parishioner who disburses and
accounts for church revenues (traditionally a tithe, or tenth, of the income of
members of the parish).

————It is as hairy as I am; said *Obadiah*.————*Obadiah* had not been shaved for three weeks————Wheu - - u - - - - u - - - - - - - cried my father; beginning the sentence with an exclamatory whistle———— and so, brother *Toby*, this poor Bull of mine, who is as good a Bull as ever p——ss'd, and might have done for *Europa*[7] herself in purer times————had he but two legs less, might have been driven into Doctors Commons[8] and lost his character————which to a Town Bull, brother *Toby*, is the very same thing as his life————

L - - d! said my mother, what is all this story about?————

A COCK and a BULL, said *Yorick*————And one of the best of its kind, I ever heard.

The END of the NINTH VOLUME.

---

7. Zeus transformed himself into a bull to carry off the princess Europa to Crete, where she bore him several children, among them the bull-like Minos.

8. The College of Doctors of Civil Law, where divorces, and other civil legal matters, were handled.

The Author on the Novel

To Robert Dodsley†

May 23, 1759

With this You will rec^ve the Life & Opinions of Tristram Shandy, wch I choose to offer to You first—and put into your hands without any kind of Distrust both from your general good Character, & the very handsome Recommendation of Mr Hinksman. The Plan, as you will perceive, is a most extensive one,—taking in, not only, the Weak part of the Sciences, in wch the true point of Ridicule lies—but every Thing else, which I find Laugh-at-able in my way—.

* * *

To a Friend.[1]

Summer, 1759

* * * I will use all reasonable caution—Only with this caution along with it, not to spoil My Book;—that is the air and originality of it, which must resemble the Author—& I fear 'tis a Number of these slighter touches which Mark this resemblance & Identify it from all Others of the [same] Stamp—Which this understrapping Virtue of Prudence would Oblige Me to strike out.—A Very Able Critick & One of My Colour too—who has Read Over tristram—Made Answer Upon My saying I Would consider the colour of My Coat, as I corrected it—That that very Idea in My head would render My Book not worth a groat—still I promise to be Cautious —but I deny I have gone as farr as Swift—He keeps a due distance from Rabelais—& I keep a due distance from him—Swift has said a hundred things I durst Not Say—Unless I was Dean of St. Patricks—

I like Your Caution of the Ambitiosa recidet ornamenta[2]—as I revise My book, I will shrive My conscience upon that sin & What ever Ornaments are of that kind shall be defac'd Without Mercy.

Ovid is justly condemn'd in being Ingenij sui Amator[3]—and it is a seasonable hint to Me, as I am Not sure I am clear of it—to Sport too Much with Your wit—or the Game that wit has pointed is surfeiting—like toying with a Mans Mistress—it may be a Very delightful Solacement to the Inamorato—tho little to the bystander.

Tho I plead guilty to a part of this Charge Yet would greatly alleviate the Crime—If My Readers knew how Much I suppress'd of

† All letters in this section can be found in *Letters of Laurance Sterne*, ed. Lewis P. Curtis (Oxford: Oxford University Press, 1935). This is the letter in which Sterne offers the first two volumes to Dodsley for publication.
1. The friend had found Sterne's manu-
script inadvisable for a clergyman to publish.
2. "Delete unnecessary ornaments." Horace, *De arte poetica*, ll. 447–48.
3. "In love with his own abilities." Quintilian, *Institutio Oratoria*, X.i.88.

this desire—I have Burn'd More wit, then I have publish'd upon that very Acc^t—since I began to Avoid the Very fault I fear I may have Yet given Proofs of. I will reconsider Slops fall & my too Minute Account of it^4—but in general I am perswaded that the happiness of the Cervantic humour arises from this very thing—of describing silly and trifling Events, with the Circumstantial Pomp of great Ones—perhaps this is Overloaded—& I can soon ease it—

I have a project of getting Tristram put into the ABishops^5 hands, if he comes down this Autumn, Which will ease my conscience of all troubles Upon the Topick of Discretion—.

* * *

To Robert Dodsley^6

October, 1759

* * * All locality is taken out of the book—the satire general; notes are added where wanted, and the whole made more saleable— about a hundred and fifty pages added—and to conclude, a strong interest formed and forming in its behalf, which I hope will soon take off the few I shall print on this *coup d'essai.*^{7} * * *

To Dr. Noah Thomas [?]^8

Jan. 30, 1760

Dear Sir,

—*De mortuis nil nisi bonum*, is a maxim which you have so often of late urged in conversation, and in your letters, (but in your last especially) with such seriousness, and severity against me, as the supposed transgressor of the rule;—that you have made me at length as serious and severe as yourself:—but that the humours you have stirred up might not work too potently within me, I have waited four days to cool myself, before I would set pen to paper to answer you, '*de mortuis nil nisi bonum.*' I declare I have considered the wisdom, and foundation of it over and over again, as dispassionately and charitably as a good Christian can, and, after all, I can find nothing in it, or make more of it, than a nonsensical lullaby of some nurse, put into Latin by some pedant, to be chanted by some hypocrite to the end of the world, for the consolation of departing lechers.—'Tis, I own, Latin; and I think that is all the weight it has—for, in plain English, 'tis a loose and futile position

---

4. *Tristram Shandy*, II.ix.
5. John Gilbert, Archbishop of York.
6. This is a response to Dodsley's refusal of Sterne's original offer, describing changes he has made and proposing to print the book at his own expense.
7. Effort.
8. This letter may be addressed to Dr. Noah Thomas of Scarborough, who appears to have disapproved of Sterne's satire on Dr. Richard Mead, the Kunastrokius of *Tristram Shandy*.

below a dispute—'*you are not to speak any thing of the dead, but what is good.*' Why so?—Who says so? neither reason or scripture. —Inspired authors have done otherwise—and reason and common sense tell me, that if the characters of past ages and men are to be drawn at all, they are to be drawn like themselves; that is, with their excellencies, and with their foibles—and it is as much a piece of justice to the world, and to virtue too, to do the one, as the other.— The ruleing passion *et les egarements du coeur,*[9] are the very things which mark, and distinguish a man's character;—in which I would as soon leave out a man's head as his hobby-horse.—However, if like the poor devil of a painter, we must conform to this pious canon, *de mortuis, &c.* which I own has a spice of piety in the *sound* of it, and be obliged to paint both our angels and our devils out of the same pot—I then infer that our Sydenhams, and Sangrados,[1] our Lucretias,—and Massalinas, our Sommers, and our Bolingbrokes—are alike entitled to statues, and all the historians, or satirists who have said otherwise since they departed this life, from Sallust, to S[tern]e, are guilty of the crimes you charge me with, 'cowardice and injustice.'

But why cowardice? 'because 'tis not courage to attack a dead man who can't defend himself.'—But why do you doctors of the faculty attack such a one with your incision knife? Oh! for the good of the living.—'Tis my plea.—But I have something more to say in my behalf—and it is this—I am not guilty of the charge—tho' defensible. I have not cut up Doctor Kunastrokius at all—I have just scratch'd him—and that scarce skin-deep.—I do him first all honour—speak of Kunastrokius as a great man—(be he who he will) and then most distantly hint at a drole foible in his character[2] —and that not first reported (to the few who can even understand the hint) by me—but known before by every chamber-maid and footman within the bills of mortality—but Kunastrokius, you say, was a great man—'tis that very circumstance which makes the pleasantry—for I could name at this instant a score of honest gentlemen who might have done the very thing which Kunastrokius did, and seen no joke in it at all—as to the failing of Kun[a]strokius, which you say can only be imputed to his friends as a misfortune—I see nothing like a misfortune in it to any friend or relation of Kunastrokius—that Kunastrokius upon occasions should sit with ******* and *******—I have put these stars not *to hurt your worship's delicacy*—If Kunastrokius after all is too sacred a

9. "The wanderings of the heart" is a translation of *Les Egarements du coeur,* the title of a novel by Crébillon published in 1736–38.
1. This is a list of contrasting types: good and bad doctors (Sydenham vs. Sangrado), wives (Lucretia vs. Messalina), and statesmen (Somers vs. Bolingbroke). Sallust was a Roman historian whose moral standards operated more strongly in his writings than in his own life.
2. *Tristram Shandy,* I.ii.

character to be even smiled at, (which is all I have done) he has had better luck than his betters:—In the same page (without imputations of cowardice) I have said as much of a man of twice his wisdom—and that is Solomon, of whom I have made the same remark 'That they were both great men—and like all mortal men had each their ruling passion.'

—The consolation you give me, 'That my book however will be read enough to answer my design of raising a tax upon the public' —is very unconsolatory—to say nothing how very mortifying! by h[eave]n! an author is worse treated than a common ***** at this rate—'*You will get a penny by your sins, and that's enough.*' Upon this chapter let me comment.—That I proposed laying the world under contribution when I set pen to paper—is what I own, and I suppose I may be allow'd to have that view in my head in common with every other writer, to make my labour of advantage to myself.

Do not you do the same? but I beg I may add, that whatever views I had of that kind, I had other views—the first of which was, the hopes of doing the world good by ridiculing what I thought deserving of it—or of disservice to sound learning, &c.—how I have succeeded my book must shew—and this I leave entirely to the world—but not to that little world *of your acquaintance,* whose opinion, and sentiments you call the general opinion of the best judges *without exception,* who all affirm (you say) that my book cannot be put into the hands of any woman of *character.* (I hope you except widows, doctor—for they are not *all* so squeamish—but I am told they are all really of my party in return for some good offices done their interests in the 176th page of my second volume.[3] But for the chaste married, and chaste unmarried part of the sex— they must not read my book! Heaven forbid the stock of chastity should be lessen'd by the life and opinions of Tristram Shandy— yes, his opinions—it would certainly debauch 'em! God take them under his protection in this fiery trial, and send us plenty of Duenas to watch the workings of their humours, 'till they have safely got thro' the whole work.—If this will not be sufficient, may we have plenty of Sangrados to pour in plenty of cold water, till this terrible fermentation is over—as for the *nummum in loculo,*[4] which you mention to me a second time, I fear you think me very poor, or in debt—I thank God tho' I don't abound—that I have enough for a clean shirt every day—and a mutton chop—and my contentment with this, has thus far (and I hope ever will) put me above stooping an inch for it, for—estate.—Curse on it, I like it not to that degree, nor envy (*you may be sure*) any man who kneels in the dirt for

---

3. Widows are not referred to on this page (in II.xix), but Tristram does argue that children other than a woman's first are in less danger of damage from pressure in passing through the birth canal.
4. "Pocket money."

it—so that howsoever I may fall short of the ends proposed in commencing author—I enter this *protest*, first that my end was *honest,* and secondly, that I wrote not [to] be *fed,* but to be *famous.*[5] I am much obliged to Mr. Garrick for his very favourable opinion—but why, dear Sir, had he done better in finding fault with it than in commending it? to humble me? an author is not so soon humbled as you imagine—no, but to make the book better by castrations—that is still *sub judice,*[6] and I can assure you upon this chapter, that the very passages, and descriptions you propose, that I should sacrifice in my second edition, are what are best relish'd by men of wit, and some others whom I esteem as sound criticks—so that upon the whole, I am still kept up, if not above fear, at least above despair, and have seen enough to shew me the folly of an attempt of castrating my book to the prudish humours of particulars. I believe the short cut would be to publish this letter at the beginning of the third volume, as an apology for the first and second. I was sorry to find a censure upon the insincerity of some of my friends—I have no reason myself to reproach any one man—my friends have continued in the same opinions of my books which they first gave me of it—many indeed have thought better of 'em, by considering them more; few worse.

I am, Sir,

Your humble servant,

LAURENCE STERNE

To Jane [?] Fenton

August 3, 1760

* * * I have just finished one volume of *Shandy,* and I want to read it to some one who I know can taste and rellish humour—this by the way, is a little impudent in me—for I take the thing for granted, which their high Mightinesses the World have yet to determine—but I mean no such thing—I could wish only to have your opinion—shall I, in truth, give you mine?—I dare not—but I will; provided you keep it to yourself—know then, that I think there is more laughable humour,—with equal degree of Cervantik Satyr[7]—if not more than in the last—but we are bad Judges of the merit of our Children.

* * *

---

5. Colley Cibber, a notoriously bad actor and writer often attacked by other writers in the 1730s and 40s, had made the opposite claim in defending himself.

6. "Still undecided."

7. That is, good-natured satire in the manner of Cervantes' *Don Quixote.*

To Stephen Croft

December 25, 1760

* * * I am not much in pain upon what gives my kind friends at Stillington so much on the chapter of Noses[8]—because, as the principal satire throughout that part is levelled at those learned blockheads who, in all ages, have wasted their time and much learning upon points as foolish—it shifts off the idea of what you fear, to another point—and 'tis thought here very good—'twill pass muster—I mean not with all—no—no! I shall be attacked and pelted, either from cellars or garrets, write what I will—and besides, must expect to have a party against me of many hundreds—who either do not—or will not laugh.—'Tis enough if I divide the world; —at least I will rest contented with it. * * *

To John Hall-Stevenson

[June, 1761]

To-morrow morning, (if Heaven permit) I begin the fifth volume of Shandy—I care not a curse for the critics—I'll load my vehicle with what goods *he* sends me, and they may take 'em off my hands, or let them alone—I am very valourous—and 'tis in proportion as we retire from the world and see it in its true dimensions, that we despise it—no bad rant! * * *

To Lady Anna Dacre [?]

September 21, 1761

* * * I am scribbling away at my Tristram. These two volumes[9] are, I think, the best.—I shall write as long as I live, 'tis, in fact, my hobby-horse: and so much am I delighted with my uncle Toby's imaginary character, that I am become an enthusiast. * * *

To Robert Foley

November 9, 1762

I am got pretty well, and sport much with my uncle Toby in the volume I am now fabricating for the laughing part of the world— for the melancholy part of it, I have nothing but my prayers—so God help them. * * *

8. Sterne's friends, the Crofts of Stillington, would have had a chance to read Volumes III and IV as they were being written.
9. Volumes V and VI.

To Elizabeth Montagu

[June, 1764]

I am going down to write a world of Nonsense—if possible like a man of *Sense*—but there is the *Rub*.[1] Would Apollo, or the fates, or any body else, had planted me within a League of Mrs Mountague this Summer, I could have taken my horse & gone & fetch'd Wit & Wisdome as I wanted them—as for nonsense—I am pretty well provided myself both by nature & Travel. * * *

To Robert Foley

November 11, 1764

* * * I will contrive to send you these 2 new Vol^s of *Tristram*,[2] as soon as ever I get them from the press—You will read as odd a Tour thro' france, as ever was projected or executed by traveller or travell Writer, since the world began—

—tis a laughing good temperd Satyr against Traveling (as puppies travel). * * *

---

1. *Hamlet*, III.i.65.   2. Volumes VII and VIII.

Criticism

Contemporary Responses

WILLIAM KENRICK

Review of *Tristram Shandy*†

* * * Of Lives and *Adventures* the public have had enough, and, perhaps, more than enough, long ago. A consideration that probably induced the droll Mr. Tristram Shandy to entitle the performance before us, his Life and *Opinions*. Perhaps also, he had, in this, a view to the design he professes, of giving the world two such volumes every year, during the remainder of his life. Now, adventures worth relating, are not every day to be met with, so that, in time, his budget might be exhausted; but his opinions will, in all probability, afford him matter enough to write about, tho' he should live to the age of Methusalem. Not but that our Author husbands his adventures with great œconomy, and sows them so extremely thin, that, in the manner he has begun, his narrative may very well last as long as he lives; nor, if that be long, and he as good as his word, will his history make an inconsiderable figure among the numerous diminutive tomes of a modern library.

But, indeed, Mr. Shandy seems so extremely fond of digressions, and of giving his historical Readers the slip on all occasions,[1] that we are not a little apprehensive he may, some time or other, give them the slip in good earnest, and leave the work before his story be finished. And, to say the truth, we should, for our own parts, be sorry to lose him in that manner; as we have no reason to think that we shall not be very willing to accompany him to the end of his tale, notwithstanding all his denunciations of prolixity. For, if we were sure he would not serve us this trick, we have no objection to his telling his story his own way, tho' he went as far about to come to the point, as Sancho Pancha[2] himself. Every Author, as the present justly observes, has a way of his own, in bringing his points to bear; and every man to his own taste. . . .

---

† From an unsigned review in the *Monthly Review*, appendix to xxi (July–December 1759), 561–71. This is the first review of *Tristram Shandy*.
1. We must do Mr. Tristram the Justice, however, to confess, that he generally carries his excuse for rambling along with him; and tho' he be not always hammering at his tale, yet he is busy enough: . . . in so much that we are apt to believe

him, when he protests he makes all the speed he possibly can. It would not be amiss, however, if, for the future, he paid a little more regard to going straight forward, lest the generality of his Readers, despairing of ever seeing the end of their journey, should tire, and leave him to jog on by himself. [*Kenrick's note.*]
2. Don Quixote's servant Sancho is notorious for long-winded stories.

But to return to our hero himself, whom we shall next consider and take leave of, as an Author; in which character we cannot help expressing, on many accounts, a particular approbation of him. The address with which he has introduced an excellent moral sermon, into a work of this nature (by which expedient, it will probably be read by many who would peruse a sermon in no other form) is masterly.

There prevails, indeed, a certain quaintness, and something like an affectation of being immoderately witty, throughout the whole work. But this is perhaps the Author's *manner*. Be that, however, as it will, it is generally attended with spirit and humour enough to render it entertaining. . . .

On the whole, we will venture to recommend Mr. Tristram Shandy, as a writer infinitely more ingenious and entertaining than any other of the present race of novelists. His characters are striking and singular, his observations shrewd and pertinent; and, making a few exceptions, his humour is easy and genuine.

* * *

From the *Critical Review*†

* * * This is a humorous performance, of which we are unable to convey any distinct ideas to our readers. The whole is composed of digressions, divertingly enough introduced, and characters which we think well supported. For instance, uncle *Toby*, corporal *Trim*, and Dr. *Slop*, are excellent imitations of certain characters in a modern truly Cervantic performance, which we avoid naming, out of regard to the author's delicacy.[1] Nothing can be more ridiculous than uncle *Toby*'s embarrassment in describing the siege of Namur, *Trim*'s attitude reading aloud a sermon, and Dr. *Slop*'s overthrow in the rencounter with Obadiah the coachman. To those, however, who have perused this performance, specifying particulars will be unnecessary, and to those readers who have not, it would be unentertaining. We therefore refer them to the work itself, desiring they will suspend their judgment till they have dipt into the second volume. * * *

From the *London Magazine*†

* * * Oh rare Tristram Shandy!—Thou very sensible—humorous —pathetick—humane—unaccountable!—what shall we call thee?— Rabelais, Cervantes, What?—Thou hast afforded us so much real

---

† From an unsigned notice in the *Critical Review*, ix (January 1760), 73–74.
1. The reviewer may be glancing at *Peregrine Pickle*, by Smollett, who was editor of the *Critical Review*.
† From an unsigned notice in the *London Magazine*, xxix (February 1760), 111.

pleasure in perusing thy life,—we can't call it thy life neither, since thy mother is still in labour of thee,—as demands our gratitude for the entertainment. Thy uncle Toby—Thy Yorick—thy father—Dr. Slop—corporal Trim; all thy characters are excellent, and thy opinions amiable! If thou publishest fifty volumes, all abounding with the profitable and pleasant, like these, we will venture to say thou wilt be read and admir'd,—Admir'd! by whom? Why, Sir, by the best, if not the most numerous class of mankind. * * *

From the *Royal Female Magazine*†

* * * *The Life and Opinions of Tristram Shandy* . . . affects (and not unsuccessfully) to please, by a contempt of all the rules observed in other writings, and therefore cannot justly have its merit measured by them. It were to be wished though, that the wantonness of the author's wit had been tempered with a little more regard to delicacy, throughout the greatest part of his work. * * *

HORACE WALPOLE

Letter to Sir David Dalrymple†

* * * At present nothing is talked of, nothing admired, but what I cannot help calling a very insipid and tedious performance: it is a kind of novel called, *The Life and Opinions of Tristram Shandy*; the great humour of which consists in the whole narration always going backwards. I can conceive a man saying that it would be droll to write a book in that manner, but have no notion of his persevering in executing it. It makes one smile two or three times at the beginning, but in recompense makes one yawn for two hours. The characters are tolerably kept up; but the humour is forever attempted and missed. The best thing in it is a sermon—oddly coupled with a good deal of bawdy, and both the composition of a clergyman. The man's head indeed was a little turned before, now topsyturvy with his success and fame. Dodsley has given him £650 for the second edition and two more volumes (which I suppose will reach backwards to his great-grandfather); Lord Falconberg[1] a donative of

† From an unsigned notice in the *Royal Female Magazine*, i (February 1760), 56.
† From *Horace Walpole's Correspondence with Sir David Dalrymple*, ed. W. S. Lewis, Charles H. Bennett, and Andrew G. Hoover (New Haven: Yale University Press, 1951), pp. 66–67. Walpole, the son of the Prime Minister, was himself for a time in politics, but achieved more importance as an antiquarian and taste-setter.

1. Earl Fauconberg of Newburgh enlarged Sterne's income by making him curate of Coxwold in March 1760, shortly after publication of the first volumes of *Tristram Shandy*.

£160 a year; and Bishop Warburton[2] gave him a purse of gold and this compliment (which happened to be a contradiction) *that it was quite an original composition, and in the true Cervantic vein*—the only copy that ever was an original except in painting, where they all pretend to be so. Warburton, however, not content with this, recommended the book to the bench of bishops and told them Mr Sterne, the author, was the English Rabelais—they had never heard of such a writer. * * *

Letter to the *Universal Magazine of Knowledge and Pleasure*†

Immodest Words admit of no Defence,
For Want of Decency is Want of Sense.
—POPE[1]

Whether the using of immodest words, and the want of decency, always imply want of sense; according to the motto; or whether, on the contrary, such freedom, may not, on certain occasions, be the result of good sense; I will not take upon me absolutely to determine. I know very well that a skilful physician can manage and compound some of the rankest and most deadly poisons in such a manner, that they shall answer very salutary purposes. Perhaps a writer, in compliance with a public corruption of taste, may be able so to blend and intermix the broad hint, and double entendre, with the moral and useful part of his work, as to engage the attention of such readers as would not otherwise look into his book; and by this means he insensibly leads them on, and agreeably deceives them at last, by leaving their hearts better than he found them. When this is the aim of an author, it is truly laudable; but it requires so much art and skill in the execution of this design, that very few, if any, meet with the desired success. If the author is a person whose character and influence may be of some weight, his using liberties of this kind, unless under proper restrictions, may be attended with pernicious consequences on the morals of his readers; for the world is very apt to use the sanction of such a person's authority, who, though contrary to his intention, is thus made to patronise and promote the reigning practice of immodest conversation, and the evil spreads in proportion as his works gain credit and acceptance.

I have been led into these reflections by the perusal of a book lately published, which meets with abundance of admirers, I mean

2. Warburton's relations with Sterne were at first friendly, but later cooled, perhaps because of rumors that Sterne intended to satirize him in *Tristram Shandy*.
† From an unidentified correspondent's letter to the *Universal Magazine of Knowledge and Pleasure*, xxvi (April 1760), 189–90.
1. The quotation is not from Pope but from the *Essay on Translated Verse* (1684), ll. 113–14, by Wentworth Dillon, Earl of Roscommon.

Tristram Shandy. Far be it from me to detract from the credit of an author, who has discovered such original and uncommon abilities in that manner of writing. I shall only beg leave to observe, that it were greatly to be wished, he had been more sparing in the use of indecent expressions. Indecent! did I say? Nay, even downright gross and obscene expressions are frequently to be met with throughout the book. . . . It is generally observable that the play-houses are most crouded, when any thing smutty is to be brought on the stage; and the reverend author of this ingenious performance has no doubt used this method as the most effectual, by making it as universally acceptable as possible. But how far it is excusable in any author, especially one who wears the gown, to gratify and promote a prevailing corrupted taste, either directly or indirectly, let himself and the world judge. I again repeat that it is really great pity he has not shewn more delicacy in this particular, for otherwise the book is truly excellent in its kind.

JAMES BOSWELL

From "A Poetical Epistle" †

*In nova fert animus mutatas dicere formas
Corpora: Di coeptis, nam vos mutastis et illas,
Favete.*

—Ovid.1

Dear Sir! if you're in mood to whistle
As Prologue to my poor Epistle—
I beg your audience for a minute,
In favour of the stuff that's in it.
  'What does the Dog by whistle mean?'
Methinks you say—good future Dean
My meaning Sir is very plain;
I mean if you've a vacant brain.
  For without question it would be
Just downright sacriledge in me
To interrupt one single thought
Of your's with—we shall call it nought.

---

† From "A Poetical Epistle to Doctor Sterne, Parson Yorick, and Tristram Shandy," Bodleian Library Manuscript, Douce 193. James Boswell (1740–95), the Scotsman who became friend and biographer to Samuel Johnson, met Sterne in London in 1760 and composed the "poetical epistle" from which these passages are drawn at about that time. Its existence, however, was not known until this century.

1. Dryden translates these lines from Book I of the *Metamorphoses* as follows:

Of bodies chang'd to various forms,
  I sing.
Ye gods, from whom these miracles
  did spring,
Inspire my numbers with celestial
  heat. . . .

Permitt me, Doctor, then, to show
A certain Genius whom you know,
A mortal enemy to strife,
At different periods of his life.
  To Country Curacy confin'd,
Ah! how unlike his soaring mind,
Poor Yorick stuck for many a day,
Like David in the miry clay.
  There for his constant occupation
He had the duties of his station;
Sundays and Holidays to Him
Were times on which he was in trim;
When with Ecclesiastic Gown
Of colour dubious, black or brown,
And wig centauric, form'd with care
From human & equestrian hair,
Thro' shades of which appear'd the caul;
Nay, some affirm his pate & all,
And band well starch'd by faithfull John,
For, to be sure, Maids he had none,
He solemn walk'd in grand Procession,
Like Justice to a Country Session,
To Church—'You'll step in there, I hope?'
No, Sir, excuse me—there I stop.

  In his retirement time was spent
So calm he knew not how it went
To murm'ring envy quite a Stranger
Nor of the spleen in the least danger.
For ease he would his head enwrap
In party-colour'd woolen Cap;
A threadbare Coat with sleeves full wide
A formal nightgown's place supply'd.
He wore, his new ones not t' abuse,
A pair of ancient, downheel'd shoes;
He roll'd his stockings 'bove his knees,
And was as *dégagé*'s you please.

  Now, God of love or God of wine,
Or muse, whichever of the nine
That erst blithe Ovid's tunefull tongue
Touch'd till he fancifully sung
Of Transformation's wondrous Power,
Such as Jove turn'd to Golden Shower,
O! to my Supplication list!
I will describe, if you assist,
As strange a metamorphosis,
I'm sure, as any one of his.
  Who has not *Tristram Shandy* read?

Is any mortal so ill bred?
If so, don't dare your birth to boast,
Nor give fam'd C[hu]dl[eig]h[2] for your toast.
This much about the time of lent,
His Harbinger to town he sent;
Procur'd Bob Dodsley for his friend,
Dodsley, who lives at the Court end—
A Circumstance which, Sir, I say't,
Must be allow'd to have some weight.
So soon as its reception kind
Was known, on swiftest wings of wind,
To reap a crop of fame and Pelf
Up comes th' original himself.

By Fashion's hands compleatly drest,
He's everywhere a wellcome Guest:
He runs about from place to place,
Now with my Lord, then with his Grace,
And, mixing with the brilliant throng,
He straight commences *Beau Garcon*.[3]
In Ranelagh's[4] delightfull round
Squire Tristram oft is flaunting found;
A buzzing whisper flys about;
Where'er he comes they point him out;
Each Waiter with an eager eye
Observes him as he passes by;
'That there is he, do, Thomas! look,
Who's wrote such a damn'd clever book.'

Next from the press there issues forth
A sage divine fresh from the north;
On Sterne's discourses we grew mad,
Sermons! where are they to be had?
Then with the fashionable Guards
The Psalms supply the place of Cards
A strange enthusiastic rage
For sacred text now seis'd the age;
Arround St. Jamess[5] every table
Was partly gay & partly sable,
The manners by old Noll[6] defended
Were with our modern chitte chat blended.
'Give me some maccaroni pray,'
'Be wise while it is call'd today;'
'Heavns! how Mingotti[7] sung last Monday'

2. Elizabeth Chudleigh was mistress to the Duke of Kingston.
3. "Handsome young man."
4. A fashionable pleasure garden on the Thames providing entertainment and refreshments.
5. A fashionable park in London's West End.
6. Oliver Cromwell.
7. An Italian opera singer popular in London.

'—Alas how we profane the Sunday.'
'My Lady Betty! hob or nob!—'[8]
'Great was the patience of old Job,'
Sir Smart breaks out & one & all
Adore S.ͭ Peter & S.ͭ Paul.

Now Sir! when I am in the cue
I wou'd not worship but praise you.
You need not try to shake your head
Or with Hawks eye strike me w.ͭʰ dread;
For as your uncle Toby stout,
What I incline I will have out.
Truth with a look of Approbation
Calls him t' encrease our Admiration:
This Sovreign's fav'rite, Edward's frien[d],[9]
Could Sycophants him more commend?
Sweet Sentiment, the certain test;
Of Goodness, commendation best!

I will admire and will pretend
To taste while I your works commend.

Yes, Sir, from partial motives free,
Which while I live I hope to be—
Your various meri[t]s sollid light:
Judgment, Imagination bright,
Great erudition, polish'd taste,
Pure language tho' you write in haste,
Sweet sentiments on Human life—
This I am sure, tis not for gain—
I firmly promise to maintain
Altho the public voice should fail
And envious Grubs[1] should half prevail,
Who swear like Shuttlecock they'll bandy
This upstart Willing Tristram Shandy.

O thou! whose quick-discerning eye
The nicest strokes of wit can spy;
Whose sterling jests, a sportive strain,
How warmly-genuine from the brain
And with bright poignancy appear,
Original to ev'ry ear!
Whose heart is all Benevolence;
Whose constant leader is good sense,
Who very seldom makes a real slip,
Altho at times he take[s] a trip
To frolic's lightsom regions where

8. A toast.
9. Prince Edward Augustus, Duke of York and Albany.

1. Many hack writers for money lived in Grub Street.

Mirth dissipates the dregs of care.
　To hear a fellow talk away
Who has not got a Word to say
Is of all things the most provoking:
Don't you think so too without joking?
Such now am I who can [no] more,
Having exhausted all my Store;
Therefore to shun your smarting Scoff
I without more ado break off.

Letter to *Lloyd's Evening Post*†

[June 4–6, 1760]

Sir,

So great an out cry is there in the world against the performance of the Author of *Tristram Shandy,* that, tho' I have only just looked into it, I am entirely convinced 'tis a smart satyrical piece on the vices of the age, particularly of that part of the Creation, which were designed for the pleasure and happiness of man. But this is not an age for wit and humour: arms and military atchievements engross the attention of one part of the public; pleasure and luxury occupy the minds of the other: So that neither Gentlemen nor Ladies have leisure to inspect their own conduct. But, notwithstanding all the clamours against this excellent production of *Tristram Shandy,* I would only beg leave to observe, that the Author has made use of a very proper expedient to put vice to the blush, and to restore to the Belle-monde, that innocency and virtue which can be their only ornaments. Perhaps, in some particular passages, he may seem to savour too much of the Libertine and Infidel; but let me recommend such nice and delicate Critics to the perusal of the sixth satyr of Juvenal,[1] which, if they be able to read and understand it, they will find was wrote with the same virtuous view, as the most abused *Tristram Shandy* is, and will be applauded as long as literature exists.

Your's,

W. K.

THOMAS GRAY

Letter to Thomas Warton the Younger†

[c. June 20, 1760]

* * *If I did not mention *Tristram* to you, it was because I

† From an unidentified correspondent to *Lloyd's Evening Post,* vi (June 4–6 1760), 539.
1. An attack on women by the Roman satirist.

† From *Correspondence of Thomas Gray,* ed. Paget Toynbee and Leonard Whibley (Oxford: The Clarendon Press, 1935), ii.681.

thought I had done so before. there is much good fun in it, & humour sometimes hit & sometimes mist. I agree with your opinion of it, & shall see the two future volumes with pleasure. have you read his Sermons (with his own comic figure at the head of them)?[1] they are in the style I think most proper for the Pulpit, & shew a very strong imagination & a sensible heart: but you see him often tottering on the verge of laughter, & ready to throw his perriwig in the face of his audience. * * *

OLIVER GOLDSMITH

From *The Citizen of the World*†

June 30, 1760

From Lien Chi Altangi, to Fum Hoam, first president of the Ceremonial Academy at Pekin, in China.

How often have we admired the eloquence of Europe! That strength of thinking, that delicacy of imagination, even beyond the efforts of the Chinese themselves. How were we enraptured with those bold figures which sent every sentiment with force to the heart. How have we spent whole days together in learning those arts by which European writers got within the passions, and led the reader as if by enchantment.

But though we have learned most of the rhetorical figures of the last age, yet there seems to be one or two of great use here, which have not yet travelled to China. The figures I mean are called *Bawdy* and *Pertness*; none are more fashionable; none so sure of admirers; they are of such a nature, that the merest blockhead, by a proper use of them, shall have the reputation of a wit; they lie level to the meanest capacities, and address those passions which all have, or would be ashamed to disown.

It has been observed, and I believe with some truth, that it is very difficult for a dunce to obtain the reputation of a wit; yet by the assistance of the figure *Baudy*, this may be easily effected, and a bawdy blockhead often passes for a fellow of smart parts and pretensions. Every object in nature helps the jokes forward, without scarce

1. An engraving from the portrait painted by Sir Joshua Reynolds in 1760.
† From *Collected Works of Oliver Goldsmith*, ed. Arthur Friedman (Oxford: The Clarendon Press, 1966), ii.221–25. "Letter liii" (above) was part of *The Citizen of The World*, which appeared as a serial in the *Public Ledger* during 1760–61. In these letters, Goldsmith speaks as a Chinese visitor writing about England to a friend at home. Though Sterne is not mentioned in the letter, he is here (as in some other letters of the *Citizen*) the main object of attack.

any effort of the imagination. If a lady stands, something very good may be said upon that, if she happens to fall, with the help of a little fashionable Pruriency, there are forty sly things ready on the occasion. But a prurient jest has always been found to give most pleasure to a few very old gentlemen, who being in some measure dead to other sensations, feel the force of the allusion with double violence on the organs of risibility.

An author who writes in this manner is generally sure therefore of having the very old and the impotent among his admirers; for these he may properly be said to write, and from these he ought to expect his reward, his works being often a very proper succedaneum to cantharides, or an assa foetida pill. His pen should be considered in the same light as the squirt of an apothecary, both being directed to the same generous end.

* * *

EDMUND BURKE

Review of *Tristram Shandy*†

* * *It is almost needless to observe of a book so universally read, that the story of the hero's life is the smallest part of the author's concern. The story is in reality made nothing more than a vehicle for satire on a great variety of subjects. Most of these satirical strokes are introduced with little regard to any connexion, either with the principal story or with each other. The author perpetually digresses; or rather having no determined end in view, he runs from object to object, as they happen to strike a very lively and very irregular imagination. These digressions so frequently repeated, instead of relieving the reader, become at length tiresome. The book is a perpetual series of disappointments. However, with this, and some other blemishes, the life of *Tristram Shandy* has uncommon merit. The faults of an original work are always pardoned; and it is not surprizing, that at a time, when a tame imitation makes almost the whole merit of so many books, so happy an attempt at novelty should have been so well received.

The satire with which· this work abounds, though not always happily introduced, is spirited, poignant, and often extremely just. The characters, though somewhat overcharged, are lively, and in nature. The author possesses in an high degree, the talent of catch-

† From a review of *Tristram Shandy*, *Annual Register*, iii (1760), 247. Burke, most famous for his political career and writings, earlier wrote literary criticism. Although he never acknowledged his editorship of the *Annual Register*, it is quite certain that he wrote this review.

ing the ridiculous in every thing that comes before him. The principal figure, old Shandy, is an humourist; full of good nature; full of whims; full of learning, which for want of being ballanced by good sense, runs him into an innumerable multitude of absurdities, in all affairs of life, and disquisitions of science. A character well imagined; and not uncommon in the world. The character of Yorick is supposed to be that of the author himself. There is none in which he has succeeded better; it is indeed conceived and executed with great skill and happiness. * * *

SAMUEL RICHARDSON

Letter to Mark Hildesley†

[January-February, 1761]
* * *Who is this Yorick? you are pleased to ask me. You cannot, I imagine have looked into his books: execrable I cannot but call them; for I am told that the third and fourth volumes are worse, if possible, than the two first; which, only, I have had the patience to run through. One extenuating circumstance attends his works, that they are too gross to be inflaming.

My daughter shall transcribe for me the sentiments of a young lady, as written to another lady, her friend in the country, on the publication of the two first volumes only.

'Happy are you in your retirement, where you read what books you choose, either for instruction or entertainment; but in this foolish town, we are obliged to read every foolish book that fashion renders prevalent in conversation; and I am horribly out of humour with the present taste, which makes people ashamed to own they have not read, what if fashion did not authorise, they would with more reason blush to say they had read! Perhaps some polite person from London, may have forced this piece into your hands, but give it not a place in your library; let not Tristram Shandy be ranked among the well chosen authors there. It is, indeed, a little book, and little is its merit, though great has been the writer's reward! Unaccountable wildness; whimsical digressions; comical incoherencies; uncommon indecencies; all with an air of novelty, has catched the reader's attention, and applause has flown from one to another, till it is almost singular to disapprove: even the bishops admire, and recompense his wit, though his own character as a clergyman seems

---

† From *Selected Letters of Samuel Richardson*, ed. John Carroll (Oxford: The Clarendon Press, 1964), pp. 341–42. Richardson was the author of *Pamela*, *Clarissa*, and *Sir Charles Grandison*—great novels which do not share the humor of *Tristram Shandy*. Hildesley was the Bishop of Sodor and Man.

much impeached by printing such gross and vulgar tales, as no decent mind can endure without extreme disgust! Yet I will do him justice; and, if forced by friends, or led by curiosity, you have read, and laughed, and almost cried at Tristram, I will agree with you that there is subject for mirth, and some affecting strokes; Yorick, Uncle Toby, and Trim are admirably characterised, and very interesting, and an excellent sermon of a perculiar kind, on conscience, is introduced; and I most admire the author for his judgment in seeing the town's folly in the extravagant praises and favours heaped on him; for he says, he passed unnoticed by the world till he put on a fool's coat, and since that every body admires him!

But mark my prophecy, that by another season, this performance will be as much decryed, as it is now extolled; for it has not intrinsic merit sufficient to prevent its sinking, when no longer upheld by the short-lived breath of fashion: and yet another prophecy I utter, that this ridiculous compound will be the cause of many more productions, witless and humourless, perhaps, but indecent and absurd; till the town will be punished for undue encouragement, by being poisoned with disgustful nonsense.' * * *

JOHN LANGHORNE

Review of *Tristram Shandy*†

* * *The Authors of the Monthly Review being determined never to lose sight of truth and candour, are neither to be misled by favour, nor irritated by reproach; neither perverted by prejudice, nor borne down with the current of popular opinion. The books that come under their cognizance will be considered with the same impartiality, whether the Authors be their friends or foes, in plain cloaths or prunella, in power or in prison. They would willingly, indeed, have their censure fall upon books only, without any regard to their Authors; but it is certain that a man may be immoral in his Writings as well as in his Actions, and in that respect he will always be liable to the censure of those, who consider themselves not only as judges in the Republic of Letters, but as members of society, and the servants of their country.

Upon these considerations, in reviewing the works of the learned, we are not only to observe their literary excellencies or defects, not merely to point out their faults or beauties, but to consider their moral tendency; and this more particularly, as it is of greater conse-

† From an unsigned review in the *Monthly Review*, xxvi (January 1762), 31–41.

quence to society that the heart be mended, than that the mind be entertained. . . .

Had we not then a right to complain, if a person, by profession obliged to discountenance indecency, and expressly commanded by those pure and divine doctrines he teaches, to avoid it; ought we not to have censured such a one, if he introduced obscenity as wit, and encouraged the depravity of young and unfledged vice, by libidinous ideas and indecent allusions?

In reviewing the *Life and Opinions of Tristram Shandy*, we have hitherto had occasion to lament, that, while the Author was exerting his talents to maintain the humour and consistency of his characters, he himself was so much out of character; and we could wish sincerely that we had now no farther reason for complaints of that kind.

The fifth and sixth volumes of this work, indeed, are not so much interlarded with obscenity as the former; yet they are not without their stars and dashes, their hints and whiskers: but, in point of true humour, they are much superior to the third and fourth, if not to the first and second. Some of the characters too are placed in a new light, and the rest are humorously supported. Uncle *Toby* is a considerable gainer by this continuation of his Nephew's Life and Opinions. In the story of *Le Fever* the old Captain appears in a most amiable light; and as this little episode does greater honour to the abilities and disposition of the Author, than any other part of his work, we shall quote it at large, as well for his sake, as for the entertainment of such of our Readers as may not have seen the original. [Quotes the Le Fever episode.]

Since Mr. Sterne published his Sermons, we have been of opinion, that his excellence lay not so much in the humorous as in the pathetic; and in this opinion we have been confirmed by the above story of Le Fever. We appeal to the Heart of every reader whether our judgment is not right?

SAMUEL JOHNSON

Conversation with Boswell (March 20, 1776) †

* * *I censured some ludicrous fantastick dialogues between two coach-horses, and other such stuff, which Baretti had lately published. He joined with me, and said, 'Nothing odd will do long. *Tristram Shandy* did not last.'* * *

† From *Boswell's Life of Johnson*, ed. George B. Hill and L. F. Powell (Oxford: The Clarendon Press, 1934–50), ii. 449. Johnson was the most important literary critic of the later eighteenth century. His literary standards were not particularly hospitable to Sterne's humor, and he especially disapproved of the fact that it emanated from a clergyman.

Early-Nineteenth-Century Criticism

SAMUEL TAYLOR COLERIDGE

[Sterne's Wit and Humor] †

* * *The pure unmixed ludicrous or laughable belongs exclusively to the understanding plus the senses of eye and ear; hence to the fancy. Not to the reason or the moral sense. . . .[1]

Hence too, that the laughable is its *own end*. When serious satire commences, or satire that is felt as serious, however comically drest, the free laughter ceases; it becomes sardonic. Felt in Young's satire —not uninstanced in Butler.[2] The truly comic is the *blossom of the nettle*.

In the simply laughable, there is a mere disproportion between a definite act and a definite purpose or end, or a disproportion of the end itself to the rank of the definite person; but when we contemplate a finite in reference to the infinite, consciously or unconsciously, *humor*. So says Jean Paul Richter.

Humorous writers, therefore, as Sterne in particular, delight to end in nothing, or a direct contradiction.

That there is something in this is evident; for you cannot conceive a humorous man who does not give some disproportionate *generality*, universality, to his hobbyhorse, as Mr. Shandy; or at least [there is] an absence of any interest but what arises from the humor itself, as in Uncle Toby. There is *the idea* of the soul in its undefined capacity and dignity that gives the sting to any absorption of it by any one pursuit, and this not as a member of society for any particular, however mistaken, interest, but as man. Hence in humor the little is made great, and the great little, in order to destroy both, because all is equal in contrast with the infinite.

† From *Coleridge's Miscellaneous Criticism*, ed. Thomas Middleton Raysor (Cambridge: Harvard University Press, 1936), pp. 117–26. Taken from Coleridge's MS notes for a lecture on "Wit and Humour," delivered February 24, 1818. The emendations in the text are Raysor's. Samuel Taylor Coleridge was a poet, philosopher, and the foremost literary critic of the English Romantic period.

1. Coleridge makes use of the work of his contemporary, Jean Paul Richter, *Vorschule der Aesthetik* (1804), including sections, 26, 28, 29, 32, 33.
2. Edward Young's *Love of Fame, or the Universal Passion* (1725–28); Samuel Butler's *Hudibras* (1663–78).

Hence the tender feeling connected with the *humors* or hobby-horses of a man.

1. Respect, for there is absence of any interest as the ground-work, tho' the imagination of a[n] *interest* by the humorist may exist, as if a remarkably simple-hearted man should pride himself on his knowledge of the world, and how well he can manage it.

2. Acknowledgement of the hollowness and farce of the world, and its disproportion to the godlike within us.

Hence when particular *acts* have reference to particular *selfish* motives, the humorous bursts into the indignant and abhorring. All follies *not selfish*, it pardons or palliates. The danger of this [is] exemplified in Sterne. . . .

Sterne

A sort of *knowingness*, the wit of which depends, first on the modesty it gives pain to; or secondly, the innocence and innocent ignorance over which it triumphs; or thirdly, on a certain oscillation in the individual's own mind between the remaining good and the encroaching evil of his nature, a sort of dallying with the devil, a fluxionary act of combining courage and cowardice, as when a man snuffs a candle with his fingers for the first time, or better still, perhaps, that tremulous daring with which a child touches a hot tea urn, because it had been forbidden—so that the mind has in its own white and black angel the same or similar amusements as might be supposed to take place between an old debauchee and a prude—[her] resentment from the prudential anxiety to preserve appearances, and have a character, and an inward sympathy with the enemy. We have only to suppose society *innocent*—and [this sort of wit] is equal to a stone that falls in snow; it makes no sound because it excites no resistance. [This accounts] for nine tenths [of its effect]; the remainder rests on its being an offence against the good manners of human nature itself. . . .

This source, unworthy as it is, may doubtless be combined with wit, drollery, fancy, and even humour,—and we have only to regret the *mésalliance*; but that the latter are quite distinct from the former may be made evident by abstracting in our imagination the *characters* of Mr. Shandy, my Uncle Toby, and Trim, which are all *antagonists* to this wit, and suppose instead of them two or three callous debauchees, and the result will be pure disgust. Sterne cannot be too severely censured for this, for he makes the best dispositions of our nature the pandars and condiments for the basest.

EXCELLENCES

1. The bringing forward into distinct consciousness those minutiae of thought and feeling which appear trifles, have an importance [only] for the moment, and yet almost every man feels in one way or other. Thus it has the novelty of an individual peculiarity, and yet the interest of a something that belongs to our common nature. In short, to seize happily on those points in which every man is more or less a *humorist*. And the propensity to notice these things does itself constitute a humorist, and the superadded power of so presenting them to men in general gives us the man of humor. Hence the difference of the man of humor, the effect of whose portraits does not depend on the felt presence of himself as a humorist, as Cervantes and Shakespeare, nay, Rabelais—and those in whom the effect is in the humorist's own oddity—Sterne (and *Swift?*).

2. Traits of *human* nature, which so easily assume a particular cast and color from individual character. Hence this, and the pathos connected with it, quickly passes into *humor*, and forms the ground of it—[as in] the story of the Fly. Character [is created] by a delicacy and higher degree of a good quality. [Refers to *Tristram Shandy*, II. xii: 'Go, says he . . . both thee and me.']

3. In Mr. Shandy's character, as of all Mr. Shandys, a craving for sympathy in exact proportion to the oddity and unsympathizability; next to this, [craving] to be at least disputed with, or rather both in one, [to] dispute and yet agree; but [holding] worst of all, to acquiesce without either resistance or sympathy—[all this is] most happily conceived.

Contrasts sometimes increasing the love between the brothers— and always either balanced or remedied.
Drollery in Obadiah.

4. No writer so happy as Sterne in the unexaggerated and truly natural representation of that species of slander which consists in gossiping about our neighbors, as *whetstones* of our moral discrimination—as if they were conscience-blocks which we used in our apprenticeship, not to waste such precious materials as our own consciences in the trimming and shaping by self-examination. [Refers to *Tristram Shandy*, I. xviii: 'Alas o'day . . . alive at this hour.']

5. When you have secured a man's likings and prejudices in your favor, you may then safely appeal to his impartial judgement. [The following passage is full of] acute sense in ironical wit, but now add *life* to it and *character*—and it becomes *dramatic*. [Refers to *Tristram Shandy*, I. xix: 'I see plainly, Sir . . . of your example.']

6. The physiognomic tact common, in very different degrees in-

deed, to us all, [is] gratified in Dr. Slop. And in general, [note] all that happiest use of drapery and attitude, which at once gives the *reality* by individualizing, and the vividness by unusual, yet probable combinations. [Refers to *Tristram Shandy*, II. ix: 'Imagine to yourself . . . in the horse-guards. . . . Imagine such a one . . . speed the adverse way.']

7. More humor in the single remark, 'Learned men, Brother Toby, do not write dialogues on long noses for nothing,'[3] than in the whole Slawkenburghian tale that follows, which is oddity interspersed with drollery.

8. The moral *good* of Sterne in the characters of Trim, etc., as contrasted with Jacobinism. [Refers to Trim mourning the death of Bobby, *Tristram Shandy*, V. vii.]

9. Each part by right of humoristic universality, a whole. Hence the digressive spirit [is] not wantonness, but the *very form* of his genius. The connection is given by the continuity of the characters.

WILLIAM HAZLITT

[Sterne's Style] †

* * *

It remains to speak of Sterne; and I shall do it in few words. There is more of *mannerism* and affectation in him, and a more immediate reference to preceding authors; but his excellences, where he is excellent, are of the first order. His characters are intellectual and inventive, like Richardson's; but totally opposite in the execution. The one are made out by continuity, and patient repetition of touches: the others, by glancing transitions and graceful apposition. His style is equally different from Richardson's: it is at times the most rapid, the most happy, the most idiomatic of any that is to be found. It is the pure essence of English conversational style. His works consist only of *morceaux*[1]—of brilliant passages. I wonder that Goldsmith, who ought to have known better, should call him 'a dull fellow.'[2] His wit is poignant, though artificial; and his characters (though the groundwork of some of them had been laid before) have yet invaluable original differences; and the spirit of the execution, the master-strokes constantly thrown into them, are

---

3. III.xxxvii.
† From *Sterne: The Critical Heritage*, ed. Alan B. Howes (London: Routledge and Kegan Paul, 1974), pp. 360–61. This was part of William Hazlitt's *Lectures on the English Comic Writers*, delivered in the winter of 1818–19 and published in 1819.

Hazlitt was a literary critic and essayist of the Enigsh Romantic period.
1. "Fragments."
2. In a conversation with Dr. Johnson—who did not agree with Goldsmith (*Boswell's Life of Johnson*, ii. 222).

not to be surpassed. It is sufficient to name them;—Yorick, Dr. Slop, Mr. Shandy, My Uncle Toby, Trim, Susanna, and the Widow Wadman. In these he has contrived to ·oppose, with equal felicity and originality, two characters, one of pure intellect, and the other of pure good nature, in My Father and My Uncle Toby. There appears to have been in Sterne a vein of dry, sarcastic humour, and of extreme tenderness of feeling; the latter sometimes carried to affectation, as in the tale of Maria, and the apostrophe to the recording angel: but at other times pure, and without blemish. The story of Le Fevre is perhaps the finest in the English language. My Father's restlessness, both of body and mind, is inimitable. It is the model from which all those despicable performances against modern philosophy ought to have been copied, if their authors had known anything of the subject they were writing about. My Uncle Toby is one of the finest compliments ever paid to human nature. He is the most unoffending of God's creatures; or, as the French express it, *un tel petit bon homme!*[3] Of his bowling green, his sieges, and his amours, who would say or think anything amiss! * * *

SIR WALTER SCOTT

Laurence Sterne†

* * *If we consider Sterne's reputation as chiefly founded on *Tristram Shandy*, he must be regarded as liable to two severe charges;—those, namely, of indecency, and of affectation.[1] Upon the first accusation Sterne was himself peculiarly sore, and used to justify the licentiousness of his humour by representing it as a mere breach of decorum, which had no perilous consequence to morals. The following anecdote we have from a sure source:—Soon after *Tristram* had appeared, Sterne asked a Yorkshire lady of fortune and condition whether she had read his book. 'I have not, Mr Sterne,' was the answer; 'and, to be plain with you, I am informed it is not proper for female perusal.'—'My dear good lady,' replied the author, 'do not be gulled by such stories; the book is like your young heir there,' (pointing to a child of three years old, who was rolling on the carpet in his white tunics,) 'he shows at times a good deal that is usually concealed, but it is all in perfect innocence!'

---

3. "Such a simple little man."
† From *Sterne: The Critical Heritage*, ed. Alan B. Howes (London: Routledge and Kegan Paul, 1974), pp. 371–74. This was part of *Miscellaneous Prose Works of Sir Walter Scott* (1834). Scott, the most successful novelist of the early nineteenth century in England, wrote this essay as one of a series of introductions to a set of standard novels.
1. See Goldsmith's attack on Sterne in this edition.

This witty excuse may be so far admitted; for it cannot be said that the licentious humour of *Tristram Shandy* is of the kind which applies itself to the passions, or is calculated to corrupt society. But it is a sin against taste, if allowed to be harmless as to morals. A handful of mud is neither a firebrand nor a stone; but to fling it about in sport, argues coarseness of mind, and want of common manners.

Sterne, however, began and ended by braving the censure of the world in this particular. . . .

In like manner, the greatest admirers of Sterne must own, that his style is affected, eminently, and in a degree which even his wit and pathos are inadequate to support. The style of Rabelais, which he assumed for his model, is to the highest excess rambling, excursive, and intermingled with the greatest absurdities. But Rabelais was in some measure compelled to adopt this Harlequin's habit, in order that, like licensed jesters, he might, under the cover of his folly, have permission to vent his satire against church and state. Sterne assumed the manner of his master, only as a mode of attracting attention, and of making the public stare; and, therefore, his extravagancies, like those of a feigned madman, are cold and forced, even in the midst of his most irregular flights. A man may, in the present day, be, with perfect impunity, as wise or as witty, nay, as satirical, as he can, without assuming the cap and bells of the ancient jester as an apology; and that Sterne chose voluntarily to appear under such a disguise, must be set down as mere affectation, and ranked with his unmeaning tricks of black or marbled pages, employed merely *ad captandum vulgus*.[2] All popularity thus founded, carries in it the seeds of decay; for eccentricity in composition, like fantastic modes of dress, however attractive when first introduced, is sure to be caricatured by stupid imitators, to become soon unfashionable, and of course to be neglected.

If we proceed to look more closely into the manner of composition which Sterne thought proper to adopt, we find a sure guide in the ingenious Dr Ferriar of Manchester,[3] who, with most singular patience, has traced our author through the hidden sources whence he borrowed most of his learning, and many of his more striking and peculiar expressions. . . . For proofs of this sweeping charge we must refer the reader to Dr Ferriar's well-known Essay, and *Illustrations*, as he delicately terms them, *of Sterne's Writings*; in which it is clearly shown, that he, whose manner and style were so long thought original, was, in fact, the most unhesitating plagiarist who ever cribbed from his predecessors in order to garnish his own

2. "To try to win the public."
3. John Ferriar in his *Illustrations of Sterne* (1798) laboriously traced Sterne's borrowings, thus providing evidence for those who wished to argue that Sterne was not very original.

pages. It must be owned, at the same time, that Sterne selects the materials of his mosaic work with so much art, places them so well, and polishes them so highly, that in most cases we are disposed to pardon the want of originality, in consideration of the exquisite talent with which the borrowed materials are wrought up into the new form. . . .

Much has been said about the right of an author to avail himself of his predecessors' labours; and certainly, in a general sense, he that revives the wit and learning of a former age, and puts it into the form likely to captivate his own, confers a benefit on his contemporaries. But to plume himself with the very language and phrases of former writers, and to pass their wit and learning for his own, was the more unworthy in Sterne, as he had enough of original talent, had he chosen to exert it, to have dispensed with all such acts of literary petty larceny.

Tristram Shandy is no narrative, but a collection of scenes, dialogues, and portraits, humorous or affecting, intermixed with much wit, and with much learning, original or borrowed. It resembles the irregularities of a Gothic room, built by some fanciful collector, to contain the miscellaneous remnants of antiquity which his pains have accumulated, and bearing as little proportion in its parts as there is connexion between the pieces of rusty armour with which it is decorated. Viewing it in this light, the principal figure is Mr Shandy the elder, whose character is formed in many respects upon that of Martinus Scriblerus.[4] The history of Martin was designed by the celebrated club of wits, by whom it was commenced, as a satire upon the ordinary pursuits of learning and science. Sterne, on the contrary, had no particular object of ridicule; his business was only to create a person, to whom he could attach the great quantity of extraordinary reading, and antiquated learning, which he had collected. He, therefore, supposed in Mr Shandy a man of an active and metaphysical, but at the same time a whimsical cast of mind, whom too much and too miscellaneous learning had brought within a step or two of madness, and who acted in the ordinary affairs of life upon the absurd theories adopted by the pedants of past ages. He is most admirably contrasted with his wife, well described as a good lady of the true poco-curante school, who neither obstructed the progress of her husband's *hobby-horse*, to use a phrase which Sterne has rendered classical, nor could be prevailed upon to spare him the least admiration for the grace and dexterity with which he managed it. . . .

Uncle Toby and his faithful squire, the most delightful characters

4. *The Memoirs of Martinus Scriblerus*, published in 1741 as part of Pope's *Works*, were the result of cooperation by a club that included not only Pope but also Swith, Dr. John Arbuthnot (probably the main author), John Gay, Thomas Parnell, and Robert Harley.

in the work, or perhaps in any other, are drawn with such a pleasing force and discrimination, that they more than entitle the author to a free pardon for his literary peculations, his indecorum, and his affectation; may authorize him to leave the court of criticism not forgiven only, but applauded and rewarded as one who has exalted and honoured humanity, and impressed upon his readers such a lively picture of kindness and benevolence, blended with courage, gallantry, and simplicity, that their hearts must be warmed whenever it is recalled to memory. Sterne, indeed, might boldly plead in his own behalf, that the passages which he borrowed from others were of little value, in comparison to those which are exclusively original; and that the former might have been written by many persons, while in his own proper line he stands alone and inimitable. Something of extravagance may, perhaps, attach to Uncle Toby's favourite amusements. Yet in England, where men think and act with little regard to ridicule or censure of their neighbours, there is no impossibility, perhaps no great improbability in supposing, that a humorist might employ such a mechanical aid as my Uncle's bowling-green, in order to encourage and assist his imagination, in the pleasing but delusive task of castle-building. Men have been called children of larger growth, and among the antic toys and devices with which they are amused, the device of my Uncle, with whose pleasures we are so much disposed to sympathize, does not seem so unnatural upon reflection as it may appear at first sight. . . .

It is needless to dwell longer on a work so generally known. The style employed by Sterne is fancifully ornamented, but at the same time vigorous and masculine, and full of that animation and force which can only be derived by an intimate acquaintance with the early English prose-writers. In the power of approaching and touching the finer feelings of the heart, he has never been excelled, if indeed he has ever been equalled; and may be at once recorded as one of the most affected, and one of the most simple writers,—as one of the greatest plagiarists, and one of the most original geniuses, whom England has produced.

WILLIAM MAKEPEACE THACKERAY

Sterne and Goldsmith†

* * * In 1765, three years before the publication of the 'Sentimental Journey,' the seventh and eighth volumes of 'Tristram Shandy' were given to the world, and the famous Lyons donkey makes his entry in those volumes.[1]

* * *

A critic who refuses to see in this charming description wit, humour, pathos, a kind nature speaking, and a real sentiment, must be hard indeed to move and to please. A page or two farther we come to a description not less beautiful—a landscape and figures, deliciously painted by one who had the keenest enjoyment and the most tremulous sensibility:—[2]

* * *

And with this pretty dance and chorus, the volume artfully concludes. Even here one can't give the whole description. There is not a page in Sterne's writing but has something that were better away, a latent corruption—a hint, as of an impure presence.

Some of that dreary *double entendre* may be attributed to freer times and manners than ours, but not all. The foul satyr's eyes leer out of the leaves constantly: the last words the famous author wrote were bad and wicked—the last lines the poor stricken wretch penned were for pity and pardon. I think of these past writers and of one who lives amongst us now, and am grateful for the innocent laughter and the sweet and unsullied page which the author of 'David Copperfield' gives to my children. * * *

† From *The English Humorists of the Eighteenth Century* (London: Smith and Elder, 1853), pp. 287–92. Thackeray was already established as one of the leading novelists of the mid-nineteenth century when in 1851 he delivered a series of lectures on the English humorists of a hundred years before.
1. Thackeray quotes most of VII.xxxii.
2. Thackeray quotes most of the conclusion of VII.xliii.

Twentieth-Century Studies

LODWICK HARTLEY

[The Genius of Laurence Sterne] †

It has been recognized for a long time that *Tristram Shandy* is in one sense a long monologue or, in another, a dialogue between the narrator and a complex of readers or hearers—being in the latter sense both like and unlike the later nineteenth-century dramatic monologue in which a "hearer" is developed often as an effectively realized character. The basic elements of this device are not peculiar to Sterne. Fielding and other contemporaries used it extensively. But no other writer of fiction in the century was able to engage and, further, to exploit the reader in the same way that Sterne does. It is no secret that a large part of the suspense and, therefore, the attraction of the novel lies in our wondering not merely what the narrator is going to do next but also into what role he is going to trick the reader—whose sex, status, and point of view are changeable at the narrator's whim. Thus the device of the shifting putative reader or hearer becomes a kind of game that the author-narrator (it is often difficult to tell which is which) plays with the one who actually has the novel in his hands.

In the space of four chapters (vii–x) in Book I, it may be quickly seen, this putative reader or hearer is addressed as "your worship," "Sir," "my Lord," and "madam." In a single chapter of Book IV (xvii), the range is considerably greater: from "dear Sir" to "madam" to "your reverences and your worships" back to "Sir." Numerous times the reader must assume the part of "madam" not to mention that of the more familial and intimate "dear girl" or "Jenny." Less frequently he is merely "gentle reader" or "Sir Critick" or "you gentry with the great beards"; or he may be asked to assume the role of a real person like "my dear Garrick." Most frequently he is "your worship" or "your worships," or "my brethren," or "your reverences and worships." In some of these parts he must sense (and in time does sense instinctively) the deprecation

† From Lodwick Hartley, "A Chapter of Conclusions" in *Laurence Sterne in the Twentieth Century: An Essay and a* *Bibliography of Sternean Studies 1900–1965* (Chapel Hill: University of North Carolina Press, 1966), pp. 65–74.

that is subtly limned and in which he is just as subtly involved. In this connection, Sterne's statement in III, xx, "As for the great wigs, upon which I may be thought to have spoken my mind too freely . . . I write not for them" can strike one as being highly ironical. Indeed, the reader may find himself breaking silence and exclaiming to the narrator, "Then you write not *for*, but *to* them." If it is always possible to put *Tristram Shandy* down, it is not possible to read it without some definite sort of engagement.

The ways indicated above are, of course, not the only ones through which the reader is entrapped and exploited. The multiple uses of a character like Uncle Toby, for example, to engage the reader's identity and empathy go rather far beyond the usual exploitation that the "dramatic" or self-conscious narrator, or any other kind of narrator for that matter, is expected to make of his audience. In no other work of fiction than in *Tristram Shandy* is the reader so often and so delightfully caught off guard—that is, if he is willing to commit himself to the game. Those who are not willing are simply those who for one reason or another do not like the book. They had better go their own way and leave *Tristram Shandy* alone. As in the instance of the "great wigs," Sterne writes not for them.

In a novel about the writing of a novel, the reader should not be surprised to be ushered frequently into the writer's study. But only in *Tristram Shandy* is the reader likely to find himself so suddenly and so intimately there:

> It is not half an hour ago, when (in the great hurry and precipitation of a poor devil's writing for daily bread) I threw a fair sheet, which I had just finished and carefully wrote out, slap into the fire, instead of a foul one.

The crinkled black ashes are still on the hearth in evidence!

Thus the game not only of *who* the reader is but also *where* he is is played against a background of people, ideas, and things that are themselves shifting but have for their moment (and after) a vivid conviction of reality.

It hardly needs to be said that as a narrator Tristram succeeds where his counterpart in real life most often fails miserably. Who can tolerate the person who in ordinary conversation is forever backing and filling, embroidering and elaborating, detailing and digressing in such a way as never to get his story told—or almost never? The secret is, again, the game—the subtle engagement.

But even to those who are willing to commit themselves, the charm does not always work. Eventually the reader may become wary. Finally he may tire. No one can argue sensibly that the novel is of a piece. The brilliance of the first four books shows some signs of wavering even as early as the third. And for all the choice materials of the fifth and sixth books—the circumstances around Bobby's death, the accidental circumcision of Tristram, Mr. Shandy's system of auxiliary verbs, the story of Le Fever—the Sternean manner (as others have noticed) at times becomes a kind of parody of itself. The announced digressive-progressive movement of the book is not always so progressive as it might be. The return to Uncle Toby's affair with the Widow Wadman in the two final books has been adjudged by some to be inconclusive and unsatisfactory but by others to offer a successful completion of what Tristram said he was going to do.

The rather recent contention, indeed, that the book is complete with the final chapter may suggest that criticism abhors a fragment in the same way that nature abhors a vacuum; and the argument may fail not because it is less than admirably pursued but because in a novel like *Tristram Shandy* it may seem irrelevant. Had not Tristram early threatened that he could go on turning out two volumes a year as long as he lived and could he not have done so had he lived? ("I have forty volumes to write and forty thousand things to say.") To what useful end can this kind of debate be taken?

The arguments for the unity of the book may also strike one as irrelevant. Still the idea that there is a palpable force holding the book together in spite of all its tendencies to fly apart is tantalizingly undeniable. The feeling of inward cohesion has a way of running in counterpoint to the outward evidence of chaos. It may be wise, when all the evidence is in, to conclude that the various arguments for the unity of the novel are useful chiefly to balance a less perceptive and less thoughtful judgment of disorder and that a settlement for an ineffable combination of plan and caprice is about as much as we can do. One may, of course, fall back ultimately on the simplicity of statement in a critic like Coleridge, whose well demonstrated skill and profundity might have been expected to allow him to come up with a better principle of unity if there was one: "Hence the digressive spirit is not mere wantonness but in fact the very form and vehicle of [Rabelais's and Sterne's] genius. The connection, such as was needed, is given by the continuity of the characters."

After all, the true genius of *Tristram Shandy* is (in a sense at least obliquely suggested by Coleridge) not so much in its unity as in its flexibility. The remarkable thing about most of the contemporary attempts to find principles of unity in structure, rhetoric, theme, or philosophic background is that such a variety of arguments is admissible—even when some of them tend to be contradictory. And if the novel can be variously interpreted in terms of the physico-theological, the Neo-Platonic, the Newtonian, the Lockean, the Hutchensonian, the Shaftesburian, the Humean thought of the eighteenth century, and even the Hegelian dialectic of the nineteenth, it can also be interpreted according to the Freudian psychoanalytical, the Camusian Existential, or perhaps even the Dalian Surrealistic "systems" of the twentieth.

The irony is that the critic who attempts to impose any kind of system on *Tristram Shandy* immediately assumes the role of Tristram's father. (This is one of the traps that Sterne himself has laid). And the critic should not be astonished if the normative reader tends to react somewhat in the role of Mr. Shandy's less systematic brother: "You puzzle me to death, cried my uncle *Toby*."

As a healthful corrective to any tendency to make an excessively academic critical treatment of the novel, one may well keep its domestic and local origins in mind. It began—and to a degree remains—as what Sir Herbert Read has called a Yorkshire epic. It is also in part an obstetrical romance. (Does not recent investigation indicate that Sterne knew the midwifery of his time at least as well as he knew Lockean psychology?) Dr. Slop, Didius, Kysarcius, Kunastrokius, Phutatorious are all disguises for real Yorkshire people—most of them involved with Sterne in the politics of the Shire or in the quarrels around the chapter house of the York Cathedral. The satire here is as sharply personal (though perhaps on a slightly different plane) as that to be found in Pope's portraits of Atticus and Sporus—a fact, incidentally, that is too often forgotten when Sterne's satire is adjudged to be closer to Swift's than to Pope's.

However, if the matter simply ended here, *Tristram Shandy* might well have gone the way of the ill-fated *Political Romance*. All the minor satirical portraits are, of course, overshadowed by those of that most remarkable Yorkshire family, the Shandys, who are just as limited geographically and ethnically as the characters in a novel by Jane Austen. They achieve their universality, in at least one way shared by the creations of Miss Austen, simply by coming vividly alive.

In this regard the testimony of a distinguished novelist and short story writer is interesting if it does nothing else than reassert the continued validity of reading *Tristram Shandy* in terms of the direct communication of the printed page to the reader. "That novel," Katherine Anne Porter has written, "contains more living breathing people you can see and hear, whose garments have texture between your finger and thumb, whose flesh is knit firmly to their bones, who walk about their affairs with audible footsteps, than any other one novel in the world." The Shandys, she goes on, "all live in one house with floor boards under their bootsoles, a roof over their heads, the fire burning and giving off real smoke, cooking smells coming from the kitchen, real weather outside and air blowing through the windows. [Miss Porter leaves out a real sash that unexpectedly falls and a real door hinge that chronically squeaks; but no matter!] When Dr. Slop cuts his thumb real blood issues from it, and everybody has a navel and his proper distribution of his vital organs."

This may all sound like the obvious. Is not the least one can say for great fiction that it creates believable people? Yet there is need for frequent repetition of such a statement chiefly because from the outset critical efforts toward evaluation of the novel have, whether for a worse or a better final judgment, been adulterated by moral, aesthetic, and philosophical issues tangential to the main business.

But however successful Sterne may have been in creating believable characters, what he was able to do with the novel as a form has a significance all its own.

The fact that he has been acclaimed a great force for Romanticism may be more important to the literary historian than it is to the contemporary critic or reader. If he was such a force, it was not because he "liberated" the novel as a form but chiefly because he seemed to elevate Feeling above Reason. And though *Tristram Shandy* played its part in spreading Sterne's influence in this respect, the most immediately effective agent (as we have already seen) was *A Sentimental Journey*. The evidence of this influence is abundant and undeniable. The true nature of Sterne's own sentimentality and sensibility is another matter. Could he possibly have tricked a generation or two of German, French, Italian, English, and American sentimental novelists into another one of his traps? The answer is far from simple. If the novelist could use and exploit a single reader, he could presumably do the same thing for many readers. It is not difficult to see that Sterne was just as fond of educing feeling as he was of giving expression to it—very likely more so. In everything that he did—his novels, his sermons, his letters—he gives constant indication of keen relish in his ability to play upon his audience, to mold, shape, and control its reactions not entirely unlike the way in which a masterful conductor "plays" an orchestra. But are we to assume that he was always the jester, that he was never capable of real feeling? "Every thing in this world, said my father, is big with jest,—and has wit in it, and instruction, too,—if we can but find it out." This is Tristram's report of what Walter Shandy observed. It cannot be taken as an easy generalization of the novelist's own attitude. It answers the basic question neither one way nor the other.

One may not be able, it is true, to dismiss altogether considerations of Sterne's morality or his "sincerity" as irrelevancies in the consideration of his art, but the question of what he did to the form of the novel is of far more importance to the twentieth century. If in *Tristram Shandy* he did not "destroy" the structural conventions that had grown up before he began writing, he did not passively accept them. And if his innovations were not actually so original as they may have seemed to be, the form that he arrived at was (beyond question) different. However he may have used, dramatized, and burlesqued ideas from Locke's *Essay concerning Human Understanding,* however much he may have been influenced by the tradition of the familiar essay as it had come down from Montaigne, or that of the satires of "learned wit," or that of the self-conscious narrator in antecedent fiction, he nevertheless evolved an architectonic all his own—far too subtle for his imitators to follow effectively and subtle enough to keep fluid our own efforts to define it. His ability to discover as early as he did that he did not have to conform to an artificial and restrictive "unilinear view of experience" in fiction enabled him to strike a blow for individualism and freedom worthy of any Romanticist. And if *Tristram Shandy* did not have the kind of immediate influence upon the form and content of the English novel as such a revolutionary volume, let us say, as *Lyrical Ballads* had on English poetry, it may have been for no other reason than that for its own time the novel was so ineluctably *sui generis.*

Sterne himself did not fail to recognize this fact. On February 9, 1768, only a little more than a month before he died, the novelist wrote a letter of thanks to Dr. John Eustace of Wilmington, North Carolina. This gentleman had sent Sterne "a piece of shandean statuary" in the form of a curious walking stick formerly owned by a Colonial governor of North Carolina named Arthur Dobbs.

"Your walking stick is in no sense more *shandaic* than in that of its having *more handles than one,*" Sterne wrote. "—The parallel breaks only in this, that in using the stick everyone will take the handle which suits his convenience. In *Tristram Shandy,* the handle is taken which suits their passions, their ignorance or sensibility. . . . It is too much to write books and find heads to understand them."

The weariness of the writer and his pathetic need for appreciation and affection are evident; but also, as we proceed, is his graciousness: "I am very proud, sir, to have a man like you, on my side from the beginning." And there is more than a spark of pride and confidence in the feeling that the "people of genius" in England are, after all, on his side and that the reception of his novel in France, Italy, and Germany has been gratifying.

What any book needs, Sterne goes on to say, is a sympathetic reader: ". . . a true feeler always brings half the entertainment along with him. His own ideas are only call'd forth by what he reads, and the vibrations within, so entirely correspond with those excited, 'tis like reading *himself* and not the *book*." Not everyone can appreciate humor, Sterne asserts "—'tis the gift of God."

The various "handles" that Sterne had admittedly given his book had too frequently led to misunderstanding and condemnation rather than to appreciation. And except for the support of people of sufficient "genius," Sterne can find reason for feeling that he has been victimized by his own cleverness, his own ambiguities, his own ambivalences, his own "negative capability." Being something like all things to all people may be a virtue in a work of art, but it is not always tolerated in the human being, the artist. And when the work of art and the artist are not dissociated, the real burden of the intolerance seems to fall on the latter. This was and has been a basic problem of criticism from the time that the first two volumes of *Tristram Shandy* appeared in the bookshop of John Hinxman in York (late in December, 1759) almost to the present.

The attempt to make this dissociation and to allow the work of art to stand on its own has been one of the major achievements of twentieth-century criticism of Sterne. The various "handles" have been used to probe the secrets of his acknowledged genius, not to oversentimentalize or to denigrate his character, his mind, or his literary product. The fact that all the investigation has failed to solve the final mystery and that his genius still remains elusive and undefined should add not so much to our despair as to Sterne's credit.

The narrator of *Tristram Shandy* believes that in order properly to set forth his life and opinions he must consider all possible systems of thinking (educational, physiological, cosmological, domestic) focalized by that fascinating and complex "Little Gentleman," the Homunculus. Through such a narrator Sterne has woven an intricte web leading to the kind of picture of the human situation (elaborately involved in impulses, obsessions, sensations, associations, "hobby-horses") that may better be apprehended than understood. Thus, as Sterne himself suggested, the most confident approach to understanding may be that of the "true feeler"—that particular type of "man of feeling" who, willing to enter the game, "always brings half of the entertainment with him" and trusts to the author and God Almighty for the rest.

D. W. JEFFERSON

Tristram Shandy and the Tradition of Learned Wit†

I

Tristram Shandy, though a much-loved work, is in many respects misunderstood. It is a pity to have to quarrel with Mr. E. M. Forster's engaging description of it:

> There is a charmed stagnation about the whole epic—the more the characters do the less gets done, the less they have to say the more they talk, the harder they think the softer they get, facts have an unholy tendency to unwind and trip up the past instead of begetting the future, as in well-conducted books . . . Obviously a god is hidden in Tristram Shandy and his name is Muddle, and some readers cannot accept him.[1]

Tristram Shandy certainly does not satisfy the usual expectations as to how a novel should be organized, but that is because it is not the usual sort of novel. The tendency among critics has been to comment on its structural oddities without first discovering to what literary kind it belongs and what its author was trying to do. Some attempt will be made in this essay to show that it has traditional form and a thematic pattern. Perfect fidelity to an artistic scheme would be too much to claim for Sterne, but it is important to realize that he had one. The view that Tristram Shandy is a muddle is related to a tendency to approach Sterne in the light of his affinities with certain later writers, exponents of the eccentric or the nonsensical. Mr. Graham Greene says that 'his whimsicality was inherited by the essayists, by Lamb in particular'.[2] Whatever his relations with the whimsical school—'whimsicality' is rather a damaging word today—he differs fundamentally from these writers in being also of an older and better school. He belongs to a tradition of wit to which they had no access. It is in relation to this background that we must place Tristram Shandy, if we are to appreciate fully its point and structure.

II

We are confronted not with one kind of wit but with several related kinds. They are sufficiently related to be seen as one tradi-

---

† From Essays in Criticism, I (1951). 225–48. Footnotes are by Jefferson unless otherwise noted.
1. Aspects of the Novel, 1927, p. 146.

2. From an essay on Fielding and Sterne in From Anne to Victoria, ed. B. Dobrée, 1937, p. 282.

tion, though the points which unite them would be difficult to state with absolute precision. It is also difficult to give the tradition a suitable label. The word 'scholastic' covers certain examples and could, with a little elasticity, be extended to cover others, but as the tradition moves further and further away from scholasticism without ceasing to be a tradition the problem of terminology becomes increasingly embarrassing. Donne's use of Thomist metaphysics in 'Air and Angels' is scholastic wit in the strictest sense. Where he uses materials which were not actually taught in the schools but which belong to some branch of medieval learning, as in his exploitation of legal expressions in 'Lovers' Infiniteness', the term is perhaps permissible. But the ratiocinative ingenuity which writers of the Renaissance and later inherited from the schoolmen was liable to be applied to all kinds of ideas, even to those of the new science and philosophy; and the result, for our purpose, is a species of wit essentially similar to that based on scholastic ideas. Some of Sterne's material may be labelled scholastic, but he also used ideas from Descartes and Locke.

There is something in the scholastic approach to intellectual issues—a speculative freedom, a dialectical ingenuity—which lends itself to witty development. And there is something in the empiricist's approach—a puritanical restriction on speculation, a plodding regard for truth—which is alien to wit. We do not look for jokes among the serious students of Newton and Locke, but a person brought up in the old tradition of wit might well find that some of the new ideas of Newton and Locke suited his purpose. When this happens the spirit of scholastic wit is still alive, though whether it is convenient to use that term is another question. Some of the most interesting types of wit which concern us have no direct connection with learning. It may be claimed that they are traceable ultimately to a mentality formed under scholastic or quasi-scholastic influences, but it is in the field of imagery not of ideas that the indebtedness is revealed. Here again, the term 'scholastic wit' might cause misunderstanding, though not much more perhaps than the term 'metaphysical image'.

By way of summing up, it may be said in general that the types of wit which come within our survey owe their character to intellectual habits belonging to the pre-Enlightenment world of thought, and that the habits were those against which the Enlightenment set its face. This kind of wit is found in considerable quantity in Augustan comic and satirical writing: for example, in Swift's *Tale of a Tub*, in Pope's *Art of Sinking in Poetry*, and in the *Memoirs of Scriblerus*. Sterne is perhaps the last great writer in the tradition. It is not enough to argue that the comic use of old-fashioned ideas or ratiocinative techniques is merely a symptom of satirical reaction against them. That they should have been matter for comedy is a sign that they were not dead. To be matter for comedy they had to be matter for the imagination. We know that Swift despised the old pedantic learning, but it provided him with excellent comic material, and the discipline of the disputation did much to mould his art. No writer has ever excelled him in the exploitation of dialectical stratagems.

The survival of this type of learned wit in the eighteenth century may be attributed partly to an isolated event in literary history: the publication of the English Rabelais. The first two books of Urquhart's translation appeared in 1653; but the wonderful third book, which we shall find most significant in relation to Sterne, was not published until 1693. The remaining books appeared in the following year. Rabelais was known to English writers before he appeared in translation, but Urquhart and Motteux made an enormous difference to his influence. It is noteworthy that the completed work was a new book when Swift began to write his early satires. Rabelais was the greatest of all masters of the comic use of scholastic wit.

I propose to review the main types of wit belonging to this tradition. When we have the tradition as a whole to refer to, we shall be in a position to concentrate on *Tristram Shandy*.

It is not to be expected that all the materials of medieval thought should survive as themes for wit into the eighteenth century. The outer framework of the medieval world-picture, the cosmological system, survived less well than other elements.

The 'determinate, humanly comprehensible universe' of medieval and Renaissance man gave opportunities to the imagination which are not afforded by the 'unrepresentable, inconceivable, affrighting universe of contemporary science'.[3] There was an all-embracing scheme of facts and meanings in which any particular matter for inquiry could always be placed. It was possible to pass from the particular event to the general cosmic pattern and *vice versa* with an easy, assured sweep of the mind such as modern man can never enjoy. This opened up huge possibilities to a comic genius. Thus with a single stroke of facile logic Panurge invokes the entire cosmic order in support of borrowing and lending without which (he argues) the relations of the planets would fall into disorder, the sun would no longer give light, there would be an end to seasons, and within man's body there would be no co-operation of the different members.[4] Comedy depends on pattern and order, on something which can stand distortion and yet retain its essential nature, like a human figure in a caricature. In some periods this is supplied by a social structure with its systems of manners and morals, but with a

3. J. L. Lowes, *Geoffrey Chaucer*, 1932, p. 21.
4. *Gargantua and Pantagruel*, III, 2–4.

cosmic structure to play with comedy can attain to the colossal. Rabelais's comedy is of this order and it is more than comedy, for into Panurge's praise of the cosmic order he puts all his poetic sense of the goodness of creation.

Ideas relating to physiology and medicine survived better. Medieval learning gave the artist many things which modern learning, with its greater store and greater accuracy of information, cannot give. One of these was a rational, readily intelligible and complete conception of the nature of man. The Galenic physiology, which contained the elements of a psychology, was, from the modern scientific standpoint, quite inaccurate, but it was a considerable achievement of speculative intelligence. If it did not explain the workings of the human organism correctly, it explained them plausibly. And physiological theory was related to other parts of the medieval world-picture. One could pass quite naturally from the question of man's organic nature to that of his place in the Christian universe. The system did not burden the imagination with too much detail, and it left a great deal to rational conjecture. The problems of modern medicine are too technical for the nonspecialist, but it was open to anyone to discuss the influence of radical heat and radical moisture on bodily health. The points of the system lent themselves to ingenious handling. One could manipulate them to provide an amusing explanation for any eccentricity of character. This made the old physiology an excellent basis for theories of character: for example, the 'Humours' theory of Ben Jonson.

A pleasing example of this exploitation of physiological ideas is found in the third section of *The Art of Sinking in Poetry*. Pope is explaining the process of creating bad poetry:

> Farthermore, it were great cruelty and injustice, if all such Authors as cannot write in the other way, were prohibited from writing at all. Against this I draw an argument from what seems to me an undoubted physical Maxim, That Poetry is a natural or morbid Secretion from the Brain. As I would not suddenly stop a cold in the head, or dry up my neighbour's Issue, I would as little hinder him from necessary writing. It may be affirmed with great truth that there is hardly any human creature past childhood, but at one time or other has had some Poetical Evacuation, and, no question, was much the better for it in his health; so true is the saying, *Nascimur Poetae*. Therefore is the Desire of Writing properly term'd *Pruritus*, the 'Titillation of the Generative Faculty of the Brain', and the Person is said to conceive; now such as conceive must bring forth. I have known a man thoughtful, melancholy and raving for divers days, who forthwith grew wonderfully easy, lightsome and cheerful, upon the discharge of the peccant humour, in exceeding purulent metre.[5]

5. *The Art of Sinking*, III.

Another characteristic of the old physiology is that it could be concretely visualized. It could become material for poetic imagery. There is a most eloquent account, in Panurge's defence of borrowing and lending, of the co-operation of the members of the body in the work of making blood.[6] As physiology and medicine became more scientific and less speculative these subjects became less available for imaginative treatment. Physiological wit, some of it based on old ideas and some on new, is found in abundance in *Tristram Shandy*.

From the materials of medicine we turn to those of law. 'Justice entangled in her web of law', writes an historian of English legal institutions, 'is a familiar figure in poetry from Sophocles to Pope and in philosophy from Aristotle to Kant.'[7] But the idea of law as a kind of net through which the undeserving, if sufficiently supple, may escape and in which the deserving may be ensnared, has less point today than in earlier periods. The old pedantic rigidity of the forms of action has gone, and the reforms of the utilitarians have tended to make the legal system correspond more to what ordinary human nature sees as reasonable and just. *Ubi Remedium ibi ius* has become *ubi ius ibi remedium*.[8] Fewer people need to go to law today, so we are all less legally minded; and in becoming more efficient the law has become less picturesque. The community has benefited from these reforms, but a theme for wit has been lost.[9] Under the old regime the legal system, in real life as in literature, was a field for playful invention, some of the fictitious proceedings which were used to manipulate the law, such as those involved in 'barring the entail', having for us the qualities of ingenious farce. The primitive concreteness of the law, as exemplified in such ceremonies of 'livery of seisin' (the handling over by feoffor to feoffee of the symbolic clod of earth) made it also a natural source of poetic imagery.

The art of the legal quibble is one application of that art of logic-chopping for which the schoolmen were chiefly renowned. The power to use logic to give a show of plausibility to an absurd or unreasonable argument is, in general, one of the distinguishing marks of the writers in the tradition of wit which we are examining. Legal quibbles are common in seventeenth-century literature. Donne, in 'Woman's Constancy' cynically invents for his mistress a far-fetched excuse in legal terms for infidelity. Dryden's Almanzor, confronted with Almahide's betrothal to Boabdelin, seeks for a

6. Rabelais, op. cit., III, 4.
7. C. H. S. Fifoot, *English Law and its Background*, 1932, p. 5.
8. *Ubi remedium ibi ius*: "Where there is remedy there is law." *Ubi ius ibi remedium*: "Where there is law there is remedy." [Editor].
9. Sir Alan Herbert's *Misleading Cases* are a reminder that the legal quibble can still be a source of light entertainment, but it no longer provides a major theme for literature.

quasi-legal basis for his own claim to her.[1] *The Merchant of Venice* is a simple example of a story which turns on a legal technicality; but there is more play with the learned materials of law, more of the scholastic spirit, in Jonson's *Silent Woman*, where the bogus canonist and divine discuss the possibilities of a divorce for the unfortunate Morose. The impeachment of Bridlegoose in Rabelais, and the interpretation by the three brothers of their father's will in the *Tale of a Tub*, may also be cited as further examples of legal wit. It is hardly necessary to mention that *Tristram Shandy* is full of it: the 'petite *canulle*' joke,[2] the 'innomine patriae'[3] dispute, the debate as to whether Mr. Shandy is of kin to his own child,[4] are delightful examples.

If legal wit has declined it does not mean that law has ceased to provide comic situations. A distinction is necessary here between legal wit, which depends on the manipulation of the logic of law and is an intellectual thing, and what may be termed the comedy of the law-court, which is simply a form of comedy of manners depending on human idiosyncrasies in a special setting. Legal situations, in so far as they are human situations, are always liable to give rise to comedy of this kind. The Bardell *v.* Pickwick trial comes mainly in the latter category.

Something must be said concerning the central subject-matter of scholastic thought: religion. But religion comes too near to the thought-life of the common man to be typical material for learned wit. Learned jokes about religion can often be classified under some other subject, such as canon law. The medieval habit of referring to religion as the supreme arbiter on all matters, however secular and commonplace, continued among writers during and after the Renaissance. It was quite natural in the *Compleat Angler* for Piscator and his friends to use scriptural arguments in defence of their favourite forms of sport, and convention allowed them to do this without destroying the essentially social and practical character of their discussion. It is a feature of conventions that they can be accommodated to more than one level of attitude. A reference to Christian doctrine could be a gesture of piety or of polite conformity, or it could be a stroke of wit. The Wife of Bath quotes patriarchal authority in defence of a promiscuous love-life and Panurge appeals to Genesis in support of his theory of codpieces.[5]

Under medieval Catholicism a good deal of joking on or near the subject of religion was habitual, while the courtly love poet travestied the materials of religion for serious purposes. Boldness in the

1. The *Conquest of Granada*, III.
2. I.xx.
3. IV.xxix.
4. IV.xxix.
5. Rabelais, op. cit., III, 8.

treatment of this subject is one of the general characteristics of those writers who come within our survey: Rabelais, Swift, Sterne. Modern readers, especially those of puritan or rationalist mentality, often misunderstand this freedom, because we have lost the idea of a Christian tradition within which so much latitude is possible. Any view we take of Rabelais is incomplete if we forget that he had moments of tender piety, which give way, however, almost without pause to his usual ribald gaiety. It is characteristic of the tradition that the little company which sits waiting for Tristram's birth should hear Trim's reading of a sermon as well as Dr. Slop's reading of the Ernulphus curse.

This elasticity in moving from the serious to the flippant is parallel to the capacity to alternate between the romantic and the improper in the treatment of sex. The gradual encroachment in the eighteenth century of a middle-class spirit in religion and morals destroyed both.

Certain types of wit within this tradition take their character not so much from any specific materials of the pre-scientific era of learning as from its procedures and habits. Modern science, with its more exacting standards of certainty and accuracy, and its specialization, imposes conditions which did not exist for such studious inquiries as Sir Thomas Browne and Mr. Walter Shandy, to whom the whole universe lay open for learned exploration. There was no question for them which they might not hopefully tackle by relying on their two principal methods: abstract reasoning and the consultation of erudite authorities.

The 'unbridled rationalism' (to use Whitehead's phrase) of the scholastic mentality, the complete absence of such restraint upon abstract speculation as scientific principles impose, led to much eccentricity and extravagance. Browne's *Vulgar Errors* is fertile in examples. On the question of whether, 'a Bear brings forth her young informous and unshapen, which she fashioneth after by licking them over', he concludes that it is, 'injurious to Reason, and much impugneth the course and providence of Nature, to conceive a birth should be ordained before there is a formation'. In Mr. Shandy this speculative freedom is carried to its limits.

The second method, the consultation of learned authorities, must be dwelt on rather longer. Under the regime of modern science it is not necessary to know all the views of one's predecessors; it is possible to say quite definitely that certain theories have had their day and can safely be forgotten. They remain of interest only as part of the history of science, a subject in which scientists are not always interested. For Sir Thomas Browne it was otherwise. In any learned inquiry—on the legs of the badger, for example, or of the elephant—reference would normally be made to a number of authorities, ancient and modern, the more the better. When one man's opinion might be quoted against another's without the question arising of a decision by experiment, it was honourable and useful to know all the best opinions. The list of authorities was the measure of a scholar's range of learning. Along with lists of authorities went lists of facts and materials culled from the authorities. Modern works of science and learning run to lists only for specific utilitarian purposes. The list has lost its rhetorical value. But in works like the *Anatomy of Melancholy* it is a thing of glory, the inventory of a treasure-house. When the facts are numerous, but not too numerous, there is some point in trying to know them all. There is a place for the gargantuan appetite of a Burton. Learning of this kind has a personal flavour: it represents individual achievement. Modern learning, with its infinitely greater array of facts and formidable mechanical organization of them, is inevitably more impersonal.

In Burton and other scholars and wits of his school we find two qualities combined: a pedantic thoroughness in the listing of authorities and facts, and a lively grasp of everyday things. The piling on of learned detail does not choke the human interest, while the materials of concrete experience are ordered with a learned thoroughness. In the following passage Pantagruel gives advice to Panurge on what to eat and what to abstain from in order to avoid fallacious dreams:

> You may take a little supper, but thereat must you not eat of a hare, nor of any other Flesh: you are likewise to abstain from beans, from the *Preak* (by some called the *Polyp*) as also from Coleworts, cabbage, and all other such like windy victuals, which may endanger the troubling of your brains, and the dimming or casting a kind of mist over your Animal Spirits . . . You shall eat good *Eusebian* and Bergamot-Pears, one apple of the short-shank Pepin-kind, a parcel of the little plums of *Tours*, and some few cherries of the growth of my orchard.[6]

We are given the impression here that behind the choosing of Panurge's supper lies a vast body of theory on the dietetic properties of all the meats, vegetables and fruits. Yet accompanying this is a personal knowledge of a particular fruit grown in a particular place. From an almost limitless world of possibilities everything is most studiously hand-picked.

In Rabelais's third book, from which this passage is taken, stupendous quantities of information, with authorities and *exempla*, are poured forth, and one source of wisdom after another is consulted, all to the end that Panurge—literature's most irresponsible

6. Rabelais, op. cit., III, 13.

figure—might be correctly advised about marriage. There is a huge comic disproportion, which is also a noble disproportion, between Pantagruel's unflagging helpfulness and its object. Only in an age which believed in princely magnificence and courtesy (and, higher than that, in the overwhelming bounty of God to undeserving man) could such a situation be created and sustained. Only in an age which believed in the nobility of learning could the materials of erudition be raised to such rhetorical heights.

A passage, similar to the last, may be quoted from *Tristram Shandy*. It is from Mr. Shandy's letter to Uncle Toby, in which he recommends a suitable diet for a wooer. It is hardly necessary to comment on the solemn absurdity of the advice, which contrasts oddly with the sardonic good sense shown earlier in the letter ('. . . and thou knowest, dear Toby, that there is no passion so serious as lust').

> But thou must eat little or no goat's flesh, nor red deer—nor even foal's flesh, by any means; and carefully abstain—that is, as much as thou canst, from peacocks, cranes, coots, didappers, and water-hens. . . .
> As for thy drink—I need not tell thee, it must be the infusion of Vervain and the herb Hanea, of which Aelian relates such effects —but if thy stomach palls with it—discontinue it from time to time, taking cucumbers, melons, purslane, water-lilies, woodbine and lettuce, in the stead of them.[7]

The attempt to exploit the list for rhetorical or comic purposes is not, as a rule, successful in modern writers. The list has almost ceased to be an expressive form, and the mere piling on of words and names with what is sometimes called 'cumulative effect' is liable to become a cheap trick.

All these types of wit hang together in that they depend for their character on intellectual materials and habits belonging to what may be roughly labelled a pre-Enlightenment world (pre-Utilitarian, in the case of legal wit). In some cases the term 'scholastic' may be used with differing degrees of justification. This tradition, as we have indicated earlier, has no clearly marked frontiers and it is difficult to decide whether some kinds of learned wit may conveniently be regarded as in it or not. Wit based on the exploitation of rhetoric is a case in point. As rhetoric was taught in the medieval schools, the case for including it would seem to be strong. The possible objection that rhetoric was much more important to the humanists than to the medieval educationists need not trouble us at all: this is a case where differences between medieval and Renais-

7. VIII.xxxiv.

sance phenomena are less important for us than differences between
phenomena belonging to both the Middle Ages and the Renaissance
on the one hand and those due to the Enlightenment on the other.
A more valid reason, it may be urged, for excluding rhetorical wit is
that it is concerned merely with means of expression while the other
types which we have considered are all related to ways of thinking.
The sort of wit which consists only in the parodying of rhetorical
figures (*Love's Labour's Lost* abounds in it) would seem not to
belong in spirit to the tradition we are studying. But rhetoric does
not deal only with manner; matter also comes within its province.
That branch of it which is called *inventio* is concerned with the
finding of the right things to say on a given topic. Panurge's defence
of borrowing is, among other things, a rhetorical performance. He
follows the conventional recommendations relating to *inventio*; for
instance, in the passage where borrowing is associated with the Four
Cardinal Virtues, which are considered in turn. In so far as the
mock disputation called for rhetorical as well as dialectical pro-
ficiency, rhetoric must be regarded as part of our subject, though
not perhaps very central to it. The formal rhetorical handling of a
theme meant an ordered copiousness, a systematic treatment of all
the conceivable aspects, with tedious consequences in many writers,
but offering a genius like Rabelais scope and warrant for a generous
display of his powers.

There is a certain amount of play with the terms of rhetoric in
Tristram Shandy; for example, in the passage where it is left open to
dispute whether Uncle Toby had really finished a certain sentence
or not:

> If, on the contrary, my uncle Toby had not fully arrived at the
> period's end—then the world stands indebted to the snapping of
> my father's tobacco-pipe for one of the neatest examples of that
> ornamental figure in oratory, which Rhetoricians style the
> Aposiopesis. . . .[8]

Mention may be made in this context of Mr. Shandy's lamentation
over his eldest son, with its Ciceronian and other borrowings. His
use of a literary model in so personal a matter is akin to his use of
learned authorities in other personal matters relating to his concrete
problems as a parent. Both point to the same sort of intellectual
eccentricity.

It was claimed earlier that the mentality formed by the old learning expressed itself in the treatment not merely of intellectual ma-

8. II.vi. Other examples may be found
in I.xix; I.xxi and elsewhere. I am indebted to Mr. F. W. Bateson for the
suggestion that the blank pages, wriggly
lines, patterns of asterisks, etc., in *Tris-*
tram Shandy are a parody of the poems
in the shape of hearts and other objects
commended in some Renaissance hand-
books of rhetoric.

terials but also of concrete things. The result was metaphysical imagery in poetry and certain uses of descriptive detail in writers like Jonson and Swift and, as we shall see later, Sterne.

One of the accepted characteristics of metaphysical imagery is its ability to embody or at least to heighten ideas. The loss of this quality, attributed by Mr. Eliot to a 'dissociation of sensibility', is obviously a complex matter, but the intellectual changes of the seventeenth century clearly have a great deal to do with it. The repudiation by the scientists of the study of final causes involved a splitting of the unity of reality: without metaphysics facts lose their roundness. The scientist ceases to be concerned with things as they enter into common human experience, but only with specific manageable aspects of things; a feat of abstraction which, affecting the general consciousness, imposes a serious deprivation on the sensibility of poets. Medieval thought knew no such schism: metaphysical principle had the ascendancy and the world of fact was kept in its place, the individual fact or thing being all the more solidly realizable for being clothed with a meaning which covered all its aspects. This harmony between the concrete and the abstract, the thing and the meaning, becoming a habit of the imagination, manifested itself in poetry; on the highest level in the imagery of Dante, the clear, living expression of the idea; on lower levels in the more mechanical type of allegory, that of Deguileville and others, in which every aspect of the spiritual meaning is given its corresponding concrete symbol *ad nauseam*. In both cases the quality which imagery acquires is that of *order*, which may be subtle or commonplace. The habit of ordered schematization of imagery and material detail was inveterate among medieval poets, in allegory or otherwise. It was natural for the medieval imagination to grasp the material world in terms of ordered patterns of particulars. An exciting play of idea and image is not common in medieval poetry: the well-designed scholastic universe tended to be accepted rather stolidly by an age which did not contemplate the possibility of losing it. Those effects in imagery which we call 'metaphysical' are found mainly at a later period, when Renaissance thought was destroying the traditional world-picture, and the old integration was threatened. The inherited habit of co-ordinating the thing and the meaning served the poet well in an age when both things and meanings were in the melting pot.

When this use of imagery departed from poetry it was not altogether lost to other forms of literature. An excellent example in Swift is the episode of the spider and the bee in the *Battle of the Books*, where the argument as to which insect has the better way of life becomes, by a nice manipulation of terms, a debate concerning the relative merits of ancients and moderns. In replacing the two

types of intellect by two types of organism Swift is able to opera,
on the imagination by imagery.

When we speak of imagery it is usually to the metaphor and the
simile that we refer, but there are other ways in which ideas may
take concrete shape: for example, in the laborious detail of medieval allegorical description, to which we have already referred.
There are descriptive passages in Swift and Sterne where the selec-
tion and ordering of the detail play an artistic role oddly reminis-
cent of that of the metaphysical image: a pointedness, a sharpness
of outline, seem to suggest an insidious intention. One of Swift's
favourite devices is the use of the learned idea with the image, the
pseudo-scholarly preamble providing the logical preparation for the
embodied monstrosity. The account of the Aeolists is a most brilliant example of this technique, and a similar example occurs in the
Introduction to the *Tale of a Tub*, where arguments are given in
favour of an elevated position for an orator, and the posture of the
hearers is described with an awful precision. These passages in Swift
have features in common. A schematization is imposed upon the
physical elements to create the appearance of ritual. But the grotesque position and grouping of the figures only *seem* to be significant: the suggestion of significance produced by the precision and
pointedness of the description serves simply to give heightening to
gross absurdity. It is Swift's imaginative response to the uncomely
posturings of religious fanaticism.

Sterne's use of similar techniques will be more conveniently discussed when we examine *Tristram Shandy* by itself.

III

It is one of the good jokes of literature that we reach the third
book of *Tristram Shandy* before the hero is born. But not all readers see why the joke is good. The entire structure of the work
depends on the fact that the starting-point is not Tristram's birth but
his begetting. At the outset Sterne declares his purpose, which is to
begin literally *ab Ovo*:

> For which cause, right glad I am, that I have begun the history of
> myself in the way I have done; and that I am able to go on, tracing
> everything in it, as Horace says, *ab Ovo*.

Between begetting and birth much may happen. It is, from the
point of view of medicine and psychology, a most important period
in a person's life. But it does not offer the kind of material which
the historian or novelist can normally handle. A modern novel
dealing with so early a phase in the career of its hero would have to
be something in the nature of a scientific fantasy, and although

,orary ideas could be exploited for such a purpose we
d expect them to undergo a cheapening process. In the intel-
ctual tradition available to Sterne ideas were not rendered crude
through being familiar. *Tristram Shandy* breaks off before the hero
is mature enough to become what in literature is recognized as a
character. Of his history we know only what the influences of the
pre-natal period and early infancy have done for him. From the
point of view of the ordinary historian or novelist very little has
happened. But from the point of view of Mr. Shandy and the
modern psychologist most of the really decisive things have happened. Tristram's character and fortune have been more or less
settled by the sequence of events beginning with the unfortunate
circumstances of his begetting and culminating in the sash-window
tragedy. In this sequence of events lies the pattern of the novel.

We cannot accuse Sterne of not announcing his theme promptly.
The first chapter is all about the perils which attend one's begetting.

> I wish either my father or my mother, or indeed both of them,
> as they were in duty both equally bound to it, had minded what
> they were about when they begot me; had they duly considered
> how much depended upon what they were then doing;—that not
> only the production of a rational Being was concerned in it, but
> that possibly the happy formation and temperature of his body,
> perhaps his genius and the very cast of his mind;—and, for aught
> they knew to the contrary, even the fortunes of his whole house
> might take their turn from the humours and dispositions which
> were then uppermost;—Had they duly weighed and considered
> all this, and proceeded accordingly,—I am verily persuaded I
> should have made a quite different figure in the world, from that
> in which the reader is likely to see me.—Believe me, good folks,
> this is not so inconsiderable a thing as many of you may think
> it;—you have all, I dare say, heard of the animal spirits, as how
> they are transfused from father to son etc. etc.—and a great deal
> to that purpose:—Well, you may take my word, that nine parts
> in ten of a man's sense or his nonsense, his successes and mis-
> carriages in this world depend upon their motions and activity,
> and the different tracts and trains you put them into, so that
> when they are once set a-going, whether right or wrong, 'tis not
> a halfpenny matter,—away they go cluttering like hey-go mad;
> and by treading the same steps over and over again, they presently
> make a road of it, as plain and as smooth as a garden-walk, which,
> when they are once used to, the Devil himself sometimes shall
> not be able to drive them off.[9]

From this introduction we pass to the concrete scene: Mr. and
Mrs. Shandy are about to perform their function. At the critical

9. I.i.

moment Mr. Shandy is interrupted by his wife's question about winding up the clock, and so occurs the first of Tristram's misfortunes. The question, coming at that moment, 'scattered and dispersed the animal spirits, whose business it was to have escorted and gone hand in hand with the HOMUNCULUS, and conducted him safe to the place destined for his reception.'

The misfortune takes place before conception, so the identity of the victim would seem to be a rather delicate metaphysical problem. Sterne, however, gives him metaphysical status and a living shape:

> The Homunculus, Sir, in however low and ludicrous a light he may appear, in this age of levity, to the eye of folly or prejudice;— to the eye of reason in scientific research, he stands confessed— a Being guarded and circumscribed with rights.—The minutest philosophers, who, by the bye, have the most enlarged understandings, (their souls being inversely as their enquiries) shew us incontestably, that the Homunculus is created by the same hand, —engendered in the same course of nature,—endowed with the same locomotive powers and faculties with us;—That he consists as we do, of skin, hair, fat, flesh, veins, arteries, ligaments, nerves, cartilages, bones, marrow, brains, glands, genitals, humours, and articulations . . . .
> Now, dear Sir, what if any accident had befallen him in his way alone!—or that, through terror of it, natural to so young a traveller, my little Gentleman had got to his journey's end miserably spent;—his muscular strength and virility worn down to a thread; —his own animal spirits ruffled beyond description,—and that in this sad disordered state of nerves, he had lain down a prey to sudden starts, or a series of melancholy dreams and fancies, for nine long, long months together.—I tremble to think what a foundation had been laid for a thousand weaknesses both of body and of mind, which no skill of the physician or the philosopher could ever afterwards have set thoroughly to rights.[1]

Tristram's second misfortune takes us into the sphere of legal entanglements. It is because Mr. Shandy insists on the terms of his wife's marriage settlement that Tristram is born in the country, not in London. Mrs. Shandy, unable to have the best professional attendance, insists on having the worst; and the result is the tragedy of Tristram's nose.

Mr. Shandy's theory, reached after much elaborate physiological speculation, is that, 'the excellency of the nose is in a direct arithmetical proportion to the excellency of the wearer's fancy'.[2] The flattening of Tristram's nose is therefore a cruel blow to his parental hopes. He falls back on the theory of names, and is again thwarted, by a mistake which causes his child to be given the name which he

1. I.ii.   2. III.xxxviii.

ndemned as the worst possible. He inquires into the possibil-
of changing it, and this leads to a great orgy of legal quibbling
ding in the decision that the parents have no rights in the matter,
not being of kin to their own child! Opportunities continue to
present themselves, however, for applying learning to his parental
responsibilities. He composes a *Tristrapaedia*, or system of education: he interests himself in theories of bodily health: *à propos* of
putting the child into breeches he makes careful researches into the
wardrobe of the ancients. Meanwhile Tristram has encountered further disaster through the fall of a sash-window.

The theme of *Tristram Shandy* may be seen in terms of a comic
clash between the world of learning and that of human affairs. On
the level of theory Mr. Shandy makes formidable preparations for
his child's welfare, but partly through his own folly or inattention in
practical matters, and partly through unlucky accident, his schemes
are frustrated. It is Mr. Shandy's perverse insistence on legal principle that is responsible for Tristram's being born in the country: he
is therefore to blame for the flattened nose. As for the mistake over
the name, fortune is cruel in making him just too late to prevent it:
the finding and donning of a pair of breeches causes the fatal delay.
The sash-window accident is not his fault directly; it is due to the
intemperate zeal of Corporal Trim in the service of Uncle Toby's
hobby-horse that, 'nothing in the Shandy household is well hung',
but it is typical of Mr. Shandy's character that he should be un-
aware, in his philosophical absorption, of what is going on in his
own house.

Was Sterne indebted for this theme to any of his predecessors in
the tradition to which we are trying to relate him? Cornelius Scriblerus's grotesque application of pedantic learning to the education
of his son Martinus in the *Memoirs of Scriblerus* may have suggested something to him, but the comedy here is not rich enough in
human values to count as a major inspiration. A more significant
parallel is provided by the third book of Rabelais, from which a
number of passages were quoted in the previous section. As these
two works are, in certain obvious ways, unlike, let us enumerate the
pointes of resemblance. In each there is a central human problem,
for the solving of which an immense body of knowledge is assembled: the question of how to give the infant hero the best start in
life, the question of whether Panurge should marry. In each there is
unquenchable faith in the validity of learning in its application to
life. In each there is a series of phases or episodes in which one
form of learning after another is brought to bear on the problem. In
each the well-meant efforts are frustrated, in the one case by a
mixture of human frailty and the cussedness of things, in the other
by perversity in its most pronounced form.

The comedy depends on the play between two things: a traditional order of ideas and beliefs, and human folly or mishap. It is essential to the effect that the ideas and beliefs should have a basis of seriousness in the mind of the author, though they are made to serve a comic purpose. The attitude of the author was, no doubt, rather mixed. We know that Sterne intended the theory of noses to be a piece of absurdity, but we cannot say the same of all the physiological lore in which *Tristram Shandy* abounds. Sterne was immersed in physiological ideas. It was a material which meant much to his imagination. It is appropriate that the Shandean philosophy should be stated in these terms:

> True Shandeism, think what you will against it, opens the heart and lungs, and like all those affections which partake of its nature, it forces the blood and other vital fluids of the body to run freely through its channels, makes the wheel of life run long and cheerfully round.[3]

The pattern of learned wit suggested above is not the only one to be found in *Tristram Shandy*. Wilbur L. Cross, the most eminent of all Sterne scholars, said that the whole work was organized in terms of Locke's doctrine of association of ideas. That this is an important structural principle is certainly true: it governs his use of digressions, and it manifests itself sometimes in the behavior of the characters; for example, when Mrs. Shandy inopportunely remembers the clock-winding ritual. Two comments need to be made on Cross's views. The first is that Sterne, unlike most eighteenth-century writers who were influenced by Locke, exploited his ideas freely as opportunities for wit, playing with them in a manner quite unlike that of their original begetter. His was the old spirit at work upon new materials. The second is that Cross is untrue to the spirit of *Tristram Shandy* in saying that 'Sterne assumes Locke's attitude towards scholastic and theological pedantry'. Sterne's attitude was, to say the least, one of humorous interest; Locke's that of the serious reformer, the ideas he attacked making no appeal to his fancy.

The learned wit in *Tristram Shandy* would be all the less interesting if the intellectual tradition to which Sterne was indebted did not exert some influence on the imagination, discernible in his treatment of concrete, everyday things. His descriptive passages are full of effects which recall that pointedness in the ordering of detail which we noted in Swift and for which kinship was claimed, at a humbler, prose level, with the union of idea and image in metaphysical poetry.

3. IV.xxxii.

...ne had a curious feeling for order which expressed itself in a ...mber of ways. In one of its manifestations it is accompanied by what would appear to be its opposite, a delight in confusion; but in Sterne these things are not opposites. To dwell upon disorder, reducing it to its particulars and bringing out its perversely twisted pattern, involves the introduction of an element of order. The complicated description of how Obadiah tied up Dr. Slop's bag of instruments is a good example.[4] Another manifestation of his sense of order is an insistence on relating happenings to their causes. Causation works in very odd ways in *Tristram Shandy*, curious devices being used for holding the structure of events together, so that one is reminded of some contraption designed by Heath Robinson. Obadiah's entanglement is itself one of the obstacles to Tristram's smooth passage into the world. ('Sport of small accidents, Tristram Shandy! that thou art, and ever will be!') The sash-window disaster is originally due to Uncle Toby's need for lead for his miniature field-pieces. The first and aboriginal mishap is associated with the winding of a clock. In a delightful passage illustrating the queer mechanisms of family life in the Shandy household Sterne dwells on the importance of a faulty hinge on the parlour door.[5] Another of his habits is to give a studied precision to descriptions of physical postures in scenes where the composed effect is grotesque rather than dignified. The spotlight is directed in such a way as to heighten the trivial. Mr. Shandy prostrate with grief on hearing of his child's flattened nose,[6] Corporal Trim as he takes his stance to read the sermon,[7] are notable examples of this type of effect. In another passage Sterne catches Mr. Shandy trying to put his left hand into his right hand coat pocket, and dwells with a connoisseur's finesse on the result.[8] Sometimes there is the odd suggestion, or the parody of a suggestion, that the detail is significant, that there is a meaning embodied in the pattern. If there is any it is, perhaps, that of 'order in disorder'. It seems to be characteristic of the Shandy world that the things belonging to order are sabotaged by human muddle, while order and exactness are imposed quite arbitrarily upon the unimportant and the incidental.

Uncle Toby's hobby-horse is the most interesting example of Sterne's idiosyncratic ordering of detail, but it is interesting for other reasons as well. It brings us back to learned wit, for military science was a form of learning like any other, and took similar forms to those of Mr. Shandy's intellectual interests. It had a relatively clear-cut system, with an ordered grouping of particulars, but

4. III.viii.
5. V.vi.
6. III.xxiv.
7. II.xvii.
8. III.ii.

with just enough complication to provide a pleasing muddle. It had its lists of learned authorities and a terminology with rhetorical possibilities: *scarp, counterscarp, glacis, covered way, half-moon* and *ravelin*. It was, in fact, good material for the kind of artistic exploitation which we have been studying.

In his discourse on hobby-horses[9] Sterne puts forward a theory of characterization, the point of which is that when a man becomes deeply attached to a favourite occupation, his character gradually takes on a shape and colouring derived from the materials belonging to that occupation. There is another side to this process, which Sterne does not mention, though his art illustrates it. If the man's nature is changed by the materials acting upon it, the materials themselves are changed by their association with the man. All organized pursuits or subjects for study may be said to have their abstract, impersonal character—their 'text-book' character, let us say—and also a variable 'human' character imposed upon them by the different sorts of treatment which they receive when human beings have to do with them. Whenever the human factor enters in there is modification and distortion. The materials of military science, entering so deeply into Uncle Toby's mind and giving him a medium through which to express himself, take on new shapes in the process.

Uncle Toby's hobby-horse arises, as Sterne explains most fully, out of a difficulty he experiences in making himself clear when he tries to tell the tale of the siege of Namur, where he received his wound. Partly because his hearers do not understand the technical terms, and partly because the terrain was somewhat complicated, he gets tied up in his narration, and this (Sterne indulges in some medical speculation here) by irritating him, adversely affects his recovery from the wound. In his account of Uncle Toby's efforts,[1] Sterne achieves the effect of 'order in disorder', the element of clear, circumstantial detail enhancing the confusion. The search for clarity leads Uncle Toby to the study of maps and text-books. But now he becomes so full of his theme that he has to find other, more elaborate, ways of expressing himself through it, so he builds miniature fortifications on a bowling-green and fights mock battles with field artillery made from leaden gutters, a melted-down pewter shaving-basin and the weights from sash-windows.

There is a quality about Uncle Toby's hobby-horse which places it on a different imaginative level from other examples in fiction of make-believe and eccentric preoccupation. The difference is one of intensity. Sterne's art manifests itself in the transformation of the concrete objects so that they become completely assimilated to

9. I.xxiv.   1. II.i.

ncle Toby's all-absorbing idea. A peculiar concentration and control of detail create the spell which we feel, as it were, objectively. The make-believe is not for us, there is no dubious invitation to fantasy:

> The corporal, who the night before had resolved in his mind to supply the grand *desideratum*, of keeping up something like an incessant firing upon the enemy during the heat of the attack, —had no further idea in his fancy at that time, than a contrivance of smoking tobacco against the town, out of one of my uncle Toby's six field-pieces, which were planted on each side of his sentry-box . . . Upon turning it this way, and that, a little in his mind, he soon began to find out, that by means of his two Turkish tobacco-pipes, with the supplement of three smaller tubes of wash-leather at each of their lower ends, to be tagged by the same number of tin-pipes fitted to the touch-holes, and sealed with clay next the cannon, and then tied hermetically with waxed silk at their several insertions into the Moroccan tube,—he should be able to fire the six field-pieces all together, and with the same ease as to fire one.[2]

Uncle Toby's hobby-horse differs from that of (say) Commodore Trunnion or Mr. Wemmick[3] not only in intensity but in the fact that it refuses to keep within its allotted boundaries. It spreads, it gets mixed up with other parts of the novel. The toys, straying from their places, contribute to the complicated system of traps and obstacles in which the characters, bodily or mentally, are caught. There is the sash-window episode: the drawbridge broken accidentally by Trim is confused—only momentarily, but the explanation takes time—with the bridge of Tristram's nose: Mr. Shandy's mention of a train of ideas makes Uncle Toby think of a train of artillery.

The phrase 'order in disorder' is also applicable to the external structure of *Tristram Shandy*. On the element of disorder it is unnecessary to dwell: it is this which strikes one most on a first reading. Sterne took pleasure in destroying the normal order of things and in creating an exaggerated appearance of disorder, but only to link up the pieces in another and more interesting way.

Sterne's treatment of sentiment is an example of the remoter operation of the 'wit' tradition. The charge of false feeling, of indulgence in sentiment, has frequently been levelled against him. But may it not be said in reply that his indulgence is always allied to a self-knowledge, that an ironical consciousness of the limitations of

---

2. VI.xxvi.
3. Commodore Trunnion is a character in Smollett's *Peregrine Pickle*; Mr. Wemmick appears in Dickens's *Great Expectations*. [*Editor.*]

his feelings adds just the right flavour to his presentation of them?[4] We understand this better when we are aware of the tradition of wit to which Sterne belonged, with its devices for keeping the comic and the serious worlds of feeling on the right terms with each other, and for allowing a writer to reveal the play of opposites in his own character. Sterne's suavely controlled treatment of a sentimental situation may have little in common technically with the blend of emotion and irony in Donne or Marvell, but both are examples of wit acting as a corrective to feeling or giving edge to it. It was Sterne's link with this tradition which enabled him to handle the new fashionable material of 'sensibility' with adroitness and sophistication.

TOBY A. OLSHIN

Genre and *Tristram Shandy*: The Novel of Quickness†

In an essay summarizing recent critical trends in Sterne scholarship, Lodwick Hartley gives much attention to what he calls "the vexed question of the *genre* of *Tristram Shandy*." There has been, as Sterne predicted there would be, a diversity of critical opinion on this subject.[1] On the one hand, some scholars have made attempts to classify *Tristram Shandy* by placing it within known genres. Northrop Frye, for instance, sees the work as an anatomy, a genre descending from Menippean satire.[2] Theodore Baird, who has discovered a source for the historical events described in *Tristram Shandy*, calls it "an exactly executed historical novel."[3] Most recently, Melvyn New has placed Sterne squarely in the tradition of the Augustan satirists.[4]

On the other hand, certain critics have found neat generic classification difficult, if not impossible. John Traugott, in considering

4. Mr. Herbert Read has written well on Sterne's sentimentality in *The Sense of Glory*, 1929, p. 140.
† From *Genre*, 4 (1971), 360–75. Footnotes are by Olshin.
1. Lodwick Hartley, "Yorick Redivivus: A Bicentenary Review of Studies on Laurence Sterne," *Studies in the Novel*, 1 (Spring 1969), 81–87; see also Hartley's excellent survey of genre studies in *Laurence Sterne in the Twentieth Century: An Essay and a Bibliography of Sternean Studies, 1900–1965* (Chapel Hill, 1966), pp. 21–23. Seeing *Tristram Shandy* as a work which had "more handles than one," Sterne commented that "every one will take the handle which suits his convenience" (Letter to Dr. John Eustace, February 9, 1768; *Letters of Laurence Sterne*, ed. Lewis Perry Curtis [Oxford, 1935; repr. 1965], p. 411.).
2. *Anatomy of Criticism: Four Essays* (Princeton, 1957), pp. 303–8.
3. "The Time-Scheme of *Tristram Shandy* and a Source," *PMLA*, 51 (1946), 803–20.
4. *Laurence Sterne as Satirist: A Reading of "Tristram Shandy"* (Gainesville, 1969); New sees Tristram as an ironic persona distinctly separate from Sterne and finds Yorick's point of view the normative one.

Sterne's relationship to Lockean psychology, remarks: "Sterne created his own genre."[5] John M. Stedmond solved the problem by referring to something he calls the *"Tristram Shandy* genre," and more than one critic has felt that Sterne established a literary form which others would copy.[6] Evaluating past genre criticism, Hartley appears reluctant to make a tidy categorization: Sterne, he notes, "evolved an architectonic all his own."[7] Finally, a position which unites both views has been taken by Wayne C. Booth. He sees *Tristram Shandy* both as a novelistic innovation and as the inheritor of three generic traditions: the comic novel, the speculative essay, and the satire in the tradition of *A Tale of A Tub*.[8]

It is from this last point of view that I should like to begin my consideration of the genre of *Tristram Shandy*. What Booth has observed in the tripartite ancestry of Sterne's work is, I think, the dissolution of the established genres and the creation, in *Tristram Shandy*, of a new and highly individual form suited to the needs of a contemporary audience. The dissolution of traditional genres in the later eighteenth century signified, of course, a dissolution of meaning, a gradual crumbling of established forms of thought, chains of causation, and moral values.[9] We can infer from the rhetoric of *Tristram Shandy* (that is, its method of presentation) that Sterne found the older literary forms inadequate for the expression of the new meanings he perceived and the values he held.[1] These meanings, which are themselves his values, should be most clearly revealed to us from a study of the way in which *Tristram Shandy* is, in effect, served up to the reader. Why, for instance,

5. *Tristram Shandy's World: Sterne's Philosophical Rhetoric* (Berkeley and Los Angeles, 1954), p. 148.
6. *The Comic Art of Laurence Sterne* (Toronto, 1967), p. 13. For views on Sterne as the founder of a new genre, see René Wellek and Austin Warren, *Theory of Literature* (New York, 1942), pp. 212–13; and David Lodge, *The Language of Fiction: Essays in Criticism and Verbal Analysis of the English Novel* (New York, 1966), p. 261.
7. *Laurence Sterne in the Twentieth Century*, p. 72.
8. *The Rhetoric of Fiction* (Chicago, 1961). For Sterne as innovator, see Booth's comment: "When I begin what I think is a novel, I expect to read a novel throughout, unless the author can, like Sterne, transform my idea of what a novel can be" (p. 127). For Sterne as inheritor of traditions, see pp. 224–29.
9. The most recent study of this aspect of the period has been made by W. B. Carnochan, "Satire, Sublimity, and Sentiment: Theory and Practice in Post-Augustan Satire," *PMLA*, 85 (March 1970), 260–67. See also the discussions

by Martin Price in *To the Palace of Wisdom: Studies in Order and Energy from Dryden to Blake* (Garden City, 1964), pp. 312–41, and Earl R. Wasserman, *The Subtler Language: Critical Readings of Neoclassic and Romantic Poems* (Baltimore, 1959), pp. 169–88.
1. I am not persuaded by the argument of Graham Petrie, "Rhetoric as Fictional Technique in *Tristram Shandy*," *PQ*, 8 (October 1969), 479–93. Although his study documents his (and Sterne's) knowledge of classical rhetorical devices, it does not support his claim that those devices induce the reader "to adopt the attitude to the events and characters of the novel which the Narrator wishes him to have" (493). I shall argue that Sterne was forced to invent a new rhetorical mode to express a new philosophy; he was, in a sense, prefiguring the function of the dramatic monologue as it has been interpreted by Robert Langbaum in *The Poetry of Experience: The Dramatic Monologue in Modern Literary Tradition* (New York, 1957). See Langbaum's discussion of the dissolution of genres, pp. 226–35.

should Sterne's satire on pedantry not have been carried out without the use of lengthy quoted documents? Why could Uncle Toby not have fought, been wounded, and retired to his hobby-horse in the chronological sequence in which those events actually occurred?[2] Or, why could not Sterne have used third-person narration to describe the erratic Shandy household? The answer in every case is that only the rhetorical methods Sterne chose are adequately suited to the persuasive function of his novel: the reader is forced to accept the highly individual ethics of the implied author only in this particular vehicle.

This vehicle, then, fits none of the traditional genres for, were it to do so, its form would compel it to make rather more traditional statements than Sterne has in mind. Instead of demanding of the work the characteristics of known genres, I should like to call *Tristram Shandy* a "novel of quickness" since it is an organic work in the Coleridgean sense: it derives its unity from the one living presence whose unity informs it, the writer himself.[3] The narrative voice of Tristram, through which Sterne projects aspects of himself, is only the largest visible symbol of that unity, and because of the periodic unreliability and characteristic inadequacy of that voice, the reader is forced past it to Sterne and the common life they share.[4] It is this self-justifying surge of life, independent of all need for external meaning, that Sterne celebrates. Moreover, because the life surge *is* self-justifying, it needs only to be affirmed by the reader who, Sterne believes, has been left isolated by an outworn set of meanings and the demise of an older value system. This affirmation of life, then, is Sterne's ethical statement, and it was eminently suited to the needs of his contemporaries: the New Science was making a once-ordered existence into a set of shifting perspectives,[5]

2. Sterne has long been thought to have been primarily interested in the subjective aspects of time; see A. A. Mendilow, *Time and the Novel* (London, 1952), pp. 158–99, and B. H. Lehman, "Of Time, Personality, and the Author: A Study of *Tristram Shandy:* Comedy" in *Studies in the Comic, University of California Studies in English*, 8, No. 2 (1941), 233–50.
3. See Coleridge's discussion of the poet as one who "diffuses a tone and spirit of unity" (*Biographia Literaria*, Chap. 14, ed. J. Shawcross [London, 1907], II, 12). The same may, I think, be said of the novelist who allows his presence to be felt in the novel. See also Langbaum, pp. 233–34. In relating *Tristram Shandy's* serial publication to Sterne's own development, Stedmond notes: "*Tristram Shandy* might be said to have grown 'organically'—to be in fact an early example of the dynamic organicism often associated with Romanticism" (p. 25).

4. Tristram has been seen as the unifying factor by Booth, p. 22; see also Ian Watt, "The Comic Syntax of *Tristram Shandy*." *Studies in Criticism and Aesthetics, 1660–1800: Essays in Honor of Samuel Holt Monk*, ed. Howard Anderson and John S. Shea (Minneapolis, 1967), pp. 315–31: "If we muse decide not so much the fictional category, as the primary principle of unity, of *Tristram Shandy*, it must surely be Tristram's voice" (p. 330).
5. The fragment, usually accepted as Sterne's, which dramatizes this point of view was published by Paul Stapfer, *Laurence Sterne* (Paris, 1870). See also Sterne's comment in a letter to Robert Dodsley: "The plan [of *Tristram Shandy*] . . . is a most extensive one,—taking in, not only, the Weak part of the Sciences, in which the True Point of Ridicule lies —but every Thing else, which I find Laugh-at-able in my way—" (May 23, 1759; *Letters*, pp. 74–75).

and the old scholasticism had lost its authority, becoming little more than a rather desiccated pedantry.

To begin to see *Tristram Shandy* as a novel of quickness, we should note how rapidly Sterne's relationship with the reader is established and how, at the same time, Sterne's attitudes are made manifest so that he may begin his work of persuasion. The novel opens:

> I Wish either my father or my mother, or indeed both of them, as they were in duty both equally bound to it, had minded what they were about when they begot me; had they duly consider'd how much depended upon what they were then doing;——that not only the production of a rational Being was concern'd in it, but that possibly the happy formation and temperature of his body, perhaps his genius and the very cast of his mind;—and, for aught they knew to the contrary, even the fortunes of his whole house might take their turn from the humours and dispositions which were then uppermost:——Had they duly weighed and considered all this, and proceeded accordingly,——I am verily persuaded I should have made quite a different figure in the world, from that, in which the reader is likely to see me.—Believe me, good folks, this is not so inconsiderable a thing as many of you may think it. . . . (I.i.)

The phrase "when they begot me," which is the chief subject of the whole chapter, is placed so that it will jolt the reader to attention: it precedes the first major stop. The incongruity of the point of view has, by this time, already been firmly established. Because we have had talk of "duty," of being "bound" to do something, we are surprised to discover, as the clause ends, that what is being discussed is an act which is nothing if not natural and spontaneous.[6] Tristram goes on to offer ostensibly logical reasons for his "wish" by contending that his parents' thoughts and un-"duly considered" actions at that time are distinctly related to his current state. As his reasoning builds towards its climax, psychology and philosophy are brought to bear on the problem. With the first mention of how the narrator appears at the moment to the reader, even a tinge of self-pity is evident. As he continues, he makes his most dramatic attempt thus far to get us to share his views: he allows us to experience the scene of his conception. Only if we are present, presumably, will we agree that he has been unjustly treated by his thoughtless parents. The crucial moment is then dramatized as con-

6. Discussing "the hero's begetting," Ian Watt notes: "We are unaccustomed to thinking about this particular action from the point of view of the end product . . ." ("The Comic Syntax of *Tristram Shandy*," p. 316). It is, I think, precisely because Sterne knows that we are "unaccustomed" to such thinking that the scene is so effective. The reader's entanglement is both unwitting and inescapable.

versation, and the reader is even given a line to speak. He becomes, whether or not he wishes to, the observer at the bedside.[7]

The apparent purpose for all of this, of course, is to render us sympathetic to Tristram so that we may come to agree with his assertions about the rational goals of sexual activity. Do we agree? Can there have been, in the whole history of readers of *Tristram Shandy*, a single reader whose intrinsic views on that subject were in any way changed by Tristram's reasoning and complaining? It seems unlikely. The reason, obviously, is that the entire opening chapter is an accomplished piece of satiric rhetoric: Sterne's intention is to undermine such views as Tristram espouses, not to support them. Sterne is not seriously proposing the importance of dutifully rational thought at a time like that; instead, he is saying that—at a time like that—rational thinking simply stops; to ask, then, for a "rational Being" as the product of such a process is to be indeed crack-brained.[8]

Moreover, Sterne is ridiculing the Lockean doctrine in which the association of ideas is considered to be aberrational and individualistic. In place of this belief, Sterne posits an associationism which is at once universal and natural.[9] Thus, while attacking the belief in the primacy of conscious, rational thought, Sterne is simultaneously revealing a seemingly new pattern of unity which is, surprisingly, not new but as old as humanity: the organic pattern of all life. When the despairing Tristram insists that concern for progeny should have been the subject of his parents' thoughts, Sterne is mocking him and those readers who consider rationality man's characteristic trait. This mockery, though, is benevolent be-

---

7. The questions of "inside" readers and "outside" readers has been discussed most recently by Arthur Sherbo, *Studies in the Eighteenth Century English Novel* (East Lansing, 1969), pp. 35–57. While the issue is too large to take on in a footnote, suffice it is to say that I feel Sterne correctly prefigures (or echoes) the responses of his "outside" readers in the comments of his "inside" ones. A comparison of the responses made by "inside" readers with those recorded by Alan B. Howes in the first chapter of *Yorick and the Critics* (New Haven, 1958) shows that Sterne was not purely fanciful in his creation of lines for the readers to speak. Furthermore, the presence of "inside" readers is another device for the entanglement of those outside: particularly where the interpolated comment is assigned to no one, we are forced to make it our own.

8. As Wilbur L. Cross has pointed out, "*Shan* or *Shandy* is still a dialectical word in parts of Yorkshire for gay, unsteady, or crack-brained" (*The Life and*

Times of Laurence Sterne [New Haven, 1929], p. 200). Ian Watt, *The Rise of the Novel* (Berkeley and Los Angeles, 1957), feels that Sterne is carefully "pursuing the naming-convention of formal realism [in telling] us exactly how his character was named" (p. 291). Cf., though, Booth on authorial commentary through titles, p. 198, n. 25; the distance between titles and character names is not a long one.

9. Note the distinction made by Howard Anderson between Locke's concept of aberrational association and Sterne's idea of "the common characteristics which lead to their association in a man's mind," "Associationism and Wit in *Tristram Shandy*," *PQ*, 48 (January 1969), 28–29. See also George Goodin, "The Comic as Critique of Reason: *Tristram Shandy*," *CE*, 29 (1967), 217: "Sterne's frequent use of phallic references and puns should make it clear that he was not altogether serious in referring to this association of ideas as having 'no connection in nature' " (I, 5.).

cause the reader is involved in the satire not only as the target but also as the ideal. Sterne as satirist relies on our *intuitively* realizing the norm he will later propound in greater detail: a recognition of man's physical aspects and an affirmation of their value. The contrast between the norm we instinctively know, and the various theories Tristram voices, becomes, then, the source of both comedy and irony. Behind Tristram's back, the reader discovers Sterne, a fellow human being who knows him at his worst and doesn't mind.

Sterne's rhetorical genius lies in the fact that he has opened his novel with the scene basic to all life, the one scene which needs no commentary. When the narrator "helpfully" provides commentary by weaving elaborate theories and reminding us of moral obligations, we are invariably kept from investing our full sympathy in his position. Because the reader shares unwittingly in the force of life which has produced him and which will drive him to reproduce himself, he must inevitably dismiss the rationalizing commentary and affirm sexual activity for the pleasure it affords. In an intuitive flash, Sterne's chief lesson has been learned, but it has happened with deceptive ease only because Sterne knows he can count on the reader's innate vitality to do part of the teaching. The living writer behind the characterized writer, then, is the one on whom the reader can rely since the organic life they share has formed a bond of quickness between them.

If this analysis has begun to account for the reader's relationship with Sterne, it must also account for the pull of sympathy Tristram exerts despite his deluded opinions. We should note that what Tristram is actually doing in his discussion of his parents' activities is searching for logical causation in a known sequence of events: conception precedes birth; *ergo*, the manner of the conceiving affects the nature of the product. It is in this search for logical meaning that we find ourselves attracted to Tristram. While the answer at which he arrives may, indeed, not be our own, the process is all too familiar. The fact that the search for meaning through logic fails this first time (and will indeed fail throughout the book) reinforces what has already been said about Sterne's belief in an intuited pattern of natural association, rather than an artificially imposed one of ostensibly rational thought. With the opening chapter, then, a double sympathy has attached the reader to the work through the "twin" narrators: first, the attraction to the living writer, Sterne, who represents the surge of actual or organic life in which all meaning and value now lie, and second, the association with Tristram through whom we experience Sterne and in whom we see a part of ourselves.

After the opening chapter, the fusing of form and theme can be demonstrated by considering the novel from three other aspects:

(1) the antichronological time-scheme, (2) the digressions which progress, and (3) the characterization of Tristram. First, what is achieved through telling of the events in an order in which they did *not* occur? Sterne could, of course, write perfect sequential narrative as a glance at his concise, highly concentrated "Memoirs" makes clear.[1] Were the events in *Tristram Shandy* told that way, however, the reader's belief in chronological order and known causation would be reinforced rather than impaired. As Wayne C. Booth has pointed out, Tristram's narrative voice succeeds in "holding together materials which, were it not for his scatterbrained presence, would never have seemed to be separated in the first place."[2] That we can come to understand Tristram, indeed, that we can know him intimately *despite* the shattered time sequence shows us just how meaningless time sequence is. And we must remember that this intimate knowing is a large part of what Tristram intends:

> I have undertaken, you see, to write not only my life, but my opinions also; hoping and expecting that your knowledge of my character, and of what kind of a mortal I am, by the one, would give you a better relish for the other: As you proceed further with me, the slight acquaintance which is now beginning betwixt us, will grow into familiarity; and that, unless one of us is in fault, will terminate in friendship. (I. vi.)

Because of this emphasis on sympathy with the living individual, the novel of quickness is an imitation of character rather than of action. Imitation of action depends on chronological sequence, an ordering which forces the reader to infer causality and to make judgments on events; imitation of character asks only that we find the character living and, consequently, sympathetic. The whole matter of causality, as Tristram says, "is an equivocation" (VIII. vi.). The shattered time scheme, then, is a rhetorical means of presenting disequilibrium: we cannot look for meaning in the order of events so we are *forced* to look elsewhere, to concentrate on the teller and not the tale. Were the events to be narrated in sequential order, this would in fact distract us from the novel's point that clock time is problematical, not to say false. The reality which Sterne wishes to recognize, the "genuine" reality of the eternal life surge, has no measured time but is, instead, timeless flux.

---

1. "Memoirs of the Life and Family of the Late Rev. Mr. Laurence Sterne" was first published in Lydia Sterne Medalle's edition of her father's letters which appeared in October, 1775; it is reprinted and annotated by Curtis, pp. 1–10. Howes points out: "The memoir, the first biographical material for Sterne to bear the stamp of complete authenticity, was widely reprinted in the periodicals of the day, and all the reviewers agreed that it was a valuable source of information" (p. 50). No doubt the coherent point of view and the sequential time-scheme established the speaker of the "Memoirs" as a reliable narrator.

2. Booth, p. 222.

Moreover, the Tristram who would speak to us in a sequentially ordered work would be one whom the author intended to show as *truly* the product of his upbringing, as is, for instance, Esther Summerson in *Bleak House*. Dickens makes the adult Esther Summerson a reliable narrator, and the maturity of her point of view permeates what she tells us of her past and the carefully ordered way in which she tells it. In using the distorted time-scheme, Sterne takes stress away from a belief in phenomena and places it on essence; in other words, experience replaces situation. What Sterne achieves, then, is a portrait of a universe where events and objects take on meaning from their relationships to human life. It is a universe where real causation can only be speculated upon with the aid of faulty and highly selective hindsight. In Tristram's world, subjectivity and objectivity fuse because an objective world, one where situations and objects have their own independent meanings, is no longer tenable. By re-shaping the time-scheme, Sterne acts to prohibit the reader from envisioning a sequentially ordered fictional world. In its place, he demonstrates the presence of a vital, organically connected world which can exist in the novel *because it already exists in the reader*.

If we have seen that the rhetorical re-ordering of events informs the theme of *Tristram Shandy*, we should also consider those passages which are not "events" in the true sense: the digressions. It has been argued that the digressions are of two kinds, explanatory and opinionative, and that one of their chief functions is to involve various types of readers.[3] On one level, this is quite true, and an author who makes his own rules as Tristram insists he does (I. v.) should certainly be allowed to give explanations and opinions at will. But this does not account for the fact that these passages are indeed, as Tristram also insists, digressive and progressive simultaneously. Let us examine the origin Tristram gives for his procedure:

> By this contrivance the machinery of my work is of a species by itself; two contrary motions are introduced into it, and reconciled, which were thought to be at variance with each other. In a word, my work is digressive and it is progressive too,—and at the same time. ·
> This, Sir, is a very different story from that of the earth's moving round her axis, in her diurnal rotation, with her progress in her elliptick orbit which brings about the year, and constitutes that variety and vicissitude of seasons we enjoy; though I own it suggested the thought,—as I believe the greatest of our boasted improvements and discoveries have come from some such trifling hints.

3. William Bowman Piper, *Laurence Sterne* (New York, 1965), pp. 31–46.

> Digressions, incontestably, are the sunshine,—they are the life, the soul of reading;—take them out of.this book for instance,—you might as well take the book along with them;—one cold eternal winter would reign in every page of it; restore them to the writer;——he steps forth like a bridegroom,—bids All hail; brings in variety, and forbids the appetite to fail. (I. xxii.)

Significantly, the digression-progression is an imitation of life: the orbit of the earth around the sun, as Tristram says, "suggested the thought." "That variety . . . of seasons we enjoy," then becomes the progress of the work, and digressions are the pleasurable "sunshine," as well as "the life, the soul of reading." But the seasons have a peculiar simultaneity of movement: at the same time as they are cyclically repetitive, they also go forward to complete the year in the linear progression known as chronological time. In short, nature repeats itself only for mankind; individual men grow older.

Tristram's intentional analogy between the sun's year and the movement of the novel helps to explain the simultaneity. On the one hand, the digression is *progressive* in that it contributes to the work's linear or developing pattern. We know that it is always connected to the subject of the incident which suggested it and, in one way or another, it tells more about that incident than we knew before. The interpolated description of Walter Shandy's coat pocket (III. ii.), for instance, makes clear the reason for his gesticulations, and Uncle Toby's misunderstanding of the word "bridge" (III. xxiii.) is well explained by the lengthy passage about Trim, Bridget, and the bridge across the fossé (III. xxiv.). Thus the seemingly unrelated "digression" serves, in reality, to push the reader *progressively* forward through the book.[4]

At the same time, though, such passages are *digressive* in the way they relieve the reader from this same forward movement. Only in a merging with timeless life, as it is artistically represented in digressions, can one forget aging, that "cold eternal winter" of progressive linear movement. The digressions, then, are "the life, the soul of reading" since they are the rhetorical means of bodying forth the life common to us all. Like the bridegroom of Tristram's simile, the digressing writer celebrates and affirms this existential surge of life by encouraging his readers (wedding guests) to have an "appetite" as large as his own.[5] Again like the bridegroom, the writer affords others the opportunity of a vicarious experience: because they know

---

4. Another way in which the reader is urged forward through the book has been suggested by Wayne C. Booth, "Did Sterne Complete *Tristram Shandy?*" *MP*, 48 (February 1951), 172–73. Ensnared by Sterne's promises, the reader finds them all fulfilled by the time the work ends with Uncle Toby's amours.

5. A Biblical source for the bridegroom image has been suggested by Arthur Sherbo, p. 130. Rather tentatively, Sherbo points out that " 'he steps forth like a bridegroom' may or may not be an echo of Psalm 19:5."

him, they can participate through him. Such participation is achieved in *Tristram Shandy* because the digressions function, as do the plot events discussed earlier, in the continuing exhibition of Tristram's personality. The digressions, like the events, become an imitation of character, enabling the reader to become ever more familiar with Tristram, the medium through whom life is being communicated. Now, the distinctions begin to break down: story and inserted passage, digression and progression, reader and writer, Tristram and Sterne. Life and art seem somehow to have become inextricably intertwined; indeed, Sterne appears to have forced down all divisive boundaries to show the universe as a mass of organic connections.[6] The digression which seemed irrelevant to Tristram's impatient reader has instead been shown to be needful: in the unity-in-diversity of subjective life, there are no irrelevancies.

We can now consider the third way in which *Tristram Shandy* is best seen as a novel of quickness, a work in which sympathy is both the method and the message. I said above that the continuing exhibition of Tristram's personality is made through the events of plot as they relate to Tristram, and that the same may be said of the content of the digressions: both function to make the reader increasingly familiar with Tristram. However, in a conventional novel, the writer would ask us to watch the hero-narrator develop and change over the course of his life. Here, Sterne speaks through a narrator who is equally Shandaic when, in his childhood, he attempts to justify the "unaccountable obliquity" of his top (I. iii.), and when, in his adulthood, he attempts to justify the erratic nature of his writing (I. xiv.). The point is that Tristram remains essentially, idiosyncratically himself at all times, and it is the reader who develops through the course of the novel.

How this happens will be clear if we envision sympathy as a force which rushes in to replace the vacuum left by moral judgment. When we find Tristram foolish, as in his careless loss of his MS (VII. xxxvi.) or too dogmatic, as in his writing of the last chapter of the *Tristra-paedia* (V. xxvi.), we reject him as someone with whom we can agree on a rational level. But—as Sterne knows—it is too late. Tristram has already become a pole for sympathy; he has, from the first sentence, forced us to say "I." Through the rhetoric of first person narrative and the reinforcement of a story-line which places the emphasis on him rather than events, his is the only point of view which can serve to get us through the novel. *Unless* we agree to learn of life from his point of view, there will be no learning at all.

6. Sterne's view of a harmonious organic cosmos depicted in *Tristram Shandy* has been discussed by A. D. Mc-Killop, *Early Masters of English Fiction* (Lawrence, Kan.), pp. 196–200.

How our sympathy with Tristram prevents us from adopting an attitude other than his own deserves attention; in a supposed conversation with a critic, Sterne anticipates and echoes contemporary criticism:

——And how did *Garrick* speak the soliloquy last night? . . . In suspending his voice——was the sense suspended likewise? Did no expression of attitude or countenance fill up the chasm?—— Was the eye silent: Did you narrowly look?—I look'd only at the stopwatch, my Lord.——Excellent observer! (III. xii.)

The critic's error lies in trying to "fill up the chasm" by using the mechanical stop watch of judgment rather than the human eye of sympathy. *Tristram Shandy*, as Tristram self-consciously points out, needs a similar living participation:

And what of this new book the whole world makes such a rout about?—Oh! 'tis out of all plumb, my Lord,——quite an irregular thing!—not one of the angles at the four corners was a right angle.—I had my rule and compasses, &c, my Lord, in my pocket, ——Excellent critic. (III. xii.)

Even if we agreed with the critic through the use of our judgment, Sterne has carefully made him a "flat" character so that he can never become Tristram's rival as a pole for sympathy. Consequently, we turn against his point of view and rely on Tristram as our guide.

Sterne, then, forces the reader to give up one external prop after another in order to continue a developing relationship with Tristram: the reader surrenders his prudery (I. xviii.), his Christianity (VII. xv.) and perhaps some of his favorite hypotheses (III. xii.) only because the rhetorical device of the Shandaic narrator sweeps all before it. Larger than Walter Shandy, larger even than Uncle Toby, Tristram is, in fact, larger than the sum of the events of the novel. It is because of this size that he quickens and makes himself the sole meaning of the novel. By the time we reach the last volume, it is clear that Tristram is no different but we, having been through the experience of his articulation, certainly are. Through sympathy with this most idiosyncratic of beings, we have been enlarged, persuaded (Sterne hopes) of the need for sympathy with all of life. The world's only pattern, according to Sterne, lies in that web of sympathetic interconnections which links us to our fellow beings, the short-lived representations of that timeless surge of life in which we are united.

It is to this end that Sterne has created the novel of quickness, a most effective vehicle for the enlargement of understanding. As form and theme fuse, the reader is shown a work where sympathy is both method and message, where the emphasis is on imitation of character rather than imitation of action. The novel of quickness, then, is achieved through combining at least five devices: (1) making the narrator the satiric object so that the reader's sympathy flows to the living writer; (2) making the narrator enough like us—particularly in his search for causation—so that he, too, gains our sympathy; (3) using an anti-chronological time scheme in order to convince us of the presence of the timeless surge of life; (4) dramatizing that surge of life through digressions which progress; and (5) forcing the reader to enter the novel through a most unlikely hero and to recognize in him the humanity we all share. The seeming disparities of life-affirmation and cynical satire, of sentiment and bawdry, and of realistic detail and surrealistic chronology are explained when *Tristram Shandy* is seen as the founder of a new genre, the novel of quickness.

WAYNE BOOTH

Did Sterne Complete *Tristram Shandy?*†

Until recently, nearly everyone has assumed that *Tristram Shandy* is a careless, haphazard book, with little or no deliberate structure. Sterne's contemporaries established the tradition by praising or blaming the book in terms of its oddity and the eccentricity of its author. Goldsmith, for example, said that the book "had no other merit upon earth than nine hundred and ninety-five breaks, seventy-two ha ha's, three good things, and a garter," and, speaking indirectly of Sterne himself, whom he clearly confused with Tristram, he said: "in one page the author [makes] . . . them [the readers] a low bow, and in the next [pulls] . . . them by the nose; he must talk in riddles, and then send them to bed to dream of the solution."[1]

In the nineteenth century, even those critics who liked Sterne's works perpetuated the standard opinion about the book as a whole; as Bagehot said, *Tristram Shandy* is "a book without plan or order," whose greatest defect is "the fantastic disorder of the form."[2] And even today it is fairly common to read fresh statements of the old judgment.[3] There are, of course, many seemingly valid reasons for this belief that Sterne produced a "salmagundi of odds and ends

† From *Modern Philology*, XLVII, iii (February 1951), 172–83. Footnotes are by Booth.
1. *The Citizen of the World*, Letter LIII (*Public Ledger*, June 30, 1760).
2. Walter Bagehot, *Literary Studies* (4th ed.; London, 1891), II, 104.
3. Arthur Calder-Marshall, "Laurence Sterne," *The English Novelists* (London, 1936), p. 90: "*Tristram Shandy* is technically a hotch-potch, without even the unity of mood in Burton's *Anatomy of Melancholy*."

recklessly compounded."[4] Tristram Shandy, the narrator, says that he never revises, that he has no control over his pen, that whatever pops into his head goes into his book; and the book reads, from page to page, as if his statements about it were certainly true. Digression upon digression, afterthoughts, delays, apologies—if, with all this, the reader is bombarded with claims that all is chaos, he can hardly believe otherwise.

Perhaps even more responsible for the traditional criticism of the work is the history of its composition and publication, coupled with Sterne's statements about his writing methods and future intentions. It was published in five parts over a period of more than seven years. Some of the later volumes contain materials that Sterne could not have known when he began to write, and thus could not have planned to put into his book. What is more, the narrator repeatedly tell us that he intends to go on publishing two volumes a year until death overtakes him, or "for the next forty years," and Sterne repeated this claim in letters and conversations outside the work. Yet his fifth instalment consisted of only one volume, the ninth, and within a few months after its publication Sterne died, If, as he said, he really saw the possibility of eighty volumes or more and if he wrote everything into his book that came to mind, it would be foolish to claim that the result is anything other than a hodge-podge.

Some recent critics have discovered, however, that Sterne planned at least large parts of the book with more care than his public attitude would suggest. Perhaps the best summary of this tendency to discover method in Sterne's madness is that of James Aiken Work, in his edition of *Tristram Shandy*:

> The book was planned and written, for the most part, slowly and with care.
> It actually employs several structural devices of importance (aside from the "continuity of characters" which Coleridge has noted), and in the development of its matter is frequently quite . . . logical.
>   The most obvious structural device in *Shandy* is the simple one of veritable chronology. . . . Anyone who chooses may search out a complete time-scheme extending with but one or two negligible inconsistencies from 1680 . . . to 1766.
>   And the leading overt actions of the story, developed through two overlapping sequences, are arranged within each sequence in perfectly chronological order. In the first sequence, which deals with my father and his household, Tristram is begot, born, and baptized. . . . The scene then [in the middle of Vol. VI] changes to the bowling-green, whence . . . we follow to the end of the book the fortunes of my Uncle Toby.

4. Ernest A. Baker, *The History of the English Novel*, IV (London, 1930), 244.

There is . . . evidence of his foresighted planning of many of the incidents of his story. My father's theory of geniture, for example, was clearly in his mind when he wrote the opening chapter of the book. My father's theory of names, developed in the first volume, demands the complementary incident of Tristram's unfortunate christening in the fourth; and his theory of noses, first hinted in volume two, makes imperative the catastrophe in volume three and the exposition of the theory which follows in volume four. My uncle Toby's hobby horse is ridden a well-planned course throughout the whole of the book; and his unfortunate amours, with which the unfinished work closes, are frequently alluded to in earlier volumes and were clear in Sterne's mind at the outset of his work.

But the most important structural device is the principle of the association of ideas upon which the whole progression of the book is based.

Amusing but precarious . . . is the reader's pursuit of the devious but almost unexceptionably logical sequence—by association —of ideas in *Tristram Shandy*.[5]

That no one has cared to go beyond this statement to discover more evidence of planning or structure is not in the least surprising, since it has been universally assumed that "Sterne did not live to continue the book."[6] If it is unfinished, the basic judgment of the book's form must always remain about as Work leaves it. Sterne's work was not so haphazard as has been believed, but questions of form and unity of the kind one asks about more conventional works are not relevant. The book's chief element of cohesion is the "association of the author's ideas"; and even if, as is unlikely, Sterne planned the pattern of associations far in advance of his actual writing, the pattern remained incomplete at his death. *Tristram Shandy* could have ended with any volume just as well as with Volume IX or could have gone on after Volume IX to an indefinite number of volumes. Thus from this point of view the critical problem of the book can, with justification, be reduced, as it invariably has been reduced, to praising the "good" parts and condemning the "bad" parts or to showing that what others have taken for bad parts are really good parts, and so on.

Fortunately, however, there is no need to be satisfied with this kind of criticism of the book, because in all probability the assumption on which it is based is not true. If one forgets about the traditional attacks, one finds every reason to believe not only that Sterne worked with some care to tie his major episodes together but that, with his ninth volume, he completed the book as he had originally conceived it. Although there is no way of knowing how

5. *Tristram Shandy*, ed. James Aiken Work (New York, 1940), pp. xlvi–li.
6. *Ibid.*, p. 647, n. 5.

many volumes he originally intended to write, there can be little question that even as he wrote the first volume he had a fairly clear idea of what his final volume—whatever its eventual number—would contain.

There is, one must begin by admitting, ample external evidence in his letters that Sterne originally intended to use more than nine volumes in the narration of his materials. Even as late as July 23, 1766—that is, a little more than five months before he actually completed the ninth volume—he wrote to a friend: "At present I am in my peaceful retreat, writing the ninth volume of Tristram—I shall publish but one this year, and the next I shall begin a new work of four volumes, which when finished, I shall continue Tristram with fresh spirit."[7] One month later, on August 30, he wrote to his publisher, "I shall publish the 9th and 10 of Shandy the next winter."[8] And, finally, a laconic statement to "***" on the sixth of January, 1767: "I miscarried of my tenth volume by the violence of a fever I just got through."[9]

It would be impossible to argue, in the light of these statements, that Sterne intended only nine volumes, unless he changed his plans after the letter of August 30. The statement made on January 6, after completion, is, of course, equivocal. It could mean, "I miscarried permanently" or "temporarily." If we had no other evidence, we should have to conclude that he meant temporarily.

But there is one bit of external evidence which argues the possibility of a change of plan between August 30 and the completion of the ninth volume sometime late in December (publication date, January 30, 1767). In September, 1767, Sterne met Richard Griffith at Scarborough, and they became rather close friends.[1] Griffith, who later was to write the *Koran* in imitation of Sterne, wrote to a friend on September 10, 1767—that is, nine months after Volume IX was completed: "Tristram and Triglyph [Griffith's narrator's name] have entered into a League offensive and defensive, against all opponents in Literature. We have, at the same time, agreed never to write any more *Tristrams* or *Triglyphs*. I am to stick to *Andrews* and he to *Yoric*."[2]

All this certainly suggests the possibility of such a change of intention before completion of the ninth volume: Sterne said in July, 1766, that he would write one more volume, then write four of *A sentimental journey*, then go back to *Tristram Shandy*; in August he said he would write *two* more volumes first; in September of the following year he swore to write no more *Tristrams*. It is also perhaps significant that between August 30 and his death he never

7. *Letters of Laurence Sterne*, ed. Lewis P. Curtis (Oxford, 1935), p. 284.
8. *Ibid.*, p. 288.
9. *Ibid.*, p. 294.

1. See J. M. S. Tomkins, "Triglyph and Tristram," *TLS*, July 11, 1929.
2. Curtis, p. 398.

mentions any possibilities of continuation, although he mentions *A sentimental journey* frequently. There is no comparable period of silence about future plans at any time between 1759 and 1767.

The fact that Sterne showed signs of growing tired of *Tristram* and that he was repeatedly advised to drop his comic vein and do more with his pathetic line corroborates this possibility. In reviewing Volumes VII and VIII, the *Monthly review* (February, 1765) said, "The public, if I guess right, will have had enough, by the time they get to the end of your eighth volume"; and the reviewer went on to urge a return to the pathetic and moral vein. Curtis interprets this[3] as a possible incentive for a *temporary* shift, but it might just as well have made him decide to complete *Tristram Shandy* and drop it permanently. And the only statements we have from Sterne about the writing of Volume IX indicate that it went very hard and that he was growing tired of the book.[4]

Finally, it should be noted that for seven years Sterne produced no real literary work other than his instalments of *Tristram Shandy*. Although there was one period of three years in which no volumes were published, during a large part of that time we know he was trying to write Volumes VII and VIII and not succeeding. His entire creative effort for seven years, then, went into this book. Yet with the publication of the last volume we have, he stopped completely any effort to write further, began another novel some time within the next five months, and published two out of the intended four volumes just before his death. There are no remains or fragments of further volumes of *Tristram Shandy*, as there would have been had he died a few months after published any one of the preceding instalments. With all this in mind, one is certainly justified in looking rather closely at the nine volumes for internal evidence of Sterne's intentions.

We may consider first Sterne's instalment conclusions. Even unskilful writers who publish serially usually concentrate at the end of each instalment whatever suspense may lead the reader to buy and read further instalments. It seems initially significant, then, though certainly not conclusive, that, of Sterne's five instalments, all but the last conclude with chapters concerned primarily with promises for future material. Sterne thus concluded each of four instalments with chapters containing general promises of difficulties and hazards, beauties and blemishes, and, more important, particular promises for further events of his own life or of Uncle Toby's amours. Then he wrote an instalment and concluded it with no promise, either general or particular. So that the last chapter—the one which, if the book was really unfinished, should conclude nothing and leave us waiting for another instalment—contains nothing but Obadiah's in-

3. *Ibid.*, p. 285.   4. *Ibid.*, p. 290.

terruption of Walter's tirade against lust, leading to my mother's question:

> L——d! said my mother, what is all this story about?——
> A cock and a bull, said *Yorick*——And one of the best of its kind, I ever heard.

There is no indication whatever of any further possibility for the story, no play upon expectations of the kind to be found in all the conclusions of the other instalments. What is more, in the entire last instalment there are absolutely none of the promises that fill the rest of the book. If Sterne intended to write further volumes, it seems rather curious that, having shown through eight volumes his knowledge of how to titillate his readers' curiosity, he should suddenly lose that knowledge or decide not to apply it.

There are many other features about this last volume which suggest that it was intended to be the last. For instance, in the last chapter, for the first time in the whole work, all the major characters are brought together in one room, to listen to the final statement about a cock-and-bull story: Mother, Father, Uncle Toby, Dr. Slop, Obadiah, Trim, and Yorick—all except the Widow Wadman, who is by now doubly an outsider, and Tristram, who is not born yet. The whole scene is thus strikingly like a parody of the conventional conclusion with a comic *éclaircissement*. Again, the dedication of Volume IX begins:

> Having, *a priori*, intended to dedicate *The Amours of my uncle Toby* to Mr. ***[Pitt]——I see more reasons, *a posteriori*, for doing it to Lord ******* [Chatham].
>
> *   *   *
>
> The same good-will that made me think of offering up half an hours' amusement to Mr. *** when out of place—operates more forcibly at present, as half an hour's amusement will be more serviceable . . . after labour and sorrow, than after a philosophical repast.

Sterne had dedicated the second edition of the first instalment to Pitt. Certainly, the use of *a priori* and *a posteriori*, in connection with the first and last instalments, seems rather peculiar if no conclusion is intended.

Once one starts to look for them, such details begin to pop up in really surprising numbers. But since in themselves they are at best inconclusive and would perhaps continue to be so even if collected by the hundreds, it will be necessary before assembling them to get at more important and more difficult matters. The crucial question about Volume IX concerns Uncle Toby's amours: his affair with the Widow Wadman, which has been our major concern for several volumes, is permanently completed just three chapters before the book closes. If one is to go beyond the relatively unimportant problem of whether or not Sterne grew tired of his book and got rid of it, and treat the fundamental problem of whether or not he wrote a book which is in any sense a completed whole, it will be necessary to consider in some detail just what significance the completion of these amours has in terms of the book as a whole.

For those who view the novel in the conventional manner, this must seem a fantastic pursuit. It is, for them, the very nature of *Tristram Shandy* that its parts do not relate in any fundamental way to one another. Sterne (and, for them, Sterne and Tristram are the same) cavorts along his planless way and talks of whatever he stumbles upon. When he grows tired of Tristram's misadventures, he takes up with Uncle Toby. Thus Cross, speaking of the beginning of Volume V, says:

> At the outset of his work, Sterne was uncertain, any reader may see, as to the course his story was to run. . . . The narrative moved on heavily.
> Sterne knew instinctively that he could not continue longer on the oddities of Mr. Shandy, and escape the danger of writing himself out. . . . He therefore passed to the kitchen of Shandy Hall and over to my uncle Toby's bowling green for a set of characters not yet so far exhausted.[5]

Remnants of this attitude persist even among critics who have spent a good deal of time and energy opposing it. Putney, for example, who has done perhaps more than any other one man to restore Sterne's reputation as a conscious comic artist, nevertheless sees Uncle Toby's story as an excrescence on an otherwise impeccable *Tristram Shandy*:

> The assumption of Tristram's mind provides also the chief structural device of the book. In the fragment we possess, very little of Tristram's life is narrated, but he was once destined to play a larger part than Sterne's fate allowed him to fulfill. Up to chapter xx of Volume VI, the misadventures of Tristram's life provided the skeleton on which the digressions are hung. . . . This [a passage promising an account of the troubles resulting from Tristram's flattened nose] and other passages in the novel make it clear that as he commenced the book Sterne intended to follow Tristram's career into manhood with a series of humiliations and petty disasters.
> The abandonment of this scheme in the middle of Volume VI for the interpolation of Uncle Toby's wars, his amour with the Widow Wadman, and Tristram's travels has obscured the structural unity (on the principle of the association of ideas) that pre-

5. Wilbur L. Cross, *The Life and Times of Laurence Sterne* (3d ed.; New Haven: Yale University Press, 1929), pp. 278–79.

vailed for the first five and a half volumes. All but a few brief and unimportant digressions are connected with the accidents that befall Tristram.[6]

There follows an excellent account of the interconnections of the first five and a half volumes, with perhaps the strongest praise for Sterne's structural gifts ever made: "Up to this point *Tristram Shandy* is as thoughtfully constructed and as unified as *Tom Jones.*" Then the man with the structural gifts of a Fielding is made to change his fundamental design to satisfy a few prudes:

> The probable cause for the alteration in Sterne's design was the clamor against the double entendre and downright indecencies of the second installment. Possibly he also realized that Walter's hypotheses were growing slightly stale. Still the compromise he made was minor. He shifted his subject to the more poignant humor of Uncle Toby's activities, but the consistency of Tristram's character as narrator and consequently the tone and comedy were scrupulously maintained.[7]

The assumption that the book is less bawdy after Volume VI than before, although a somewhat amusing one in the light of the sustained bawdry of the courtships of Corporal Trim and Uncle Toby, does not concern us primarily here. But the assumption that the shift Tristram announces in chapter xx of this volume was not planned from the very beginning of Sterne's writing is of primary concern, particularly since it comes in a passage the main point of which is to declare Sterne's structural artistry. Our attitude toward the book as a whole and toward the problem of its completion depends on what we think is happening when Tristram announces that he is dropping *his* story and taking up the story of his Uncle Toby. And if Sterne is really as skilful a craftsman as Putney says, one is certainly justified in looking rather closely at the claim that suddenly, after five and a half volumes of superb artistry, he became a bumbler.

Actually, it does not take very careful reading to discover that, as Work dimly suggests in the passage quoted above, there are only two main story-threads in *Tristram Shandy*: the story of the young Tristram, before and after birth, and the story of Uncle Toby. More important, they run simultaneously; there is no real shift of direction to match the announced shift in the sixth volume. The details of Uncle Toby's campaigns and amours have been promised again and again, beginning in Volume I, and the misfortunes of Tristram's youth pervade the remainder of the book (to say nothing of the fact which Putney does notice—that Tristram, the adult narrator, per-

6. Rufus D. S. Putney, "Laurence Sterne, Apostle of Laughter," *The Age of Johnson: Essays Presented to C. B. Tinker* (New Haven, 1949), p. 163.
7. *Ibid.*, pp. 164–65.

sists as one of the central interests fully as much after the "shift" as before).

The first volume has not been long under way before we are introduced to Uncle Toby's campaigns, which ostensibly do not begin until Volume VI. But even before his Hobby-Horse, which *is* his campaigning, is presented to us, we are given a passage on his modesty:

> My uncle TOBY SHANDY, Madam, was a gentleman, who . . . possessed . . . a most extreme and unparallel'd modesty of nature; ——tho' I correct the word nature, for this reason, that I may not prejudge a point which must shortly come to a hearing, and that is, Whether this modesty of his was natural or acquir'd.—— Whichever way my uncle *Toby* came by it, 'twas nevertheless modesty in the truest sense of it. . . .
>
> * * *
>
> . . . [H]e got it, Madam, by a blow . . . from a stone, broke off by a ball from the parapet of a horn-work at the siege of Namur, which struck full upon my uncle *Toby's* groin.——Which way could that affect it? The story of that, Madam, is long and interesting;——but it would be running my history all upon heaps to give it you here.——'Tis for an episode hereafter; and every circumstance relating to it, in its proper place, shall be faithfully laid before you [Vol. I, chap. xxi].

Thus when this first volume ends with a description of Uncle Toby's wound and of its effects on his Hobby-Horse, the attentive reader already suspects that Toby is to figure as prominently in the book as Tristram, and, without knowing it, he has been given the basic facts of the Toby-Wadman denouement.

The first five chapters of Volume II deal with further background events of the campaigns, concluding:

> How my uncle *Toby* and Corporal *Trim* managed this matter, ——with the history of their campaigns, which were no way barren of events,——may make no uninteresting underplot in the epitasis and working-up of this drama.——At present the scene must drop,——and change for the parlour fire-side.

And we go to the parlor fireside to await the birth of Tristram. But the many exigencies surrounding his delivery are interspersed with hints and promises of what is to come, with ever increasing allusions to Uncle Toby's hobby and amours and with perhaps even more suspense concerning Uncle Toby than concerning Tristram, whenever promises of future volumes and chapters are made. For example:

> I know nothing at all about them [women],——replied my uncle *Toby*: And I think, continued he, that the shock I received the

year after the demolition of Dunkirk, in my affair with widow Wadman;——which shock you know I should not have received, but from my total ignorance of the sex——has given me just cause to say, That I neither know nor do pretend to know any thing about 'em or their concerns either [Vol. II, chap. vii].

The first instalment (January, 1760) then concludes with these two paragraphs:

> In what manner a plain man, with nothing but common sense, could bear up against two such allies in science,——is hard to conceive.——You may conjecture upon it, if you please,——and whilst your imagination is in motion, you may encourage it to go on, and discover by what causes and effects in nature it could come to pass, that my uncle *Toby* got his modesty by the wound he received upon his groin.——You may raise a system to account for the loss of my nose by marriage articles,——and shew the world how it could happen, that I should have the misfortune to be called TRISTRAM, in opposition to my father's hypothesis, and the wish of the whole family, God-fathers and God-mothers not excepted.——These, with fifty other points left yet unraveled, you may endeavour to solve if you have time;——but I tell you before-hand it will be in vain, for not the sage *Alquife*, the magician in Don *Belianis* of *Greece* . . . could pretend to come within a league of the truth.
>
> The reader will be content to wait for a full explanation of these matters till the next year,——when a series of things will be laid open which he little expects.

Now besides the resolution of the immediate scene, there are only three events explicitly promised in this conclusion. Two of them concern the young Tristram, and they are given in Volumes III and IV. The other concerns Uncle Toby's modesty: the reader discovers how Uncle Toby got his modesty as a result of his wound only in the third to the last chapter of Volume IX!

In the second instalment, Volumes III and IV (January, 1761), Tristram tells the story of Trim's affair with the Widow Wadman's servant, Bridget, pretending that it must be told to make clear the incident of the broken nose-bridge. He says:

> The story, in one sense, is certainly out of its place here; for by right it should come in, either amongst the anecdotes of my uncle *Toby's* amours with widow *Wadman*, in which corporal *Trim* was no mean actor,——or else in the middle of his and my uncle *Toby's* campaigns on the bowling-green——for it will do very well in either place;——but then if I reserve it for either of those parts of my story,——I ruin the story I'm upon,——and if I tell it here——I anticipate matters, and ruin it there [Vol. III, chap. xxiii].

And Tristram gives an even more explicit prediction of the events of Volume IX in the succeeding chapter:

> Tho' the shock my uncle *Toby* received the year after the demolition of *Dunkirk*, in his affair with widow *Wadman*, had fixed him in a resolution never more to think of the sex. . . .
> After a series of attacks and repulses in a course of nine months on my uncle *Toby's* quarter, a most minute account of every particular of which shall be given in its proper place, my uncle *Toby*, honest man! found it necessary to draw off his forces and raise the siege somewhat indignantly [Vol. III, chap. xxiv].

The fourth volume concludes thus:

> In less than five minutes I shall have thrown my pen into the fire ——I have but half a score things to do in the time——I have a thing to name——a thing to lament——a thing to hope . . . and a thing to pray for.——This chapter, therefore, I *name* the chapter of THINGS——and my next chapter to it, that is, the first chapter of my next volume, if I live, shall be my chapter upon WHISKERS, in order to keep up some sort of connection in my works.
> The thing I lament is, that things have crowded in so thick upon me, that I have not been able to get into that part of my work, towards which I have all the way looked forwards, with so much earnest desire; and that is the campaigns, but especially the amours of my uncle *Toby*, the events of which are of so singular a nature, and so Cervantick a cast, that if I can so manage it, as to convey but the same impressions to every other brain, which the occurrences themselves excite in my own——I will answer for it the book shall make its way in the world, much better than its master has done before it——Oh *Tristram! Tristram!* can this but be once brought about——the credit, which will attend thee as an author, shall counterbalance the many evils which have befallen thee as a man——thou wilt feast upon the one—— when thou hast lost all sense and remembrance of the other!——
> No wonder I itch so much as I do, to get at these amours—— They are the choicest morsel of my whole story! and when I do get at 'em——assure yourselves, good folks,——(nor do I value whose squeamish stomach takes offence at it) I shall not be at all nice in the choice of my words; . . . the thing I *hope* is, that your worships and reverences are not offended——if you are, depend upon't I'll give you something, my good gentry, next year, to be offended at——that's my dear *Jenny's* way——but who my *Jenny* is——and which is the right and which the wrong end of a woman, is the thing to be *concealed*——it shall be told you the next chapter but one, to my chapter of button-holes,——and not one chapter before.

Here the only long-range promise that has anything to do with what has gone before or that is ever mentioned again is the promise of the "choicest morsel of my whole story," Uncle Toby's amours. This choicest morsel is what we are given in the ninth volume. When it comes, Sterne is careful to remind us of its central importance: he has been hastening all along toward it, Tristram says, knowing "it to be the choicest morsel of what I had to offer to the world."

It should perhaps be emphasized that all these explicit promises have been given to us long before the "interpolation" of Uncle Toby's amours into the story, in Volume VI. And they are explicitly for the exact event as it occurs in the ninth volume. No other future events are promised nearly so often or with such consistency and particularity.[8] And, as we would expect from these promises, there is an ever increasing concentration on Uncle Toby in the remainder of the book. The third instalment, Volumes V and VI (January, 1762), contains the beginning of Uncle Toby's amours: he falls in love in the last four chapters, and we are told to expect the descriptive details in later chapters. The last chapter, the famous chapter on narrative lines, contains only one explicit promise for future material of any kind, except for the promise to try harder to tell the story in a straight line: "I am now beginning to get fairly into my work; and by the help of a vegitable diet, with a few of the cold seeds, I make no doubt but I shall be able to go on with my uncle *Toby*'s story, and my own, in a tolerable straight line."

In the fourth instalment (January, 1765), after the trip abroad in Volume VII, which fulfils his promise to go on with his *own* story, Volume VIII begins the amours in earnest, though of course in the same playful, disgressive manner that has been used throughout, circling about the subject, telling first of Trim's amours, and concluding with the elaborate preparations for "the attack" by Uncle Toby and Trim, and the preparations of my father and my mother to walk down to the Widow Wadman's, "to countenance him in this attack of his":

> My uncle *Toby* and the corporal had been accoutred both some time, when my father and mother enter'd, and the clock striking eleven, were that moment in motion to sally forth——— but the account of this is worth more, than to be wove into the fag end of the eighth volume of such a work as this.———

Thus each of the first four instalments concludes with a chapter in which the promises concern either Uncle Toby's amours and Tristram's life or, once the events of that "life" are completed and dropped, Uncle Toby's amours alone. The ninth volume (January, 1767) is almost entirely concerned with these amours and describes

8. There are, of course, some unfulfilled "promises" when the book closes. But a careful tabulation of them, too lengthy to insert here, shows that none of them is ever made in such a way as to arouse serious expectations. Practically all of them are, in fact, imitations of similar kinds of promises made in the precursors of *Tristram Shandy* (see n. 3 below).

them *in their entirety*. Once Uncle Toby "receives his modesty," his story is completely exhausted; our long-range interest in him has been gratified and all particular expectations fulfilled. This happens in the third to the last chapter: the amours are completed with Uncle Toby's discovery of the source for the Widow Wadman's "humanity."

It thus seems thoroughly plausible that, from the beginning, Sterne planned the structure of the book as an elaborate and prolonged contradiction of its title-page. For this purpose, one major shift of attention, if sufficiently surrounded with a multiplicity of minor shifts, is all that is needed: begin by pretending to tell the life and opinions of Tristram Shandy and end by telling the amours and campaigns of Uncle Toby, concluding the whole account four years before the birth of your original hero. Whether, as Putney suggests, Sterne originally intended to do a lot of other things besides is hard to determine. It does seem likely that he considered many possible alternative digressions on his main line; for example, it is probable that he once contemplated following Tristram's father and the family on a fairly detailed journey through Europe, and later, as a result of his own trip abroad, substituted an account of Tristram's journey alone. But his main line remained unchanged. As Putney shows, Tristram's misadventures dominate the first few volumes; all the "digressions" of these volumes cohere as tightly as Tristram, in his more sanguine moments, claims. And, as we have seen, the only sizable body of material in the first part not dependent upon Tristram's story is the account of Uncle Toby's Hobby-Horse, which, with his amours, dominates the *last* part of the book. What seems to have been his abiding intention has been carried out; there are no unexhausted lines of expectation, once Trim reveals the truth about the Widow's humanity.[9]

Once we accept this hypothesis as plausible, the signs of finality

9. There are two possible exceptions to this. It is seemingly probable that the narrator will be unpredictable, and it might be argued that, with Sterne, anything goes. However, this is never more than a superficial probability, since part of the pleasure of the work depends on our recognition that Tristram seems not to know, yet does know, where he is going. In practically every case of Tristram's "irresponsibility," as far as narrative devices are concerned, the reader in the long run finds himself fooled; the caprice was not caprice after all. Similarly, it might be argued that Sterne could have gone on with his own youthful misadventures or, as Putney suggests, using as evidence Tristram's early statement, with the troubles that resulted from the flattening of his nose. But as for other youthful troubles, it would be

hard to think of any that would lend themselves to Sterne's manner so well as conception, birth, naming, circumcision, and breeching; and as for the troubles resulting from the flattened nose, we have certainly been given them aplenty by the end of Vol. IX (one should note, too, that the promise for these troubles is made in the same general terms as his many other promises for chapters and anecdotes that never materialize). I don't doubt that Sterne could have managed to make us accept almost anything, had he decided early enough to do so. But only by planning whatever was to follow Uncle Toby's amours *before writing the first instalment* could he write a book which belonged as well with the continuing material as the entire present book belongs with the present conclusion.

in the last volume itself, and particularly in the last chapters, are much more striking. For example, in each of the first two instalments we are promised the story of Trim's brother's courtship of the Jew's widow, in Spain.[1] In both cases the seemingly pointless detail is stressed that the Jew's wife "sold sausages." Only when the story is finally told to us in Volume IX do we learn why. The account comes as a preliminary to Uncle Toby's visit to the Widow's, and with its bawdy scene of courtship over a sausage machine—a scene which could not take place without the sausage machine—it is a perfect buildup to the more "delicate" bawdry of the scenes with the Widow. It thus seems very likely that Sterne planned from the beginning to juxtapose Toby's and Trim's stories at the end of his novel. At the very least, it is clear that Sterne is here, as elsewhere throughout the last volume, using up whatever good materials his earlier promises make available.

Similarly, the *éclaircissement*-like scene at the conclusion, which is hard to justify if we assume that the novel is to continue, makes very good sense as a summation of the whole novel. Yorick's final statement to the assembled cast of characters is that the "story" is about "A COCK and a BULL." The "story" as a whole consists, as we have seen, of the substitution of one story-thread for another— Toby's for Tristram's. Yorick's phrase thus refers not only to Obadiah's immediate problem, which it neatly summarizes, but also to the whole book, the first word epitomizing the whole story of Uncle Toby's amours, centering as they do in the Widow's concern about the extent of the damage to his groin, and the last word referring to the trick of the belied title and the topsy-turvy novel that results.[2] What is more, it was common for earlier facetious writers to call their entire books "cock-and-bull stories" (in French, *coq-à-l'âne*).[3] Sterne, who knew many of these works well, can hardly have failed to intend this meaning for the phrase when he wrote that final line. Furthermore, the materials out of which Obadiah's problem in this last chapter is built are the same materials out of which the first few chapters of the whole book are built: sexual intercourse, gestation periods, fertility and sterility, and, of course, birth itself. The materials of my father's oration, also in the last chapter, are even more explicitly similar; it is a lament that generation must take place in sordid conditions, with sordid instruments:

> I still think and do maintain it to be a pity, that it should be done by means of a passion which bends down the faculties, and

---

1. Vol. II. chap. xvii; Vol. IV. chap. iv.

2. "Bull," according to the *OED*, was used in the sense of "ludicrous jest" as late as 1695; as a verb, it meant "to make a fool of, to mock, to cheat out of," at least as late as 1674.

3. For substantiation of this and other points about *Tristram Shandy*'s precursors in this paper see my unpublished University of Chicago dissertation, *"Tristram Shandy* and Its Precursors: The Self-Conscious Narrator" (1950).

turns all the wisdom, contemplations, and operations of the soul backwards——a passion, my dear, continued my father, addressing himself to my mother, which couples and equals wise men with fools.

It is as if he were lamenting four years in advance the manner of Tristram's begetting and reprimanding his wife in advance for her foolish question about the clock in chapter i. In short, we have a thematic return which seems deliberate, since no other chapter in the whole work resembles so completely the first five chapters of Volume I.

What is more, the subject matter and the allusions of the entire final volume are more closely parallel to those of the first volume than are those of any other volume of the work. Chapter i consists of a lengthy discussion of Tristram's mother's lack of pruriency, the quality which caused the initial incident of the book and thus indirectly produced Tristram's capriciousness and the kind of book he writes. Her deficiency has never been discussed at such length before; only the first few chapters of the whole book approach it. Tristram even quotes the exact words of the earlier discussion:

> And here am I sitting, this 12th day of August, 1766, in a purple jerkin and yellow pair of slippers, without either wig or cap on, a most tragicomical completion of his [Walter's] prediction [in Vol. I, chap. iii], "That I should neither think, nor act like any other man's child, upon that very account."[4]

Chapter xi consists of a joke on my father, the point of which depends on our remembering his sacrament-day regularities—the regularities which we learned about in the very first chapter and which led to Tristram's downfall:

> ——Though if it comes to persuasion——said my father
> ——Lord have mercy upon them.
> Amen: said my mother, *piano*
> Amen: cried my father, *fortissimè*
> Amen: said my mother again——but with such a sighing cadence of personal pity at the end of it, as discomfited every fibre about my father——he instantly took out his almanack; but before he could untie it, *Yorick's* congregation coming out of church, became a full answer to one half of his business with it ——and my mother telling him it was a sacrament day——left him as little in doubt, as to the other part——He put his almanack into his pocket.

---

4. There is a similar echo in chap. xxv of this last volume: "All I wish is, that it may be a lesson to the world, *'to let people tell their stories their own way'* "; cf. Vol. I, chap. vi: ". . . bear with me, ——and let me go on, and tell my story my own way."

The first Lord of the Treasury thinking of *ways and means,*
could not have returned home, with a more embarrassed look.

And there are other passages in Volume IX which would be very
strange indeed if taken as mere stages in a much longer journey.
For instance, the transition between chapter xxiii, which deals with
a very close assault by the Widow Wadman, and chapter xxiv is as
follows:

Let us drop the metaphor.

CHAPTER XXIV

——And the story too——if you please: for though I have all
along been hastening towards this part of it, with so much earnest
desire, as well knowing it to be the choicest morsel of what I had
to offer to the world, yet now that I am got to it, any one is
welcome to take my pen, and go on with the story for me that
will.

In the light of everything else. Tristram can hardly be understood as
dropping only a small part of his story; he is dropping what has
gone on "all along." He could indeed hardly give us a plainer
indication of his intention to quit than the echo of the concluding
promise ("choicest morsel") of Volume IV. One must think Sterne
very clumsy indeed to suppose that he intended to continue beyond
his announced choicest morsel, after all this buildup through eight
volumes toward it and after the final explicit pronouncement that
this morsel and no other is what he has "all the time" been hastening to tell. If this pronouncement were an isolated one, we might
perhaps question its importance. He might indeed have a dozen
"choicest morsels." We might even say, if we had no other evidence,
that all these echoes of earlier phrases and situations merely indicate
that Sterne, tired of writing, decided to quit and pillaged his earlier
work in order to make some semblance of a concluding gesture.
Even the fact that one finds more "fulfilments" of earlier facetious
promises (a chapter on the right end of a woman, a chapter on
pishes, etc.) in Volume IX than in Volumes V, Vi, VII, and VIII
together might be similarly dismissed as a valiant, but rather unimpressive, last-minute effort at tying up the loose ends. But as we
have seen, he *has* all along been "hastening towards" this part, and
he has been liberally dropping clues to his whole plan all along the
way.

If, in the light of these converging probabilities, one can accept at
least tentatively not only the fact that Sterne was through with his
book when he sent Volume IX to the printer sometime late in
December, 1766, but also that the book he had completed represented the completion of a plan, however rough, which was present
in his mind from the beginning, then the book as a whole begins to
come into focus. Questions about the form of this "formless work,"

questions which have until now been ignored and which I have scarcely touched on here, can now for the first time receive adequate consideration.

WILLIAM BOWMAN PIPER

Tristram's Digressive Artistry†

Tristram Shandy hopes, as he says to Sir, that "nothing which has touched me will be thought trifling in its nature, or tedious in its telling" (I. vi). But he knows that the figures and events which have touched him decisively, although not really trifling, are yet peculiar enough to seem so: his father was possessed by "an infinitude of oddities" (V. xxiv.); his Uncle Toby was a man of "great singularity" (I. xxiv.); his whole family, indeed, was "of an original character throughout" (I. xxi.). And the crucial events of his life, with their deep family involvement, are naturally peculiar too. Tristram must preserve this peculiarity of his life and of his family to preserve their truth; but, if he is to make them interesting and important to society, he must also make them generally understandable and generally significant.

That he has succeeded in doing so we have the valuable testimony of Samuel Taylor Coleridge, who wrote that Sterne had achieved in *Tristram Shandy* "the novelty of an individual peculiarity together with the interest of a something that belongs to our common nature."[1] He has observed, particularly, in Toby's freeing of the fly "how individual character may be given . . . humanity." In this case Coleridge seems to have laid the interpenetration of the peculiar and the general to "the mere delicacy of the presentation"; but elsewhere he has spoken more suggestively: he detected in Sterne, as in other great humorists, "a certain reference to the general and the universal" which Sterne had achieved by bringing "the finite great . . . into identity with the little, or the little with the finite great." Applying these terms particularly to *Tristram Shandy*, we may say that Tristram has brought "the little," which was his peculiar life, into variously significant relationships with "the finite great," which was his wide social audience. In this chapter we must try to see how he has done this, and how it has affected the quality of Sterne's novel.

It is chiefly through Tristram's two main kinds of digression, explanatory and opinionative, that Tristram makes his peculiar life

---

† From William Bowman Piper, *Laurence Sterne* (New York: Twayne, 1966), pp. 31–46. Reprinted by permission of the publisher. Footnotes are by Piper.

1. See *Complete Works*, IV (New York, 1871), 275–85 for all the material referred to in this paragraph.

generally clear and broadly interesting. With his explanatory digressions, he defines his story's connections and fills in its background so that society can follow its crucial events and understand their Shandy importance. With his opinionative digressions, he derives from these events the widely relevant wit and instruction that will hold society's interest and attention. To understand this use of the digressions, which Sterne's critics have variously misunderstood,[2] we must analyze, first, their external references and, second, their internal forms.

I. The Digressions' External References

Tristram generally introduces his explanatory digressions, to begin with these, just where they are needed, starting some of them, such as his description of Toby's character (I. xxi.), in the middle of story sentences. And he usually asserts their explanatory value right away, stating that they will explain, translate, or give reasons (III. ii., III. xxxi., IV. xxvii., VI. xvi., VII. xxx., IX. xx.; etc.). We take, for instance, this introduction to an explanatory digression: "What was the cause of this movement, and why I took such long strides in uttering this—I might leave to the curious too; but as no principle of clock-work is concern'd in it—'twill be as well for the reader if I explain it myself" (VII. xxx.). Tristram uses here not only "explain" but also the logical term "cause": he will explain the cause of his long strides. Tristram commonly concludes his explanatory digressions with a similarly formal assertion of their relationship, as in his conclusion to the digression whose introduction has just been quoted: "In my list, therefore, of *Videnda* at *Lyons*, this [the tomb of the two lovers], tho' *last*—was not, you see, *least*; so taking a dozen or two of longer strides than usual across my room, just whilst it passed my brain, I walked down calmly into the *Basse Cour*, in order to sally forth" (VII. xxxi.). "Therefore" here reflects "cause" in the introduction. Tristram has further defined the use and the extent of this digression by repeating the "long strides" which it has been explaining. He introduces his digression on Phutatorius's exclamation (IV. xxvii.) also to "explain" the "cause"; and he concludes it by repeating that exclamation which was the "effect" of this cause. Although his terms are not always so philosophical as this, Tristram generally brackets his explanatory digressions with assertions of their value and with definitive repetition.

These digressions have, moreover, the explanatory values Tristram claims for them. Tristram explains his long strides "to the curious," for instance, as a sign of his great desire to walk out to the

2. See, for instance, Alan B. Howes, *Yorick and the Critics* (New Haven, 1958), pp. 35–37 and Arthur Cash, "The Lockean Psychology of *Tristram Shandy*," *ELH*, XII (1955), 131 for fairly representative explanations of the digressions.

tomb of the two lovers. Trim's make-believe artillery, again, which Tristram set off to explain "as I generally do, at a little distance from the subject" (IV. xxiv.–xxvii.), has been vividly, unforgettably realized by the time Tristram brings in Uncle Toby to direct its fire. Tristram likewise explains in detail Trim's feeling of guilt over the window-sash accident (V. xix.) which, as he said, his readers could never imagine on their own. And he presents the background and nature of Walter's two beds of justice in his digression on that subject (VI. xvii.) better, perhaps, than Madam, for whose sake he has taken the trouble, could wish. There are a few digressions, explanatory of Shandy life, whose actual explanatory connections are weak. The long digression filling his readers in on Toby's character (I. xxi.–II. v.), for instance, holds up nothing more characteristic of Toby than his suggestion to ring the bell; and that on Yorick (I. x.–xii.) explains, as Tristram admits, very little of the action at Shandy Hall. But these early digressions are exceptions to Tristram's explanatory rule. Tristram generally introduces explanatory digressions where they are needed to explain to his audience just what he says they need to have explained.

He is sometimes tardy in telling his audience the exact narrative relevance of an explanatory digression. He has started on the digression about his father's concern for names (I. xix.), for instance, without making it clear to the reader how this information, which explains events his narrative has not yet reached, will apply. He has likewise introduced the digression on his father's weakness for his own eloquence (V. iii.) merely by asking Your Worships' leave "to squeeze in a story between these two pages." But Tristram makes the explanatory relevance of these digressions perfectly clear before he concludes them. In these cases, as in the others, Tristram has paused to explain the odd elements of his story, knowing full well that he "is obliged continually to be going backwards and forwards to keep all tight together in the reader's fancy" (VI. xxxiii.).

Tristram's opinionative digressions are introduced to generalize the odd events of his life, that is, to draw from these events lessons and applications of broadly human value, and thus to make them meaningful to his audience. Tristram takes his mother's insistence on the midwife, for instance, as an example of a common trait in human psychology (I. xviii.). He finds evidence in Dr. Slop's rehearsal of Ernulphus's curse for the opinion that none of us invents his own curses (III. xii.). From his own tearing out of a chapter (IV. xxv.), again, and his struggle to raise his imaginative powers (IX. xii.–xiv.), Tristram derives generally applicable opinions on literary composition. Opinionative digressions follow immediately the narrative matter from which they derive; and their connections are always clear. Tristram's opinion of curses comes right after Dr.

Slop's rendering of Ernulphus's curse (III. xi.–xii.); his opinion on the tearing out of chapters follows hard on the chapter (xxiv of Volume IV) which Tristram has just torn out. To be sure that we recognize this chapter's omission and, thus, the present relevance of his opinion, Tristram begins: "—No doubt, Sir—there is a whole chapter wanting here."

Tristram directs each of these opinionative digressions, by which he hopes to deepen his audience's sense of involvement in his life story (I. vi.), toward those people most likely to benefit from it. Trim's hat dropping, for instance, leads Tristram to an opinion beneficial to "Ye who govern this mighty world [etc.]" (V. vii.). He aims his opinion on the homunculus (I. ii.) at the gentlemen in his audience, his opinions on wishes (III. i.) and feminine vanity (V. ix.) at the ladies, and his opinion on baptism at them both (I. xx.). He directs his opinion on the dangers to total literary effects of brilliant episodes, more pointedly, at Your Reverences (IV. xxv.), his opinion on the causes of mental confusion at Sir Critic (II. ii.), and his opinion on the dangers of the erotic imagination at My Dear Girl (III. xxxvi.).

Many of Tristram's digressions have values for his audience both as explanation and opinion; they explain a Shandy event and suggest a lesson or example of general applicability. In Toby's peculiar kindness toward the fly (II. xii.), for example, which was introduced merely to illustrate Toby's remarkable goodness of heart, Tristram finds an example which will serve "parents and governors instead of a whole volume upon the subject." His account of Trim's oratorical stance (II. xvii.), which he introduced merely to "give you a description of his attitude," Tristram concludes by addressing more sharply to artists and orators as a model for such attitudes. His explanation of Dr. Slop's* * * * * * (III. xiv.) allows Tristram to give Your Worships and Reverences, the usual recipients of such opinions, a point on the decline of oratory and, having done that, to illuminate for them a moment in the drama on his birthday at Shandy Hall.

There is one further type of digression, the interlude, which we must notice before concluding this part of our analysis. Tristram's digressive interludes do not explain events of Tristram's life; nor do they derive from it as his opinionative digressions do: they are, rather, separate items of public discourse. Accordingly, Tristram introduces them only at major breaks in his narrative—at the termini of volumes, as in the case of the Slawkenbergius (beginning of IV.) and Whiskers anecdotes (V. i.), or at the natural breaks in his story, as in the case of the violin recital which punctuates what Tristram has called his life's first act (V. xv.). The interludes refer only to Tristram's audience, not to his story—as he perfectly understands. With some of them, such as the Preface (III. xx.) and the salutations at the ends of volumes, Tristram fulfills customary obligations; others, like the Chapters (IV. x.) and Whiskers interludes, he presents as special courtesies. The Whiskers anecdote, indeed, he has revealed, much against his will, only because he made the world a promise of it (IV. xxxii., V. i.). Tristram has made the most of his interludes' social appeal: he flirts with his audience's prudery in the Green Gowns (V. viii.) and Whiskers interludes; carries his point with an *ad hominem* argument in the Preface; and puts his dedication (I. viii.–ix.) up for public sale.

We may now say that all of Tristram's digressions—all except for a very few transparent, emotional ones (II. iii., III. viii., beginning of IV.)—were introduced to attract and hold Tristram's audience. He has explained his story and derived opinions from it to make it clear to his audience and to give its odd items a generally didactic or edifying value. And he has so defined and presented his digressions that his audience should have no trouble in understanding the special relevance of every one to itself. We must now turn to the internal forms of Tristram's digressions to make sure that he has composed them simply and clearly enough for Madam, Sir, and others like them to follow.

II. *The Digressions' Internal Forms*

Tristram's many short digressions, which perform such common narrative functions as asking for attention, filling in background, and voicing asides, are easy to follow. So are his long chronological digressions, such as the story of Lefever or the tale from Slawkenbergius. It is the long non-chronological, or partly chronological, digressions, which are the most peculiar to Tristram's art, that must be examined. We will find that virtually all of them fall into two or three clearly defined and related sections.

Digressions of two balanced, parallel sections are common. In one of these (II. viii–ix.), for instance, Tristram has a point to remind his readers of and a point to inform them about. He is careful, not only in introducing this digression, but also in shifting from its first to its second point, to assert its two-part form. He likewise separates his digression on his troubles (VIII. vi.) into two parts: there is, first, his trouble as an author and, second, his trouble as a man. He sees, on another occasion (V. xii.), two ways by which Eleazer may have received from the East his opinion that none of us is born to be a slave: there is, first, the water way and, second, the land way. He develops several digressions by telling, first, what is not the case and, second, what is the case. He gives in one digression (II. ii.), for instance, what did not cause Toby's confusion and then what did cause it. And in another (VIII. v.–vi.) he tells what causes of sexual attraction do not account for Mrs. Wadman's attraction to Toby and then, as he is able, what cause does account for it.

Most of these clear and simply formed digressions, despite their formal balance, move toward communicative climaxes, toward main points. That the negative-to-positive digressions should do so is obvious; but others also rise to their closes. What Tristram reminds his audience of, for instance, is merely his father's eccentricity in general; what he informs them about is that particular eccentricity, Walter's concern for the cerebella of emergent fœtuses, which his story is now coming to. Tristram's trouble as an author, again, is merely the slow sales of his book; his trouble as a man is a recent great loss of blood. And Tristram concludes the two ways by which Eleazer may have got his opinion by exclaiming, no matter which way the opinion came, what a time of it the learned had in Eleazer's day. A most striking case of parallel construction and rhetorical climax is furnished by Tristram's argument for believing that his father did not write the chapter on window sashes in the *Tristrapœdia* before his own window sash accident (V. xxvi.). Tristram gives two reasons: the first is that, had his father written the chapter before the accident, it would surely have been averted; the second is that he has written this chapter of his father's book himself. Thus Tristram can lead his audience through two balanced sections of digression in a pointed and emphatic fashion which his conversational ease may disguise but does not nullify.

The parts of Tristram's longer bipartite digressions are often more tightly related than this. Tristram is very fond, for instance, of the general statement and its exception. He will prove to everybody except a connoisseur, he says on one occasion (III. xii.), that we have not invented our own oaths. He starts with the exception, satirically obliterating all connoisseurs, and, having done that, he makes his proof to everybody else. The proof, by the way, is developed in two balancing sections: it is developed by the artistic argument, which Tristram himself professes, and by the scholarly argument, attributed to Walter. Tristram's digression on sleep (IV. xv.) also contains a point, that bookish men can say nothing good on the subject, and then an exception, something pretty good from Montaigne. In the dedicatory chapter on hobby horses (I. viii.), Tristram has given the exception a graceful complimentary emphasis. No man's riding of his own hobby horse hurts anyone else *except* in the case of your Lordship (the prospective purchaser of the dedication) who may be neglecting the high callings of patriotism and glory.

Tristram's most difficult digressions, when subjected to analysis, will be seen to fall into structures of closely related parts. His curious explanation of his way with his life's little misfortunes (V. xxix.), for instance, is made up of an ambiguously beasterisked anecdote which illustrates his way of "making a penny of every one of 'em' " and of an argument in which he makes literally this idea of making pennies and claims that he would make pounds out of "good cursed bouncing losses." Tristram concludes this digression by defining just the good bouncing loss, that is, just the financially valuable one, he desires: it is one worth "a hundred [pounds] a year or so." Tristram's argumentative Preface on wit and judgment (III. xx.) is also composed of two sections: there is a minor point—that wit and judgment are in somewhat short supply; and a major point—that each man has been endowed with just the amount of judgment that his amount of wit requires.[3] The late digression by

3. Here is a fuller analysis of Tristram's Preface for those who may need or desire it.

Tristram's Preface on the distribution of wit and judgment (III.xx.) is composed of a main point and a subordinate point. The subordinate point, which Tristram argues first, asserts the lack of a plenitude of wit and judgment. It is divided into three parts: the first and third argue logically, the second by a climate analogy. The first and third parts argue that we would act in certain ways if we had plenty of wit and judgment, that we do not act in these ways, and, therefore, that we do not have plenty. The first part, which tells how sharply we would all attack one another with our plentitude of wit and then how graciously we would smooth things over with our plenitude of judgment, seems largely fanciful at first. Tristram has called it "the first insinuating *How d'ye* of a caressing prefacer." The third part, which describes how odd the conduct of different professions would be if their practitioners had a plenitude of wit and judgment, is admittedly satirical. The second part of this section describes a tour from the icy wastes of Lapland and Nova Zembla, where there is the least wit and judgment and the least need of them, to the erratic climate of England with its erratic outbursts and absences of wit and judgment. The lack of general plenitude, argued by all three parts, is explicitly stated between the first and second parts and again between the second and third.

Having made this subordinate point, Tristram formally turns to "the main and principal point I have taken to clear up." It is: "How it comes to pass, that your men of least *wit* are reported to be men of most *judgment*." His attack on this report has two parts. In the first, Tristram argues that the report is false by establishing that there is a balance

of wit and judgment in every man. He does this by referring to the two knobs of his chair; but he is actually arguing from his unstated certainty in God's wisdom and orderliness. In the second part, he explains how the false report of inbalances in the distribution of wit and judgment, whose falsity he has just shown, got started.

Tristram has asserted a strong connection between the two points of his Preface: "by the help of the observations already premised [in making the subordinate point], and I hope already weighed and perpended by your reverences and worships," he says, "I shall forthwith make [the main point] appear." This help is not a logically necessary one. For, although we must be certain of a lack of wit and judgment to argue their distribution, the mere lack does not certify the distribution Tristram is arguing for any more that it does the distribution he opposes. We can, however, see a strong conversational *ad hominem* help for the main point in Tristram's conduct of the subordinate one. His easy joining of wit and judgment in the second and third parts of the subordinate section would accustom Tristram's audience to think of them together and thus to think of them as going together. The second part, which makes both equally dependent on climate, would be especially effective in asserting their proper union. This sub-rational joining of the two, before rationally arguing for their joining, would be strengthened by the first part of the subordinate section which has, by separating wit and judgment, made a joke out of perfect wittiness with no judgment to restrain it and perfect restraint with nothing to restrain. Even more important, perhaps, is the strong assertion of a wise God, who gives us all the wit and judgment we need, with which Tristram concludes

which Tristram has recommended his way of raising his creative powers (IX. xii.–xiv.) contains not two but three main parts: the first, on poor methods for raising one's powers; the second, on Tristram's good method (shaving); the third, on objections to this method. Tristram has developed it by variously using almost every formal device we have uncovered: the parallel, the negative-to-positive, the illustration and the exception; and he works the whole wonderfully fluid passage into an almost Scholastic form of argument.

The digression introducing, first, Uncle Toby's minor traits and, second, his major ones (I. xxi.–II. vi.) is probably the most difficult and involved in the novel. Indeed, its first part is briefly marred by a confusion. Tristram should have introduced Toby's and Walter's argument over Aunt Dinah into this first part merely as an illustration of Toby's minor traits of modesty and family pride. But he has actually presented this argument as a matter of the first communicative importance, to which the revelation of Toby's traits is ancillary. The story of the argument has come up at the mention of Aunt Dinah in the introductory paragraph on the family or blood origins of Toby's character, before any of Toby's minor traits has been mentioned. In the next two paragraphs Tristram dedicates himself solely to getting his story straight. Thus when Toby's modesty and family pride are finally discovered, they seem like mere background material to the story of the argument, both of them being required if the audience is to understand the argument. It is by following the argument over Aunt Dinah, moreover, that Tristram will get to Toby's third minor trait, his argumentative whistling.

There is reason to believe that Sterne saw that in allowing such formal confusion as this, into which the Dinah story has led his narrator, he was flirting with communicative chaos and thus with the ruin of his novel. The most immediate sign of his awareness is the complete chapter which divides this long digression's two main parts. It is a whole chapter of formal clarification disguised as self praise. In it Tristram says:

---

his verbal tour from Lapland to England. It makes Tristram's dependence on a wise God in his crucial argument for the balance of wit and judgment in every man seem natural and right.

The relationship between these two sections of the Preface is, then, not a logical one. Nor is any part of the Preface philosophically binding, not even the key argument. An argument based on the wisdom of a creator, when neither his wisdom nor even his existence has been established, has no philosophical validity. It is thus an error to speak of this Preface of Tristram's as a corrective to Locke. Tristram is here in a public argument with Your Reverences and Worships, with men, we may say, who profess belief in a wise and orderly creator and yet defend the odd distribution of wit and judgment which, of course, allows them to claim the latter. As an effort to laugh and argue away their continued holding to the odd distribution (if, as Tristram does not insist, they now hold to it) and as a revelation to the rest of society of their absurdity in holding to it, the Preface is wonderfully trenchant and effective. And that, of course, is its purpose in Tristram's discourse.

I was just going . . . to have given you the great outlines of my uncle *Toby's* most whimsical character;—when my aunt *Dinah* and the coachman came a-cross us, and led us a vagary some millions of miles into the very heart of the planetary system: Notwithstanding all this you perceive that the drawing of my uncle *Toby's* character went on gently all the time;—not the great contours of it,—that was impossible,—but some familiar strokes and faint designations of it, were here and there touch'd in, as we went along, so that you are much better acquainted with my uncle *Toby* now than you was before. (I. xxii.)

This does more than admit the confusion: it settles the confusion, subordinating the Aunt Dinah argument and reasserting the proper primacy of Toby's character. It re-establishes the integrity of the digression, which any audience would have come to doubt.

Another sign of Sterne's awareness of the danger of this confusion is the clarity with which he has pursued Toby's character in the rest of this digression and his general avoidance of such confusion hereafter. Future digressions will be digressive and progressive too, explaining a main point of Shandy life, say, by revealing another point of Shandy life or a relevant opinion; and there will always be in Tristram's digressive practice many conversational freedoms; but the confusion of main and interruptive matter will not be repeated. We might notice in this connection the late digression Tristram will call "the most puzzled skein of all" (VII. xxvii.–xxviii.): this is his weaving into the story of his recent French travels "a small thread or two" from his earlier French travels. That small digressive thread Tristram will introduce quite formally to explain why he could go on forever about Auxerre; he will develop it with perfect lucidity; and he will close it with precision by distinguishing between the threads of his different travels and by taking up again the one which is his chief concern. But even in this early digressive adventure on Toby's character, which Sterne wrote when he was still working out his style, he has finally achieved coherence and allowed Tristram to impress on his audience a clear and pointed digressive order.

Tristram has generally helped his audience follow his digressions, especially the harder ones, by the emphatic use of paragraphs and chapters. Paragraphs, for instance, divide the exception from the rule in the digressions on sleep and on swearing. Paragraphs divide Tristram's general statement of his troubles and the two points, as an author and as a man, by which he develops it. Paragraphs and transitional paragraphing define the sections of the Preface; and paragraphing sets off the section on Tristram's own travel problems from his opinion of travels in his Invocation (IX. xxiv.). A complete chapter of clarification divides the digression on Uncle Toby, as we have just seen. A chapter break separates Tristram's statement of the historian's problems from the quotation of his mother's marriage settlement, which led Tristram to make this statement (I. xiv.–xv.). And the digression which tells how not to raise creative powers, then how to raise them, and then faces objections is properly parcelled into three chapters. This formal punctuation of digressions does not follow any mechanical rule, and not every paragraph or chapter unit in a digression is so significant as these I have mentioned. However, the patterns of all of Tristram's extended digressions have been sufficiently punctuated for the members of his audience—if they are as attentive as he asks them to be—to have a clear notion of every digression's parts and structure.

Tristram, then, has composed his digressions with great care, using them quite explicitly to help him accommodate his peculiar narrative material to his social situation. We must not be led to miss the care with which he has composed them or their relevance to his discourse by his passing admissions of whimsy or carelessness. Most of these, like his saying that he writes his first sentence and trusts to Almighty God for his second (VIII. ii.), are equivocal, reversible. This most famous admission, for instance, Tristram has followed by saying that it would cure an author of writing any other way to see how orderly and coherent his writing comes out. Nor should we overemphasize Tristram's few artistic failures, such as his very few emotional digressions (III. xxxiv.; VI. xxv.), in which he turns his back on his audience, as it were; or his once or twice briefly losing his way (VI. xxxiii.). These flawed passages, all of which are perfectly understandable, should rather underscore the nearly perfect skill with which Tristram has projected his peculiar, oddly involved story as an object of general entertainment and instruction.

III. *The Digressions' Quality and Effect*

But what has Sterne achieved beyond making Tristram's story socially understandable and edifying by working out this hard won solution to a hard pressed problem? He has achieved, to use Tristram's word (IX. xii.), a "texture," a web of life and opinion, of particular story and general statement which involves the trivial items of Shandy experience with general human truths in a fabric of great richness and density. It is with his opinionative digressions, especially, and with those explanatory ones which contain interweavings of opinion that Tristram has accomplished this texture. We can best approach its nature and value by working through a few examples.

We take, first, Tristram's effort to generalize Walter's response to the news of his son's unlucky misnaming (IV. xvi.–xvii.): Walter "took down his hat with the gentlest movement of limbs, that ever affliction harmonized and attuned together . . . [and] walked composedly . . . to the fish-pond." Tristram has drawn three opinions from this, two from Walter's oddly gentle bearing and one from the pond. The first, that "the different weight, dear Sir,—nay even the different package of two vexations of the same weight,—makes a very wide difference in our manners of bearing and getting through with them," he treats before mentioning Walter's walk to the pond. He has developed it by a particular description of the way he recently bore and got through one of his own vexations by throwing his wig violently at the ceiling; and he further develops it by deriving from that violent action of his a second general opinion: we cannot understand the various peculiar actions by which Nature allows us to relieve our various peculiar griefs. This second opinion gives new meaning to the two odd responses to vexation of Walter and Tristram, taking them both as examples, and refines the first opinion. Thus, Tristram's action is doubly valuable, exemplifying two different if related opinions; and Walter's action is trebly so since it is important as an item of Tristram's story as well as being doubly exemplary.

But the texture of this passage is richer still since the second opinion gives and receives meanings from the matter following it as well as from that which has preceded. It helps explain Walter's walk to the pond, by which it receives further exemplification; for Walter's relief is, like Tristram's wig throwing, another of Nature's mysterious workings; and it is refined and focussed by the general opinion Tristram dedices from Walter's relief, that "there is something, Sir, in fish-ponds . . . under the first disorderly transport of the humours . . . unaccountably becalming." The general truths stated in this passage, then, are variously broadened and refined by their relationship to one another and strengthened by their rootedness in particular Shandy actions; and Walter's action, with which this passage begins and ends, comes, for all its oddity, to represent the variety of mankind's response to grief.

Tristram has had a harder time involving Walter's odd opinion on the importance of free-swinging door hinges with generally relevant truth (III. xxi.). To manage this, indeed, he has first had to tie Walter's odd notion to Walter's failure to oil the squeaky hinge to his own parlor door. Having asserted that connection, he can rise to a general statement on Walter's nature: "his rhetoric and conduct were at perpetual handy-cuffs." And then he goes on to a universally applicable utterance: "Inconsistent soul that man is . . . his whole life a contradiction to his knowledge!" Walter, in his inconsistency over the door hinge and in his generally inconsistent nature, thus stands once again for all mankind. But Tristram does not stop with Walter. Rather, he applies this universal truth, which he has derived from Walter's peculiar concern with the parlor-door hinge, to his own concern with the very same thing: "The parlour-door shall be mended this reign." He thus unwittingly offers himself as a further example of the inconsistency between man's knowledge and his conduct; and he shows himself to be, at one and the same time, a normal member of the human race and the peculiar Walter Shandy's true and resembling heir.

Tristram works out an extremely ambiguous particular-general texture in his account of Walter's opinion that a man's Christian name determines his destiny (I. xix.). This, like all of Walter's opinions, seems at first to be in itself both general and particular: it is general in Walter's application of it but totally particular to Walter as a belief, being just one more odd element of Shandy history. In developing it, however, Tristram shakes this interpretation of the opinion. He does this, after first particularizing it with a few names Walter approved and a few he abhorred, by giving Walter's argument for it. This wonderful *ad hominem* argument, which depends on the opponent's admission that he would not name a son Judas, strongly suggests that the opinion is not so peculiar to Walter after all. It leads Tristram on to a general statement about Walter— that he was eloquent and that he had to be so to defend such peculiar opinions as he took up. In explaining Walter's odd opinions, Tristram throws out a warning "to the learned reader against the indiscreet reception of such guests." This discussion of Walter's generally odd opinions leads Tristram back to Walter's opinion of Christian names, which now stands as an example of Walter's peculiarity in his opinions. We must notice the ambiguity here: Walter's opinion of names has been suggested to be, on the one hand, more generally held than is admitted and presented, on the other, as a particular example of Walter's peculiarity in opinions. Tristram does nothing to resolve this ambiguity: "Whether this [that his opinions began in jest and ended in earnest as he has been conjecturing] was the case of the singularity of my father's notions,—or that his judgment, at length, became the dupe of his wit;—or how far, in many of his notions, he might, tho' odd, be absolutely right; —the reader, as he comes at them, shall decide."

Tristram concludes his account of Walter's opinion by giving more names that Walter had fit into his system and by ending with the name Walter most abhorred, Tristram; and thus he draws his reader's attention with tremendous force to those particular events by which he himself came to receive that most hopeless name. But how will the reader take the story now? He may take it as sheer comedy, as an example of much ado about nothing, only remembering that, as Tristram has reminded him, he too is susceptible to such odd opinions and such absurd sorrows. Or he may take his part in Walter's defeat more to heart, admitting that he too worries about names, that he would suffer, some at least, if his son had the name he most abhors affixed to him forever. This passage, then, has given the whole story of Tristram's misnaming an ambiguous general value. It is, at least, an example of Walter's opinions and of the sorrows they led him into. It may be, also, an example of the odd misfortunes all of us, all learned readers anyway, are susceptible to; and it may be, still further, an instance of the miseries all mankind faces because of its (absurd?) concern for names. And, thus, one who came to scoff at Walter's oddity may remain to sympathize. But, as Tristram says, the reader shall decide.

This sort of narrative texture is not peculiar to *Tristram Shandy* in the eighteenth century. *Tom Jones*,[4] which has been shown to share the use of a self-conscious narrator with our novel,[5] also shares this. Fielding's narrator, also, must often stop to explain or generalize an event in his story. He explains the general belief that Tom was born to hang, for instance, by giving three cases of Tom's youthful thievery (77), and explains the high bill Tom got at the inn before Gloucester by giving his readers some maxims on inn-keeping (360); he introduces Miss Bridget Allworthy's middle-aged passion for Captain Blifil, again, with some general remarks on the love of middle-aged women, asserting that Miss Bridget will serve as "an example of all these observations" (30). He gives a particular account of Mr. Northerton's escape from the inn where he was confined, first, to clear the character of the sentinel who had been on guard (327) and, second, to explain the compassion of the inn's landlady (328). Fielding's narrator also habitually relates the particular events of his story to general opinions and truths. Sometimes he takes the events merely as occasions, concluding his account of Jones's fight with Thwackum and Blifil, for instance, with the wish that all battles could be settled, as this one has been, without deadly weapons (211). But usually his opinions derive from particular events which reflect on them as examples. In Sophia Western's changing of her hair bow and thus missing her meeting with Tom, the narrator finds a general lesson for all young ladies (236). In the love Sophia felt for Tom after he had saved her from being thrown from her horse, the narrator found particular evidence that bravery endears a man to the hearts of women (152). Jones's drunkenness serves as an example that liquor exaggerates a man's real nature rather than reversing it (199–200); and Jones's gullible belief in Partridge's professions of friendship underlies the narrator's opinion

4. The Modern Library edition (New York, 1950) which is the source of my quotations and to which my parenthetical pagination refers.

5. Wayne C. Booth, "The Self-conscious Narrator in Prose Fiction before *Tristram Shandy*," *PMLA*, LXVII (1952), 175–80.

of the two ways by which such incautious trust in others may be overcome (358). Both of these last two opinions, by the way, are developed in little bipartite essays, like so many of Tristram Shandy's.

Fielding's novel naturally has something of the texture of Sterne's. Take, for example, the narrator's explanation of Mr. Allworthy's lessening of affection for Tom (97). There are two reasons for it: one is Tom's receiving more affection than Blifil from Mrs. Bridget; the other is Tom's own wildness. The first both explains Mr. Allworthy's feelings and serves as an example of his general habit of mind. The second and, indeed, all those wild actions it introduces not only explain Allworthy's lessening of affection but also exemplify a general lesson, that "Prudence and circumspection are necessary to the best of men." Thus this considerable element of the novel, the story of Tom's wildness, is presented to the reader both as an affective narrative and as a didactic example.

These explanatory and opinionative digressions, which the narrator explicitly describes as digressions (5;224), are often directed explicitly at his reading public, much as Tristram's have been. The example of Tom's wildness is addressed "to all those well-disposed youths who shall hereafter be our readers." The example of Sophia's untimely vanity the narrator has drawn up "only for the sake of the ladies." His report of Mr. Northerton's escape was due to his desire that "the reader" would not damn the sentinel and that "our reader" would not mistake the landlady's compassion. Thus Fielding's narrator has engaged in some of the same digressive practices as Tristram Shandy and for something like the same reason, that is, to attach and to instruct society. Moreover, he has achieved a similar, if not as thick and complex, a discursive texture as Tristram has.

The texture in *Tristram Shandy* is thicker partly because Sterne's narrator must include himself in his story, being the last member of the family he is describing, whereas Fielding's narrator can maintain a kind of divine distance from his. More important than this is the difference in the two narrators' materials. The particular characters and events of *Tom Jones* are so typical of mankind that the connection between them and general human nature is broad and firm. In asserting it, Fielding's narrator needed merely to weave the simple, sturdy fabric he has woven. But Tristram has had to bind his general lessons and applications to an almost impossibly peculiar and atypical narrative; and this has required of him the imaginative variety and dexterity that we have been examining.

The texture of Tristram's discourse is thicker, finally, because Tristram has attempted to involve all possible elements of society in it as deeply as he could (I. iv.). Fielding's narrator wished to give a generally true account of human nature to those who could relish it

(1–3). He confidently dismissed those who could not (1;216–217), willing to satisfy himself, if necessary, with fit audience though few. He had, therefore, no need of pointed attentions or elaborate courtesies. But Tristram, with his desire to keep all segments of society vividly and personally attentive, has had "to consult everyone a little in his turn" (I. iv.). This explains the pointedness and the variety of his vast system of explanations, entertainments, and opinions.

Every reader will determine for himself the effect of Tristram's discursive texture of life and opinions, as Tristram has often acknowledged (I. iv.; I. vi.; I. xviii.–xix.; I. xx.; II. xi.; III. xx.). But attentive readers may well find themselves so involved that "nothing which has touched [Tristram] will be thought trifling in its nature, or tedious in its telling" (I. vi.)—just as Tristram hoped they would. They may come to feel that every most peculiar Shandy item is pregnant with general truth and that every general truth is radiant with life. As they weigh Walter's opinions of noses and names and follow his defeats; as they weigh Toby's opinions of marriage and love and follow the failure of his courtship; as they weigh Tristram's opinions on literature and follow his hopeless struggle to describe his whole life: sensitive readers may feel the absurd peculiarity of their own opinions and the narrow scope of all human actions.

MARTIN PRICE

[The Art of the Natural] †

At the heart of Sterne's work is a central paradox that runs through the eighteenth century and receives its fullest statement in Denis Diderot's *Paradoxe sur le comédien* (written in the 1770s and published in 1830). Diderot's actor is the man who must be free of emotion in order to call up emotion in others:

> At the very moment when he touches your heart he is listening to his own voice: his talent depends not, as you think, upon feeling, but upon rendering so exactly the outward signs of feeling, that you fall into the trap. He has rehearsed to himself every note of his passion. He had learnt before a mirror every particle of his despair (trans. W. H. Pollock, as *The Paradox of Acting*, New York, 1957, p. 19).

---

† From Martin Price, "Sterne: Art and Nature" in *To the Palace of Wisdom* (New York: Doubleday & Co., 1964), pp. 327–36. Footnotes are by Price.

Diderot's paradox is the culmination of a dialectical process one can see in his *Salons* and even more clearly in *Rameau's Nephew* and *Jacques the Fatalist*, a dialectic of art and nature.[1]

Rameau's nephew is the intransigent "natural" man, who insists upon his selfishness and uncontrollable passions. He makes the point that moral restraint and dedication are unnatural; they require a position—as he puts it—"which would cause me trouble and which I could not hold" (88). His energies are enormous and undisciplined; his talents are spilled in vile pantomime; his art is an unstable mixture of brilliance and nonsense. He challenges the decorum of moral men: "Just imagine the universe philosophical and wise, and tell me if it would not be devilishly dull" (35). At least he is nakedly what he is: "Neither more nor less detestable than other men, he was franker than they, more logical, and thus often profound in his depravity" (76). "The important point is that you and I should exist, and that we should be you and I. . . . The best order, for me, is that in which I had to exist—and a fig for the most perfect world if I am not of it" (16).

The music the young Rameau defends against his uncle's is a "natural" music in which "the animal cry of the passions [dictates] the melodic line":

> We call out, invoke, clamor, groan, weep, and laugh openly. No more witticisms, epigrams, neat thoughts—they are too unlike nature. And don't get it into your head that the old theatrical acting and declamation can give us a pattern to follow. Not likely! We want it more energetic, less mannered, more genuine (71).

Rameau's nephew represents the vitality and the formlessness of the natural, both its honesty and its shabby cruelty. The *Moi* who confronts him may be somewhat stuffy in contrast, but he defends the freedom of Diogenes the Cynic, "the philosopher who has nothing and asks for nothing." Art holds its own against nature.

Diderot is fond of pushing to extremes the unnaturalness of morality, and he draws from that demonstration an ambiguous conclusion. In the *Conversation between a Father and His Children* (1772), the father insists upon maintaining the law even when to do so creates unhappiness for everyone; and his son, the philosopher, argues against him for the "natural": "Isn't the natural wisdom of humanity many times more sacred than that of some lawgiver? We call ourselves civilized, yet often we behave worse than savages. . . . Pure instinct, unhindered, would have led us

1. For Diderot, I have cited J. Robert Loy's translation of *Jacques the Fatalist and His Master*, New York, 1959, and the translations of Jacques Barzun and Ralph H. Bowen in *Rameau's Nephew and Other Works*, Anchor Edition, 1956. These are cited by page numbers. The *Salons* are given in the translation of Beatrix L. Tollemache.

straight to our goal" (283). The issue is drawn but hardly settled; the father's moral simplicity, unnaturally devoted as it is to law, has a strength that the son's arguments hardly damage.

In *Jacques the Fatalist* this problematic relation of morality and nature is presented differently. Jacques professes a doctrine that denies all meaning to morality, but he cannot live by it. Jacques is persuaded that actions follow inevitably from their causes, that whatever will happen is written in the Great Scroll, and that no action, therefore, has moral value.

> According to such a system, one might imagine that Jacques rejoiced and sorrowed about nothing. Such, however, was not the case. He behaved very much as you and I. . . . Often he was inconsistent, like you and me, and subject to forgetting his principles, save in those few circumstances where his philosophy clearly dominated him. It was then he would say: "That had to be, for that was written up yonder." He tried to prevent evil; he was prudent, yet all the while he had the greatest scorn for prudence. When the inevitable accident happened, he reverted to his old refrain, and was consoled by it. For the rest, he was a good fellow, frank, honest, brave, affectionate, faithful, strong-headed, but more than all these, talkative . . . (167).

Here unhindered instinct, for all the overlay of doctrine, has its own morality, more active and energetic than that of the master, who insists upon his freedom but hardly acts.

In *Jacques the Fatalist*, which resembles *Tristram Shandy* in several important respects and borrows from it, Diderot is exploring several problems in which ethics shades off into metaphysics. Jacques, like Voltaire's Candide, acts well when he acts without regard for his theories. And through Jacques and his master, we explore the issues of freedom, and especially men's habit "of confusing the voluntary with the free" (as Diderot put it in a letter of 1756 to Landois). Diderot wants to preserve an inclusive and problematic view of choice. Its role is crucial even though it is determined by all that a man has been and known. Diderot tries to avoid the fatalism that denies that man can ever be a moral agent and the radical libertarianism that separates a decision from its conditions and sees it as a pure act of will.

Related to this problem of man's nature is that of the world's order. Pangloss, with his doctrine of "sufficient reason," finds a tight causal sequence in all events that conforms to human values and produces good out of evil. He vulgarizes the optimism we see in Pope's *Essay on Man* by insisting that the good is an external, tangible one, realized in the world. (Pope insists only upon the necessary limitations on any one individual's external happiness in a design that must sacrifice each individual in some degree to every other, and he tries to induce the contentment that can arise from identifying the will of the self with the welfare of the whole.) Diderot and Sterne do not present in their fiction the possible Order that lies behind apparent disorder, but, like Pope, they study the pathology of false expectation.

In Pope it is pride that lies behind the demands of selfhood; in Diderot and Sterne, the error is not moral failure but simply the limitations of man's categories of thought. Both writers are willing to acknowledge a rightness of choice that rises out of the "heart" when thought is suppressed or side-stepped. Both are willing to recognize the dangers of formal thinking, where all is "reasoned, formal, stiff, academic, and flat" in contrast to the exuberance of natural energy finding its own form. "The license of his style," Diderot says of Montaigne, "is practically a guarantee to me of the purity of his habits" (*Jacques*, 206). And this license of style—the subversion of narrative or discursive forms—makes, in turn, for the celebration of those non-verbal, spontaneous movements of psychosomatic wisdom—gestures.

Neither Diderot nor Sterne, it should be noted, is content to give unqualified trust to the heart or to the natural. Both see something ludicrous and unstable (and Diderot also something terrible) in the natural, and both insist on the paradox of nature and art. The natural heart can achieve a spontaneous artistry that puts to shame all deliberate endeavors; yet, it may turn out, in another view, that the natural can be attained only by the calculated surprises of art, the deliberate disordering of forms and the artful pretense of spontaneity. The balance the Augustans tried to hold between the natural and the artificial, the "true" and the histrionic, breaks down in Sterne; there is interplay but hardly fusion. In this respect Sterne recalls some of the qualities of baroque art.

It was F. W. Bateson who first applied the term "baroque" to English literature of the later eighteenth century. Like the baroque art of the century before, the art of Sterne (and others of his age) deliberately splits open the harmonies of classical form. High baroque art in Italy leaves nothing undone "to draw the beholder into the orbit of the work of art."[2] Bernini's statues, in Rudolf Wittkower's words, "breathe, as it were, the same air as the beholder, are so 'real' that they even share the space continuum with him, and yet remain picture-like works of art in a specific and limited sense" (101). In Bernini's bust of Scopione Borghese (1632) "the head is shown in momentary movement, the lively eye seems to fix the beholder, and the half-open mouth, as if about to speak, engages him in conversation" (98). The effect is a break-

2. Rudolf Wittkower, *Art and Architecture in Italy, 1600 to 1750*, London and Baltimore, 1958, p. 92.

down of familiar limits. As the beholder finds himself "drawn into the orbit of the work," he asks himself, "What is image, what is reality? The very borderline between the one and the other seems to be obliterated" (106).

Inevitably, when realism is so intense that it has become illusionistic we become aware of its artifice and theatricality. Illusionism breaks through the familar conventions, stable and unobtrusive as they often remain, upon which most art depends; and in doing so, it calls up awareness of the conventionality of all art. Sterne's age is far different from Bernini's, however. The breakdown of artistic distance in Bernini becomes an approach to religious mystery, a disolution of rational coolness and an involvement of the sense in the full experience of ecstatic transcendence. The theatricality we see in Sterne is turned upon itself, and it is closer to what Wittkower sees in the late baroque, where we find an interesting double movement—in one direction toward the example of stage design, in the other toward the new celebration of the sketch as opposed to the finished work. Wittkower also draws a connection between the new interest in the sketch and the new taste for painters, like Magnasco in the eighteenth century, who use a broad brush and depart from the conventional realism of the finished surface. We have moved from art as illusion to concern with the processes of art.

Diderot in his *Salon* of 1767 treats the question of our pleasure in the sketch. It has, he begins, "more life and less defined forms. As forms become more accurately defined life departs. In dead animals, dreadful objects to our sight, the forms are there, but life is gone." He tries that most common of explanations: the sketch pleases us because "it leaves our imagination free to see what we like in it, just as children see shapes in the clouds, and we are all more or less children." He goes on, however, to make a significant comparison, to which I shall return in connection with Sterne's use of music: "It is the same difference as that between vocal and instrumental music; in the former we listen to what it says, but in the latter we make it say what we choose." When he turns to Greuze, Diderot considers the problem again. "A sketch is generally more spirited than a picture. It is the artist's work when he is full of inspiration and ardor, when reflection has toned down nothing, it is the artist's work when he is full of inspiration and ardor, when reflection has toned down nothing, it is the artist's soul expressing itself freely on the canvas. His pen or skilful pencil seems to sport and play; a few strokes express the rapid fancy, and the more vaguely art embodies itself the more room is there for the play of imagination." And once more Diderot turns to the example of instrumental music.

What matters for Sterne is the shift of attention from the embodied work to the energy of the artist, from the formed—in Shaftesbury's distinction—to the forming, from the creation to the immanent creator. It is this concern, I think, that accounts for the double interest in the artifice of art and the process of artistic creation. In the eighteenth century, a number of instances come to mind—some of which I deal with in the next chapter—like Hogarth's device of formal notation reducing human postures or frames to geometrical forms, out of whose suggestions figures could be formed anew; Gainsborough's gathering of rocks and bits of moss from which to paint full landscape scenes in his studio; Alexander Cozens' method of developing a landscape drawing from an ink blot. In all these cases the artist cultivates an arbitrary beginning, suggestive but vague, from which the inventive process can take its start. Or one can cite Reynolds' use of "quotations," partly witty allusion, partly suggestive model—Mrs. Siddons as a Michelangelo Sibyl or prophet, Garrick between Tragedy and Comedy like Hercules at the Crossroads, infants in the grand postures of prophets and judges. In the case of Reynolds we can see most clearly the link between awareness of the artificial and the arbitrary and the double vision of the mock form, where the Augustans had allowed artifice freest and most conspicuous play. The divorce between apparent form and apparent subject was at the heart of the mock form, and the play of imagination was therefore most frankly play.

Sterne's interest in gesture draws together many of the tendencies of the age. It led, first of all, to his being likened (by Ralph Griffiths) to "the delicate, the circumstantial Richardson himself." Sterne's gestures, so meticulously presented, allow the reader that "play of imagination" Diderot valued in the sketch. Sterne himself wrote of the "true feeler": "His own ideas are only called forth by what he reads, and the vibrations within, so entirely correspond with those excited, 'tis like reading *himself* and not the book." The gesture, like music, combines formal clarity with suggestiveness; it gives the reader the experience of having his unconscious movement sharply defined before him. Gestures have much the same function for the artistry of feeling that suggestive forms may have for the painter. This artistry of the heart is an essential theme in *Tristram Shandy*, and we see it most clearly in the untutored movements of Corporal Trim. As he prepares to read the sermon aloud, he assumes precisely the posture that reveals Hogarth's "line of beauty," the serpentine curve whose movement "along the continuity of its variety" Hogarth had praised in *The Analysis of Beauty* (1753) and presented on his title page (where he also cited Milton's "Curl'd many a wanton wreath," the description of Eve's hair).

Sterne ponders Trim's curious infallibility:

> How the duce Corporal *Trim*, who knew not so much as an acute angle from an obtuse one, came to hit it so exactly;—or whether it was chance or nature, or good sense or imitation. . . .

The description is minute and fussy:

> He stood,—for I repeat it, to take the picture of him in at one view, with his body sway'd, and somewhat bent forwards,—his right-leg firm under him, sustaining seven-eights of his whole weight,—the foot of his left-leg, the defect of which was no disadvantage to his attitude, advanced a little,—not laterally, nor forwards, but in a line betwixt them;—his knee bent, but that not violently,—but so as to fall within the limits of the line of beauty; —and I add, of the line of science too;—for consider, it had one eighth part of his body to bear up;—so that in this case the position of the leg is determined,—because the foot could be no further advanced, or the knee more bent, than what would allow him mechanically, to receive an eighth part of his whole weight under it,—and to carry it too.

The full account of Trim's stance makes clear the holistic nature of Sterne's concern with gesture. The gestures become part of a composition:

> Corporal *Trim's* eyes and the muscles of his face were in full harmony with the other parts of him;—he look'd frank,—unconstrained,—something assured,—but not bordering upon assurance.

We see Trim at last "with such an oratorical sweep *throughout the whole figure*,—a statuary might have modell'd from it" (II. xvii).

This feeling for the *gestalt* of the whole figure is important in Sterne. In the account of the Monk of Calais in *A Sentimental Journey* we have an artistic rendering again:

> The rest of his outline may be given in a few strokes; one might put it into the hands of any one to design; for 'twas neither elegant or otherwise, but as character and expression made it so. . . .

When the Monk pleads the poverty of his order, he does it with "so simple a grace, and such an air of depreciation was there in *the whole cast of his look* and figure, I was bewitch'd not to have been struck by it—"

In the phrases I have set in italics, we can see the emphasis upon the unifying power of expression. Gesture, by its very muteness, calls forth sympathetic imagination and demands an attention to the whole figure. "There are a thousand unnoticed openings," says Walter Shandy, "which let a penetrating eye at once into a man's soul; and I maintain it, added he, that a man of sense does not lay down his hat in coming into a room,—or take it up in going out of it, but something escapes, which discovers him" (VI. v).

Trim's funeral sermon on Bobby provides another instance of the eloquence of gesture:

—'Are we not here now';—continued the corporal, 'and are we not'—(dropping his hat plumb upon the ground—and pausing, before he pronounced the word)—'gone! in a moment?' The descent of the hat was as if a heavy lump of clay had been kneaded into the crown of it.—Nothing could have expressed the sentiment of mortality, of which it was the type and fore-runner, like it,—his hand seemed to vanish from under it,—it fell dead,—the corporal's eye fix'd upon it, as upon a corps,—and *Susannah* burst into a flood of tears.

Now—Ten thousand, and ten thousand times ten thousand (for matter and motion are infinite) are the ways by which a hat may be dropped upon the ground, without any effect.—Had he flung it, or thrown it, or cast it, or skimmed it, or squirted, or let it slip or fall in any possible direction under heaven,—or in the best direction that could be given to it,—had he dropped it like a goose—like a puppy—like an ass—or in doing it, or even after he had done, had he looked like a fool,—like a ninny—like a nincompoop—it had fail'd, and the effect upon the heart had been lost.

What is clear in these brilliant descriptions of gesture is that Sterne is more than a realist. He records them with an exactness that goes far beyond the demands of conventional realism, and he brings to description the analytic apparatus of the art or drama critic, as if he were judging the performances by their effect. Scattered through the book are allusions to the formal criteria of criticism:

My father instantly exchanged the attitude he was in, for that in which Socrates is so finely painted by Raffael in his School of Athens; which your connoisseurship knows is so exquisitely imagined, that even the particular manner of the reasoning of Socrates is expressed by it (IV. vii).

The formal categories of criticism are necessary to express the exquisite rightness of the least detail. Yet, as usual, the critics are too clumsy and arrogant to do justice to their subject; their heads are "stuck so full of rules and compasses." When Garrick suspends his voice in the epilogue, he breaks the rules of the "grammarian."

But in suspending his voice—was the sense suspended likewise? Did no expression of attitude or countenance fill up the chasm? —Was the eye silent? Did you narrowly look?—I look'd only at the stopwatch, my Lord.—Excellent observer!

And what of this new book the world makes such a rout about? [i.e., *Tristram Shandy*]—oh! 'tis out of all plumb, my Lord,—quite an irregular thing!—not one of the angles at the four corners was a right angle.—I had my rule and compasses, &c. my Lord, in my pocket.—Excellent critic! (III. xii.)

But the language of criticism, for all its limitations, is necessary to show the artless art of Walter's rhetoric or Trim's oratorical postures, to catch Toby's benign oval of a face, or the eloquent "venereal" eyes of the Widow Wadman. The author may be forced to translate gesture into words, as he paraphrases the Widow's blushes "for the sake of the unlearned reader" (IX. xx.). Still, words and critical categories can only approximate the supple expressiveness of Nature:

> She, dear Goddess, by an instantaneous impulse, in all *provoking cases*, determines us to a sally of this or that member—or else she thrusts us into this or that place, or posture of body, we know not why—But mark, madam, we live amongst riddles and mysteries —The most obvious things . . . have dark sides . . . and even the clearest and most exalted understandings amongst us find ourselves puzzled and at a loss in almost every cranny of nature's works (IV. xvii).

What Sterne does with gestures, he does again with sound. Walter's rational systems prove to be eccentric twistings of thought and language, but his earnest sophistry becomes effective in its musicality. When he argues down an opponent, he falls into "that soft and irresistible *piano* of voice, which the nature of the *argumentum ad hominem* absolutely requires" (I. xix). It is language that has become expressive sound that fascinates Sterne. Phutatorius' reaction to the hot chestnut in his breeches produces "Zounds," conveyed in "a tone of voice, somewhat between that of a man in amazement, and of one in bodily pain." Those with "nice ears" can "distinguish the expression and mixture of the two tones as plainly as a *third* or a *fifth*, or any other chord in musick" (IV. xxvii). Dr. Slop's assertion that there are seven sacraments produces Toby's "Humph!"— "not accented as a note of acquiescence,—but as an interjection of that particular species of surprize, when a man, in looking into a drawer, finds more of a thing than he expected." And Dr. Slop "who had an ear, understood my uncle Toby as well as if he had wrote a whole volume against the seven sacraments" (II. xvii). The Widow Wadman's eye, finally, recalls those nuances of expression that turn words to music:

> 'twas an eye full of gentle salutations—and soft responses—speaking—not like the trumpet-stop of some ill-made organ, in which many an eye I talk to, holds coarse converse—but whispering soft —like the last low accents of an expiring saint (VIII. xxv).

JEAN-JACQUES MAYOUX

Variations on the Time-Sense in *Tristram Shandy*†

The Novelist, so Forster says, must tell a story. A story can do, in theory and perhaps even in practice, without space. It cannot do without time. Time belongs, ineluctably, to the story telling as much as it would to the structure of a piece of music, and more than it would, for instance to a philosophical essay, or even to a poem. The essay has taken time to write, takes time to read, but does not incorporate, *need* not at any rate, a time-structure. If all writing belongs to the arts of time, narrative writing differs radically from the rest: in it the time which literally it takes, say if we read it aloud, or the time which was taken in the writing, in both cases objective clock-time, is hopelessly tangled, inexorably overwhelmed and superseded, by the evocation of the factitious, fictitious time supposedly taken by the series of events in the story. In the creative imagination, I mean that of the ideal reader as well as the writer's, there is little awareness of this dual time-structure. Spontaneously, the imagination tends to ignore the props and the scaffoldings of the story telling so that it may concentrate on the effect of the story told. Willing suspension of disbelief is at that price. It was Sterne's invention, the product of his genius, helped I suppose by his total indifference to the creation of belief, to reverse this habit of fiction-writing and fiction-reading. It has been the characteristic effort of his admirable willfulness to blend and confuse the time-structure of the story with the time-infrastructure of the writing, for the delight of extricating them again, of analyzing their relations, of arranging them into telling patterns.

Moreover it has been his historic choice to concentrate on the subjectivity, on the workings of the mind where the primary integration of the several time-structures had occurred. Of all of Sterne's erratic or obsessive book-reading, nothing perhaps should be retained as essential, not even Rabelais or Cervantes, except Locke, whose importance concerning the genesis and conduct of this book Professor Traugott was the first to stress and analyze. Fielding was interested in Hume's ethics. Sterne was concerned by the problem of existence, of, let us be more precise, intellectual existence in relation to literary creation; and the key to it was provided by Locke's *Essay*, which he terms, so aptly to his purpose, "a history-book . . . of what passes in a man's own mind" (II. ii.). How does Sterne see the Lockian succession of ideas and its equation to subjective time?

† From *The Winged Skull,* ed. Arthur Cash and John Stedmond (London: Methuen, 1971), pp. 3–18.

We might say *where*, instead of *how*, for the context and situation are very relevant. While Walter and Toby are waiting anxiously for news of Tristram's birth, Walter discovers that in terms of clock-time they have remained thus for only two hours and ten minutes. "But," he remarks, "it seems an age" (III. xviii.). It is then that my uncle Toby stumbles on the Lockian definition by remarking that their impression is due to the succession of their ideas; and Walter, much piqued because he meant to be the one to give the formula, proceeds to ascertain that Toby does not know what he is talking about, and to secure compensation for his injured vanity by bringing out a lengthy near-quotation from Locke. The episode is helpful, if less than illuminating. Clock-time and mental time, it might be said, follow after all parallel roads, the one with necessarily even pace, the other at a more erratic and fanciful gait according to the rhythms, currents, wanderings generated (to retain our instance) in and between those two heads. Each consciousness is double; it carries the sense of one's own existence, with all its concerns butting in, and a vague, discontinuous awareness of the external world implying external time. The resulting impression is a cross-product of the two systems, creating a particular tempo. The tempo here was sluggish, as slowed down by anxiety and absence of mind.

The main revelation or confirmation, due to Locke or upheld by Locke, was that life was lived in the mind. The old vision of the microcosm was as important again to Sterne as it could have been to Donne; and Sterne may well be termed a metaphysical novelist. We hear his frequent echoes in those metaphysical writers of our own times, Virginia Woolf and James Joyce.

In this vision, each living person, even the humblest, down to Susannah or Obadiah, is such a microcosm, whose stream of consciousness reacts to the death of Bobby in its own way: green satin nightgown to be had from the mourning, or pasture land not to be sold but to be put into shape. And each microcosm has its own time-dimension, enclosed and separate, with its own structure, rhythm, and flow. Life, Sterne has discovered, as it is lived mostly inside, is carried on in solitude. He is less dramatic about it than his modern successors and does not emphasize or sentimentalize the point. What he gives us is a comedy of absurdities which can be equated with the effects of the singular, individual, time-dimension being brought up against the plurality of individuals. It takes place when, from his own private path, the individual emerges into the common way, clad in his oddity, having pursued his own trend up to the precise instant of his emerging, and meeting on the one hand what we term objective reality, on the other hand, other microcosms. Then bridge meets bridge, Dr Slop's bridge for a crushed nose is mistaken for my uncle Toby's bridge for military transit, and *quid pro quos* soon build up. Not all microcosms, of course, are equally fruitful; not all are equal to showing this dominant seclusion in such a manner as to remain interesting. Joyce has only granted interior monologues to three characters. Similarly, of his own obsessive tendencies subdued by humorous self-awareness, Sterne has made up his two humorists, of whom one, my uncle Toby, must be our special concern, for his very special and revealing time dimension.

* * *

After receiving his wound, which owing to its obvious although uncertain sexual character we may term a trauma, the existence of this active and unimaginative spirit seems to have fallen into a sluggish flow, as of a slowly moving backwater, its proper current having stopped on that fatal day. Another of those modern writers that I find myself so frequently quoting, William Faulkner, has, in *Light in August,* created a near-tragic yet grotesque character, the Reverend Hightower, whose personal time-flow has been stopped, it would seem, before it could have started in his proper person with his individual life, by fantastic inherited memories of the civil war which also amount to a decisive, inhibiting trauma, so that he can only rehearse and repeat indefinitely that ghostly scene, that heroic vision, perhaps of a merely grotesque reality—the ride of his ancestor through the town.

My uncle Toby, in the long monotonous days of his sick bed, has been put suddenly on to the plan of recalling in infinite detail the military events of his own campaigns and service that led to his disablement. The normal life movement which carries a thick past towards the open future to which it is connected by some active project has become altered to a closed world of memories.

That is the first stage of my uncle Toby's diseased time. It becomes a subsidiary element of a second stage characterized by what we may term parodic time. For now Toby has left his own past behind without returning to a present of his own. The succession of his ideas is in abeyance, and has been replaced by the succession of the news brought by the *Gazette.* Inspired by Trim's invention, he follows and repeats, on the absurd mirror of his bowling green, the campaigns, sieges, and conquests of the Allies. Yet, however insignificantly, he goes on living in his own right, I mean in his own body, going through the day's physiological quota of sensations and actions, and his assuming also the large burden of collective history in his own single person makes up a comically double time-dimension. We read that the siege of Dendermond by the Allies went so fast "that they scarce allowed him time to get his dinner" (VI. viii.), or again, we see him, "after passing the French lines, *as he eat his egg at supper,* from *thence* [i.e. both from supper and the French lines] break into the heart of France" (xxxv.). In these two significantly similar instances, time in the head is willfully brought up against what we may term time in the body, or may prefer to term objective reality.

And then suddenly, the widow Wadman appears, and compels my uncle Toby to notice her and finally to fall in love with her; and he rediscovers living time; his time-sense is again activated; the world of memories is again subjected to present awareness and, existentially speaking, to a project looking towards the future. The life rhythm is shown by Sterne as quickened almost to the point of impatience and fretfulness. My uncle Toby can thus be taken as a case-study of the time-sense.

He has been held to be a mask for Sterne's sentiment. Is he not also a light caricature of the artist's way, of Sterne's way, as an artist, of finding substitutes for the reality of life? What I have termed his parodic time could then be seen as clumsy and home-made, but of a type with the artist's re-creation of time. My uncle Toby is a bad or at least an inferior artist, being, if I may risk this anachronism, a photographic imitator or illustrator of time. Sterne's reflecting memory, rearranged in ingenious patterns, takes its own time-substitutes on an altogether higher level.

* * *

There is among these various microcosms a master-mind at work, that of the author, self-built and projected into one of them, that of the narrator. Tristram's head includes all that is to be found in a book truly presented in the title, whatever obtuse or cavilling critics may have said to the contrary, as giving his "life and opinions." He, Tristram, it is, whether we take him as author or narrator, who has the ordering of everything. He is a genial conjurer calling forth whom or what he wants when he wants, and showing a vivid consciousness of his power, a firm intent to make full use of it, to disturb the film of appearances or the dull routine of pseudo-objectivity. He will arrange instead a complicated system or interstructuration, of significant relations which will be found to be, almost entirely, time-relations. He does it most successfully—triumphantly —but rather in the manner of a skillful clown, pretending to be perplexed, tangled even, by the difficulties that he himself has created. He it is who directs the game, and very carefully engineers its turns and hesitations, all hanging round the absurd encounters that we have described above. But if he gives us in full the comedy of broken solitudes, he is no less fascinated by the way in which, in the prevailing separateness, these private worlds have been shaped, organized, developed, each according to its special pattern or system, building up a human memory, which receives a constant influx of "ideas" stored in readiness for future recombination and re-appearance.

Again, at work and prevailing on those several memories, Sterne, or Tristram, is a master-memory. Sterne the artist is aware that there, in this complexus of memories, under this pleasant guise or disguise of plurality, rests his inspiration. His consciousness of this is the source of a new vision, one which is revealed when Sterne writes: "*I have got* entirely out of Auxerre in this journey *which I am writing now,* and I am got half way out of Auxerre in that *which I shall write hereafter.*" And further down, "*I am this moment* walking across the market place of Auxerre with my father and my uncle Toby" (VII. xxviii.).

Let us pay all due attention to this grammar, which we might call the living grammar of literary creation—to these challenging present tenses referring us to the non-present of memory; and to the more challenging blend of past and future in one sentence: the past of the remembered, the future of the unwritten intention, already sketchily present before the creative mind. How clearly this lucid description shifts the burden of reality from the event to the recalling, from the recalling to the telling. The second half of the first sentence—"I am got half way out of Auxerre in that which I shall write hereafter" —invites special analysis because at first sight it appears a meaningless paradox. It means in fact that a memory (or what the writer asks us to take as a memory) related to this further journey has crossed his mind, and temporarily interfered with the other journey. It could have been pushed aside. But it is Sterne's way to welcome mental interference and to make of it all he can.

* * *

We may add that in willful confusion he frequently pretends to believe that the future of the yet untold, that is, the future in his mind, is the objective future of the not yet occurred in reality, which allows him to say in Chapter xxxix of Volume VI that owing to the servants' premature passing on of the news he will be able to enter upon my uncle Toby's amours a fortnight before their existence.

With perhaps a little overmuch eighteenth-century showmanship, a little over-stressing and yet a little summariness, Sterne or his Tristram opens up in the end the world of private time where Lockian ideas have become part of a thick, obscurely organized coexistence, any fragment of which is ready, at the beck and call of very capricious chains of associations, to emerge as memory manifest in the stream of consciousness as we know it. With Sterne we enter at one leap yet somehow decisively the world of memory which was only to become ours by general consent in Romantic times.

Memory is ambiguous: it originates in the past but it is only known in the present. There is no conscious reality that is not present, that is not part of this thick present which the creative imagination may organize and display. Again, this was one of Sterne's new interests: the mind, caught and held in a unit of its living processes, with all its intricate relations and the constant interchange between the inner and the outer world—precisely what Virginia Woolf will define as the moment. The substance of her essay under that title is, potentially, to be found in Sterne.

In this vision, what is real, what counts, is the activity, the movement of the living mind between points, the drama, the vividness of its jumps, the strange states in which we can perceive the fascinating Janus-like alternation of its workings. The inner, subjective world is enclosed, but it is a vast universe, the possession of which, with freedom to range through it, far from inducing claustrophobia, as it will in Samuel Beckett, is exhilarating. There is a joy in the freedom of this inner world, and Sterne's very grammar proclaims it. It puts us in the mood to understand and to accept what is the key to the narrative method in *Tristram Shandy*: that the writer may go backward and forward along the line of his story. These dips, then these returns, from points of memory to the present, are no accident: they give, within the uncertain dimensions of the consciousness, the time-depth and relief required also by Sterne's vision.

* * *

From his vantage points—the present and a human head—Sterne orders and constructs all times and their relations to ensure the utmost intellectual interest. Not until our own day was so much interest to be taken in those relations. Let us take as an instance the invention of ways to suggest simultaneousness. Time must be left at a standstill and then be found again precisely as it was, where it was. So we read: "I think, replied my uncle Toby, taking his pipe from his mouth . . ." (I. xxi.). Two pages further on, we read of my uncle Toby, "whom *all this while* we have left knocking the ashes out of his tobacco pipe"; and lastly, *thirty-three pages later*, we have, "I think, replied my uncle Toby,——taking, *as I told you*, his pipe from his mouth . . ." (II. vi.). There has been, and he wants us conscious of it, a considerable time lapse in *the telling* of the story, in the writing, and it was marked in the middle-reference by "*all this while*." But there has been no corresponding time, no time at all, in the story told. So certain films, like Buñuel's *Angel of Death*, come suddenly to a standstill because time has stopped; we may then hear a comment or shift scene until it starts again.

Thus there has been created by Sterne's ingenuity what we may term a comic suspense. Not until De Quincey's compositions of time in *Murder Considered as One of the Fine Arts*, or *The English Mail Coach*, shall we find anything so precisely and finely engineered.

Moreover, while my uncle Toby's advance in time has thus been stopped, it is obvious that the writer is free to take us anywhere else, to bring before us any other character. The principle of simultaneousness has been established as soon as means have been found to make it manifest: while story-time is not moving on, the people in the story remain available in suspended activity. Sterne has made full and manifold use of the distinction that he has been so careful to establish between his own or his narrator's time and that of the story. It does more than give him this extraordinary freedom to digress, which he rather stresses and exaggerates than conceals. It gives the characters a corresponding freedom to live on while the author chooses to forget about them. The effects can be of something more important in *Tristram Shandy* than simultaneousness, and that is continuity. It is one of the great and fascinating paradoxes of the book that out of a willful discontinuity this continuity is born. The mother-cat gaily lives her own life: the kittens seem forgotten; but she knows that when she comes back to them she will find that they are still there, or in serial terms, are there again, having quietly lived on. Sterne is absolutely conscious of his method, and duly stresses this point, that his story with the characters living in it goes on without him while he is indulging in digression: "I constantly take care to order affairs so, that my main business does not stand still in my absence" (I. xxii.). For playful safety's sake, he can wait till they are steadily employed or asleep before he turns to his Preface. But the point is, once you, the creative writer, that is, the creator of time, have set time going—the separate time of a story—the separate time-dimension of its characters—you cannot stop it, except by your own obtuseness. Existence, if you have believed in it enough, if you trust it, shows in your creatures its well-known tendency to persevere in existing. This is possible, even natural, precisely because what interests Sterne is not the singularity of any action but just such a daily continuity, almost indifferent or undifferentiated, of existence.

In the narrative, continuity through the discontinuous can be seen, for intsance, in a passage which looks at first sight strikingly similar to the one about my uncle Toby and his pipe. It again relates to Toby's slow-witted efforts to communicate. "I wish, quoth my uncle Toby, you had seen what prodigious armies we had in Flanders" (II. xviii.). After eleven pages of quite other matter, " 'I wish, Dr Slop,' quoth my uncle Toby (*repeating his wish* for Dr Slop *a second time*, and with a degree of more zeal and earnestness in his manner of wishing, than he had wished it at first)——'I wish, Dr Slop,' quoth my uncle Toby . . ." (III. i.).

And in the next page, Walter takes up the topic: "What prodigious armies. . . ." Here we see that between the broaching and the resumption of the topic, there has been, however small, a real lapse of story-time, of living time: the characters have lived *on*, be it a few minutes. In such a way, by such means, a continuity has been established. In a remarkable manner, Sterne's world is a world of bodies alive; and they are in touch with objects which also have their strong inanimate continuity. Prostrate on the bed in despair, Walter lets his hand rest on the handle of the chamber-pot, of which he remains vaguely çonscious until he begins to rally and shift his position. Meanwhile my uncle Toby remains seated "in his old fringed chair, valanced around with party-coloured worsted bobs" (IV. vii.; III. xxix.; IV. iii.). Thus carefully defined, thus present before us, the chair remains, to be called up again, later in the same passage: it is an element of the dimension of the moment, which is yet another novelty of the Sternian time-vision.

* * *

Thus the time-sense has appeared dispersed between the creation and the creator. Knowing Sterne, we must be aware, and I stressed it from the first, that the creator is the more, the essentially important. Time as construction, time as play of the mind belongs to the writer. True, time is time and a story is a story. But all of the story-time is his to play with *from the start*; or rather it can be seen as all past from the first—if it is the usual type of a story and relates to a now closed cycle of events. But conversely, in this creator's vision, what of it has not yet been written about partakes of a double aspect: it is both past and future. Hence the challenging phrase, "a cow *broke* in (*to-morrow morning*) to my uncle Toby's fortifications" (III. xxxviii.), wherein at any rate we keep to one definition of time——to external time, if anything can be termed external that has been produced by the writer's imagination. In Volume III, Chapter ii, we had an even bolder statement of the turning of matter into mind, of a length of time into a spread of words: "when the door hastily opening *in the next chapter but one.*" Once again the fantastic language and jarring grammar reveal the true seat, the purely mental reality of time.

Yet I suppose that this freedom, not so much of reality as of unreality, palls. For in the passage of challenging paradox about Auxerre, an end is put to it. I may be invited to mix in my mental cocktail-shaker three Auxerres and one Lyons, but finally a compelling awareness gets hold of me and substitutes for the phantoms and fantasms of memory the truth, the only absolute truth, of the present instant in which the inky pen touches paper—not the remembered or the imagined, but the writer at the writing of it in the Toulouse pavilion, not in a thick present any more, but in an absolute present. "Time: the Present"—the *present*, as Joyce might say—such could be Sterne's prevailing stage-direction.

In the end, time as a thick present is the overall dominant, burdened with all the remembered past and pregnant with all the intended future in the writer's imagination; a present in which, in contrast with the ordinary novelist, Sterne dwells complacently, and which eventually narrows down to the sharp bodily present of the moving hand and the beating heart. His writing, he states early on, is a sort of conversation, not so much between the characters as between the author and the reader in yet another present, the time of their imaginary meeting. Before that there is something touching in his frequent insistence on his physical presence on the day, hour, instant, at which the pen, ink-laden, scratches the paper. His humanity, open and defenseless, is entrusted to ours, now, beyond the absurd grave. We read, "this very day, in which I am now writing this book . . . which is March 9, 1759" (I. xxi.). Then, "this very rainy day, March 26, 1759, and betwixt the hours of nine and ten in the morning." Is it by chance that the last reference of this sort insists so much more on the living person? In Volume IX, Chapter i, we read, "here am I sitting, this 12th day of August, 1766, in a purple jerkin and yellow pair of slippers, without either wig or cap on." There is a strange and disturbing magic in his sitting thus, so clear, for two centuries. Even the past that he writes about is referred to this absolute present: "the door . . . somewhat a-jar——*as it stands just now*" (V. vi.). The determination to maintain in a future present his living dialogue with the reader is everywhere. We need not be surprised if it includes a little philandering, if the ideal reader is a fair lady whom he scolds amicably for not being aware of theological implications: "How could you, Madam, be so inattentive . . . ?" (I. xx.).

* * *

On the outer side the book is a conversation; but on the inner, it is difficult to ignore Sterne's own musical images, which go so well with the musical aspects of his genius. As he says "to write a book is for all the world like humming a song——be but in tune with yourself . . . 'tis no matter how high or how low you take it" (IV, xxv.). Thus, from time used up and, as it were, wasted in chronological sequences of events, we see, separating itself by nature and quality, what we may term pure time, or what Gertrude Stein would have termed time as composition: not external any more but a representation, or, in Stein language again, an arrangement. The finest expression of this is where Sterne begins with the reader's time—"It is about an hour and a half's tolerable good reading since my uncle Toby rung the bell"—then takes in the time of the event under consideration (Obadiah's expedition to fetch Dr Slop), finally the time that the writer's imagination has meanwhile expounded and organized round the figure of my uncle Toby, brought "from Namur, quite across all Flanders, into England," to be "*ill upon my hands near four years,"* then to be set down in Yorkshire, "all which," Sterne ends, bringing together at last in the game of representation the writer's and the reader's time, "all which put together, must have prepared the reader's imagination for the entrance of Dr Slop upon the stage,——as much, at least . . . as a dance, a song, or a concerto *between the acts"* (II. viii.)—an admirable sentence which I have always conjectured must have given Virginia Woolf the title (and more) of her last novel, and which insists on the musical character, the musical rhythms, and tempos, and movements, of literary creation.

* * *

Thus the writer feels himself to be free and master of time—until he sets himself the impossible aim, which was to be pursued by Proust in other ways, of regaining lost time, or, in Sterne's view, of equating and synchronizing primary reality and its representation, life and recollection, living time and writing time. Never was hare more perplexed by the tortoise-race of life, or more willful in his musings by the way, but never was willfulness better grounded on the consciousness that the musings made no difference. While we still hear from chapter to chapter many a triumphant assertion of the writer's freedom, the first hint of concern about the problem of getting the writing abreast of the living is heard as early as Volume I, Chapter xiv: "I have been at it these six weeks, making all the speed I possibly could,——and am not yet born." It is heard again, very similarly, in Chapter xxxviii of Volume III: "I have left my father lying across his bed, and my uncle Toby in his old fringed chair . . . and promised I would go back to them in half an hour, and five and thirty minutes are laps'd already." Playing his usual game, of pretending that imaginary time and his relation to it are real, he professes himself sadly perplexed, having so many things to tell, including the cow's future conduct, all "in five minutes less, than no time at all." The problem, if it were less palpably fanciful, would be merely technical. Sterne, at his happy gambols between his two worlds, does not yet take himself seriously. In Volume IV, Chapter xiii, is to be found the first passage in which the problem is more firmly and simply faced, in which the flippancy seems barely to cover with the appearance of comic despair, his anxiety at the impossibility of bringing finally together in chronological coincidence life as it has been lived and the story of it—because life goes too fast.

> I am this month one whole year older than I was this time twelve-month; and having got . . . almost into the middle of my fourth volume——and no farther than to my first day's life—— 'tis demonstrative that I have three hundred and sixty-four days more life to write just now, than when I first set out; so that

instead of advancing, as a common writer, in my work with what I have been doing at it——on the contrary, I am just thrown so many volumes back. . . .
——I shall never overtake myself. . . .

The game is hopeless, and increasingly so, in a monstrously growing ratio. It is the writer's duty, the mark of his honesty, not to abridge or omit anything that is significant; and nothing is more significant than the insignificant. It may take two chapters to do justice to the talk of Walter and Toby going down the stairs, but justice must be done, and the consequences faced.

Yes, of course, all this is said in a flippant and jesting tone. Can we fail, however, to perceive that the theme is becoming obsessive, and to detect under the surface what I have termed anxiety and might perhaps term anguish? Do we not perceive a change of tempo, almost imperceptible perhaps until we reach Volume VII, and then suddenly overwhelming? Can we ignore the urgency in that first chapter, the all-too-real panting for breath, the frightened heartbeat, and the fascinating adaptation of the language to the condition, the ending of the amused rococo twists and flourishes, the short sentences and the frequent staccato rhythms? "For I have forty volumes to write, and forty thousand things to say and do, which no body in the world will say and do for me. . . ." ("except thyself," he adds for his friend Eugenius, but we need not take *that* seriously). Here again what we have heard is the voice of the passionate individualism that we connect with our own century, the voice of André Gide about "l'individu irremplaçable."[1] So that this unchristian pastor can feel honest despair about the brevity of his life: as "I who must be cut short in the midst of my days . . ." (VII. xiv.).

Synchronizing is hopeless, but as much truth of oneself as possible should be given "*whilst* these few scatter'd spirits *remain*" (VII. i.). The *whilst* and the *remain* show the awareness of time the destroyer to the full. Until Sterne turns again to my uncle Toby, it will not cease. There is a little self-pity in this fourteenth chapter, in this "I who must be cut short in the midst of my days," in the wistful evocation of the times fifty years hence that he will not see; but there is much more human tenderness, much more pity for the general human plight, for the horrible equation in it of time and change, ceaseless, ruthless change and decay. "Aimez ce que jamais on ne verra deux fois,"[2] Vigny the Romantic will say, turning away from nature to woman. And here we have, peeping below the jests, a Romantic Sterne, in the choice at Montreuil of Janatone before the church of St Austreberte, which will be there and the same these

1. "The irreplaceable individual." [*Editor.*]

2. "You love what you'll never see a second time." [*Editor.*]

fifty years to come to be admired or measured—"but he who measures thee, Janatone, but do it now——thou carriest the principles
of change within thy frame" (VII. ix.).

Now this cruel awareness of time as change gets such a hold of
his imagination that in a remarkable manner he adapts himself to its
rhythms so as once more to master it: he turns inevitable change
into the free creation of change by speed. It may be that as long as
the horror of change as a premise of dissolution has been with
mankind, mankind has also known, within its technical means, this
passion for speed, this urge to outrun its own predetermined, ruthless movement onwards and downwards. We forget about the panting and the heartbeat. Death may pursue, but we can race faster;
and again in speed joy is with us. "So much of motion," we read in
Chapter xiii, "is so much of life, and so much of joy . . . to stand
still, or get on *but slowly*, is death and the devil——" (VII. xiii.).

Yet in the midst of this proclaimed elation we may hear the
reality of the flight in the breathless rhythms, in the very system of
dashes: "——No;——I cannot stop a moment to give you the
character of the people——their genius——their manners——their
customs——their laws——their religion——their government——
their manufactures——their commerce——their finances . . ."
(Chapter xix.).

And in Chapter xvii we had "Crack, crack——crack, crack——
crack, crack——so this is Paris." That much repeated noise is
merely the postilion's whip's; yet somehow in this atmosphere of
Volume VII, we hear something like the rattle of bones in Bürger's
Lenore, we feel that this was asking at least for Rowlandson's
illustrations to the *English Dance of Death* and its grim merriment.
We must remember Sterne's own life and condition, and as we
commemorate both his genius and the date of his death, recall his
awareness, at the time that he was writing this book, that it was
impending. His correspondence tells the tale, as in the letter of
1765, written after three hemorrhages: "I find I must once more fly
from death whilst I have strength . . ."[3] Regain lost time when life
is lost—it cannot be done. He knows, and with that newly gained
purity of style, he addresses his "dear Jenny" in unforgettable
terms: "Time wastes too fast: every letter I trace tells me with what
rapidity Life follows my pen; the days and hours of it . . . are flying
over our heads like light clouds of a windy day, never to return
more——every thing presses on——whilst thou art twisting that
lock,——see! it grows grey" (IX. viii.).

Sterne was aware before Beckett of the fantastic nullity of time,
of its compressibility, so total that as Pozzo reminds us in *Waiting*

---

3. Letter to John Wodehouse, Sept. 20,
1765, *The Letters of Laurence Sterne*,
ed. Lewis P. Curtis (Oxford University
Press, 1935), p. 257. [*Editor.*]

for Godot, a life can be said to begin and to end on the same day, the same instant.

* * *

This, then, is my construction of time and the time-sense in *Tristram Shandy.* It may be said against it that it is highly subjective. It would be the less Sternian if it were not. Yes, admittedly, my ideas got up with me and were clad in my clothes. I have, however, attempted to transcend subjectivity by seeking coherence. My system, that is, was meant to take in and to bring together in unified or at least cohesive meaning most if not all relevant facts and points in the book. The resulting view could be said to present the dialectics of freedom and necessity. The first proposition, which could be put almost better in Leibnitzian than in Lockian terms (bating pre-established harmony), is that the human world is made up of microcosmic, enclosed units, of windowless monads, which, forming as they proceed and pursuing a private time-dimension, bump clumsily again and again against each other or the world of objects and circumstances in the process of what is fondly termed communication. This is all haphazard, but Sterne the artist sees his chance in this mischance, instead of ignoring it, as was the custom of his fellow-novelists. Out of the comic absurdities he makes a pattern, he produces a design.

The second essential point is that his perhaps crowning inspiration has been to fling himself into his own stew in the guise of the narrator, Tristram, the like of whom had never been seen, and was not to be seen again until Proust's Marcel. He orders and directs the patterns and his own place in them; he inserts into their already considerable intricacy his own double time-dimension, that of Tristram the man and that of Tristram the artist. While the other microcosmic units were bound by necessity, the artist recaptures freedom through composition: all times, as he finds several occasions to say, belong to him. He takes his stand in the present, wherefrom he juggles triumphantly with all past. The present is his strong anchorage in reality.

The third point is, as it seems to me, that his constant stressing and over-stressing of his freedom covers an anxiety. At any rate, if all time belongs to him, he belongs to time, and he knows it. Volume VII is perhaps a break and perhaps merely a belated admission into the consciousness of the fear that had been there obscurely from the beginning, the fear that time was prevailing against him, irresistibly, and that the recovery of lost time was doomed. All that the artist can do is, like the musician, to *compose* time from this piling waste. If Sterne so frequently brings in musical references, it is because he was knowingly musical; it is also because music is the most perfect, freest triumph over time. But both his imagination and his technique, so modern when not hopelessly rococo, suggest to us striking affinities with that art of our time, perhaps the best endowed with means to manipulate time in all manners and directions, I mean the cinema. Ellipse and montage are here everywhere. We have seen simultaneousness putting in an appearance, continuity asserted. Volume VII, at the end of its anxious tussle with time, has one more, the most vivid, cinematic device. As my tentative fabric is about to dissolve, I cannot do better than recall the most graceful and tenderly wistful "dissolve," or "fade-out-fade-in," of all time. It is found in Tristram's encounter with Nannette:

> Capriciously did she bend her head on one side, and dance up insiduous——Then 'tis time to dance off, quoth I; so changing only partners and tunes, I danced it away from Lunel to Montpellier——from thence to Pescnas, Beziers——I danced it along through Narbonne, Carcasson, and Castle Naudiary, till at last I danced myself into Perdrillo's pavillion . . . (VII. xliii.).

Where we shall leave him to escape from time in the composition of my uncle Toby's amours.

RICHARD A. LANHAM

Games, Play, Seriousness†

"I will draw my uncle *Toby*'s character," Tristram tells us, "from his HOBBY-HORSE" (I. xxiii.). And at times he seems to draw everything else from hobbyhorses, too. The metaphor suffuses the book like one of the controlling images Gilbert Norwood finds in Pindar's odes. The play atmosphere it creates has been widely recognized[1] but description of it has not gone beyond the theory of humors. Since there does exist today a body of knowledge called "game theory," it seems reasonable to ask what light it sheds on the game sphere of *Tristram Shandy*. For the kind of seriousness Sterne's *ludus* offers clearly is the seriousness of the gamesman and the game. A satisfactory mapping of the game sphere might grant us common cause with the Victorians, unite the two ways of looking at the novel, the serious and the frivolous. It might explain what high seriousness means in the case of Sterne, and what pleasure means as well. It might even betray how Sterne really offended the Victorians,

† From Richard A. Lanham, *"Tristram Shandy" and the Games of Pleasure* (Berkeley and Los Angeles: University of California Press, 1973), pp. 37–51. Footnotes are by Lanham unless otherwise noted.

1. John M. Stedmond, for example, treats it as a commonplace: *The Comic Art of Laurence Sterne* (Toronto, 1967), p. 100, n. 12.

prompted the immoderate denunciations of Thackeray and Bagehot.

Game theory is not so coherent a body of knowledge as the literary student might wish. It splits into two quite different groups. First we have game theory, properly speaking, invented by the mathematicians and taken over by the social scientists specializing in conflict-resolution and decision-making.[2] It provides some beguiling metaphors for the literary critic, infinitely expandable yet never so precise as to constrict. But precisely for these reasons, it sometimes only seems to describe, defeats its own purpose. As the mathematicians invented and use it, it provides a consistent body of knowledge. When it is applied to social concerns it becomes tricky, and applied to literature trickier still. Like rhetorical theory, one of its principal contributions to *literary* conflict is in rendering us self-conscious about it. Standing near this internally consistent body of theorizing we have a second group which is anything but.[3] One

2. Probability theory deals with games of chance. Mathematical game theory deals with games of strategy. Games of strategy are games where the player must decide what to do rather than let chance decide for him. So we have the definition: "Game theory is a method for the study of decision making in situations of conflict." (Martin Shubik, *Game Theory and Related Approaches to Social Behavior* [New York, 1964], p. 8.) But it works in a carefully defined, very narrow sphere. I have neither space nor competence here to explain game theory even in its simplest outlines. (See, as a beginning, Anatol Rapoport's *Two-Person Game Theory: The Essential Ideas* [Ann Arbor, 1966], and his *Fights, Games, and Debates* [Ann Arbor, 1960].) We must simply state that it tries to provide mathematical models for *rational* conflict. It *assumes* perfectly rational players and, as a cardinal principle, that all players are the same (Rapoport, *Two-Person Game Theory*, p. 126). Every game must have players, payoff, rules. It has six essential features: (1) At least two players; (2) One player begins by moving, this leading to a new situation; (3) New situation determines who moves next and what he can do; (4) Other player's choice is either known or not; if known, the game is one of "perfect information"; (5) There is a termination of the game role; (6) Each player must get a payoff. There are two-person games. There are n-person (more than two-person) games. The second kind is obviously more complex than the first. A zero-sum game is one in which the interests of the two players vary inversely. A non-zero-sum game is one in which the interests of the two or more players may at least partially coincide. Mathematical games exist in two forms, an extensive form (written out rules), and a matrix form (charted on a matrix, a mathematical diagram). To be reducible to a matrix and hence to fit into game theory, a game must be very simple. Most of what the layman would call games are far too complicated for treatment by game theory. Special games, in fact, are usually invented for it, the most complicated being the simple kind of dilemma most of us had in our elementary logic class at school. With conflict as it occurs either in ordinary life or in imaginative literature, it cannot deal at all, "because there is no room in that theory for the psychological make up of the participants." (Rapoport, *Two-Person Game Theory*, p. 206.)

3. Perhaps the relation between the two may be clarified by this discussion of the limits of mathematical game theory: "The lesson to be derived [from modern game-theory] is that many of our cherished notions about every problem having an 'answer,' about the existence of a 'best' choice among a set of courses of action, about the power of rational analysis itself, must be relegated to the growing collection of shattered illusions. Rational analysis, for all its inadequacy, is indeed the best instrument of cognition we have. But it often is at its best when it reveals to us the nature of the situation we find ourselves in, even though it may have nothing to tell us about how we ought to behave in this situation. Too much depends on our choice of values, criteria, notions of what is 'rational,' and, last but by no means least, the sort of relationship and communication we establish with the other parties of the 'game.' These choices have nothing to do with the particular game we are playing. They are not *strategic* choices, i.e., choices rationalized in terms of advantages they

hardly knows what to call it. Anthropologists had cataloged games before *Homo Ludens* but Huizinga's great books seemed to put minds in several disciplines to work in a new way. Jean Piaget had been philosophizing about the role of game but in the relatively narrow arena of child psychology. (See most importantly, *Play, Dreams and Imitation in Childhood.*) Huizinga made the concept as wide as human culture. As a result, we have an important book by Roger Caillois,[4] the more philosophic side of Anatol Rapoport's work (in the volumes cited in n. 2), and recently some literary studies.[5] And, finally, the concept of game has been made into the center of an existential view of the universe.[6]

Definitions of play by the nonmathematical theorists are apt to be broad and blurry. *Homo Ludens* offers this one:

> Play is a voluntary activity or occupation executed within certain fixed limits of time and place, according to rules freely accepted but absolutely binding, having its aim in itself and accompanied by a feeling of tension, joy and the consciousness that it is "different" from "ordinary life." Thus defined, the concept seemed capable of embracing everything we call "play" in animals, children and grown-ups: games of strength and skill, inventing games, guessing games, games of chance, exhibitions and performances of all kinds.[7]

But how little this excludes! Anything fits. Even so, how nicely the concept of play fits the unbreachable chasm between Sterne the philosopher and Sterne the jester. The game is utterly frivolous to those without, utterly binding on those within. In itself, it combines the most serious concerns and the least. It manages to be both at the same time.

Caillois gives us a definition of play more immediately germane. Play has six characteristics. It is:

1. free
2. separate
3. uncertain
4. unproductive

---

bestow on us in a particular conflict. Rather they are choices which we make because of the way we view ourselves, and the world, including the other players. The great philosophical value of game theory is in its power to reveal its own incompleteness. Game theoretical analysis, if pursued to its completion, *perforce* leads us to consider other than strategic modes of thought." (*Ibid.*, p. 214.)

4. Roger Caillois, *Man, Play and Games*, trans. Meyer Barash (Glencoe, Ill., 1961).

5. See, for example, vol. 41 of *Yale French Studies*, and a challenging book by Michel Beaujour, *Le Jeu de Rabelais* (Editions de l'Herne, n.p., n.d.).

6. See, for example, two books of oracular—and opaque—wisdom by Kostas Axelos, *Vers la Pensée Planétaire* (Paris, 1964), and *Le Jeu du Monde* (Paris, 1969).

7. J. Huizinga, *Homo Ludens* (Boston, 1955), p. 28.

5. governed by rules
6. make-believe[8]

The internal conflicts, the seeming inconsistencies, in a definition like this parallel those in *Tristram Shandy*: the combination of freedom and governance; unproductivity and high emotional yield; uncertainty and the predictability rules supply; separateness yet the constant need for an audience.

The seeming inconsistencies have not gone unchallenged. R. Ehrmann, in a carefully reasoned reappraisal of Huizinga and Caillois, attacks both for conceiving play in cultural isolation.

> Their formulation of the problem of play makes no allowance for the problem of understanding culture. Culture, *their* idea of culture, is at no time called into question by play. On the contrary, it is *given*: a fixed, stable, pre-existent element, serving as a frame of reference in the evaluation of play. . . . In other words, in an anthropology of play, play cannot be defined by isolating it on the basis of its relationship to an *a priori* reality and culture. To define play is *at the same time* and *in the same movement* to define reality and to define culture.[9]

Ehrmann stresses the social use of play, sees the play-work antithesis as a product of industrialism. The separation of play and culture once denied, it easily follows that "the distinguishing characteristic of reality is that it is played. Play, reality, culture are synonymous and interchangeable. . . . All of our critical methods must be reconsidered according to these new norms." Under such an extension art becomes simply another kind of play.[1] Such amplification of the game concept destroys its usefulness. Why not call it culture and be done with it? The difference between the two spheres Ehrmann never admits: games are played self-consciously, culture is not. The more self-conscious we are about the restraints of culture, its rules, the more like a game it seems, of course, and the more game can function as absurdist model for culture. But even in advanced existential circles the two stay a long way apart. Culture has, in the long run, its goals determined for it by time and circumstance. Play exists for its own sake. It may, of course, serve a long-range cultural function, but it does so in virtue of serving an arbitrary short-range one decided on by itself. "The time has come," the editor of the *Yale French Studies* volume noted earlier announces, "to treat play

---

8. Caillois, *Man, Play, and Games*, pp. 9–10. A less full definition, offered in a paper by John M. Roberts, Malcolm J. Arth, and Robert R. Bush, "Games and Culture" (*American Anthropologist*, n.s. 61 [1959], 597–605) lists four criteria; (1) competition; (2) two or more sides; (3) criteria for choosing a winner; (4) agreed-on rules.

9. R. Ehrmann, "*Homo Ludens* Revisited," in *Yale French Studies*, 41 (1968), 55.

1. So Beaujour argues in "The Game of Poetics" in the same volume of *Yale French Studies*. "I posit that poetry is a *game*, or like a game," p. 58.

seriously." But if we do so by extending it to equal culture as a whole, we distort its fundamental nature. We may synthesize thereby an agreeable existential view of the world, but we destroy play as a useful descriptive concept.

Precisely the same kind of pressure is being applied to *Tristram Shandy*. Sterne offers a series of games. The Victorians dismiss them as child's play. We insist on taking them seriously; they adumbrate a whole philosophy. The games, first reduced to triviality, are then inflated out of existence. Our problem with *Tristram Shandy*, as with game, is to preserve the middle ground. Huizinga himself, in an essay written several years before *Homo Ludens* appeared, had insisted precisely on this point, both confuting and condemning the wider philosophical view of play:

> The most fundamental characteristic of true play, whether it be a cult, a performance, a contest, or a festivity, is that at a certain moment it is *over*. The spectators go home, the players take off their masks, the performance has ended. And here the evil of our time shows itself. For nowadays play in many cases never ends and hence is not true play. A far-reaching contamination of play and serious activity has taken place. The two spheres are getting mixed. In the activities of an outwardly serious nature hides an element of play. Recognised play, on the other hand, is no longer able to maintain its true play-character as a result of being taken too seriously and being technically over-organised. The indispensable qualities of detachment, artlessness and gladness are thus lost.[2]

Play, that is, preserves its importance by *not* being serious. To take it as model, as world view, denies its nature. Its peculiar fund of seriousness demands that it not be taken seriously. Perhaps Émile Benveniste has made this point best. "Immense c'est le domaine du jeu." Yet this wide scope is not coterminous with all culture: "le jeu est de plus en plus nettement spécifié comme distinct de la réalité, comme non serieux."[3]

Mathematical game theory spans a narrow range very precisely and hypothesizes rational players. The philosophers of play cover a very wide spectrum and hypothesize irrational players, moving from there in great leaps to a universe of the existential absurd. What *Tristram Shandy* requires is a theory between these two, one that allows some of the mathematicians' schematic clarity but does not depend on their—for our purposes crippling—premise of rational players. We have, of course, already discussed just such a one— rhetorical theory.

2. Huizinga, *In the Shadow of Tomorrow* (New York, 1964 [1936]), p. 177.
3. Emile Beneveniste, "Le Jeu comme structure," *Deucalion*, no. 2 (1947), pp. 161–167. [The first French sentence may be translated: "The domain of play is immense"; the second may be translated: "Play is more and more clearly specified as distinct from reality, as not serious."—*Editor.*]

It is interesting to pair rhetorical theory for a moment with game theory as we have just described it. Both are theories of conflict-analysis and conflict-resolution. Both try to reduce conflict to pattern, defuse it by stylizing it. Both, that is, try to isolate the self-pleasing ingredient in conflict, magnify it, above all make the contending parties aware of it. Both move from persuasion to "pure persuasion." They move from aggression to pleasure, from other to self. They do so by formalizing and distancing conflict. Both move, then, toward a literary definition of reality, toward comedy. Rhetorical *topoi*[4] can, like game "strategies," be categorized. The cocktail-party games that people play, as Eric Berne sees them,[5] are really two- or three-move games from Aristotle's *Topics*. Both are founded on power; both aim to govern the decision-making process. Duncan Black talks of moving from game theory to economic theory to a theory of committee decisions, getting at the same time "sufficient means to construct a Theory of Politics."[6] And J. von Neumann and O. Morgenstern, in the classic *Theory of Games and Economic Behavior*: "Our problem is not to determine what ought to happen in pursuance of any set of—necessarily arbitrary—principles, but to investigate where the equilibrium of forces lies."[7] So Isocrates argued against Plato for a political science based on power. Both kinds of theory avoid spontaneous decisions, foresee a strategy for every situation. Rhetorical theory aims to provide strategies for the irrational player against the irrational player, for people as they are. Game theory, restricted to the rational player, can afford much more formal coherence. Both predict the future. (Someone who knows only his own strategy will know the *outcome* but not the *course* of the game. Someone who knows both strategies, however, should be able to predict the course of the game as well.[8] So the theorists at RAND chronicle a future war to avoid it, much as Thucydides chronicled a past one. And their relation to teaching lessons for the future is precisely *Tristram Shandy*'s relation to theme. They must remain wholly within the game to teach a lesson to the world outside it. *Tristram Shandy* must abjure thematic statement in order to preserve its theme.) Both equate motive with self-interest.

One is a verbal theory, one nonverbal. To see *Tristram Shandy* in terms of both may work because Sterne both sees words as absolute limit in *Tristram Shandy* and at the same time tries to see beyond

4. "Literary conventions." [*Editor.*]
5. Eric Berne, *Games People Play* (New York, 1964).
6. Duncan Black, "The Unity of Political and Economic Science," *The Economic Journal*, LX (September 1950), 506–14, reprinted Shubik, *Game Theory*, pp. 110 ff.
7. J. von Neumann and O. Morgenstern, *Theory of Games and Economic Behavior* (Princeton, 1947), p. 43.
8. Rapoport, *Two-Person Game Theory*, p. 45.

them. He tries to see beyond them by ironically juxtaposing the various verbal models of the classical rhetorical tradition: the characters of Toby and Walter; the various genres we have seen; the *topoi*; the styles. Thus from the *disjecta membra*[9] of classical narrative he builds a very modern series of games. By using both kinds of theory—and seeing their fundamental similarities—we can, in a reasonably precise way, surprise Sterne "making it new." We can see, in the narrative tradition in which he chose to write, *Tristram Shandy*'s essential *agon* or game, the struggle of the rhetorical and the philosophical views of man for dominance. We can see Sterne's persistent attempts to move games, the games of philosophy, rhetoric and war, from zero-sum to non-zero-sum (see n. 2). We can see him insisting that philosophical seriousness become rhetorical play.

How does he do so? Rapoport develops a threefold distinction in *Fights, Games and Debates*. "Fight," "game," and "debate" signal for him the three models of conflict. In a fight you try to eliminate your opponent. In a game you reach an accommodation with him— he must be preserved so that the game can continue. Debate offers you a chance to triumph over your opponent's mind, to combine with him, make him of your mind. The end here is not annihilation but absorption. In these terms, Tristram never fights. Dr. Slop must stay on the scene to be pilloried. The tolerance of *Tristram Shandy*, the geniality of the satire, deprecates fights. The novel comes closest to condemnation, as with the Roman Catholic satire surrounding Slop and his curse, when it represents people who fight rather than play, people, as it seemed to Sterne, of the Roman persuasion. The distinction between game and debate bears more centrally on our purpose. For those who seek—or deny—in *Tristram Shandy* a high seriousness, presume the novel a *debate*, Sterne working us finally toward his persuasion. Practically no one has considered the novel as a *game* in Rapoport's sense of the word, a continuing contest with, by its nature, only intermediate results.[1] We hear a great deal about the novel as process, but that this implies a new conception of thematic yield seems unconsidered. Yet the satire against learning, the inability of anyone in the novel to convince anyone else of anything, ought to prove something of Sterne's feelings about debates. He seems to have shied away as strongly as he did from fights. His locus lay in game, in the kind of contest offering no final result. The game is over only to begin again. "I shall write," he

9. "Scraps." [*Editor.*]
1. As close as anyone has come seems to me Jean Baptiste Suard's review of vols. 7 and 8 (quoted in Alan B. Howes, *Yor-ick and the Critics: Sterne's Reputation in England, 1760–1866* [New Haven, 1958], p. 18). He calls the novel "a riddle without an object."

promises us, "as long as I live."[2] Perhaps this was also what he means when he specified his range as "the laughing part of the world."[3] And when, in his discussion of Sterne, Coleridge tells us that "the laughable is its own end" perhaps he too points to Sterne's contentment with difference, with facing forever an opponent, or a reader, who might not share his mind. *Tristram Shandy*, then, resists the pressures exerted on it from either side of the game sphere. Conflict was not to become physically real (fight), or intellectually so (debate), but to remain in the center.

The best chart for this center I have found is Caillois's four types of games:

1. *agon* (games of competition).
2. *alea* (games of chance).
3. *mimicry* (games of simulation, impersonation).
4. *ilinx* (games involving loss of balance, the sensation of vertigo —drugs, for example, or a ride on a roller coaster).[4]

Surely these are controlling kinds of game in *Tristram Shandy*. Walter contends, Toby simulates a war, Yorick delivers himself to chance, Tristram, as he tells us over and over, makes us and himself giddy. The game of giddiness seems especially suggestive for Tristram, perpetually interrupting himself and yet preserving his balance; juggling his sources, yet letting us see them *as sources,* so we can appreciate the juggling; disturbing our sense of time by dragging us forward and backward in it; saying one thing to hold our attention while doing another;[5] moving us with a dislocating wrench from one style or one genre to another. ("A ride on a sort of intellectual switchback," Saintsbury calls it.) If we wished to move to biography, we might refer to the *whirl* of London and the *whirl* of Paris, as his social triumphs are described in the *Letters*; or to his continual awareness of the *motions* of his own body, of his blood flowing, his heart beating; or to his unequaled capacity to render the motion of travel, either in the *Letters, Tristram Shandy,* or the *Journey.* Always we feel the attack on our sense of gravity.

The other categories seem hardly less apt. "Agon," Caillois writes, "is a vindication of personal responsibility; *alea* is a negation of the will, a surrender to destiny."[6] Walter's struggles—what do they symbolize but the responsible personality, accountability? And Yorick's collaboration with chance in the incident of the chestnut? The

2. Laurence Sterne, *Letters of Laurence Sterne,* ed. Lewis P. Curtis (Oxford, 1935), p. 143.
3. *Ibid.,* p. 189.
4. Caillois, *Man, Play, and Games,* pp. 14 ff.
5. "Shandeism is often like a successful conjurer's trick, diverting the attention of the audience from the important part of the transaction." (W. B. C. Watkins, *Perilous Balance* [Princeton, 1939] p. 110.)
6. Caillois, *Man, Play, and Games,* p. 18.

omnipresence of chance makes the whole novel seem a kind of *alea*. Less often discussed than the role of chance in *Tristram Shandy* is the almost pastoral democracy of all those who live under its sway. Time and change do indeed happen to them all, but the conditions of play work precisely against the inequalities of fate. "*Agon* and *alea* imply opposite and somewhat complementary attitudes, but they both obey the same law—the creation for the players of conditions of pure equality denied them in real life."[7] Play both reinforces the force of chance in the novel and supplies a counterforce to it.

It may, then, be possible to view the famous hobbyhorses of *Tristram Shandy* a little more precisely than heretofore, even to chart their race. The larger implications already emerge. *Tristram Shandy* has been called a provincial epic.[8] But if it is a collection of overlapping, sometimes conflicting games or hobbies (Walter's, Toby's, Tristram's, Yorick's, Sterne's, Ours) it grows both narrower and more generalized, less localized,[9] becomes the epic of the private life. The game or hobby then becomes the symbol for the private life, and the elements in the novel which challenge and interfere with the games become, inevitably, symbolic of the public life, of duty rather than pleasure. Often comment on the hobbyhorse goes astray just here. Joan Hall remarks that "commitment in the Shandy world is by hobbyhorse."[1] But surely this is the opposite of commitment as we usually use the word. Hobby represents commitment to self, commitment, finally, to pleasure. This point could hardly be more important. If *Tristram Shandy* represents the world *sub specie ludi*, then we can expect to find a world whose pursuit is pleasure. This was, for Sterne, the essential attribute of the private life. Although Tristram asks us continually to reflect on the deal of philosophy beneath his facade of frivolity, when we try, we confront a maze of overlapping games that are nothing but surface, nothing but pleasure. Continually invited to seek the key to the novel, we are continually prevented by the horrid democracy of game. All the games are equal. We can find no *pied à terre*, no fixed point of view. The modern consensus chooses sentiment as the thread out of the maze. But as Norman Holland has pointed out, "Sterne treats sentiment just as he treats every other hobby-horse."[2] Sentiment occurs in the ironic context of the whole novel, sentiment indeed, feeling not in excess of the object but for the pleasure of feeling. Feeling, having the right feelings at the right time, becomes

7. *Ibid.*, p. 19.
8. First by H. Glaesner, "Laurence Sterne," in the *TLS* (1927), pp. 361–362, then two years later by Herbert Read in *The Sense of Glory* (Cambridge, 1929).
9. Sterne writes to Dodsley, "All locality is taken out of the book" (*Letters*, p. 81).
1. Joan Joffe Hall, "The Hobbyhorsical World of *Tristram Shandy*," *MLQ*, XXIV (1963), 132.
2. Norman O. Holland, "The Laughter of Laurence Sterne," *Hudson Review*, IX (1956), 430.

as much a game as anything else. Far from connecting man to man, it seems to act the other way, to render man content with the pleasures of his own feelings.

One critic has seen the disparity between theory and practice as central to the novel.[3] The games are in one way all theory and in another all practice. But they are not, precisely not, concerned with the clash between the two. Games stay self-contained, almost auto-erotic. They meld theory and practice. The conflict, if there is one in *Tristram Shandy*, must come between the world of individual games and an overall game sense. The crucial question remains whether this point of view exists and, if so, where? In Tristram? Sterne? Us? The search for the central point of view becomes at the last the search for seriousness. To the extent that it can be found, the novel will have a theme (and possibly a structure) in the conventional sense. The theme Tristram announces as his central one, some of the time at least, is motivation. But finding the answer in the game sense, in the private life, casts us out once again onto the opaque surface of the novel, the surface of overlapping games. Motive becomes pleasure and high seriousness is denied us once again. We are thrown back into the lap of comedy.

What kind of morality is possible in such a world? Tristram's genial tolerance seems to be as far as we can go.

> —*De gustibus non est disputandum;*—that is, there is no disputing against HOBBY-HORSES; and, for my part, I seldom do; nor could I with any sort of grace, had I been an enemy to them at the bottom. [I. viii.]

Play may sublimate aggression and release sympathy but the sympathy extends only as far as letting the other fellow play in peace. In this orchestration, the moral sense consists only in becoming aware of the role of hobbies and in the willingness to let each have his own. Some literary implications might be spelled out. Humor becomes preoccupation with a single game and Wit the ability to move with ease and tolerance from one game to another, picking up the rules of one as you let go the rules of the other. But the moral implication goes no further than we have indicated. Once the world has been subdivided into games, there is no center remaining. The logic of *Tristram Shandy* as a fictional form may go further toward solipsism than Sterne, as man or clergyman, would have gone.[4] But the logic stays there. *Really* imbued with the spirit of game

3. Robert A. Donovan, *The Shaping Vision: Imagination in the English Novel from Defoe to Dickens* (Ithaca, N.Y., 1966), p. 95.
4. Perhaps, as Reid says, "his seriousness was greater than he realized himself!" ("The Sad Hilarity of Sterne," *Virginia Quarterly Review,* XXXII [1956], 119).

(Huizinga says, after all, that the eighteenth century was the great age of play), Sterne differs from us in his stance toward reduction of the world to the private life only. Whereas the modern critic almost instinctively feels the pain of solipsism, of the really private life, Sterne sees its joy, its infinite possibilities for eccentricity. The world of a rigorous individuality his novel creates reduces a modern critic to philosophical despair. Sterne rejoices.

Perhaps we can now see the Victorians' distaste as akin to this modern despair. "Play, love, war, work," writes Kenneth Burke, "these are the names for the ways in which a man is engrossed. The putting of them all together, the 'allocating' of them, is 'religion,' leading to some manner of transcendence or other."[5] *Tristram Shandy* collapses the last three into the first, reduces them all to play, so preventing any transcendence except through it. Perhaps this is what Bagehot really meant when he called Sterne pagan. Allowing no direct access to the other elements of which a transcendence might be composed, he seems to deny seriousness at the source. Arnold observed a parallel configuration in Chaucer's poetry and so denied him a place among the highly serious immortals.[6] And Chaucer and Sterne have in this respect been compared: "Sterne in his human comedy is perhaps closer to the mood and spirit of Chaucer, who is almost always indulgent and tolerant of human frailty. . . . Chaucer, too, cannot bear remaining overserious for long."[7] The Victorians felt threatened not in their prudishness but in their sense of reality. Inasmuch as they saw him preoccupied by the idea of game, Sterne must have seemed blasphemous. Perhaps this response stands behind the long and widespread disquietude that the author of *Tristram Shandy* was a clergyman. Perhaps, too, the Victorians saw in the exhibitionism of *Tristram Shandy* (and of Sterne) a further disquieting instance of the play impulse. Sterne seemed almost to embody the spirit of display, display for its own sake, as a game. Rolling all this conjecture up into a ball, might we say that the Victorians saw what we have not, that Sterne's novel was an attack on seriousness itself, ours as well as every other kind? More than we do, they may have seen what they most disliked, unashamed addiction to the pleasure principle. If so, they were threatened more fundamentally still. *Tristram Shandy*'s elaborate game with games finally yields a conception of human identity anathema to them. For Sterne, we finally become not only insatiable pleasure-seekers but, by our nature, incurable poseurs. Such a threat to the self, looming behind the condemnation of Sterne's posing, must have seemed gravest of all.

5. Kenneth Burke, *Attitudes Toward History* (rev. ed., Boston, 1961), p. 92.
6. See Richard A. Lanham, "Games, Play, and High Seriousness in Chaucer's Poetry," *English Studies*, vol. XLVIII (1967).
7. Watkins, *Perilous Balance*, p. 129.

SIGURD BURCKHARDT

Tristram Shandy's Law of Gravity†

To look for the "law" of *Tristram Shandy* is one of the least promising enterprises in criticism. Those who have felt compelled to explain the novel's structure have usually taken refuge in the "association of ideas," a portentous term for idiosyncratic wilfulness, which, even though it can claim Locke for its father, leaves the novel an esthetic chaos. The Lockean doctrines of time yield some structural elements; but time is, at best, but one dimension, not enough to build a structure with. Rhetorical analysis may give us insight into Sterne's comic strategies, but hardly the law by which the Shandean world moves. The very point of *Tristram Shandy* seems to be that it defies all laws, that it gives unlimited scope to its author's heteroclite wit and arbitrary playfulness, that it exhibits a mind never at a loss and as sovereignly irresponsible as Haroun al Rashid.[1] Any attempt to formulate the principles it "obeys" appears from the start condemned to distortion and failure.

If this is so, to propose gravity as the law of the novel is not merely futile but perverse. Gravity, we are told almost at the outset, is "a mysterious carriage of the body to cover defects of the mind"; it is the target of Yorick's enmity and Tristram's nose-thumbing; of all imaginable laws it seems the one most obviously flouted by this lighter-than-air indirigible. But the attempt has at least one thing to be said for it: it is perverse enough to do justice to so perverse a book. And it may have another advantage: it restores to the word "gravity" the physical weight and concreteness which we too readily vaporise into the evanescence of an idea. The axiom of the following interpretation is the simple one that we must read Sterne far more literally—i.e., corporeally—than has commonly been done; we are sure to miss his meaning if we smile too quickly at his "irony." Sterne had learned from Swift; as the last irony of *A Modest Proposal* is that it is *not* ironic, that—society being what it is—Swift's ghastly humanitarianism is genuine and an ironic reading merely an evasion of his cruelly literal point, so Sterne's final joke is again and again that he is not joking. Properly read, he forbids us to take the easy way out of literalness into a knowing smile.

† From *ELH*, 28 (1961), 70–88.
1. Caliph of Bagdad, who figures in many tales of the *Arabian Nights*. [*Editor.*]

It is a terrible misfortune for this same book of mine, but more so for the Republic of Letters, so that my own is quite swallowed up in the consideration of it,—that this self-same vile pruriency for fresh adventures in all things, has got so strongly into our habit and humours,—and so wholly intent are we upon satisfying the impatience of our concupiscence that way,—that nothing but the gross and more carnal parts of a composition will go down:— The subtle hints and sly communications of science fly off, like spirits upwards;—the heavy moral escapes downwards; and both the one and the other are as much lost to the world, as if they were still left in the bottom of the ink-horn. (I. xx.)

Oh, we are clever fellows and men of the world; trust us to catch the author's wink and to return it. You won't find *us* thinking he means moral and science when he says "moral" and "science," or nose when he writes "nose," no matter how much he protests his serious intentions and the purity of his mind. So we read on, and as we stand with the expectant crowd before the gates of Strasburg, waiting for the return of the nose to an unmistakably bawdy denouement, our smile, spontaneous and genuine enough at first, turns sillier and sillier, until at last we discover (or do we?) that our gross carnality has led us by *our* noses. If Sterne, like Swift, is something less than humane, it is because he gives so much scope to our vile pruriency. He does, evidently, enjoy watching us making fools of ourselves; he is not above being sardonic. But he can justly claim that he is no more responsible for our foolishness than Yorick was for the hot chestnut's dropping, in simple obedience to the law of gravity, into Phutatorius' breeches. If we have sense enough to feel not merely the first "genial warmth" of his book, but gradually the heat and sting of it—and if then, unlike Phutatorius, we have wit enough not to blame Sterne as the malicious perpetrator, but to seek the true cause in the constitution of things—we will be entitled to share Yorick's contempt for Phutatorius' kind of wordly wisdom.

No sooner do we assume that *Tristram Shandy* is not perverse than its "carriage" becomes "mysterious" in the extreme. It is shot through with admonitions that it must be read curiously and minutely, that its message is not for the vulgar, that the tradition to which it belongs is the esoteric one. We can discount all these, and reading will be a bawdy gambol, interrupted here and there by a sentimental journey. But we can also attend to them and probe for the mystery of the very corporeal gravity which orders Sterne's strange universe. There is substance in *Tristram Shandy*, body— and we will not understand its wit unless we let it show us how it out-wits gravity by a far from ordinary obedience.

I

A messy fatality attends the falling bodies of the novel, the things that stupidly plummet: they always land on the genitals. Rocks, sash windows, chestnuts do far more damage than bullets. The rock launches Uncle Toby on his hobby-horsical career, which finally, and by a causality that will need inquiring into, brings him to Widow Wadman, disillusionment and permanent bachelorhood. By intermediate steps it also begets the fall of the sash window and Tristram's mutilation. The chestnut's fall, caused by the attempt to have Tristram's name changed, proves the undoing of poor Yorick. But it is the first fall, in Sterne as in the Bible, that demands our particular attention.

Uncle Toby, trying to recover from his wound, finds himself getting worse rather than better, because the effort to render an account of his mishap to kindly visitors proves impossibly confusing and frustrating. " 'Twas not by ideas,—by heaven! his life was put in jeopardy by words." The obvious remedy is so to devise matters as to make words superfluous; and this is what Uncle Toby does and what determines his future course. Necessity drives him to invention and invention into creativity; he hits upon the happy solution of providing himself with a map of Namur, so that henceforth, instead of talking, he can simply point with his finger and say "there!" So inspired, he creates about him a little world of things, which duly restores him to health and happiness.

It would be pleasant to continue the tale, but we are already deep in the mystery. For a long time it was a critical commonplace, now happily being abandoned, that *Tristram Shandy* was meant to be a comic illustration of Locke's doctrine of association and his criticism of language. But there can be no doubt that Sterne's frequent references to Locke, though always deferential, are in good part ironic; while he shares the philosopher's skepticism, he is far from sharing his certitudes. This is nowhere more evident than in the explicitly Lockean account of "the causes of obscurity and confusion in the mind of man." Sterne uses the homely simile of Dolly's sealing a love letter to her Robin; the only ideas needed for our comprehending the theory are those of sealing wax and thimble, and ideas can hardly be more simple and determinate than that. Locke's conditions for clarity and truth are meticulously fulfilled; the only trouble is that, in being transmitted, even these simple ideas lose their simplicity. By the time they strike our "sensorium" they have ceased to be virginal and turned bawdy. Sterne demonstrates, not the Lockean doctrine, but the naiveté of the faith on which it rests. Locke wanted to purify language and disentangle thought by making words conformable to simple ideas; Sterne shows that in any sense that is communicable—which is to say, in any *sense* at all—*ideas do not exist*; only words exist.

And words, unlike ideas, have body; that is the price we have to pay for their being communicable. Having body, they are subject to gravity, so that nothing is surer to make a man miss his target than the philosopher's notion that the only requirement is to aim straight. Sterne's sexual innuendo is an almost continuous demonstration that words in flight will curve downwards and hit the hearer's con-cupiscence instead of his reason. Concreteness and simplicity are no remedy, nor is the philosophers' other panacea against confusion: definition. For one thing, "to define,—is to distrust," and who has ever become more trustworthy for being distrusted? Moreover, for-mal definition merely adds two terms to the confusing first one, so that, instead of a bullet, one fires shrapnel. The only "pure" defini-tion is that which Tristram offers of the word "nose":

> I define a nose, as follows,—intreating only beforehand, and be-seeching my readers . . . to guard against the temptations and suggestions of the devil, and suffer him by no art or wile to put any other ideas into their minds, than what I put into my defi-nition.—For by the word *Nose*, throughout all this long chapter of noses, and in every other part of my work, where the word *Nose* occurs,—I declare, by that word I mean a Nose, and nothing more, or less. (III. xxxi.)

A nose is a nose is a nose; this is pure because it is pure tautology, mere noise, or would be if it did not awaken our suspicion by its protest of innocence. Since words are bodies, no disclaimers will reclaim them; they only make the wound nastier.

Uncle Toby, then, in reverting to the mute and unequivocal lan-guage of things and the vocable "there," is already two hundred years ahead of Locke; he builds upon the solid ground of the bowling green and confines himself to Bertrand Russell's minimum indefinable. But Sterne is ahead of Russell; Toby's later misfortune reveals the hubris of using even this most unassuming of words. In the end, "there" is no more exempt from the Fall than the proudest abstraction. The inveteracy of Mrs. Wadman's inquiries after the wound, which causes Uncle Toby to believe her tender above the common humanity of a Bridget, stems in truth from his innocent failure to understand her first periphrastic and finally "categorical" question: "Where?" "You shall see the very place," he answers at last—and sends Trim for the map of Namur. He has immersed himself so totally in his creation that words have no reference for him outside it; he lives in a metaphor so embracing and tangible that he is no longer able to see it as a metaphor. From his *hamartia*,

his wound, and its life-endangering consequences he escaped into
the innocence of things; but this innocence, though his glory, proves
his nemesis. His one moment of pride is his undoing; faithful Trim
(another Tiresias), stung by his master's deluded exaltation of Mrs.
Wadman, tells him the truth and shatters his faith in female purity.
The veil of illusion falls, and with it the curtain on the novel as a
whole; peripety and anagnoresis bring *Tristram Shandy* to a fitting
close.

I have stressed the tragic structure of Uncle Toby's amours
(Sterne calls them the "the sub-plot in the epitasis" of his drama),
because this is the only properly structured and rounded plot we
get. Being that, it offers itself as a parable, in which the mystery of
the whole assumes, for those who have eyes to see and ears to hear,
palpable form. Uncle Toby's bowling green is the parabolic equivalent of Tristram's story of his life. Wounded in more ways than
one—begotten in distraction, delivered by extraction, christened by
and reared to mutilation—the pitiful hero tries, like his uncle, to
render an account of his sufferings. But though his *Life* is quite as
much jeopardised by words as Toby's, the escape into the healing
innocence of things is forbidden him; he is tied to language. Here is
the difference between the parable and the message: Tristram must
do in words what the old soldier does in things. The esoteric mystery, as in Scripture but literally, is the Word; and the parable is not
merely one of many, but the Parable quintessentially, the attempt to
render the paradox of the Word sensible. As the end of the story
shows, Sterne knows of the final impossibility of the attempt: the
parable itself must be told in words and thus falls into the very
contradiction which it is designed to circumvent.

What contradiction? Uncle Toby is an artist, a sculptor of sorts;
the clay and sods of his bowling green are his pliable and unam-
biguous medium. Tristram's predicament can be summed up in the
obvious and unfathomable fact that "word" is a word. If all human
reasoning must ultimately end in paradox, or in that special form of
it which is infinite regression, here is the source and archetype. The
baffling fact of self-consciousness, by which the "I" ceases to be
integral and becomes the object of its own contemplation, the
shame Adam and Eve felt upon eating of the tree of knowledge, the
sundering of the paradisal wholeness: all this finds its linguistic
form and may even have its root in the ability which language
has—and which it shares with no other thing except its speakers—
to become its own object, to be something other than what it is.
Uncle Toby, trying to rescind the Fall, attempts to live by Bishop
Butler's axiom that "every thing is what it is, and not another
thing." How true and beautifully simple—if only man and the word
did not exist to give it the lie.

II

What, then, can human ingenuity devise to close the rent, to heal the wound which the law of the fall has made and continues to make? The Christian, of course, has a remedy; baptism washes away Adam's stain. But Sterne, somewhat irreverently, makes the orthodox point that even so a gap remains through which an otherwise innocent, new-born babe, weighed down by original sin, can fall straight to damnation. If, as Protestant doctrine demands, a child can be baptised only after it is fully born—if the saving name can be attached only to the fully present body—then there is always the danger of a fatal lag. If, on the other hand, the doctrine can be modified, as the Papists hold, so that the lag may be reduced, the gap narrowed, then where is modification to find its limit? Sterne's quoting the memorial of the Sorbonne doctors, according to which baptism may be administered *"par le moyen d'une petite canulle,"* is fine fooling; but it is more than that. The device is brought to its logical perfection in Tristram's scheme that there be a plenary and anticipatory baptism of all homunculi at once, administered between the marriage ceremony and the consummation. What we have here is a ludicrous counter-innocence to that of Uncle Toby, a fool-proof mechanisation of the sacrament of baptism. As Toby seeks innocence in things, so Tristram, farcically improving on the learned doctors, seeks it in names. If the sacrament of name-giving can follow immediately upon that of marriage, before man has paid tribute to his fallen estate in the sexual act and has thereby perpetuated the sin of Adam, the gap is closed. But the Protestant doctrine, backed moreover by St. Thomas, is the true one: there must be a sin-laden body to receive the sacrament; Divine Grace cannot be mechanised by human engines.

Engines and devices pervade the whole novel; they are second only to sex in supplying the metaphorical substance, and even sex appears a good deal of the time in the metaphor of the engines and mechanics of war. The flying chariot of Stevinus, the forceps of Dr. Slop, the bridge for Tristram's nose, the closely related bridge which Trim and Bridget demolish—these are some of the numerous progeny of *la petite canulle*. The mechanical turn of mind goes deeper: Walter Shandy's typically 18th-century enthusiasm for "projects" and his faith in contrivances and systems are the most obvious instances. His theory of names is of this kind; how delectably characteristic his shrewd and mechanical calculation that if the baby were sure to die, one might as well please Toby by naming it after him, but since there is a bare chance that it might live, the misfortune of the crushed nose has to be compensated for, and nothing less will do than "Trismegistus." Every one of Tristram's misfortunes is attributable to a misplaced faith in the efficacy of mechanical devices; most obviously his name and his nose, less directly his disturbed geniture (the result of the mechanical ordering of various little "family concernments") and his circumcision (the effect of trust in sash windows and of the enthusiasm for engines of war).

The discomfiture of the mechanists and project-makers is total; sex, though battered, holds its own. The *petite canulle* is the paradigm case and Ur-instrument (it also gives Sterne his first major occasion to impress on us the need for close and serious reading—cf. above). Human union, the joining of separate and incomplete halves as symbolised by marriage, has two required rites: the spiritual joining through words and the corporeal joining through the consummation. Since it is through the second that the fall is perpetuated, the end of all devices is, so to speak to "get in" first. And the hilarious paradox is that the very thing which is to render the penis harmless is a "squirt"; sex takes its revenge upon all projects for mechanical innocence and guaranteed purity.

The omnipresent sexual innuendo in the novel has, as one of its purposes, that of gaining expression for the "unmentionable" in the literal sense, for what cannot be said except by indirection. In this respect it serves as the metaphor of the unmentionable mystery of the word, of Tristram's paradoxical enterprise of accounting for his "wound" in the very medium of that wound itself. (We might call his quest for health homoeopathic, while Uncle Toby's is allopathic.) The link between Uncle Toby's story and his own is not merely in the events, but more pervasively in a constant metaphorical mirroring. The terms of military science, pure to Toby, are precisely the most ambiguous outside his little world, the most readily distorted by concupiscence, an unfailing and incessantly tapped source of bawdy. In other words: the very substance of his innocent universe of things turns, in Tristram's universe of words, into its opposite—into ambiguity, equivocation, punning. Thus the world of language becomes virtually identical with the world of sex, lies under the same curse and demands, if it is to be rendered pure by human agency, the most elaborate contriving. But the contrivance cannot come from the outside; it must be fashioned from the very substance whose tendency to fall into the regions of impurity it is meant to counteract. Tristram, as a writer, is condemned to make an instrument of his trouble, to overcome gravity through the law of gravity, to beat sex and language at their own mischievous game. And since language is by its very nature communicative and transitive, it cannot fashion itself into a self-contained little world like Uncle Toby's, a world which has its purity in simply being. It must venture forth, entrust itself to the Mrs. Wadmans; it must mean.

III

There is a seemingly negligible but nevertheless puzzling inconsistency in Uncle Toby's story. Upon first taking up military science, he studies N. Tartaglia, the authority on ballistics, "who it seems was the first man who detected the imposition of a cannonball's doing all that mischief under the notion of a right line." But this necessity for indirection proves to Toby "an impossible thing," and he dutifully goes back to Galileo and Torricellius, where

> he found the precise path [of a projectile] to be a Parabola,—or else an Hyperbola,—and that the parameter, or *latus rectum*, of the conic section of the said path . . . stop! my dear uncle *Toby*, —stop!—go not one foot further into this thorny and bewildered track . . . O my uncle!—fly—fly—fly from it as from a serpent . . . Alas! 'twill exasperate thy symptoms . . . waste thy animal strength . . . impair thy health,—and hasten all the infirmities of thy old age.—O my uncle! my uncle *Toby*! (II. iii.)

This "spirited apostrophe" (which I have greatly shortened) is curious in many respects: first, that it should be prompted by so drily abstract a matter as mathematics; second, that it warns Uncle Toby of exactly the same dangers as those which arose from his efforts to explain his wound; third, that it has some odd parallels to the apostrophe to St. Thomas, who found pre-natal baptism *"la chose impossible"* and for this earns Sterne's "O Thomas! Thomas!" But what is still odder is that a little further on, in discussing the bridge which is to be built in place of the one broken by Trim and Bridget, Tristram informs us that "my uncle *Toby* understood the nature of a parabola as well as any man in England." Since none of the dire effects of a study of ballistics have befallen Toby, we might have thought that he had remained innocent of conic sections; unless we assume that no one in England (with the exception perhaps of Tristram-Sterne?) does know anything of parabolas (or parables), the inconsistency is patent.

In the bridge-building passage, as in the ballistics episode, a problem of mathematics is taken up and then, because of Uncle Toby's inability to deal with it, dropped. Toby "was not quite such a master of the cycloid [as of the parabola];—he talked about it however every day;—the bridge went not forwards.—We'll ask somebody about it, cried my uncle *Toby* to *Trim*." And there the matter is left hanging.

The bridges themselves are of some interest. The original one, destroyed by the fall of the intertwined servants, had moved on two hinges. For the rebuilding this model is rejected on the grounds that, in case of a siege, half of such a bridge is left in the hands of the enemy—"and pray of what use is the other?" To avoid this fault, a one-hinged, one-piece bridge is suggested, but it is impracticable, because for Uncle Toby, invalid that he is, a bridge entirely of one piece is too heavy to operate. A bridge which would thrust out horizontally is rejected because "it would but perpetuate the memory of the corporal's misfortune," meaning that its sexual symbolism would provide Walter Shandy with a ready opening for his indelicate teasing. The bridge decided upon, but never built, was to be counterbalanced by lead (like the sash window), and the construction of it "was a curve-line approximating a cycloid,—if not a cycloid itself." A cycloid is a curve, in appearance quite similar to a parabolic trajectory, which is, however, generated by a point on the circumference of a circle which rolls on a straight line in its plane.

As to the destroyed bridge, it brings to mind what Sterne says of writing and conversation: "Writing . . . is but a different form of conversation. . . . The truest respect which you can pay to the reader's understanding, is to halve this matter amicably, and leave him something to imagine, as well as yourself." One might as well be amicable about it and make a virtue of necessity; as Sterne never tires of showing, the reader *will* take his half, whether the writer wants to leave it to him or not. On the principle of the two-hinged bridge—which Uncle Toby had been able to operate with his crutch, but which was destroyed by a sexual fall—harmony between speaker and hearer must be pre-established, if communication is to be possible. Wounded man is incapable of operating a communicating device hinged only on his side; the "thrusting" kind of sexual communion is repellent to his delicacy; and the principle of the cycloid, which might be the solution, is too complicated to be put into practice.

All this confusion is by no means cleared up in the following passage:

> The machinery of my work is of a species by itself; two contrary motions are introduced into it, and reconciled, which were thought to be at variance with each other. In a word, my work is digressive, and progressive too,—and at the same time. . . . For which reason, from the beginning of this, you see, I have constructed the main work and the adventitious parts of it with intersections, and have so complicated and involved the digressive and progressive movement, one wheel within another, that the whole machine, in general, has been kept a-going. (I. xxii.)

With the matter thus properly tangled, nothing remains but to add the final question of the chapter on lines, in which Tristram conscientiously (but not, I fear, honestly) diagrams his erratic story line volume by volume, hopes to achieve, in the last three books, the "moral rectitude" of a straight line, but ends:

> Pray can you tell me . . . by what mistake—who told them so— or how it has come to pass, that your men of wit and genius have all along confounded this [straight] line, with the line of Gravitation? (VI. xl.)

I am far from able to solve the vastly complicated problem of Sterne's narrative machinery, but I will try to carry it forward a step by defining the element common to bridges, ballistics, story lines and writing. This element is that of "getting something across," whether it is missiles or people or meanings. The matter is obvious enough with bridges and cannon, but Sterne also makes it clear that his story is not simply a thing, a physically existing "work of art," which has its unchallengeable being within itself, but an address, an utterance, which for its being is dependent upon the sadly unreliable, sluggish, concupiscent and even hostile understanding of the hearer. By giving words body—or rather, by showing that they *have* body—the writer exposes them to the danger of falling into the genital region; for this he has to compensate by "wit"—i.e., by devising paths for them which will get them to their true destination. The question, therefore, why men of wit and genius have all along confounded the straight line with the line of gravitation is asked by Sterne in honest bewilderment; nothing seems so obvious to him—and nothing should *be* so obvious—as that, if you want to project something over a gap, your line can never be straight, but must be indirect, parabolic, hyperbolic, cycloid.

It is for this reason that scarcely a sentence in *Tristram Shandy*, far less a chapter or an episode, and least of all the book as a whole, ever runs straight. The novel is a vast system of indirections, circuitous approaches—of parables driven to the point of hyperbole. In fact, the book ends before it began; Uncle Toby's concluding disappointment in love happens some five years before Tristram's birth. The only story that is told with reasonable (by Shandean standards) straightness and completeness is carefully placed so that it turns the whole back upon itself. No critical debate has been more idle than the one about whether *Tristram Shandy* is complete as it stands or whether Sterne simply gave it up after Book IX and left it a fragment. The novel is as carefully, as calculatedly "brought round" as so ambitious an enterprise to set forth and get the better of the mystery of language can be.

In this fact, perhaps, the secret of the cycloid lies. A circle, coming to nothing in itself, perfect but intransitive, rolls along on a straight line. But the straight line, as Tartaglia showed, is a mere "imposition," at least for things that have substance and weight and are to be got across; therefore the real line of communication must be the cycloid curve, indirect, similar to the projectile's parabola. I feel on shaky ground here; what sustains me in my speculations is the conviction that in these figures the secret of the book is hidden and revealed, and that careful reading and supple and rigorous thinking may ultimately come up with a satisfactory formulation of the law of this most curious machine. It may be that, between the passage on ballistics and that on bridges, Sterne changed his view of the nature of his task, and consequently modified his conception of the proper narrative line and with it his metaphor. It is possible that he found the metaphor of missiles and cannon too univocally militaristic, and that the more ambiguous one of a bridge—an instrument both of peace and war, of harmony and conflict—seemed more adequate to his medium. He may also have considered that there is something in the very nature of a work of art which is circular and self-defining, so that the verbal artificer's task is not the relatively simple one of aiming his missiles at the properly indirect angle to compensate for gravity, but that of managing the esthetic circle in such a way that it transmits a meaning, carries a message along a path similar to, but arising from a more complex motion than the parabola.—I hope your worships take my meaning!

IV

The ambiguity of the bridge, if I have rightly interpreted it, fits well with what is manifestly the chief structural metaphor of the novel: the interchangeability of sex and war. Its purport surely is this: direct communication between people, of the kind that would eliminate the pitfalls of language, is radically ambiguous; at this level, no distinction between love and enmity is possible. There is profound irony in the fact that Uncle Toby, the gentlest of men, who literally will not harm a fly, should find happy and complete fulfilment in the building of engines of destruction and the re-enactment of slaughter. In his innocence, he shapes the impairment of his sexual organs into a substitute embodiment of potency and, as the pervasive puns make clear, of sexual aggression. By resolutely closing his ears to the ambiguity, he manages a kind of enclosed, hermetic purity—but only for himself; his work of art is capable of the most sordid and cruel interpretations when it is taken on terms other than his. And so, as soon as the peace of Utrecht breaks out and compels Toby to break out of his artificial world into the real one of discourse and communion, the world in which marriages are made and children begotten, the artfully maintained purity is destroyed; the ambiguity which it tried to overcome by exclusion has its revenge.

Sterne, to be sure, allows Uncle Toby to retreat into innocence—but not completely. Through the mediation of the sash window, he now transmits his wound to his nephew, and the same old problem must be confronted once again. But Tristram, though likewise substituting a construct of art for the impairment of his sexual potency, chooses—or is compelled—to engage the ambiguity directly and bodily; instead of excluding, he exploits it, tries to make it into an engine of *con*struction, to turn it back upon itself.

If Sterne has "constructed the main work and the adventitious parts of it with intersections," so that the progressive and the digressive movement (as in a cycloid) are one and the same, two important points of intersection between the Toby and the Tristram stories are the episodes of the sash window and of the bridge. The first of these is clearly substantial and causative, while the second appears merely verbal and playful. (Trim reports that Dr. Slop is making a bridge, which Uncle Toby takes to be a replacement for his broken one, whereas it is intended, of course, for Tristram's broken nose.) But this is a false distinction to draw; the verbal is not only *as* substantial, but more truly substantial than mere matter. A pun—as that of the bridge—is the most serious thing there is in the world of *Tristram Shandy*. As a physical causality leads from military games to genital mutilation—a painfully tangible translation from play into earnest, and thus a figure which I hope justifies my mode of interpretation—so a verbal causality connects these games with a verbal mutilation. Sterne goes to elaborate lengths to make it unmistakable that "nose" is the *verbal* equivalent of the penis. I have italicised "verbal," because we miss the point entirely if we think—in our vile pruriency, which attends only to the grossly carnal parts of the composition—that the nose *is* the penis. As the parallel of Walter Shandy's system of names and system of noses shows, "nose" means word; and so Sterne defines it. The hero's triple mutilation, therefore—in name, in nose and in genitals—is a redundancy; but it is a redundancy with a difference.

Sash windows and genitals belong clearly to Uncle Toby's sphere, the sphere of things; consequently, the causality which applies here is the law of gravity in the simple physical sense: things *fall*. Walter's theory of names belongs to the realm of "pure" names, of verbal magic; the corresponding causality is arbitrary, erratic, at the mercy of the speaker's will; it neither has the order, nor does it the tangible damage, that characterises falling bodies; it is exempt from gravity. We are free to believe that the nominal mutilation is just that, nominal, and that it is mere caprice to think that "Tristram" is a worse name than "Trismegistus." (In fact, since it is the name of Iseult's famed lover and has attained rather more glory than that of the obscure "hermetic" philosopher and magician, we are positively encouraged to believe this.) But the nose, as Sterne introduces and carefully manages it, belongs simultaneously to both the realm of words and that of things; with it, causality crosses over from Walter's fanciful notions to physical fact (through the intermediate agency of Dr. Slop). Neither pure name nor pure thing, the nose becomes the emblem of impurity *per se*; but at the same time it "bridges"—or might, if it were accepted for what it is—the chasm between mere names and mere things. For in its own right it is a true *word*—which is to say, a pun—the mysterious union of body and name.

V

Walter Shandy's sphere is that of bodiless names and unballasted speculation. He is the tireless talker and reasoner, whose speeches commonly find a hollow echo in the void of Mrs. Shandy's mind, and whose forged chains of reasoning are broken by Uncle Toby's *argumentum fistulatorium*. His system of education is verbalism in undiluted concentration; Tristram's mind is to be stocked with ideas, through a kind of verbal parthenogenesis, by the conjugation of auxiliaries. It is curious that the system is put to a practical test when Mrs. Wadman hears Uncle Toby promise that she shall see "the very place":

> L——d! I cannot look at it—
> What would the world say, if I looked at it?
> I should drop down, if I looked at it—
> I wish I could look at it—
> There can be no sin in looking at it.—
> I will look at it. (IX. xx.)

In Walter Shandy's illustration of the system, the "idea" to be thus conjugated was "white bear"; what Mrs. Wadman does is to state the paradigm in its most general form. "It" is the algebraic noun, standing for any and all verbal quantities; it is as close as words can come to being bodiless, pure sign. But precisely for this reason the equation between Mrs. Wadman and Uncle Toby is a false one; "it" does not stand for any and all words here, but for very specific ones. To the widow it stands for "white bare—," to Toby for the map of Namur; thus the propositional calculus breaks down when it is applied to a concrete and pressing case. At the climax of the Toby parable, and so of the novel, Walter's faith in names meets with Toby's in things; by making Mrs. Wadman go, at this decisive moment, through a "Tristrapaedic" conjugation, Sterne manages to define the tragic conflict as the clash between these two mistaken faiths.

I said that Walter's system of names has no tangible ill effects on Tristram, that the act of magical naming is exempt from the law of gravity. This is not altogether true; the act does cause a fall and a misfortune—the chestnut's and Yorick's. That Walter's wish to change the name precipitates the fateful situation is evident enough; but how does Yorick get involved?

Yorick's mistake is that he picks up the chestnut after Phutatorius has extracted it from its dishonorable lodging place and flung it to the floor. As always when he wants us to pay attention, Sterne is elaborately casual about it:

> Yorick picked up the chestnut which *Phutatorius'* wrath had flung down—the action was trifling—I am ashamed to account for it—he did it, for no reason, but that he thought the chestnut not a jot worse for the adventure—and that he held a good chestnut worth stooping for.—But this incident, trifling as it was, wrought differently in *Phutatorius'* head: He considered this act of *Yorick's* . . . as a plain acknowledgment in him, that the chestnut was originally his,—and in course, that it must have been the owner of the chestnut, and no one else, who could have played him such a prank with it. (IV. xxvii.)

Thus, the consequences of this fall are set in and defined by a twofold context: first, that of an attempt to revoke a name once given, and second, that of a fallen object's being held to be the property of him who picks it up.

The second of these has been the subject of a learned dispute between Didius and Tribonius. Here the fallen object was an apple (which it is hardly far-fetched to identify with the legendary one that came off the tree of knowledge and fell onto Newton's head); the question was whether, when and how, in the state of nature, the apple would become the property of the man who picked it up. Since civil society begins with property, the debate is in fact about when and how the state of nature—and innocence—ended. Thus Sterne defines the causality which connects the mismanagement of Tristram's baptism with Yorick's misfortune as having, once again, to do with man's fall from innocence. Baptism being an acknowledgment of man's fallen estate, the attempt to revoke the baptismal name is implicitly an attempt to revoke the Fall. But the Fall cannot be revoked. The attempt has no other effect than to set things rolling and falling, to make them temporarily ownerless, and to permit false and harmful inferences about causation and proprietorship.

Yorick, who might otherwise have been an unconcerned bystander in the drama, pays the price of Walter's wilfulness, because he thinks a fallen object "not a jot worse" for having made inflammatory contact with a man's genitals. The chestnut's fall was none of his doing; the effect follows from the misguided separation of name and body and from the constitution of things. But unlike others, Yorick is willing to pick up the dishonored object and restore it to dignity and usefulness.

Tristram Shandy is full of chestnuts: "noses," "whiskers," "sausages" and "covered-ways" will do as examples of a basket full of them. The claim which Sterne here enters, but which he does not expect the Phutatoriuses, Somnolentuses and Gastriphereses among his readers to accept, is that the fall of these words—indeed of all words—is none of his doing, but that, on the contrary, he renders them nourishing and even pleasant. The objection is obvious: Can there be any doubt that Sterne is shamming when he protests his innocence, that it is he himself who has set the chestnuts to rolling? Noses and whiskers were perfectly unobjectionable until he took hold of them and aimed them. But the objection is valid only in a special sense: Sterne is responsible for the results of the fall only in the way that a physicist, setting up an experiment to demonstrate the law of gravity, is responsible for whatever object he makes fall. To make his point, Sterne must control words, and through them our minds; for his point is precisely that words do control our minds. He cannot halve the matter amicably with the reader, as in ordinary, uncontrolled conversation; if that would do his business, he need not have written his book. Simply to be circumcised by a falling sash window does not suffice to make Newtons of us.

The expression "halve the matter amicably" is used once more by Sterne, and given graphic substantiality, in the story of the Abbess of Andouillets and the novice Margarita, who between them try to make their mules go by halving the words *"fou-ter"* and *"bou-ger."* "There are two words," explains Margarita,

> which I have been told will force any horse, or ass, or mule, to go up a hill whether he will or no. . . . They are words magic! cried the abbess in the utmost horror—No; replied *Margarita*, calmly —but they are words sinful. (VII. xxv.)

Unfortunately, the attempt to cleanse the words by halving them also deprives them of their efficacy, which, it thus appears, is inseparable from their sinfulness; the story ends with the two nuns still half way up the hill and the mules immovable. The better the joke, the more graceless is it to explain it; and the story of the abbess is wonderfully funny. But Sterne is never as simple as that. It seems as though he cannot rest until he has embodied any abstract point he has made, parabolised it and thus turned it to his true purpose; his jokes are experiments. If words were magical, we may assume that they would do their business automatically; whether they are composite or integral would not matter. But words are not magical, they are sinful; somebody must accept responsibility for them. Sterne *is* responsible, but only because he is willing to accept language as in its nature it is, because he does not fling words away, but picks them up and makes them serve, as Newton made the apple serve. To speak of "Sterne's dirty mind" is as meaningful, and meaningless, as to speak of "Newton's laws of gravity."

Thus the point of the dispute between Didius and Tribonius is that it is pointless. Walter's attempt to restore the state of nature, to revoke the baptism and to reclaim the name once given creates a radically false situation. Words are not magical but sinful; they are irrevocable proof of the fact that whatever innocence there is to be had for us lies ahead and uphill and not behind and downhill. Like the abbess and the novice, we have left the purity of the convent behind us and are caught halfway up the hill, with the alternative of saying the sinful word or remaining isolated and exposed. No casuistry will help us, no halving of responsibility. Sterne picks up the apple as Yorick does the chestnut, knowing that it is the apple of Adam, but also that of Newton.

Once we accept *Tristram Shandy* as what it is—a universe of language which reveals the nature of its medium by that medium's motions—we will, I think, discover in it a causality as binding and as precise as that of classical mechanics. I have tried to show along what lines interpretation will have to proceed if the mechanics of words, as Sterne has embodied them, are to be formulated. I know that nothing could appear more foreign to the quality of the novel than the rigorism I am proposing (and which I am fully aware I have hinted at rather than practiced). But then, nothing appears more foreign to the quality of soap bubbles and aurorae boreales, of snowflakes and comets, than the description of them by the laws of physics. There is no objection to jigging through God's world, or through Sterne's, with a hey-nonny-nonny; on the contrary. But when, pursuing the soap bubble, we stumble into a ditch, we will be wiser to ponder the laws of fall than to believe that God in person has stuck His foot out to trip us up. Gravity is slavery, but since we will not grow wings by pretending that it does not exist, what little chance of freedom we have rests on our understanding; we would not be flying except that someone had the wit to discover that air is heavy. And if this is true of matter, it is much truer—or more humanly true—of words.

HOWARD ANDERSON

Tristram Shandy and the Reader's Imagination†

Very early in *Tristram Shandy*, after allowing a little time for his narrative method to intrigue and irritate his reader, the narrator pauses, ostensibly to beg our indulgence, and, in fact, to offer us some useful advice:

† From *PMLA*, 86 (October 1971), 966–73.

In the beginning of the last chapter, I inform'd you exactly *when* I was born;——but I did not inform you, *how*. No; that particular was reserved entirely for a chapter by itself;——besides, Sir, as you and I are in a manner perfect strangers to each other, it would not have been proper to have let you into too many circumstances relating to myself all at once.——You must have a little patience. . . . As you proceed further with me, the slight acquaintance which is now beginning betwixt us, will grow into familiarity; and that, unless one of us is in fault, will terminate in friendship.——O *diem præclarum!*——then nothing which has touched me will be thought trifling in its nature, or tedious in its telling. Therefore, my dear friend and companion, if you should think me somewhat sparing of my narrative on my first setting out,——bear with me,——and let me go on, and tell my story my own way:——or if I should seem now and then to trifle upon the road,——or should sometime put on a fool's cap with a bell to it, for a moment or two as we pass along,——don't fly off, ——but rather courteously give me credit for a little more wisdom than appears upon my outside;——and as we jogg on, either laugh with me, or at me, or in short, do any thing,——only keep your temper.

The rhetoric is alienating and seductive: we are at once put on guard and disarmed by Tristram's unexpected consciousness of our dawning criticism of his blatantly arbitrary narrative method (or, alternatively, by this sign that he is himself more aware than we had been of that very arbitrariness); we are both put off and attracted by the prospect of intimacy with a person of such perception. And we know too much of seduction to be entirely willing to place trust in a person who is so knowing about our responses and, at the same time, so suavely determined to follow his own intentions in spite of them.

Willingly or grudgingly, fully or partially, trust him we must— not only because we must otherwise close the book; but also because he has demonstrated a larger conception of our mutual situation than the narrow literary one we have, implicitly, been entertaining. He has suggested a way of looking at our relationship that hadn't occurred to us and which is yet plainly appropriate—he has shown that he can teach us, that his approach to this experience is freer than our own. Thus, almost at once, Tristram Shandy begins to make us aware of reductive limits that our imaginations have imposed upon a new experience. He makes us doubt the adequacy of our own imaginations to comprehend and assess accurately what is happening before our eyes. And, throughout the book, he insists, frequently and variously, that such doubt makes us dependent on *him*. He may do it with polite condescension, as here, or with despairing condescension, as when he remarks of the causes of his window-sash circumcision that "It is in vain to leave this to the Reader's imagination" (V. xviii.); or with arrogant condescension, as when he concludes his first volume with, "I set no small store by myself upon this very account, that my reader has never yet been able to guess at any thing. And in this, Sir, I am of so nice and singular a humour that if I thought you was able to form the least judgment or probable conjecture to yourself, of what was to come in the next page,——I would tear it out of my book" (I. xxv.). Condescending as such comments inevitably seem, they are as inevitably literally true.

Our response to these comments may be complicated, however, and our annoyance deepened, by the fact that they are interspersed among many contrivances that make it impossible for us not to try to guess. This is not one of those friendships in which our companion takes it as part of his duty to make perfectly clear in advance just what we are to make of any given proposal or event; on the contrary, it is apparent from the start that we are expected to do our share. In a famous passage, Tristram says that, as "Writing, when properly managed, (as you may be sure I think mine is) is but a different name for conversation: As no one, who knows what he is about in good company, would venture to talk all;——so no author, who understands the just boundaries of decorum and good breeding, would presume to think all: The truest respect which you can pay to the reader's understanding, is to halve this matter amicably, and leave him something to imagine, in his turn, as well as yourself. For my own part, I am eternally paying him compliments of this kind, and do all that lies in my power to keep his imagination as busy as my own" (II. xi.). Well before this agreeable division of responsibility, but after reprimanding his female readers for their careless reading habits, he has explicitly set forth his hope that "all good people, both male and female, . . . may be taught to think as well as read" (I. xx.).

By such apparently contradictory signs it is quickly established that Tristram has set out to educate and train our imaginations, rather than allow us the simpler pleasures of giving free rein to our own conceptions or passively relying on his. He holds out the prospect (though not the promise) of some rewards if we do in fact show ourselves capable of something more than reading "in quest of adventures" (I. xx.); we may at least hope that the author won't be in a position to laugh at us as often as he has done. The primary device of his method of instruction is to make us doubt the imaginative faculties that we have relied on to carry us through this narrative (as they've done through many others), and also to make us see that we are dominated by preconceptions that are inadequate for a full interpretation of the unfamiliar circumstances that we find ourselves in.

The episodes that Tristram recounts in his own life and in those of his relatives and acquaintances characteristically dramatize confrontations between expectation and realization in which the former is constantly disappointed: Walter Shandy's efforts to control the circumstances of his son's life through an auspicious parturition and christening, Toby's naïve assumptions about the nature of Mrs. Wadman's interest in his health, are only among the best-known instances in a continuing series of events designed to show that life, and specifically other men and women defy human assumptions about them. These repeated examples warn the wary, but as is immediately apparent to the reader of *Tristram Shandy*, Sterne is not content with the possibility that his reader will fully comprehend the follies and dangers attendant on applying old generalizations to new specifics merely through observation of examples. Personal experience is a surer teacher, and he makes certain that we will have sufficient instances of our own imaginative failures to supplement the lessons of the Shandean household.

His means for making us confront ourselves are very numerous, but I will center on the three that I have found most important. Most frequently, we cannot resist judging situations ourselves that are under analysis by characters in the novel and, as a result, we find our own deluded prejudices laid bare by the very processes that uncover theirs. Thus when we are shown the folly of their interpretation, we laugh at ourselves while we laugh at the fools and knaves in the world of the novel. Second, we are made to participate in the double meanings of words, with the effect that we find ourselves reading meanings, often unflattering ones, into situations where such meanings may be entirely mistaken. And finally, from the very first page of the novel, Sterne repeatedly manipulates us by deliberately disappointing expectations of narrative form which we have developed through our prior reading. By arbitrarily departing from conventions of customary narrative form in the epic, the novel, and the romance, Sterne insists that arbitrariness lies in the conventions themselves and that our allegiance to them is a sign of a preference for convenient artifice over inconvenient reality. Through each of these techniques, Sterne leads the reader to look first at himself so that when the reader confronts others his vision will distort less radically what he sees. By these various means Sterne leads us particularly to understand that the causes of human events are richer and more complex—more fully human—than we typically assume.

II

To begin—as the book does—with the last of these methods: Sterne is seldom willing to make his literary innovations quietly. Plunging into the opening contemplation upon his conception, he first of all ensures that the reader will find his method eccentric even to the point of aberration. But no sooner have we confidently decided that we are dealing with a mad literary *ingénu* than he pauses to point out what he has done by placing it in the context of traditional literary openings and drawing attention precisely to the intentional artfulness of his approach. Conjuring up the shade of no less than the greatest Roman critic, he remarks that he has "begun the history of myself . . . as *Horace* says, *ab Ovo*" (I. iv.). Thus enters, it would seem, the highest possible literary authority to vouch for the validity, the timeless truth, upon which this history is founded. But of course that isn't the case at all: "I know," he continues, that Horace "does not recommend this fashion [of opening a narrative] altogether." And indeed Horace does not: in the passage that Tristram alludes to, Horace commends Homer for starting the *Iliad in medias res* rather than going back, as he might have done, to its remoter cause in the emergence of Helen from the egg. But the apparently crackbrained use of authority accomplishes several purposes. It makes us doubt our first assumption that Tristram is entirely without literary sophistication. More important, it makes us aware that *where* a writer begins his story is a matter of choice and should depend upon his calculation of the most important causes of the story he is going to tell, not upon some universally recognized causes having their origins in a small set of universally recognized points of departure. In the perspective thus established, Tristram's opening is no more arbitrary than Homer's, which, he suggests, may be appropriate to an epic poem or a tragedy (p. 8). However, since he is writing neither one nor the other, he decides to ignore Horace altogether: "in writing what I have set about, I shall confine myself neither to his rules, nor to any man's rules that ever lived" (I. iv.).

By this time the reader should feel sufficiently uncomfortable about his original doubts of Tristram's literary control. His opening is surely less arbitrary than our judgment of it has been, for he has at least thought of it in relation to the particular story he is going to tell, while we have judged it on preconceptions gathered from other books. His choice has been more conscious and considered than our judgment of it. If it remains arbitrary, it is arbitrariness with a difference: with the suggestion, in short, that all attempts to trace causes may end, where Tristram begins, with a pathetic, ludicrous, but valiant effort to describe the ineffable. In any case, it is the need for such conscious consideration of the relation between generalities and particulars that he is determined to instill in us. He has chosen to begin his story at a remote and uncommon point; now that he has given us an idea of his reasons for doing so, he will go on with further details. But the reader must make up his own mind whether to follow him: "To such . . . as do not choose to go so far back into these things, I can give no better advice, than that they skip over the remaining part of this Chapter; for I declare before hand, 'tis wrote only for the curious and inquisitive" (I. iv.). Whether we now choose to ignore our narrator's obvious preference depends on whether we believe that the manner and time of a man's conception may in fact make an important contribution to his history. Or at least, he has given us the option of so choosing.

One further point should be made about this initial embarrassment of the reader through the literary preconceptions that he brings to *Tristram Shandy* before I go on to consider another instance in which the narrator expands upon and consolidates his victories along this line. Tristram's opening lesson is characteristic in that it does not so much reveal a new truth to the reader, as force him to be conscious of what he has known all along but forgets under the pressure of certain situations. To phrase the point that Tristram brings up here as I did when I said that we must decide whether it is possible that the manner and time of a man's conception may in fact make an important contribution to his history makes it obvious that he is getting us to acknowledge a truth that was hidden only by the unique and unexpected way that Tristram asserted it in his eccentric opening chapter. Thus typically it is because we are startled and defensive that we are disinclined to apply our own *experience* to a situation and resort instead to formulaic preconceived *ideas* to provide our judgments of the significance of events in this novel.

Among the many other ways in which Sterne assaults our preconceptions about what a narrative should be, and thereby gets us to reconsider what a narrative (and a life) *is*, his digressions into stories apparently unrelated to his history are the most noticeable and the most important to his purposes. In one sense, the very title of the book provides justification for any amount of deviation from the norms of narrative: if you are telling the story of your opinions as well as of your life, what authorization beyond its existence is required for the inclusion of any idea in your book? How can anything be digressive? But if Sterne's title, like his self-consciousness about his way of starting the novel, amounts to a helpful assertion of purpose, the value of the purpose nevertheless remains to be tested. If we evaluate the coherence of Tristram's narrative on the basis of apparent similarities to familiar narratives, we are certain to be embarrassed.

Sterne does all he can to ensure that we will be. Throughout the first volume he builds our conventional impatience to have the hero born and teases us with his digressive interruptions. Our hopes are foiled by the story of Yorick and the midwife, and by a copy of a learned pronouncement from the Sorbonne, by a facsimile of the Shandys' marriage contract, and by the beginning of the description of Uncle Toby's character, which in turn is interrupted by the story of Aunt Dinah and the coachman. And as we near the end of the volume with Tristram still in the womb, the story is stopped again by his bland pronouncement that these digressions "incontestibly, are the sunshine;——they are the life, the soul of reading;——take them out of this book . . . you might as well take the book along with them;——one cold eternal winter would reign in every page of it; restore them to the writer;——he steps forth like a bridegroom, ——bids All hail; brings in variety, and forbids the appetite to fail" (I. xxii.).

This assured mockery of the reader's impulse to have him get on with the central narrative line results in part from reasons that he has set forth just prior to this rhapsody on his own artistry. Worried that no one has noticed his unprecedented accomplishment, he begins the chapter by asserting that he must commend himself for his digressive skill, "the merit of which has all along, I fear, been overlooked by my reader,——not for want of penetration in him, ——but because 'tis an excellence seldom looked for, or expected indeed, in a digression;——and it is this: That tho' my digressions are all fair, as you observe,——and that I fly off from what I am about, as far and as often too as any writer in *Great-Britain*; yet I constantly take care to order affairs so, that my main business does not stand still in my absence" (I. xxiii.). Such claims, like the jaunty assurance of his early remarks about Horace, demand investigation, and this time we are far enough along in the book to use past evidence. When we look back at his title and at the long chain of digressions, we find that they do indeed bear directly though esoterically upon the conditions of his birth and, presumably, upon the formation of his opinions.

Tristram makes us aware, then, that, as Henry James was to say, "really, universally, relations stop nowhere," and he shows us that our assumption that the really important part of his history will start only when he gets out into the world is naïve and simplistic. Much of what he is to be is decided by what other people said and did long before he was born, so that the digressions which had seemed peripheral *do* further the main business of the work. But this effect in turn has a further result: given such an endless chain of causes, it becomes apparent that how he chooses to see them is as important as the fact that he sees them at all. If all such remote determinants are important, then all are meaningless—except as the narrator chooses to invest them with significance. Tristram's digressions, many of which dramatize the reasons why he has been "the continual sport of what the world calls fortune" and why that "ungracious Duchess has pelted me with a set of as pitiful misadventures and cross accidents as ever small HERO sustained" (I. v.), are nonetheless the "sunshine of this book," because he chooses to turn his misfortunes into high comic art.

This conclusion is made inescapable not only by our observation of Tristram's characteristically high-spirited response to his misfortunes and infirmities, but by those of the admirable characters whose careers he traces within the digressions. To consider only those that precede his boast about his digressive skill: the episode concerning Yorick shows him making a joke of the vicious hostility of his colleagues even when it has brought him to his deathbed; and the story of Aunt Dinah and the coachman, which Walter can never resist telling despite the pain it causes his brother, in time elicits only a song from Toby—he responds to it by whistling *Lillabulero*. The reader accustomed to the straightforward causes and effects of an "adventure" discovers that Tristram Shandy is subtly influenced not only by past actions but by past example as well: like Yorick and Toby, he turns unavoidable misfortune to his own imaginative uses. And, incidentally, in so doing, this "small hero" finds the same consolation for his woes that Alcinous in the eighth book of the *Odyssey* proposes to that greater hero: "That was all gods' work, weaving ruin there / so it should make a song for men to come."[1]

To move to the second of Sterne's devices for making us self-conscious, I will turn now from his education of his reader's imagination by disappointing and so instructing our narrative expectations to what I will call his parables of preconception. A great deal of the humor and meaning of the novel depends, of course, upon the creation of situations in which people misinterpret actions or talk because their responses are determined by dominant preexisting ideas rather than by attention to the specifics of the situation itself. Sterne distinguishes harmless hobbyhorses, which may prevent accurate comprehension of a situation but which cause no further harm, from the more self-interested predispositions which insist upon interpreting everything to someone else's disadvantage. But both kinds of episodes work to keep the reader alert to the perils involved in properly interpreting external signs. For example, when Walter Shandy assumes that Corporal Trim doesn't understand the real meaning of his catechism because he rolls off the commandments as if they were military orders, he proceeds to construct a

---

1. Trans. Robert Fitzgerald (Garden City, N.Y.: Doubleday, 1963), p. 142.

hypothesis about the differences between science and wisdom on the basis of his assumption. But when Trim aptly and touchingly glosses the fourth commandment as allowing your mother and father three halfpence a day out of your pay, when they grow old (V. xxxii.), it is *Walter's* mind that is shown to be mechanical, and he is for once effectively, if temporarily, silenced.

Such an episode certainly warns the reader to be careful about his approach to the situation he is himself involved in: we had better not assume that because Tristram's way of expressing himself in this book appears naïve that it is so in fact. (The novel's opening, already discussed, is a case in point.) But, especially in the first part of the book, when he offers his parables of preconception to the reader, Tristram usually takes pains to *ensure* that we will apply them to ourselves and not sit back and smile in amused complacency at the folly of others. Like Fielding in *Tom Jones*, Sterne uses the example of false judgments of minor characters to guide the reader's judgment of his major character in the future. One extended example will illustrate how Sterne makes it hard for us to avoid applying his parables to ourselves.

When Tristram begins to tell how Yorick came to provide a midwife for his parish, he makes us first have a look at what we assume would be likely motives for doing a woman a good turn. For my part, he says, since the parson provided the funds to set her up in business, I think he should have his share of the honor for it, but "The world at that time was pleased to determine the matter otherwise" (I. x.). The reader, not totally exempt from the world's weaknesses, at once begins to supply the lowest common denominator of dealings between men and women. And he is encouraged by Tristram: "Lay down the book, and I will allow you half a day to give a probable guess at the grounds of this procedure." Since we already assume that we know, we proceed at once to have our suspicions apparently confirmed by the information that the world's judgment resulted from the parson's having "made himself a country-talk by a breach of all decorum, which he had committed against himself, his station, and his office." And thus our assumptions trap us, and the need to rely on the narrator's fuller knowledge is confirmed, for it turns out that the breach of decorum that leads the public to be disinclined to honor Yorick for his good deed to the midwife is in fact merely his having chosen some years since to provide himself with a poorer horse than his parishioners consider appropriate to one of his station.

That is the first turn of the screw. With our own unworthy predisposition to think the worst fully exposed, Tristram next begins to build the parable of the parishioners' preconceptions. Yorick's delicacy and tact, his modesty and self-effacement, his patience and good humor, and, above all, his willingness to be laughed at, all emerge from an account of how, though "In the language of the county, where he dwelt, he was said to have loved a good horse" (I. x.), he came to prefer a poor one. Yorick's neighbors, it seems, were always borrowing his fast horses and riding them to death on one or another errand; buying new ones was ruining him. Rather than hurt their feelings by keeping the horses to himself, he chose to jog along on the equivalent of Don Quixote's Rosinante.

And rather than ascribe his choice correctly to delicacy and tact, the world preferred to explain his change of style as a ludicrous eccentricity—until the moment that he set the midwife up in business in his parish. Then the memory of their most common reason for borrowing the horses—to ride to the next town for medical aid—rushed back into their minds in time to provide a selfish motive for Yorick's action: "The parson had a returning fit of pride which had just seized him; and he was going to be well mounted once again in his life" (I. x.). Thus Tristram presents as the moral of the story the human predilection to think the worst of others whenever possible. And it would seem that with the example of ourselves and Yorick's parishioners before us, we would have sufficient lesson to ponder.

But Tristram at once prepares the third turn of the screw, whereby we are implicated in the same motive, as we had been in the same impulse, that characterized Yorick's hostile neighbors. In the two following chapters their hostility is seen to spring specifically from the parson's habit of "unwary pleasantry," his frankness, and his willingness to turn anything to a joke, "without much distinction of either personage, time, or place" (I. xi.–xii.). And so it develops that "tho' he never sought, yet, at the same time, as he seldom shun'd occasions of saying what came uppermost, and without much ceremony;——he had but too many temptations in life, of scattering his wit and his humour,——his gibes and his jests about him.——They were not lost for want of gathering." In short, his good humor and freedom make him enemies, and no one who has been the object of his wit ever forgets it. Turning to the reader, Tristram calls on us to judge for ourselves what the result would be: "As the reader (for I hate your *ifs*) has a thorough knowledge of human nature, I need not say more to satisfy him, that my Hero could not go on at this rate without some slight experience of these incidental mementos." Having made clear Yorick's generosity toward his parishioners first in loaning them his horses and then in providing them with a midwife, he has provided us with an example of demonstrably good intentions that are willfully misconstrued by people who can't bear occasionally to be laughed at: Yorick's friend Eugenius makes it explicit when he says that "I cannot suspect it in the man whom I esteem, that there is the least spur from spleen or malevolence of intent in these sallies.——I believe and know them to be truly honest and sportive:——But consider, my dear lad, that fools cannot distinguish this,——and that knaves will not; and thou knowest not what it is, either to provoke the one, or to make merry with the other,——whenever they associate for mutual defence, depend upon it, they will carry on the war in such a manner against thee, my dear friend, as to make thee heartily sick of it, and of thy life too."

The reader who by this time fails to sense that he has again fallen into a trap must be very willing indeed to be called by the former of Eugenius' epithets. From the beginning of the book we have been the objects of Tristram's humor, and therefore we stand in the position of Yorick's neighbors; and, like them, we too have doubtless been a little annoyed and insulted by gibes and jests. But, like Yorick, Tristram has effectively benefited us even while he was making jokes at our expense; thus we must be as foolish or as vicious as Yorick's parishioners if we don't comprehend the generous motive behind his honest sportiveness. At every step in this parable the reader is shown the inevitable folly and the possible vice of judging on preconceptions, and, in the last part of it, the danger of allowing injured vanity to prevail over a recognition of generous motives and beneficial actions. Patient and clear-sighted observation of his actions reveals Yorick to be eminently trustworthy; Tristram's enthusiastic approval of that example carries the clear suggestion that the reader may expect comparable benefits, along with gibes and jests, from his association with Tristram, if our patience and trust can prevail over our laziness, skepticism, and humorlessness.

The third important method that Sterne uses to make the reader aware of his common preconceptions, and the dangers of adhering to them without examination, may be the most memorable—at least to those who have tossed the book into a corner and refused to pick it up again. His double-entendre may indeed seem, in the words of F. R. Leavis' confident dismissal of *Tristram Shandy* from the great tradition of the English novel, "irresponsible (and nasty) trifling."[2] (What would we do without Leavis' convenient remark as a departure point in *Tristram Shandy* criticism?) But to readers who believe that "through imaginative play we learn about ourselves,"[3] Tristram's *noses* and *whiskers* define the rules of the games we play with ourselves in place of communicating with each other, and at the same time show how, given the inevitability of such games,

2. *The Great Tradition* (Garden City, N.Y.: Doubleday, 1954), p. 11, n. 2.
3. Ian Watt, Introd. to *Tristram Shandy* (Boston: Houghton Mifflin, 1965), p. xxxv.

we may be able to communicate both around and through them.

Once again Sterne does not teach a new truth but rather forces us to recognize the implications of something we have known all along. Of course, double-entendre exists, like beauty, in the eye of the beholder, and while Tristram may rather insistently impose certain objects to force his point, our minds would be impenetrable if they were pure. His first aim is to show us how easy it is for "little interests from below" to make us leap to conclusions on very little evidence. The leaps, we find, are inevitable: when Tristram applies the slightest pressure, our minds will supply the responses. While it is unlikely that we have been conscious of the rich possibilities of the word "nose," for example, when Trim first announces to Walter Shandy that Dr. Slop is making a bridge for Tristram's (which has been crushed "flat as a pancake to his face" by the forceps), only a little emphasis is sufficient to bring quite another appendage to mind. And once it has occurred to us, no amount of definition will stop the growth of the idea in our minds. Sterne's method here is not to make us choose which meaning we will believe but rather to force us to arrive at an impasse. Our uncertainty grows precisely in proportion to Tristram's efforts to assure us that his meaning is simple: "by the word *Nose*, throughout all this long chapter of noses, and in every other part of my work, where the word *Nose* occurs,——I declare, by that word I mean a Nose, and nothing more, or less" (III. xxxi.).

Thus our preconceptions lead to confusion. The alternatives offered are not between one or another interpretation of the word— we really can't know which is correct—but between remaining in uncertainty with the mind alert to further clues, or giving up, and, if we are consistent, closing the book. If we have by this time learned to be patient and to rely on Tristram to do his best to reward that virtue, we will be offered some help by later events. The window sash that falls some years later, for example, may help us in this case to be more certain that Tristram meant just what he said: a circumcision could scarcely have taken place otherwise.

Though such efforts are vital to our comprehension of Tristram's story, here (as in the case of the digressions) the ultimate effect of our initial confusion is the revelation of quite another kind of meaning, an effect that goes beyond the instruction in how to arrive at denotations more accurately. The decision to suspend judgment when we have no real grounds for a decision results in a considerable freedom: we need no longer act as automata imposing simplistic systems upon the world and mankind. From that result emerges the further awareness that our ambiguous responses to language represent a complexity in our response to things. The fusion between objects of our perception that Tristram makes us so unforgettably conscious of in his double-entendre originates in our sensuous perception of things, not in the words themselves. And Tristram's knowing manipulation of our responses is intended not only to arouse our fantasies but to make us certain that he shares our sense of this fusion just as we share his.

These associative fusions of things in our minds through the similarities of some of their characteristics deprive language of denotative simplicity, but at the same time endow it with a symbolism of supreme expressive power. Sterne's double-entendres amount, then, to a primer in poetry, initiating the naïve reader into the principles of the symbolism which is essential to his effort to communicate with us in *Tristram Shandy*. It is the ability to recognize and make use of this fusion of the mind and the senses that Sterne's double meanings begin to teach the reader. Out of the muddle of preconceptions which inevitably enter the mind through the senses, we may, with insight, devise a means of expressing, though not finally a means of controlling, some of the infinite ambiguity of life. It is in this limited but very real freedom that Sterne begins to instruct his reader when he first goads him into thinking about the meanings of the word *nose*.

III

When he denied that his book was "wrote against predestination, or free will," claiming instead that "If 'tis wrote against any thing, —'tis wrote, an' please your worships, against the spleen; in order, by a more frequent and a more convulsive elevation and depression of the diaphragm, and the successations of the intercostal and abdominal muscles in laughter, to drive the *gall* and other *bitter juices* from the gall bladder, liver and sweet-bread of his majesty's subjects, with all the inimicitious passions which belong to them, down into their duodenums" (IV. xxii.), Sterne was stating the truth literally. Tristram Shandy makes every possible effort to persuade his reader to be good-tempered, but in so doing he is also proving, if my reading is correct, the existence of both predestination and free will as causes of human events. For him, true good temper requires the patience to accept things and human beings as they are and to find in them sources of joy to compensate for the misfortunes imposed by "one of the vilest worlds that ever was made" (I. v.). Thus when good temper exists it makes possible precisely an escape from the universally predetermined painful brevity of life, a chance to transform suffering itself, as we have seen, into humor, and the irrevocable physicality of human nature into poetry.

Good temper, then, is the attribute that makes individual freedom possible. Through it, the determined destructive causes of what happens to us may be subordinated to the vital creative forces that *are* in our control. "Are we for ever," asks Tristram, "to be twisting, and untwisting the same rope? for ever in the same track—for ever at the same pace? Shall we be destined to the days of eternity, on holy-days, as well as working-days, to be shewing the *relicks of learning,* as monks do the relicks of their saints—without working one—one single miracle with them?" (V. i.). The answer that emerges from his example and his instruction is surely clear: we are destined to remain trapped in sterile futility only if we refuse to break barriers that our minds erect between us and the world. Sterne threatens those barriers by making us laugh good-humoredly. That kind of laughter implies that we must like and, above all, trust the person who causes it; our acceptance of Tristram becomes, in fact, the sign of our acceptance of the world. For, like the world, the very ways in which Tristram is hard on the reader allows us the options of giving up in frustration, or responding with vigor and responsibility. He tests and teaches his reader. Thus the book attempts to persuade us of the necessity and the possibility of trusting this odd narrator, and this odd world, to help us understand what our unaided preconceptions inevitably find baffling in each new experience. Thus it is written, I should say, against simple individualism and self-reliance, as it is against simple predestination and free will. As Tristram Shandy twice reminds us, "We live in a world beset on all sides with mysteries and riddles" (IX. xxi.; IV. xvii.) *"hardly do we guess aright at the things that are upon the earth"* (II. xvii.). But with the aid of the infuriating, condescending, and generous Tristram, *and* "with labour, do we find the things that are before us" (II. xvii.).

J. PAUL HUNTER ·

Response as Reformation: *Tristram Shandy* and the Art of Interruption†

I

The way *Tristram Shandy* digests bits of this and chunks of that, if does not seem surprising to find an entire Sterne sermon included, word for word (Vol. II. ch. xvii.). Looked at in one way, this stratagem is like a host of other Sternean stratagems where themes, ideas, or systems from all sorts of places are bodily taken over and

† From *Novel*, 4 (1971), 132–46. Footnotes are by Hunter.

absorbed into the Sternean purposes of the work. It happens to
Hamlet and Don Quixote, suggestively at first and then overwhelm-
ingly; it happens to Rabelais, Swift, and Fielding; to the Church
Fathers; and to learning so arcane that the standard edition of
Tristram Shandy is overwhelmed by footnote descriptions of
"sources." Such allusiveness makes fun of itself, and we are continually made wary of becoming the pedant who sees all, recognizes
all, systematizes all. Yet we are guided by a writer who does all that
but is not the prisoner of his learning—who, rather than being
confined by the borders of his predecessors, invites all learning into
his own work, there transforming it into something that fits his own
artistic needs. The omnivorous maw of Tristram Shandy devours
whatever it finds, and nothing remains undigested.

Such a work challenges us with its learning, not only to discover
its sources and recognize the allusions, but to justify the homogeni-
zations and interpret the transformations. When an eighteenth-
century writer controls tone, introduces a theme, or engages a norm
by allusion to Hamlet or Don Quixote, we are not surprised by the
technique, for it is a common one. Self-allusion may, in certain
instances, also be somewhere in this spectrum of allusive uses, as
Pope teaches us, even though such allusions turn inward toward
form, rather than outward toward the work's historical reception and
interpretation. But when an entire discrete work like Yorick's sermon is embedded whole it may seem at first untransformed, undigested. Yet whatever separate existence the sermon may have,
when it is included in Tristram Shandy it is affected by the fact that
it bears relationships to the rest of a larger work. It is another illustration (and an extreme test case) of the powers of context over
something that in another place is self-sufficient, and it is an indication of the lengths to which Sterne will go to examine the process
of transformation.[1]

Sterne himself had preached the sermon—"On the Abuses of
Conscience"—on 29 July 1750, and he published it shortly after,
ten years before he included it in Tristram Shandy; he later included
it again in The Sermons of Mr. Yorick (Vol. IV, 1766). In those
instances it asserts its relation to the eighteenth-century homiletical
tradition. There it shows us Sterne as an orthodox Anglican divine,
examining a major theological and moral issue in a way approved

---

1. The fullest examination of the sermon
itself is by Arthur Cash, "The Sermon in
Tristram Shandy," ELH, 31 (1964), 395–
417; Lansing van der Heyden Hammond
has considered its relation to the homiletical tradition in Laurence Sterne's Sermons of Mr. Yorick (Yale Studies in
English, 108: New Haven, 1948). For
examinations of the sermon in the context of Tristram Shandy, see the brief
but suggestive discussion by John M.
Stedmond, The Comic Art of Laurence
Sterne (Toronto, 1967), pp. 85ff., and
the longer but less satisfying one by
Henri Huchére, Laurence Sterne: From
Tristram to Yorick, trans. Barbara Bray
(London, 1965), pp. 225ff.

by the conventions of sermon rhetoric. Sterne's theological and moral position remains the same in *Tristram Shandy*, and the sermon asserts the stance that moral man ought to take, but the positioning of the sermon in the novel demonstrates that man does not take that stance and that he does not learn from the usual attempts to make him do so. As a sermon it is a failure in *Tristram Shandy*: Trim weeps for his brother, Walter theorizes about oratory and authorship, Uncel Toby fortifies his hobbyhorse by sorting out the military metaphors, Dr. Slop sleeps. No one whets his conscience on the sermon; in fact the sermon itself becomes an emblem of lack of conscience, for (according to Tristram's account of its genealogy) the sermon was plagiarized.[2] Yet the sermon is not a failure in the larger sense, for its reception demonstrates what will not, and what will, move the minds of men. Here is incorporated an instance of the limits of conventional rhetoric, a demonstration of the richness of human response, predictable not by the standards of conventional rhetorical theory but by the methods which take more exact account of the way the mind of perverse man works—methods explored in the human world of *Tristram Shandy*, a world which in spite of its eccentricities is far more like our own world than we care to admit.

II

No reader who navigates chapter xvii remembers much about the sermon as such. Plain solemn prose does not fare well when interrupted by the gesticulation and debate of the Shandean folk, and here it is interrupted often, sometimes for a sentence or phrase, sometimes for minutes at a time. The pattern is set at the beginning: the first seven words of the sermon are followed by a lengthy and increasingly esoteric conversation, five minutes worth, at least. The emphasis in such a presentation falls not on moral abstraction or theological argument but on the interruptions. Even the *exempla* in the sermon do not compare for liveliness to the squabbling of Walter and Dr. Slop or the tearful cries of Trim. Such upstaging of the sermon's content is no accident; it is part of the general motif in *Tristram Shandy* of watching the responder at work—of using the book's

2. Sterne is, of course, toying with his Sterne/Yorick distinction here; part of the effect is simply comic play, and part is self-mockery or an in-joke, for Sterne had in fact taken a passage on the inquisition from Richard Bentley. After Sterne's death there was quite a fuss about his supposed "plagiarism" of sermons and he may be teasing earlier rumors or engaging a "confessional" strategy that would interest his psychological critics. But the charges of plagiarism were greatly exaggerated in the late eighteenth century. Hammond (p. 105) prints the parallel Bentley passage, only a paragraph. But I think we must, in reading the history of the sermon in *Tristram Shandy*, distinguish the biographical or pseudo-biographical from the fictional strata; I wish to emphasize the effect, in context, of the fictional fact.

characters as surrogates for the reader who can learn about his own responsive process by watching the eccentric (but predictable) Shandean responses.

Given the laws of this world, the responses are all characteristic. Each character responds to the sermon exactly the way he does to anything else—in terms of his own hobbyhorsical preoccupations. The ideas of the sermon penetrate not at all; all meaning is grounded into meaninglessness on the lighting rod of the character's eccentricity. Even before the sermon begins, inevitable responses are clear; the assemblage is scouring Stevinus for a drawing of a chariot, and the whimsical Sterne has the literal-minded Trim shake the book to see if a chariot falls out (ch. xv). The sermon emerges instead, and everyone is willing to accept the substitute vehicle:

> I think 'tis a sermon, replied Trim;——but if it please your Honours, as it is a fair hand, I will read you a page;——for *Trim*, you must know, loved to hear himself read almost as well as talk.
>
> I have ever a strong propensity, said my father, to look into things which cross my way, by such strange fatalities as these;——and as we have nothing better to do, at least till *Obediah* gets back, I should be obliged to you, brother, if Dr. *Slop* has no objection to it, to order the Corporal to give us a page or two of it,—if he is able to do it, as he seems willing.

Once the sermon begins (in fact, once the text is announced) everyone falls into his predictable posture. For Walter Shandy, all responses are filtered through the meticulosities of his System. First he addresses himself to Trim's oratory ("you give that sentence a very improper accent; for you curl up your nose, man, and read it with such a sneering tone, as if the parson was going to abuse the Apostle"), and he keeps a running account of the writing and speaking style ("The language is good, and I declare *Trim* reads very well"). Later Walter debates the parson's theological stance with Dr. Slop, not because he intends to be influenced by it but simply because he is intellectually interested in deducing whether the writer is Protestant. Similarly, he deduces its occasion ("I see plainly . . . that this sermon has been composed to be preached at the Temple,———or at some Assize") and congratulates himself for seeing in advance that the Parson and St. Paul will agree ("it is now clear, that the Parson, as I thought at first, never insulted St. *Paul* in the least;———nor has there been, brother, the least difference between them"). His interest is not in what the sermon might do for him, but rather in what his mind can do with the sermon. For Walter, a sermon is as good a vehicle as a chariot and, whatever its quality, will go just as far.

For Uncle Toby, all the world is battles and fortifications, and he shows little interest in the proceedings except for a question here and there inspired by the comments of others ("Pray is the Inquisition an antient building . . . or is it a modern one?"; "Pray how many [sacraments] have you in all . . . for I always forget?"). But suddenly Toby's attention is arrested, not because the sermon's ideas move him but because its imagery touches his only responsive chord:

> "Conscience has got safely entrenched behind the Letter of the Law; sits there invulnerable, fortified with *Cases* and *Reports* so strongly on all sides;——that it is not preaching can dispossess it of its hold."
> [Here Corporal *Trim* and my uncle *Toby* exchanged looks with each other.——Aye,——aye, *Trim!* quoth my uncle *Toby*, shaking his head,——these are but sorry fortifications, *Trim*.—— O! very poor work, answered *Trim*, to what your Honour and I make of it. . . .]

Now Toby becomes enthusiastic and laments the sermon's shortness:

> I wish it was longer, quoth my uncle *Toby*, for I like it hugely.

Later, he revels again in a literal response to the military metaphors, but his enthusiasm does not extend beyond the military speculation it begets; there is no carry-over to the sermon's ideas, and Sterne gives us no hint that Toby's conscience is improved at all.

Trim shares Toby's celebratory response to the military metaphors, but his major response is an even more private one: he is moved; by the sermon's attack on Catholicism, to bewail the unknown fate of his brother at the hands of the Inquisition. Ultimately, he confuses one of the sermon's *exempla* with his brother and is overcome by anger and grief:

> [Oh! 'tis my brother, cried poor *Trim* in a most passionate exclamation, dropping the sermon upon the ground, and clapping his hands together——I fear 'tis poor *Tom*. . . .]

The other hearers comfort Trim by assuring him that the document is only a sermon:

> [Why, *Trim*, said my father, this is not a history,——'tis a sermon thou art reading;——pri'thee begin the sentence again.] . . . [I tell thee, *Trim*, again, quoth my father, 'tis not an historical account,——'tis a description.——'Tis only a description, honest man, quoth *Slop*, there's not a word of truth in it.——That's another story, replied my father. . . .]

But finally Trim is overwhelmed, and Walter must finish the reading —still punctuated by the cries of Trim who first wishes his brother alive, and then wishes him beyond the miseries of this-worldly torture. Trim purges his pity and fear in the performance, but purgation is on his own terms, not on the sermon's. His emotional response parallels Walter's intellectual one; both make the sermon answer the needs of their hobbyhorses while the sermon's subject and aims remain unregarded.

For Dr. Slop the relevant matter is his own Catholicism, and he comes the closest to grappling with the sermon because the sermon directly assaults the area of his greatest concern. Still, he does not react to the sermon as such, but rather to the topic; far from being moved either intellectually or emotionally, he is only concerned to correct it. From the beginning, he is suspicious and defensive, certain that the sermon is Protestant and therefore will attack his system of belief. He takes Trim's articulation of the text as a clue, and he is already flailing away long before the attack begins:

> . . . the writer (who I perceive is a Protestant) by the snappish manner in which he takes up the Apostle, is certainly going to abuse him,——if this treatment of him has not done it already. But from whence, replied my father, have you concluded so soon, Dr. *Slop*, that the writer is of our Church?——for aught I can see yet,——he may be of any Church:——Because, answered Dr. *Slop*, if he was of ours,——he durst no more take such a licence,——than a bear by his beard:——If, in our communion, Sir, a man was to insult an Apostle,——a saint,——or even the paring of a saint's nail,——he would have his eyes scratched out. ——What, by the saint, quoth my uncle *Toby*. No, replied Dr. *Slop*,——he would have an old house over his head.

Slop continues to interject, first to prove the correctness of his Protestant attribution, then to defend Catholic faith and practice, including the Inquisition. He is the noisiest of the interrupters, silent only when Popery is really under attack. But Slop's most significant response comes later when, upon hearing the familiar solacing word, he falls asleep:

> "Let CONSCIENCE determine the matter upon these reports;—— and then if thy heart condemns thee not, which is the case the Apostle supposes,——the rule will be infallible;" [Here Dr. Slop fell asleep]. . . .

Slop does not even wait to hear what the rule is, once he discovers it to be infallible. Ideas pass him by as they do the others; his responses are triggered only by his own expectation or by a key word which (irrespective of context or meaning) signals an automatic reaction.

Once the sermon is finished, the hearers repeat again their responsive patterns, and the inefficacy of the sermon is again underscored. The hearers engage in much theoretical speculation about the sources of homiletic effectiveness, and they assure themselves that this particular sermon, read in this particular way, is very effective indeed:

> I like the sermon well, replied my father,——'tis dramatic,—— and there is something in that way of writing, when skilfully managed, which catches the attention.

But here no attention is caught, and the speculation and assurance give themselves the lie; no one speaks of the sermon's content, and there is no later evidence that any of the hearers have improved their notions of conscience at all.

The final emphasis of the episode falls on the journey of the sermon into Uncle Toby's copy of Stevinus, a journey that underscores the impotence of the homily by implying its effect (or lack of one) on hearers beyond the Shandy household. Sterne here invokes the history-of-the-weapon convention and characteristically works curious variations upon it. One of his accomplishments is to emphasize the unusual connection of *Tristram Shandy* with Sterne himself and to toy with both the affirmation and denial of Yorick as Sterne —a toying which (like many another aspect of *Tristram Shandy*) may well raise pertinent questions for the psychological critic who is concerned with why Sterne identifies himself with a character and then insists on a distinction between them. But my concern is not with the extra-literary question here; I wish rather to emphasize the literary effect which the fictional history of the sermon produces. Never mind, for a minute, that Sterne published his own sermon, or at least one that was substantially his own. The *fictional* fact is that the sermon was preached and published by a prebendary who was *not* its author. Clearly, his conscience was not improved by hearing about abuses of conscience, or even by preaching on them, for he is able to send the sermon, first orally and then in print, into the world as his own. Such an account of where the sermon has been underscores its inefficacy and raises the question of whether any sermon, according to *Tristram Shandy*, will have its desired effect on human beings.

III

The ultimate question is whether any didactic work—sermon, tract, satire, or novel—can have the desired effect on human beings, or whether in fact all is vanity, and the didactic intentions of a moral philosopher are the greatest vanity of all. Sometimes this question has been answered with assurance about Sterne: that *Tristram Shandy* proves the vanity of all intentions, and that here we have demonstrated the total subjectivity of all men—so much so that no moralist or artist can calculate or predict the effect he may produce on men who bring their own hobbyhorses and ultimately ride away on them. I believe *Tristram Shandy* proves the opposite: that in spite of subjectivity and eccentricity, men share certain responsive patterns and that the writer or speaker in possession of this knowledge may indeed manipulate his readers or hearers in a way that he can predict and control. The comic responses to noses, hats, bridges, and hinges—induced by the associations Sterne sets up[3]—seem to suggest the possibility of controlled evocation, and the sermon episode sets up some guidelines by demonstrating pitfalls to be avoided by a would-be didacticist.

The protagonist of *Tristram Shandy*, one might argue, is the Reader.[4] Even when he is not on the printed page as "Sir," "Madam," or "Your Worship," he is present for the conception of the work, presumably working alongside Tristram and helping design the work for himself. Of course, much of this is posture, if not imposture; Sterne's calculation and control are far more comprehensive than his devices allow him to show. Yet, in a larger sense, the reader always governs the artistic choices, for, rather than giving his reader loose-leaf options as he sometimes pretends, Sterne, just like other novelists and rhetoricians continually makes those choices expressly to move a definable response. But how can he predict a general response when he so elaborately details the hobbyhorsiness of each individual? Sterne realizes that he cannot know the hobbyhorse of each reader, and that he could not appeal to them all even if he did. What he does is set up means of canceling the more circuitous travels which hobbyhorses offer. Chief among his means is exploration and exposure of the nature of response through close examination of a limited number of characters. Such examination isolates those elements which remain constant in spite of individual preoccupations and exposes all the responsive weaknesses which flesh is heir to.

If the characters are, in fact surrogates for the reader and if they expose their responsive liabilities as in the sermon episode, then the reader is jolted into a kind of awareness by observing the absurdities of the scene. He is invited to discover with what preoccupations he approached the scene, the book, or literature generally. Such an invitation, even when successful, does not guarantee correction, but it does short-circuit one of the most active enemies of response and allows a resourceful artist to attempt enlarging the areas of audience response.

3. My point is that Sterne *uses* associational psychology to set up rhetorical strategies. I do not regard Sterne as a blind mimic of the processes of the mind, conceived associationally.

4. For a related discussion, see Andrew Wright, "The Artifice of Failure in *Tristram Shandy*," NOVEL, 2 (1969), 212–20.

Awareness of the follies of others may awaken a sense of folly about one's own actions and attitudes, especially if the exposure has been relentless and all-encompassing. Watching everyone else misrespond to the sermon, a reader may well wonder how he himself misresponded, and if he is perceptive and fair he is likely to admit that his conscience was as unmoved as those of the Shandeans. Such awareness does not necessarily intensify one's engagement with Sterne's ideas on conscience, but it does broaden one's knowledge of what his responsive processes are like. A reader of the sermon episode is likely to learn that he does not respond directly to straightforward moral exhortation; such information is useful to a reader, but it is even more useful for a writer to know that readers are the way they are, especially in a time when didacticism is assumed to be a value in art, and when the relevant question is about successful methods of reaching an audience.

Tristram Shandy is about response because it is about the nature of art. Sterne's concern is not primarily to sharpen the reader's sense of awareness (although that is an important by-product of his efforts), but to describe possible ways of moving a response. To define the possible, he exposes the impossible, those straightforward methods which assume that a reader will pay attention and learn what he is told to learn. The sermon is one form that uses such methods, though it is only one. Akin to it are various panegyrical and hortatory forms, in prose and verse, which portray the ideal and assume that man, limited and fallen though he may be, will readily respond to reason and appeals to the benevolent part of his nature.

Such forms and assumptions come to eighteenth-century literature from an older and more confident age—when men could feel themselves more justified in praising and more rewarded in their direct appeals for honor and justice. Augustan writers are increasingly nervous about these forms and assumptions, not only because of their traditional Augustinian view of fallen human nature but because eighteenth-century events seemed to conspire in illustrating the depravity and perversity that man is capable of engraving on civilization. For the Augustan mind, desperate situations demanded desperate answers, and if the traditional didactic forms and methods did not work, they had to be replaced with forms and methods that did. This is but one reason that we find such a wide discrepancy between neoclassical theory of genres and the practice of the major Augustans in fusing genres and working great variations upon their conventions, not only in their play poetry but in official ministrations of their public function. Whatever the ancients might have known about proprieties, modernity had produced mutants that had to be dealt with, and in the real world which Augustan poetry engaged were grotesqueries that could not be exposed by strict adherence to rules that were premised on better times and better men. The georgic, for example, was continually merging with satire to make its didactic point, for models, imitation, directness had to be matched or superseded by spectres and indirection if real men were going to respond.[5] Of course the old forms and old methods stayed on (ironically they were engaged primarily by those most in harmony with modernity, while new methods were employed primarily by conservatives who were willing to be rash in order to provoke a return to old values), and one cannot point to a sharp end to direct moralizing; but co-existent in the early eighteenth century was the strain of didacticism which we usually associate with the great Augustan moralists—the later Dryden, Swift, Pope, Fielding, Hogarth. This strain does not usually hold up models of perfection (except as a rhetorical norm), nor rely on straight-forward exhortation (passages read that way often turn out to be ironic, as in Pope's *Essay on Man*). Rather, it attempts to laugh or frighten man from his follies and vices, and to tease him into awareness through satiric inversion and irony.

The necessity for such indirection is succinctly stated in the prefatory rationale for *Directions to Mankind in General*, a 1745 treatise which is distinguished not for its subtlety or individuality but rather its typicality in using irony to "advise" courtiers, lawyers, divines, physicians, and justices of the peace:

> There lurks in the Heart of Man so strong a Principle of Revolt against all Advice or Instruction, that there is not, perhaps, a surer Way of giving his conduct a wrong Byass, than by attempting, in that Way, to guide and set him right.
>
> This Waywardness, so conspicuous in Childhood, strengthens with Years; and all that is got by teazing pretty Master or Miss, with sage Council, is, that they hate you, stick the closer to their innate ruling Passion, and as they grow up, according to their Capacities, acquire more Art to cover, or excuse it.
>
> Hence that constant State of Hostility between Principle and Practice, which bewilders and puzzles so much the Unacquainted with the *actual* System of Human Life, opposed to that of speculative Morality; which, one would imagine, was only so well known, so strongly inculcated, and so inwardly approved, that it might be the more splendid Sacrifice, in practice, to our Vices and Passions.[6]

Such a passage clarifies not only the didactic grounds of irony but helps to define the suspicion that some didacticists had of other

5. The most suggestive recent account of such genre-crossing is by Ralph Cohen, "The Augustan Mode in English Poetry," *Eighteenth-Century Studies*, 1 (1967), 3–32.

6. Pp. 3–4. The treatise is attributed to "Dr. Fitzpatrick."

didacticists, such as Swift's distrust of Defoe and Fielding's of Richardson. For if perverse men refused to follow straightforward advice and imitate ideal models, such straightforwardness might actually encourage folly and vice.

I have briefly (and simplistically) sketched some eighteenth-century disagreements about didacticism because in reading Sterne we need to be reminded that denigration of a didactic method does not necessarily equal anti-didactic and amoral (or immoral) sentiments. Such a reminder would not be necessary if we were to think of Sterne in terms of his Augustan predecessors, but critical predilection with his modernity, rebellion, sentimentality, and pre-Romanticism are apt to cast his exposures of didactic inefficacy into an eerie and misleading light as anti-didactic, cynical, amoral. Sterne *is* often concerned to correct his predecessors, but theirs is the context he chooses. In many ways, *Tristram Shandy* is a very old-fashioned book, not only in terms of the battlegrounds it chooses, but in terms of the aims it espouses; only the rules of battle are varied to meet the needs of his situation and even the rules are not as different as they first seem to be. As the great Augustans teach us, literature may be sharply innovative and still preach the old verities; it may be highly unconventional and still depend crucially on convention and a presumed response. *Tristram Shandy* is old-fashioned just as *A Tale of a Tub* is old-fashioned and Wotton and Bentley are not, just as *The Dunciad* is, and Cibber and Theobald are not.

IV

The sermon episode offers us perspective on *Tristram Shandy*'s place in the eighteenth-century debate about didactic methods, showing Sterne not to be eccentric and unorthodox, but rather to be traditional in his skepticism of human nature and suspicion of human response. The method of exposure in the episode is similarly traditional, for the dramatic portrayal of garbled response to moral exhortation is not as original as Sterne makes it seem. Such a portrayal is part of what we might call the "whole-as-observed-part" tradition, a tradition related to the "play-within-a-play" and previously used in eighteenth-century prose fiction. Its fundamental characteristic is the use of an interpolated tale to show how characters react to it. I do not here propose to offer a detailed account of that tradition but I do wish to point up its prominence and to indicate the variations that Sterne works upon its conventions.

Interpolated tales are common in eighteenth-century novels, as they had been in earlier fiction; *Don Quixote* is only the most famous instance. But many such tales participate in the "whole-as-observed-part" tradition. We have not usually paid attention to how they are received in the action of a fictional work, because our recent penchant for "unity" has turned attention to their content—especially their themes and their parallels to the main action. Many interpolated tales may need to be approached in terms of content, but in Sterne (as in Fielding before him) it is the response of the hearers that deserves our real attention, for we are not dealing with an insert or a simple parallel, but with a major demonstration of how such interpolations are received into the novel's main action.

Tom Jones makes perhaps the most prominent use of the "whole-as-observed-part" tradition, and Sterne may well have taken his cue there for the sermon episode, as he did for many other strategies in *Tristram Shandy.* Fielding's novels include several tales where the main narrative action is interrupted to hear a shorter narrative, complete in itself. Such are the tales of Leonora and Mr. Wilson in *Joseph Andrews,* and those of Mrs. Fitzpatrick and the Man of the Hill in *Tom Jones;* closely related are the puppet show and the London performance of *Hamlet.* The frequency and density of audience interruption varies widely in these tales and performances, but one major interest of the digressions lies in what we learn about response from watching the digression interrupted.[7]

The tale of the Man of the Hill is one of the most significant of these; it is near both the spatial and artistic centers of *Tom Jones.* This narrative and the response it provokes help to focus the novel's concern with how an audience is made to respond to a didactic work. Fielding is not perhaps so skeptical as Swift or Pope of human nature, but neither is he so easily persuaded as Defoe and Richardson that man, presented with appropriate models and corrective exhortation, will follow the good, the true, and the beautiful. Thus he complicates Tom as an object for emulation and even slightly humanizes Sophia, though for Fielding humanizing women too much is a somewhat different matter.

Fielding's incorporation of the Man of the Hill parodies the

---

7. Howard Weinbrot's fine essay, "Chastity and Interpolation: Two Aspects of *Joseph Andrews* (*JEGP,* 69 [1970], 26n) conveniently lists most standard discussions of interpolation. Also relevant are Douglas Brooks, "The Interpolated Tales in *Joseph Andrews* Again," *MP,* 65 (1968), 203–13; Glenn W. Hatfield, *Henry Fielding and the Language of Irony* (Chicago and London, 1968), 201ff.; Robert Alter, *Fielding and the Nature of the Novel* (Cambridge, Mass., 1968), pp. 108ff.; Leon V. Driskell, "Interpolated Tales in *Joseph Andrews* and *Don Quixote:* The Dramatic Method as Instruction," *South Atlantic Bulletin,* 33 (1968), 5–8; and Manuel Schonhorn, "Fielding's Digressive-Parodic Artistry: *Tom Jones* and The Man of the Hill," *TSLL,* 10 (1968–69), 207–14. From different perspectives, Weinbrot and Driskell share my concerns with in-the-novel responses. The most suggestive recent discussion is by Martin C. Battestin, "*Tom Jones* and 'His Egyptian Majesty': Fielding's Parable of Government," *PMLA,* 82 (1967), 68–77, an essay which has implications far beyond the episode which it examines.

straightforward moralizers. The Man's name "sounds" allegorical,[8] and his tale is shaped like the spiritual biographies and autobiographies which were popular in the late seventeenth and early eighteenth centuries, especially among Puritans—a shape that was imitated in much didactic fiction.[9] The Man begins with an account of his birth and early life of degradation, salvaged at last by his repentance and disillusioned withdrawal from society. He is a mixture of Robinson Crusoe, Lord B, and Gulliver, and his voluntary isolation as a hermit seems excessive and stupid in the joyful, life-loving world of *Tom Jones*. Much of this effect is produced by the Man's manner—solemn, egocentric, and ultimately boring; he self-righteously recounts details calculated to justify his Timon-like misanthropy. His performance seems especially humorless and tedious because of its contrast with the rest of *Tom Jones*, and a reader is apt to conclude that one would need to desire edification very badly, perhaps desperately, to profit from the autobiography of the Man of the Hill.

Fielding's handling of the tale underscores its inefficacy. Not only is the teller made to seem unattractive, misguided, and dull, but the tale itself—set as it is in the midst of a lively, spirited, engaged pursuit of a moral standard to fit the needs of man in society—seems ponderous and irrelevant, and it is presented in a stark, pseudo-allegorical style that contrasts sharply with the basic style of *Tom Jones*. As an alternative to the ethic Tom is working out, it is simplistic and unpersuasive, for it emphasizes disenchantments rather than solutions and ignores the complex responsibilities of social man. The Man's *method* of moralizing is equally inadequate, compared with Fielding's own. The Man relies upon the simple recounting of an individual experience to make a universal point; Fielding vividly portrays moral anxieties and complexities, and he reasons with his reader, using the full resources of his ironic stance to invite the reader to watch, evaluate and decide for himself. Fielding's narrator is no less certain of his own morality, but he reasons and cajoles, while the Man dogmatizes, expecting a straightforward, automatic response.

But it is the in-the-novel response to the Man's tale which ultimately makes Fielding's point. Tom is the most important member of the audience, but Partridge is more active during the tale and Fielding uses him for a greater variety of purposes. His role resem-

8. The name seems to derive from the "Lord of the Hill," who prepared a refuge for sojourners in *The Pilgrim's Progress*. I think Fielding expected his readers to recognize the name as allusion and thus find the Man's lack of hospitality an inversion of expected and approved behavior. One might further regard the Man as Fielding's anti-Puritan version of what Christianity becomes when it follows the Calvinistic vision of man's lonely pilgrimage.

9. I have discussed such shapes more fully in *The Reluctant Pilgrim* (Baltimore, 1966).

bles that of the collective hearers in *Tristram Shandy*, for Fielding is working on a smaller stage (in this particular scene) and he lets Partridge perform functions which Sterne parcels among a number of characters. Partridge continually interrupts to footnote or comment, demonstrating from the beginning that his major interest is not in hearing what the Man has to say. His first interruption comes before a word of the Man's tale (end of ch. x, Book VIII), and scarcely a paragraph goes by when Partridge interrupts again. The Man has described his industrious father and now begins to portray his mother as an "arrant vixen," and a queen shrew:

> But though this circumstance perhaps made him miserable, it did not make him poor; for he confined her almost entirely at home, and rather chose to bear eternal upbraidings in his own house, than to injure his fortune by indulging her in the extravagances she desired abroad.
>
> "By this Xanthippe" (so was the wife of Socrates called, said Partridge)—"by this Xanthippe he had two sons, of which I was the younger. . . ."

This interruption is ostensibly a kindness to Tom, for Partridge offers a "learned" footnote; but actually, while trying to show off his knowledge, he merely demonstrates his ignorance of how words work. Unable to understand figurative language, he assumes Xanthippe to be the name of the Man's mother; his footnote thus "explains" what the teller assumes will be immediately understood as allusion. A paragraph later, Partridge interrupts again to assure the Man that he understands his point because of an analogous personal experience. This time "Jones chid the pedagogue for his interruption," and the Man proceeds for several minutes before Partridge again intrudes, curious about a detail. Now Tom begins to be embarrassed and "begged the gentleman to proceed without regarding any impertinent questions." And so it goes. Sometimes Partridge questions ("Nubbing cheat! . . . pray, sir, what is that?"; "Pray, sir, where was the wound?"), sometimes he comments (". . . evil spirits can carry away anything without being seen . . ."). Once he interjects a long story of his own, prompted only by the slightest of topical similarities. Several times Tom shows his annoyance at Partridge's responses, but efforts to quiet him do not avail.

Some of Partridge's impertinencies arise from his being typed as a schoolmaster; his explication of Xanthippe, his injection of a Latin phrase and his detailing of the translating ability of a character in his story all show this preoccupation. But many of the other interruptions are less specific; more than a schoolmaster he becomes a type of the impertinent reader who feigns interest only to exercise his own ingenuities. Partridge means well enough (or thinks he does), and when the Man fears that his tale is getting too long and his philosophizing too boring, Partridge assures us of his interest:

> "Philosophy elevates and steels the mind, Christianity softens and sweetens it. The former makes us the objects of human admiration, the latter of Divine love. That ensures us a temporal, but this an eternal happiness. But I am afraid I tire you with my rhapsody."
>
> "Not at all," cries Partridge; "Lud forbid we should be tired with good things."

But the nature of his interruptions suggests that Partridge had learned little. Although he is a closer listener than anyone Sterne offers us, he does not profit much:

> Partridge . . . had fallen into a profound repose just as the stranger had finished his story; for his curiosity was satisfied, and the subsequent discourse was not forcible enough in its operation to conjure down the charms of sleep. Jones therefore left him to enjoy his nap; . . .

Tom is more polite during the whole lengthy story and probably more attentive, but his response is hardly what the Man might wish for. Tom begins predisposed to hear of the Man's life; in fact, it is at Tom's urging that the tale gets told at all. But though Tom appears moved by the Man's misfortunes, he is not attracted to the Man's conclusions; misanthropic isolation holds no more charm for Tom at the end of the tale than at the beginning.

Fielding contrives events to make the point clear. The episode of the Man of the Hill begins with Tom rescuing the man from thieves —a rescue which demonstrates the necessity of human acceptance of social responsibility. Without Tom's social concern, the Man would not have been left to tell his tale. And when the tale is over, there is another rescue, just as Tom and the Man have climbed Mazard Hill and taken a prospect both backward and forward. (This passage seems to derive its power from the space/time prospect tradition used by Denham and Pope, and points to the figurative dimensions which Fielding's work sometimes engages.) Tom does not hesitate when a woman screams; immediately perceiving his responsibility, he rescues Mrs. Waters and subdues her attacker, Ensign Northerton. For Tom, the depravity of human nature requires not isolation but involvement, the Man's story, together with his passive conduct during Tom's struggle with Northerton, only underscores the inadequacy of a philosophy which allows man to think of himself as self-satisfied—free from the brutal confrontations of human interaction and social reality.

Interpolations may offer alternatives to the implications of the main action, or they may parody the main action on another level, or they may simply provide resting places for the weary reader. But in the Man of the Hill episode, it is the responses to the tale—immediate and ultimate—which "place" the tale in *Tom Jones*. The rejection of the tale, first by an enthusiastic listener who can't keep his mind attentive, and second by one who reflects carefully and finds its message inadequate, primarily means a rejection of an outlook on life; but the moral method, because of its parodic basis and its ill success in the arena, comes in for critical glances as well.

Fielding's use of the interruptions is more than comic relief from the solemnity of a long, tedious story, and what he does with the episode relates to one of his central concerns in *Tom Jones*—defining not only an acceptable morality but describing a successful method of inculcating morality. Partridge is a surrogate for the typical reader, good-natured in his intention to learn but ultimately more anxious to justify himself and preserve his own views and his own comfort. Tom, more like the ideal, attentive reader Fielding wants for his own novels, finally evaluates the morality and efficacy of a tale not in terms of abstract belief but in terms of its ethical application.

Sterne's use of the "whole-as-observed-part" is thus not focused exactly as it is in Fielding, but Sterne follows him (and the tradition) in using the responses of the in-the-book hearers to make this point. For Sterne, the point is more rigorously argued than in Fielding or in any other example of the tradition that I know. Sterne strips bare the pretense that readers will learn anything at all from straightforward moral discourse; Fielding had merely, in the process of exposing an inadequate moral system, cast some glances at inadequate methods and implied that bad morality uses bad methods. But he is more sanguine that men can see through such methods; his is a "softer" view of humanity than Sterne's, for he is confident that bad morality is ineffectual by any method, whereas Sterne finds that even good morality will not be persuasive when supported only by conventional methods. Sterne splits Partridge's role among the responses of four characters, and emphasizes that the more individual the responses, the more they are alike: there is no Tom in *Tristram Shandy*.

V

If my analysis of the sermon episode is correct and if Sterne's artistic concerns are really with methodology more than with ideology, then the central problem of *Tristram Shandy* is to set up some positive possibilities for the rhetorician—possibilities that conform to the realities of human response. These positive possibilities are a highly complicated matter, worthy of extended discussion, and here I can only hope to cite a few examples of Sterne's moralizing and sketch briefly the grounds of his method.

Sterne is full of sign-posts, strategies verbal and non-verbal which underscore this and point to that. Such sign-posts ostensibly tell us what to watch for and what to look at with care. There are hands, italics, underscoring phrases ("This is to serve for parents and governors instead of a whole volume on the subject"), and we soon learn to smile at them in our superior way—rejecting their satiric target, the pointed moral. Yet there is finally something troubling about the sign-posts, for oftener than not it turns out that the sign *does* point to something and that when we are through smiling at the device we are left with the fact that the device, though improperly thought out in conventional didactic rhetoric, was properly employed by Sterne. We are permitted (or forced to) the "double take." First, it seems absurd for anyone to be so grossly straightforward and direct (exaggerating to its logical conclusion the openness of a sermon or moral tract); then, when the device is dismissed, the passage seems worth another look.

A great many things in *Tristram Shandy* derive their ultimate effect through the double take (which seems to be produced by double mirrors), for the device frees the reader from blatant absurdity through a glorified self-consciousness which works via the same in-group principle as does Augustan satire. Then he is "free" to see matters as they are, not through a set of preconceived stereotypes. The joke often turns out to be that the stereotypes represent matters as they are, but when a reader gets there by a method which convinces him of its own honesty, he does not mind learning something he would have been unwilling to accept had it been told to him straight. Sterne is concerned with the fact that stereotypes are worn out; his target is not what the stereotypes represent.

The black page bemoaning the death of Yorick is an early example of the double take. There (Vol. I. ch. xii.) Sterne sets up his death's head, and he does it comically. The page is black because that is the conventional color for death and sadness. So far as I know, no one has ever cried much over this page, and when a reader first comes upon it he is likely to laugh in surprise at the blatant and simplistic reduction of symbol. Yet ultimately the absurd black page is one of many sign-posts that underscore the way we respond to Yorick, for once all the kidding is done—with sorry nags, threadbare clothes, tombstones, stolen sermons, and gimmicks to say that Yorick is now among the dear departed—we are back to the figure from *Hamlet* who shows us just where we stand in relation to a topsy-turvy, scurvy, mutable world that includes Dr. Slop and Tristram as well as Trismegistus and Alexander the Great. If pride is the great enemy, Yorick (alas) is the great moral warrior, and black pages and pointed fingers (as well as words that turn back on themselves) are among the weapons that Sterne can give him.

The didacticism in *Tristram Shandy* is like the bawdiness. It is carefully set up so that no one can say that the teller is responsible. If you, dear sir and madam, think of something else when Sterne narrates of the Slawkenbergius nose, then it is you who have the dirty mind. Similarly, if you contemplate your own mortality when you see a black page, or hear the name "Yorick," it is you who make the association and are responsible for the thoughts that follow. Of course, it is Sterne who has dismantled the hobbyhorses and replaced them with his own rhetorical patterns so that a sensitive reader cannot help himself, but Sterne has an alibi by normal didactic standards. No court in the literate world can convict; the guilt is clear, though not demonstrable. Sterne thumbs his nose at us, but the gesture turns out not to be what it seems.

Two-level self-consciousness (one dismissive, the other assertive —and in this order) is characteristic of Sterne. It is annoying and sometimes infuriating because not only are things not what they seem; they are not the opposite of what they seem either, and a good deal of attentive engagement is necessary to sort things out. While a reader may puzzle and tie himself in knots over *Tristram Shandy*, he can hardly use the book for his own purposes, or fall asleep where its words assert their authority. If he finds it (like life) too complicated, too difficult, too infuriating, he can abandon it; but if he stays with it he will (especially if he is an artist) leave a wiser man. The process is everything, and it is enough.

CHARLES PARISH

A Table of Contents for *Tristram Shandy*†

Book I

(1) The author reflects upon the sad circumstances of his conception. (2) The author bemoans the vitiated homunculus and animal spirit. (3) How the preceding has been told to the author by his Uncle Toby. (4) Formal statement of the above for the benefit of readers who "find themselves ill at ease, unless they are let into

† From *College English*, 22 (December 1960), 143–50.

the whole secret from first to last." (5) The author says he was born November 5, 1718. (6) The author prepares the reader for his donning the "fools-cap." (7) The installation of the midwife by the parson's wife. (8) A statement on hobby-horses, plus a Dedication. (9) Remarks on the preceding Dedication, its virginity and its value. (10) Fruitless return to the midwife; the story of Yorick's fine horses. (11) Yorick the jester and Yorick the parson. (12) Yorick's humor, its consequences, and his sad death (1748). (13) Second fruitless return to the midwife. (14) Difficulties of an author; despair at ever catching up: "I have been at it these six weeks, and am not yet born." (15) Mrs. Shandy's marriage settlement; her right to lie-in in London. (16) False-alarm and the return from London. (17) Consolation for Walter Shandy: Lying-in in the country. (18) Anticipations of Walter Shandy on his wife's lying-in in the country; his measures against careless delivery. (19) Walter Shandy on names good and evil; his unconquerable aversion for "Tristram." (20) The author on careless readers; "Les Docteurs de Sorbonne" on baptism. (21) First chapter on Tristram's birth; Uncle Toby knocks out his ashes, and says "I think—"; Uncle Toby's modesty concerning Aunt Dinah. (22) The author's statement on his work: "In a word, my work is digressive, and it is progressive too,——and at the same time." (23) Reasons for drawing Uncle Toby's character from his hobby-horse. (24) The fact that Uncle Toby had a strange hobby-horse. (25) Uncle Toby's wound; the ease gained through telling about it. The author says that the reader cannot guess what he is about to say.

Book II

(1) King William's Wars; Uncle Toby's idea of a map of Namur. (2) The author answers his critics; he says that his book, like Locke's, is a "history of what passes in a man's mind." (3) Uncle Toby's map; the broadening of his knowledge of fortifications. (4) The author explains why he ended the previous chapter "at the last spirited apostrophe"; how Uncle Toby mightily desires his health. (5) Trim incites Uncle Toby to go down to the country to build fortifications. (6) The end of Uncle Toby's sentence, "I think——" which began in I, 21; a talk on modesty as a reason for Mrs. Shandy's preferring the midwife to Dr. Slop. (7) Modesty, cont'd; the right and wrong ends of a woman; Uncle Toby mentions his unfortunate experience with the Widow Wadman. (8) Concerning time (1½ hours' "tolerable good reading"), and the hypercritic's pendulum. (9) Obadiah's collision with Dr. Slop. (10) Enter Dr. Slop; on Uncle Toby's train of thought (connecting Stevinus with the ring of the bell). (11) "Writing is but a different name for

conversation." Dr. Slop has forgotten his bag. (12) Why Stevinus
came into Uncle Toby's mind; patience and placidity of Uncle Toby
shown by the episode of the fly; Walter repents his baiting of Uncle
Toby and is forgiven. (13) " 'Tis not worth talking of." (14)
Stevinus, cont'd. (15) The discovery of the Sermon upon Conscience. (16) How *Conscience* is upon neither side,—neither Catholic nor Protestant. (17) Trim's stance and posture; the Sermon,
with many interruptions; Trim's brother, Tom. (18) Obadiah's entrance with the bag; Uncle Toby's "I wish you had seen what
prodigious armies we had in Flanders." (19) "I have dropped the
curtain over this scene for a minute." Mr. Shandy's nicety in reasoning; the center of the brain is the medulla oblongata—proved at
length.

Book III

(1) Uncle Toby's wish, cont'd; Dr. Slop's "confusion." (2) Walter's challenging of the wish, and the reaching for a handkerchief.
(3) Reaching for the handkerchief, cont'd. (4) The author on the
relation of body and mind. (5) Reaching for the handkerchief,
cont'd. (6) Walter's challenging of the wish, cont'd; Uncle Toby
whistles *Lillabullero*. (7) How the green bag was knotted because
Obadiah could not hear himself whistle. (8) The knotting of the
green bag, cont'd; how this was a link in the concatenation of events
against the fortunes of Tristram Shandy. (9) The knotted bag,
cont'd. (10) The cutting of the knots; on curses. (11) The curse of
Ernulphus. (12) On exactitude, illustrated by Garrick's *Hamlet*; the
inclusiveness of Ernulphus's curse—how all others derive from it.
(13) In which Tristram Shandy begins to be born; the midwife's
accident; Dr. Slop's "the subordination of fingers and thumbs to
******." (14) A discussion of Dr. Slop's "singular stroke of
eloquence" compared to one of Cicero's. (15) Dr. Slop draws from
his bag forceps and squirt; Uncle Toby's advantage. (16) Demonstration of the forceps on Uncle Toby. (17) Danger of the
forceps mistaking the hip for the head. (18) Lecture on Duration:
Walter to Uncle Toby; the chagrin of Walter. (19) The author
regrets that the lecture was ended by Walter's petulance. (20) Sleep
descends on Walter and Uncle Toby, whereupon the author finds
time to write his Preface; the Preface: concerning Locke's favoring
Judgment over Wit and how he was bubbled. (21) How the parlor
door hinge has squeaked for ten years. (22) Rude awakening by
squeaking hinges; how heirloom boots become mortars. (23) Tristram Shandy has been born, and Dr. Slop builds a bridge. (24)
How this bridge is mistaken for the one destroyed by Trim and
Bridget. (25) How the destroyed bridge was to be rebuilt. (26)

Return to the "present"; Uncle Toby sends thanks to Dr. Slop for rebuilding the bridge. (27) The enlightenment about the bridge; Walter is led to his room by Uncle Toby. (28) The author shows respect for the tribulations of his father. (29) Man bears pain and sorrow best in a horizontal position. (30) Why Walter's affliction was extravagant; "To explain this, I must leave him upon the bed for half an hour." (31) Discussion between Tristram's great-grandfather and great-grandmother on noses. (32) The same, cont'd. (33) Discussion between Tristram's grandfather and grandmother on noses. (34) Walter's concern with the literature on noses. (35) Walter's collection of this literature. (36) A warning by the author to the female reader. (37) Noses, cont'd. (38) In praise of Hafen Slawkenbergius. (39) Conflict between Walter and Uncle Toby on noses. (40) Locke and noses. (41) Noses, cont'd. (42) Further praise of Slawkenbergius by the author.

Book IV

The ninth tale of the tenth decad of Slawkenbergius, translated from the original Latin by the author. (1) Cautious hints concerning the untranslated tenth tale of the tenth decad. (2) Back to Walter Shandy, who is still prostrate. (3) Lashes, metaphorical and literal: Walter Shandy vs. "a grenadier in Makay's Regiment." (4) Trim's memory and his brother in Portugal. (5) A very short aside by Walter. (6) How Walter Shandy rises from his bed of grief. (7) Walter on misfortune. (8) How "Trismegistus" will counteract a crushed nose. (9) Walter on the laws of chance. (10) The author writes a chapter on "chapters," while his father and uncle are still on the stairs. (11) The greatness of "Trismegistus": antiphon by Walter and Uncle Toby. (12) How husbands are ignored during childbirth. (13) How the author gets his father and uncle off the stairs at last, as he despairs of ever catching up with the story of his life. (14) Time has truly passed; Walter is awakened by the maid; the leaky vessel carries away "Trismegistus," part of which seeps out. (15) The author writes his chapter on sleep. (16) Walter remains calm. (17) The author's explanation of this calmness. (18) Uncle Toby and Trim regret the misnaming, musing however upon the uselessness of names in battle. (19) The belated Lamentation of Walter. (20) The author on the dangerous and devious turnings of his book. (21) Digression upon kings: how Francis I solved a knotty problem satisfactorily. (22) The author explains that his book is written against nothing but spleen. (23) Walter and Yorick discuss un-naming; Yorick suggests a dinner with learned men. (25) A chapter has been torn out, and the author explains what was in that chapter: the coach with the erroneous bend sinister in the Shandy arms. (26) The dinner of learned men (The "Visitation Dinner"). (27) The same, cont'd. A misplaced chestnut. (28) Treatment of a chestnut burn. (29) Discussion by the learned men on the naming of a child; how a mother has no relation to her child. (30) On the latter point, between Uncle Toby and Yorick. (31) Walter Shandy's legacy—the ox-moor or Bobby's "grand tour"; how the matter is settled by the death of Bobby. (32) The author: how true Shandeism opens the heart and the lungs.

Book V

(1) The author inveighs against plagiarism; his digression on whiskers with the story of the Lady Baussière. (2) Walter is informed of the death of his son Bobby. (3) How Walter carried on: consolation in rhetoric. (4) Containing a choice anecdote: a culmination of Walter's carryings-on. (5) How the author leaves his mother standing outside the parlor door. (6) In the kitchen: a parallel to the parlor declamation. (7) Trim the orator: on Death. (8) In which the author remembers his debt of a chapter on chambermaids and buttonholes. (9) Trim continues: on Death. (10) The same, cont'd. (11) The author remembers his mother outside the parlor door. (12) The author returns to his mother—but does not. (13) What Mrs. Shandy had heard. (14) The matter of Socrates' children, cleared up. (15) The author digresses with "Had this volume been a farce. . . ." (16) Walter writes a Tristra-paedia. (17) Tristram has an accident, *ætat*[1]5. (18) Susannah confides in Trim. (19) Digression: Uncle Toby wishes for more cannon; Trim removes the window sashes. (20) Trim champions Susannah. (21) How Trim's succoring Susannah suggests the Battle of Steenkirk to Uncle Toby. (22) The Battle of Steenkirk, cont'd. (23) Susannah, Trim, Uncle Toby, and Yorick advance on Shandy Hall. (24) The author on his father's variousness. (25) The author mentions his right to go backwards. (26) Walter is informed of the accident. (27) Walter finds a certain good in the accident: on circumcision. (28) Walter Shandy: On the Good. (29) A story by Yorick: the battle between Gymnast and Tripet. (30) Walter on the merits of the Tristra-paedia. (31) Tristra-paedia: the origins of society and the rights of the parents (an echo of IV, 29). (32) Trim is catechized. (33) Tristra-paedia: Walter Shandy on radical heat and radical moisture. (34) The same, cont'd. (35) The same, cont'd. (36) The same, cont'd. (37) Uncle Toby and Trim on radical heat and radical moisture. (38) The same, cont'd. (39) Dr. Slop delivers a prognosis on the results of the accident. (40) Radical heat and moisture, resumed. (41) The author shouts encouragement and

---

1. "Aged." [*Editor.*]

choice of three roads to Paris. (4) The flight: should one describe Calais? (5) The flight: the author describes Calais. (6) The flight: on to Boulogne. (7) The flight: delays on the road; the passengers' speculations on the author. (8) The flight: to Montreuil; the author's patience with French coaches and drivers. (9) The flight: Montreuil: Janatone, the innkeeper's daughter, and the transience of her beauty. (10) French postroads and distances. (11) "One gets heated traveling." (12) Abbeville and the inn not fit to die in. (13) On wagon wheels. (14) On Lessius's and Ribbera's estimates of the size of the soul; the author's sense of his death. (15) En route. (16) Reflections on how to pay the post charges and still sleep; the author sees Chantilly (hurriedly). (17) First view of Paris: "So this is *Paris*! quoth I." (18) Enumeration of the streets of Paris, quarter by quarter. (19) En route. (20) How French post-horses are urged on. (21) The above illustrated by the story of the Abbess of Andoüillets. (22) The same, cont'd. (23) The same, cont'd. (24) The same, cont'd. (25) The same, cont'd. (26) The author looks back upon the distance he has covered. (27) Trips are interchanged: Tristram's grand tour with his father and his uncle; their visit to the mummies at Auxerre. (28) The author comes to his senses and resumes the first journey. (29) The wrecked coach is sold in Lyons; "Every thing is good for something." (30) "Vexation upon vexation" in Lyons. (31) The story of Amandus and Amanda. (32) The interlude with the ass of Lyons: the author gives "Honesty" a macaroon. (33) Tristram and the Commissary. (34) The same, cont'd. (35) Tristram scores on the Commissary but pays nonetheless. (36) The loss of the "remarks." (37) Back to the coachpurchaser. (38) The "remarks," used as curl-papers, "will be worse twisted still." (39) Sight-seeing in Lyons: "Lippius's clock" and the "Chinese history." (40) No tomb to drop tears on. (41) At Avignon: its windiness and its nobility. (42) En route: the author begins to believe that he has outrun Death. (43) The author, while en route, promises the continuation of the story of Uncle Toby's amours; he stops to dance with happy country-people; Nanette.

Book VIII

(1) Further statement on the necessity of going forwards and backwards. (2) The author expresses confidence in his method of writing a book. (3) The effect of velvet masks on the Shandy lineage. (4) How Uncle Toby finally heard that he was in love. (5) On drinking water. (6) How Uncle Toby's being a water drinker would have explained Mrs. Wadman's feelings toward him; the author expresses difficulty with this chapter. (7) The author, impatient, points out the care required in telling his story. (8) How

Uncle Toby lacked a bed when he first came down to Shandy Hall; how he accepted a bed at the Widow Wadman's. (9) Widow Wadman's nightgowns and cold feet. (10) How Uncle Toby did not learn of her love for him until eleven years later, at the demolition of Dunkirk. (11) The author curses women who don't care whether he eats his breakfast or not; he also curses furred caps. (12) He is struck by his extravagant metaphor. (13) An alphabetical damning of love. (14) How the position of Widow Wadman's house enabled her to attack. (15) The author prefers to be burned from the top down; on the "blind gut." (16) The attack: Mrs. Wadman and Uncle Toby look at maps in the sentry-box. (17) The author treasures a map with their thumbprints. (18) "Dunkirk" is finally destroyed: a continuation of the action first mentioned in VI, 34; Uncle Toby is sad. (19) To divert him, Trim essays the story of the King of Bohemia and his Seven Castles; Uncle Toby's argumentativeness. (20) Trim's tale of the wound on his knee and of the fair Beguine who nursed him. (21) The same, cont'd. (22) The same, cont'd; Uncle Toby finishes Trim's story for him. (23) Widow Wadman attacks again. (24) How she gets something in her eye. (25) How Uncle Toby does not get it out; a description of Widow Wadman's eye. (26) Uncle Toby breaks a blister and realizes that his wound is not merely skin-deep. (27) Uncle Toby announces to Trim that he is in love. (28) Discussion between Mrs. Wadman and Bridget about Uncle Toby's wound. (29) How a sword gets in one's way. (30) Plans of action by Uncle Toby and Trim. (31) Preparations for Walter Shandy's laugh. (32) Walter laughs; Uncle Toby's blister and Hilarion's ass. (33) Altercations in the Shandy family concerning love. (34) The same, cont'd; Trim's wager; Walter's letter of advice to Uncle Toby. (35) Uncle Toby and Trim are ready to attack; Mr. and Mrs. Shandy stroll down to observe the campaign.

Book IX

(1) Mr. and Mrs. Shandy; her placidity and lack of prurience. (2) Uncle Toby's battle array: how his tarnished gold-laced hat became him. (3) Uncle Toby's fear of the attack. (4) Trim assures Uncle Toby that the Widow Wadman will accept him as readily as the Jew's widow accepted Tom, Trim's brother. (5) The story of Tom and the widow, told outside Mrs. Wadman's house. (6) The same, cont'd. (7) The same, cont'd. (8) Trim and Uncle Toby are seen by Mr. and Mrs. Shandy still standing and talking; the author's sense of the speed of time. (9) The author's comment on the reader's reaction to "that ejaculation." (10) Mr. and Mrs. Shandy await events, as Trim tells his story to Uncle Toby. (11) They agree

about the nonsense of fortifications; Mrs. Shandy's agreeableness and Walter's chagrin about the date. (12) The author pauses to balance folly with wisdom to assure the success of his book. (13) The author's method of overcoming dullness while writing; how his laundry bills will prove the cleanness of his writing. (14) The author continues killing time, waiting for Chapter 15. (15) The author realizes that in talking about his digression he has actually made it; his surprise at this fact. (16) Trim and Uncle Toby finally knock at the front door. (17) The front door is opened with great dispatch; the author on finances. (18)   (19)

(20) Uncle Toby assures Mrs. Wadman that she shall see and touch the very spot where he received his wound. (21) How a woman chooses a husband, illustrated from Slawkenbergius. (22) How all Uncle Toby's virtues are nothing to Mrs. Wadman. (23) Bridget's determination to get the truth out of Trim. (24) The author feels his "want of powers" to continue the story; the Invocation to the gentle imbecile, Maria. (25) In which the author explains the necessity of having written Chapter 25 before he could write Chapters 18 and 19 (18) Uncle Toby informs Mrs. Wadman that he loves her; the thanklessness of children and the burden. (19) Mrs. Wadman's "fiddlestick"; Uncle Toby's confusion and the siege of Jericho. (26) Mrs. Wadman's past concern about Uncle Toby's wound; she asks him where he received the sad blow; Uncle Toby sends for the map. (27) After Mrs. Wadman has put her hand on the spot where Uncle Toby was wounded, the map is sent to the kitchen. (28) Trim explains the siege of Namur to Bridget; her charge and his refutation. (29) Trim learns the story of Mrs. Wadman's concern from Bridget. (30) How Uncle Toby and Trim had carried on separate attacks. (31) Trim tells Uncle Toby of the widow's concern, apropos of her "Humanity"; Uncle Toby is disillusioned. (32) The Shandy family convenes; Walter Shandy on women's lust. (33) Walter on the "provision . . . for continuing the race"; Obadiah's child and the Shandy bull ("a story about a cock and a bull").

Bibliography

BIOGRAPHICAL WORKS

Wilbur L. Cross, *The Life and Times of Laurence Sterne*, 3rd ed. (New Haven: Yale University Press; London: Oxford University Press, 1929) remains the complete critical biography. The first volume of Arthur Cash's biography, *Laurence Sterne: The Early and Middle Years* (London: Methuen, 1975) provides much new information and is likely to supersede Cross when it is complete. Lewis P. Curtis, *The Politics of Laurence Sterne* (Oxford: Oxford University Press, 1929) provided facts about Sterne's early career that made this study valuable in itself and also contributed to Cross's revisions for his definitive third edition. Lodwick Hartley, *This Is Lorence: A Narrative of Laurence Sterne* (Chapel Hill: University of North Carolina Press, 1943) centers on the complexity of Sterne's character and its relation to his work, as does Margaret R. B. Shaw, *Laurence Sterne: The Making of a Humorist, 1713–1762* (London: Richards Press, 1957). The fullest recent treatment of Sterne's life and its relations to his works is Henri Fluchère, *Laurence Sterne, de l'homme à l'oevre: Biographie critique et essai d'interpretation de "Tristram Shandy"* (Paris: Editions Gallimard, 1961); the English translation (abridged) is by Barbara Bray (Oxford: Oxford University Press, 1965).

GENERAL STUDIES

The following general studies are useful: D. W. Jefferson, *Laurence Sterne*, Writers and Their Work, No. 52 (London: Longmans, Green, 1954); A. D. McKillop, "Laurence Sterne," in *The Early Masters of English Fiction* (Lawrence: University of Kansas Press, 1956); Alan B. Howes, *Yorick and the Critics: Sterne's Reputation in England, 1760–1868*, Yale Studies in English, Vol. 139 (New Haven: Yale University Press, 1958); and Howes' collection of comments and criticism, *Sterne: The Critical Heritage* (London: Routledge & Kegan Paul, 1974).

THEORETICAL STUDIES

Theoretical studies include the following books: Ernest Dilworth, *The Unsentimental Journey of Laurence Sterne* (New York: King's Crown Press, 1948); Alice Green Fredman, *Diderot and Sterne* (New York: King's Crown Press, 1955); William V. Holtz, *Image and Immortality: A Study of "Tristram Shandy"* (Providence: Brown University Press, 1970); Helene Moglen, *The Philosophical Irony of Laurence Sterne* (Gainesville: The University Presses of Florida, 1975); Melvyn New, *Laurence Sterne as Satirist* (Gainesville: University of Florida Press, 1969); John M. Stedmond, *The Comic Art of Laurence Sterne* (Toronto: University of Toronto Press, 1967); James E. Swearingen, *Reflexivity in "Tristram Shandy": An Essay in Phenomenological Criticism* (New Haven: Yale University Press, 1977); John Traugott, *Tristram Shandy's World: Sterne's Philosophical Rhetoric* (Berkeley and Los Angeles: University of California Press, 1954).

Significant chapters on or relating to Sterne appear in: Walter Allen, *The English Novel: A Short Critical History* (New York: Dutton, 1955); Ernest A. Baker, *The History of the English Novel* (London: Witherby, 1924; New York: Barnes & Noble, 1950); Wayne Booth, *The Rhetoric of Fiction* (Chicago: University of Chicago Press, 1961); David Daiches, *A Critical History of English Literature* (New York: Ronald Press, 1960); Michael DePorte, *Nightmares and Hobbyhorses: Swift, Sterne, and Augustan Ideas of Madness* (San Marino, Calif.: Huntington Library, 1974); Northrop Frye, *Anatomy of Criticism: Four Essays* (Princeton: Princeton University Press, 1957); Edwin Muir, *Essays on Literature and Society* (London: Hogarth Press, 1949); John Preston, *The Created Self: The Reader's Role in Eighteenth-Century Fiction* (London: Butler & Tanner; New York: Barnes & Noble, 1970); Herbert Read, *The Sense of Glory* (New York: Harcourt, Brace, 1930); Arthur Sherbo, *Studies in the Eighteenth Century English Novel*

(East Lansing: Michigan State University Press, 1969); Stuart Tave, *The Amiable Humorist: A Study in the Comic Theory and Criticism of the Eighteenth and Early Nineteenth Century* (Chicago: University of Chicago Press, 1960); Dorothy Van Ghent, *The English Novel, Form and Function* (New York: Rinehart, 1953); W. B. C. Watkins, *Perilous Balance: The Tragic Genius of Swift, Johnson, and Sterne* (Princeton: Princeton University Press, 1939).

Some useful essays on various aspects of Sterne are: A. E. Dyson, "Sterne: The Novelist as Jester," *Critical Quarterly*, IV (1962), 309–20; Norman N. Holland, "The Laughter of Laurence Sterne," *Hudson Review*, IX (1956), 422–30; Ernest H. Lockridge, "A View of the Sentimental Absurd: Sterne and Camus," *Sewanee Review*, LXXII (1964), 652–67; A. D. McKillop, "The Reinterpretation of Laurence Sterne," *Etudes Anglaises*, VII (1954), 36–47; Ernest Tuveson, "Locke and Sterne," in *Reason and Imagination: Studies in the History of Ideas, 1600–1800*, ed. J. A. Mazzeo (New York: Columbia University Press, 1962), pp. 255–77.

In addition to the articles reprinted here, the following studies of *Tristram Shandy* are significant: Robert Alter, "*Tristram Shandy* and the Game of Love," *American Scholar*, XXXVII (1968), 316–23; Howard Anderson, "Associationism and Wit in *Tristram Shandy*," *Philological Quarterly*, XLVIII (1969), 27–41; Theodore Baird, "The Time-Scheme of *Tristram Shandy* and a Source," *PMLA*, LI (1936), 803–20; Frank Brady, "*Tristram Shandy:* Sexuality, Morality, and Sensibility," *Eighteenth-Century Studies*, 4 (1970), 41–56; Arthur H. Cash, "The Lockean Psychology of *Tristram Shandy*," *ELH*, XXII (1955), 125–35; William J. Farrell, "Nature Versus Art as Comic Pattern in *Tristram Shandy*," *ELH*, XXX (1963), 16–35; Eugene Hnatko, "*Tristram Shandy*'s Wit," *Journal of English and Germanic Philology*, LXIV (1965), 47–64; Ian Watt, "The Comic Syntax of *Tristram Shandy*," in *Studies in Criticism and Aesthetics, 1660–1800*, ed. Howard Anderson and John S. Shea (Minneapolis: University of Minnesota Press, 1967), 315–31; Andrew Wright, "The Artifice of Failure in *Tristram Shandy*," *Novel*, II (1969), 212–20.